THEY MADE LOVE, WAR AND HISTORY. THEY LIVED, DIED AND GAVE THEIR ALL FOR ... *LOVE AND GLORY.*

Bunny Palermo—a pushover for passion, with a heart of gold and a mouth of brass. In the hot Pacific jungle, she's safe in the arms of a stuffy colonel—until she falls for a smooth, sexy sergeant. . . .

Page Hannaday—a general's daughter, she yearns for a brilliant career in the WACs ... and for the passionate embrace of a handsome intelligence officer. Torn between two loves, she must abandon one. . . .

Jill Hammersmith—daughter of a Southern belle, she's a pint-sized rebel who wins a Bronze Star. Trapped by a doomed and tragic love, she battles her desire for the one man who can set her free. . . .

Elisabeth Gardner—a gorgeous New York model fleeing a shady past. She betrays her patrician husband for the fierce sensuality of a man she cannot resist—a ruthless war profiteer. . . .

A BOOK-OF-THE-MONTH CLUB SELECTION
THE CRITICS CHEER *LOVE AND GLORY*!

(see next page ...)

Books by Jeane Westin

The Coming Parent Revolution
Love and Glory

Published by POCKET BOOKS

LOVE AND GLORY

★ ★ ★ ★

Jeane Westin

PUBLISHED BY POCKET BOOKS NEW YORK

To my dear friends
Irma Ruth Walker and the late Teri Shapiro,
who believed I could, thought I should,
and encouraged until I did write this book.

POCKET BOOKS, a division of Simon & Schuster, Inc.
1230 Avenue of the Americas, New York, N.Y. 10020

Copyright © 1985 by Jeane Westin
Cover artwork copyright © 1986 Ron Lesser

Published by arrangement with Simon & Schuster, Inc.
Library of Congress Catalog Card Number: 85-18422

ISBN: 0-671-62910-7

First Pocket Books printing November, 1986

10 9 8 7 6 5 4 3 2 1

POCKET and colophon are registered trademarks
of Simon & Schuster, Inc.

Printed in the U.S.A.

ACKNOWLEDGMENTS

In particular I wish to thank Eleanor Fait, member of the First WAAC Officer Candidate Class, and Betty Coyle, member of the Fifth OC Class. Both gave valuable criticism and insight into the early days of women's wartime military service.

Grateful acknowledgment is also made to Colonel Bettie Morden, current WAC historian, and to Mattie E. Treadwell's official history *The Women's Army Corps* for factual information about the Corps during World War II.

Grateful acknowledgment is made to the following authors and publishers for permission to reprint the following materials:

"All or Nothing at All" by Jack Lawrence (words) and Arthur Altman (music) © copyright 1940 by MCA Music, A Division of MCA Inc., New York, N.Y. Copyright renewed and assigned to MCA Music, A Division of MCA Inc., and MPL Communications, Inc., for USA. Used by permission. All rights reserved. (p. 15)

"Bless 'em All" by Jimmy Hughes and Frank Lake © 1940 reproduced by permission of Keith Prowse Music Co., Ltd., London. (p. 314)

"Don't Sit Under the Apple Tree (with Anyone Else but Me)" by Lew Brown, Charlie Tobias and Sam H. Stept © 1942, 1954 Robbins Music Corporation. © renewed 1970, 1982 Robbins Music Corporation & Ched Music Corporation. Rights assigned to CBS Catalogue Partnership. All rights controlled and administered by CBS Robbins Catalog Inc. & Ched Music. All rights reserved. International copyright secured. Used by permission. (p. 140)

BOOK ONE

1942: FROM SILK TO KHAKI

PROLOGUE

ALL THAT HOT July 19th morning the women had come, 440 of them, out of the mainstream of America to the old cavalry post, their bright dresses, spectator pumps and Sunday hats almost garish against a background of khaki uniforms and precise rows of green barracks. They clambered down from canvas-covered six-by-sixes onto the manicured, tree-ringed Dewy Parade Ground of Fort Des Moines, Iowa, to begin a new experiment called the Women's Army Auxiliary Corps.

All that summer Sunday morning in 1942 the women had come, the cream of thirty thousand applicants drawn to their country's military services during wartime, not knowing what to expect, or what would be expected of them. One thing they knew: Women had no military history; they would have to make their own.

U.S. WOMEN TROOP TO ENLIST IN
ARMY'S FIRST ALL-FEMALE FORCE

On May 27, for the first time in history, the U.S. Army began general recruiting of women. The response was terrific. Before the day was ended, 13,208 had applied.
                                        —*Life, May 29, 1942*

TWO SERGEANTS, THEIR starched-stiff cotton twill wilting in the humid Iowa heat, stood watching the women as they descended from trucks in front of the reception center.

"Damned if I don't believe it now," muttered the one with hash marks to his elbow.

"Believe what?"

"Believe we're gonna lose this war, that's what." He frowned, deepening the layers of wrinkles on his weather-beaten face, as the last four women were helped to the ground by MPs. "No sirree, I didn't believe it—not when Corregidor fell, not even when we lost Guam. Now, by God, I do," he said, finality adding to the rasp in his command-coarsened voice. "If it don't beat all when they put women in this man's army."

"You said it, pal." His younger companion shook his head in disgust. "Women soldiers? Kee-rist! When I heard they was comin' here, I didn't believe it. What'll the big brass think of next? Hey—" he ran to catch the other man moving away swiftly along the perimeter of the manicured parade ground— "hey, Wolford, do ya s'pose they'll put us all in khaki kilts?"

A perspiring young second lieutenant skirted the crowd of milling women exchanging their first shy confidences, and

3

moved toward the last four arrivals, standing uncertainly in a jumble of suitcases. "Your name, miss?" he asked the first one, resting his clipboard on his hip.

"Page Hannaday, Lieutenant." Her eyes followed his pencil down the roster.

"Washington, D.C.?" he asked.

"That's right."

"Any relation to the General Hannaday on Marshall's staff?"

She hesitated for a moment and dropped her voice. "Yes, he's my father."

At that point a group of off-duty soldiers began to chant from across the road that ran along the west side of the parade ground, "You'll be sorry. You'll be sor-ry."

Page saw the last woman off the truck, dark-haired and busty, in her late twenties, grin and wave to them. They answered with several loud wolf whistles, and the woman laughed out loud.

The lieutenant motioned them off. "*Your* name, miss," he asked the woman irritably.

"Call me Bunny."

"No, miss, your full name."

"All of them?"

He nodded, a trickle of sweat appearing from under his sideburn and sliding slowly toward his neck.

"Okay, Captain, you asked for it. Let's see . . . there's Barbara Eugenia Rose-Marie Patra—that's my maiden name. Then I married Johnny LaMonica, and then I married Johnny Palermo, but—" she stopped, grinning, as the man flushed red—"of course, not before I divorced the first Johnny. But then I divorced the second Johnny too. See why you just better call me Bunny?"

Page pressed her lips hard together to keep from smiling. What a clown! Pulling an officer's leg like that during her first hour in the Army. She saw the second lieutenant shift his clipboard uneasily, since the other two women standing close by had overheard the exchange and were smothering snickers.

"Miss," he said, his voice edged with impatience, "first, I'm not a captain, I'm a lieutenant, and, second, I need to know the name you enlisted under so I can check you present on this roster."

4

"Why didn't you *say* so?" the woman called Bunny asked, smiling teasingly up at him.

Then Page saw a tiny woman in a red peplum dress, whom she had first noticed on the truck coming from the troop train, step up boldly and hand the lieutenant her travel orders. "Jill Hammersmith. My middle name—" she began and then moved to the officer's side to look at the roster—"it's Henry," she said, pointing. "That's a family name. Anything else you want to know, just ask."

The lieutenant located her name on the list. "California?"

"Right. I enlisted in Sacramento, but I live outside—"

"Are you the vet?" He looked down at her, more than a little disbelief in his voice.

"I was studying veterinary medicine, but I'm not a graduate vet," she offered. "I just finished my first year last month, and—"

"Excuse me, miss, you can tell all that to the classification people tomorrow."

Page watched as he stepped in front of a stunningly beautiful blonde standing slightly apart from the others.

"Mrs. Marne Pershing Gardner—Elisabeth, that's spelled Elisabeth," she said, her voice husky and cool despite the heat. "New York City."

"Okay, that's it, ladies," he said, eying both his completed roster and Elisabeth Gardner with satisfaction. "Hannaday, Palermo, Hammersmith, Gardner—you four wait over there"—he pointed to one of the giant elms surrounding the parade ground—"until I can figure out what company you've been assigned to. We didn't have much time to get ready for you girls—I mean you WAAC officer candidates."

Now that she was officially checked into the Army, Page eagerly picked up her small valise, containing the one change of clothing she had been told to bring, and carried it into the shade. She did not need a second invitation. Quickly undoing her hatpin, she removed her wide-brimmed straw to catch a stray breeze, fanning herself to move the humid air about her face.

"Hi," the smiling dark-haired woman said, joining her. "Is this shade taken or can anybody melt here?"

"It's the Army's shade—everyone's welcome," Page said and extended her hand in introduction. "Page Hannaday."

5

"Yes, I heard. Mine's—"

Page laughed now. "Yes, *I* heard—Barbara-Eugenia-Rose-Marie . . ."

Bunny spoke up when Page's memory faltered. "Patra-La-Monica-Palermo," and they finished in singsong unison, "Just-call-me-Bunny."

The other two women had moved into the shade, and they joined in the laughter, awkwardly, since they'd barely met. Page saw in their three faces that they were evaluating one another, as she was them, but not as total strangers. It was as if being among the first women in the Army they were already linked to one another by the act of enlisting. Their conversation was casual—they could have been four women meeting anywhere—but underneath, Page felt, they all sensed the adventure of this moment.

Bunny broke the mood. "I thought an army traveled on its stomach. When are they going to feed us?"

Page smiled at her. "You sound like a regular-army chowhound already."

"Is it always this hot?" Elisabeth asked, smoothing the folds of her emerald-green silk dress.

"Probably," Page said. "At least a summer I spent at Fort Sill was this hot, or even worse."

Jill bounced up from her perch on a suitcase. "It's not so bad," she said, looking around. "I think it's kind of pretty—all those old trees and those white-columned buildings over there beyond the cannon and the flag. It's like one of those covers on *The Saturday Evening Post*—you know, to remind us what we're fighting for."

Bunny shook her head. "I'm not sure, kiddo. We may have another war on our hands. Did you see those two grizzled warriors looking like they could bite nails as we got off the truck? If that's the welcoming committee—well, I'll just turn around and get myself back to good ol' Bloomfield, New Jersey."

Jill shook her head, a determined, even grim set to her mouth. "Nothing could make me leave." Then her face lightened. "Elisabeth, I really love your dress. It's so neat. I couldn't keep mine from wrinkling on the train."

"Small girls should never wear peplums."

Page saw that Jill had been hurt, but that Elisabeth had not meant her remark to wound. The pronouncement had been delivered in the matter-of-fact tone of an authority. Jill ducked her head, busying herself with her suitcase lock, and when she looked up again Page could see in the set of her mouth that the hurt had been dismissed. It was obvious Jill was not going to let anything or anyone get in her way. With a wink, Bunny offered Jill a Lucky and then lit it for her.

Page had expected a disparate group, maybe not quite the standard Hollywood film soldier mix, but different backgrounds and certainly different reasons for joining the Army. It was already apparent that Bunny with her wry outlook, delivered in flattened New Jersey vowels, was the group joker; tiny Jill with a giant's optimism written on her gamin face was the gung-ho type; and Elisabeth, with her intriguing elegance and reserve, was the cool one—with a hint of mystery wafting about her like the expensive perfume she wore.

As for herself, she was the army brat. General Dalton C. Hannaday's little girl had been fed to bugle calls and put to bed at the sound of the retreat cannon. But most of her life Page had watched soldiers from reviewing stands. She had never dreamed she'd be part of the parade.

Jill was talking to Bunny. "What do you mean about the sergeants? You don't think they like us, is that it?"

Bunny shrugged. "Ask our expert here," she said, indicating Page.

"I wouldn't call myself an expert."

"You seem to know your way around this Army better than we do. Come on, give out."

With everything in her, Page knew that until the Women's Army Auxiliary Corps proved itself to men like the two sergeants they would be invaders in this ancient male bastion, more feared than Japs or Nazis.

She had been in the gallery in early May when the bill to establish the Corps had been argued in the House of Representatives. She had listened in dismay as Hoffman of Michigan had asked from the floor in ringingly righteous tones, "Take the women into the armed forces, who then will maintain the home fires; who will do the cooking, the washing, the mending, the humble homey tasks to which every woman has devoted herself?" Men around the chamber had nodded in agreement, but it had been New York's Congressman Somers who had voiced the most vehement protest: "Think of the humiliation! What has become of the manhood of America? The thing is revolting to me." That the bill passed was due to three forces: the tenacity of its author, Representative Edith Nourse Rogers, General George C. Marshall lobbying behind the scenes, and unexpected support from chivalrous Southern legislators who wanted to humor the ladies.

"Well," Jill asked Page impatiently, "do the sergeants like us or not?"

"I can't give you a yes or no. I was a volunteer at WAAC headquarters with Director Hobby—"

Jill jumped in. "Oveta Culp Hobby—I saw a picture of her last May in *Time* magazine taking the oath."

"Yes, that's right—and we learned that nearly everybody, Army, government and the public, thought we were a crazy wartime experiment. These next six weeks are crucial for the WAAC. We're all in the spotlight, especially Director Hobby. As the first women officer candidates, we're going to have to give her something to convince them with or ..." She didn't know what might happen.

"You mean," Jill said, biting her lower lip, "they could send us home."

The girl looked so disturbed that Page put a friendly arm around Jill's shoulder. "Don't worry, I'm betting on us."

"That's right, kid," Bunny said, "we signed up for the duration plus six months, and they'd better get used to it."

Jill shyly looked up at Elisabeth. "What do you say?"

"Of course, we can do whatever we must—" Elisabeth shrugged as she said it—"how difficult could it be, after all?"

Jill brightened. "Say, maybe we four could kind of stick together—at least for today."

The lieutenant who had checked them in reappeared and handed each of them a piece of paper. "Candidates, this is your meal chit. If you'll form up with the women behind Sergeant Wolford over there—"

Jill asked, "The one with all the stripes on his sleeve?"

He nodded, frowning. "—he'll take you across the parade ground to your quarters, where you can leave your duffle. Then you'll proceed to the mess hall. After chow, you'll have the rest of the day free to settle in."

Jill whispered as the lieutenant walked away, "Did you hear that? He called us candidates."

The four women joined almost a hundred others straggling across the close-cropped grass, hurrying to keep up with the sergeant's rigid khaki-covered back, and headed toward rose-colored brick barracks stretching on each side of the white-pillared headquarters building.

"Somehow lunch and a Sunday nap isn't what I expected," Bunny said. "A soldier's life might not be so bad, after all."

Page smiled to herself as she helped Elisabeth, who was struggling with a large Bonwit's hatbox. She remembered the extensive training schedules she had seen at WAAC headquarters. The women were facing weeks of drill and calisthenics, courses in map reading, military courtesy and field sanitation. They would have to master a long list of skills before they could truly call themselves women soldiers.

No one had been more against the idea of women as soldiers than Page's father. At first he had been only amused, until she volunteered to work at the WAAC planning office in Temporary M Building on Constitution Avenue. But his amusement faded when she became engrossed in the work of preparing the Army for its first women recruits.

"Damn it all, Page," her father would begin his nightly debriefing, "what do you *do,* anyway? You're spending entirely too much time down there—I won't even dignify that place as a headquarters—with those loonies who think the Army needs women soldiers. And don't remind me that they're there because of an act of Congress. Since when have those dumb civilian bastards on the Hill known how to run an army?"

Page had known he was missing the personal attention that had been his and the knowledge that she was in her place, at home, whenever he took a break in his twelve-hour staff-planning workday. In the ten years since her mother died, she had been the woman of the house, the one who smoothed out the wrinkles of his off-duty life.

"Anyway, what about Randy?" he'd say, playing on her big-sister conscience. "He'll be coming from the Point for his second-year leave, and his sister won't have the home fires burning for him."

"Dad, Randy doesn't need me to play housemother. I'd be in his way. Besides, Randy wrote that he thought the WAAC was an exciting new idea as long as I didn't turn into an amazon and beat him on the tennis court."

At that he had focused his commanding general's eye on her and stiffened to attention. "You wouldn't be thinking of *joining* this fool adventure, would you?"

"I don't know, Dad," she had answered, honestly at the time. She had never had the last word with him. He had always appealed to her sense of family duty, rolling over her ideas of independence with as much ease as he had rolled his tank over German trenches in the World War. "Would it surprise you," she had asked cautiously, "if I had inherited the same soldier genes from you that Randy did?"

He had laughed then, and it had hurt her more than his anger could have. "My dear little girl, surprise me, no, but horrify me—most emphatically, *yes*. I can't imagine a Hannaday woman in uniform any more than I can imagine a Hannaday man out of uniform." With the assurance of a lifetime of command, he had dismissed any further dialogue. "Jimmy's death is what all this WAAC business is about"—and then he had dismissed Jimmy—"but it's been six months since Pearl Harbor. Time to end mourning and get back into circulation."

Page looked around her at the other women as they passed into the ground floor of Company One barracks. Not exactly the kind of circulation her father had in mind, but then she knew she must stop thinking of her father, and especially of those last horrible days. He had all but disowned her, refusing to acknowledge her enlistment and, finally, not even seeing her off at Union Station. His last words to her were burned into her consciousness: "It's a man's duty to serve his country; it's a woman's duty to raise sons to serve. Only traitors deny their duty."

Bunny unrolled her mattress, let it fall on the bare wire of the gray metal bed, and sat down. Her feet were killing her, and she kicked off her sling-back platforms and rubbed first one instep, then the other. How had her feet ever passed the army physical?

So far the Army seemed to be a succession of lines to stand in: at the train depot, at the reception building, and now one was forming at the bathroom—latrine, as they were already beginning to call it. Across the aisle, Elisabeth and Jill began to unpack. Up and down the room that Sergeant Wolford had called a bay, she saw thirty-five other women of all sizes and ages survey their new home, place their belongings about them in the particular way that was each woman's signature, and wonder aloud how they'd fit everything into such a small space.

Next to her she saw Page placing her clothes neatly in the wall locker behind her bed, a look of exhilaration on her lovely face. Easy to tell that Page Hannaday had class. She seemed to have an air of surety that came only after long years of knowing and doing and wearing exactly the right thing until poise had become an unconscious part of her. Her thick chestnut hair fell to her shoulders, and her tawny skin, Bunny was willing to bet, looked tan even in midwinter. Both hair and skin framed intense wide-set green eyes. The woman had the clean long-limbed look that most people thought of as "all-American girl," but that was, Bunny knew, quite rare outside magazine covers.

Unpacking her traveling bag and cosmetic case, Bunny remembered the young lieutenant at the reception area. "I want the name you enlisted under," he'd said. She'd given him the name then, Barbara LaMonica Palermo; the first one she had been born with, and the second and third she kept to remind her that loving a man was either all-taking or all-giving.

She had grown up in a brick row house in Bloomfield, New Jersey, the oldest of four girls, and the only one to go to Sacred Heart College. Like a parent in most second-generation Italian families, her mother had hoped one daughter would find a vocation in the church, and she fixed on Bunny, her oldest, to fulfill this ambition.

But her mother had hardly laid her white confirmation dress away in mothballs when Bunny had changed almost overnight from a skinny carbon copy of every other little girl in the parish into a voluptuous, cocoa-eyed beauty. From that time on, every warm evening found boys draped over her porch rail, elbowing one another, faking jabs to the midsection and other excesses of hormonal zeal that they hoped would bring them to her notice, all under the unblinking eye of Mama Patra.

During Bunny's senior year at Sacred Heart College, the woman who, for years, had given her an after-school job at La Jeunesse Beauty Parlor decided to retire and offered to sell her the business. With her savings and a loan from her Uncle Sal, Bunny made a down payment and became the owner. It was 1936, she was about to marry Johnny LaMonica, and life was more exciting than she had ever dreamed it could be.

He was easy to fall in love with; in fact, it was probably inevitable. Their mothers were friends, and the youngsters had grown up in the same parish youth hall. They knew the same people, liked the same food and had the same memories. He had clear skin, a fine job selling Chryslers and had always been in her life. During their courtship, she thought she read in his eyes a thousand well-bred invitations to sex, and at twenty-one she was tremblingly overdue for physical love and dying to go to bed with him. She knew that happy marriages all around her had grown from worse beginnings.

But not this one. It did not take her long to realize that she was number two in his life. His mother had first call on his time and energy and, what was a greater disappointment, filled all his needs, except, of course, the sexual one, for which, she discovered on her honeymoon, he had a low appetite.

All this she could have forgiven him, as women before her had forgiven, but Johnny LaMonica had one overwhelming, teeth-grating trait that drove her wild. Having defined weekend sex as the only kind permissible to a hard-working Chrysler salesman, he answered every hesitant overture testily, "Not now, Bunny"—and this in an aggrieved tone— "you know we always read the Sunday funnies on Saturday night!"

In his own way, he had been thoughtful, pampering her, giving her whatever money could buy. But it became increasingly plain, and at the end unbearable, that she had nothing he wanted, nothing at all of her specialness that he would take. *Any* woman could have been his wife. Despite her mother's hysterics and innumerable sessions with the priest who had married them, she could not spend her life with a man who compromised her ability to love.

After the divorce she immersed herself in work, hiring and training her three sisters as they grew old enough, on the latest permanent-wave machines. By the summer of 1940 she owned three shops, and marriage was something she thought she'd left far behind her, until she took a short vacation in Atlantic City.

On her first night, she had been drawn from the boardwalk

into the Uptown Club by the sound of a drummer who got more out of a snare-drum riff than Gene Krupa.

Johnny Palermo was everything Johnny LaMonica had not been. Having no family ties, he moved restlessly from band to band. He drank too much, but he was intensely sensual. There was never any doubt in Bunny's mind that this Johnny wanted her body. She held him off until, during her last night on the boardwalk, he had flashed a tiny diamond ring at her.

"Baby, let's go to Elkton and get married," he whispered in her ear. "I guess I got it bad this time. I'll play your tune and sing your lyrics, if that's what it takes to get you into bed."

"Maryland?"

"They don't have a waiting period. I'm no good at waiting."

She hadn't trusted herself to speak; she was afraid she might tell him how close she had come to playing it his way. She was determined to make marriage work this time. Sure, she had her eyes open; Johnny was wild, but he was an antidote to the first Johnny. She would settle him down. She would give him the love that was missing from his life, that had made him run away from a brutal father at fifteen, that had made his life so mean and empty. For a single moment, she felt reason grapple with her reckless passion for him, the overwhelming physical urge to belong to him, to merge into him that gave him power over her life. But the moment passed and they spun on through the night toward Maryland.

Later in an auto-court cabin next to the office of the justice of the peace who married them, under a blinking sign that said "We Never Close," he undressed her and made love to her with the same virtuosity that had brought the patrons of the Uptown Club to their feet. He knew how to light little pyres of pleasure that sent heat racing through her until her skin glowed pink and hot. The relentless rhythm of his mouth devouring hers, of his hands evoking exquisite sensations from her taut body, and finally his body inside hers, released a crescendo of dammed-up passion. Breathless, helpless, she gave herself to each shuddering, rolling convulsion, all her senses melding into a cry of love that had been gathering in her throat for a lifetime, "Johnny!"

She had taken him home the next morning. "Mama," she pleaded, "try to understand."

But her mother had cried, wretched as only a mother who

dreams for a perfect daughter can cry. "I understand that you're living in sin, that's what I understand. My baby! My Barbara!"

"What can I do, Mama? You went with me to the monsignor for an annulment. You heard what he said: five years— maybe. Or never."

"He was a good man, your first Johnny. He worked hard. He didn't drink. He didn't chase other women. What more did you want?"

"He didn't want to be a *husband* to me, Mama."

"I don't want to hear that kinda talk. What kinda thing is that for a girl to tell her mama? All I know is that now you bring this strange Johnny home, and you can't take communion no more. How can I leave your confirmation picture up here on the mantel next to your sisters'?"

Bunny, hurt and frustrated, left her mother cradling the gold-framed picture to her breast, tears dropping on the green felt backing.

That night Johnny asked her for five hundred dollars. She gave it without question. She would have given him her soul if he'd had a use for it. It wasn't the last time he asked for money, and when, months later, she had no more to give and all three shops were mortgaged, he stole from the till and lied about it. By winter 1941, he was drinking heavily and disappearing for days. One cold Saturday evening in early December after she locked up at La Jeunesse, she found him parked outside in her car with a whore.

Walking through the snow to their apartment, she was numbed, not from cold, but from betrayal; stunned by the realization that all loving was a lie. One man had not wanted her love, another had taken it all and then deliberately tossed it away.

Bunny packed in a frenzy, fearful that Johnny would return to arouse her natural instinct of generous love, the part of her that needed to understand him no matter what he had done. But he had not returned.

She walked out without a backward look, then dropped her suitcase at the head of the stairs. Shouldn't she leave him a message? She went back inside the hollow room, lifted the lid on his Crosley and dropped a record on manual. It would play until he turned it off. Music was the only message Johnny could understand. As she made her way down the wooden stairs, heavy suitcase banging against the railing, Frank Sinatra's voice followed her out the door and into the winter night.

> *"All or nothing at all—*
> *Half a love never appealed to me.*
> *If your heart never could yield to me,*
> *Then I'd rather have nothing at all. . . ."*

She had always assumed that feelings were truth; now she found that they were lies, and she couldn't trust feelings anymore.

Her first months without him were full of little terrors. He followed her, telephoned her, gave her no time to retrain her senses to act independent of his touch or his pleasure. Even the divorce hadn't freed her of wanting him, of being afraid that one day, in a moment of remembered passion, she'd run to him. When the call came for women to join the WAAC, she made her youngest sister, Angela, manager of what was left of La Jeunesse, and enlisted. Like some men before her, Bunny saw the Army as a haven from the disappointment of love—her own personal French Foreign Legion.

And now here she was, in the middle of an Iowa heat wave, a thousand miles from home, surrounded by new faces and the challenge of being one of the first women soldiers in America. What surprised her, since the visible parts of her life had changed so drastically, was how little her desire for Johnny Palermo had faded—as if it fought even harder for existence in alien territory.

2

Once her Mommie made her bed,
Cleaned her clothes and buttered her bread,
And her favorite dress was red—
Oh me, oh my, that ain't G.I.
 —"The G.I. Song," *Lieutenant June Morhman*

" 'TAKE ALL YOU Want, But Eat All You Take,' " Jill Henry Hammersmith read aloud the sign posted just inside the mess-hall screen door. She had changed into a blue jersey dress and self-consciously tugged at the belt, glancing in Elisabeth's direction. "Sounds like my mother," she said, pursing her lips.

Page nodded, smiling. "The Army *is* your mother. It nurtures you with food and clothing, teaches you how to act properly in a military society, and chastises you if you misbehave."

"That's Mother, all right."

"Now I know where I've seen you before," Bunny said to Page, snapping her fingers. "*Life* magazine—at some swank Washington party with your father. That's it! He's a general or something."

Before Page could answer, the mess sergeant asked for their chits and pushed his hand-held counter four times. They picked up metal compartmented trays and joined a long line of women making choices from laden steam tables.

"Since your father's a general," Jill took up the conversation once they'd found seats together at a long trestle table away from the roar of the tall floor fans, "he must be so proud of you."

Page looked at Jill and her eyes clouded. "I hope that someday he will be."

"You mean he didn't want you to join up?"

16

Page bent forward. "No, but we Hannadays have always been regular army since the Revolution." The intensity of her own response surprised and embarrassed her. She smiled apologetically and added lightly, "I may have to arrange to fight in a separate war than my father—"

Bunny interrupted. "That explains what you're doing here, Page. But what about the rest of you?"

"You first, Bunny." Page looked up, interested.

"It's this way, kiddo. People used to stop me on the street in Bloomfield and ask me, 'How's your husband Johnny?' Then I'd have to ask, 'Which one?'" They all laughed at her—even Elisabeth Gardner, although Bunny could see that the laugh never quite reached her eyes. Good! She invited their laughter; it was exactly what she wanted. She had learned that a quip was the best way to divert questions that came dangerously close to her emotions. "Your turn, Jill—although I don't know how a mite like you passed the physical. Don't you have to be at least five foot tall and weigh a hundred pounds to join the WAAC?"

"I am five foot tall," Jill snapped.

"A hundred pounds?" Bunny teased, eying her small frame.

"Well, okay," Jill admitted reluctantly, "maybe not all the time. I spent the morning of my physical stuffing myself with bananas and Baby Ruth candy bars. I just *had* to get in. I'd already dropped out of vet school to enlist. You see, I just had to after Neil—he's my fiancé—joined up last January. And besides, this war is going to be the biggest thing that happens in my whole life. I couldn't stay at home and miss a chance to be part of it."

"Ah ha," Bunny said, "we have a gentlewoman adventurer, if a rather small one. When Adolf and Il Duce hear you're coming, they'll just beg us to let them surrender."

Page said, "I think Jill will give a good account of herself."

"Of course," Bunny said seriously, and placed the palm of her hand against her heart. "I swear, Jill—no kiddin' now—I didn't mean to get out of line. I've got a big mouth, that's all. Have I told you about the time that my first husband . . ."

But Jill wasn't really listening. She could see that Bunny was only joking, but still she disliked being teased about her size. She didn't mind not being beautiful in the usual sense. What she minded—hated, even—was always being too small and too young for her brains. Cute, everyone called her. Being cute *and* smart was a tremendous burden that weighed down her small frame and made her try all the harder to measure up to the tallest people she could find—like Page. And she could beat Page at this army game even if she didn't have a general for a father. Worried, Jill looked sidewise at Page listening to Bunny, embarrassed at her unworthy thoughts, and with Page so swell and friendly, not high hat at all.

Sometimes Jill knew she was too competitive, but she hadn't had much choice. Her determination to win had pushed her through high school by age sixteen, and had sustained her through college until she fought her way into veterinary school when everyone had been sure she wasn't strong enough to do large-animal work. It had helped her persuade Neil Martin to postpone marriage when he had been insistent. And now it had brought her to Iowa with the first contingent of women accepted by the Army.

Had it been only a month since the enlistment party—that fateful day? She had relived the scene so often, the smell, the heat, the hurt of those few devastating minutes. Suddenly she was there again in her mind, every detail sharply in focus.

"Please, Jill," her mother was saying, "come out of the shade so that I can get some Kodak pictures. I want to send one to your Aunt Celia in Charlottesville."

Complying reluctantly, Jill had fussed, "Hurry, Mother, I'm roasting!" She hated cameras. Her curly auburn hair frizzled in the heat or hung limp in winter, and her brown eyes—the only large thing about her—never seemed to show to advantage.

"Stand still, dear, and pat your hair down. After all, it's not every day a Henry girl enlists in the Army." Jill remembered how pleased she'd been that her mother seemed to accept her enlistment when just last year she had insisted veterinary medicine was no place for a lady. Her dad said it was the Henry patriotism overwhelming her mother's sense of ladylike propriety.

Poor Dad. An ordinary doughboy with a battlefield commission, he'd married a Virginia belle in 1918 and now found his life defined by her aristocratic ancestors. Well, she'd be damned if hers would be!

Out of the corner of her eye, Jill had seen Mrs. Martin rushing into the yard with Mr. Martin close behind. She was glad to see them, glad they had been invited to her party, since her mother thought of them as hired hands, not social equals. But wait—there was something strange about Mrs. Martin's walk. The top of her body was bent over as if it was more anxious to reach its destination than the bottom half. Her face was swollen and mottled red.

"Congratulations!" The word made no sense, coming as it did from between tightly clenched teeth.

"Well, ah—thank you, Mrs. Mar—"

"Now you've got—everything," the distraught woman interrupted, waving a yellow piece of paper in Jill's face. "He's wounded. My boy's wounded. Maybe bad. *Now* are you satisfied?"

"Neil—wounded—oh, God, *no!* Mrs. Martin—please believe me, I—"

"You got your way," Neil's mother sobbed, tears running into her mouth, blurring her words. "He didn't want to go—to disobey the Lord's Commandment," she said, appealing, with wild swings of her head, to the crowd of neighbors and friends standing in stunned silence. "It was her—" she turned back and pointed to Jill—"she talked him into it with her fine-sounding ideas, and now—now—the judgment of the Almighty . . ." She broke into a fresh spasm of sobs.

"Mother, Mother," Mr. Martin said, pulling her backward out of the yard with both arms, throwing apologetic looks toward the group in the courtyard. "Please don't mind her none," he pleaded. "She's just beside herself since the telegram came from the Navy Department."

Mrs. Martin strained to break out of her husband's arms. "Don't you tell me to be quiet. It *is*—it's all her fault, just as much as the Jap who pulled the trigger. As God will judge me on the final day, I'll bless no union 'twixt my boy and her. Never as long as I draw breath!"

For some minutes Jill stood scarcely breathing, listening to the sobs retreating through the warm June afternoon.

"Well!" Jill's mother expelled the word. "What can one expect from such common folk?" Pushing the guests toward the buffet laid out on the patio, she refused to comment further.

To May Henry Hammersmith every one of life's crises was a matter of a violated tenet of decorum. In her the sense of proper and improper, right and wrong, had descended direct from the old Virginia Henrys and reached its genealogical zenith. She had taught Jill a list of absolutes that were never to be questioned.

Most of these rules had to do with the requirements of being a Virginia lady, requirements so rigid that even Virginia ladies no longer adhered to them, let alone young California girls in the summer of 1942.

From her earliest remembrances, Jill had been caught between her desire to please her mother—no matter how impossible that seemed—and the fury engendered by her own emerging personality yearning to be itself. As adolescence faded into young womanhood, she dated Neil, an "Okie" boy whose parents worked for her parents and who drove a truck with the legend "Jesus Saves" painted on the sides. Then she decided to become a veterinarian—an occupation, her mother reminded her in subtle ways every day for months, that was not a fit one for a Henry woman.

Matching her mother will for will, she swore she would be the person *she* wanted to be. But Jill was wrong. She could not, as she matured, belie her own inheritance. The result was standards so high she could never quite live up to them. Until now, that is. Today, at Fort Des Moines, she knew she had become a pioneer, one of the first women in the Army, a woman whom others would follow. No one would ever be able to take that away from her. Here in the WAAC she would prove her worth not only to others, but finally to herself.

" . . . and that was the end of that marriage, so be warned, my children," Bunny was saying through the giggles around her. "I swear," she went on in mock bewilderment, "every word is God's truth."

"Attention to orders!" The words came from Sergeant Wolford, who was holding the mess-hall door open. Through it marched a tall officer dressed in riding boots and breeches, with a crop tucked under his arm. Jill thought he was the most magnificently handsome soldier she had ever seen.

"Candidates," he said, and the women fell silent, "my name

is Lieutenant Stratton, officer in charge of Second Platoon, Company One. I will also be responsible for Company One's training in military customs, leadership and close-order drill. But for today I am detailed to assist the reporters and newsreel people who want to interview you and take your pictures. I'm sure all of you realize how important it is to the Army that you cooperate—within reason. Now, I have a request here from the *Herald-American* for New York City girls and one from the *Los Angeles Times* for California girls to meet with the reporters in the Company Two dayroom. Questions?" The lieutenant looked balefully out over the crowded mess hall, and no one dared ask anything. He turned smartly, slapping his riding crop against his shiny boots, and left the mess hall.

"Dismissed!" yelled Wolford.

A voice across the mess hall called after the sergeant, who was already out the door, "Doesn't anybody want to talk to women from the rest of the country?"

An answering voice yelled, "There *is* no country between New York and Los Angeles," followed by applause and boos.

"Wow," Jill said, finishing her dessert. "Did you see him? What a swell-looking guy."

"You poor kid," Bunny said with mock seriousness, "less than one day in this women's army and already you're khaki-wacky and man-starved."

"Maybe some of us have not had your generous portion, Bunny."

"Ouch! Touché, kiddo."

"Aren't you ever serious, Bunny?" Jill asked.

"Never," Bunny laughed lightly, but Jill noticed a pensive tightness in her tone. For a moment Jill wondered what it could mean. Then, remembering what the lieutenant had said about the reporters, she started to suggest that she and Elisabeth meet them together, when the other woman jumped up.

"I don't want to talk to them," Elisabeth said and was pushing her way toward the rear door of the mess hall before Jill could answer.

How strange *she* should be shy, Jill thought. She sighed. If she had Elisabeth's height and looks—well, those haughty cheekbones and that tall, gorgeous figure that clothes looked positively molded to . . . Jill sighed again at the impossibility and walked toward the barracks with Page and Bunny.

"What got into our glamour puss?" Bunny asked.

Elisabeth Koszivak Gardner hurried into the three-story brick barracks building and sat down on a gray metal bed halfway down the first-floor bay. She had to admit that, stupidly perhaps, she had not foreseen the possibility that this army post in the middle of the Iowa nowhere would be swarming with press. But she had been in tight spots all her life and got out of them. She would get out of this one too.

Out of habit she opened her purse and snapped open her compact. She dusted her nose with the puff lightly, added a touch of lipstick and was satisfied. She had the look she had worked hard for over so many years—the soaring cheekbones, heightened by just the right application of darker powder, the narrow Anglo-Saxon nose that had cost her five hundred dollars, and lustrously blond upswept hair that she vowed not to cut even if General Marshall himself ordered it. The muscles around her lips were drawn into a tight look of self-protection, learned in childhood and deliberately perfected to heighten the dramatic tension in her face. Her blue eyes were remote, like shuttered windows. She liked her look because she alone had made it.

She had not always been Elisabeth. As Mareska Koszivak, she had run away from her home in the Pennsylvania coal country when she was fifteen after one of her father's drunken rages. He had whipped her savagely again, not because she had disobeyed him but because she was there and she was weak. But the beatings had not been the worst of it. From as early as she could remember, he had crept back to her room after the beating to fondle her, until, lost between hurtful bruises and hate-filled pleasure, she could no longer distinguish between them.

Later she was to learn from her psychology classes at City College that the loss of innocent trust was a far more serious loss to her ego than mere virginity. By then she had learned to live, and live very well, without either.

Elisabeth had discovered easily what impressed people. Scarcely fifteen, a runaway in Depression-ridden New York City, she had rid herself first of her nasal western-Pennsylvania twang. After working in ever more exclusive dress shops along Fifth Avenue, she had at last acquired the drawling vocal mannerisms of café society.

She knew she could be somebody if she tried. This ambition drove her to finish a high-school correspondence course and enroll in night college. Altogether she packaged her own makeshift finishing school. Leaving Mareska behind to become Elisabeth filled her life so completely that she never made friends, not with co-workers or with fellow students. Being alone was what she wanted; it was the way she knew she was meant to be.

From selling expensive clothes she advanced by the time she was nineteen to modeling them—not in the top fashion houses, but in the second echelon of fashion, the manufacturing houses. Here the boss worked out of his wallet, cheating one supplier to pay another. It was crazy and frenetic, but here Elisabeth learned the reality of her world: she was sent to steal designs and cheat department stores, and she proved adept at it. At Saks or Peck and Peck she would charge an elegant, expensive dress, which she then took back to Marco's Fashions. The dress would be taken apart and a pattern cut from it, and the resewn dress could be returned the next day for credit. At the next market week, a cheap version of the dress would be on its way to stores all over the country and Elisabeth would be fifty dollars richer.

Another kind of reality Elisabeth learned was that during the flurry of market week she was often the sweetener that softened the buyer's bill. All the short, fat out-of-town buyers in hundred-dollar suits were promised a date with a model—and they all wanted a tall, slender blonde to show off in front-row theater seats at a current Broadway hit. Her ambitions made her a willing partner, ready to entertain in public or in bed, and yet she managed to keep her essential self shrouded and aloof.

After two years of this life, a chance meeting changed her direction.

She had been loaned for a day to model lingerie, when she heard a heavily accented voice straight out of an old vaudeville bedroom farce. Phony or not the voice was talking about her. *"Incroyable!* Look—zee legs of a colt wiz zee face of a Titian madonna. Tell me, *ma chère,* have you ever thought of working for me?" The speaker was Madame Gabriella, a holy name in fashion, with her black hair pulled strictly back into a bun, those great heavy tortoiseshell glasses perched on her imperious nose, and the ever present pretty boy.

"I have thought of little else, madame," she lied. Truthfully, she had fancied herself as wearing Gabriella originals purchased for her by an adoring millionaire, but she was not blind to the opportunity Madame presented her.

She left that moment with Madame's entourage, without a word to Marco even though it was a few days before the fall market. She owed him nothing. He had used her and she had used him. They were even.

Men of consequence—with power and money—came into her life then. She made it a practice never to go out with a man who did not buy the gown she was modeling. It was her way of ensuring solvency, her very own Dun & Bradstreet rating system. It bothered her not at all that they usually bought the gowns for the women they were with or for some unseen woman. Her turn, she knew, would come. She was momentarily content with the world of long-stemmed roses, jewels from Cartier, Worth perfume and evenings at the Colony Club, Maxie's Bar or 21.

That is, she had been content until First Lieutenant Marne Pershing Gardner had walked into the salon, and into her life. He was simply the biggest man—a Viking of a man—she had ever seen. Redheaded, with sea-green eyes, he stood a head above even the tallest man in the room and weighed more than two hundred pounds. With all his bigness he had an agile figure, thin-hipped and long-legged, which was accented by the perfect cut of his Faber "pinks." Marne had been the model of military presence from his erect bearing to his 1940 West Point class ring, and he drew every female eye in the showroom. He reeked of "old money," and Elisabeth was on his scent from the first moment she saw him. He was the challenge she had unerringly groomed herself to meet.

Within weeks they were married. She had known he would ask and she had known she would say yes. He had what she wanted, and a lot of it—a respected Boston Brahmin name, money, powerful friends and a future. It did not matter that he planned to make the Army his career; she would change his mind about that quickly enough once the war was over. Like a drowning woman, she could foresee her life with Marne before her eyes: a stately home, social influence, her own lovely designer clothes—security, respect.

Never again would she smell the acrid odor of coal soot or be a prisoner of poverty and ugliness. It was odd that she had been able to tell him about her childhood, not the whole story—she knew too much about men to be sexually honest with him—but enough so that he knew her fears. From the first, she had intuited that her poor-but-honest-girl-from-the-wrong-part-of-town tale was the perfect way to manipulate his latent socialist tendencies. Most of the monied people she met had them, and she knew that raising her from poverty made Marne feel like a savior, and his money less a guilty burden. She had been right. And to the point, which made everything logical: he was very much in love with her.

After an afternoon City Hall ceremony, they drove up to Newport in his yellow Cord convertible for the four days' leave Marne had wangled before his transfer to the 2nd Armored Division in Texas, a transfer he had initiated. His decision made without telling her, when she had dreamed of Washington duty for him, with elegant dinner parties and dances for her, had pitched her on her wedding day into a rage which she had barely managed to hide.

"But why, Marne?" she had asked again that night in the huge Newport home lent for the occasion by friends of his family. She could not comprehend his answer that armor was going to win the war, or what that had to do with her.

"We're going to start fighting them back soon—the Nazis and the Japs," he said patiently, "and when we do, armor is going to be in the forefront of the fighting. Any first lieutenant is going to come out of this war a major or maybe even a lieutenant colonel. I don't want to spend fifteen years in a company grade the way some of the men did after the last war."

There was nothing she could do but play the loving wife and bide her time. But it was harder than she'd bargained.

Marne was an ardent but immensely ordinary lover. That she could have borne, after the succession of Broadway trophy hunters she'd been "nice" to. What she couldn't bear was his tenderness. He treated her like some fragile porcelain doll, gently stroking, exploring, exposing, without taking her to any heights she had not climbed a dozen times before with other men.

"You're so good for me," Marne said. "I want to be so good for you."

"You are darling—so good," she automatically repeated the familiar lie.

On the last night of their short honeymoon, he had talked about his father and how he had died in France at only twenty-four. "He was just my age, Elisabeth. They had only a few days before he left, but Mother told me all my life that Father had left her with me and that he would never be dead to her. I hate to ask you to quit your job with Gabriella, but I want you to think about going up to live with Mother while I'm gone. I know she'd love you to come."

She had been genuinely alarmed at his obvious purpose. She refused to consider the tiresome possibility of burying herself with an old lady, and having his baby in exchange for a moment of half-satisfied passion. How could she allow Marne's need for immortality to enslave her body? She had no intention of rocking away her youth, knitting booties for a tiny bit of protoplasm he had insisted on implanting in her womb. Fortunately she had taken precautions because he refused to use a condom.

During one climax he cried, his voice romantically prayerful, "Oh, God, I want to leave you with something of me!"

To herself she said a quite different prayer, *Thank God, these are my safe days.*

She was relieved when he left for Texas, but her relief was short-lived. A few nights later as she stepped from a cab onto the sidewalk, a black Cadillac limousine idled in front of her apartment building.

"Hey ya, Liz. Come 'ere."

"What do you want?" she said, recognizing Marco's brother, a two-bit mobster named Joe Bonine, at the car window.

"Get in. Let's go around the block."

She hesitated, then took a step back away from the curb.

"Get in!" There was no mistaking the menace in his voice.

"Well, well," he said when she was inside, "I hear you really come up in the fashion world, Liz—and I have to say it couldn'ta happened to a nicer broad."

"What's this all about, Joe?"

"Now, didn't they teach you no better manners midtown? Don't you remember how friendly you and me used to be?"

The bastard! What did he want? She didn't owe him anything.

"Okay. Okay. I can see you don't wanna talk, so here's the deal. We want you to do a little job for us just like the old days. We want a few little drawings—not even the patterns."

"That's crazy!" she said, suddenly colder than she had ever been. "Steal Gabriella's fall line? I can't do it, Joe. She's no twenty-five-dollar-a-week salesgirl. She'd know in an instant. No, you can't make me pull a dumb stunt like that."

She put her hand on the door—would he let her go? And then she caught sight of the photos in his lap and dropped her hand.

"Wanna see some pretty pictures, Liz?" his slimy voice oozed through her. "Or maybe youse'd rather I showed 'em to that new husband of yours or his high-class family up in Boston—Gardners, ain't they? Wonder how much these'd be worth to them."

She knew instinctively what was in the photos: documentation of every rotten thing she'd ever done to get where she was. They must have spied on her, taken pictures through peepholes—hell, sold tickets, for all she knew. Marco and Joe had just been waiting for her to have something to protect before they pounced. God, if Marne ever learned of their existence . . .

She had stolen the drawings then, and waited, resigned to being discovered, wondering if Madame would call the police, planning to threaten to spread a bit of nasty business about her latest boy who wore Gabriella's lingerie under his tight suits. The tension was almost unbearable, so the call from Madame's office had come almost as a relief.

Madame's face sagged when she saw her. "Eleesabet, in this business you can be forgiven a *petit* larceny, but no one in fashion wants a thief who stole a whole collection. You are *finie*. You will never work again as a model in this town. Be assured, I will see to it. Now go!"

At first she was relieved to escape so easily, but then she realized that every door in New York she had pushed open had closed behind her. She didn't know what to do, where to go. Under no circumstances could Marne find out the truth. She couldn't even tell him she was out of a job or he'd insist she go to his mother. Then she'd sit out the war in some Back Bay backwater, growing babies and growing old.

On the second morning after leaving Gabriella's salon, she was walking the Manhattan streets, trying to think of a way out of the trap she was caught in, when she saw a poster in a recruiting-office window: "RELEASE MEN TO FIGHT! SERVE IN THE WAAC," and underneath it the legend "New Faces, New Places, Excitement, Good Pay." A new start, *that's* what she needed. Then again, maybe she was a bit taken in by Marne's flag waving or she outsmarted herself in a scheme to get out of trouble and at the same time to impress him and bind him more tightly to her. When you don't love a man, she instinctively knew, you're always afraid of losing him. Whatever jumble of desperate reasons she had, they all came together in front of that poster.

At the last minute before boarding the train for Fort Des Moines, she wrote to him. By that time, Elisabeth had been sworn in and there was nothing either of them could have done to change things.

"There you are, Elisabeth," Jill called merrily as she and Page and Bunny came into the barracks. "You didn't miss anything much with those reporters. They just wanted to know what our first impressions of army life were. I told them I thought the Army always ate beans, but we'd had a swell lunch, except for the bologna—and, oh yes, I said the women I'd met so far were great. The reporters kept asking if we'd been issued olive-drab underwear. They made a big thing out of whether the Army was going to supply girdles or not. Pretty goofy stuff."

"I'm sorry I ran out that way," Elisabeth said when Jill sat down on the bed next to hers. "You see, my husband's with the Second Armored Division training in Texas right now, and there are no reporters down there asking him how he feels about it. I just didn't want any special treatment."

Elisabeth saw that Jill had admiration in her eyes, and for a moment she half believed her own nobility. A tiny part of her wanted to believe. . . .

ARMY'S MOST UNUSUAL ROOKIES ARE "PROCESSED" INTO WAACs

On Monday, the dreary treatment known to the Army as "processing" began. The recruits were tagged, inoculated, inspected, measured, and given their uniforms. They drew the strangest assortment of equipment that a supply sergeant ever saw. Each issue included: three brassieres, two girdles . . .

—Newsweek, *July 27, 1942*

HUP, TUP, TH-RIP, four! Company One, First WAAC Officer Candidate Training Regiment, marched toward the quartermaster clothing-supply building to a cadence that only two days earlier had been unintelligible to most of them. Page thrilled to hear the concert of footsteps, the rhythmic, light march step of women stretching to meet a regulation thirty-inch army stride.

The first full day in the Army had been like a summer camp and sorority hell week lumped together. They had been given follow-up physicals, dental checks, the first round of shots—Page felt the aching soreness of both arms as she swung them—and been taught how to make an army bed with hospital corners, white collars and sheets stretched so tight, according to Sergeant Wolford, they should hum the "Colonel Bogey March." The women were barely dismissed from one formation when the call "Fall In!" echoed down the barracks, and the sound of running feet with an accompanying chorus of groans and gripes began to mark them as real soldiers. Page knew it was a good sign. She had heard her father say it often enough, "If they don't gripe, they aren't regular army."

For their first thirty-six hours in the WAAC they had retained the vestiges of their civilian identities. They were still newspaperwomen, teachers, lawyers, artists, housewives, secretaries, wearing frilly dresses and open-toed pumps. Page knew that in the next few hours all that would change. Putting on the WAAC uniform would begin the process of turning them into the first women soldiers the country had ever seen.

Page was so busy sorting her first feelings about the Corps that she didn't hear the order to halt and stumbled into the woman at the head of her squad. "Pardon me," she said automatically.

"Quiet in ranks," ordered Sergeant Wolford, glaring at her. "This ain't no ladies' tea party, *this is the Army*. You women wanted to be soldiers, and soldiers you're gonna be."

Page felt her face burn red with indignation and bit her lip.

"Don't mind him," Bunny said moments later after they broke ranks. "The old boy hasn't got used to an army without horses yet. Now here we women come, and it's just too much for him."

In a way Page felt sorry for men like Wolford and her father. It must be dreadful to be unchanged in a changed world.

Jill agreed with Bunny, dabbing with her handkerchief at the perspiration on her face. "I heard that all the cadre are being paid extra to train us."

"Hazardous duty pay?" Elisabeth asked sarcastically.

"In a way you're right, Elisabeth," Page said, voicing a feeling that had been strong in her since she arrived at the fort. "We Waacs are like combat for Sergeant Wolford. He's forced to change his whole idea of what a soldier is—even his idea of himself. I've thought a lot about this," she told the others, "and it may sound odd, but, look, men have been putting on armor and going out to meet dragons for thousands of years. Before they'll accept us, we women will have to slay a few dragons of our own."

"A pretty metaphor," Elisabeth said. "But we enlisted to release a man to fight, not to do the fighting."

"She's right," Jill said. "What do you mean?"

"Oh, I don't know," Page answered. "It's just a feeling. For now, maybe we just have to outsoldier men where we can—be more spit-and-polish, march better, respond to orders more promptly."

Bunny squealed. "You mean I have to use more starch than the sarge? But he positively crackles!"

A solid-looking young woman called Kansas joined them. "Hey, I don't mind the starch, it's this reveille business. How can I get my eight-hour beauty sleep between eleven P.M. and five A.M.?"

A woman in her thirties named Smitty—Page recognized her from the third floor of their barracks—spoke up next. "We'll have to learn to do what my students used to do—sleep in class."

Sergeant Wolford came out of the QM building. "Form a single line," he yelled, "and keep it moving."

The line began to inch slowly up the wooden steps, and they entered the building one by one. A row of men stood behind the counter handing out uniform parts and checking a form that followed each candidate down the line. A barracks bag came first, to hold what followed.

"Six pair panties, brown," sang out the second supply clerk.

Bunny whispered behind Page, "Ahh—the elusive WAAC lingerie. It's a good thing they closed the fort to the press for the next two weeks, or they'd be sneaking pictures through the barracks windows."

"You said it," said Kansas testily from behind Bunny. "I was beginning to feel like a freak. First they stared at me in my hometown when I enlisted, then they pointed me out on the train, and when I got here some guy was always shoving a camera in my face."

"Quiet there! Four shirtwaists, tan," the next clerk said, shoving them toward Page as she walked along.

"One blouse, cotton twill." A belted jacket plopped into the bulging bag.

"Move to the next area for your fittings," ordered the supply sergeant at the end of the counter.

Page saw Elisabeth and Jill already standing on boxes being measured by a swarm of fitters from Younkers department store in Des Moines.

"Can't you move this fourth button higher to give a better line to the jacket?" Elisabeth asked.

"We are only authorized to fit the uniform as it is to the figure, miss," one fitter answered.

Elisabeth's face was set. "Can't you see that this fourth button will pull the jacket as I sit, giving it a pouched look across the stomach? I'll look pregnant!" Since this was a fate she had gone to some trouble to avoid, she thought the point worth pressing.

"We're not allowed to alter the design."

"Who made this idiotic design?"

"I believe it was the Quartermaster Corps in Philadelphia. *We* certainly had nothing to do with it," the fitter answered in a huff of injured professionalism. "Please don't move while I pin your skirt."

"Imagine," Elisabeth said as she and Page sat down to be measured for their shoes, "that hick seamstress tried to tell *me* how to do a fitting."

"You obviously know clothes," Page said. "Were you in sales or a model?"

"A model," Elisabeth answered without pursuing the conversation. She'd said too much already.

How odd she was, Page thought. Sophisticated, cold, and yet she had patriotically joined the WAAC to help her soldier husband. Elisabeth was a contradiction. Her worldliness, even her polished accent, was something she seemed to wear like a borrowed gown; it did not hang comfortably about her like garments she had worn all her life.

"Lights out," Wolford called through the barracks door that night, setting off a scramble for one last visit to the latrine or a final sentence on the first letters home.

Page, with freshly pressed uniforms hanging in her wall locker, and her foot locker neatly arranged at the foot of her bed, sat cross-legged on top of her blankets, feeling that outer transformation from civilian to soldier was complete. The first clear notes of Taps drifted through windows open to catch a night breeze—the sweet, sad melody that signaled the death of an army day.

"Did you hear that?" Bunny whispered across the six feet that separated their cots, after the last note had faded.

"Yes, I heard it," Page said softly. "I've heard it thousands of times, but tonight it's different. Tonight, it's for me."

"I've been watching you; you're really in love with all of this, aren't you?"

Page didn't answer. She didn't know what to say. She was as patriotic as the next woman, but love . . .

"Page," Jill called drowsily across the aisle.

"Yes, Jill."

"The dragon you were talking about before—you know, the one we Waacs have to fight. Do you think we'll be able to do it—slay the dragon, I mean?"

"I'm sure of it, Jill. Now get some sleep."

Page heard Jill say something to Elisabeth and Elisabeth answer, "Yes, I'm all right, but I can't sleep because those damned shots are throbbing."

Page rolled over and pushed the brown blankets stenciled with the U.S. Army logo to the bottom of her cot. Something had happened between the four of them in the past two days. Pure chance had placed them in the last truck from the train station, in the same barracks and squad, but something more than that had made them care about one another. It was as if each of them knew that the time ahead would try them as no challenge ever had, and that they would need to be friends, a circle, a band of sisters.

Page kicked off the top sheet. It was so humid. She and Bunny and Elisabeth, being Easterners, were used to it, but not the California girls. Poor little Jill was white from near heat exhaustion.

In the cot on the other side of Jill, Elisabeth stared into the dark, slowly rubbing the fevered, swollen lumps in her arms where the needles had penetrated. She had to admit that she had made a horrendous mistake joining the WAAC. She didn't belong here, not like Page and Jill. Even Bunny seemed to adapt to this women's army better then she did. She shifted the thin pillow under her neck. Why had she panicked? Certainly she was clever enough to think of a dozen logical reasons to tell Marne why she had left Madame Gabriella's, and an equal number why she couldn't possibly move to Boston just yet, although, of course, she was dying to. But joining the Army? She must have been temporarily insane. Damn! Damn! She beat her fist silently against the mattress. Whatever the reason, she had been right about one thing: she had to get away from New York City—fast. When the time came, she'd know how to get out of the WAAC too. She turned to a cooler spot on the sheets and fell asleep.

4

HEADLINE NEWS:
HITLER ORDERS STALINGRAD ATTACK.

This Is the Army *opens July 27, 1942, on Broadway with an all-soldier cast and a new Irving Berlin song, "I Left My Heart at the Stage Door Canteen."*

The individual sugar ration is set at eight ounces per week.

"You've met Director Hobby. What's she like?" Bunny asked Page as they filed into the Fort Des Moines theater on the fourth morning of training.

"Very determined, a great organizer, but always a Southern lady. You'll see," Page whispered, since Colonel Faith, the post commandant, had mounted the stage to introduce Oveta Culp Hobby, the Director of the WAAC.

"She'd have to be Scarlett O'Hara to take my mind off my hot, tired feet," Bunny said. She saw a small, pretty woman with upswept graying pompadour step to the podium. Her uniform and bearing were impeccably military although she had had no training. All the candidates in the room knew she had begged to be allowed to go through with this first OC group but had been turned down by General Marshall. They had glimpsed her looking on longingly as they practiced close-order drill and double-timed between classes. But orders from a four-star general took precedence over desire. As director she wore a colonel's golden eagles on her shoulder, and it was against army policy to train bird colonels with lowly officer candidates.

A riffle of excitement swept along rows of assembled women as the Director's voice reached them. "You are the first women to serve," she began. "Never forget it. . . ,"

Bunny felt Elisabeth stiffen in the seat beside her and heard her mutter, "The hell—I'll forget it first chance I get."

A woman in the row ahead turned and glared at her.

The Director's soft Texas accent reached to the far end of the now hushed auditorium. "You have just made the change from peacetime pursuits to wartime tasks—from the individualism of civilian life to the anonymity of mass military life. You have given up comfortable homes, highly paid positions, leisure. You have taken off silk and put on khaki. And all for essentially the same reason—you have a debt and a date. A debt to democracy, a date with destiny."

No one breathed in the stillness of the theater while those sentences echoed and reechoed. Bunny saw that even Elisabeth was paying attention to words no other women had ever heard.

"You do not come into a corps," the Director went on, "that has an established tradition. You must make your own. But in making your own, you do have one tradition—the integrity of all the brave American women of all time who have loved their country. You, as you gather here, are living history."

Suddenly, Bunny realized that for the past few minutes she'd forgotten her sore feet and the heat. The Director's determined voice reached inside her and touched a love of country she had not known was there.

"From now on you are soldiers, defending a free way of life. You are no longer individuals. You wear the uniform of the Army of the United States. Respect that uniform. Respect all that it stands for. Then the world will respect all that the Corps stands for."

Page felt a thrill of belonging that she had never experienced before. She looked around the room and saw other women, their faces filled with new pride and sense of mission. They shared in that moment what no other American women had ever shared. They were comrades. Now, she knew, that word belonged to women too.

Filing out, Jill whispered with tears in her eyes, "I was getting a little homesick. I wasn't sure I'd done the right thing by signing up. Now I'm sure."

As they formed up outside the theater, Sergeant Wolford yelled with his rising inflection, "Comp'ny One! Dress right, *dress!* Straighten those lines, people, this is no conga dance."

Bunny heard a new snap to their execution of his commands. Even Elisabeth seemed to drop her model's glide and step off the cadence smartly.

Officer Candidate Hannaday. Page, keeping the correct distance from the women in front of her, turned this new appellation over in her mind. She had been daughter, friend, sorority sister, fiancée and now she was Candidate Hannaday. All those other selves now seemed like ghosts. As they marched to their next class, Director Hobby's words echoed in her ears: "You have a date with destiny."

The next morning Company One was issued gas masks and marched to its first chemical-warfare training class. By the time they broke formation and scrambled into the bleachers, Page was clammy with apprehension.

"What's wrong, Page?" Bunny asked as they took their seats for the lecture. "You seen a spook—or an old boyfriend?"

"No, it's nothing, really—I mean, yes, there is something. Do you think we'll have to put on these masks?"

"Not only put them on, but yesterday Company Two had to walk in there"—Bunny pointed to a small windowless cinderblock bunker—"and take them off in front of an open canister of tear gas."

Page's worst imaginings had been confirmed. Her palms perspired, and the humid air blowing across the open field crept along her neck, leaving behind prickly sensations of damp fear. It wasn't that she was just afraid of suffocating under the mask. Mostly, she was afraid of being afraid, of going out of control and making a fool of herself. No one else could possibly understand how she felt when her face was covered. She didn't understand it herself. Maybe such an unreasonable fear had as harmless a beginning as a childish pillow fight that had got out of hand, or maybe she'd become entangled with her baby blankets in her crib. Whatever it had been, for years now she had awakened shrieking if bed covers had slipped over her face. She'd taken elaborate precautions, pinning blankets low on the mattress ... But a gas mask, covering, smothering—there was no way out. She tried to slow her breathing, but she was already giddy from gulping air.

A Chemical Corps sergeant, standing on the first bleacher seat below the seated Waacs, held up a gas mask and identified its parts, pointing out the breathing hose attached to purifiers that filtered out small particles of dust, smoke or harmful gases. "The mask must fit tightly over your head and face," he said, "or you could breathe poison fumes. Don't think you'll be safe because you women won't be in the trenches. Modern gases can reach you by bomber or long-range artillery."

Next he demonstrated the proper way to don the gas mask. "Now I want each of you candidates to put on your masks and check the straps of the woman on your left and right to see that they are tight. We'll spend about fifteen minutes practicing before you get your first exposure to real gas." He looked at his watch. "Begin!"

There was a flurry of activity all around her, and soon Page heard the mask-muffled voices of the other candidates. She saw Bunny, looking like a Buck Rogers character, motion for her to put on her own mask, but her hands were frozen at her side.

"Candidate!"

The instructor was calling her.

"Yes, Sergeant."

"Why isn't your mask on?"

"I—I want to put it on, but ... there's a problem."

"What's the problem?"

"I can't breathe with it on."

"What do you mean? All these women are breathing. You've got five minutes to put it on and prepare for gas drill. What's your name?"

"Hannaday, Sergeant."

"Well, Candidate Hannaday, this drill is a must. Either you accomplish it or you're a washout. I'm giving you a direct order to *put on your gas mask.*"

"Page!" Jill's blurred voice came through to her. "Do it—for God's sake ..."

Bunny shook Page's arm, eyes wide behind the eyepieces. "We're all in this together. Come on, don't let us down."

Page picked up the floppy rubber-and-fabric mask and watched it as it closed in upon her face. Her hands seemed to be responding to something beyond her fear, while the rest of her body tried to shrink away and become invisible. Suddenly, the bitter smell of rubber was in her nose and the sharp taste of it in her mouth, yet she managed to pull the webbing tight on either side. Swallowing compulsively, she pushed down the rising waves of panic and forced herself to breathe slowly so she wouldn't faint. Now her hands dug into the wooden bleacher where she sat. She could feel her fingernails snap off to the quick, but she held on tight to keep from ripping off the mask.

Satisfied, the sergeant nodded at her. "Form a single line behind me," he ordered Company One.

They climbed down the rows of seats and marched in a single line toward the cinder-block building. An officer put on his gas mask, opened the door and stepped into the billowing white smoke, shutting the door behind him.

The sergeant spoke, his words terrifying to Page, who experienced an almost continuous sensation of pitching forward. "One by one you will enter the building. I want you to walk to the officer at the table, take a big breath, remove your mask and give him your name, rank and serial number. Have you got that?" The women nodded, their air hoses wobbling up and down. "Got that, Hannaday?"

Page nodded, the movement increasing her lightheadedness. She felt Jill's hand steadying her from behind.

"One more thing, Candidates," the sergeant said. "Leave by the door on the other side of the building and *don't* breathe till you're outside. Go!" He opened the door and tapped the first woman on the shoulder.

The line half-stepped forward. First one woman, then the next disappeared inside until it was Bunny's turn. Page saw Bunny give her a cocky thumbs-up before stepping into the tear gas. Then it was Page's turn.

Jill squeezed her arm. "We're with you." The words came to Page as a far-off whisper.

Page was no longer thinking of escape as her fear told her she must. She was acting automatically now, acting out some ancient military instinct, the same instinct that had made the Light Brigade charge at Balaklava, the Texans remain in a doomed Alamo, the army nurses stick it out on Corregidor. It wasn't just bravery and patriotism. It was an intense feeling that grew with every test they faced together: the knowledge that, as soldiers, they could count on one another. They had to. There was no one else.

Page felt the sergeant's hand push her shoulder hard, and she stumbled inside the bunker. The tear gas was so thick she could scarcely make out the outline of the officer who motioned her forward. He was seated at a small table, his gas mask on. Page knew there was no chance now for a reprieve. She had to come through or admit to her friends, herself and her father that she was unfit to be a woman soldier. Her father . . . She could hear his voice—half amused, half angry. "Damned if it doesn't sound like you had your date with destiny, Page—and stood him up!"

The officer rose from behind the table and pointed to her gas mask.

Taking a breath so deep it hurt her lungs, Page ripped off her mask. "Hannaday, Page, Candidate L205720."

The acrid fumes swirled like a hot fog about her face, creeping into her throat and nostrils, burning, stinging like hundreds of insect bites. Her tear ducts opened, and water cascaded down her cheeks. She flailed at the noxious cloud until she found the door and threw herself near-blind outside, gasping, choking, sucking at the pure air.

Bunny, tears streaming down her own face, grabbed her by the arm and led her away from the blockhouse, from which tear gas escaped every time the door opened. A few feet distant, they stopped, chests heaving, and waited until both Jill and Elisabeth ran out.

Elisabeth looked as wretched as Page felt. "Are they going to let us go back to the barracks and bathe?" she asked. "I don't think I can stand to walk around smelling like Chemistry 201 all day. Ugh! My mouth tastes like rotten eggs."

Jill, wiping her eyes, looked closely at Page. "Are you all right?"

Taking a lovely, deep breath, Page said, "Yes, Jill, I'm fine."

"Well, you sure had me going. I was so scared you were going to goof up."

"Sorry. I won't ever frighten you like that again."

* * *

That night the foursome nursed Cokes in the PX, too tired to talk or even take off their floppy fatigue hats.

"You ought to have seen them," they overheard a GI at the next table saying. "Like a bunch of pigeons in gas masks, flapping around and giggling." By the time he had finished they knew he was talking about them, and loudly enough so they'd be sure to hear.

Jill, her lower lip thrust out, her cheeks hot with resentment, spoke up for all of them. "It must be great being a jeep jockey all day. Nothing to do but drive the major's wife to the grocery store."

Page shushed her. "Just ignore them."

"I won't," Jill said stubbornly. "If there's one thing I know, it's about bullies like that. You let them think you're scared and they never let up."

Page's shoulder and neck muscles ached from tensed nerves. She didn't think she could stand another scene.

The GI got up and swept Jill an exaggerated bow. "Begging my *lady's* pardon," he said, smirking at his friends.

"That's enough, Burt," one of them, a corporal, said.

Burt looked almost ready to challenge him, but sneered and swaggered away.

"I'm sorry," their rescuer said. "He's a show-off."

Page answered for the still-angry Jill, "That's all right. Forget it."

"Can we buy you another Coke—just to apologize?"

When they put it that way, it seemed ungracious to refuse them. "Okay, guys," Bunny said.

Returning with the drinks, the corporal turned his chair to face them, as did the two privates he was with. "We're in finance, not jeeps," he said, smiling at Jill. "Payroll division. You'll like us a lot better next month when you get to salute the paymaster for the first time."

But Jill was only slightly mollified. "Tell me," she asked him, "why don't you guys like us Waacs?"

He seemed astonished more than embarrassed. "That's not true. Oh, maybe some of the sergeants—the cadre—are pushed out of joint, but we lower ranks don't dislike you. It's—" he frowned, searching for the right words—"it's just that we don't understand how you can replace us."

"Replace you—what do you mean?" Elisabeth asked.

"Well—by the way, my name's Jerry and this is Ben and Leonard—I mean the posters and the slogan. You know— there's a WAAC recruiting poster at headquarters building that shows a buck sergeant with a typewriter chained to his back. It says, 'Replace a Man for Combat.' I'll tell you, some of us don't want our sisters and our girlfriends to put on a uniform so we can get sent overseas."

Bunny grinned. "Well, fellas, *I* won't take the typewriter off your back—not even if you give it to me."

Ben and Leonard laughed, and even Jerry joined in.

Bless Bunny, Page thought. Always a quip in time.

Soon all seven chairs were crowded around the Waacs' table and they were trading training stories as soldiers do.

"Did you really have to go through the gas bunker today?" Jerry asked.

"That's not Chanel Number Five wafting over the table." Elisabeth sniffed the air.

"I didn't know they'd make you girls do that," Ben said.

Leonard, the shy one, spoke up. "Have you had your supply class yet?"

"Not yet," Page said.

Jerry laughed and slapped the table. "Boy, are you in for it if you get old Baker, the top S-three noncom. He's a bear on requisition forms."

Page watched them. We just need to get to know each other, she thought. We have so much in common; it's just the little things that divide us.

5

U.S. marines land on Guadalcanal and Tulagi in the Solomon Islands, the opening round of the fight to roll back the Japanese offensive.

OFFICER CANDIDATE JILL Henry Hammersmith hid in a latrine stall after lights out, her stationery folio on her lap. She chewed on the top of her pen, then wrote:

> *7 August, 1942*
> *WAAC Training Center*
> *Fort Des Moines, Iowa*

DEAREST, DARLING NEIL,

Tomorrow is our first big command inspection. It's so important that 2nd Platoon do well. I'd just die if I got a gig, but I had my friend Page go over my area and she said even her father (who's a general) would find it strictly GI.

We get our first overnight pass after inspection and we're all heading for a hotel in Des Moines. I'm planning to spend the entire thirty-six hours in a tub.

Do everything the doctors tell you to do, and please write. I understand that you may not be up to it yet, but ask the Red Cross volunteers to write for you. I do need to know how you are.

I know you weren't feeling well when I came to Oak Knoll hospital, but you must believe that I still want to marry you after this war is over. I know you still love me, and you'll see—we can make it work.

* * *

She signed the letter, thought about adding a P.S., rejected several, then fished in the folds of the folio for a three-cent stamp.

"I thought I'd find you in here, Candidate Hammersmith," Bunny said, peeking over the stall door.

"What! Is there no time a girl can call her own?"

"Rules are rules, as you're always reminding me. Come on, Mother Bunny will tuck you in bed."

"*Mother* Bunny?" Jill giggled. "You're not like any mother I've ever seen."

"No arguments, kiddo. You work harder than any of us, so hit the sack."

"Quiet in the latrine," yelled an irritated voice. "*Some* of us need our sleep."

Both women put their forefingers to their lips and grinned.

"That's the dean," Bunny whispered. "She still thinks we're freshmen in her dormitory."

Jill made a face, but tiptoed quietly through the darkened barracks. During the past weeks she had learned what a swell gal Bunny was. Sure, she was a kidder, but there was no malice in her. Just the opposite. When their muscles ached after hours of drill and physical-training jumping jacks, and their heads throbbed from classes on morning reports and supply requisitions, she made them laugh in spite of themselves —even when her own poor feet were in the sorest shape of all.

Jill climbed into bed, careful not to step on her shined shoes, their toes aligned in perfect flank formation. All her clothes in the wall locker were on hangers exactly one inch apart, buttons buttoned, all turned one way. At the foot of her bed, her foot locker held rows of neatly rolled bras, hose and panties. She was strictly GI. If only her college roommates could see her now, they wouldn't believe how neat she was.

What would Neil say if *he* could see her? Would he be proud of her or . . . How could she know *what* he was feeling after that horrible day in the hospital?

In late June he had been flown from Hawaii to Oak Knoll in San Francisco. When she visited him on her way to Des Moines—she'd worn that damned red peplum dress because it was his favorite—well, she'd hoped with all her heart that he would understand why she had enlisted, partly for him, partly for herself. But he hadn't seemed to understand anything.

Jill had waited an hour outside the office of the chief of nurses before she was admitted.

"I'm sorry," the woman in white had said from behind her desk, "I'm deluged with family requests—who was it you wished to see?"

"Seaman First Neil G. Martin, in Ward Ten."

"Ward Ten? Are you his wife—sister?"

"His fiancée."

The nurse consulted a folder and then looked up at Jill, her voice compassionate. "I don't see your name on the visitors' list. Did Seaman Martin write and ask you to come?"

"Not exactly—no, but, you see, I've joined the WAAC and I'm on my way to the Midwest for training. It might be months before I can get back. He *needs* to see me. I know he does. There is something that I must explain."

"Miss, er—" the chief of nurses looked down at the appointment slip Jill had handed her—"Hammersmith, you should know that Ward Ten is reserved for our most serious cases. You are not prepared for what you will see—and I can't take the chance that you'll make things worse for this sailor."

"I won't—I promise I won't. I can take whatever there is to take. You must understand—if I don't see him today he might think . . . I . . . I don't know what."

The woman was obviously sympathetic to Jill's request. "The regs say no—but wait here and I'll check with the doctor. It may take a few minutes."

As soon as the office door closed behind the nurse, Jill knew what the doctor's answer would be. What could she do? If she didn't see Neil today . . . It was then that she saw the pad of signed passes on the desk. Recklessly, she tore off the top one and quickly left the room.

Neil's lanky body looked incredibly young huddled under a blanket in the wheelchair at the opposite end of Ward 10. Walking toward him, Jill thought that he had not aged in combat as men were supposed to do, but gone backward in time. It was a small-size boy's face he turned toward her—a half-face drawn tight and shriveled by a cockpit fire as his torpedo plane dived into the sea at Midway—a little blank-faced boy with unfathomably sad, lashless eyes.

Suddenly, she was fighting to keep her own eyes steady, to reject the rising nausea as she came closer and saw that he had no mouth where it once had been. She had never realized how important a mouth was. It's not the eyes that are a beacon for the face, she thought, it's a mouth that gives a face life and humanity.

When she was midway down the ward, he saw her and violently thrust out both bandaged hands to fend her off, as if she were a new fire coming to threaten him. "Nurse! *Nurse!*" The words were all throat sounds, like shattered gargles.

"Neil, it's me, JILL. Don't—please don't turn away. I love you." She was faint at the sight of him like this, but she stepped forward, her hand, palm up, held out to him. He screamed and kept on screaming, clawing with his hands against the wheels of his wheelchair, trying to make them roll backward away from her, until red splotches began to spread on the white gauze wrappings. Never in all her life had she felt so helpless, so frozen in uselessness. Oh, God—why hadn't she listened? From far off, she saw the chief of nurses, followed by a ward nurse, run toward her and felt them take her roughly by an arm. "You have to leave *now,* miss," Jill heard them shouting.

Dazed, Jill allowed herself to be propelled rapidly back down the aisle between the rows of white beds where limbless men lay, their eyes full of intolerance at this intrusion into their despair. Later, as she stood outside Oak Knoll looking up at the windows of Ward 10, she thought she saw Neil watching. Taking a deep, determined breath, she waved and smiled so he would know that nothing had changed, that everything was going to be all right.

A slight Iowa breeze stirred the limp air in Company One's barracks as, sleepless, Jill slipped out of bed and padded across the bay to Bunny's area. She whispered, "Bunny—you awake?"

"Uh-huh."

Jill sat down quietly on Bunny's foot locker. "I was writing to Neil—you know, my fiancé."

"Yes."

"I—I keep writing, but he doesn't answer."

"He was badly wounded, wasn't he?"

"Yes, but it's more than that. He hasn't said so, but I think he blames me." Jill waited, but Bunny was silent. "You see, he didn't want to go. Oh, he's not a coward or anything, but he was going to register as a conscientious objector. It's his religion, but—well, I told him I'd be ashamed of him, and our children would be, too. Bunny, I forced him, and now he . . . he's terribly scarred—his face . . . "

"Kid, you're not to blame for this war." Bunny's voice came softly to her in the dark. "Everything that happens is not your fault. Jill, you've got to learn to trust yourself, to forgive yourself for what you can't change, or the world will eat you up."

Back on her cot, Jill wondered about what Bunny had said. Maybe it was true, maybe she had never learned how to be a friend to herself. And because she didn't know how, every human mistake she made caused a nagging whisper to rise inside her that said, "You see, you can't do anything right."

"Second 'toon!" Wolford yelled. "Attention to roll call. Adams."

"Present."

"Fair."

"Present."

"Gardner."

"Present."

His voice droned on past Hammersmith, Hannaday and Strayhorn to Thorpe, and then with an about-face he turned to give the all-present-and-accounted-for response to the inspection party. "Parade *rest!*" Sergeant Wolford projected his voice down the long line of the Company One formation in front of their barracks.

Each woman immediately moved her right foot one step to the right and snapped her arms behind her, hands clasped. Jill was very careful to keep her eyes focused in front, since she knew that this order did not mean she could stand easy. Please, God, don't let them find anything wrong with my work detail, she prayed as the inspecting party passed into the barracks, and knew that all the other women were sending up the same silent plea.

She was sure that her toilet bowls were spotless, all six of them. She had asked Page to check them for her and had stood over them until the last minute to make sure no one used them. Then she had double-checked Page's mop-rack detail for her. The mops were hung on their hooks at attention, bleached white, with the strings cut to uniform length.

What time was it? She strained her eyes to see Elisabeth's watch in the front rank, but couldn't. It must be at least ten o'clock, and she had been on her feet since the reveille cannon went off at 0530. Even though the inspection party had been late arriving, there was no way she could have sat down without putting a crease in her heavy chino skirt.

"I feel like a wooden soldier," Bunny had said. "Can't even bend my arms."

Jill knew Bunny was not really complaining. None of them was. It was just that everyone—the press, Congress, but most of all the Army—was watching the first women soldiers. She only hoped she could stay off the gig sheet, so that Lieutenant Stratton and the others would believe she was mature enough to be an army officer. All her life there had been someone telling her she was too small for this or too young for that. This was her chance to prove them wrong.

"Comp—ny. *Attention!*" Captain Burchette, their CO and an old-time line officer, took the all-present-and-accounted-for report, executed an about-face and gave the same report to Colonel Faith.

This is it, Jill thought, our first training-center commandant's inspection, and she crossed her fingers quickly for luck.

"Open ranks, harch!" ordered Lieutenant Stratton, and the inspection party started down the front rank, the commandant first, then the CO and Stratton, followed by Sergeant Wolford with a little black notebook. She could see them coming along the first rank, Colonel Faith making a left-angle turn in front of each OC. She could see him talking to each in turn, probably asking them their general orders or which poison gas smelled like apple blossoms. Her knees felt wobbly, and she realized she couldn't remember anything she had learned. Not one damn thing!

Straining to hear as the commandant turned into her rank, she heard him ask Page, "Who is the WAAC training-center commandant?"

"Colonel Faith, sir."

And then he was in front of Bunny, next to her.

47

"Who is the WAAC training-center commandant?" he said.

"Colonel Faith, sir," Bunny answered.

Jill stiffened into rigid attention: knees straight, hips tucked under, chest out, arms straight—but not stiff—feet at a forty-five degree angle.

He made a left-face—in front of her now. The rest of the inspection party, sun glinting off their brass, trailed behind. "And what," he said to Jill, "is your name?"

"Colonel Faith, sir," Jill said in her deepest voice before she could stop herself. "I mean it's Jill—er, I mean, Candidate Hammersmith, J., sir!" She was fairly shouting in his face by the time she got it out. He nodded and moved on. She wished with the fervency of all her twenty-one years that she could simply shrivel up and disappear.

"Jill—it's not the end of the world," Page argued.

Jill refused to be comforted. "Didn't you see them? They were laughing at me."

"No they weren't." Bunny said, "They could see how hard you were trying. All except for Stratton. He's so anxious to get out of here, he'd love to see the WAAC fail."

"Come on," Page said, "they're posting the gig sheet."

Jill's face fell even farther. "Oh, I know I'll get a personal gig."

They joined the first-floor squads crowding around the bulletin board. A woman from first platoon let out a wail. "No! It can't be. I remember tying all my shoelaces. I distinctly remember . . . "

Jill saw her name with a lovely round zero next to it. "I can't believe it. No gigs!"

"Damn!" Elisabeth said aloud. After all her hard work, there was one gig next to her name on the detail roster, with the explanation "Laundry tubs with cleaning powder residue." "Damn!" she repeated. "What do they want? Those tubs are to wash clothes in, not to do brain surgery."

"Don't worry, Elisabeth," Page said, eying the commendation for her mop rack, "there were only two gigs in the barracks. That's one short of being restricted to post. We'll all get our passes."

"I don't know about the rest of you," Elisabeth said, anger

distorting her usually controlled voice, "but I had no plans to remain in this hellhole another weekend if we'd got a hundred gigs."

"You don't mean you'd have gone AWOL," Jill said, disbelief written on her face.

But Elisabeth, already on her way back to her area, didn't answer.

"Candidate Hammersmith." Jill saw Sergeant Wolford standing by the screened front door. "Report to Lieutenant Stratton in the orderly room."

She felt her knees weaken. "Oh God, Bunny," she said, turning to the older woman, "I knew it! Oh God—they wouldn't wash me out for a dumb mistake, would they?"

"Of course not, kiddo," Bunny said and gave Jill's arm a reassuring pat. "Maybe ten lashes with the cat-o'-nine-tails in the PX at high noon."

Jill, her teeth biting into her lower lip, relaxed somewhat. "Damn it—be serious?"

"I am, Jill. The best thing you could do for yourself is to let up. You're wound so tight you're going to pop a spring. Now go see what Lieutenant Riding Crop wants so that we can catch the noon trolley to the big city of Des Moines."

"Wait for me," Jill called back just before the screen slammed behind her.

Later, on the trolley crowded with Waacs on their first overnight pass, Jill recalled the kindness in Lieutenant Stratton's voice. "He's not as bad as he seems," she told her three friends.

"But what did he want?" Page asked.

"He just told me not to worry. Asked me why I enlisted, how I liked the WAAC so far—personal questions like that."

Elisabeth stared at the track ahead, a slight smile playing about her lips. Bunny looked at Page, one eyebrow raised.

"I saw that," Jill spoke rapidly. "Have you forgotten I'm engaged? Besides, he's not like that." She was surprised at her own vehemence.

"I'm sure he's not, Jill," Page said, "but be careful. You know they can wash out an OC who fraternizes with an officer."

Bunny rolled her eyes. "And if he's her own *platoon officer* they stand her against the wall and call the firing squad!"

6

WAAC days, WAAC days,
Dear old break-your-back-days . . .
  —Barracks ditty sung to the tune of "School Days"

"*FALL OUT* IN five minutes!" Sergeant Wolford's command voice filled the barracks. "Dress for the afternoon is Class-A uniform and raincoats."

Bunny slammed her fist against the foot locker she was sitting on. "Damned if I'm going to ruin a starched uniform under that rubber steam bath they call a raincoat, then have to wash and iron all night." She quickly stripped to her bra and OD panties and slipped into the heavy rubber coat.

Page laughed in spite of herself. "Bunny, you can't do that."

"Watch me! I've found the perfect way to stay cool and get out of all that laundry."

The platoon snapped to under Sergeant Wolford's baleful eye. "Straighten up those ranks."

In the midst of their minute shuffling to the right and front, and without warning, the rain that had been falling steadily for an hour suddenly stopped, and the sun came out bright and hot. Stratocirrus clouds of steam swirled about the platoon.

"*Take off raincoats!*" Wolford boomed.

Bunny felt every eye on her and heard some hastily swallowed snickers. Damn!

"Palermo, would you like to join the rest of us?"

"No, Sergeant. I don't think I'd better."

Wolford was apoplectic. "I've had just about enough of your—"

"Sergeant, I'm out of uniform—I mean *really* out."

The suppressed snickers erupted now from every rank.

Wolford's face was red. "Platoon, '*ten-hut!* Candidate, you've got three minutes to get into Class A."

Bunny raced to the barracks, threw on her uniform and ran as fast as her sore feet allowed back to the formation. Damn! How was she to know the rain would stop at that very minute?

"Candidate Palermo, you'll walk extra fire patrol for two hours a day in full Class A for the rest of the week. '*Toon!* Double time—*harch!*"

Sergeant Wolford's command brought an involuntary groan from half of Second Platoon.

"You're at attention in ranks," his voice grated over them. "The next time you don't like an order, the whole platoon can spend Sunday afternoon policing the post. Is that all right with you, Hammersmith, if that's still your name?"

Page ground her teeth. The sarge was in a foul mood today. He had pounced on Bunny—but she had pulled a dumb stunt. Still, picking on Jill by reminding her of that silly mistake she'd made during command inspection was just plain mean.

Wolford sang out the fast pace, "Hut-hut-hut-hut."

Page settled into the cadence, legs and arms pumping. She knew she had stretched her body beyond any physical endurance level she had ever needed before. How much more could she expect of herself? This morning Second Platoon had completed an hour of close-order drill, an hour of physical training which had left their seersucker PT dresses and fatigue hats limp with perspiration. Jumping jacks, toe touches, knee bends. Now they were being double-timed to class and were expected to be mentally sharp for the next three hours.

Didn't the sarge ever wear out? He seemed to have a body like an iron rod, always straight, always strong.

"Pick 'em up, Palermo," Wolford ordered.

Out of the corner of her eye, Page saw Bunny skip to get back into step, her face distorted from the pain of pounding her badly swollen feet against the hard-packed earth.

Another brief afternoon shower drenched them as they reached the classroom area, and made everything worse. Humidity. Uniforms. Tempers.

"Got a cigarette, Hannaday?" Henrietta Hawks, a woman from First Platoon, asked, irritation creeping into her tone.

"Sure, Hank." Page extended the pack. "Keep it. It's too hot to inhale."

"When I think I could be sitting in Seattle right now trying to keep warm ... "

Page nodded. The heat was everybody's favorite gripe; even mess-hall food ran a poor second.

She heard a man clearing his throat around the corner of the classroom building. "My God, Sergeant, these women are making better grades in Company Administration than West Point cadets!"

It was Lieutenant Stratton's voice.

"Lieutenant," Wolford's unmistakable voice spoke next, "women just naturally take to paperwork, but that don't mean they should be officers, same as men. Come right down to it, sir, they won't cut it in your Principles of Leadership class."

Page leaned exhausted against the side of the building. She didn't mean to eavesdrop, but she was too tired to move out of range—and now too angry at what she'd overheard.

"I don't know," the lieutenant was saying good-naturedly. Page had the feeling that he enjoyed the sergeant's ill humor and egged him on.

"Lieutenant," Wolford said irritably, "do you want to spend the rest of the war nursemaiding a bunch of women playing soldiers? It's just like when we was kids and our sisters was always pestering to play our games—only this time we can't keep them out." Page saw Wolford's hand squash a cigarette in the butt can attached to the corner of the building.

"I understand what you're saying, Sergeant, but some of them are kinda cute—that little one from California especially ... "

" 'scuse me, sir." Wolford blew his whistle. "Break's over," he yelled.

Page watched the Waacs field-strip their cigarettes, grind the tobacco into the dirt with their heels and roll the paper into tiny white balls which they tucked into the corners of their shirt pockets. She was curious to hear what the lieutenant would have said about Jill, although Jill ignored any warnings against the handsome officer. Wolford was another matter. She had thought that by excellent work the Waacs would win him over. Instead, the better they marched on the drill field, the higher grades they made in their classes, the sharper their skirt creases, the more he resented them. She wanted to shout at him, We don't want to take anything away from you—we want to add a new dimension to army life. Instead, she wearily took her place in line and marched in to her squad seat next to Jill, Bunny and Elisabeth at one of the front tables.

The windows were open, but not a whisper of fresh air stirred through them. She looked at her friends, all of them hot and tired. She realized that the physical and mental stress of the past three weeks had been the most exhausting period of their lives and that the next three weeks of OC would be even worse. They were cramming three months of training into half that time—up before dawn, working until late at night. The WAAC was on trial, she knew, and Director Hobby needed trained women soldiers to show to the world—and soon. The only thing that made it bearable was the feeling that every woman in Company One and the rest of the OC companies was in the same boat with her.

This military experience with other women was different from any other, she thought, different from boarding school and college, different from civilian friendships. During training the polite barriers of ordinary friendship tumbled and each woman quickly got to know the others' most intimate secrets. It happened to everyone, even Elisabeth. Her cool, aloof manner had not changed much, but since she had shared the same marching, calisthenics and tear-gas drills she had become, not popular in the platoon, but less unpopular than she might have been.

Bunny, with her self-deprecation and the nurturing she disguised as wisecracks, was easily the most popular woman in the barracks.

And Jill? It was just heartbreaking to see how she pushed herself, always demanding so much. She had the rigid determination of the youthful idealist who tried to make wishes become facts through the sheer force of desire. She did not have the self-confidence yet to appear even a little confused. Page hoped with all her heart that Jill would never fall; she might not be able to get up again.

Page looked around the crowded room at the familiar faces of her barrack mates, and outside another WAAC Company passed, their guidon preceding them. All of these women were meeting physical stress—some for the first time in their lives. Girls in America weren't raised to accept sore muscles, fevers from tetanus shots, sprains and bruises, too little sleep, all without quitting. And yet these women were doing just that, and some were doing it while wondering if their men—at Guadalcanal or on the North Atlantic—were still alive. *Oh God, she was proud to be one of them.*

And what about her own evaluation? Everyone assumed for her a worldly competence she knew she did not possess, just because she was an army brat. Nothing substituted for experience, and General Hannaday's little girl had never lived on her own away from her father's plan for her life—to marry a military man and settle into being a professional officer's wife. She had heard so many of the other OCs worry about losing their independence in the women's army, of having to suppress the qualities that gave them their special identity. She almost laughed when she listened to them. These last few weeks had given her the only unobstructed view she had ever had of what Page Hannaday was really like.

She felt like an eyewitness at her own baptism. And she was pleased—thrilled, even—with what she saw. She had learned that she could accept army discipline, that she could march another hour longer than her body told her she could, that she could have a claustrophobic attack and leave her gas mask on anyway—out of loyalty to comrades, but partly because she gloried in following orders, especially difficult ones. All the superficial things had gone: silly prejudices, the need for personal luxuries—all had melted away, and she discovered that they had really meant nothing to her, less than nothing.

Page recognized the meaning of this new idea of herself. She ought to; she'd heard her father lecture dinner parties, cronies and his son often enough. A soldier's personal pride, he'd called it. He'd never included her in his philosophizing. Women weren't supposed to understand. Would she ever be able to tell him that she understood—no, that *she* had what he admired?

A nudge on her arm erased her father's image and brought her back to the converted barrack classroom. "Wake up, Page," Bunny murmured beside her, rubbing her sore feet under the table.

Page whispered back, "Thanks—but I'm awake." The classrooms were so hot they took turns keeping each other awake.

Stratton droned on, reading an army manual, which Page had practically memorized the night before. Her mind wandered, and her father returned unbidden to her thoughts. What would he say if he could see his pretty green-eyed daughter with perspiration dripping off the end of her chin, her uniform sodden? She knew better than to wish it. He would not like what he saw. He wasn't opposed to hard work, but he wouldn't understand the self-control she was beginning to exert on her life—a control quite as strong as his own. What a paradox, she thought. Here, in this women's army, she was seemingly totally controlled—marched from one place to another—and yet had more self-control than she had ever had. She had lost her privacy in this mob of women, but she was now more intimately alone with herself than she had ever been in her father's house with a bedroom of her own.

"Candidate Hannaday!"

Page jumped to her feet, realizing by the lieutenant's tone that she must have been called on before but hadn't heard. "Sir!"

Stratton was striding up and down the front of the classroom as he talked, but the riding crop was no longer part of his outfit. "Tell us, Candidate Hannaday, what do you think the first duty of a WAAC officer is?"

"To get the job done, sir," she said, standing to attention. "To see that the army mission assigned to her and her enlisted women is carried out as swiftly and completely as possible."

Stratton smiled faintly. "You can stand easy, Candidate; this isn't a ladies' West Point." He looked around the room, and his eyes circled back and rested on Jill, although he spoke to Page. "That sounds like a good book answer, Hannaday, but how does the WAAC officer accomplish this swift, complete mission?"

"Sir, through good leadership. It's easy to give orders, but I don't believe women can be driven, they have to be led. I would treat enlisted Waacs like adult women instead of children, women I expected to do their best. I think people quite often give back just what is expected of them."

She was surprised at the confidence in her own voice. But she hadn't meant to sound like a know-it-all either. She hadn't known what she believed until he asked her. How much more knowing, she wondered, was there in her that had not been prodded to the surface?

Stratton, his face intent, did not move on to question another candidate. "Tell me, Candidate Hannaday," he said, facing her, "what would you do if you were to find that one of your women disobeyed your orders, but you could not determine which one was guilty?"

"Sir, I would use every means to discover the identity of that individual. Wrongdoing that is not punished is bad for everyone's morale." *Bless you, Father, for teaching me that,* she thought, gazing steadily at him.

A gravelly cough from the rear of the room reminded her that Sergeant Wolford was an interested onlooker.

"But suppose," Lieutenant Stratton persisted, "that you investigate without success. Would you then punish the entire platoon to get to the guilty one?"

"No, sir, I would not." This time she answered from her own feeling. Her father had often punished whole companies—once a battalion—knowing that the outraged soldiers would take care of the guilty man in their own way. Some instinct told her this would work badly with women. "I think women rebel at unjust treatment. As a woman, I respond better to positive leadership."

"Is that right?" the lieutenant answered with a hint of a teacher's sarcasm at being instructed by a student in front of the class. "And just how would you accomplish this miracle of feminine leadership?"

She could see she had offended him. "Sir, I'm here to learn. Perhaps I've—"

"No, no, Candidate, please go on and enlighten me—indeed, all of us."

Page knew there was no retreat possible. She hadn't wanted to seem like the new girl who wants to change everything, but the lieutenant was not going to let her back down.

"For example, sir," she plunged ahead, "I've noticed that when you needle men they become more competitive, but with women—well, the same treatment can frighten them into giving up. I see women responding to firm leadership with lots of praise and encouragement." From the impatient look on Lieutenant Stratton's face, she knew she was going on too long, but it was as if an idea in the pupal stage had suddenly spread wings, carrying her along with it. "A leader of women must be a *caring* officer—and show it. That doesn't mean she can't be tough, yes, when the mission demands it, and tough on herself too. But along with toughness a WAAC officer must show compassion and understanding to her troops. I think she must also keep a light touch—humor would help; women tend to see humor as caring not weakness."

An hour later, Page was lying on her bed, her heart thumping wearily in her chest. She was sure her outspokenness had marked her a show-off in Lieutenant Stratton's eyes. God alone knew what Sergeant Wolford thought. She had probably confirmed every one of his Waac-hating views.

"Bravo, Page," Bunny said, raising herself on one elbow, her feet elevated on her pillow. "I think you gave our little tin soldier a lesson in leadership today."

"I didn't mean to do that."

Bunny shrugged. "At this point, Page, I think your idea of WAAC leadership is just as good as his. Somebody better tell the lad that women and men are different." Bunny laughed, her voice just loud enough to tease Jill, who was bent over her foot locker, cleaning her lapel insignia. "And I know who that someone could be."

"Say what you want," Jill said, looking at them from under her lashes, "I think he's really very nice." She and Lieutenant Stratton had bumped into each other near the Iowa Hotel last Saturday night, and had met later in an obscure little bar for a drink. She remembered every moment of it, every word he'd said, but most of all she remembered when he had casually covered her small hand with his long fingers. Something had happened then, something physical, warm and wonderful, a feeling she had pulled back from because she knew instinctively that it threatened her plan to devote her life to Neil after the war. Jill felt the remembered warmth return.

"Why, Jill," Bunny said, "you're blushing."

After lights out, Page remembered the look on Jill's face. Surely the girl wasn't falling in love with Stratton. But she'd seen the signs, the unmistakable flush when Jill looked at him, the look of longing instantly suppressed that one woman can read in another woman's face. She met Jill's eyes for a moment, then looked away. The sudden tensing of Jill's cheek muscle made Page feel like an eavesdropper spying on a painful private hurt. How hellish to feel responsible for the crippled shell of one man while falling in love with another—this one quite definitely a whole man.

At least Page had been spared that awful conflict, and then she felt ashamed of the thought. Her feeling for Jimmy Southworth had been more like a passionate friendship than love. When he asked her to marry him at the Annapolis June Week dance, she had said yes without thinking about it too deeply. This was her life, playing itself out as she had always known it must. Her healthy young body responded to his that night. She had halfheartedly tried to twist out of his arms when he took her back to the hotel, but he stepped into her room, held her and kissed her hard, not pulling away until near dawn.

They had announced their engagement and chosen their silver and china patterns. After a month's leave, he had gone off to Pearl Harbor as the newest ensign on the battleship *Arizona.* Then she entered a new and equally predictable phase, months of planning for a June 1942 wedding—the great rite of passage of every woman's life.

When she learned of his death a week after the attack, learned that he would spend eternity sealed inside the hull of the capsized *Arizona,* she had cried for him. She had cried for James Ridgely Southworth III, remembering him, long-legged, suntanned, missing easy tennis forehands because he watched her at courtside instead of the ball. She remembered he loved her in blue; she remembered and cried for the end of a young life.

But she had not cried for Page. In her deepest self, as far inside as she had penetrated in twenty-three years, she knew she felt no deep loss. That inner Page was intact, untouched. Only then had she faced the feeling of relief; she fought it down— but it came back again and again. Something deep inside her hoped that her obligation to fill a role ordained for her at birth had been fulfilled with Jimmy's death. She had done what she had been raised to do, what every young woman of her generation was expected to do. And now why couldn't she be free, free to use her life as she wanted? No answer came to her, so the question remained a question.

7

DIEPPE RAID: On August 19, 1942, some 6,100 British and Canadian commandos with thirty tanks stage a trial invasion of France, but are pinned down on the beaches; 1,179 die, 2,190 are taken prisoner by the Germans.

THE FOLLOWING SATURDAY, after inspection, Elisabeth stood at the registration desk in the Iowa Hotel, oblivious to the stares of the other Waacs and the male officers crowding the counter, hoping to get a room.

"Good afternoon, Mrs. Gardner," the desk clerk said with exaggerated politeness, handing over her key. "Your room is ready as usual," he added.

"I hope not, since last weekend the room had not been properly cleaned."

"My apologies, Mrs. Gardner," the clerk said, half bowing and muttering something about all the good help quitting to go into war work. "Today I checked your room myself, and if there is any little thing you need—day or night, mind—please don't hesitate to call on me."

"Thank you," she said, ignoring his oily eagerness.

"Oh, Mrs. Gardner, don't forget your messages," he said, stretching over the counter.

She felt his fingertips under the pieces of paper lightly brush across her breast. He was one of those sly, sleazy men who touched women's bodies under the guise of accident. A more naïve woman, seeing his friendly manner, would have felt guilty about her suspicions, but Elisabeth knew such men for what they were, and used their weakness for her own benefit. She smiled slightly. Better to let the clerk win a little and hope to win more. It did her no harm, since she had long ago learned to separate her feelings from her body, and it did wonders for prompt room service.

In her room, she removed her uniform and slipped into a light silk kimono she had purchased locally and kept in the closet, just for the few weekend hours when she could escape from Fort Des Moines. She picked up the phone, ordered ice and took a precious bottle of scotch from her night-table drawer. When the ice arrived, she poured herself a double.

Fluffing the pillows, she propped herself on the bed and took a large, thirsty swallow from the glass, glancing briefly at her messages. All three were calls from Marne in Texas, as she had known they would be. She tossed them on the bed covers. The thought that now consumed her was an idea that had been growing since her first days at Fort Des Moines. Somehow she must find a way to get back to the life she had earned, back to comfort, beautiful clothes and freedom where she belonged, and she had a wild plan that just might get her—well, halfway back. At least it was worth a try.

The phone rang, and she reached for it.

"Hello," she said.

"Hold the li-on," intoned the operator. "That will be one dollar and fifteen cents for the first three minutes, Lieutenant."

Elisabeth heard the deep bong of the quarters, the clunk of a nickel and the ping-ping of a dime.

"Elisabeth, are you there?"

"Oh, darling, how *wonderful* to hear your voice," she said. "I've been waiting here wishing you'd call again." She did not think of it as lying. She merely gave men what she knew they wanted.

"I can see you now, sweetheart," Marne said, his voice the musky tenor of some big men, "and thinking of you drives me crazy. Just a minute," he said, noise and music temporarily overwhelming his voice. "Pipe down, you guys," he yelled.

"Marne, I can't hear you very well."

"Sorry, honey, just a few of the guys—but how are you? I called your orderly room, and the charge of quarters gave me this number. Said you were signed out for the weekend on a pass."

"I've taken a hotel room in Des Moines. I know it's horribly expensive—"

"Darling, I've set up a trust fund with my lawyers. You'll be getting a check every month—but only if you promise to buy yourself pretty things."

"I'm so glad you don't mind. I had to get away from all those women, Marne. There's no privacy, no quiet—everything's so public."

"I know the Army, darling," he said, and she heard him take a deep breath. "I still can't understand why you quit Madame Gabriella's and joined the WAAC. Mother is sick over it. She wrote me that she's heartbroken you didn't come to her."

Elisabeth sighed and expertly punctuated the next sentence with a tremor. "Please don't be angry with me," she said. "I know it was a terrible mistake, but I—I so much wanted you to be proud of me. It sounds silly now, but I thought if I was in the WAAC I would be closer to you."

"It doesn't sound silly, sweetheart. It's exactly what a wonderful woman like you would think."

Elisabeth held the telephone tightly. "Please, please, darling, can't you help me get out of here?"

"How, Elisabeth? How could I do that?"

Then she laid out the plan that had taken shape in her mind. "Marne, your family has connections in Washington," she began in a rush, afraid he would interrupt, "I know you wouldn't ask favors for yourself. But ask for *me*—not to get me out of the Army, I know you can't do that, but to get me somewhere I can do what I was meant to do." She began to sob, and this time the tears were full of real frustration.

His voice faded in a storm of crackling noises as the operator came back on the line. "Your three minutes are up. Please signal when through."

"Don't cry, darling. What do you want me to do?"

"Marne, I'm going to write to the Quartermaster Corps in Washington and outline what I think is wrong with the WAAC uniform and what I could do to help make it right if I was transferred to the QM department. My letter might get lost at headquarters unless someone saw that it got into the right hands."

"I've got to go, darling." His voice was clear again.

"Will you do it, Marne?"

"I'll try. Please stop crying, Elisabeth."

"Darling," she said, "I think of you every minute."

More atmospheric disturbances, and his voice faded in and out. " . . . hellish field training . . . love you . . . "

Elisabeth replaced the telephone on its cradle, rolled over and immediately fell asleep.

She was aroused by a knock at her door. "Who's there?"

Jill's voice answered, "Second Squad, Second Platoon, Company One, First WAAC Officer Candidate Training Regiment."

Elisabeth unlocked the door, and Jill, Page and Bunny crowded in.

"Wow," Jill said, looking around curiously, "a bathroom all to yourself. How do you rate? I have to share one with these two," she added, plopping onto the bed. "Do you know that I had to bribe Bunny with my last Baby Ruth to get her out of our tub?"

"And mighty good it was, too," Bunny grinned. "There are three wonders of the modern world—bathtubs and chocolate."

Page laughed. "That's only two wonders, Bunny."

"Is it?" Bunny said, looking puzzled. "Sounds good enough for three."

"You know, Elisabeth," Page said, smiling, "if you listen to her long enough, she begins to make sense."

Elisabeth offered them a scotch and water, and stepped into the bathroom to wash the glasses. She felt strange—lost—in the midst of their camaraderie. She had lived two separate lives, the first in the dark shadow of her father's needs, the second in a scramble through the lower layers of New York's fashion world. She had never had the kind of confidences she could share with other women without risking their disgust.

"We're going to have dinner and a drink at Babe's," Page told Elisabeth, "and maybe take in a movie."

"Noel Coward's *In Which We Serve* is playing at the Rivoli," Bunny said.

Elisabeth started to say no.

"Or if you want to forget the war," Page said, "*The Road to Morocco* is at the theater across the street, and it's Bank Night too. Come on—go with us if you have no plans."

"Come on," Jill said, bouncing on the bed, "we'll stick together."

Elisabeth hesitated by the bathroom door. "It would take me time to get ready . . . "

"We'll wait," Bunny said with an engaging smile, "at least as long as your scotch holds out."

Suddenly Elisabeth wanted very much to go with them.

With the exception of a few bemused civilians, both floors of Babe's restaurant had almost been taken over by contingents of Waacs on weekend pass.

Genuinely puzzled, Elisabeth asked Page, "Why do they come here? These are the same women they see every weary day—don't they want to get away?"

"I've wondered, too," Page answered slowly, frowning a bit in an effort to make her words mean what she wanted them to mean. "I think it's because we all share the same purpose in life. It's a special feeling—more than family, even—but it's a separateness too, a knowing that no one but another Waac can possibly understand what we understand. We're in another world that outsiders can never be a part of. Male soldiers share this intense comradeship, especially in combat, and now I think we women share it."

"See, Elisabeth," Bunny said, "you ask Page a question about the WAAC and you get a whole damned parade."

Elisabeth laughed aloud. She leaned against the back of the wooden booth and watched the three of them talking, and realized they had drawn a circle of friendship that included her.

8

When I hear that Serenade in Blue,
I'm somewhere in another world alone with you,
Sharing all the joys we used to know
Many moons ago.
Once again your face comes back to me,
Just like the theme of some forgotten melody
In the album of my memory,
Serenade in Blue.
It seems like only yesterday,
A small café, a crowded floor,
And as we dance the night away,
I hear you say "Forever more";
And then the song became a sigh, forevermore became
    goodbye,
But you remained in my heart.
So tell me, darling, is there still a spark,
Or only lonely ashes of the flame we knew;
Should I go on whistling in the dark?
Serenade in Blue.
—"Serenade in Blue," Harry Warren and Mack Gordon

DESMOND STRATTON WAITED impatiently across the street
from the Iowa Hotel. It was nearly eleven o'clock at night and
Jill had not yet shown up. Each time a group of uniformed
women approached the door, he looked for a small figure incongruously clothed in belted khaki. He was not exactly sure
why he was waiting for this particular Waac, there were

dozens of women around, but each time he thought he would not wait any longer he extended the time for another five minutes.

At last he saw her preceded by her three friends. They were the real lookers in second platoon. If he was going to get into trouble with an OC, why not one of them—Gardner was married, but the other two? Oh, to hell with it, Stratton, he chided himself, you were never good at picking the right woman.

Jill saw him as soon as he saw her. "Wait for me," she told her friends, and crossed the street. She saluted, and he returned her salute.

"If you were wearing civvies," he said, "I'd risk taking you for a nightcap."

"I have a dress up in the room." The words were out of her mouth before she could stop them.

"You game?" he asked.

She nodded yes, a kind of stubborn wildness seizing her. Because she was always proving herself, she was particularly vulnerable to dares. "Wait around the corner," she told him.

Up in the room Page and Bunny watched her change into civilian clothes.

"Jill," Page began, "if you want to go out with him, just wait until you graduate."

"Listen, kid," Bunny agreed, "you know officer country is off limits."

But Jill closed her ears to what she didn't want to hear. When she was down on the street again, out of sight of the Iowa Hotel, he took her arm and walked her down a side alley to a dimly lit bar decorated in South Sea murals and fake palms.

Finding a small table against the wall, he asked her, "What'll you have?"

"I had some good scotch earlier," she answered, as if it were her usual drink, when in fact it had been her first taste of scotch.

"I'll try," he said, "but we may have to settle for blended whiskey. There's a war on, you know, and all the good stuff goes to our boys in uniform—and girls."

Her large dark eyes smiled up at him from under thick lashes, and she pursed her lips self-consciously over a faint overbite into one of the most kissable mouths he had ever seen. Nice going, chum, he thought, she likes you. Now what?

She watched him walk toward the bar, his tall, slim figure trim in summer tropical worsted. He had a boy's narrow hips, but a man's broad shoulders. She could see that other women's eyes followed him approvingly. Why had he asked her for a drink, when he could have asked Bunny, Page or even Elisabeth? She was puzzled by his attention, and maybe—she was reluctant to admit it—a little frightened.

"Here you are," he said, putting her drink on a cocktail napkin just as the pianist at the other end of the bar began to play and sing "Serenade in Blue." "I wangled some scotch from under the bar."

"I'm engaged to be married, Lieutenant Stratton," she announced, unable to completely understand why she was making such an uncalled-for statement, but making it nonetheless.

He was startled for a moment, then threw back his head and laughed. She was absolutely without guile. That must be why he was attracted to her. She was not at all like his ex-wife, Lois—knowing, cold, grasping and, almost incidentally after that, unfaithful.

Jabbing the air with his swizzle stick, he launched into his autobiography. "I'm divorced, no children, twenty-nine years old, my parents are dead, I have a degree in electrical engineering, I was a reserve officer called up last March, and, oh yes, I like clam chowder—the red, not the white—Humphrey Bogart movies and women, in reverse order."

Jill was embarrassed at first by her sudden outburst, but by the time he had finished she was angry that he was making fun of her. She might have left him laughing there had he not put out a hand to stop her.

"Truce, Jill," he said, serious now, "let's just enjoy a drink together. You needn't worry that I'll carry you off, or try to marry you." He took his hand away and lit a Camel, inhaling deeply, his mouth twisting sardonically. "In fact, Jill, if you *don't* want romance, I'm the safest guy in this room—hell, in the whole Army."

His words, meant to reassure, disappointed her—more than that, made her feel a strange kind of emptiness as if something struggling for life had aborted.

"I wish you happiness with— What's his name?"

"Neil."

"With Neil, but as for me, I tried love and discovered I was a hell of a lot happier without it. I live for the moment now, not tomorrow, but tonight—" almost automatically he gave her his standard make-out line and didn't like himself much for it—"tonight is all you have, too, Jill."

She felt the sensual power of male sadness, and came to the brink of agreeing before she pulled back.

"I don't think I could live that way, Lieutenant."

"Call me Des, Jill, short for Desmond—my mother's idea. It's a name only a woman would pick for a man."

"I like it."

He took her hand again. "I'm glad, because I like you—engaged and all." He smiled across the table. "Now," he said, "it's your turn. Tell me about Jill Hammersmith."

She told him then about growing up on a peach ranch in California; about her college years and her fight to be accepted in veterinary school.

He shook his head in mock wonderment. "I couldn't believe it when I read your 201 file. I never met a lady veterinarian. You must love animals."

Jill waited for a moment, then said in a soft voice, "I do." She paused again, aware that her answer was trite but, even more, was incomplete. "But it's more than loving animals. I—I trust them to love me just as I am." Again she felt a flush of embarrassment creep into her face. She seemed always to tell this man more than she intended.

Christ, Des thought, why was he trying to seduce such an innocent? He stood up abruptly. "It's late—finish your drink and I'll take you back to your hotel."

Jill was wounded. She must have said something to offend him, or he had decided she was too silly and not worth his time. Maybe he was one of those men who couldn't stand the idea of a woman having a profession, even one she hadn't yet qualified for.

They separated a half block from the hotel and appeared to meet by accident in the lobby.

"What floor?" he asked her as they crossed to the elevators.

"Four."

"Four, please," he told the elevator operator.

"You don't need to come to the door with me," she told him stiffly as the elevator opened onto the fourth floor.

"I'll see you safe, then I won't have you on my conscience," he said, his voice gruff now because he was angry and ashamed of himself. What had he been thinking? She was a child-woman, sweet and uncomplicated, and thus far more dangerous to play around with than an experienced woman. Even an obvious cobra like her friend Elisabeth would have been safer.

"I can take care of myself," she said for the second time that evening, not understanding his sudden emotional withdrawal.

"Sure you can," he said, walking fast, forcing her to half-run down the corridor. "Okay, here you are. Where's your key?"

Her lower lip trembled as she fumbled with her purse, and her vision was suddenly blurred. "I'm sorry," she said, looking up at him.

"For what?"

"Whatever I did that made you so mad at me."

He could take only so much, he thought, and in equal parts of frustration, anger and desire he pulled her to him.

"Des—" His name came in a rush from her mouth, and he caught the sweet breath of it as he bent to kiss her, his lips trying to match the hardness of his angry heart—trying, but failing. He ached with the taste of her, hungry to learn more, plunge deeper, and for a brief moment he wavered, but finally he thrust her firmly away from him and walked swiftly back toward the safety of the elevator. With each step the distance between them widened and he became more determined never to run the risk of falling in love with her.

"Back so soon, Lieutenant?" the elevator operator snickered, an adolescent leer pulling at his mouth, as the car started down.

"Yes, I'm back, kid, and I'll give you some free advice."

"Yeah, I get lots of that."

"Stay away from the good girls, sonny. They're more trouble than a guy can handle."

From down the corridor, Jill watched him until the elevator doors shut behind him. She was not sophisticated enough to see his anguish, or to guess at its origin. She only knew that this man's kiss had awakened a need to melt into him, a need that Neil's kiss never had touched and now—oh, his poor scarred face—never could touch. She could only believe that having awakened this need, Des had found it uninviting and rejected it.

Fumbling for the lock, she tiptoed into the room where Bunny and Page were sleeping. She undressed, and burrowed miserably into her pillow.

Bunny heard Jill come in, and guessed at the cause of the muffled sobs. She thought about going to the girl and telling her that no man was worth even one of her tears. But she didn't move.

How could she help the kid? Trying would only stir memories of Johnny P.—all her memories—until she ached and throbbed inside and out with them.

She lay there awake, remembering him, long after the girl in the next bed had ceased her tears and fallen into a restless sleep.

9

If incendiary bombs fall, play a spray from a garden hose (never splash or stream) of water on the bomb ... A jet splash, stream or bucket of water will make it explode.
—OFFICE OF CIVIL DEFENSE MANUAL

"MAN IN THE barracks!"

Jill heard the cry and grabbed her fatigue dress to cover her khaki-colored slip.

"All right, people, *listen up!*" Wolford's gruff croak echoed down the first-floor squad room.

A collective sigh went up from thirty-five throats. They had hoped to spend their study hour under cover from the relentless Midwest sunshine.

"Second Platoon, fall out for an extra drill period in Class-A uniform. Five minutes!"

The sigh grew to be a groan.

Jill knew why. Class A meant nine layers of soggy material belted around each waist—heavy jersey panties, girdle, slip, cotton shirt, double chino skirt waistband, heavy cotton jacket, double jacket belt.

An inspection was always imminent; they were ready for that. No Waac ever sat on her bed until after retreat call at 1730 hours. Latrine basins were carefully wiped after daytime use. But extra drill under the midday sun!

"There's a special place for guys like Wolford—" Bunny puffed, struggling into a uniform that almost refused to slide over her damp body and pushing her chronically swollen feet into dry service shoes—"but unfortunately it's not as hot there as Iowa in August."

"Knock it off, Palermo," Hank Hawks yelled from the other end of the barracks. "He's just doing his job."

"Damned apple polisher," Bunny muttered.

"It's the green guidon," Jill said. "He wants to win it this Saturday at the graduation parade."

"We ought to complain about such treatment," Elisabeth said, gingerly rubbing her sculptured nose, now tipped a sunburned red.

"And confirm his opinion of us. Never!" Page said, knotting her tie. "If we do nothing else in the WAAC, let's show Wolford—"

"It won't be easy," Bunny said, her face pink from exertion.

"Nothing in the Army is easy," Elisabeth said, wondering how she ever thought it could be. Even Gabriella, a tyrant in her showroom, had been a sweetheart compared to Wolford on the drill field.

Jill smoothed the wrinkles from her skirt just as the whistle blew. The sun was high overhead when she reached the formation. Lights danced in from the side of her vision, and her head spun slowly like a spent top.

Five minutes later, Sergeant Wolford, wearing his usual sour expression, marched them down the broad street past Officers' Row. As the column turned onto the grass of the parade ground, Jill stumbled, then caught herself.

"Pick 'em up and put 'em down," Wolford roared and glared straight at Jill. "Hell," he muttered loud enough for the whole platoon to hear, "what can you expect of a candidate who doesn't even know her own name?"

Damn him! What did he *want* from her? Jill fixed her eyes on the back of the woman in front of her and tried to count cadence in her mind, but she had trouble concentrating. Her head was whirling faster, and now nausea gripped her.

"'Toon, halt!" Wolford yelled. "Left face! Hammersmith, front and center!"

Somehow Jill marched to the front of the platoon and faced him.

"What's the matter with you, Candidate Hammersmith?"

"Just a bit dizzy, Sergeant." Thank God, he had seen she wasn't feeling well. She wouldn't have to fall out on her own and prove to him that she couldn't take it.

"Hammersmith, do you want to go on sick call?" His skeptical tone said more than the words. He didn't believe her!

"No, Sergeant, I don't *want* to go, but—" she began, hoping he would insist.

"Then get back in ranks, Hammersmith," he barked, "and we'll find out if you're any kind of officer material."

"Yes, Sergeant."

Somehow she bumbled through the drill and back to the barracks.

"Jill—my God," Page said, helping her to her bed. "You're positively green, and shivering. Lie down and I'll make a cold compress. No," Page ordered as Jill struggled to get up, "down you go and don't worry about the bed. I'll make it again."

"What's wrong with Jill?" Elisabeth asked, tossing her hat and gloves onto her bed.

"Heat exhaustion, I think." Page bathed Jill's face and pressed the cool cloth against her temples.

Elisabeth loosened Jill's tie and jacket belt. "What was it they said in First Aid class about salt?"

Page checked Jill's clammy skin. "Have you been taking your salt tablets regularly, Jill?"

"I—I may have forgotten once or twice . . . "

Bunny rushed up. "Page, what's wrong with the kid?"

"Heat has her down. Bunny, get a glass of salty water for her."

Jill, fighting the dizziness, tried to focus her eyes. "Did I show him, Page?"

Page's lips were pressed together in a stubborn line. "He's not the kind that learns easily, Jill. The sergeant doesn't want us in his Army; I guess we'll never prove to him that women belong here."

"Page, he has no human sympathy," Jill whispered, the words an effort. "Surely, he wouldn't have let one of his men . . ."

"It's obvious he thought you were goldbricking."

"But, Page," Jill struggled on, her words mixed with tears, "I've heard him say that half of us aren't going to make it, that we'll wash out when it gets tough."

Bunny came back carrying a glass of salt-clouded water. "Here, drink this."

Elisabeth came around to the other side of Jill's bed and awkwardly patted her head. "Don't worry about the sergeant. He's mad because he can't get a reassignment. I saw him almost on his knees to Stratton this morning."

"I—I don't think I could take washing out with only a week to go." Jill was scarcely listening to the other women. "I know that sounds odd, since I took such a stupid chance with Lieutenant Stratton last Saturday, but . . ." Another Waac had just been discharged by the "murder board." Kansas had been the fourth OC to wash out since training began. Jill would never forget how frighteningly empty her bed had looked, mattress rolled slackly to the top, lockers open, clothes gone. Where once had been an OC—someone Jill had spent every minute of training with—there was within the space of a few minutes absolutely nothing left to show that Kansas had ever existed. Why? Nobody knew or was saying. "That's the awful part, Page—not knowing what they want from us."

"Ssshh." Page placed the compress over her eyes. "You must stop flagellating yourself. You're not going to wash out. Everything's all right now. Save your energy."

"That's right, kiddo," Bunny said. "Just get through the afternoon classes and then you stay flat on that bed tonight—we'll do your detail for you."

Jill knew that her friends made sense, but she struggled to sit up anyway. "I can't just *lie* here. I've got my shoes and brass to shine, and—"

"Down on that bed, Candidate Hammersmith—" Bunny's voice was a perfect imitation of Sergeant Wolford's gravel-flecked growl—"and that's an order."

"You two stay with her," Elisabeth said, a crazy scheme forming in the back of her mind. "I'll be back."

"Where are you going?" Bunny asked.

"I've had enough of a certain sergeant," Elisabeth said, squaring her Hobby hat. "I'll see you at the mess hall." She ignored them when they called her back.

Elisabeth was furious as she crunched up the gravel path to the orderly room. She marveled at how angry she was, not the cool controlled anger she had always used to bend others to her will, but the hot anger of injustice. How dare Wolford treat Jill this way! Of course, she thought, her mouth curving up the tiniest bit, even this sudden concern for fair play had its uses.

She opened the OR door and stopped in front of the company clerk's desk. "Candidate Gardner requests permission to speak to Sergeant Wolford."

"Just a minute," the corporal said, "and I'll see if the sergeant is in his cubicle." A minute later he returned. "Yeah, Candidate—go on in."

Elisabeth found herself facing a puzzled Sergeant Wolford. "What is it, Gardner?"

"Lay off Hammersmith, Wolford." She meant to push him as far as she needed to. *Come on, you bastard, wash me out!* How could she lose? When the word got around, she'd be the heroine, but most of all she'd be out of this women's army.

"What did you say?"

She spoke the words slowly. "I said lay off Jill Hammersmith or I'll go over your head to Marshall himself if I need to."

"Candidate, you're insubordinate. When you speak to me you call me Sergeant. I don't give a good goddamn what you think of me, but you will respect these stripes." He tapped the stripes and hash marks that covered his right sleeve. "And, another thing, *you* don't give *me* orders. Until you have bars on your shoulders, I give you orders—and you jump."

"You heard me. If you don't lay off Hammersmith, I'll go to Hobby, Colonel Faith and throw in *Life* magazine. You can kiss your pension goodbye—*Sergeant*," she added with pointed sarcasm.

He got up slowly from his desk and walked around behind her, but she had played this game of nerves before and remained facing away from him.

Wolford walked back behind his desk and thrust his face toward Elisabeth's. "Gardner, you're not the smart gal you think you are, even with your high and mighty ways. Do you take me for a sap? I know why you're here. You don't give a small shit about Hammersmith; you want to take a hike through the main gate at high noon." He smiled, relaxing. Even though he had to admit he might have been riding Hammersmith too hard—tryin' to toughen her up—damned if he didn't enjoy taking the haughty Gardner dame down a peg or two. "Let me tell you the order of the day. You are *not* gonna wash out for insubordination. You are *not* gonna get another gig, or I'll restrict you to the post till you get your detail right. And don't try to report on sick call too much, 'cause I'll have you recycled, and you can repeat OCS—in my platoon—till the war's over if needs be. Is that clear, Gardner? I'm makin' it my *personal* duty to see you stay in this WAAC for the duration. We didn't want you women, but here you are, and, by God, you're gonna *keep* your oath of enlistment just like the rest of us. Dismissed!"

Elisabeth shrugged, swung on her heel, and left. Her plan had misfired. She'd done no good for herself—or even Jill. How could anyone figure this damned army? None of these dumb jerks played by the rules of probability.

Sergeant Wolford stared at the gorgeous figure in full retreat. Whew! What was a woman like that doin' in this man's army? But the others, now—well, they hadn't whined, and he had been pushing them plenty hard. Maybe they had the makings of good soldiers after all—even that half-pint Hammersmith.

By Wednesday of their last week in OCS, Jill had recovered. And Sergeant Wolford wasn't riding her anymore, thanks to Elisabeth. The story of how she had faced down the sarge for Jill's sake was being retold and embellished in every barrack and dayroom. No matter how many times Elisabeth waved her off, Jill would never forget what a pal she'd been.

Jill felt so much better, she was even alert in the most boring afternoon class of all. She was actually listening intently to Master Sergeant Baker of S-3 drone on about the correct distribution of property accounting forms when he stopped to read a note handed to him.

"Candidate Hammersmith, report to the OC Review Board at headquarters building on the double."

The shock of it rooted her momentarily to the bench. Page, Bunny and Elisabeth turned apprehensive faces toward her. Jill felt their concern, but she knew they could not help her. This was something she had to face alone. She gripped the table, rose and walked the gauntlet of eyes, some compassionate, some curious, to the rear of the room and out of the building.

The thing she had feared most had happened to her. Washout! She had worked so hard only to have her effort despised in the end. Had Wolford turned her in for heat prostration? Why would he, when it had been his fault? Des, then? She couldn't believe they would kick her out for spending an off-duty hour with Des, no matter what her friends said. The sound of her mother's voice kept time with her hurrying footsteps: "Jill, you take after the Hammersmiths all right, just can't seem to do anything right."

She caught sight of herself in a window as she entered the building, shoulders slumped, face contorted. What a sight she was. Unmilitary. Straighten those shoulders, Candidate! She did not know exactly what she faced, but she was certain she would not help her case if she lost her military bearing.

She reported to the counter clerk and was told to sit down and wait. That's the Army, she thought, hurry up and wait. Don't panic, she told herself again; and again, like a silent, tuneless whistle in the cemetery, the words were a litany of comfort. To be on the safe side, she invoked the protection of Pallas Athene, the WAAC symbol borrowed from the Greek goddess of femininity and war. It couldn't hurt, she thought defiantly, as if to silence her Episcopalian forebears.

"This way, Candidate," the clerk said.

She knocked on the closed door and responded to a muffled "Enter."

"Candidate Hammersmith, Jill H., reporting as requested,

sir," she said smartly, saluting the senior officer and ordering her voice to be firm. They must see her as self-confident and under control.

"Candidate, you don't have to be nervous. The purpose of this hearing is not to hurt you, but to listen to your side in this matter."

"Yes, sir. I'm eager to answer any questions you might have." She was pleased with her words and her tone. They showed appropriate military bearing.

"Good."

He introduced himself as Captain Dawson on Colonel Faith's staff, and then introduced next to him a Lieutenant Giles of Infantry. "And of course," he added, "you know your platoon officer, Lieutenant Stratton."

Jill felt her head jerk around. She had been so intent on making a good impression she hadn't noticed him at the far end of the table, sitting apart from the others. Relief filled her. They couldn't have been caught or Des wouldn't be here. Whatever this was about, she could count on him. For the first moment in the last hellish half hour she could swallow past the lump in her throat.

The captain, after what seemed an eternity but could not have been more than two minutes passing while he flipped through her 201 personnel file, finally said, "Candidate, your academic record during officers' training has been outstanding. You deserve congratulations for your intellectual achievements—" he coughed into his hand—"but there are some questions about your fitness for a commission." He turned to the lieutenant of infantry and nodded.

"Candidate," Lieutenant Giles began, "you're very young. Of course, your age is not your fault, but it does have a bearing on your maturity." The lieutenant looked at Des.

Des looked up from the papers in front of him, a glint of warning in his eyes, a muscle pulsing in his cheek. He was trying to tell her something, but she didn't know what. "Candidate—" his voice thin and flat—"we have an MP report here that you were seen in Des Moines last Saturday night, fraternizing with an unidentified officer." He looked at her steadily, his eyes flashing messages she could only guess at. "Are you prepared to name the officer?"

The captain's curt voice interrupted Des. "It will go easier with you if you do, Candidate."

Jill's heart beat loud enough for the whole board to hear. Dazed, she wanted to believe that Des wasn't a coward, but she could allow herself no time to think about it. All her energy must be spent in a desperate attempt to save herself from the ax. "I admit I had a brief social encounter with an officer"—she willed her voice to remain steady—"but I will not name him. I cannot believe this would bear more on my fitness to command than the record I've made since I've been here."

A faint note of pride crept into her voice. She had stood up to them. The best thing, her father had always told her, was to meet every problem head on. She couldn't fight their intangible attitudes toward her age and size and maturity, but she would adopt a firm attitude of her own that they could not change. The idea was to be sure about herself. She would have to be stronger in her feelings than they were in theirs.

"Of course, your abilities are not in question." Des looked directly at her now, his eyes clouded and miserable.

The captain interrupted again, impatiently. "Lieutenant Stratton, let's not get off target here." He extracted a sheet from the table and waved it at her. "Candidate, you are here to answer a specific report, which bears on your ability to accept army discipline. You've already admitted a breach of military custom."

Jill was enough of a soldier to know that any excuse she offered a superior would go hard on her. No excuse, sir, was the standard military response.

"Sir, I don't question the Army's right to judge me"—all her will went into an effort to keep her voice controlled, knowing that everything depended on the impression she left with them—"but, Captain, let me say something more for the record." She forced herself to look them in the eye, one after another. "I admit my mistake, but I think there's more to judge here today than an off-duty drink with a superior officer. We Waacs need time to learn about the Army, but the Army needs time to learn about us, too—and maybe about the new Army men *and* women must create together. Can the Army really expect its soldiers to deny they are men and women, especially off duty?"

The captain cleared his throat, but Jill plunged ahead. "Sir, please think about this too: maybe the old ways of evaluating soldiers don't fit women. It's not how tall we are—why, I'm only a little shorter than Napoleon—or how rugged, or whether our voice is deep and loud, that fits us for leadership."

The captain shifted uncomfortably in his chair. "Is that all?"

"One thing more, sir." She felt strong and bold for just a moment, but it was long enough. "I'll take whatever punishment you order. But I beg you to give me one more chance to make good. When the war's over, and the Allies have won, then, sir, I want you to decide whether I was a good woman soldier, but not now—not before I've shown you what I can do."

"Wait in the anteroom, Candidate, until we call you."

"Yes, sir, thank you, sir." She performed a perfect about-face, her heels coming together with a click after a precise 180-degree turn, which faced her toward the door. As she turned to close it behind her, she saw Des staring at her.

Outside, the seconds on the twenty-four-hour clock ticked so slowly that they appeared to go backward. No wonder they called the OC Review Board the "murder board." This *was* murder. She went over her statements compulsively and thought of a dozen better ways to answer each question. Of course she had told no lies. It was stupid to lie when the truth, told with confidence, was so much more effective. Oh, why were they taking so long? What were they saying about her? What was Des saying? Was he telling the truth?

"Candidate Hammersmith?" The infantry lieutenant called her from the door. Jill rose and followed him.

"No need to report again," the captain told her with a grim look.

It was all so obvious. They were going to wash her out. But she wouldn't break down. Damn it—she wouldn't! Resigned, she waited for the ax to fall.

"Candidate Hammersmith," the captain intoned, sounding for all the world as if he were sentencing her to death and dis-memberment, "it is the judgment of this board that you have answered the questions put to you in a full and unique, if not necessarily a military, manner and should be given another chance to prove your worth—"

Jill could hardly believe what she heard. "Thank you, sir!" she said, trying to hold herself at attention when she wanted to jump and shout with relief.

He held his hand to stop her. "—but the decision is not clear cut. Lieutenant Stratton voted for your dismissal from the service, and—"

Jill swayed, scarcely believing the words she heard, but she forced herself to concentrate as the captain read from the paper in front of him.

"—Lieutenant Giles voted to drop the charges. And I was undecided, so I had to rule in your favor. Therefore, it is my duty to warn you that if there is ever one minor question of fitness to reach your file—even if it is in the last hour of training—I will personally see to it that you are recalled before the board, at which time the results may be quite different. Have I made myself clear?"

Numbly she said, "Yes, sir."

The ax had fallen, and its blade still rested squarely against her neck. But she knew she would be absolutely perfect for the next four days. No one could keep her from her bars now, not the captain, not Sergeant Wolford—not even Des. Suddenly, she allowed her full fury at his betrayal to emerge. Coward! Traitor! Although he had obviously decided he wasn't interested in her as a woman, somehow she had felt she could trust him. She would never forgive him for not revealing himself, for covering his guilt at her expense. Not that her lack of forgiveness mattered to him. That was obvious now. Repeating the military formalities, she left the room without looking back.

10

In backyards and communal plots, twenty million Victory Gardens produce 40 percent of the vegetables eaten in the United States during the first summer of war.

THE FINAL AUGUST week of the first WAAC OCS was filled with assignment rumors. On Tuesday, Elisabeth overheard the company clerk say that the whole of Company One would be shipped "out" somewhere, probably to England. On Wednesday, Bunny saw Jerry again at the PX and he said that Personnel was talking about a big shipment of WAAC officers going to the Pentagon, the new Washington, D.C., military complex due to be completed in October.

"Guess what," announced a breathless Jill, bouncing into the dayroom Thursday night.

"If it's another latrine rumor," groaned Bunny, who was toughening her feet in a brine soak, "I don't want to hear it."

"No, honest. I got this straight from a guy who's cutting the orders."

"Okay, give."

"Half of us are going to stay right here as cadre and station complement."

Elisabeth walked in at the end of Jill's announcement. "Who's going to stay here?"

"About half of us, according to the latest rumor," Jill answered her. "I'm sorry, Elisabeth. I know you're disappointed." Then she brightened. "But at least we'll all stay together."

How did Jill do it? Elisabeth wondered. She'd just had a tremendous scare at her murder board hearing, and here she was as optimistic as a puppy dog. There was something about

Jill that reminded her of Marne. Hopeless romantics, the two of them, weaned on Hollywood musicals, happy endings and Horatio Alger platitudes. Those things were illusions. She had none, particularly about the WAAC—although she wouldn't argue about the women's army with Page around. For Elisabeth this was just a period of craziness she had to get beyond. She shrugged. "We'll all know soon enough, Jill."

Page had listened intently. "We really shouldn't be surprised to get orders for troop duty, at least for a few training cycles. Since we're the first class to finish, we're going to have to take over training the OCs and Auxiliaries who come after us, at least until there are enough qualified WAAC cadre to do the job."

"I think it's a good thing, too," Jill said. "At least we know what to expect of women."

The pain of Des's betrayal was subsiding, because she pushed it aside whenever she saw him; she was determined to put him out of her mind. He had tried to talk to her alone twice yesterday, but she had been so militarily formal he had backed off.

Hawks spoke up across the dayroom behind her inevitable Coke. "Use your heads, Candidates. This is where all the rank will be made. I bet I make captain before the year's out."

"You're right, Jill," Bunny said, lowering her voice and ignoring Hawks, who always seemed to invite herself into every conversation, "we do know more about women than some of our officers do, but let's be fair. The guys aren't all bad. Wolford is hopeless, but Captain Burchette is a good egg—even Stratton tries after his fashion. That Stratton—can you beat what that guy did? I thought he was a skirt-chaser, but I didn't figure him for—" Bunny looked in Jill's direction, realizing she'd said too much again. At the mention of Stratton's name Jill's face had frozen into a mask of unconcern. Bunny pulled her feet from the basin and dried them. She knew what it was like to be Jill, in love with a man who could only hurt her. "Sorry, kiddo, you know I shoot off my mouth too much."

A woman from Company Two drifted over to the piano and picked through the sheet music on top, then sat down and began playing a labored version of "Elmer's Tune." Other Waacs gathered behind her to sing. "The hurdy gurdy, the birdy, the cop on the beat/ All sing Elmer's tune—yeah . . . "

A tall, slender Waac stopped by Jill's chair. Jill stood up. "Hi, Eleanor, I've been waiting for you," she said and, turning to the others, added, "This is Eleanor Douglas from Third Platoon—used to be a radio announcer. She's going to help me practice my command voice. Anybody else want to come?"

Bunny grinned. "I'm beyond help."

"Of course you aren't," Douglas said, taking her seriously. "Any woman can project if she knows breathing, and tongue placement."

Bunny smiled up at her. "Thanks, but no, thanks. The spirit is willing, but the feet won't move."

"You need to relax sometime, too, Jill," Page said.

"I'll relax after I get my bars."

Page sighed after Jill and Eleanor had left. "Jill's so hard on herself."

"I give up. I can't understand this crazy army," Elisabeth said, leaning back languorously in her wicker chair. "I've had more gigs than anyone, and there's no question about my graduating, while Jill even irons her shoelaces. It doesn't make sense, does it?"

Page smiled. "It doesn't have to make sense. Remember what we were told the first day of training: there's the right way, the wrong way and the army way."

"I have a better theory," Elisabeth said. "Jill's so intense, like electricity, she attracts a kind of negative charge."

"You mean she's so hard on herself that she invites others to join in," Bunny said.

"Something like that. People with everything to lose seem to bring out the worst in human nature. The trick is never to let anyone know you care about anything."

Now she tells me, Bunny thought, a half-sad smile twisting her mouth. Changing the subject, she asked, "Either of you got a nickel for a Coke?"

That night, Elisabeth heard rain tapping insistently on the barrack's windows as she prepared for bed. She remembered her nightly routine before joining the WAAC. Had she ever really soaked in a hot tub with expensive bath oils, instead of grabbing a shower on the run? Had she really worn filmy silk gowns and peignoirs instead of blue flannelette pajamas? Had she once had soft, white skin instead of drying, sunburned skin, and creamed it in a beveled mirror—one that reflected only *her* face? Now, morning and night, she stood in front of one of twelve washbasins in the Company One latrine with a dozen images reflected. She hated it, hated having nowhere to hide when she needed to hide.

She sat on the edge of her bed, lit a Chesterfield and pulled the soothing smoke deep into her lungs. Ordinary barracks noise subsided. Women padded toward the latrine, toiletries bulging from their pockets; others called to one another, some already slept, a few read letters whose creases had frayed from repeated foldings. So many of them had husbands or boyfriends fighting, perhaps at this moment, dying. Strange how sharing their uniform brought women closer to their men. To her own astonishment, she had thought more often and more tenderly of Marne since she arrived at Fort Des Moines.

For a moment she felt discomfort at the change, frightened by a suspicion of weakness, of an unsuspected need within her. For the first time in her life, other people counted on her, listened to her opinions, even liked her—not because of what they might take from her, but because— She stopped, unable to go further. Her wildest imaginings could not explain a relationship that did not cost her. Elisabeth had no experience in being accepted for herself.

The final day of OC training was a whirl of last-minute testing in each of nine courses to determine that the first women soldiers were ready to be launched into the Army as officers and gentlewomen. OCs were called out of ranks during drill to put their platoons through column rights and left flanking movements, counting cadence with the perfectly imitated nasal tones of their male instructors. Even Jill began to sound more like Sergeant Wolford than the sarge himself. OCs could locate an azimuth on a military map, knew how far to place tents from a slit trench for field sanitation, and that they should send the pink, not the yellow, clothing-requisition copy to S-3 post supply. Every woman had crammed far into the night that last week memorizing military customs, defense against air attack, company administration and mess management, and they had quizzed each other incessantly on field first aid.

The Friday night before the last white-glove inspection and the graduation day parade, barracks details were done until they shone. Though the OCs worked hard, there was an air of manic silliness in the barracks, the natural result of weeks of hard work and tension. After the last rousing chorus of the WAAC marching song, "Duty," rang through the downstairs bay, Eleanor Douglas hopped atop a foot locker and recited her grammar-school Rudyard Kipling prize-winner to generous applause. Then the clapping had become rhythmic and half the barracks had chanted, "Robust-and-No-Bust, Robust-and-No-Bust!"

String mops at right shoulder arms, Bunny and Jill broke into a little time step down the bay while onlookers sang "Through Fort Des Moines, No Mother to Guide Us."

Laughing and out of breath, they collapsed against the wall near the door. Bunny asked, gasping, "You really don't mind that silly No-Bust nickname, do you? They wouldn't bother to tease you if they didn't like you."

"No. I'd rather be No-Bust than Robust."

"Oh, you would, would you?" Bunny said, thrusting her mop at Jill. *"En garde!"*

"Got any more dandruff shampoo, Bunny?" Elisabeth asked from down on her hands and knees over a bucket and brush.

Bunny passed her a bottle, which Elisabeth up-ended into the bucket. "This is the last of Mr. Fitch's secret weapon. I hope he never finds out what we did with his gift."

Page, on all fours in her khaki-colored slip, strands of hair escaping her fatigue cap, looked up from her scrub brush and said, "I can hear the Fitch Bandwagon ad now." She began to sing, "When you go to war, use your head, save the floor, use Fitch Shampoo."

"Well, what did he expect?" Bunny laughed. "He sent so many cases of the stuff, we couldn't possibly use it all on our hair. I think I was damned ingenious to think of it. None of the cadre have the faintest idea how we get our floors so clean. Besides, I guarantee this floor will never get dandruff." She ducked as Page sent a wet scrub cloth flying down the bay. "Missed me!" she taunted.

"Man in barracks!"

There was a rush for robes, and they scrambled to their feet.

"At ease, Candidates," Sergeant Wolford said, climbing onto a foot locker at one end of the bay.

"Oh, my achin' GI feet, what now?" Bunny stage-whispered. "Is he going to drill us by moonlight?"

Wolford cleared his throat and examined some papers he had in his hands. "Anyone here interested in her assignment?" Fifty women shouted, "Yes!" "I'll post it on the bulletin board as I leave."

He stopped and looked at the papers again, but he didn't get down from his perch. "Okay, people, listen up, because I'm only gonna say this once," he began, his voice lacking the familiar gruffness they knew only too well. "Some of you—" Wolford stopped again.

Bunny looked at Page, her eyebrows raised, her shoulders lifted in a questioning shrug.

Up and down the First Platoon bay, women turned to their neighbors and whispered about Wolford's uncertainty. Even Elisabeth looked interested.

Finally, with the expression of a man about to dive into icy waters, Wolford said, "No use beatin' around the bush with you. Guess ya know I never thought this women's-army idea would work out. But I'm a man to admit a mistake when I make one—and I *may* have made one. You troops"—and here his voice broke almost imperceptibly—"have done . . . okay."

"Well, I'll be damned," Bunny said aloud.

Wolford ignored her. "Now go out on that parade ground tomorrow and be the best," he said, his voice grating again. "Go out and bring me back the green guidon—or, by God, don't come back without it!"

He stepped down in the hushed barracks, pinned a sheet of paper on the bulletin board and left without a backward glance.

No one spoke as the screen door slammed behind Sergeant Wolford. Then Bunny broke the stunned silence. "You know, they say if you live long enough you see everything. I think we can all die happy now."

"Don't you know what it means?" Page said, smiling broadly. "We won."

Jill nodded, repeating, "We won. We won."

"To hell with Wolford," Elisabeth said, "let's look at that assignment sheet."

"I can't believe it!" Bunny said over her shoulder to Page. "I'm going to an Auxiliary training company at the Stables.

God, why couldn't they give me a nice desk job so I can rest these poor doggies of mine?"

"You'll be a wonderful troop officer," Page said. "You know, they're already calling the Auxies at the converted stables 'Hobby's horses.'"

"That's clever. Just so they don't try to throw a saddle on me."

A shout went up from several women in Third Platoon. "Daytona Beach. Wow! That means overseas!"

Page looked for her name and followed it across the page. "'Training Center Public Information Office,'" she read out loud. "Oh!" Her shoulders sagged with disappointment. "I really wanted troop work."

"But you're a natural for PIO, Page," Bunny said. "Who better to give all the visiting brass a first-rate impression of the WAAC?"

Elisabeth called from the back of the crowd, "Page, I can't see. What's my assignment?"

Page read, "'Gardner, Elisabeth K., Training Center Quartermaster.'"

The crowd thinned and Jill made her way to the assignment sheet. As she read the words beside her name, her eyes widened.

"What is it?" Bunny asked. "Where are you going?"

"Nowhere."

"What!"

"Nowhere," Jill said, a look of pure triumph on her face. "I'm staying right here. I'm the new Second Platoon officer for Company One." A pure look of glee swept her face. "That makes Wolford my noncom."

"What happens to Stratton?" Page asked her.

"I don't care."

11

Duty is calling you and me,
We have a date with destiny.
Ready, the Waacs are ready,
Their pulses steady the world to set free.
Service, we're in it heart and soul,
Victory is our only goal,
We love our country's honor
And will defend it against every foe.
—"Duty," unofficial WAAC marching song, sung to
the tune of the "Colonel Bogey March"; lyrics by
Dorothy Nielsen

AT LAST, AUGUST 29, 1942, the first WAAC OC graduation day, dawned—bright, clear and hot. Page glanced quickly down the squad room for one last check just as the inspection party arrived. Every OC stood straight and still, her starched khaki uniform wrinkle-free. The harsh smells of Brasso, saddle soap and Clorox perfumed the air, now as familiar to her nostrils as Coty and Yardley once had been. She watched out of the corner of her eye as the colonel's glove whisked along a rafter and came away as white as ever. The women soldiers had learned the Army's first lesson well—that dirt was as desecrating to a barrack as a Christian was to Mecca.

They had shined their shoes with two layers of brown and cordovan paste wax heated in a tin over a cigarette lighter and then applied and brushed vigorously. After the polish had thoroughly dried, they had achieved a final glassy finish by buffing each shoe with a precious nylon. The WAAC OCs had become so famous for their shoeshines that half the GIs on the post were begging for their used stockings.

The inspecting officers passed quickly along the bay, looking at the clothing alignment in one woman's wall locker, the rolled underwear in another's foot locker, testing a bed for tightness, pinching a barracks bag for more than one day's laundry or contraband food, and on into the latrine and laundry areas where dirt could hide in far corners. Page knew that the colonel's eye had not missed much, and what he had not seen the captain had.

As the inspection party mounted the stairs to the second floor, Sergeant Wolford called, "Stand easy."

"How'd we do?" Jill whispered.

Bunny answered. "I didn't see Wolford write in his little black book, not even once. You can stop worrying, Jill. It's all over."

"It's *not* over," Jill said softly between clenched teeth, "not until graduation parade, not until those bars are on my shoulders."

Ten minutes later they heard the inspection party descend the outside fire stairs, and soon Wolford stuck his head in the door. "Get ready to fall out for parade in five minutes. Hammersmith, report to the orderly room on the double."

Instinctively, Page moved toward Jill, but not in time to catch her. Bunny grabbed her before she fell, and eased her down onto her foot locker.

"It's too cruel," Jill said weakly, her head spinning. "The last day—the last minute—they *couldn't* wash me out. Not now, not after all we've been through!"

Page knew that Jill was close to a breakdown. None of them had the strength left to deal with such a blow. "It's not what you're thinking," she insisted over and over, not at all sure she believed what she was saying, but knowing that she had to say it. "Hang on to yourself."

Wolford was at the door again, shielding his eyes, unable to adjust from the outside glare to the ordinary light of the barracks. "Hammersmith," he called down the bay. "Orderly room!"

"Yes, Sergeant," she answered him from behind the screen of friends shielding her from his view, her voice quavering imperceptibly.

"On the double, unless you want me to recommend someone else to carry the company guidon at graduation parade. Now *move!*" He slammed the door.

Jill exhaled a long shuddering breath. "*Me*—carry the guidon," she said, her voice now full of wonder at such an honor.

"See—what did we tell you, kid?" Bunny said, obviously relieved.

"Congratulations, Jill," said Page. "You deserve it."

Elisabeth looked down at the little woman and pushed a lock of Jill's hair up under her Hobby hat, a caring gesture that had come on her so quickly she had not had time to pull it back. "That means," she told Jill admiringly, "you had the highest academic standing of any OC in Company One."

Jill smiled gratefully at Elisabeth, shook her head to clear it, and felt a surge of energy. "I'm all right now. I'd better go, but I'll see you right after the ceremony, won't I?" She grabbed her dress gloves from her foot locker and took a deep breath, calling on reserves of energy she hadn't known she possessed. "Thanks—all of you. I couldn't have done it without you."

As they watched her run from the barracks, Page knew none of them could have completed OCS without the others. They had been stretched to their physical and emotional limits, and they had learned what few of them could ever have learned outside the Army—that the job, whatever it was, had to be done right; there were no second bests and very few second chances.

Grasping the yellow flag with the big black "1," Jill remembered Sergeant Wolford's admonition. "Now step out, Candidate," he had said, shaking his head at her short legs. "Watch your distance, or the tall girls will climb right up your back."

From the direction of the Dewy Parade Ground, she could hear the band playing the "Washington Post March." The company moved off down the road, while other companies from the OC and Auxiliary training regiments marched before and after them. From each compass point, the first massed units of women soldiers converged on the place where the Army, the press and the public would view the results of their training.

Every cell in Jill's body was keyed to execute all the commands along the line of march as if she had stepped out of the army manual of close-order drill—the perfect soldier. She had failed Neil, and someday she would make up for that failure; but today was special. This was the recognition she had craved all her life. She had shown them, shown them all.

As they approached Dewy, the color guard stepped off, the first time in history that women had carried the colors in a military review. Right behind them, exactly at 1000 hours, Company One swung onto the close-clipped grass, the OC regiment forming behind. Jill tingled to the sound of hundreds of feet meeting the turf simultaneously, the rasp of chino on chino as arms swung, the concert of heartbeats keeping time to the four-beat cadence sung by sergeants on their companies' flanks.

Approaching the tall white reviewing stand, Jill heard Des give the "Eyes right!" order and snapped the company standard to horizontal salute. The weight of the flag at full extension rested along her right arm. She realized with a happy start that OC training had made her small arms stronger than their size had ever meant them to be.

Page marched behind and to the left of Jill in the third rank. The band was playing her favorite "Colonel Bogey March," which every Waac now called "Duty," when she heard an intense whisper sweeping down the ranks behind her: *"Dress and cover!"* Each woman moved slightly to synchronize exactly with the woman in front and the one on her right. As they passed the stand, flashbulbs popped and the crowd applauded. A sad little shiver shook her. How could any moment in her life ever equal this one? She was a part of the parade at last, a part of the Army, a part of something infinitely greater than anything she had ever experienced.

On the far-left flank, Elisabeth marched, shoulders back, head high. She hadn't expected to feel anything, but the music, the flags flying—all of it must have hypnotized her.

In the middle file, Bunny marched on ravaged feet. She knew this was a moment she would remember for the rest of her life. She may have joined the WAAC to get away from Johnny, but sometime during these past weeks she had begun to believe in what women were doing in the Army.

Company by company, they lined up in front of the reviewing stand. Long trails of packed grass still wet from a morning shower stretched from one end of the parade field to the other, marking their passage.

Colonel Faith's voice carried clearly to the rear ranks. "You are all a credit to your training cadre and to the Women's Army Auxiliary Corps. Your performance today has set standards for those women who come after you." After a consultation with other members of the reviewing party, he announced, "The green guidon for best marching company goes to—OC Company One!"

Jill could hardly believe what she had heard. They had done it! *She* had done it! If only her mother could see her now. And Neil. Even Mrs. Martin might forgive . . .

She marched forward alone to the base of the stand, received the green guidon and stepped smartly back to her place in front of the company, her head high.

Colonel Faith commanded, "Company One, pass in review!"

Once again they wheeled past the reviewing stand, taking their victory turn around the field, the green guidon with the golden-helmeted head of Pallas Athene floating above their heads.

Again they stopped in front of the reviewing stand crammed with general officers, Director Hobby and Congresswoman Edith Nourse Rogers, the tall gray grandmotherly woman who had introduced and fought for the WAAC bill. "You are soldiers," she told them, "and belong to America. Every hour must be your finest hour."

Page knew that the first WAAC OCS was almost over. The weeks of marching, exercising and studying in almost unbearable heat, under the charge of men who almost dared them to become soldiers, had come to an end—and they had succeeded. *She* had made it on her own, without her father's help or influence. This was one accomplishment even he would have to recognize.

The WAAC band played "Auld Lang Syne," and the commandant shouted, "Pin 'em on!"

A shout escaped from 436 throats, new third officers of the Women's Army Auxiliary Corps. There was a mad scramble of new officers looking for friends and relatives. Page grabbed Jill and hugged her, guidon and all.

"I can't believe it," Jill said over and over, reluctantly handing the guidon to the Company One clerk. "We made it. We actually made it."

Elisabeth and Bunny joined them, holding boxes containing the shiny gold bars that they had all purchased at the PX the night before.

Elisabeth held her two bars out to Page. "Will you pin mine on?" she asked, her expression shy and haughty at the same time, as if she expected to be refused and intended not to care if she was.

"Of course," Page said, taking the proffered bars, "if you'll pin mine."

"Okay, kid," Bunny said, grinning at Jill, "I'll kneel down and you can—"

Jill pulled back a fist in mock anger.

Bunny raised her hand in the truce sign: "Okay, okay—no teasing. I forgot you're not the kid anymore, but an officer and a gentlewoman. Hey," she said as the thought struck her, "so am I!"

Jill placed one gold bar on each one of Bunny's epaulets.

Bunny held out her hand for Jill's bars. "Now I'll pin yours for you."

"I'd love that, but I have another plan."

Bunny watched as Jill walked rigidly erect toward Lieutenant Stratton, saluted and held out the box containing her new golden bars. Bunny saw the lieutenant hesitate, then, without speaking, accept the outstretched box and bend to pin Jill's bars on her shoulder. She saw Jill salute, about-face and walk away without a word.

"Oh God," Bunny said to Page and Elisabeth, "would you look at that. Sometimes Jill is an insufferable perfectionist, but you have to say one thing—she has guts. Look at her facing down Stratton—after the guy almost threw her to the wolves. He must feel like two cents right about now." Too bad, Bunny thought, but didn't say aloud, because it was plain that Jill was trying to compel Stratton's admiration when what she clearly wanted—plain as anything—was his affection. Bunny wondered if Jill would regret this moment she had used for revenge, but there was nothing in Jill's face to indicate regret when she rejoined them, nothing in her face at all.

Page saw Sergeant Wolford then, shouldering through the

crowd of excited new WAAC officers. He looked much the same as the first day she had seen him, starched and grim, but with the slightest softening of his uncompromising glare when he looked at them.

"So," he boomed, facing them, his hands on his hips, "you're second louies now."

"Third officers," Page corrected him with their WAAC ranks.

"Get used to lieutenant, Hannaday. No one can remember those Girl Scout ranks the War Department dreamed up. I still don't think this women's-army idea will work out in the field, but shavetails you are, and shavetails I'll call ya'."

"Not quite yet, Sergeant Wolford," Page said.

"What?" he boomed.

She smiled at him, no longer awed by his drill-sergeant demeanor. "It's not official until we receive our first salute and give that person a one-dollar bill."

He drew himself to magnificent attention and saluted each of them in turn, with all the formality invested in him by a thousand command inspections and his thirty years as a line-company noncom.

Solemnly, they returned the salute as he had taught them to, and each handed him a crisp new dollar bill.

After that, Page knew, no bars had ever rested more firmly on any officer's shoulders. But as the four of them turned toward the barracks and their first weekend pass as WAAC officers, Bunny walked up to Sergeant Wolford and, with a wink, kissed him.

Glancing behind her, Page saw the hand in the hash-marked sleeve reach to touch his cheek, a flush growing under the weathered wrinkles and something close to moisture in the hard gaze that had shriveled the inside of more than one WAAC OC.

Jill looked back, too, but beyond the sergeant to the place where Des had stood a few minutes ago. He was gone, but it made no difference to her where he went. She wanted never to see him again as long as she lived.

12

By early November, requests for more than 400,000 Waacs lie on Director Hobby's desk. Lieutenant General Eisenhower has requisitioned two WAAC companies to be sent to him overseas, and estimates of 1 million women in uniform by 1946 are being bandied about the Pentagon.

ON A COLD but clear Sunday, November 8, Page, Jill and Bunny lounged in the Fort Des Moines WAAC officers' club.

Bunny asked, "Remember Smitty from Company Two? She wrote from Washington that Services of Supply recommended the War Department draft a half-million women next year. Can you believe that?"

Page said, passing a hand over her eyes, which had suddenly blurred, "That would mean ten new training centers instead of just the new one in Daytona Beach."

"Page, are you sick?" Jill asked.

"No, just tired."

"Good. Anyway, as I was saying, we can't train officers any faster than we're doing." Jill spooned up the last of her hot-fudge sundae.

"Hi." Elisabeth slid her tailor-made uniform into the booth. "Jill, how can you eat that goo? Your figure will positively balloon."

"Gosh, do you think so?" Jill put the spoon down as if it had burned her hand. "I *am* having trouble keeping my girdle snapped."

Bunny laughed. "That's not you kid. It's these damned wartime girdles. You know how they're saving rubber by putting only one supporter on each side. Well, the other day I'm in the

94

middle of Dewy with my Auxie platoon, double-timing to keep them from freezing to death, when both my supporters popped and my hose dropped like a shot. I tripped and went head first into a snowbank."

They all laughed at the ridiculous picture she painted.

"Oh, that's not all." Bunny built the suspense. "Who should come along just then but the new commandant, Colonel Hoag, with some visiting firemen—or rather, I should say clergy—who politely looked the other way while I snapped them back in place and double-timed out of there."

"Listen, everybody," shouted the bartender, "we've invaded North Africa!"

He turned up the volume of the radio in back of the bar, and a somber voice intoned, advancing and receding with the strength of the transmission, "Hello, everybody. This is Lowell Thomas in London." The familiar voice filled the O club. "Prime Minister Churchill announced this afternoon that a combined U.S.–British force of four hundred thousand men has landed at Casablanca, Oran and Algiers in North Africa. The troops, transported by an armada of five hundred ships convoyed by three hundred fifty naval vessels, surprised the Vichy French garrisons and overpowered them after brief fighting."

A spontaneous cheer went up, and someone struck the first chords of "Over There" on the bandstand piano. Page found herself with Bunny, Jill and Elisabeth shouting a chorus of "The Waacs are coming, the Waacs are coming . . ." "Tomorrow I'm going to walk into the Chief's office and put in for overseas duty."

"That's easy for you, Page," Jill said, "you have a public-relations skill they want. What about me? Have you heard about any requisitions for training officers with one year of vet school? No, you haven't, because there aren't any, and there won't be any."

"I thought you loved training OCs," Bunny said.

"I do, but I want to get over there where the war is." Determination firmed her small mouth. "What should I do, Page? You must know what skill can get me overseas."

Without hesitating, Page said, "Communications. That's what they're going to want from us—telephone operators, radio operators and cryptographers."

"You mean breaking secret codes? That's for me! Tomorrow *I'm* going to put in for cryptography school."

Bunny scooted her chair back. "This is depressing. Look, the bar's finally open. Anybody want a drink?"

Elisabeth ordered a Brandy Alexander. "And tell them use real cream or forget it."

"Why depressing?" Jill asked Bunny when she got back with the drinks.

The older woman looked downcast. "Mother Bunny hoped we'd all stay together, kid, at least for a while longer."

"If they open several new training centers, you know we'll be scattered," Page said. "We're lucky one of us didn't have to go when they opened Daytona Beach."

"Bunny, why not put in for code school with me?" Jill asked.

"You go to it, kid. You go slay Page's dragon. Not me! I'll stay right here in the dull old U.S. of A. hutting my Auxies around Dewy."

"Elisabeth, have you heard anything about your request for the QM office in the Pentagon?" Page asked.

"Nothing," Elisabeth said. Almost four months had gone by since she had written to the Quartermaster General detailing the problems Waacs had with the uniform and her suggestion that someone from the field with a model's training—namely Elisabeth Gardner—would be of inestimable help in solving those problems. She knew she should have followed up with a formal request—maybe put more pressure on Marne—but for some reason she had allowed the matter to slide. It wasn't like her to drag her feet about anything. She could hardly put a word to it, but if she must she had to admit that it was out of loyalty to these women. She had grown, in her own reserved way, so close to Page and Jill and Bunny that the thought of leaving them was troubling to her.

"Did I tell you," Bunny asked between sips of her Tom Collins, "about this latest crop of Auxies? Some bunch! We've got a concert pianist—she's good, too. Even I can tell that, and I'm boogie, not Bach."

"What's her name?" Page asked.

"Annaliese Kaplan. She escaped from Nazi Germany in 1939, lost her fiancé, her family, everything, and yet she works as hard as anyone—harder, maybe. There's something very intense about her. She reminds me a bit of you, Page."

"I can't imagine why," Page said.

"Now, don't take this wrong, but—gee, how can I put this?—she knows herself too well, like you do, and so she's never surprised. She's like you, but not—or maybe like you could be."

"Bunny, what *are* you rattling on about? Anyway, I'd like to meet her sometime."

"Sure, anytime," Bunny said, relieved that Page wasn't angry at her rantings, and she went immediately into one of her funny monologues about her Auxie platoon. "We've got this kid, Victoria Hansen, from Parker's Prairie, Minnesota, in this cycle. She makes Jill here sound like Mae West in heat. Talk about innocent! You wouldn't believe the questions Mother Bunny has to answer. The other day she asked me if a girl could have a baby after kissing a boy. Would you believe that—in 1942? I think the kid's a case of arrested development!"

Jill scoffed, miffed because Bunny thought her innocent. "You're making that up, Bunny!"

" 's truth, so help me. But that's not the best of this new lot. We have an ex-Carmelite nun—name's Kathryn Mary O'Conners—and she absolutely refused the captain's direct order to take down a large crucifix she'd hung on the locker in back of her bed. Now, aren't you dying to see how the Army deals with *that?*"

Elisabeth smiled and sipped her drink. "That's a classic confrontation all right—army standard operating procedures versus God. If she wins, let me know. I could use someone with her connections to cut through red tape at Supply."

"Which reminds me," Bunny said, "of the uniform shortage. Elisabeth, something's got to be done. I know *you're* concerned with how it fits, but damn it all, recruits are pouring into the Stables and the new Boom Town barracks every week, and there aren't any uniforms for them." Bunny bent over the table toward Elisabeth. "Look, I've got some of the Southern and West Coast women marching about in flimsy shoes and lightweight dresses."

"Didn't the coats help?" Elisabeth asked. She knew that

Director Hobby had ordered men's winter overcoats issued until supply caught up with the overwhelming demand for WAAC uniforms.

"You mean those old World War One coats? Yes, they helped, but not enough small sizes are available. I've got some recruits who look like vaudeville comics out on Dewy—empty sleeves flapping and hems dragging to their ankles. Some show for visiting VIPs we make!"

Jill nodded. "It's not just the Auxies, but the OCs too. The last class had to take all *left* galoshes—you know, the ones they call arctics, with the big buckles. Both feet went sideways. How do you think that looks on parade?"

Elisabeth tapped the table impatiently. "Yes, yes, I know. But it's not my fault. S-3 says it's Hobby's fault—some snafu at WAAC headquarters."

"That's not fair, Elisabeth," Page said, coming to the Director's rescue. "I hear this all the time, from press and parents. You've got to remember that Director Hobby's caught up in the army bureaucracy just as we are. One day she's told the WAAC is authorized a strength of a thousand recruits a week, a few weeks later the figure jumps to five thousand a week, and a month after that the General Staff's talking about drafting hundreds of thousands of women. Can't you guess what happens to supply? Original clothing requisitions go in to the Quartermaster Corps, then they're doubled and redoubled within weeks. Each time, contracts are let and then recalled. It gets to be an awful supply tangle, worse than anything we can imagine. And on top of all this, there are still those people who are just waiting to say we made a mess of our chance."

"Want another drink?" Bunny asked.

"Not for me," Page answered. "I've got letters and laundry."

Bunny gulped the last of her drink. "Letters? Gee, sorry, Jill, I almost forgot. This came for you at headquarters, and I picked it up." She reached into her purse and pulled out a slim airmail letter. Teasing, she held it up to the light. "Looks like it's another one from your old friend Stratton."

Jill picked up the letter lying between them on the table and without looking at it tore it in two pieces. Then she placed the two pieces together and tore through them again, repeating the process until she dropped the confetti into the ashtray. "I've got some duty rosters to make out." Abruptly, she put on her coat and left.

"Whew," Bunny said. "I sure wouldn't want Jill mad at *me*. She's got a stubborn streak that's almost frightening."

"It's not stubbornness," Page said thoughtfully. "She's trapped by her own standards. She can't allow herself a mistake, so she's never learned to forgive other people's."

Elisabeth raised an eyebrow. "Nothing wrong with that. You make a mistake in this world and you get eaten alive."

They walked in silence back to the WAAC BOQ. Page felt the forces of change moving in on them. The Corps was growing rapidly, and they would be obliged to grow with it. Their private lives would have to be put on hold for the duration. For a moment, the thought was comforting, but only for a moment. That's nonsense, she thought. Life doesn't wait, not even for a world war. Even love cannot be denied; not the ache-all-over love that Bunny tried to forget, not the love-hate that Jill rejected, not even the married love that Elisabeth seemed to feel very little. Love. She turned the word over and over again in her mind, examining it. Love was something Lieutenant Page Hannaday could postpone for now. Suddenly Page felt dizzy. She stumbled, and Bunny grabbed her arm.

"Thought you were going to do a good imitation of my girdle dance." Then Bunny grew serious. "What is it, Page? Your skin is positively gray."

"Just tired," Page mumbled, "just tired."

"You better go on sick call tomorrow. Get some of those little all-purpose capsules. You know what Sergeant Wolford says. If APCs won't cure it . . ." Bunny's voice trailed off as Page turned an anxious, angry face toward her.

"Don't you *dare* say anything about this to anyone," Page yelled at Bunny, who had never seen her angry before.

13

K rations are packed by Chicago's Wrigley Company and contain compressed graham crackers, canned meat or meat substitute, three tablets of sugar, four cigarettes and a stick of Wrigley's chewing gum. For breakfast a fruit bar and soluble coffee are added; for dinner, bouillon powder and a bar of concentrated chocolate.

BY THE FIRST anniversary of Pearl Harbor, Page was on orders for an undisclosed overseas destination.

"Lieutenant Hannaday."

The nurse at the hospital dispensary window was calling her name. "Report back to Dr. Carter in Examining Room Three."

"Yes, ma'am," Page answered quietly, longing to ask why she had been asked to wait when all the other officers on overseas orders had been released back to duty.

A major in a white coat with the sewn-on caduceus insignia of the Army Medical Corps stood by the examining table, another army nurse behind him. "Remove your blouse and unbutton your shirt, please, Lieutenant." He patted the table. "Sit right here."

He considerately rubbed the stethoscope to warm it and then moved it from between Page's breasts to under her left breast and then around to her back. "Experienced any dizziness lately?"

She hesitated. "Just a little," she answered, not quite truthfully, "but I'm sure it's overwork. We've all worked hard, first in officers' training and then getting the training center going."

"Tell me," he said in a quiet, even tone from over her shoul-

der, "have you ever had any heart trouble?" Page could feel
her heart hammering in her ears.

"Absolutely not, Doctor. I've led an active life—played on
my college tennis team—and I've been an A club player since
then."

"Any family history of heart problems?"

"My mother—she died of an aneurysm. They said it was
congenital." She heard the panic rising in her voice. "What is
it? What do you hear?"

"Please don't excite yourself. That's the worst thing you can
do. Before I sent you out to the waiting room, I heard an irregular heartbeat—it's called arrhythmia. That's why I asked you
to wait. Occasionally, I find that physical examinations are
stressful for women, and some men too—that they have elevated blood pressure or unusual heart reactions." He stopped
talking and listened again.

Page stood his silence as long as she could. "For God's sake,
Doctor . . ."

The major shushed her and continued listening. "It's there
all right—a fluttering sound," he said, removing the stethoscope from his ears and hooking it on his neck. "I'm sorry,
Lieutenant, but I have to mark you unfit for duty."

"If you do that, I'll be off the overseas shipment."

"Yes, that's true, and . . ."

Something about his eyes told her that the worst news was
yet to come. "What else?"

"I may have to recommend you for discharge."

She heard her own dazed voice, thin and frightened, pleading, "Doctor, isn't there anything—a cure, or some medica-
tion?"

He shook his head. "I'll review your chart, and if hospital
rest is indicated, perhaps we'll try that first before I make a
recommendation for discharge."

Page felt abandoned. The Army did not want her, after all.
Craziness surfaced in her usually logical mind—maybe the
fates had found a Hannaday woman in uniform to be the
anathema her father had predicted. She could see his knowing
face before her. If she had to go home like this, not good
enough for the WAAC, she'd never be able to leave again.
He'd see to that, and she wouldn't have the strength to defy

him. She felt her world crumbling beneath her. Sitting slumped on the examining table, mourning, she hardly noticed the nurse gently helping her into her uniform.

"Page," Jill ranted and beat one size-five-and-a-half fist against the other, "they *can't* do this to you!"

"I'm afraid they can and they did," Page answered the circle of faces hovering over her hospital bed. "I'm out of the first overseas shipment. The question is, will they let me stay in the WAAC?"

"Damn and hell!" Bunny said, her dark-lashed eyes blue-ringed after twenty-four hours as training-center duty officer. "It's not fair. No," she said emphatically, "not you, Page. You're the best—the best."

"Oh—" Page realized that tears were gathering and there was no way she could stop them—"please, just leave now. They're going to try isolation. Complete rest—no visitors, no reading, nothing but sleeping and eating."

Bunny laughed, a strained laugh. "Sounds like heaven, you lucky gal."

Page managed a smile. "I'll see you in two weeks—one way or the other."

Elisabeth opened her mouth, and then quickly closed it. She had no words to heal this grief she could not even understand. Page's dedication to the women's army embarrassed her and made her feel an unaccustomed shyness. She knew she would have taken any way out of the WAAC, even this way.

That afternoon Major Carter came to see Page. "How are you doing, Lieutenant?"

"I'm feeling stronger, Doctor," she said sitting up, hoping it was true.

He gently pushed her shoulder back to the pillow. "Well, now, don't expect a miracle in one day. It would be unfair to you to get your hopes up unnecessarily. But I'll tell you one thing, young lady. If your friends have anything to say about it—"

"My friends?"

"Yes, I received an earnest deputation this afternoon at the dispensary, three young women, who tried to persuade me that the WAAC would fall apart if you weren't part of it. Damned near convinced me, too."

Page could only nod, for once excused of military etiquette; she could not trust the huge lump in her throat to allow the passage of grateful words.

The next two weeks in isolation were the longest Page had ever lived. Cut off from everything—friends, work, war news—she concentrated on ways to help herself. Listening to her heartbeat pounding through the silence, she tried to regulate the echo bouncing off the chambers of her heart.

At night she thought of positive, pleasant things. A long-ago memory, a fuzzy image of her mother, gradually formed in her mind. A pretty, dressed-up lady hovered over her bed, saying, "Think, little love, of fluffy blue clouds, and when they have passed, every tiny one, Mommy will be home again and come in to kiss you good night."

She could scarcely remember now what her mother looked like outside of the family photograph her father had kept in his den: he was holding her, Page, in an ages-ago Panama summer, her long legs dangling down the front of his tropical worsted summer uniform; her mother, young and beautiful, was holding baby Randy.

But every night that December her mother came to the Fort Des Moines hospital, bending over her bed, repeating the childhood reassurance. Then Page would drop into a deep and even sleep, the blue clouds passing over, one by one.

Page walked slowly down Des Moines' Walnut Street and headed east past Younkers department store. Despite the late-December cold, the night was clear. Iowa's sometime blustery wind was calm, and she was only one of many men and women in uniform celebrating this second Christmas Eve of the war.

The clock in Davidson's window across the street pointed to eight, reminding her that she had eaten little from the lunch tray at the hospital. Not that eating mattered much to her tonight.

She turned into Babe's, walked through the downstairs restaurant full of civilians, who paid no attention to the now familiar uniform, and climbed the stairs to the second-floor banquet room.

Bunny saw her first and waved her to the table. "You look fantastic, Page," she said, hugging her.

"Absolutely healthy!" Jill said.

"Well, are you cured?" Elisabeth bluntly asked the question that was on all of their minds.

Page, relief written plainly on her face, nodded happily. "Dr. Carter marked me fit for duty." Suddenly she stopped. What she had to tell them was happy news for her, but sad too, since it meant she would be separated from them. "I got word this afternoon that I'm shipping out tomorrow—to the Pentagon. Director Hobby requested me."

Bunny raised the glass. "You'll soon get that place organized." She hid her feelings behind the joke.

Page laughed. "I can't promise we'll win the war this month—maybe next month."

Jill picked up her drink and raised it. "Here's to all of us, Page."

"What?"

"We're all on orders."

"Oh—" she forced herself to be happy for them, even though she knew that an important part of her life had come to an end—"it had to come, didn't it?"

Bunny said, "Me to the Air WAAC in Texas—the new CO of a photographic unit. Can you imagine me as a field company commander?"

"And you, Jill?" Page asked.

"Just what I wanted," Jill answered, her voice happy. "Cryptography school at Fort Monmouth, New Jersey."

"And you, Elisabeth?"

Bunny interrupted. "Where else but—"

Page asked, "Not to Washington with me?"

Elisabeth shook her head. "Not the Pentagon, Page, but the big QM depot in Philadelphia. Back to the *fringes* of civilization, at least."

The jukebox played the "Warsaw Concerto," its smashing chords a melodramatic underlining to the friendship that had grown into an intimacy stronger than sisterhood. Page wondered if they would ever see one another again after tomorrow.

Bunny ordered a bottle of champagne, but when it came Jill grabbed it before it could be opened. "Let's all sign the label and leave it at the bar, then when the war is over we can come back here and drink it—and swap war stories. Come on," she said, excited, "I saw Gary Cooper do it in a movie once."

Elisabeth shrugged. "Jill, that's silly—schoolgirl stuff."

"No it isn't," Jill said, determined now. "It's called the 'last survivor' bottle. Let's make a pact to return here—say, the Christmas Eve after the war is over. Whoever shows up gets to drink the bottle in memory of the others."

Bunny grinned. "You've got some imagination, kid. We're all coming back."

But the idea appealed to them after all, and they signed their names and the date, December 24, 1942, on the bottle's label.

"Still seems like a waste of good champagne to me," Bunny grumbled after they had deposited the bottle with the bartender and watched him put it on a shelf high above the rest of the stock.

"No such thing," Jill said, pleased with the high drama of it all. "Tell you what. If I don't come back, Bunny, you can have my share."

"Praise the lord and pass the ammunition . . ." the jukebox blared out the big hit song.

But Bunny wasn't listening to the music. A sudden chill—a draft from somewhere—gripped her and she wished she'd never heard of a damned "last survivor" bottle.

The Des Moines taxi moved through the storm-slowed Christmas Day traffic down Walnut Street.

"I wish we could stop at Babe's one last time," Jill said, torn between nostalgia for the good times already rapidly receding and excitement over the unknown adventures ahead.

"We will one day," Bunny said, her voice full of unaccustomed determination. "We *all* will."

"Promise, Mother Bunny?" Jill said, laughing.

"Promise."

Page heard Jill and Bunny's exchange, and saw Elisabeth holding her tightly packed duffle bag, staring out the window, smiling, her blond hair wreathed in sunlight. The smile was strange, because the rest of them were so close to tears. She never would understand Elisabeth; then, maybe she didn't need to. They had worked together the past five months as no women ever had, suffered identical hardships and forged a bond that would continue even if they never saw one another again.

The taxi pulled up in front of the Rock Island train station, and they gave each other a lift with the heavy bags.

A group of women in civvies huddled under a huge sign on the platform that read: "WAAC REPORT HERE." The new recruits stared at the four WAAC officers.

"Remember when we were that green?" Bunny asked. "A hundred years ago."

In some way the new Waacs comforted Page. She and her friends had been the first women soldiers, but now that they were moving into the field, others were taking their place—and others after them—assuring a continuity of women soldiers.

They checked the call board for their trains. Jill would be leaving first.

"If any of you ever get up to Monmouth—" she began.

"We'll look you up," Page said what they were all thinking. "And if you're ever in Washington—"

"I'll look you up," Jill finished the thought.

"We won't ever lose touch with each other," Bunny said. "Promise?" She stuck out her hand.

Like the old children's game of one-potato-two-potato they piled one hand on top of the other until all four of them had promised.

This must be what it's like to have sisters, Page thought, watching Jill's small figure in the olive-drab coat walk away down Track 5.

"Page, I'm really no good at this," Bunny said, her eyes glistening. "Now, don't argue, you two—I'm going over to my gate and wait alone."

"Write when you get to Texas," Page called after her.

The two of them, Page and Elisabeth, stood there a moment, watching Bunny walk away.

Elisabeth said, "I must be off myself, Page, but first I'd like to tell you—" She stopped.

"Tell me what?"

"I haven't made it a secret that I don't like the WAAC, and yet, you were my friend. No—don't say anything. I'm not fishing for compliments. I don't understand it myself, but knowing you and Bunny and Jill has made these the happiest months of my life." Elisabeth picked up her bag and turned a haunted face toward Page. "I haven't deserved it, you know," she said, her usually cultured voice flat with a western-Pennsylvania twang. "If you knew me, *really* knew me—who I am, where I come from, what I've been—"

Page stopped her. "I know all I need to know. You're one of us, and if you ever need a friend . . . "

Page watched Elisabeth's tall elegant figure walk toward her gate, hand her ticket to the conductor and turn once again to wave. The smile she had seen on Elisabeth's face in the taxi had returned even more triumphantly. Suddenly and irrevocably Page knew what that smile meant. Elisabeth, at last, had people in her life to care about—and to miss.

Whoo-sh sh-oo. The rush of released air echoed from brakes all along the length of the sleek *Silver Rocket* as Page swung aboard. The diesel engine whirred, the huge wheels churned, and she took a seat facing forward. The four of them were moving in different directions. She felt regret and the poignant feeling of being alone for the first time since they had all stepped off the truck that hot July Sunday, in what seemed now like another age. But she couldn't quite suppress her anticipation of the adventure that lay ahead of her.

BOOK TWO

1943: A DATE WITH DESTINY

14

In 1943, the tide of war begins to turn against the Axis Powers. In the Pacific, Allied forces capture Buna in New Guinea, freeing Australia from the threat of Japanese attack. In North Africa, the U.S. Fifth Army and the British Eighth Army drive forward in Tunisia. On the Russian front, the Germans start a retreat from the Caucasus.

The Waacs are on the move from their Fort Des Moines training center. Nine full companies have been delivered to commands in the Zone of the Interior, two units are secretly training with antiaircraft artillery that rings Washington, D.C., in case women have to replace men in defending the capital from Nazi planes. Another large unit is on its way to England. It follows in the wake of a torpedoed ship carrying five WAAC officers, who are rescued and delivered to Eisenhower's North Africa GHQ, begrimed and in rags.

ON A BLUSTERY Sunday morning, January 3, WAAC Third Officer Elisabeth Gardner arrived at the billet address on her travel orders, a run-down hotel in central Philadelphia, home of one of twenty-seven WAAC Aircraft Warning Service units trained at Fort Des Moines and now spread along the East Coast.

"You're lucky, ma'am," the first sergeant at the Franklin Hotel WAAC detachment said, consulting her room roster. "Let's see, now—all the aircraft warning officers are shift workers and you'll be straight day shift, so you've got a single room."

Lucky! Lucky to be playing soldier in a third-rate hotel?

She glanced down the roster and recognized no names from her OC company. Alone again.

"Go on up to Room 301 at the head of the landing, ma'am, and when you've unpacked I'll show you the ropes," the sergeant was saying. "You're only attached to us for quarters and rations, but the CO wants you to rotate duty officer with the others. I'll have the new DO roster posted this afternoon."

Elisabeth picked up her duffle bag. "Is that all, Sergeant?"

"We have no mess here, ma'am, so you'll get a dollar twenty-five a day to eat at any restaurant that accepts government chits. It's not much, but the others can tell you where the good but cheap meals are."

Two minutes later, Elisabeth opened the door on a room the size of her closet at Madame Gabriella's, dropped her bags and collapsed onto the unmade bed. She stretched her cramped leg muscles, sore after days of travel on a crowded day coach. There had been no roomettes available, not even an upper berth although her ticket called for one. The Pullman conductor had taken a twenty-dollar bribe, then pretended he didn't remember it. The war had ruined men. Or rather, the war had almost ruined her. How could she have been so taken in by Page's noble rhetoric, Jill's heroic determination, even Bunny's good-sport resilience? High ideals were possible in a small enclave of patriotism like the WAAC training center, but the real world outside hadn't changed. Everybody would cheat you if you didn't cheat him first.

It would have been bad enough if she had just had to sit up in a day coach all the way to Philadelphia, but her coach had been uncoupled somewhere in Indiana and left for an entire night. After that, everything had happened to that damned train. Between Des Moines and Philadelphia it was sidetracked for troop trains, freight trains, probably even milk trains—a half-dozen or more long, frustrating delays. Even a two-day rest at a hotel in Pittsburgh hadn't lightened her mood.

Those days on the train hadn't resembled any travel she'd ever known. As 1942 turned into 1943, everyone in the country seemed to be on the move to somewhere else: older men and boys heading toward war plants and shipyards; young men in uniform trying desperately to get home for the holidays; young wives with screaming babies following husbands some of them hardly knew; even younger girls in Sloppy Joe sweaters and bobby sox trailing anything in khaki pants.

Elisabeth stretched, dismissing those scenes from her mind. She could sleep for a week, but she didn't have a week. Tomorrow she must report to the quartermaster depot. She wondered what job they wanted her to fill. Perhaps it didn't matter. Wasn't this supposedly the culmination of all that marching and those tin-soldier inspections? She was ready to do her bit for victory against the Axis, wasn't she?

Elisabeth smiled ruefully at the ceiling. Some of the gung-ho at Fort Des Moines had infected her for a time—or maybe it had been knowing Page and Bunny and Jill. All through the long train journey, she had examined the past months in her mind. Something wonderful, strangely wonderful, had happened to her, and she would store the memory of it away in a special part of her. With these women who had become her friends, what was honest in her nature had come forth. For a few months, she had thought that the rest of her life might be different, that she might be like them.

She rolled onto her side and stared out at the snow falling past her third-floor window into the alley below, and her smile disappeared. Now that she was alone again, she could see more clearly. She had wanted to be liked by them, but not to be like them. They were nice girls who lived by all the nice-girl rules. Now that she was back in her world, she had to make her own rules to survive. Still, she knew, she would always have three friends who had shared a strange new life with her. Nothing could ever take that away.

The next morning she boarded the stubby olive-drab army bus that pulled up promptly at 0810 in front of the frayed awning of the Franklin's Broad Street entrance. After a twenty-minute ride, she reported to the administration building at the depot.

"You're to see Colonel Nickolson—uhh, Lieutenant," a young corporal with a GI haircut growing in a half-dozen directions informed her, his voice trailing off into openmouthed awe. She could feel his eyes following her as she walked between the rows of scarred oak desks manned by enlisted men. Several low wolf whistles erupted behind her.

Elisabeth was herself again. All the indecision and self-doubt she had experienced at Fort Des Moines was gone.

Again she reveled in what she was, a beautiful, desirable woman, but she was not for the likes of these enlisted men.

She let them know it. The subtle way she moved her body with the conscious grace of a trained model captured their eyes, but she was as untouchable as a crown jewel under glass. And that was the way she had always wanted it and now wanted it again—admiration with no strings.

Nickolson ushered her into his office and held his desk side chair for her. "Well, well—Lieutenant." He cleared his throat. "It's so damned hard to get used to calling a woman by a military title. And I'll never get used to all those made-up WAAC ranks—third officer, second leader and so forth. You understand?"

"Of course, Colonel." She used her pleasant, deferential tone. "I'm here to help in any way I can." Next Elisabeth put on her demure face—the most difficult one for her. "I have given up my career for the duration, so titles aren't in the least important to me." She had determined what he wanted to hear and said it.

"Admirable," the colonel said, pulling a paper from a stack in his in basket. "Now, this was quite an impressive letter you wrote the Quartermaster General while you were taking your training. After I saw it, I put in a personal request for you through the OQMG in Washington. . . . "

Elisabeth smiled. *Who's he kidding? He got orders to request me.*

". . . You sounded like you had the kind of specialized knowledge we can use here. We'll carry you on the table of organization as my secretary, but I have something else in mind for you."

At first she thought he was making a pass. Even though his hair was thin enough to show most of his scalp and his waist had slipped over his web belt, he was a man, after all.

"Lieutenant," he went on, his mind evidently on business, "do you know the last Gallup poll revealed that women prospects for recruitment rated the WAAC uniform last after all the women's services? Waves, Spars, Women Marines all scored far higher."

"No, sir, I didn't know that, but I'm not at all surprised," she answered bluntly. "I would have voted the same way."

"Good! We'll get along. I hoped you'd be as direct as your

letter." He lit a cigarette, after offering Elisabeth one. "Let me tell you, we've had our problems with allocations from the War Manpower Board—you'll learn about these—but we do want to turn this situation around. Everybody's on my neck about it from your WAAC Director to the General Staff. What I need from you is a detailed report of what a woman of your experience finds wrong with every item of WAAC issue. And *why*—give me the why of it! I'll expect your recommendations in this office by the first week of February 1943. That's just a month. Can you do it?"

"Yes, sir, this is the chance I've been hoping for." Jill could not have said it better, she told herself.

The next few weeks Elisabeth found surprisingly interesting. January flew by. Her days were as full as they had ever been at Gabriella's in the busiest season—fuller, perhaps, because she was now much more than a mere mannequin; she was working with cloth, design and the details of procurement. And the wonder of it was, she was good at it. She felt—well, she could only call it excited, as if she had suddenly discovered a lost twin, Elisabeth still but a more perfect Elisabeth.

Although she found that the Quartermaster Corps had legitimate gripes to level at the Requirements Division in the Services of Supply (Requirements seemed completely incapable of approving proposals without lengthy debate over possible cost discrimination *in favor* of women), still the real problem lay, she could plainly see, in the inability of the Army to believe that there were really female bodies in their uniforms, and that female bodies were different from male bodies.

She was shocked to find that a male form had been used for the WAAC uniform's master pattern. "This alone would account for many of the complaints I heard at Fort Des Moines," she told Corporal Danny Barnes, a slightly built young tailor on the uniform specialists' team she had joined. "Look at this," she said to him after several days of taking uniforms apart. "All these jackets have been cut with wide collars and narrow hips as if for men."

"They've used men's short, regular and long sizing too," Barnes said. "The shirts are just as bad. Take a look."

"This is crazy. They go by neck sizes instead of bust sizes. No wonder I never saw a Waac whose collar wasn't too big or whose shirt wasn't pulling across the bust."

Barnes was a valuable co-worker. From the first day, he was at her elbow, anticipating her wishes. She soon found he was an indispensable cutter of red tape. He could get her an item she needed when no one else could. It was only slightly inconvenient that he obviously had a crush on her.

At night she returned to the Franklin Hotel, stopping first at a small out-of-the-way family restaurant off Vine Street near the Betsy Ross House. The food was plain but well-prepared, and the papa fussed over her table, giving her extras without charging for them. Best of all, to her mind, she almost never saw other Waacs there, and she took care not to share her discovery with them. Why should she? They talked of nothing but the incessant boredom of their work plotting unidentified planes on the central eastern corridor filter board, of their dreary boyfriends and their equally dreary postwar marriage prospects. Most of all she avoided them because they wanted from her the intimacy they had come to expect from one another at Fort Des Moines, and she had determined she would never succumb to that need again.

Often there were letters from Marne waiting in the orderly room for her, and she methodically answered them letter for letter. He wrote with the same mindless contentment she had observed in people who were sure of their past and of their future and sure, so very sure, of themselves.

The closeness to him that sharing a uniform had first made her feel had passed.

By late January, Elisabeth was putting the finishing touches on her report for Colonel Nickolson, which included a model uniform incorporating all her changes. The idea had been Elisabeth's, but the rest of the team had gone along, especially Barnes, whose talent as a tailor had shown her how to translate her ideas to paper patterns and then into material.

"Let's do one more fitting to make sure we have it perfect," she said and slipped behind the dressing screen.

Emerging a few minutes later, she smoothed the skirt and well-fitted jacket that no longer flattened her full breasts or bulged over her flat stomach. She looked in the mirror and with her hand smoothed her hair into the elegant wraparound roll that kept it off her collar. Under the overhead lights her hair took on a summer gloss, and her skin, she was pleased to see, was once again ivory with a healthy rose blush. She carefully scrutinized her face with a professional's care, looking routinely for the faint lines and shadows that would mark the end of youth. Then, satisfied, she became aware that two dark eyes were regarding her with a professionalism of their own.

"Who is that?" she whispered to Barnes, motioning imperceptibly toward a powerfully built man of moderate height detached from a group near the colonel's office.

"You don't know Max Stryker? He's Mr. Big in clothing manufacture. Besides that, I think he owns half the Philadelphia waterfront."

He must also own a resort in Florida, she thought, looking at the tanned face, handsome in a leonine way, but too knowing, secretive, full of the old anger of self-invented men. His iron-gray hair still streaked with black swept back from his high forehead. She saw that he knew he'd been observed, but instead of looking away his appraising eyes slowly traveled along her entire body, a faint smile on his wide, sensual mouth.

Elisabeth had been stared at like some prize thoroughbred before and had a standard put-down, but she chose not to turn him away—she could recognize an important man when she saw one. Instead she returned his gaze, her eyes level with his.

She had heard his name around the QM depot. Who hadn't? His critics, and there seemed to be quite a few of them, portrayed him as a rogue Frankenstein's monster who left bloody footprints in the snow. It was common knowledge that he had broken his partner and then bought him out for pennies on the dollar. Yet, far from this making him *persona non grata,* the gossips adored him, reported him squire for half the Philadelphia lovelies, including one Biddle. Altogether a fascinating predator, she decided, excited at the prospect of the old man–woman game she hadn't played for a while.

Max Stryker crossed the open warehouse floor to where Elisabeth stood. "Lieutenant Gardner," he said in a baritone but rather breathy voice, "my friend Nick Nickolson tells me you don't think much of my uniforms. I'd like to hear more, but I haven't time now. Over dinner tonight?"

The question held a hint of command, and she had it on her tongue to refuse. Experience made her stop. She could scarcely refuse a man who was the colonel's friend. She nodded yes.

"It's settled, then," he said as if he'd been in no doubt. "My car will call for you at seven." He walked away, the sound of his heels falling abruptly on her ears. So that's the awesome Max Stryker. She shrugged, but the amazing vibrance of his person hung in the air about her.

Elisabeth knew men, and she realized she had just been in the presence of raw masculine power—some primitive sexuality that took her unawares and caused the hair at the nape of her neck to tingle its ancient warning. Max Stryker was obviously a man who took what he wanted. She wondered what it was like never to see anyone's needs but one's own, and then, in a flash of insight, she realized that she herself was such a person or would be. Ah, but the difference between them was his money, which he had wrested from lesser men, while she'd been forced to mortgage her body for everything she got.

15

More than 280,000 jobseekers, most of them young women, pour into wartime Washington, D.C., lured by high government wages which pay typists $1,600 a year. As many as 35,000 of these workers fill the newly completed labyrinth across the Potomac called the Pentagon. People wonder what the War Department will do with such a huge building after the war, but President Roosevelt explains that it will be used to house government records and store quartermaster supplies.

A COLD DRIZZLE greeted Page's return to Washington. In the taxi from Union Station to the Pentagon, she made an effort to repair the ravages of a long train trip, tucking her chestnut hair up under her hat and putting a touch of Coty powder on the circles under her tired green eyes before reporting to the Director's office for duty. She almost wished she had time to stop for some of the new pancake makeup everybody was talking about.

"Third Officer Hannaday, Page—reporting as ordered, ma'am." Page snapped a precision salute, shoulders straight, eyes front, left hand touching the side seam of her skirt.

"Welcome back to WAAC headquarters, Hannaday," the duty officer said. "We're on a six-day week now, sometimes more. A word of advice," she went on, not unkindly. "Carry your rank easily here. You're just in from the training center, and—well, you may be a bit too military for some of the men. Relax a little, and you'll do well."

In crowded Washington, Page had the incredible luck to arrange a three-room apartment sublet, for a very reasonable fifty-five dollars a month. Its present occupant, a Finance Corps Waac, had put in for troop duty at the newly activated training center of Fort Oglethorpe, Georgia. Page arrived on the pleasant residential street just as the woman was packing.

"Come on in," a pleasant voice called when she knocked on the open door, "but leave the door open, so I can hear the taxi driver."

"I don't want to barge in before you're out," Page replied.

"Nonsense." The voice came from the bathroom. "Grab some coffee in the kitchen and come help me sit on this bag. I can't even get the darned strap around it."

"Hi," Page said, carefully placing her hot coffee cup on the dresser scarf. "Want me to hold the lock while you pull?"

"Would you?" the woman said, pushing away the hair falling in front of her eyes, to reveal a mass of freckles. "I'll die if I miss my train."

Page steadied the duffle bag while the woman hauled on the webbed strapping. At last the clasp clicked into place around irregular bulges that were obviously not army issue.

"Your name must be Hannaday. First OC, wasn't it? My name's Georgie Morris—and—I was—in the third—class," the woman puffed. "Got enough candy bars and nylons in here to last a year," she said, looking at her watch. "Good! Five minutes left—just time for a quick tour of the palace."

They walked through the small apartment, Georgie pointing out its idiosyncrasies—a faucet handle that came off in her hand, an ancient GE refrigerator that ran better if one leg had a small block under it, throwing it off balance.

"Guess that's it," Georgie said. "I better get downstairs. D.C. taxis won't wait for Eleanor Roosevelt herself."

"Good luck," Page said, holding out her hand.

"Thanks," Georgie said, shaking hands, "but you better keep your luck, friend, 'cause you're going to need it. Myself, I can't wait to get out of this town."

"Why?"

"Why? It's a man's town, that's why. The place is jammed full of little frilly things who just *l-o-v-e* a man in uniform. Now, we Waac officers can't wear civvies or have a drink in public, and we work late hours and weekends. We're no guy's idea of a party girl—no matter what you've heard. Let me tell you, this town's a WAAC purgatory. Anyway," she said, giving Page an appraising look, "maybe *you'll* do better. Now I really gotta run." And she rushed, breathless, through the door, her bag bumping behind her down the stairs.

After the first-floor door slammed, Page surveyed her new home. Drab and small though it was, with a splash of color and a little imagination it wouldn't be half bad, she told herself. She unpacked, pressed her uniforms and placed her cosmetics and toiletries neatly on the dresser and in the tiny bathroom. Actually, this was the first place all her own she had ever had. Why, then, did she feel so glum, so much a visitor, like a small child sent away to school?

She missed Bunny and Jill and Elisabeth, but it was more than that. She missed the staccato bugle notes that signaled the passage of army time, the banging trays in the officers' mess; she even missed the incessant borrowing that was part of life in the WAAC BOQ, the gripe sessions, the rush to the PX when a shipment of scarce items was rumored—the whole rhythm of a soldier's life. She knew now that she had always longed for it. Even as a child when she had gone away to boarding school, she had missed the ceremony of a military post. She remembered trying to hold fast to those ceremonies, of saluting the school flag on the stroke of five (while her roommates giggled), just as she had with her father at Command Retreat. She had never done it again, but at five every afternoon she had thought herself back to Fort Sam Houston or Fort Sill or to any one of the other posts where her father was serving. Page had always supposed she was missing her father, but now she knew it had been more than homesickness, because that feeling had returned full force to the adult Page now.

Finally settled into her new apartment, but without dinner because she couldn't shop until she had been issued ration books, Page fell asleep hungry.

It was dark when a knock at the door awakened her. She turned on the small lamp by her bed and squinted at her alarm. One o'clock! Who could be—? She heard the faint knock again. Slipping on her robe, she went to the door. "Who is it?"

"Georgie, it's Paul Burkhardt."

"I'm not Georgie," she said.

"Are you a new roommate?" asked the male voice.

"No, I'm Lieutenant Hannaday, but . . ." she began to explain, then stopped. She couldn't carry on a loud conversation at this time of the night.

Opening the door, she saw a major's gold leaves before she saw his face. "Major?"

"I'm sorry to disturb you," he said, peering into the room behind her, "but is Georgie here?"

"Georgie's been transferred to Oglethorpe. I've sublet the apartment."

"Oh," he said, "I didn't know—then I owe you an apology. You see, I've been at the Farm for over a week, and . . ." He was obviously embarrassed, and held up the grocery bag he was carrying. "Food," he explained. "When I can get away, Georgie lets me cook home style. But I'm keeping you up," he added, backing toward the stairs in confusion. "So sorry."

"Wait," she said, wondering for a moment how she could even consider inviting a strange man into her apartment to cook for her. But she wasn't the least frightened of him. He had confident, compelling eyes, dark, yet full of light; not a classically handsome face, but one that was wonderfully self-contained, almost serene. "As long as you're here, Major Burkhardt," she said, smiling, "I must admit I'm famished, if you'd like to practice your culinary art on me."

"Oh, I couldn't . . ." he began. "Are you sure I wouldn't . . ." he asked, but took off his hat and stepped through the door that Page opened wider.

"I'll dress while you get started," she said. "You know your way around the kitchen?" Page put it in the form of a question, but it was obvious that he did. She supposed all those spices and condiments she had noticed earlier in the cupboard had been his and not Georgie's.

Later, when she came to the kitchen, he had set the small table and decanted a bottle of red wine, and the smell of sizzling steaks made her ravenous. "Major, may I do something to help?"

"You can call me Paul," he said, smiling at her. "I think cooking for a lady in the small hours qualifies for a suspension of military etiquette."

"My name's Page Hannaday."

He nodded. "Yes, I know. You don't remember, but we've met."

"Really?"

"At the Army-Navy Club," he said, flipping the steaks he was frying and handed her a knife, after he pointed toward a large loaf of bread. "You were there with your father—last April it was—and I delivered a message to him from General Willis. I was on Willis' staff at the time."

"I'm sorry," she said honestly, slicing the bread, "I don't remember, but I promise I won't forget you again—my mouth is absolutely watering."

"Sit down, then," he said, putting on his uniform jacket and holding her chair.

He poured her wine and courteously lifted his glass, which she touched with hers, and then they ate in silence, occasionally smiling across the table, not flirtatiously but comfortably, as if they'd been having late-night suppers like this for years.

"You're really a lifesaver, Paul," she said, sighing contentedly at her empty plate. "I won't be able to shop for groceries until tomorrow night. But, tell me, is your farm near here?"

He laughed. "It's not *my* farm," he said, "and it's not that kind of farm."

She looked at him, puzzled.

"I know it doesn't make sense," he said, pouring more wine into her glass. "I can't tell you much, except that I've been working in intelligence since I left Willis' staff. The Farm— with a capital *F*—is a training station we have over the line in Maryland. I have an arrangement with a mess sergeant who supplies me with the basics for meals such as this one in exchange for my helping him with his German out of class."

Page knew enough not to probe into why he was teaching German at a curious place called the Farm. "I could have guessed you were a teacher," she told him. "Even in that uniform you have a professorial air."

Paul smiled. "I'm disappointed," he said, his voice a pleasing baritone. "I hoped I'd left my tweedy look back at Rutgers."

"Don't be disappointed. I meant it as a compliment."

He lit her cigarette and took short puffs on his pipe. "I should be going. You must be on duty tomorrow."

"Yes, soon you really must, but finish your pipe first."

He asked her about her training and her new assignment. She was aware of his controlled interest in her, and in a comfortable way she returned it. Here was a strong man, not in the muscular sense, although he was tall and well built, but in the sense of a man who had claimed his piece of the world and was content. He was like her father in that way, and just for a moment she feared this peculiarly male strength, feared being folded again into a man's life until what was beginning to be Page disappeared again.

"Now I really must go," Paul was saying. "Thank you so much for sharing this late supper with me," he said at the door.

She held out her hand and he took it.

"I hope you'll let me cook for you again," he said, small lines radiating from the corners of his eyes in a friendly way.

"I'd like that—but just a bit earlier." She returned his smile.

"Next Saturday—about eight then?"

"Yes, that would be fine," she said as he stepped onto the landing. "I'm sorry you missed Georgie," she called after him softly.

Paul stopped and moved one step back toward her, "Yes, she was a nice girl—but we were just . . ." he paused and answered her unasked question, "dinner partners."

Waving then, he went quietly down the stairs.

Page undressed and went back to bed. She could sleep three more hours before her alarm went off. Paul. What a sweet man he was, she thought, tucking the covers tight under the mattress. Imagine meeting him before and not remembering. They had probably only spoken briefly to each other, acknowledging an introduction.

Page turned to her side and tucked her knees into her stomach. Most of her life since adolescence she had been her father's hostess, greeting people for him and never really meeting them for herself. She had a feeling that with Paul, this time, it would be different.

"Georgie Morris," she whispered into her pillow, "I think Washington is a wonderful town."

16

All motorists are assigned gasoline ration stickers. Those with A stickers are allowed four gallons a week; with B or C stickers they are entitled to extra gasoline because their driving is essential to the war effort or to public health. Unlimited gasoline supplies go to motorists with X stickers. Pleasure driving is banned, and a 35-mile-per-hour speed limit is enforced.

PROMPTLY AT SEVEN on the evening she was to dine at Max Stryker's house, Elisabeth walked through the rococo lobby that served as the detachment dayroom. It was filled with Waacs listening to the *Hit Parade* on a Stromberg-Carlson console radio, writing letters and gossiping.

Past the beveled-glass doors, a black limousine with an X gasoline sticker affixed to the window waited, purring, at the curb. It was a bright, sharply cold night—no snow—and Elisabeth hugged her WAAC winter-issue coat about her body while the uniformed chauffeur opened the car door for her. After stepping in she could see with some satisfaction that a windowful of Waacs peered out at her with intense curiosity. Elisabeth smiled at the idea that she might be the object of their gossip for the rest of the evening.

She ran her hand over the deep pile upholstery, luxuriating in the space and comfort of the limousine. Tucked in the corner she saw a fur lap robe which she recognized as mink. She spread it across her legs with a shuddering sigh at its sensuous embrace.

"Mr. Max say to keep you warm all the way to Drexel Hill, miss," the driver called through a window he had cranked down. "Help yourself to some refreshment."

Elisabeth opened the door of the cabinet located between the two jump seats, to reveal a well-stocked miniature bar, complete with Venetian crystal stemware.

"There's a thermos of coffee, miss, or you can have a brandy."

She couldn't resist having a cup of coffee with the smallest jigger of brandy in it. It would have been unbearable to have such an opportunity and not take advantage of it. Few of the men she had known in New York had had such a car. She could see she would have to raise her sights.

The tires crunched up the long, curving drive through a park of old elm trees to the largest Colonial Revival house that Elisabeth had ever seen outside the movies.

A houseman met her at the door, took her coat and ushered her into a large room on the right halfway down the tiled foyer. A wood fire burned in the huge stone fireplace, and Elisabeth thought it was the most consciously masculine room she had ever seen—rubbed wood and soft dark leather permeated with the smell of good Havana cigars; it simply reeked of male virility. She couldn't help but think that in another man she might think it all a pose, but with Max Stryker the room was obviously an unconscious extension of himself.

He left a group about the fireplace and walked quickly toward her, his hand extended. "Mrs. Gardner—it is Mrs., isn't it?" He lifted her ring hand and nodded. "How nice of you to come. May I tell you how very attractive you look in my uniform." He smiled, a sardonic but not unpleasant twist to his full mouth.

Elisabeth began to apologize, breaking one of her few rules. "Oh, I didn't mean your uniform was—"

"Of course you didn't," he said, holding up his hand to stop her apology, appearing the gracious host. "Forgive my bad joke. Come. Let me introduce you to my friends."

Elisabeth was not used to being bullied by a man—indeed,

just the opposite—and she did not intend to give him any further chances. She nodded coolly when introduced to Kit Longley, an attractive if no longer young woman in a Trigère gown, prewar no doubt, but timeless in its classic lines.

"My dear, how sweet of you to actually *join* the woman's army," the woman said, placing a proprietary hand on Max Stryker's arm. He bent attentively and kissed the back of the hand.

One of the men, who had been introduced as Clay something or other, brought Elisabeth a martini. "Isn't it awfully hard on a woman—I mean all the marching and living in tents and all? I'd be in it myself but for a perforated eardrum."

She was bored with his fatuous questions, but as Max's guest she had to be nice to his friends. "Yes, it's hard," she answered. "No, we don't live in tents. Yes, it's too bad about your eardrum." She wished they could forget she was in uniform, but apparently she was such an oddity they were going to spend the evening examining her like some Barnum and Bailey freak.

"Well, Max," Elisabeth overheard Clay say a bit tipsily, "if all our women soldiers look like Mrs. Gardner does in their uniforms, the Army should give you a bonus."

Max replied loudly enough for everyone to hear, "Mrs. Gardner complements the uniform, Clay. She's a former Gabriella model—one of her best, as I understand it."

"Beg pardon," Clay mumbled into his glass. "Thought she looked too good to be just . . . Max, old boy—" he raised his glass in a mock toast—"leave it to you to find a diamond in an army uniform."

At dinner, Kit Longley stared openly and none too happily at Elisabeth from across the table at Max's left. It pleased Elisabeth that she made the other woman nervous. Spoiled rich bitch! Most of all Elisabeth enjoyed the attention of a man like Max. During the months she had played soldier she had forgotten how satisfying it could be. Anyway, this was more like it. For one evening at least she had succeeded in rendering her natural enemy, a patrician woman like Kit Longley, absolutely harmless.

After a dinner of rare roast beef followed by the airiest of chocolate mousses, Max imperiously rushed his guests through their brandy. "You must excuse us. Mrs. Gardner and I have some business to discuss," he said, signaling the butler to bring his guests' coats.

Kit paused at the door, a full-length sable thrown casually about her shoulders despite the cold. "I doubt that we'll meet again, Mrs. Gardner, but I do hope you'll take care of yourself and not get into any trouble—a young girl in a hungry lion's den, you know."

"Thank you, Miss Longley, but please don't concern yourself," Elisabeth replied with matching hauteur. "I have always enjoyed taming the male animal." Thrust, parry and touché, Elisabeth thought, not bothering to hide her satisfaction at the riposte. If there was one thing Elisabeth recognized it was a hands-off warning—she had had enough of them delivered in her direction over the years.

"Call me tomorrow, Max," Kit said, without another glance at Elisabeth. "I have a darling little Maryland property in mind that I want your advice about—it's so near your own Whiskey Hill."

When the other guests had left, Elisabeth braced herself—for what, she wasn't precisely sure. Max took her arm and propelled her toward his study. Damn it! She didn't like being treated like a dog on a leash. He had been all solicitous attention while Kit Longley was watching; now he acted as if he owned her. If he thought he could use her to make another woman jealous, he was badly mistaken. She would never let a man use her again.

"Sit there," he said, pointing to a sofa in front of the smoldering fire, and without actually meaning to she found herself doing as she was told. She was shocked at how naturally she obeyed his commands. "Now tell me," he said and lit a cigar, "what's wrong with my uniforms."

She spared him no detail of the problems she had identified, enjoying her moment in Max's spotlight. He listened attentively, and slowly the anger that had fueled so much of the evening drained away from her.

"Is this the substance of the report you're going to give Nick—Colonel Nickolson?"

"That's most of it, plus, of course, my recommendations for a new uniform."

Elisabeth could not tell if he was upset with her. He had

hardly stopped moving—pacing up and down in front of her with a relentless energy that was indisputably charming. He moved to the bar enclosed on three sides by glass mirrors, which reflected every angle of his handsome head, and poured two small snifters.

"Here," he said, "you've earned part of my last bottle of prewar Courvoisier. It comes from the Charente region; a special white wine grape is grown there and in no other spot on the earth. Do you know France?"

"Madame Gabriella told me a great deal about it," Elisabeth answered untruthfully, and then said honestly, "but I haven't been myself—yet."

"Interesting—since Madame was born and raised in the Bronx and her accent is as phony as a three-franc note." He waved his hand abruptly to dismiss the subject. "Nevertheless, my dear, as soon as this war is over you must go abroad." He said it as conversationally as if he were suggesting she visit Baltimore. "Would you like that?"

Yes, she would like that very much. Elisabeth felt the soft sensuousness of the leather sofa gather her body into it as the brandy warmed her blood. It was late. She had only a midnight pass, but she knew she did not want to leave this place or this presence.

He sat down beside her. "You may be right about some of the problems you cite, but you're incredibly naïve to think they'll remake the entire uniform on your say-so, not with the enormous stockpile they're building. On the other hand, minor pattern alterations are another matter. I'll have something to say about that—don't think I mean to keep my mouth shut and lose a very large contract. I mean to fight you for it—and I mean to win!" He paused, then smiled. "But I'd so much prefer we work together."

Elisabeth was off balance. Max Stryker seemed to hold out a mysterious threat and then to change it into a promise. She was aware that he was close to her and that the heat of his body was getting all mixed up with the hot embers in the fireplace and the brandy. Suddenly her head was too heavy to remain erect and she rested it on the back of the sofa; her hair uncoiled its tightly controlled roll and spread across her shoulders, falling as if she had planned it—and for once she hadn't—next to his hand.

He twisted his fingers in her hair and gently, but relentlessly, pulled her head closer to his. He sought her hand, turned it over and kissed the soft fleshy place under the thumb. His strangely breathy voice excited her.

"Elisabeth, tell me if I'm wrong, but I think you and I would know how to work together."

For a moment she held her breath. Did he somehow know what she had done at Gabriella's? Was this entire evening a threat? Was he another Joe Bonine, only with fancier tastes?

She reclaimed the hair he had been holding spread between his fingers like the reins to a balky mare. Some primal instinct overtook her, and she stood up abruptly, ready to flee. Slowly, without loosing her hand, Max rose, too, his eyes locked on hers. The fading firelight dancing across the angles of his face, now sinister with the power she suddenly knew he exerted over her.

"You see," he was saying with a disarming smile, pointing toward the wall, "I do cast a shadow, so I must not be a vampire after all."

She was hardly aware of his words. All her energy flowed to her legs, telling them to carry her to safe ground.

In a low voice, with just a hint of uncharacteristic sadness, he was saying, "Don't believe the gossips, Elisabeth. You must have been their target more than once, so you can understand how I've been misunderstood."

She nodded, drawn now to his steady gaze. Against her will, a will she no longer seemed able to control, she moved an involuntary step closer to him. He was right, of course. She did feel she understood him. The person she didn't understand was herself. Whatever she had been, she knew she had never been a self-deceiver; she had always been on to herself, but here she was ready to fall into this man's arms, to throw herself into his bed. And who was he? A tough amoral bastard who would forget her as soon as the door closed behind her. Besides, it was quite possible, in spite of the passion her practiced eye read in his face, that he would use her simply to keep his lucrative uniform contract.

"The next time you come, Elisabeth," Max was saying, as if she had been a part of his life always, "I want you to wear one of the gowns I have upstairs. There are several that would suit you well."

With her last strength she flung a question at him. "What makes you think there will be a next time?"

He sighed impatiently, his hand tracing the curve of her shoulder, "Elisabeth, you are the last woman in the world I would expect to play childish games."

It was no declaration, simply an attitude that made instant sense to her. And then she stepped into his kiss, and was suffused in the glow of his sensuous approval. For the first time in her life she was perfectly honest, not faking her response.

"You're coming with me to my place in Maryland next weekend," he murmured, his hot breath almost melting her ear.

He walked with her to the portico and stood framed in the double doors as the limousine bore Elisabeth away down the curving drive, a light snowfall glistening in the headlights. She hugged the dark image of him standing there throughout the ride back to the Franklin Hotel, beating back the warnings that every man-knowing cell of her mind screamed out. She willed herself to forget about Marne, about the WAAC, about Page and Jill and Bunny—to forget about anything that might stop her from having Max Stryker. As she climbed the stairs to the orderly room, the shabby carpet suddenly looked as colorful as a just-woven Persian rug.

"Ma'am," the CO said after she signed in at the pass book, "your husband called earlier this evening from Texas. He said to tell you he'd be here on leave next weekend."

17

The Battle of Kasserine Pass in Tunisia pits inexperienced American troops against Rommel's Afrika Korps. Luftwaffe Stuka dive bombers create confusion in the Allied ranks, resulting in ten thousand casualties.

AAF Navigation School
Hondo, Texas
Sunday, 14 Feb. 1943

HELLO KID,

I know that Mother Bunny has been rotten in the letter writing department, but you should see my schedule. At least, you get Sundays off in code school (Jill, did you get over to see my mama yet? She's expecting you for dinner) but for us poor troop officers there ain't no such thing as a day off. I've written WAAC HQ & they promised me an exec, but they're so busy staffing new training centers, I'm at the bottom of their list.

Later

Sorry—had to stop for an emergency. No heat in one of the barracks. We can't stoke the coal furnace ourselves because we women are too weak (?) so we have to send for two firemen, who have to call for an MP guard before they can enter the WAAC area & on and on. Who dreams up these regs?

I missed Elisabeth's husband last Wednesday. He called to say he was passing through (on leave & on his way to Philly. Overseas?) and asked me to meet him at the O club for a drink. Wouldn't you know that was the afternoon I'd get stuck at the Red Cross because one of my Auxies wasn't writing home—which brought the Post Chaplain & the Gray Ladies roaring to the rescue of

American motherhood. By the time I'd called the woman on the carpet, extracted a properly contrite letter, taken it to the Red Cross & dashed to the club, he'd gone. There goes my last chance to see the big guy who talked our glamour queen into marriage. Speaking of E., thanks for the news. Leave it to her to get a cozy set-up like a hotel with civvy chow. Maybe the army does know what it's doing sometimes. I can't imagine *her* here in a Texas sandstorm!

Speaking of husbands (?), I got letters from both of my exs (or it that exes). I've heard men say that putting on a uniform brings old girlfriends out of the woodwork—Allotment Annies, ya know. Guess there's nothing like a girl in khaki to make a guy straighten up and fly right.

Which reminds me about the latest latrine rumor—next time you hear from me I may be a fly girl on a real air base instead of a school. Talk is they're going to move photo lab tech school to Lowry Field in Colorado.

Take it easy kiddo—AND DON'T TRY TO WIN THE WAR SINGLE-HANDED.

MOTHER BUNNY

Bunny folded the tissue-thin stationery into the matching envelope, licked it thoughtfully and dropped it into the mail clerk's out box. *Damn it!* She missed the kid, and Page too, even Elisabeth—why, she'd give a month's pay just to see that dazzling model's smile of hers, the one she could turn on and off at will.

For a few minutes Bunny allowed herself a reverie back to her OC days when all four of them had been outsiders in the Army, clinging together, overwhelmed by a sense that every day they had to get up and make history.

There was no camaraderie now for Bunny. She was the lone WAAC officer on the post. Another woman in uniform at the officers' club was either Red Cross, USO or a nurse from the post hospital—hardly the same thing at all.

Not that companionship was any problem—especially the male variety. If anything, she felt that she stood at the head of a long line of men, all of them wanting something from her—wanting her to be their lover, their sister, their sweetheart and, at times, their mother. No, the worst part of this duty, she had to admit, wasn't the loneliness. The worst part was that Johnny Palermo had begun to write to her (she had her sister Angela to thank for giving him her address), not the kind of letter that Johnny LaMonica and his mother had written, with "patriotic duty" spelled out all over it, but love letters that interrupted the healing process, a process Bunny knew hadn't progressed as far as it should have. Of course, the simplest solution was to send them back unopened so that he got the idea she was out of his reach. But she hadn't done that.

Outside her office, Bunny heard the orderly room radio blaring reports about a big battle in North Africa. Her head ached—she'd been on duty every day for a month—but she hadn't the heart to tell the first sergeant to turn the news down. The sergeant's son was with the First Infantry Division right in the thick of things.

Bunny opened her desk drawer and saw Johnny's letters lying on top of a pile of requisition forms. For weeks she had read them over and over without answering. What could she say? *Glad you know you made a mistake. Wish you were here.* It was much too late for regrets. It was too late to reinvest the real Johnny with the dreams of perfect physical love she'd had; too late since the night he'd turned on her. How could she ever go back to trusting him? Even if she could trust him—and she knew she would be a fool to try—she was in the Army for the duration.

Bunny sat there in the winter day's half-light. Outside her window she saw the detachment flag tugging against its halyard, as if it was trying to break away.

Her fingers, inside the drawer, traced the stamp on his last letter, circled it compulsively, felt its rough edges and then moved on to outline the letters of his name in the upper left corner—the name he wrote in an awkward boy's script that used no capital letters.

Memories rushed through her fingers. Bunny saw his eyes gleaming darkly up at her from a white pillow as he propelled exciting rhythms from her body. The memory was too vivid. She closed her eyes and, in response to a sudden rush of feeling, pressed her legs together and buried her face in her hands. *Oh, God, all this agony from a few letters!* She'd be crazy to actually see him again.

A knock on her open door caused her to drag her head

quickly erect. The mail clerk was eying her quizzically. "Yes, Corporal. What is it?"

"I've got the jeep now, ma'am, so I'm going to run the mail over to the post office," she said, holding up the contents of her out box. "Is this it?"

Bunny hesitated for so long the corporal shifted her weight and looked embarrassed.

"No, Corporal. Give me fifteen minutes. There'll be one more letter to go."

18

President Franklin D. Roosevelt submitted a whopping $109-billion 1943 budget to Congress, $100 billion earmarked for the war effort.

ON A SNOWY Saturday in mid-February, Marne Wilson Gardner burst from the crowd at the main Philadelphia Greyhound depot, his duffle bag slung under one muscular arm, his great green eyes roving the milling crowd of soldiers, sailors and civilians like searchlights at a movie premier.

What if Elisabeth hadn't received his telegram? *Oh Jesus!* There wasn't one precious minute to waste. Maybe she had duty. Seven months was a long time to be away from any wife—but a wife like his! Christ, he'd driven himself half crazy on the bus remembering her body—every inch of it. It was the kind of memory that made a man clench his fists and dig them self-consciously deeper into his pockets so as not to betray their longing. She has *got* to be here, he thought, then stopped his undisciplined searching and began, like any trained combat armor officer, a sector-by-sector survey of the waiting room jammed with uniforms. Suddenly, he saw her coming through the revolving doors from the street outside.

He pushed his way through the crowd to her, oblivious of the men in overalls chewing tobacco, girls in slacks with their hair piled in ringlets on top of their heads and tired women with kids in tow—oblivious of everything until he felt his arms around her, the familiar smell of Worth perfume in his nostrils and her body filling the aching hollows of his own.

"I've never kissed a lieutenant before," he said after a long embrace, which only intensified his need for her, "or is that an old joke for a Waac?" He saw that people had stopped in their rush to their own destinations to stare sentimentally at the uniformed man and woman greeting each other. Before she could answer, he rushed on. "Listen, darling—" he took charge with an urgency born of empty months—"let's get out of here."

He took her straight to the hotel where she had booked a room, passing Independence Hall with scarcely a glance at its perfectly balanced Georgian façade. He held her hand firmly but gently, the words tumbling from him, words he couldn't write in letters or say over the telephone.

Elisabeth's mind, as she sat next to Marne, was engaged with his on a conscious level, acting as a mediator between her husband's need for her and her own deeper needs. That deeper self was thinking of Max, not deliberately, but compulsively, and angrily viewed Marne as an intruder.

He wondered that she was so quiet, almost shy with him. But he could understand. They'd had such a little time together after their wedding. She didn't know him as her husband, but her letters had been so sweet, so loving.

Marne ordered a bottle of champagne sent to their room and tipped the departing bellboy extravagantly.

"Elisabeth, you don't know how many times I've thought of you like this," he said, drawing her down on the bed beside him, kissing her neck, her eyes, her lips.

She winced and turned her face away from his. "Your beard, Marne . . ."

What an oaf he was! "Of course," he said, scrambling to his feet, longing for these next hours to be perfection. "I'm sorry, Elisabeth. I've been on maneuvers so long, it's hard to behave like a civilized man." He rummaged in his bag, extracted his robe and headed for the shower. "Darling, will you order dinner sent up?" he called over his shoulder. "I'm not going to share you with a roomful of strangers. Not tonight."

Elisabeth watched him step into the shower. Less than a year ago, she had been so willing, even eager, to barter her body for the life Marne Gardner offered her. Something in her had changed and she did not understand it. This lack of perception frightened her. She had always been self-knowing, able to trust her own motives, and she had based this trust on her faultlessly realistic outlook.

After he had showered and shaved, they drank champagne while they waited for dinner. He told her about the months of training and more months of teaching others what he himself had learned. "I'm up for my captaincy. It's hard to believe—less than three years out of the Point. There's no stopping me now." He covered her hand with his. "How would you like to be a general's lady someday?"

"That would be nice," she agreed with measured enthusiasm.

He reasoned that her coldness to the idea of being a general's wife was due to her hatred for the WAAC.

"I missed seeing your friend Bunny."

"Didn't you get my letter with the directions?"

"Yes, but she was on duty and couldn't get away. Too bad, I really wanted to meet her because she was your friend."

"You would have liked her, Marne." Elisabeth had no doubt about that. The two of them were a type. Bunny carrying that huge torch for her ex-husband, and Marne encasing his wife in marble and imprisoning her on a pedestal.

"Marne darling, do you know where you're going?" she asked, and to him her voice was wonderful even when it questioned him.

"I've a pretty good idea it'll be North Africa. That's where armor is being tested so far in this war."

"But isn't it almost over in Africa? Rommel will be beaten soon."

"You can never count the old Desert Fox out. But Rommel's not why we're going to North Africa now. Rumor has it there'll be a second front soon, either through southern France or along the Baltic coast. We've got to be ready to jump off no matter where the Allies decide to go in."

Dinner arrived, late. Good service was one of the first casualties in wartime, he told her. He didn't mind that the entree was not steak, but turkey. "Sorry," the waiter had said pointedly, "but we're sending all the steaks to our boys in uniform." Smart-aleck kid!

Elisabeth had taken off her jacket and tie and loosed her glorious hair. He was still not used to seeing her in uniform—still a bit stunned, really. He preferred her in one of the fashionable gowns he had first seen her wear, the ones that draped around every curve and hollow of her.

He still could not understand why she had so suddenly left Gabriella's. It was unlike Elisabeth to be impulsive. He decided against bringing up the subject again, since she had written that she was happy with this posting. Still—his Elisabeth with second lieutenant's bars on her shoulders . . .

Marne saw that their windows looked out on a block-square park, two walks crossing in the middle to form an X. A few shipyard workers, from the look of their lunch pails, hurried toward home in the dusk to beat the dimout. One lone lost man stood at the center where the paths crossed, seeming not to know which to take. A slight shiver shook him, but he shrugged if off. He hated indecision.

Gently, he leaned across the table and covered her smooth hands with his maneuver-hardened ones. He could not wait for dessert, or for brandy. He could wait no longer—surely civilized behavior demanded no more of him than the seven-month sentence he had served. Scooping her into his arms, he carried her to the bed, set her carefully down on the coverlet, threw off his robe, and began fumbling with the buttons on her shirt. Always in his daydreams he was the suave lover, whisking a woman's clothes off without her even being aware they were gone. But when he was with Elisabeth, he was no better at it than he had been the first time he'd got a girl to go all the way in his roommate's Ford runabout.

At last he had her underwear off, her skin shivering under his fingers. He kissed her hard, and his memory of the problems of the past months—of tank tactics, gun trajectories and armored firepower—was forgotten in the sweet rush of his erection, and the male pride he felt in giving it to her. He determined to keep his eyes upon her face as he took her; he wanted to watch her beautifully curving lips part in an agony of passionate pleading, to see her head arch against the pillow for that uncontrollable moment before she collapsed after climax. He wanted this picture indelibly engraved in his memory, to be called forth at will during the days and nights of combat he knew he would soon face.

Elisabeth lay under the burden of his loving, formless—a mouth, breasts, legs, all unconnected to her feelings. Only one man in her life so far had excited her sexually, and he had shamed her forever in the doing. Since her father, the rest had given her no more than mild exercise. "I love you, darling," she told him, more or less automatically.

Later he lay on the rumpled bed, the top sheet pulled across his hard-muscled abdomen, and watched her brush her hair at the dressing table. Something bothered him, something elusive that he tried to grasp but could not. Elisabeth was willing in bed, compliant and yet? "Tell me darling," he said and watched her eyes to see if they turned to scorn, "did you like it?"

"Like what?" she asked, her own eyes foglike as if she were seeing another room altogether.

Ignoring the warning bell that tolled his own contempt for men who begged women for sexual compliments, he repeated, "Like it? You know—like it when I make love to you?"

She hated it when men behaved like little boys with a crush on the teacher, wheedling compliments after school. "Of course, darling," she said and continued brushing her hair.

Her answer wasn't enough for him. Heedlessly he rushed on, knowing he would never trust an answer he had coaxed, but helpless to stop now he'd started. "Then why do I feel you didn't like it—that something was, well, missing for you?"

She brushed on, but her lips stopped counting the strokes. "Have I ever said that I didn't like it? Have I ever refused you?"

"It's not that, Elisabeth. *Christ!* It's not anything you've done. It's a feeling I have."

He saw her eyes lose their private dream and focus on him. "What makes you think I'm responsible for your feelings, especially when you can't put a name to them?"

This was going badly. He had only wanted her to reassure him of her love and desire for him, and now the thin thread that held them together after so many months apart was coming unraveled. He plunged on, knowing it was no longer possible to recall any of their words. "Did you . . . did you . . . uh, climax?"

She swung about on the dressing-table bench until she faced him, her beautiful features the reality of every dream of woman he had ever had since he was a boy. "Yes," she said, her voice plainly bored, which was worse to him than her anger. "Of course I climaxed. Why do you men always seem to think orgasm is so difficult for women? The truth is, Marne, that there's really not much I can do to stop it if I have a reasonably adequate lover."

He did not mention their lovemaking to her again. In a way, he almost wished she had lied to him. He would have known it, but somehow the lie would have been better than the truth. At least he could have had something to work toward, to make better. When he made love to her again that night and the next day, it felt stripped of all specialness; and he felt like some cashiered frontier soldier of old, with buttons and medals ripped off, marching out the fort gate—a man in love still, but less than the man he wanted to be.

During the last of their brief hours together, she was as attentive as he could wish. He began to think that he had pushed her too hard and that her response had been what any normally spirited girl would have made. It had probably been his fault. After all, his wife had been one of New York's top models, not a nun. He'd known that—he was no kid—but he also believed she had a loyal heart. Other men looked at her; the poor bastards almost drooled. But she never gave them any cause. He had watched her covertly since the day they met: she never gave other men a tumble. She was absolutely faithful to him; he was sure of it. For God's sake, she'd even joined the Army to share his life as best she could. He felt rotten. How could he have doubted the best wife a guy ever had?

Finally there was an hour left to catch the bus for the ninety-mile trip to the New York port of embarkation. "Darling," he said and gave his tie one last tug, "I want to spare you a goodbye at the station. I couldn't bear to leave you standing on the platform alone."

"But I do want to see you off, Marne," she said, a soft protest in her tone. "I don't know when I'll see you again." Real tears gathered under her lashes and were swept away by the back of her hand in a little-girl gesture that imprinted on his memory, wiping away any small lingering doubt.

"Don't worry about me. I'm not a dogface on foot. Remember, I'll be surrounded by two inches of armor plate." He captured her inside his arms one last time. "And remember, too, darling, I know what I'm fighting for. I'll have you to come back to and our life together—and the family we'll have. Just knowing you're here, waiting for me . . ." He couldn't go on, the words wouldn't move past the huge lump in his throat.

After one last, long look, a look to memorize the tiniest details of her, he closed the door and, taking the steps two at a time, rushed down the stairs, through the lobby and out to the taxi stand near the little park.

Elisabeth saw Marne turn and stare up at the hotel, searching for the window to their room. She sensed the hurt he'd tried to hide, and she was uncomfortable, but she did not accept responsibility for his pain. Whether he knew it or not, she always retained with every man the freedom to leave him emotionally just as she had been left on her own in the emotional limbo of her childhood experience. She pulled back the flowered yellow chintz curtain and waved until he saw her. From the fifth floor she noticed he did not look as tall, his massive shoulders became quite ordinary. She would have to be more careful of his male ego. The bigger they come . . .

More importantly, she would have to rethink her marriage to Marne. It had become terribly clear to her during the last two days that she had made a bargain she no longer wanted to keep.

Idly she ran her fingers down the curtain draw cord as she watched his taxi pull away, and for a moment she resisted the feelings that had been building barriers to rational thought all weekend. Then she swept her mind of all interfering images, walked to the night table and picked up the phone. She dialed DRexel 5-1025. "Hello, will you please tell Mr. Stryker that Mrs. Gardner is on the line?"

"Mr. Max and his party just comin' in from Maryland now, madam."

She heard receding footsteps and then the sound of a telephone being picked up.

"Good evening, Elisabeth," Max Stryker said with no hint of surprise in his voice.

She felt an unfamiliar thrill of excitement that was decidedly physical, more so because these last hours with Marne had been so devoid of real physicality.

Max went right to the point. "When I didn't hear from you about this weekend, naturally I thought—"

"My husband was here on overseas leave."

"I see."

"Max—" she chose her words deliberately—"I've been thinking. About my report to Colonel Nickolson, perhaps I've been too hasty."

19

Don't sit under the apple tree with anyone else but me,
Anyone else but me, anyone else but me,
No, no, no,
Don't sit under the apple tree with anyone else but me
Till I come marching home. . . .
I just got word from a guy who heard
From the guy next door to me
The girl he met just loves to pet
And it fits you to a "T"
So don't sit under the apple tree with anyone else but me
Till I come marching home.
—"Don't Sit Under the Apple Tree," words and music by
  Lew Brown, Charlie Tobias and Sam H. Stept

"IT'S GOING TO be a thirty-minute wait for West Coast circuits, Lieutenant Hammersmith," the woman at the Red Cross office told her, "and then there are three others ahead of you."

"I'll wait," Jill said, the balmy early-April Sunday adding to the natural lethargy of a duty-free afternoon.

For Jill Henry Hammersmith the months at Fort Monmouth had passed swiftly. The first part of code school had been devoted to learning the endless details of unclassified communications-center procedure, Teletype sending and receiving, message routing and punch-tape reading. Often she had sent coded traffic on its way, wondering at the mystery behind the jumbled five-letter groups.

Now at last the waiting was over. Her top-secret clearance had been approved and tomorrow she would enter the code room, a guarded windowless vault in the middle of the com-center—a place of mystery to the uninitiated. After three more months of cryptographic training, she would be eligible for an overseas levy. She just *had* to go! If she couldn't get over there where the war was actually happening, all her efforts in the WAAC, her desire to take Neil's place and show him she hadn't asked him to suffer something she wasn't willing to undergo herself—all of it would count for nothing.

Page had agreed that getting overseas was important, last Sunday when Jill called her from one of the pay phones at the O club, hoping Page could put in a word for her.

"But, Jill, it's not that easy to get overseas," Page had said. "Director Hobby insists that only volunteers go until Congress changes our auxiliary status. I realize you'd gladly volunteer, but that's not the big problem. As long as we're only *with* the Army and not *in* it, a Waac is not legally eligible to be treated in a military hospital if she's wounded, and if she's killed there's no insurance."

"I know that, Page, but what about the bill Representative Rogers introduced last January to make the WAAC a part of the Army?"

"It hasn't passed yet," Page answered.

"Where does that leave us?"

Page had been frank. "I don't know. Anything can happen. Congress is uncertain, as usual. They're arguing now that if women aren't in the front lines they don't deserve soldiers' benefits. We asked them if they would then deny military status to General Eisenhower and his headquarters staff, but who knows whether logic will work with the men on Capitol Hill."

"Damn it! I don't know why I'm beating my brains out up here at Monmouth."

"Yes, you do, Jill. Our orders from Marshall here in the Director's office are to forge ahead as if the Women's Army Corps bill will pass. We all have to keep going, especially now that . . ." Page's voice had suddenly grown sad and trailed off.

"Especially now that what?"

At first Page hadn't wanted to tell her, but she had wheedled it out of her.

"There's just a lot of gossip about the WAAC, Jill. Bad stuff—organized slander, really. We're all supposed to be pregnant or lesbians, or both—which tells you how crazy the talk is. We've tried to counter with positive stories, but it just keeps coming from everywhere. G-2 thinks it might be Nazi sabotage."

"Oh, that old stuff," Jill had said. She had dealt with attitudes like that when she decided to pursue a career in veterinary medicine. When a woman stepped out of the kitchen, the whole world thought something must be wrong with her. The talk had got worse, she remembered, when her paper on chicken pneumonitis had won a national prize. *If the gossips are after the WAAC, it must mean we're doing a hell of a job,* she thought, and made a mental note to say so the next time she wrote to Page.

"Lieutenant, you're next," the woman in Red Cross gray told her. In the game room next door, Jill could hear the click of billiard balls and over that the jukebox playing the Andrews Sisters' big hit "Don't Sit Under the Apple Tree."

She gave the operator her home number and heard it ring.

"Hello," a familiar male voice answered.

"Hi Daddy, it's me, Jill."

"Jewel!" He used his pet name for her. "How are you?"

"I'm fine, Daddy, just fine. How's everybody there?"

"Everybody's well. Your mother's at the church now—there's a special service tonight for the boys."

They both fell silent then as people do when they know each other so well they don't need words.

Her father broke the silence. "You ought to see the trees this year, Jewel—early spring, no late frost. They're all in bloom, especially the ones down by the Martins' house. Looks like a heavy crop of Albertas."

She had wondered if he would mention Neil first, or if she would have to. "Daddy, has Mr. Martin told you how Neil . . . how he's getting along?"

"Better than that. I saw him two or three days ago."

"You saw Neil?"

"He's on convalescent leave—between operations, his dad told me."

"Did you talk to him? Did he ask about me?"

"Well, Jewel, I wouldn't call it a conversation—he a . . . he has a speech problem—but I said hello and he said hello."

"Are you implying he didn't ask about me?"

"I'm sorry, honey."

"Oh . . . "

"Give him time."

"How much time? I've been writing to him for eight months and he hasn't answered once, Daddy—not once. And when I went to see him at Oak Knoll, he . . . I can't describe it, Daddy."

"Bear's down there with him. Neil seemed to want him to stay, and I couldn't see harm in it."

"No—I mean of course. No harm at all."

Why not? Bear was her dog, but Neil had loved him since the day her father had rescued the roly-poly albino German-shepherd puppy from a breeder determined to kill it to keep his kennel strain pure. They had named him Polar Bear, soon shortened to Bear, because he looked so much like the cub they'd seen at San Francisco's Fleishacker Zoo on her thirteenth birthday.

Neil and Bear had looked so odd together—like brothers, really: Bear with his thick white coat and pale eyes; Neil, fair and sun-blond, his eyelashes so white they disappeared in the light, leaving his blue eyes unprotected.

Neil had laughed when she mentioned it. "Maybe in my next life I'll come back as Bear."

"Jewel?" her father was saying.

"Yes, Daddy, I'm here."

"I'll go get the dog and bring him home if you want me to."

"No—leave him for as long as Neil wants him. And Daddy, tell Neil I said so."

"I will, Jewel. I'll tell him, but . . . "

"But what?"

"He's changed, honey."

"I know, but they can do marvels of reconstructive surgery—"

"No, that's not the kind of change I mean. He's different inside too, Jewel. The Neil you knew is gone—"

"Oh . . . "

"—and I don't think he's coming back."

Although she didn't tell her father, Jill rejected what he said. If Neil blamed her for his wounds, he'd get over it. He had to. Her mother had taught her that everything in life works out for those who try hard enough and long enough. She'd just have to be patient and keep trying. Maybe Bear could do what her letters couldn't do—remind Neil that she was coming back to him.

For a moment, Des Stratton's face floated unsuppressed to the surface of her mind.

You can't take what you dish out to me, the image said.

It's not the same thing at all, she defended herself. *Neil and I grew up together, while you only pretended to be my friend.*

But her vision of Des wasn't listening to her. He smiled, and said—it was funny how well she remembered his smile—*Answer me, Jill, if you could go back and do it all over again, would you marry Neil?*

But she didn't answer, because she forced him out of her mind, and she didn't have to answer.

Jill paid her telephone bill and started back toward the BOQ. The streets were almost empty. Sunday afternoon was a quiet time on a military post. Dayrooms and service clubs were full of lounging Waacs. In the barracks, laundry and ironing, letters home and gripe sessions spun out the daylight hours until the post theaters opened after chow, which was usually cold cuts.

Jill knew she should get some rest. Tomorrow was a big day—her first inside the code room—and she wanted to be sharp. She really had nothing to worry about. Neil would write soon—Bear would do that for her. As for Des Stratton, she had forced herself not to look at his return address on that last letter she'd torn up, and so now she didn't know where he was.

20

April 17, 1943: One hundred fifteen B-17s bomb the Bremen aircraft plant, shooting down ten German fighters; sixteen U.S. bombers are lost.

A Young & Rubicam advertising campaign designed to boost sagging WAAC recruiting changes the unpopular "Release a Man for Combat" theme to pretty Waacs saying, "I joined to serve my country and am having the time of my life."

BUNNY FELT THE C-47 bank in a wide arc on its approach to Bolling Field. Through the forward window she saw small parks and the Capitol dome slide past below, followed moments later by the Washington Monument.

"Fasten your harness, honey," the co-pilot yelled back through the open cockpit door.

"Sure thing, Lieutenant." She shrugged into the webbing buckled to the metal seats along the plane's bulkhead, adjusting the straps which had never been meant to accommodate a generous female bosom.

They had been five hours out of Dayton's Wright Field, fighting April head winds all the way. More than once Bunny had wondered if she had saved herself several days of furlough travel time only to be turned into a permanent ice cube. If the crew hadn't shared an enormous thermos of hot coffee with her, she would have been frozen solid after the heater had gone out somewhere over Pittsburgh.

The wheels touched down and screeched along the tarmac; her teeth rattled as the pilot throttled back and braked to a stop in front of a hangar. The guy must have raced jalopies as a civilian.

"Thanks for the ride, fellas," she said, grinning, as they elbowed each other to help her down the short metal stairs.

"How about meeting me for a drink tonight, Lieutenant?" said the co-pilot, who couldn't have been much more than twenty by the sparseness of his mustache. Why did the young ones always seem to go for her? Mother Bunny's fatal charm for children, no doubt.

"I'll take a rain check, guys. See you back at Lowry in ten days." She didn't want to hurt their feelings—men of any age never could understand a woman wanting to be by herself—but she had a heavy date with a tub bath and room service.

She walked toward the ops hut, put down her flight bag and looked up Page's number at the Pentagon.

"WAAC headquarters. Office of the Director," a voice answered.

"Second Leader Hannaday, please. Say that Bunny Palermo is on the wire."

A moment later a familiar voice was calling her name. "Bunny! Where *are* you?"

"I'm at Bolling—or what's left of me is. Arrgh! The C-47 hasn't been built yet with my anatomy in mind."

Page laughed. "Same old Bunny. You never change." She was glad. The whole world was falling apart, but if Bunny stayed the same . . .

Bunny snorted. "Of course I've changed. It's been five months, one birthday and two gray hairs since we left Fort Des Moines." She shifted the telephone to the far end of the counter, making room for a crew studying weather maps. "Right now, Page, I need a room. Can you tell me a hotel that won't cost me a month's pay?"

"Hotel?" Page repeated. "There's not a room to be had anywhere in Washington. Besides, I wouldn't hear of it. I have an apartment with the only unrented sofa in town. Have you got a pencil? Take this down. Tell the cabbie to go to 210 Nineteenth Street—that's off Connecticut Avenue near the Mayflower Hotel. When you get there, tell my landlady, Mrs. Mallory, that you're a friend of mine and she'll let you in. I'll call ahead so she'll be expecting you. Have you got all that?"

"Sure thing."

"I'll try to get home as soon after six as I can make it."

Later, Bunny's taxi crossed the Potomac and was immediately snarled in traffic. She nervously saw the meter edging past the dollar mark. At this rate the money she'd saved for her first leave wouldn't go far.

They passed the Tidal Basin and she drew in her breath sharply at the sight of three thousand Japanese cherry trees in gorgeous blossom.

"Some guys chopped four of them down after Pearl Harbor," the cabbie told her over his shoulder. "Shoulda chopped 'em all down."

Oh no, she thought, they're too beautiful, although she understood his anger. How could a country that sent such a gift, a gift that carpeted Washington with pink-and-white petals every April, drop bombs on a peaceful Sunday morning? It hadn't made any sense on December 7, 1941, and in the spring of 1943 it still didn't.

Three GIs heading for Union Station crowded into the cab on Massachusetts Avenue. As soldiers do, she exchanged names and duty stations with them.

Uniforms jammed the downtown area—olive drab, navy blue, marine green—as they turned into Nineteenth Street.

"Okay, soldier lady, here you are," the driver said and stopped midway down the block. "That'll be a dollar eighty-five."

She took out two one-dollar bills and handed them to him. "Keep the change."

"Nothin' doin'." He handed her a dime and a nickel. "You keep it. Makes me feel like a million bucks just hauling you girls in uniform."

"Thanks." She'd heard so many unflattering stories about D.C. cabbies since the war started. Bad news traveled fast and good news not at all. She made a mental note to relate what the cabbie had done.

Waving goodbye to her fellow passengers, she walked up the wide steps of the white stone building and rang the bell button marked "Mrs. Mallory, Manager."

"Right this way," the manager said after Bunny explained who she was. "Miss Hannaday's rooms are off the second landing, facing the garden in the rear. The garden is lovely this spring. It doesn't know there's a war on. Now, mind that bucket of sand and the shovel in the foyer. Mr. Byron, the block warden, is a stickler for all that air raid paraphernalia. But then you army girls know all about that, don't you?"

Mrs. Mallory chattered on. She reminded Bunny of her mama, who filled the empty air with words, not to get answers but to occupy space with the familiar and comforting sound of her own voice saying things she could believe. After thanking her for her trouble, Bunny put her bag down in Page's living room. The sun-splashed room full of bulky oak furniture was not up to Page's easy sophistication, but was comfortable and heavenly quiet after hours of thundering airplane engines. The windows looked out over a brick courtyard of clipped privet hedges, blooming ranunculus and anemones. After months of Army Air Forces green and gray, on a base where the only flower beds surrounded the reveille cannon in front of the headquarters building, this patch of color looked to Bunny like the Garden of Eden. She opened the windows to let in the fresh late-April breeze, took off her shoes and promptly fell sound asleep curled up on the sofa.

"Fall out!"

Bunny's feet hit the floor before she opened her eyes to see a laughing Page standing over her. "Damn it," she said in mock anger, "there ought to be a regulation against barrack jokes when a body's on furlough."

"I couldn't resist. How are you, Bunny?" Page gave her a welcoming hug.

"They're making one helluva photographer out of me, Page. I wouldn't have believed it, but I'm not bad at it, not half bad."

Page nodded. "I knew you must be good when you got out of troop work to train as an instructor. How do you like it?"

"Well enough—no, I'll be honest, I'm crazy about it, especially when I get to go up with the aerial reconnaissance camera." Then she asked Page the question most on her mind. "Do you think that means I'll have to go overseas? You know I've never been gung-ho to go—not like Jill."

"Not much chance of overseas, Bunny. Although the requests are flooding in, it looks like only about fifteen percent of the WAAC will get out of the States."

"I hope you're right. I was never one for camping out. The

last time I tried it I was six and I peed in my blanket and ran home crying in the middle of the night."

Page smiled at the image of a small soggy Bunny dashing through the New Jersey night. "I'm telling you not to worry. There are plenty of officers who *want* to go," she said, removing her uniform jacket and undoing her tie. "More than we can ever use."

Page bent to pick up a box of groceries. "Look what I found for us at the corner butcher—lovely thick pork chops, and only seven red points. Mmmm! Come on into the kitchen and keep me company."

Bunny followed her into the small kitchenette. "I'm good for more than chitchat. Remember me—Home-and-Hearth Bunny? I come from a big family, and Mama wanted all her girls to be good cooks." She rolled up her khaki shirtsleeves and set the table, snapped the green beans and blended the orange vegetable coloring into the white margarine. "It's good to be in a kitchen again, Page. I never knew what a little homebody I was when I was a civilian."

"The grass is always greener . . . I miss the BOQ and the mess hall. I even miss SOS—mmmh—creamed chipped beef on toast."

"Shit-on-a-shingle?" Bunny rolled her eyes. "Next you'll be telling me you miss the coffee?"

"Yes, the coffee too."

"God, Page, that's carrying nostalgia too far even for you. Have you forgotten how bitter it was?"

Spontaneously they began to sing, lustily, a song from OC days they had often marched to:

"The coffee in the Army they say is mighty fine,
It's good for cuts and bruises and tastes like iodine.
Oh, I don't want no more of army life.
Gee Mom, I wanna go, but they won't let me go—HOME!"

They laughed uproariously at the memories the song evoked, feeling silly and carefree.

"Bunny, I can't tell you—it's just so *damned* good to see you in this crazy town. Did I ever tell you that you're the sanest person I know?"

As they talked, Bunny was aware that the feeling of specialness she, Page, Jill and Elisabeth had felt for each other was still there. She knew that no matter how often or for how long they were separated, when they came together it was as if they had only stepped apart for five minutes. They had a seventh sense of understanding that neither absence nor distance could erase. "Wish Jill and Elisabeth were here," Bunny said. "Wouldn't it be great if we were all together again—even for an hour?"

Page nodded. "Elisabeth isn't so far, but her weekends are tied up every time I call her."

"Uh-oh, sounds like a man."

"Don't be hard on her, Bunny."

"No, it's nothing like that. We both know she didn't care a fig about that husband of hers. I've seen her type before, so cool and safe within themselves. But watch out when they fall for some bozo—they take a real nose dive."

"Hope you're wrong." Page searched her cupboard for the right condiments, wishing Paul was here to do the cooking. "There was always something so lost and easy to hurt right under Elisabeth's surface."

"Page, you always saw more in her than I did, although she *was* absolutely fascinating. Speaking of man trouble—tell me about that new hunk of man you wrote me about. Do you see much of him?"

"Paul? Yes, a great deal." Page stooped to light the gas under the oven grill, plopping the salted and peppered chops on the tray. "We'll both be seeing him for dinner tomorrow night. He's so eager to meet you. But I must warn you, I've told him outrageous stories about you."

"Thanks a lot! A girl can't have any war secrets."

"He'll adore you, Bunny. I hope you like him. He's the calm, silent professor type—pipe and all."

"Grab him, Page. Believe me, steady is everything." Bunny's mouth twisted in a wry grin. "Well, nearly everything."

After dinner they settled deep into the living-room chairs, lit cigarettes and sipped V.O. on the rocks.

"Now," Page said, contentedly exhaling, "tell me about you. A handsome flyboy in your life?"

"About a dozen at last count."

"Any one special man?" Page probed.

"One who thinks he is, but I'm not falling for his line—you know the one, 'Just be patient and I'll divorce my wife.' "

Page frowned, suddenly worried. "Careful Bunny—you're more love's lemming than butterfly."

Bunny looked up sharply, "You see that, huh?" She sensed a chance to share a secret part of her life for the first time. "I don't fool you for a minute, do I?"

"At first, maybe. But gradually I knew that some one man must have hurt you badly. It was your last husband, wasn't it? I don't know—something about you changed when you talked about him, even when you joked."

Bunny shifted in her chair and lifted her glass to study the amber liquid in the glow of a lamp. "I've never talked about it to anyone before, but I'd like to tell you." She spoke, haltingly at first, and then in a torrent of words, about the real Johnny Palermo, not the fun-loving satyr she'd made up a joke to cover the deep scar, but the real Johnny, the one who had squeezed her heart dry and left her empty, unable to trust any man's love, unable even to trust her own sense of love. Finishing, she stared at Page. "He only wanted my money," she said bitterly. "Why did his weakness win out, Page? I thought my love would prop *him* up; I didn't know he'd end up knocking the pins out from under *me*." Tears threatened to overwhelm her.

Page was silent for a moment and looked down at her hands resting in her lap, trying to give her friend privacy. "Stop blaming yourself. *You* did nothing wrong." She was surprised at the words of comfort that tumbled out as if she'd always known them. "You're not the first woman, and certainly not the last, to confuse physical need with loving some man forever. Bunny, listen, if you blame yourself you'll not be able to recognize the real thing when it comes your way—and it *will*. You don't know what a truly good person you are. Given any chance at all, the right man can and will love you for yourself if you let him."

Bunny listlessly pulled her hands away from her face. "I wish it was that simple."

"It is."

"No it isn't. He's writing to me."

"So what?"

"He's asked me to see him when I get home on leave."

"Are you going to?"

"Page—please don't be disappointed in me . . . "

"Of course not. How could I be?"

"Then yes—yes, I'm going to see him. I have to know, don't you see?"

The next morning was Saturday, and Page asked her section chief for an hour off. "Bunny, now I've got time to drop you downtown if you want to see some of the sights."

"Wonderful! Do you know it's been ages since I felt so good? Even my GI achin' feet feel fine."

"That's good, because you'll have to walk everywhere. The buses are jammed." She handed Bunny another breakfast dish to dry. "They've even taken the seats out so they can cram more people in."

Bunny stacked the dried bowl with the others in the cupboard. "Now tell me what's going on at WAAC headquarters. There are all kindsa rumors floating around Lowry."

"What kind of rumors?"

"For instance, that the Corps is going to be dissolved."

Page bit her lip. "That's one of many possibilities, Bunny."

"You can't mean it!" Bunny felt more shock than upset.

Page nodded, her face grim. "This spring has been an awful time for all of us at headquarters. Forgive me if I get on my soapbox, but—" she wiped her hands and took their refilled coffee cups to the table—"Bunny, it seems that the press of the whole damned country is on our backs. Director Hobby is so distressed by stories that call us 'a Corps of whores,' enlisted only to service the troops."

Bunny interrupted, "I had one mother who called me and told me to send her daughter home. Some of the young kids were afraid even to go home on furlough, because they'd have to face all the dirty stories."

Page smashed her cigarette in an ashtray. "We fight them all the time, but they crop up everywhere. One writer in the *Washington Times-Herald* wrote a column about how we Waacs were all going to be secretly issued prophylactics. He thinks we're some kind of New Deal scheme of Mrs. Roosevelt's. It's crazy! The press just can't seem to understand that any group of women soldiers might have a serious, patriotic purpose. The WAAC defies their definition of what women are supposed to be—so the only way they can explain us is to make us promiscuous."

Bunny swiped angrily at the coffee ring her cup had made on the table. "Is this what we joined the Army for? How can they print that kind of trash?"

"Oh, they're not singling us out—it's happened before. The nurse corps was vilified, and the British military women." Page's hands unconsciously were fists. "Bunny, the worst of it doesn't even *get* into print. We've been fighting one slander all spring—you know, the one about Eisenhower expelling a whole shipload of pregnant Waacs from North Africa. The latest wrinkle is that armed guards supposedly had to stand over them to keep them from jumping overboard. If that ridiculous rumor was true, every one of the two hundred Waacs in North Africa would have been shipped back ten times over."

"Nobody believes that—do they?"

Page clenched her teeth. "I wish I could say no, but . . . G-2 is busy running every one of these rumors to ground because they're devastating our recruiting campaigns, not to mention morale."

Page was now so angry her hand shook lighting another cigarette she didn't really want. "You know what the truth is? We've had exactly one pregnant Waac in North Africa so far—and she was married. But does *that* rumor get around? No! The truth is not nearly so exciting. Do you know that General Eisenhower wants hundreds more of us? He's putting through priority requisitions every week. I won't argue that Waacs are saints—after all, we're mature women, not girls— but our VD and pregnancy rates overseas and stateside are *lower* than the civilian population's."

Bunny hated to see Page taking it all so personally. "Page, a lot of it could be Nazi propaganda."

A haunted look came over Page's face. "I wish it was. I *really* wish it was." For a moment she twisted her hands in front of her. "But most of the rumors G-2 runs down were started by GIs writing from overseas, passing on jokes and stories—and, Bunny, most of *them* never so much as *saw* a Waac. Or by parents of boys sent to the front lines—that damned 'Release a Man to Fight' campaign backfired on us.

It's gossips in barber and beauty shops; it's disgruntled and discharged Waacs trying to justify themselves. No, it's not Nazis, Bunny—it's *us*."

Bunny frowned. How can we fight everybody?—it's hopeless, she thought, but she couldn't bring herself to say so out loud. Instead she asked, "What's being done?"

"Director Hobby's so distressed by these slanders that she's assigned me full time to counter them with positive publicity about the Corps."

"That's tough. You can't go around saying, 'Hey, look here, we're not pregnant.'"

"You're right. It only allows people to hear the slander twice. What I try to do is show who Waacs really are—forty-five-year-old grandmothers, wives and sisters of heroes, J.P. Morgan's granddaughter, farm girls—the diversity of the Corps, the next-door realness of these women."

"*Now* you're cookin'." Bunny was quiet for a moment while they finished their coffee. Then she said softly, "Will this country ever accept a woman in uniform?"

"Maybe after we've slain our dragons."

For the first time Bunny recognized the true depth of Page's devotion to the Corps. It's like a one-sided love affair, she thought. No wonder Page understands me—she's in love and she's rejected.

With a sigh Page stood up, collected their empty cups and put them into the sink. "You know, Bunny, there will always be a few who will *want* to believe we're fallen women. I have a nightmare that forty years from now I'll be at a cocktail party and I'll hear these same lies repeated."

"Stand easy, Lieutenant. You're beginning to sound like Jill, trying to win the war single-handed. Remember you're doing everything you can."

Page shook her head. "It's not enough. We're fighting to save the Corps. We must be completely taken into the Army with the same ranks and privileges for women as for men. We can't be an auxiliary any longer—it's not working."

When Page said that, she seemed even more agitated. Bunny didn't understand. "But isn't that what you want?"

"Yes, but don't you see the problem? That means every officer and Auxie will have a chance to get out or reenlist in the new Corps. We're so afraid this slander campaign will cause most of them to take a discharge, and then the Corps will be ruined anyway."

The idea hit Bunny hard. Johnny's last letter had begged her to try to get out, and suddenly here was an opportunity she'd never have again. But she couldn't bring herself to say so to Page.

An hour later, Bunny was being jostled by off-duty night-shift workers and by clerks from the Office of Price Administration who worked around the clock. She wandered from monument to monument and stopped in front of Farragut's statue. "Damn the torpedos," she read on the pedestal, "full steam ahead." This guy sounded a lot like Page.

She enjoyed a day that did not begin with a bugle call and end with the smell of photographic fixative on her clothes. As much as she loved her work as an Army Air Forces photographer and instructor, this furlough had reminded her that at heart she was a civilian.

By midafternoon she was starved, and she found a Rexall drugstore lunch counter where she watched women her age in a marathon search for scarce bobby pins and their favorite soap or shampoo. Everywhere there were lines—lines for cigarettes, for a small shipment of boxed Whitman's candy which was whisked off the shelf in minutes, for a few rare nylon stockings. Bunny saw one woman take her precious new hose, sit down on the curb and put them on while a couple of sailors ogled her legs.

Ah, Saturday. She had always loved Saturday for the air of anticipation about it. Anything *could* happen on Saturday night, she remembered telling her first husband. No matter how many Saturday nights she spent when not one thing occurred, like a compulsive gambler she could never escape the feeling that the next time it would. Tonight she knew would be special. Page's major was taking them to dinner at the Shoreham Hotel. Some class! Mama and her sisters would be impressed when she told them she'd dined and danced at the famous Shoreham, rubbing shoulders with congressmen, White House people and military brass from all over the world.

Then she made up her mind. Hang the money! She would have to look special for the occasion. She finished her Coke and rushed out to Garfinckel's for a knock-their-eyes-out dress. She barely heard the headlines being hawked from the corner newsstand. Something about American and British forces in North Africa closing the ring around Rommel's armies at Tunis. She wondered which OC she'd known at Fort Des Moines was in North Africa.

When she left the department store carrying a dress box under her arm, the late-afternoon editions headlined the battle Polish Jews were fighting against the Germans in the Warsaw Ghetto.

21

Nightclub business booms—up 40 percent over prewar years—despite food, liquor and gas rationing. Long lines form in blacked-out New York City to see Frank Sinatra at the Waldorf-Astoria's Wedgwood Room, Hildegarde at the Persian Room and Danny Thomas at La Martinique.

SATURDAY NIGHT BUNNY sang as she gave herself a last-minute check in the full-length mirror. It was so strange to see herself in a dress that she looked again to make sure it was really she. The blue shantung with padded shoulders and fitted sleeves clung to her body in just the right places to accentuate the curves that were undeniably there—a few more than she wanted, since she'd lost only three of the ten extra pounds gained at OC. Her breasts pushed against the dress bodice, their fullness accented by a centered sequin clip. Although she felt strange out of uniform, as if she had shed her skin, it was wonderful to feel something next to her body besides wool, barathea cloth and starched cotton poplin.

"Bunny, you're a knockout," Page said, smiling, from the bathroom doorway.

"Does it really look as good as it feels?"

"Better—and I have some earrings that will complement the clip perfectly."

The doorbell rang and Page left to answer it. Slipping into wonderfully soft elbow-length gloves and placing a single white gardenia just so above her left ear, Bunny went in to meet Paul, feeling a little nervous. What would she talk about? She'd never been much of a scholar.

"Bunny," Paul said warmly, taking both her hands. "Page has told me how your wit saved her many times during your training together."

Before she could stop herself, she said, "Only half the time."

He laughed delightedly at her joke. "Oh, I would never call you a half-wit."

She liked him for laughing. Not every man, she'd discovered, felt comfortable when a woman joked. He was the kind of cultivated man she had never known outside of the movies. That's it, she thought, he's Ronald Colman with muscles. It was plain to see, from the way his eyes constantly returned to Page, that he cared for her. And it was just as plain to Bunny that Page returned his affection, although in a way Bunny couldn't quite fathom. There was passion all right, but no belonging. Could a woman love and still belong to herself? Bunny knew she herself never could.

On the way to the Shoreham, Paul drove through nighttime Washington to show Bunny the sights. The streets were crowded like Times Square on New Year's Eve. There was a festive, even frantic party atmosphere which seemed not to belong in the same town where soldiers with steel helmets and fixed bayonets patrolled the White House and antiaircraft guns were camouflaged behind foliage in the parks.

"I may be the most envied man in Washington tonight," Paul said as they passed into the lobby of the Shoreham. "I could cause a riot squiring the two most beautiful girls in town."

Bunny laughed at his obvious gallantry, since everybody knew there were eight girls to every man in Washington. "I hope I'm not caught out of uniform," she whispered to Page. "My arm keeps wanting to salute all this brass. I held on to it so hard back there at the entrance, I thought I'd break it."

After dinner they were seated at a table in a ballroom jammed with men in uniform on the move, who had just arrived in Washington or were telling their friends goodbye. Bunny had never felt such a concentrated sense of excitement in one room before, a sense of a moment being lived and of its supreme importance over any other moment. There was a palpable vibration between men and women, a sexual hum that pervaded the music, the conversation, the camaraderie.

Paul ordered champagne, apologizing because it was Australian Syspelt. "That's just one more reason to hate the Nazis."

"Major," she heard a voice say from behind her, "it's absolutely unpatriotic to keep *two* lovely ladies off the dance floor." A hand seemed to be attached to the voice, and it touched Bunny's shoulder. "Wanna dance?"

Bunny turned to see a nice-looking young captain smiling down at her. They exchanged names.

"Page, do I dare? It's been ages. Besides, my feet grew two sizes in OC."

Page laughed. "They'll give you better balance. Get out there and show them how it's done."

"Okay, Captain," Bunny said as he helped her with her chair, "if you're willing to take a chance."

The band was playing a hot version of "I Want to Be Happy," and other couples were tearing up the dance floor. The eager captain pushed through the crowd and the closely packed tables, half dragging Bunny behind him. In a few minutes they had made their way to a spot on the floor where the crowd was thinner.

"Say, you're a swell dancer," the captain shouted in her ear, throwing her out and pulling her back. "Let's show these people how to cut a rug. Where I'm going there won't be any gorgeous gals like you."

The captain did a hot jitterbug with a little Balboa and Jersey Bounce thrown in. They shagged and trucked-on-down, way down, until Bunny laughed out loud with the delight of moving her body to an upbeat rhythm once again. And he was a sweet young guy even if he did chew a huge wad of Dentyne gum in her ear, and swing her into a back-breaking dip at the end of the slow numbers. She was flattered that he would want to have his last stateside dances with her, although she knew that any girl would have served to provide him with the memory he was trying to create for the days and months ahead.

This was going to be a great Saturday night. The band really swung! A great beat! So familiar—she must have heard it on the radio.

"Cutting in, Captain."

"Nothing doin', Lieutenant," he said, shrugging off another of the stags hungrily prowling the dance floor.

His grip on her waist showed her he had no intention of sharing his dancing partner with his fellow officers. She was content to alternately gyrate and glide in his arms, the music pulsing through her feet. The misery of her life with Johnny P., the regrets and the self-blame resurrected last night with Page, seemed to fade in the glow of present friendship, and laughter; in this place, her problems seemed small compared to those men going off to war, possibly to die.

Bunny cringed involuntarily as the band began to play the familiar first notes of "All or Nothing at All," and her partner's arms circled her more tightly. The girl singer stepped to the microphone after a trombone intro. "This is for Bunny from a friend," the singer said and started the lyric.

"Hey, there's another Bunny here," the captain said.

For answer, she grabbed his hand. "Please, let's go back to the table—right now!"

But she was too late. The hand that tapped the captain on his shoulder was one she knew too well.

"Captain, can a guy get a dance with his ex-wife?"

"Uhh . . ." the captain said, turning from one to the other, "is that right, Bunny?"

But she didn't have to answer. Her face gave her away, and the captain reluctantly released her to the darkly handsome man in the white dinner jacket with the Shoreham crest on its breast pocket.

As she'd dreamed for a hundred nights, she was in Johnny's arms again, gliding across the floor to the tune she knew only too well. What was he doing here? She had not expected to have to face him quite so soon.

"So you decided to come," he said, the voice quieter than she remembered.

She was puzzled. "Decided to come?" she repeated his statement, making it a question.

"I wrote as soon as I knew I had this gig. Isn't that why *you're* here?"

"I never got your letter. I just came with friends." Suddenly a feeling flooded her, washing away acquiescence, and that feeling was anger. "You think that song is a joke, Johnny?" she asked, her right hand clenched inside his hand.

"No. Can't you see what I'm trying to tell you? You were right all along. I see now that it has to be all or nothing with us, babe." His voice was low next to her ear, sending waves of longing through her body. "Bunny, I'm trying to tell you I was wrong. And I ain't never said that to a girl in my life."

She didn't trust the music; she didn't trust herself; she didn't trust him. "The band—that's why it sounded so familiar," she said, the truth dawning.

"I saw you when you came in with that army guy and the other girl. In that dress, I coulda picked you out of any crowd." He drew her tense body into his. "I may not be as smooth as your new friends, but, Jesus, Bunny, don't you know when a guy is saying he still loves you?"

She heard his voice, his low earnest words, but they were strained as if through a vision, a dream of what might have been. He was from her yesterdays. How could she return there with him? Even if it was possible . . . Her thoughts trailed off as her body responded to his as if it had no connection to her brain. It had been so long. . . .

Some survival instinct made her try again to reject her feelings. "Johnny, there was too much—too much that was bad between us."

He was as hard to convince as ever. "It wasn't all bad, Bunny," he insisted, his mouth moving against her ear. Wave upon sensate wave pulsed through her body. "Don't you remember our place and how it was when we made love together? All I'm asking is for a chance to show you how much I've changed."

This was a Johnny she'd never seen before. All the mean cocksureness was gone, leaving only the brilliant smile and the sensual insinuation of his voice into memories that were all at once incredibly fresh. The physical yearning of the past months almost overwhelmed her. But something in her, some sanity, resisted this spell he was weaving. Why—why did he want her after all the past hurt? Did it appeal to his male vanity to regain her lost love? Could the Johnny she had known ever be a straight shooter with any girl? How could she even be here dancing with him after what he had done?

He turned her expertly around the floor. Unlike most professional musicians, Johnny had always been a wonderful dancer.

"I'm on the level, Bunny. We need to go somewhere for a quiet drink and talk. Just for old times' sake, baby—the good times."

She had to know if she could ever be truly free of him—the old Johnny who had hurt her so terribly, or even this new Johnny, humble and loving but with his sex appeal very much intact.

She walked back to the table, where Page and Paul were deep in conversation, their foreheads touching.

"Page—Paul—I'm sorry, but—" She stopped, not wanting to say too much in front of Paul. "Johnny P. is here and—I'll catch a cab back to the apartment later. Paul, will you please excuse me? Page will explain."

Page said, "Are you sure? Is there anything we can . . . ?"

Reassuring Page that she would be all right, she thanked Paul for the evening and met Johnny at the ballroom door. They walked through the lobby and took the elevator to his room. There was no more pretense of talking. She knew what he wanted, and she had to admit she wanted it, too. Didn't she owe it to herself to find out if there was any chance for a new start?

Inside the room, an ordinary Washington hotel room with two cityscapes over the bed, Johnny quickly got two glasses, poured two fingers of South African brandy into each, warmed them in his hand and handed one to her. She accepted the drink, but it was the first one in months she hadn't needed. Johnny was here in front of her. She didn't need alcohol to conjure him. While she sipped he moved about the room picking up his possessions, in an effort to make his life tidy for her.

Edging closer to where she sat, he stopped in front of her chair and slid to his knees, burying his head in her lap, like a hurt little boy. "Baby, I've missed you." His voice was husky with wanting. "I've really kicked myself for the way I treated you. I've done a lot of growing up in the past two years. You do believe me, don't you?"

She felt his hands slide up her body and cup her breasts, strong fingers moving over her nipples, while his eyes searched her face for a sign of the old surrender.

Bunny knew that if she had any sense she would leap to her feet and run, fast and far, that she would never stop running. What was it Page had called her? She struggled to remember. A love lemming, that was it, someone who committed emotional suicide.

He stood, pulled her up, turned her around and unzipped her dress.

This is a dream, she thought as she shrugged out of her dress and let it fall to the floor. But she didn't want to wake up. She pulled her slip over her head past his hands, which were now everywhere caressing her. She unfastened her nylons, pulled off her garter belt, stepped out of her panties and lay down on the rumpled bed. These were practiced movements, but all done as if in a vision of herself doing them. This was not real. Soon she would wake and know it had all been a dream.

She saw his eyes on her, never leaving her while he threw off his clothes. The room was softly lit and warm as he slipped into the bed and straddled her.

"I'll show you what you've missed, baby," he said, his voice issuing from between her breasts now shuddering because she was gasping for breath.

She felt his two hands lock tight around her wrists and lift them over her head, pinning her hands to the pillow and simultaneously imprisoning his own. Using his tongue as a third hand, he began to work on the roundness of her breasts, making smaller and smaller circles until his greedy lips covered each nipple in turn. He moved up to her hot, dry mouth and used his tongue to moisten her lips and finally to thrust inside slyly, insinuating a much deeper thrust to come.

Bunny longed for the exquisite moment when she would be filled by him. She no longer cared if there was trust between them. It would grow again. It had to.

He fell upon her then, and to prolong the sweet agony she clamped her legs shut, forcing him to plunge repeatedly between, the friction sending her into a series of rhythmic moans she could hardly recognize as her own music. He released her wrists and with his hands relentlessly parted her legs, which she threw about his back in a total physical embrace. He thrust inside her, steadily, completely, in one deep drive, and with his exquisite sense of drummer's timing he gradually picked up the beat, sending flashes of sensation through her that climaxed in frenzy. He rolled off her, exhausted, while she still throbbed helplessly.

"Baby," he said, catching his breath, "there's never been anyone like you for me. See how good we do it together?" He threw one dark leg over her, and the weight of him caused the heat inside to rise again. "Just tell me what you want, and I'll do it for ya."

She saw, and felt, and heard. Johnny was not perfect, but he had changed, was still trying to change, was willing to change even more. Maybe they *could* make a fresh beginning. Maybe they could live as if these past months hadn't happened.

Johnny turned her face—warm, with a film of moisture—toward his own. "Can we try again? I'm gonna get outa the band business—settle down and get a steady job. Maybe you could even teach me to give permanents." He laughed, his white even teeth flashing in the dim light. He reached over and turned on the radio on the nightstand, and the low, lovely strains of Miller's "Skylark" filled the room. "Yeah, baby, permanents—Angela says I'd be good at it."

"When did you see Angela?"

"I just bumped into her once. I was asking all about you." He explained that that was how he had got her address in Texas. "Just ran into her on the street by accident."

He kissed her, a sweetly questioning kiss that drew every bit of the poison he'd placed there out of her system. She knew he was waiting for her answer, but she hardly knew what that answer would be until she heard it herself. "I want you, Johnny, and I want us to have a second chance. Give me two or three months and I think I'll be getting out of the Army."

He pulled her close and she could feel he wanted her again. And oh how she wanted him, passion overwhelming a final, too late instinct that told her to escape. She had been starving and Johnny was feeding her. Just for a moment she remembered what Page had said about the Corps and felt like a deserter, but then his body recaptured her memory and she thought of nothing but what he was doing to her.

22

Admiral Isoroku Yamamoto, planner of the surprise Pearl Harbor attack, is shot down April 18, 1943, when American fighters intercept his plane over Bougainville Island.

FOR THE THIRD time, Page, thinking she'd heard Bunny knocking, tiptoed down the stairs to the front door, which was locked at this time of night, stared up and down the street, and returned to Paul, seated on her living-room sofa.

"Paul, it's nearly two o'clock. Do you think Bunny will be able to find her way back here?"

"Bunny's a big girl."

"But that ex-husband of hers is pretty awful."

"Page," Paul said, removing his pipe, "Bunny strikes me as a down-to-earth sort—a realist."

"She is, but that only makes her more vulnerable to a man like that. Don't you see? Realists think they're so safe they never learn to make good judgments about romance." She saw that Paul, condescending, smiled at her woman's reasoning. "Besides," she went on stubbornly, "Bunny's realism didn't stop her from falling for the wrong man, a weak, manipulative man. She thought she'd gotten away from him when she joined the WAAC, but now he's after her again." Page sighed, and looked at her watch. It was well after 2 A.M. now. "Paul, she's given that man so much of her life already. If she starts again, I'm afraid she could be so badly hurt she'd never get over it."

Paul ran both hands back through his hair. "Giving and love aren't the same things at all, Page. Giving feels like love, but too much—well, it can stifle a man."

"You men all stick together, don't you?" It wasn't exactly a question she wanted him to answer. She was really a little angry because she'd expected agreement from Paul and she wasn't getting it.

Paul frowned. "Page, this is not what I'd planned for tonight, but if we must talk about this, I'll tell you what I think. For most men, love is only part of their experience. They run from women who want to monopolize their lives." He had said too much and not what he'd meant at all. What he'd meant to say was that he could understand a man who needed his freedom, but as for him, he would like to be monopolized by Page's love. But something in her eyes warned him this was not the time to say so.

Page shrugged. "I guess I'm just worried that Bunny will get out of the Corps when the changeover comes."

Paul tapped the ashes from his pipe into an ashtray and, after sucking on the pipe to make certain it was out, dropped it into the ashtray on the end table. "Page, you know I'm all for the women's army, but if Bunny wants out, then perhaps you shouldn't try to pressure her to stay in. After all, she's older than you are and maybe she should get started on the rest of her life."

He moved closer to her, and Page saw the antimacassars Mrs. Mallory insisted on draping over the dilapidated sofa slipping down behind him as they always did. "You mean Bunny should think about marriage and a family?"

"Frankly, yes. Isn't that what a woman in her middle to late twenties should be doing?"

Page knew Paul was talking as much about her as he was about Bunny. He was asking *her* to think about marriage, a home and children in a quiet college town after the war—a life so different from her own childhood as an army brat, dragged from post to post and shunted off to lonely schools between times, that she had only a dreamy idea of what it would be like. The stable life he seemed to offer was what a part of Page had always yearned for.

"Page," Paul's voice insistently responded to her silence, "as important as the WAAC is now to the war effort, it's only symbolic of the unlimited expansion of wartime. Once the war's over there'll be no need for a *women's* army. In peacetime, women will want to lead their normal lives, to make homes and raise families. There's no place for women in the regular peacetime service. You do see that, don't you, Page?"

"But, Paul, it would be such a shame to throw away everything that women have accomplished in the Army."

"It wouldn't be throwing it away. You'd always have your niche in history." He kissed her then and she felt the heat of his hands through her dressing gown. She couldn't think what to answer him when they were together like this. She always felt so much stronger and safer when she put on her uniform.

23

A slip of the lip will sink a ship.
                                  —*Espionage warning poster*

Italy faces collapse, but the Italians, bargaining for better than unconditional-surrender terms, delay laying down their arms, allowing the Germans to pour in troops and take up strong defensive positions.

JILL HAD BEEN sweltering in August humidity close to one hundred all afternoon, but she wouldn't have traded places with an Eskimo. At last the 59th WAC Signal Company was at Camp Shanks outside New York City, waiting to embark for overseas.

"Want a Coke, Lieutenant?"

"Thanks, Sergeant," Jill said, shoving a nickel across the duty officer's desk.

Until the sergeant had interrupted her, Jill had been immersed in a waking dream of imaginary heroism. In her mind, she stood at the head of her platoon while a crusty French *maréchal* pinned the Croix de Guerre on her blouse and bent, while tears of gratitude welled in his rheumy old eyes, to kiss her on both her desert-tanned cheeks. Flashbulbs popped. Legionnaires in white kepis held back a surging crowd, which included her mother and Neil. "What has she done?" the crowd asked. *"Mon Dieu"* the Frenchman said, "she has broken the German diplomatic code—a numerical double substitution system that has baffled the great cryptanalytic minds of the entire world!"

Drinking her Coke, Jill let her mind linger on the scene, savoring the triumph. She wondered if she would ever really show them—all those people who had doubted her ability. There was little to do *but* dream. As Sunday-afternoon duty officer in a staging area, she had no detail rosters to make up, no weekly training schedules to prepare. After the rush of shipping the entire company with equipment from Fort Monmouth to Shanks in a few days, she now had empty hours—who knew how many?—to fill. She decided, moving the small electric fan in front of the window, that hurry-up-and-wait was no empty army irony.

She had acquired new skills during her eight months at Monmouth. Learning to type on the clunky electric code machine with its sets of rotating drums marked with numbers and letters, she was now at forty words per minute. Pretty respectable, she thought, for someone who only last year had done all her term papers with two fingers.

At the same time, she had learned to be a field-company troop officer, attending to the welfare and training of Second Platoon, which often meant counseling or meting out discipline to women ten or fifteen years her senior, but more often meant listening to gripes about the mess hall or managing emergencies peculiar to the Army, as she was today.

The great galoshes controversy had erupted three times during the afternoon. The first sergeant had told her that all packing had come to a halt until the women knew whether galoshes were to be worn, or packed in the A bag, which was to be carried on board ship, or in the B bag, which went into the ship's hold. Jill guessed that until final orders came down—to wear or not to wear—the question would ricochet back and forth between barracks and orderly room.

Jill felt she couldn't wait to write Bunny about this one. But she'd have to. No mail could go out now that they were in a total communications blackout.

"Lieutenant Hammersmith," the CQ announced, standing at the open door. "PFC Brodzinsky requests permission to speak to you about a personal matter."

Jill nodded. Here it came again. It seemed to her that every woman in her platoon was in a personal crisis since they had been locked up in Camp Shanks.

"Yes, Private," she said and returned the salute, "what can I do for you?"

"Lieutenant," Marie Brodzinsky said, holding out a letter, "I got this letter from home just before we left Fort Monmouth, telling me that my fiancé will be in New York City on convalescent leave this weekend. I only want to see him for a few hours—" she saw Jill start to refuse—"just for one hour then."

"But that's impossible, Brodzinsky. We could be alerted for immediate shipment at any hour of the day or night."

"I haven't talked to Bill for over a year, Lieutenant," Brodzinsky said, her eyes filled with tears. "Just let me call him, then."

"I can't authorize a telephone call, not even to immediate family—you know that. As far as they're concerned, we're already at sea."

She got up, came around the desk and put her arm around the woman's shaking shoulders. "I know how you feel, Brodzinsky, but these orders apply to all of us. One woman's mother died, another's husband filed for divorce, but the blackout has to be complete for the safety of the whole company—even the whole convoy. Try to understand."

As Private Brodzinsky left, Jill could tell by her stiff gait that her logic hadn't reached the woman. She sighed and thought how different actual field command was from the paper exercises she'd worried over as an OC. Her time was spent between the sadness of such individual appeals and the silliness of the galoshes controversy, once again, apparently, in full swing.

Two standby orders had come down from battalion only minutes apart. Galoshes will be worn! Galoshes won't be worn! She suspected that the women were having a field day railing at the stupidity of the brass, herself included. She knew she had a reputation for going by the book, but she didn't think her platoon held it against her. She had to follow orders like every other Wac. Perhaps the women's obsessive concern these last hours with such piddling details was a good thing after all. At least it kept their minds off the German wolf packs lying in wait for convoys off the East Coast.

The first sergeant was again at her door. "Lieutenant?"

"Yes, Sergeant Harper."

"Are the women allowed out of the company area tonight?"

Jill nodded. "CO says they can sign out for the post theater or the enlisted service club, but everyone has to sign back in by ten o'clock."

The women deserved some distraction. They might gripe and grouse as all soldiers did from tedium or tension, but she was immensely proud of them. When the WAAC had become the Women's Army Corps by act of Congress last month, ninety percent of her platoon had reenlisted, a Fort Monmouth record.

At seven o'clock, Jill turned her OD armband over to her relief and headed for the O Club before returning to the BOQ for a peaceful evening. "Hi, Kaye, may I join you?" she asked Kaye Young, lieutenant from Third Platoon, sitting at a table alone.

"I wish you would," Kaye said in the direct manner Jill liked because it reminded her of Bunny. "I've heard so many hard-luck stories today, I'm beginning to get homesick myself. How about you?"

"I just got off OD."

"Poor child, you've had your share, then. Want a hamburger? They're not bad today."

"We'd better have one last one to remember what they taste like wherever it is we're going." As soon as the steward had taken her order, Jill bent her head close to Kaye's, whispering. "It has got to be one of two places—England or North Africa. They won't send us into Sicily even though our guys and the Tommies have just taken Messina."

"It won't be England," Kaye said, whispering back. "The First WAC Battalion landed there last month for duty with the Eighth and Ninth Air Forces. They'll wait to see how they work out before sending over any more of us. At least that's the way I've got this man's Army doped out."

Kaye was not really a man-hater—she admired a handsome face like any woman—but she acted as if she was angry at the whole opposite sex. Nobody knew why for sure, except that Jill had heard a hot latrine rumor that Kaye had been jilted during OC by a hotshot aviation cadet stationed at Randolph Field. And there were other things—snatches of conversation about her parents' divorce when she'd been in high school. Kaye had good reason not to trust two men, but evidently she'd decided not to give any of them a chance. She usually turned them away with sarcasm. Too bad. Kaye was not pretty—she still had facial scars from adolescent acne—but she was funny and interesting to be with and Jill had seen a lot of guys drawn to her. It was a darned shame. But it was Jill's good luck that Kaye made a perfect friend for her. Since she was engaged to be married, she had to be careful of her reputation around the swarms of young officers she met every day. "You think it's North Africa, then?" Jill asked her, which set them off on another round of speculation.

The hamburger was thick and juicy, like the ones her father had grilled California style on their patio of a hot summer evening when even the cool adobe had been stifling in the San Joaquin Valley heat. But the memory of her home, her parents, even Neil, was fading like her much-washed khaki shirts. That life and the girl she had been almost belonged in a story-book she had once read, not to the reality she knew now, the one of war and uncertainty and making decisions affecting other women's lives.

" . . . and I can't think why they would show it, can you?" she heard Kaye saying.

"I'm sorry Kaye—show what?"

"Action in the North Atlantic," Kaye repeated. "That's the movie playing at the post theater tonight. Whoever chose the film to play at *this* post has a high sense of gallows humor."

"What's it about?"

"Raymond Massey and Humphrey Bogart have a convoy tanker torpedoed out from under them and they float around on a raft until they're rescued."

"At least it has a happy ending."

"Not if half the company has nightmares tonight."

An enlisted steward approached the table. "Telephone call for Lieutenant Hammersmith," he said. "You can take it at the bar, Lieutenant."

She followed the steward and picked up the receiver lying on the bar. "Lieutenant Hammersmith here."

"Lieutenant, this is Captain Trueblood."

Why was the company commander calling her? This must be it. They were shoving off. "Yes, ma'am."

"There's been an accident, Lieutenant. I'd like you to come right down to the MP company. Do you know where Kaye Young is?"

"Lieutenant Young is here with me. Is it one of my women, ma'am?"

"I can't talk about it on the telephone, Lieutenant. But I need both of you down here on the double."

Hurrying back to the table, Jill reported the conversation.

Kaye took one last bite of her hamburger and picked up her purse. "The MPs are on the main post road—four or five blocks from here."

"Let's hotfoot it over there," Jill said. "The captain made it sound urgent—an accident, she said. Maybe one of the women was hit by a car."

Kaye frowned. "They'd take her to the hospital. No, it must be a security violation. Some lovesick idiot tried to get off the post."

Jill jammed her cap on her head. "If it's that damned Private Brodzinsky, I'll put her on permanent kitchen police."

By the time they arrived at the MP company, both a bit winded, they had guessed at a dozen possibilities, none as bad as the one they found.

Jill, with Kaye right behind, was ushered by a sweating corporal into a back office at MP headquarters. Captain Trueblood was there, and next to her a Wac slumped in a swivel chair, uniform torn and dirtied. Jill asked tentatively, "Private Brodzinsky—Marie?"

The woman's head rose at the sound of her voice, and Jill caught sight of her face—red welts and swollen jaw, making the woman she'd seen a few hours ago almost unrecognizable. Oh, God, she hadn't meant to be so flip about Brodzinsky—she hadn't wanted anything to . . .

"Captain?" Jill questioned, looking up.

"Private Brodzinsky claims she's been raped, Lieutenant. She requested that you be called to hear her story before I file a report."

"Marie," Jill said softly and knelt beside the chair. "What happened?"

"He raped me," Marie said in an eerie otherworldly voice that made Jill shiver.

"Did he do this to you, too?" Jill asked, gently touching her face.

"Yes, when I said I was going to turn him in," the answer came, and then an uncontrollable sob.

Captain Trueblood told them, "We know that Private Brodzinsky accepted a ride from a station-complement sergeant named Glover, went to the noncoms' club with him, had several drinks and left with him. That much has been confirmed by preliminary MP questioning. According to Brodzinsky, the man took her to a building by the rail terminal and forced her to submit to sexual advances."

The private, biting her lower lip to stop the sobs, turned to Jill. "Lieutenant, it *wasn't* that way—not the way it sounds. Three of us were on our way to the service club when this— this sergeant stopped in a jeep and told us to get in. When we got there, he asked us if we'd ever been to the noncoms' club. The other girls got out—but, well, I was mad because you wouldn't let me call Bill in New York, and . . . and I thought I could handle it." Her sobbing started again, her chest heaving; her arms hugged herself in what looked to Jill like a desperate effort to keep her body from flying apart.

"Private," the captain said, "you were off limits, then."

"Yes, but . . .." Her voice trailed off at a knock on the door. Jill opened it.

A major with military-police insignia on his collar leaned inside. "May I see you, Captain Trueblood? Out here."

The captain's voice was grim. "Lieutenant Young, you stay with her. Hammersmith, you come with me."

"Captain," the major said when they were outside, "let's try to reason this out before you go filing charges." He sat down on the edge of a desk and picked up a ruler, which he jabbed at the desk blotter, gradually shredding it as he talked. "Here are the facts as I see them. The girl had too much to drink and went with the sergeant willingly. He swears she submitted, and he's regular army, with a good record."

"Major," Captain Trueblood snapped, "what about her physical condition? She's badly bruised about the face. Did she willingly fall into the bastard's fist, too?"

Jill was amazed at the anger in the captain's voice. The women had nicknamed her "Captain Blueblood" because she was always such a lady, almost as if she were still teaching philosophy at college. Right now she didn't sound like a lady at all.

The MP major jabbed at the blotter again impatiently. "I don't think that kind of attitude will help us get to the bottom of this, Captain," he said and stood up. "You know that rape in wartime is a capital offense, don't you? The sergeant could be shot. Besides, this could be a black mark against the WAC with the troops. Where there's fire, and all that."

"I see," the CO said, her mouth twisting angrily. Then she motioned Jill to follow her and they walked back into the office.

Brodzinsky was no longer crying. Jill saw her staring out the window into the dark that was punctuated by headlights entering the post road. She started up as Jill and the CO reentered the room, and threw Jill a look of total helplessness.

For a moment Jill wanted to run from so much obvious pain, but she was conscious, as always, that she was being judged on her maturity.

The captain spoke first, her voice weary with what Jill supposed was the agony of a command decision no woman would want to make. "Private, you've had a terrible experience, but there's something you ought to know before you decide to file charges. You will be kept here and your friends who were with you will be kept here to testify at the sergeant's court-martial. I'll probably be forced to leave Lieutenant Hammersmith behind to represent you."

Jill started to object, but held her tongue. It was intolerable to think she could be yanked off the levy and forced to spend months in this backwater. After all she'd been through, to miss the war now . . .

The captain was talking. "If you lose, Private, you could be discharged for false accusation. If you win, the sergeant could get the death penalty. Is that what you want?"

Brodzinsky looked at the captain uncomprehendingly.

Kaye, with a reckless courage Jill had to admire, broke in. "Marie, that's your *right*. If you want to file charges, go ahead."

"Lieutenant Young, you're here as an observer," the captain said. "I'll explain the private's rights. Do you have anything to add, Lieutenant Hammersmith?"

"No, ma'am." Jill could see that the captain was upset but

under control, governed by the code of what was good for the service. This, then, was what that phrase *really* meant in practice.

"There's another alternative, Private," the captain went on. "I could recommend you for discharge—for emotional reasons. Did I hear you say your fiancé was nearby? This might be a good solution for you."

Brodzinsky stood. She swayed, and Kaye put out an arm to steady her. "No, thanks, Captain," she said, her voice sour with betrayal. "Go to Bill? Now? I can't ever be with him again." She looked at all of them, and her eyes, naked with rage, stopped at Jill. *"Just one phone call,* Lieutenant, and all of this wouldn't have happened."

The shock of her accusation, the unfairness of it, hit Jill hard later as she returned to the BOQ with Kaye. "I'm not to blame, Kaye," she said, and then, "but why do I feel so terribly guilty?"

"Damn it, Jill, we *should* feel guilty—all of us, including the CO. Do you know what we did to that poor girl? We let her get raped twice! We told her she should forget about the worst thing that can happen to a woman, because the man might be severely punished."

"But, Kaye, I can understand the captain's problem," Jill argued. "She has to worry about getting this company overseas intact, and besides our mission she has to think about what's good for the service."

"Jill, I like you," Kaye said, her mouth set in a harsh line, "but sometimes you're crammed full of horseshit! How can what we just did be for the good of the service? It's bad for Brodzinsky, and it's *bad* for the Corps. Christ! Don't you see that?" Kaye stalked into her room at the BOQ and slammed the door.

What could *she* have done? Jill asked herself. Stand up to the captain, who hadn't liked the whole affair any better than she had, then get left behind, stateside, while the rest of the company sailed. It was a hopeless dilemma. And what about her efficiency report coming up? A good one could mean one step nearer to first lieutenancy. Her bars had come too hard to throw them away for a rebellious private who had disobeyed orders. Maybe Brodzinsky *had* asked for it. It came down to being her word against the sergeant's, didn't it? But as she undressed for bed, none of this soothed the sick feeling Jill had or erased the memory of Brodzinsky's battered, pleading face. Page had said once that the only reason the Army needed officers was to take care of their people. One of her people had been in trouble tonight, and she hadn't stood by her.

Where, then, did her first loyalty lie—to her women or to her superior officers? Deep in her conscience, Jill knew she had been loyal to neither. She had been thinking of herself. She wondered what Page would have done, and knew the answer. Page would have spoken, like Kaye, for what was right. Why did she always seem to choose friends who were like moral watchdogs, constantly nudging her conscience in the most painful ways?

But the most troubling aspect of all was the unbidden but persistent memory of Des Stratton. After a year, his face was blurred. Sometimes she could see each individual feature, but she could no longer put them together into a single clear image. But the memory of his voice was certainly sharp enough. *Hey, Jill, how can you call me a traitor because I didn't speak up for you? Didn't you just do the same thing to that poor girl?*

After what seemed like hours of tossing in her bed, she slept fitfully. When her Big Ben alarm sounded the next morning at five, she determined to put the incident behind her. Perhaps it would be better to transfer Brodzinsky to another platoon. The private would be more comfortable with a change of bunkmates, and less embarrassed as the story got around, which it surely would.

After breakfast at the officers' mess, she arrived in the company area at 0700 to find it in turmoil.

Kaye, looking as if she'd got little sleep, rushed past her at the orderly room door. "Jill, the captain wants us to have all B bags ready for a truck pickup by 0800 hours. I think this is it!"

Making her way through the crowded OR, Jill called on the barrack's squawk box, "Sergeant Harper, assemble the platoon in the downstairs squad room. I'm coming right over."

The sudden chaos resolved all Jill's questions and confusions of the previous night as she headed for the barracks. This was what she had waited and trained for. As she entered the squad room, the sergeant shouted attention. "At ease," Jill said. "Go ahead and smoke if you want to. Sergeant Harper will read the uniform of the day and the equipment you're to fall out with when the marching order comes down."

The sergeant stepped to the center of the bay, and her loud voice droned the list in a staccato singsong. "You will fall out wearing your helmet, Class-A uniform, utility coat, pistol belt with first-aid packet and canteen. Over your right shoulder you will carry your shoulder bag, gas mask and musette bag. Over your left arm you will carry your winter topcoat. Any questions?"

"What about galoshes?" The same question erupted from all over the room, followed by a burst of laughter.

Smiling, Jill answered, "Hold them out of your B bags. As soon as we get official word, I'll tell Sergeant Harper." She walked down the aisle slowly and talked as she went. "Any of you who still has civilian clothes must box them to be sent home. The sergeant will march you to the post office at zero eight ten hours. At zero nine hundred, you may visit the PX for last-minute supplies. I'd advise you to take at least a year's supply of cosmetics, and it would be a good idea to have a couple of bars of soap. If you're lucky enough to find some nylons, I don't have to tell you to buy extra pairs. That's it. I know you're tired of waiting, but it won't be long now."

The sergeant called the platoon to attention as she headed toward the door. "Harper," Jill said, "will you see that the women with pompadours square their helmets when they fall out. I don't want to see any tin pots sitting on the backs of their heads. The men will think we don't know how to wear them."

24

On September 3, 1943, Allied forces cross from Sicily to Reggio di Calabria on the Italian toe under a nine-hundred-gun barrage.

THE EVENING HEADLINES claimed bridgeheads three miles deep into Italian soil as Bunny waited for Johnny to finish his long day shift at Bloomfield, New Jersey's, Westinghouse lamp plant. She added up the days since she'd been discharged from the WAAC. It had been one week.

She had decided that April night in Washington to get out of the Army and begin again with Johnny. Maybe she'd been planning it even before, without realizing it, but that night she knew with a certainty that she had to give the two of them another chance or she would forever wonder if it might have worked. What she hadn't planned was the sense of guilt she felt at leaving the Corps. Not just because she knew that the Army had spent $10,000 on her trainiu g or that Page had been so disappointed—even Elisabeth had written that she'd re-upped—but because she felt so useless out of uniform, as if the world was racing ahead without her.

"Sit still," Mama told her a dozen times a day while she waited at home for Johnny to finish work.

"I can't. I don't know what to do with myself. It's funny, I prayed to get out of the Army, I wanted it, but now I'm just lost."

Without looking up from her mending, Mama had said, "God doesn't give you what you want. He gives you what you need."

She'd heard that all her life, but it made no more sense to

her now than it had when she was a little girl and wanted a pony to materialize in her backyard.

"Go, Bunny—go to the shop," Mama said, exasperated, when Bunny got too restless.

"I'm taking a little vacation. Besides, Angela doesn't know what to do with me." But it was more than that. Although Bunny had tried to resume their old habits of affection, Angela was strangely distant, hardly speaking when they were together. The truth, she suspected, was that Angela didn't *want* her at the shop. All the beauticians were new since her two younger sisters had left to go into war work. And most of the customers came now from the Westinghouse plant across the street. She felt like an intruder in her own business.

She'd have to be patient, give her sister some time to get used to the idea before—

"Hi, babe."

She was swept into Johnny's arms, her face pressed against the rough material of his work clothes. This was a different Johnny from the man in the Palm Beach suit and wing-tipped shoes she'd met so long ago in Atlantic City. Not just in outward ways; he'd changed on the inside too; she was sure of it. She had to be.

"Let's go," he said. "I could eat a mountain of pasta. A sandwich doesn't go far on a twelve-hour shift."

"I'm so proud of you, Johnny," she said, motioning toward the plant. "I know you miss the guys in the band."

"Sure I do, but they're drafting musicians—hell, Glenn Miller's whole band was inducted and took some Mickey Mouse training in Atlantic City. I knew I had to get into essential war work."

"Oh, *that's* it."

"Yeah, little Miss Lieutenant, that's it. Look, one soldier in the family's enough."

He laughed, heartily for Johnny, and she managed a smile. Sometimes Johnny still said things he didn't mean; he was too wary to show his soft side. But his actions were what was important. He was doing his bit just like everybody—and, most of all, he wanted to make a new start with her.

"Listen," he said, walking her to the corner, "give me fifteen minutes, and I'll get to my room, shower and change. Be right back and we'll do the town."

"I'll be in the shop with Angela."

"Nah. Wait there—right there. I want to be able to think of you on that spot while I'm gone."

Bunny saw Angela staring at them through the plate-glass front of La Jeunesse and waved. But Angela turned away without acknowledging it. *Damn!* Bunny knew she'd have to talk with her sister about the shop, but she dreaded family fights. Besides, she could understand how Angela felt. She had put over a year of hard work into La Jeunesse and had begun to feel that it was hers, that Bunny was the usurper. Suddenly it was clear to Bunny what she had to do, and the solution was a relief. She would make Angela her equal partner instead of a paid manager. It was no more than right. Surely Johnny would agree.

But Johnny didn't. "I want to take care of you this time," he said as they ate spaghetti in a nearby restaurant.

His tone chilled her.

"Don't you see, that's what broke us up before—you had the money, and I didn't."

She didn't remind him that he had asked for money many times and then used it to betray her. Instead she said, "It was our money, Johnny."

He stabbed with his fork at his plate. "That's just supposed to make me feel good, but I don't buy it. When we're married this time, I don't want you to earn more than I do. Besides, you're going to be too busy being Mrs. Johnny P."

For a long time she had ached to hear him say that, but the ache now seemed more wonderful than the reality. When they had been separated, when she had lain alone on barrack cots, she had cherished all that was young and hurt in him and excused the way it complicated her life. Now she had to face him as he was, and more—the nagging inner voice that told her she had put personal happiness ahead of her country, and her friends.

Impulsively—just the way she liked him—Johnny reached across the table and captured her hands in his, sending shivers of memory along every nerve. Being with him was physically exhilarating, like the aftermath of a hard-fought game; her heart raced, her face flushed, and within the prison of his hands her fingers trembled.

"Well?" he asked.

"What do you want me to do with La Jeunesse? Sell it?"

"Baby, that's your decision." He looked at his watch. "Bunny, I'm beat."

"Oh. I thought we could do something tonight."

He laughed and winked. "With two graveyard-shift workers sleeping in the same room?"

"I just meant talk together, make plans . . . "

"We will." He yawned, his dark eyes drooping under their impossibly thick, curling lashes. "Tomorrow."

After he left her to go back to his boardinghouse, she walked past the darkened shop. Looking through the front window, she could see the faint shapes of chairs, bowls, dryers and the passive tentacles of permanent-wave machines. Whatever it had meant to her in the past, that feeling was gone. She would offer to sell it to Angela, then everyone would be happy.

Hurrying home, she found that Angela hadn't yet arrived, and Mama complaining about the dinner she'd prepared for two ungrateful daughters. "You off with that Johnny Palermo and Angela callin' at the last minute sayin' she's gonna work late."

"But . . ." Bunny began and then shut her mouth. If Angela was doing something she didn't want Mama to know about, it was none of her business.

It was after midnight when Bunny wakened from a half-sleep as Angela tiptoed up the stairs. "Angie, come in here."

Angela stood at her doorway, a light coat huddled around her to conceal, Bunny surmised, a wrinkled dress. She'd been crying too.

"What's the matter?"

"Nothin'."

Then softly Bunny asked, "Are you having man trouble, Angie?"

"No." The word was barely audible, and the ones that followed were scarcely more so. "Why did you have to come back, Bunny?"

There had been a time when Angela had looked up to her adoringly, trying to imitate her older sister, but it was obvious that that time was past.

"Angie, dear, listen—I've decided to sell La Jeunesse to you, if you want it. What do I need with it anymore, huh, kid? Besides, Johnny and I are going to get married again."

Angela dropped her hand, and her coat fell open. Bunny could see she had guessed right. Angela's dress was creased, hastily put on, not even buttoned.

"Listen, kiddo," Bunny began as her sister closed her coat quickly around her again, "are you sure there isn't—"

"Stay out of my business, Bunny. Take a good look—I'm all grown up. I don't need your help."

"Sorry—"

"Me too. Tired, I guess—but never mind that. What do you want for the shop?"

"I thought about two thousand—land, building, fixtures, goodwill, all of it. We can work out the payments so—"

"No payments. I'll pay you cash."

Bunny couldn't help wondering where Angela could get that much cash, unless it was from . . . Damn! It was more and more obvious she was mixed up with some man. And if she wasn't bringing him home to meet Mama, then she was probably not too proud of him.

Angela's face looked thin and tired in the dim hall light. "If you'll sign over the deed, I'll have the money for you tomorrow afternoon. Come to the shop around four."

"Angie, there's no hurry—"

"There is for me."

Long after Angela had gone to bed, Bunny lay there trying to make sense of her feelings. She had expected Angela to be excited, pleased at least, but the kid hadn't even acted surprised. Bunny shrugged against the pillow. Maybe Mama was right about the ingratitude of the young. Still, she couldn't complain. Everything seemed to be working out for her. She'd wanted out of the Army, and the conversion from auxiliary to army status last month had made that possible. She and Johnny had wanted another chance and they were to be married again. Angela had wanted La Jeunesse and she was getting it. Everyone was getting what they wanted. Then why did she have the feeling something had gone terribly wrong?

The next afternoon she went to a lawyer and had the deed transfer papers drawn up, paid the filing fee and reached La Jeunesse a few minutes after four. A "Closed" sign hung on the door.

Bunny wondered why Angela would close the shop so early on Saturday. "Angie," she called as she knocked.

Angela peeked from behind the window blind on the glass door front and opened the door. "Hi."

To Bunny her younger sister looked tense and unhappy. "I have all the papers here," Bunny said reassuringly. "The minute you sign them La Jeunesse is yours."

"Come on in the back." Shoulders sagging, Angela led the way toward the small partitioned room that first Bunny and then she had used as an office. Johnny sat behind the desk.

Bunny hadn't expected to see him until he finished his shift. "Johnny?" she said, smiling. "What are you doing here?"

Angela went around behind the desk and stood beside him. "He's here because I asked him to be here." Her eyes slid across Bunny's face and then away.

"*You* asked him?" Bunny didn't want to think. What was happening?

"Johnny and I are married."

"*No!*" The scream surprised her, frightened her, so that she forced herself to repeat Angela's words, as if by the act of repeating she could make them more knowable. "Johnny and you are married."

Johnny put his arm around Angela's shoulder, and Bunny saw each of his long fingers dig into the young flesh. "Clam up, Angie, you're talkin' too much."

"She's *got* to know. I can't stand this pretense anymore," Angie said, desperately avoiding Bunny's eyes.

Bunny looked from her sister to Johnny and back again, one question stumbling about in her head: How long had this been going on? She was suddenly aware of the overwhelming aroma of permanent-wave solution and fought down queasiness, but she could do nothing about the dizziness that made her head spin. "Johnny, can you explain—"

Angela's head jerked up defiantly now, her face red, her eyes flashing. "Johnny doesn't have to explain anything to you. You walked out on *him!*"

"Angie, you don't know what you're—"

"I *do* know. Johnny told me how you were always lording it over him with your money, making him beg for every penny. I'll never do that. This is all for Johnny. You never loved him—no, let me finish—you never loved him like I do or you wouldn't have left him alone and joined the Army."

"Angie—how could you—"

"Don't give me that big-sister stuff, Bunny. It's my turn. You always got everything. Mama spent most of the time I was growing up worrying after you. You had the shop, the money—and then you had Johnny. I had nothing, until you turned your back on all of it. Do you think you can walk back in here whenever you want and take everything away from me?"

"Angie, don't you see what he's doing? He doesn't want you. If he did this to me, he'll do it to you."

But her sister didn't see Johnny's gloating face and, most of all, didn't want to see him as he was. Angie would not know the real Johnny P. until he allowed her to, and by then it would be too late.

Bunny was trembling, but wanted to laugh at herself—at her own stupid self. She had been purposefully blind to what Johnny really was—and, to give him due credit, he'd never really pretended to be a saint. *She* had done all the pretending. Now she saw the real Johnny standing before her, clearly. The liquid black eyes were not sensuous but sly; the hands not loving and artistic but grasping; the unexpected boyishness not vulnerability but a calculated image. Oh, he hadn't lied very expertly at all, he hadn't needed to. *She* had provided the lies for herself.

Bunny closed her eyes, but the scene in front of her refused to disappear. It was like a silent movie where every gesture was exaggerated. And to think she had believed that Angela didn't want to imitate her older sister anymore, while all the time Angela was doing a perfect imitation of her own obsession with Johnny.

She wished her head would stop spinning long enough to be angry, to say to both of them the things she had a right to say. Instead, her voice flat and dry, Bunny asked, "Angie, why didn't you just write and ask me to sell the shop to you? Why this, and why—" she directed to Johnny the question her pride compelled her to ask—"why that night in Washington?"

Her fists clenched, Angela shrieked, "Go to hell! You can't make me jealous, if *that's* your game. Johnny's already told me how you threw yourself at him when he played the Shoreham."

At this, Johnny's face broke into a delighted smirk.

The pieces were falling together for Bunny now. Angela's

animosity and Johnny's charade almost made sense. "Answer me, Angie—come on, just satisfy my curiosity," she said softly, knowing her sister's pain, imagining how much more there would be in store for her. "Why didn't you just ask me, just write and ask me to sell you the damned shop?"

"Don't tell me you'd have sold it if you knew about Johnny and me."

Bunny honestly didn't know if she would have. She hardly knew anything anymore. It was as if all the truths of her life were suddenly sliding beyond her grasp. Maybe truth wasn't important now. Her eyes closed and her body swayed. Then she opened her eyes and her purse and placed the deed and the transfer papers on the desk. "Here—" and she managed a rueful smile, which she liked herself for even at that moment—"as soon as you sign it, this place is yours. Now, Angie, you've got everything you want." Want, yes, Bunny thought, but you can have no idea how much you're going to need, how much he's going to take from you.

Johnny quickly picked up the papers, took a pen from the desk and handed it to Angela. Casually, he fished a roll of bills from his pocket, peeled off twenty $100 bills and pushed them across the desk toward Bunny. "Count it."

"Why?" she asked, and some of her anger and bitterness came through. "You'll pick my pocket before I get out of here."

He threw back his head and laughed, obviously enjoying himself hugely. "Baby, your pocket's already been picked."

"Johnny, don't—" Angela said.

"Don't hell! The bitch has it coming for what she did to me." He took the signed transfer papers and put them into his jacket. "This is our ticket to California." He patted his pocket. "We've got an offer to sell this land to Westinghouse for ten times what we just paid you."

Her head stopped its incessant spinning, and she stared at the two of them, all uncertainty gone. She remembered the child Angela, tagging after her, asking her questions, so eager for her approval; she remembered Johnny on the boardwalk and how blindly she had wanted him to want her. Here were two people she had loved—two people who had ruthlessly killed a part of her. Her heart was empty now, dead.

She left them standing there and walked through the shop.

Quickly, she was out the door, walking faster, the late-afternoon September air, sharp with the smell of smoke from the nearby plants, clearing her head. All her life, it seemed, she had been in search of love, and had recklessly entangled herself with men who could not love her in return. She stopped on the corner where she had waited for Johnny last evening, and rested her aching head for a long moment against the cool metal of the signpost. *May God strike me dead if I ever let another man do this to me again!* With those words she thrust away the last flimsy illusions she had nurtured about Johnny P.

"Lady—you all right?"

Bunny looked up to see a middle-aged man in overalls, carrying a dinner pail. "Yes—yes, I'm all right."

"Sure, I can see that." He put his pail down on the sidewalk and stood there looking at her. "What is it—lose your boyfriend? Why, a great-lookin' girl like you can just whistle up a new one."

"Something like that, but really—please—I know you're trying to help, but—"

"You know what they say"—she wished he would go away and quit talking—"God sends you what you need. You'll see, it'll all come out in the wash."

She smiled up at him. "Thank you," she whispered. Then she prayed, Thank you for sending me this man, who speaks in everyday platitudes. She had needed to hear old truths and to listen to them just as she needed to see Johnny clearly so that she could know what she really needed.

The next day she caught a train to Washington to reenlist in the Women's Army Corps. For the first time in a very long time, she liked the way she felt.

25

Domestic servants have disappeared into war plants, and the classified ads are full of potent inducements. One desperate Newark, New Jersey, lady offered a potential maid a room, a radio, a good salary and the use of her full-length mink coat on days off.

STANDING NAKED AT the foot of the bed where Elisabeth lay, Max vaguely remembered some Aldington lines about a woman as lovely as gold but far colder. He stared down at her. "Do you know the poet Richard Aldington?"

"No."

"I thought not."

"Max, don't pull that to-the-manor-born shit on me."

Max clicked his tongue against the roof of his mouth. "You are a little hellion, aren't you? Maybe you *should* read some poetry, my dear. Your veneer of night-school sophistication wears very thin at times."

"That's why I'm so good for you, Max. I remind you of where you came from. I keep you honest with yourself."

The bitch was right, damn her! For these past months he had indeed felt increasingly comfortable with her in his wary sort of way. They both understood the way the world really was, and therefore he could laugh with her as with no one else. The Max Strykers of the world, he knew, rarely belonged anywhere or with anyone, and he'd known this for a long time—maybe it was the first truth he'd ever learned. For that reason alone, Elisabeth could easily become too important to him.

He had left the world of immigrant needle workers, fifth-floor cold-water flats jammed with three generations bent over their piecework—left it so long ago he had almost succeeded in erasing the memory of ever having been part of it. In thirty-five years he had recreated his identity to his own liking: Max Stryker, manufacturing tycoon and sophisticated Maryland country squire. The Philadelphia Mainliners hadn't wanted him, but they had been forced to pay him court—new money could not be ignored, especially after 1929. But belonging? No, he didn't *belong* with them, but he had discovered something better, far better. He controlled them just as he controlled this woman on the bed. Not with money alone—lots of men had money; he controlled them with his authority, because he was never in doubt. He always knew what he wanted next and went after it no matter who got in his way. Right now, he wanted this woman again.

He crossed to the empty side of the bed and tossed the wadded satin sheets aside. He must remember to tell Elisabeth to change the bed later; good maids were harder to find than good lovers these days. He stared down at her. "Now it's your turn to be honest with me. Tell me, did that hero husband of yours ever make you feel like this?" He grabbed her roughly, the welts his hands made on her buttocks thirty minutes before glowing pink on her cool white skin, already tinged with blue.

"How do you feel?" he asked, as he always did. It was part of their love ritual and she challenged him, "Empty—what are you going to do about it?"

He threw himself on his back beside her and pulled her over on him. Her flesh dominated him—breasts, hips, full lips, all yielding and yet demanding. She lay full length atop him and he could feel her body rubbing up and down, little animal sounds issuing from the back of her throat.

"Max, it's never been like this. Never!"

He grasped her long hair in both hands as the low summer Maryland sun slanting in through the window threw gold tints into its waves, and he twisted it tight, forcing her head cruelly back until her chest arched; then he lowered her slowly until her breasts fell, first one, then the other, into his waiting mouth.

Her hands frantically pushed against his chest; she was trying to slide down on him.

Christ! The woman was insatiable; she relished the pleasure of pain and love and the sadness that followed. By God, this time he'd give her a ride she'd never forget. Loosing her hair, his right hand groped beside the bed until his fingers closed around the riding crop he had dropped inside his boots earlier after their morning ride. He raised the crop and flicked it lightly against her heaving buttocks just as she slid down on him and he disappeared into her.

He saw her crouching atop him, the faultless symmetry of her magnificently proportioned body rose and fell like some mad Godiva, her close-to-golden hair a wild torrent about her shoulders, her breasts jutting insolently above him in the midst of his deepest strokes. He flicked the crop again and she laughed, a deep-in-the-throat sound of savage ecstasy.

"Post!" he commanded, slowing her down at will, wanting this moment to last. Oh God! This woman—she could give him—*ahh*—what he needed. "That's right," he gasped, "Now I'll canter for you!" He pushed upward and swung the crop again and again and at last felt the tip deflect and bite into his own leg. The pain referred in a sharp burst of pleasure to his groin and with a surge he cleared the last hurdle, exploding into her. From an incredible distance, he heard a shriek of passion escape her lips. Instantly she tensed, suspended in air above him, and clamped his thighs tightly with her knees, her whole body shuddering, releasing a cascade of fiery liquid, which enveloped his cock, mingled with his own surge, and dove into a deep, warm pool of delight; then she sprawled forward onto his chest.

He lay under her burden until his breathing slowed, then he slid her limp form off and onto the bed. It was true—goddamn her! She *was* a magnificent thoroughbred. But not for one moment could he lose sight of the danger she represented to him. He needed her on the inside of the quartermaster depot, close to the contract bids, more than he needed her in his bed, and he'd better not forget that fact no matter what a tantalizing piece of ass she was. He had enjoyed stripping away, one layer at a time, the various calculating, worldly, cold images she had shown him, until today he had reached the essential Elisabeth. She was so obvious as to be laughable, and he stretched until his joints cracked, smiling at his own cleverness. Elisabeth simply could never love any man who loved her. Received love was so foreign to her that she was suspicious—contemptuous, even—of men who offered it. That poor fool of a husband had driven her away permanently with his first act of adoration. He smiled again. It wasn't so much that he knew human nature as that he knew human suffering.

"You're smiling, Max," she said, stirring at his side. "Are you pleased? With me?"

"With you, Elisabeth?" he asked, answering her question with a question. Indeed he was pleased. She was probably the world's greatest lay, but he had to remember that her body and its pleasures were of passing importance. The important thing, he knew, was to keep her off balance, guessing and wondering how he felt about her.

Lying naked in bed, a total lassitude in her limbs, Elisabeth watched him emerge dripping from his shower. His features— no, it was his compelling expression—forced her to watch him; not that she wanted to turn away. She liked to observe him naked—stark, brutally naked. He was the only unclothed man she had ever seen who did not look less impressive than the clothed man, whose genitals did not dangle like some incongruous anatomical afterthought. Max's cock seemed always sinuous and alert. Looking at him, she felt passion stirring again, and something more, a desire to be with him, like this, forever.

Max's body betrayed to her experienced eyes the lineage of a thousand generations of European peasant toilers. He was thick through his neck and thighs, the muscles rippled across his back when he moved, like tides pounding against boulders; only determined exercise, she knew, kept his stomach muscles taut. A thick mat of black hair covered his chest and trailed in a curling, tantalizing line down to his pelvis. Elisabeth buried her head in the sheets and breathed the primitive love scent of him deep into her, a flash of intuition warning her *not* to tell him how much she wanted him, needed him, again—and now. She had learned to repress her insatiable need for him because mèn, even a powerful man like Max, saw it as a threat. She had been born with such knowledge.

Now, dressed in a Bond Street dark tweed hunting jacket, tartan tie and gray flannel slacks, his face cast in the late-afternoon shadows, Max looked to Elisabeth like a desert sheik transformed into English squire. He bent to kiss her lightly, almost, she fumed, cousinly.

"I've guests, you know," he murmured. "They'll be wondering about us."

"Will they?" she asked, an eyebrow raised.

"Perhaps not." His voice a deeper match for her irony, he laid the hand she had placed on his during the kiss firmly back upon the bed. "But they *will* be thirsty, my sweet. We'll have cocktails on the terrace in thirty minutes." As an afterthought, he added, "And wear the Mainbocher country-weekend suit. I like you in that, Mrs. Gardner," he said and flipped open the closet door. As he left he called back over his shoulder, "We're short of help this weekend. Be a sweet girl and strip the bed."

Before she could tell him to go to hell, he was gone. She swung her long legs out of bed, wincing at the bruises; applauding, she raised her hands to the door he'd just exited through. Touché. That plantation-boss routine was masterful. Max loved the last word.

She crossed to the cheval mirror in the huge bathroom and examined her buttocks with her fingers. Lovingly, she rubbed the welts and the darkening splotches on her white skin, the touch of her fingers bringing a sensation of remembered pleasure and a delayed contraction of the place Max had lately filled so completely.

Max! She rolled his name silently on her tongue and knew that she had fallen in love, totally in love like some Third Avenue shopgirl with her thirty-dollar-a-week office clerk—finally in love, forever. Every man she had ever known she measured against his power, and found them laughable. Even as she examined this new emotion, Elisabeth couldn't help but be onto herself; her feelings for Max were excessive, she knew it instinctively, but then she had been nurtured by excess—extremes of hate and love were natural to her.

He had introduced her to the world of industry and big money and leisure. She had access to everything she had ever wanted from a man—every man but this one. From Max she wanted more, and, yes, she had to admit it, shivering as she stepped into a tepid bath and shivering even more at the thought, she wanted Max. She wanted to be with him every night, to wake with his darkly bearded cheek on her pillow; she wanted him to look at no other woman, to think of nothing and no one but her, to remember no sex, no happiness, no tragedy she hadn't shared with him; she wanted to own his hands, his mouth, his memory and his future.

And why not? She was willing to do anything, to give anything and to dare anything for him. Hadn't she convinced Colonel Nickolson that the existing WAAC uniform could be salvaged with a few changes for which Max got a lucrative contract cost overrun? Hadn't she reenlisted in the new WAC, when she longed to escape the women's army, because she knew she was valuable to Max inside the QM depot? Oh, he hadn't asked her to stay. He was too clever to place himself in her debt, and she hadn't wanted to rouse his resentment by making him ask. But he had accepted her decision agreeably, and even more agreeably given her a sable cape and this wildly lovely weekend at his Maryland estate, Whiskey Hill. There had been moments during the past two days when she had been certain he would ask her to marry him, and other moments when he treated her no differently than any of his other female house guests.

"Mrs. Max Stryker." She said the words aloud and slipped the Mainbocher jacket on, pulling her near-golden hair from underneath and letting it cascade down her slender neck and over the stylishly padded shoulders. "Mrs. Max Stryker," she said again softly as she descended the staircase and walked toward the group lounging on the terrace.

26

After refitting with electronic monitoring equipment, 20mm. anti-aircraft guns and acoustic torpedos, German U-boats resume wolf pack operations against Atlantic convoys in September 1943.

INCREDULOUS, JILL TURNED toward the sound of familiar voices in the crowd on New York's Pier 90, voices she could barely hear above the noise of the band playing a booming chorus of "Pistol Packin' Mama."

"Jill Hammersmith!"

"Hey, kiddo!"

She scanned the crowd, and from behind a Red Cross worker with a donut tray two women in khaki burst out of the melee and hurried toward her.

Suddenly she was the center of their hugs and laughter. "Page—Bunny! How did you—what are you—?"

"Whoa, Lieutenant," Bunny said, saluting. "It's simple. I'm a poor enlisted woman waiting in D.C. for reassignment, and our clever PR friend"—she indicated Page—"put this bon-voyage party together."

Page nodded with mock importance. "All very official, too. Permission to photograph Wacs embarking for overseas just came down when I saw your name on the manifest—"

"Sorry, ma'am," a sergeant interrupted, "please clear the gangway."

The three moved aside as a long line of men with backpacks and rifles filed into the hold.

"This is chaos," Page said, pulling them back against a building, "but I'm glad we came. I wish Elisabeth could have made it, but . . . "

Jill smiled wistfully. "Elisabeth wouldn't bother."

As if on cue, they heard a voice calling, "Lieutenant Hammersmith!" The crowd parted, and Page saw Elisabeth walk toward them, wearing one of the new overseas caps atop a wonderfully tailored uniform.

"Wow!" Bunny murmured. "Mama always told me to perfect my whipstitch."

Shyly, Jill shook Elisabeth's hand. "How did you—?"

"It was all Page's doing. She called and talked my colonel into giving me one day of temporary duty to evaluate the condition of WAC clothing at the port of embarkation."

"One day for me too," Bunny said, "but that's all I'll need to photograph you for posterity. Why so surprised, kiddo?" Bunny grinned at Jill. "Did you think we'd let you go to the ETO without warning you about those suave European men?"

Puzzled, Jill looked at Bunny's uniform. "But why are you wearing an enlisted woman's uniform?"

"It's a long story, kiddo, I'll write you all about it." Bunny grabbed a passing GI. "Take our picture, will you?"

"Sure," he said, hoisting Bunny's big Graflex four-by-five, "where do I push?"

They posed smiling together in front of the gangway, three of them in dress uniform and the smallest of them, Jill, green-helmeted, with her musette bag strapped to her back, a blanket roll tied over it. Behind them Jill's platoon marched into the troop transport, all looking like real veterans.

"I better grab some crowd shots," Bunny said. "Be right back."

"I still can't believe you're all here," Jill said as Bunny left. "Page, you've got *some* pull with the big brass." She hoped she hadn't sounded envious, but she was afraid she had because she was, a little, and was ashamed of herself for it.

"No, really, Jill," Page answered, "this is a legitimate assignment—though maybe I wouldn't have been in such a hurry if it hadn't been for you."

"I'm glad you came. I—well I've been too busy today to be lonely, until just this minute. It's just hit me that I'm leaving home, heading for the unknown."

Page squeezed her arm. "You'll be fine, Jill. God, how I wish I were going with you."

Elisabeth snorted. "You're both bucking for a Section Eight with that kind of talk."

"Who's crazy?" Jill said, the old closeness of OC returning. "After all that big talk at Des Moines, you didn't get out of the Army when you had a chance. I think you're more gung-ho than you let on."

Elisabeth put up a hand in protest, but Jill brushed it aside, refusing to listen to her protests.

Bunny rushed up. "Did you see it?"

"See what?" Page asked.

"My God! You mean you didn't see what was going on at the other end of the pier?"

"How could we?" Page answered. "There must be a thousand people milling about. What's up?"

"Kate Smith's down there sending off the troops. She was singing 'God Bless America' at the top of her voice when right behind her Rita Rand—you know, the famous stripper—started taking it off, right there in the middle of the song.

The guys in the bow of the ship started screaming and stamping, and Kate Smith—she thought they were yelling for her—began to sing louder and louder, really throwing herself into it. Page, I'm not kiddin' you, there's a riot going on down there. I saw one GI try to get out through a porthole and get stuck—somebody said he broke some ribs. A bird colonel told me not to dare take pictures. If the newspapers got hold of them some ladies' church group will start a big stink about our boys' corrupted morals or something."

Jill grinned, shaking her head in wonder. "Leave it to you to find the joke in all this."

The last of Jill's Second Platoon had just passed up the gangplank, their galoshes making a squeaking sound on the metal stairs. Laughing, she told the others about the great galoshes controversy.

Bunny nodded knowingly. "Situation normal—all fouled up."

Jill shifted the heavy pack that was digging into her shoulders. "I wish we had hours, but . . . "

"We know," Page said. "We just wanted you to have friendly faces in the crowd."

Jill held out her hand to Bunny, who took it and then hugged her impulsively. "There's all kinds of regs against an EW hugging a platoon officer, but . . . " Bunny sniffed and blinked her eyes quickly. "Now, don't try to win the war single-handed, kid. Save something for the rest of us to do."

"You all right, Bunny?" Jill asked, suspicious, trying to catch Bunny's eye. "You weren't busted or anything?"

"No, nothing like that. And I'm very all right, kid, maybe I've never been all-righter. Don't worry about me—*you* just take care of yourself."

Jill blinked. "So long, Elisabeth. The last batch of uniforms that came through to Monmouth were first class. I knew you'd get everything straightened out down there."

"I—" Elisabeth's face flushed, and she bit her lip, "I'll write more often, Jill."

Jill set her foot on the first step and felt a loss of contact with home, a severing of roots. She was really leaving. She turned back and took Page's outstretched hand. "Remember, we've got that bottle of champagne waiting for us at Babe's."

"I won't forget, Jill."

The past fifteen months had all been such a dream—Neil's wounds, joining the women's army, getting her bars, meeting and losing Des Stratton—that somehow she had never considered the reality of going into a war zone, of putting her life into jeopardy.

"Come on up, love," she heard a singsong British accent from above her. "Don't go getting gangplankitis on us."

She stiffened and glared into the darkened gangway. She'd heard that sometimes guys simply froze on the gangplank like paratroops at the airplane door. But not Jill. Not *any* Wac in her outfit.

One last time, she turned and highballed a salute at the three women standing on the dock. "Hey, Page, I'll bring you back the dragon's tail."

Page gripped the gangplank railing. "Just bring yourself back," she called after Jill as she disappeared inside the ship.

"I hate this," Elisabeth said, her voice low and strained. "I don't know what I'm doing here."

Page felt guilty. "I'm sorry. I forgot—this must remind you of your husband."

Elisabeth closed her eyes tightly, suppressing her frustration. Why were they all so blind? Couldn't they see she was not like them?

"Come on, you two," Bunny said, linking her arms in theirs. "As soon as we launch Jill, we'll just have time for a drink before we catch the *Capitol Limited* at Grand Central. I'll tell you the real inside dope about how my second husband almost became my third. You see . . ."

On board the *Canberra Princess* Jill stowed her gear in the small cabin she was assigned to share with Kaye Young and the company's other platoon officer, Betty O'Neil, and went on deck to watch the pier slide away as the tugs nosed the ship into the river channel. Far below on the dock, she saw her friends, shouldering their way past the bandstand, turn and wave before they passed from sight.

As they picked up speed, she could see up streets running in perfect stone grids right into the heart of Manhattan; then the ship dropped down past the burned-out hulk of the liner *Normandie* lying on her side at her berth and slipped in the late-afternoon light beyond the Statue of Liberty. Jill could not shake the oppressively heavy feeling of farewell, of finality. Of course she was being silly. Page and other Wacs everywhere would give anything to trade places with her, and here she was acting like a child on the first day of school.

That evening after the second sitting, the British ship's captain, Hawkes, invited all Wacs to remain in the dining room. "Ladies, this ship is the liner, *Canberra Princess,* which before the war plied the Indian Ocean route from Australia to Southampton." Hawkes was flanked by an officer he introduced as Number One. "We are a medium-fast vessel and we will convoy during the night off Hampton Roads with other troop transport and cargo ships. Together we will pick up a heavy naval escort by dawn. We have gun emplacements on the upper deck with trained crews. I think it is safe to say that if Jerry has a go at us with his U-boats we'll give a helluva good account of ourselves."

He looked around the room at the 150 uniformed women. "By the by," he said pleasantly, "in case of emergency come here to the dining room until my officers come from their deck stations to take you to your lifeboats; I don't want you wandering about on deck. Be sure you have your helmets. And you might keep with you a small packet of essentials such as lipstick which you will require in the lifeboats." He stopped, waiting for the laugh.

"Obey orders," Captain Hawkes continued, "keep calm and be good girls."

"Yes, Daddy!" Kaye whispered fiercely in Jill's ear. "Some men are such pricks!"

On the first evening out, Jill kept busy checking her women's cabin assignments. Eighteen were packed into the former Queen's Suite all the way forward on the promenade deck. Sergeant Harper had already made a roster for the marble bathtub formerly occupied by cruising society. The women groaned when Jill informed them that there would be only two hours of hot water daily and that they were restricted to one bath every three days. She checked to see that all their musette packs contained emergency supplies. The enlisted women had already begun to call them torpedo bags, and each one had slung hers together with helmet and life preserver at the head of her bunk. Jill gave each EW her lifeboat assignment in time for the first boat drill.

Back in her cabin, she saw that another bunk had been attached to the wall, and on it lounged a woman wearing a WAC uniform with a correspondent's shoulder patch.

Kaye introduced her, "Jill Hammersmith, this is Dee Gleeson of *Ladies' Home Companion.*"

"Hi, Lieutenant," said the woman. She was in her late thirties or early forties; her hair in a neat wraparound roll peeked out from under her helmet. She picked up a pencil and a notebook. "Where are you from?"

Jill told her, and listened while Kaye and Betty recounted every funny army story they could think of. She liked Gleeson almost immediately. It didn't take long to discover that she was the kind of older woman who fit in with a group of younger ones because she never told them how much she'd learned since she was their age. She was a rare good listener. Jill supposed that was why she was one of the country's top women journalists.

"You're really interested in other people, aren't you, Mrs. Gleeson?"

"Call me Dee. And the answer is yes, I'm interested, but mostly in what they do and why they do it. Writers are observers of life, you know—we don't live it, as you gals are doing."

Jill had never seen a writer in action before. It made her realize that she rarely heard what other people had to say because she was so busy getting ready to defend herself. A banty-rooster complex, some guy in college had once called it. But she'd had to learn to defend herself. Still, she was impressed by Dee's self-assurance mixed with warm caring—so much like Page—and she determined to make these qualities part of her own personality.

Kaye and Betty liked having Gleeson in their cabin for other than her congeniality. As a certified war correspondent she had access to every part of the ship, she knew the latest scuttlebutt almost before it happened, and she even had a shortwave radio she was allowed to keep in the cabin.

At damp first light the next morning, Jill went with Dee up to the section of the promenade deck reserved for WAC use, and they took brisk turns around the deck. The wind that always blows at sea whipped Jill's auburn curls into a tangle.

"You ought to have been on the *Queen Mary* or the *Europa* before the war," Dee reminisced. "I often had a seat at the captain's table for meals. There were lounge tea dances in the afternoon and fruit baskets in all the cabins, changed daily when the steward turned down the bed." She grimaced, "This voyage will be a bit short on such amenities."

As far as Jill could see on either side of the ship there were other ships in geometric close order. "They can't be more than a half-mile apart."

"They're not, and they'll close up even more at night, although they constantly shift their sailing pattern. That's so if one of Adolf's U-boats is tracking us, it'll have a hard time slipping between us for a shot. See—" she pointed off to starboard—"there's a destroyer escort darting between those ships now."

For a civilian, Jill thought, Dee knew a lot about convoy operations, and she told her so.

"I don't mean to be such a know-it-all, Jill, but we journalists tend to sound as though we're smarter than we are. We interview so many people and write so many stories that we get to be a little expert in everything without ever really having a great deal of personal experience. That's why I'm with this convoy. I thought it was about time I saw what it was like over there for myself."

Just then Jill was startled to hear the deafening sound of short, staccato bursts of gunfire from above her on the gun deck and from everywhere around the convoy. Instinctively she flattened herself against the bulkhead, then was ashamed of her momentary panic. What if one of her platoon had seen her? Some example she'd set.

"It's okay, Jill," Delores yelled. "They're just testing the guns. The captain told me last night they . . . " Her voice was drowned by another burst that sent tracers from the port guns in a trajectory high over the ships.

After that first day's practice, Jill heard no more firing, although the ship's crew were called to battle stations several times a day. It began to look as though that was as close as she would come to the shooting war on the high seas as day melted into September day without one U-boat sighting. She wrote long letters home and to Page, Bunny and Elisabeth, although she knew Elisabeth and Bunny thought she was crazy for volunteering for overseas.

Daily shipboard routine varied little. Each WAC platoon took turns mustering on the promenade deck for exercise and

fresh air. Jill tried to ignore the notes that sailed in paper airplane form down from the upper deck, where troops from the
ship's hold lined the rail to watch her women go through the
familiar cadence of an exercise sequence.

"Where're ya from?" they yelled.

The women yelled back their home states to the inevitable
"Hey, me too—I'm from right near there."

Boat drills, chow call twice a day and even some volunteer
work in the sick bay and the transport office and regular shifts
for radio ops weren't enough to keep the women busy. To fill
their time the U-boat rumor mill began to grind at top speed,
and Jill and the other WAC officers worried that tension was
building to an almost unbearable pitch. Jill did her best to
reassure the women in her platoon, but she was on edge herself like everyone else, and she was afraid it showed.

"Lieutenant, how about coming down into men's country
with me?" Dee said one day about a week out when she was
headed for the hold.

They descended gangways until they were below the waterline. Each compartment in the lower decks had long wooden
tables with benches on each side. The place had the stale odor
of a gym; it was where the men lived, ate and—in hammocks
slung from hooks—slept.

Jill thought Dee had a marvelous way with the men. She
knew just how to talk with them to gain their confidence.

"Anybody here from Texas?" she called.

"Yo!"

And again, "How about Georgia?"

"Me, ma'am."

"What's your hometown?" she asked, drawing out their
stories.

Texas said, looking over his shoulder with a grin at his buddies, "If y'all promise you won't squeal on us, we'll show you a
stowaway."

And then, passed from one pair of hands to another over the
heads of the packed-in men, Jill saw a little furry mutt.

"This here's Princess," Texas said, holding the pup out to
the correspondent. "We named her after the ship. We all fig-
gered if they could send female soldiers on this ship"—and
here he grinned at Jill—"well, we could have us a little girl
dog."

After interviewing them, Dee promised to visit again. In the companionway outside, she put her hand on Jill's arm, "I can see the army regs whirling around in your head, Jill, but I'd appreciate it if the news of the men's dog didn't go any farther—as a personal favor to me. We journalists like to think we're as reliable as priests about our sources."

"Why would you think I'd run to the captain?"

"Look, Jill, I like you, but you've got a reputation with the women as an officer who doesn't know how to . . . "

"How to what?"

"To bend. Sometimes it's more important to care about somebody than to obey the letter of a rule."

Jill felt the disapproval in her tone. "Does that come from Private Brodzinsky?" How could she explain to a civilian woman what a tightrope she had to walk between her responsibility for the enlisted women and her duty to superior officers?

Dee shrugged off the question. "You're a sweet kid, Jill, but you've picked up the idea that rules are more important than people. I hope you don't mind my talking to you like a Dutch aunt, but I hate to see you get hurt—and you will. I know, because I . . . well, once I thought a man should live up to my ideas of perfection."

"What happened?"

"He left me flat, and I can't blame him."

Jill searched Dee's face. Did she know about Neil? How could she? "I won't report the dog, Dee. Okay?"

"Good. The men down there will appreciate it. Anyway, didn't you tell me you had a dog at home? So you know how important a companion animal can be at a time like this."

"I know. I love animals. I'll be going back to vet school after the war."

"You've never told me, Jill"—Dee took her arm and they started the climb back topside—"how you came to join the women's army."

By the time they got back to their cabin, Jill had told her how she had driven Neil to enlist and how he blamed her now for his wounds. "You were right, Dee. I forced him to live by my rules, and now . . . "

"Don't blame yourself too much for a tragedy of war."

Jill nodded, feeling miserable. "Yes, everybody says so, but oh, Dee, it's not only that. I . . . I met another man during OC training, and I . . . oh, I acted holier-than-thou—refused to listen to him." She twisted her mouth up at Dee ruefully. "You know how it is, don't you?"

"You bet I do. But don't let it get you down. Maybe you've wised up in time."

"No. I tore up his letters and now I don't even know where he is. It's too late. Sounds like the continuing drama of my life, doesn't it?"

Thirteen days out, Jill distributed a pamphlet called "Guide to North Africa" instructing male troops how to act but not mentioning female troops at all. At least their destination was no longer a secret. But if Jill was excited by this news, she was sobered by the thought that the most dangerous part of their voyage was still ahead.

"The guys in the officers' lounge say the Mediterranean is swarming with U-boats," Dee told her cabinmates as they huddled around her shortwave that night. "The sky may belong to our guys, but the Krauts have submarine pens on the French coast within easy striking distance."

"But we've got sonar and depth charges," Jill reminded her.

Betty O'Neil chimed in, "And torpedo planes will be coming out to meet us from our bases in Morocco."

"Right you are, you two, and I shouldn't—" The short wave crackled and an English voice came through strongly. "It's Lord Haw Haw," Dee said, shushing them. "We've got Berlin."

The cultured traitorous voice opened the broadcast with the familiar "Germany calling" sign-on and railed at RAF bombers who were killing innocent women and children in the Berlin raids. It gloated over the shooting down of forty-five Allied bombers by German cat's-eye night fighters.

"He's not too funny tonight," Dee said, reaching out to turn the dial.

"Greetings to the lovely ladies of the Fifty-ninth WAC Signal Company now off the Straits of Gibraltar. . . . "

"Wait, Dee," Kaye said. "That's us. Christ! Someone talked!"

"Hold it, there's more," warned Dee as the unctuous voice continued:

" . . . Your convoy is taking you into a dangerous area.

There is a great naval battle taking place all around you. Do not think that because you are women our U-boat commanders will spare you. You have been tricked by your leaders, who have used you to ensure the safety of the combat troops who cram the hold of the *Canberra Princess*. We do not want you to die and go to a watery grave. Go now to your officers and tell them to turn around and take you back to your mothers and fathers, your sweethearts and husbands, in America."

"How *dare* he think American women are cowards!" Jill said angrily.

"What scares me," Kaye said, "is how much they know—our unit number, the name of our ship . . . I would have sworn we had the tightest information blackout controls ever before we left the States."

"You probably did," Dee said. "They can take little bits of information from everywhere and put them together."

Theirs wasn't the only shortwave tuned to the Berlin frequency. Jill was called the next day to a security lecture, which she passed on to every woman in her platoon. She told them, "Double black curtains at the doors leading on deck; one has to be closed before another is opened. Keep the portholes closed. If we're hit and the ship listed even a few degrees, open portholes could flood us fast. No flashlights or cigarettes on deck after dark. Don't throw *anything* overboard—no candy wrappers or orange peels. And I don't want any of you women even in the latrine—or anywhere—without your life preserver."

That night Jill slept in her clothes. She knew half the ship was ready for the sound of a shattering explosion. She was tense and tired the next morning from waiting for it.

The next two nights they zigzagged constantly, but nothing happened to disturb the sound of waves washing past the bow and the creaks and groans of a large ship heaving and rolling.

On Monday, September 20, the news that British and American troops had linked up at a place called Eboli in Italy blared from the ship's intercom. Amidst the general celebration between the British crew and their American passengers, Jill helped her platoon trade their dollars for occupation scrip. "We'll dock in Algeria in twenty-four hours," she told them while they cheered.

"We ought to have a gala," Dee said that night. "It's a shipboard tradition on the last night before arriving in port. You gals have already got the funny hats," she laughed, picking up a Hobby hat. "Jill, why don't you see what you can rustle up at the canteen, and I'll try the male officers' lounge."

Jill arrived back from the canteen in thirty minutes with four chocolate bars and a pack of Chesterfields. "This is the best I can do. They're nearly cleaned out."

Dee showed up ten minutes later with two bottles of Guinness stout under her life preserver. "Not exactly champagne, gang, but at least it bubbles," she said. "Our American officers have no booze at all, so our handsome Captain Hawkes kindly lent me two warm bottles of beer on the condition I pay him back Saturday night at the British officers' club in Algiers."

Kaye hooted. "That's swell as long as you don't mind going out with Captain Bligh."

Jill got glasses for everyone, and Dee carefully poured four ounces into each. "To warm beer," Gleeson said, "stale chocolate, and the best damned gala night ever."

Jill raised her glass over her head in an exaggerated toast and watched it spin across the cabin and smash against the bulkhead. Only then did she hear the ear-splitting noise of a torpedo exploding.

Kaye and Betty were in a tangle on the floor; blood spattered in bright-red spots on the white sheets of the bunks. Dazed, Jill realized that the blood was pouring from a cut on her hand.

A terrifying claxon went off in the gangway outside the cabin: *WHOOP! WHOOP! WHOOP!* Jill tried to stand, but her whole body seemed to be working in slow motion as if in an escape nightmare where the unknown terror pursuing her got closer and closer while her legs pumped slower and slower.

Dee reached down and pulled her to her feet. "Let's get out of here!"

Jill grabbed her Mae West and hastily wrapped her washcloth around her bloody hand. "The torpedo bags—get 'em!" she called over her shoulder and wrenched the cabin door open, feeling the pain in her right hand now for the first time. Once outside, she saw that the deck listed in the direction of the stern.

The women in her platoon moved quickly toward the dining room. "Sergeant Harper!" Jill called in what she hoped was a near-normal voice to the noncom hurrying toward her against the stream of women. "Check each starboard cabin to make sure all our people are out. I'll check the port side."

Kaye and Betty rushed past her to see to their own platoons. Dee had already disappeared up the gangway toward the deck. Jill quickly made her way down the passage, opening each stateroom door to see that everyone had gone and that no life preservers remained in the cabins. Satisfied, she rushed breathless to the dining room. Hours seemed to have elapsed, but the big wall clock told her that only four minutes had actually passed.

Captain Trueblood was walking from table to table with a first-aid kit, ministering to cuts and sprains. Jill saw one of her women crying, but the woman smiled as Jill approached. "I feel so silly, Lieutenant—just give me a minute to stop."

"Take it easy," Jill said, patting her heaving shoulder. Not one Wac was hysterical, Jill saw with pride, despite the steady sound of exploding depth charges trying to force the submarine to the surface.

"Lieutenant," Captain Trueblood said, pulling her aside, "you're hurt."

"Just a slight cut. Nothing serious."

"Private Brodzinsky is missing. No one has seen her since we were hit. She must be found."

A depth-charge explosion closer than the others shook the ship and told Jill they must be right on top of the submarine. Gripping the rail, she descended to the promenade deck and again checked all cabin doors until she reached the Queen's Suite. She swung open the big double doors and saw that the room was empty. Damn! Where could Brodzinsky be? It was then she heard the sound of running water from the bathroom. She rattled the door. Good God! It was locked. "Who's in there?" She could hear the shrill panic in her own voice.

"I knew the captain would send you."

There was no mistaking Marie Brodzinsky's sarcasm-laden voice.

"Marie—for God's sake, get out of there. We're under attack—unlock this door!"

A moment passed. Jill could hear the incongruously merry sounds of splashing water.

"Ya' know, Lieutenant, every time you want to stop me from doing what I want to do you give me that chummy 'Marie this' and 'Marie that' line."

"Private Brodzinsky, you're forcing me to give you a direct order to come out of there—*now!*"

"You see that roster on the door, Lieutenant? Well, this is my first bath in three days and I'm damn sure gonna have it. So call out the MPs. What can you do to me that would make any difference in my life now? I'd just as soon go straight down to hell on this ship."

"We're not going down." Jill was not sure she wasn't lying. The deck seemed to be listing even more than a few minutes earlier.

Marie was talking, the bitterness of her words coming clearly through the door. "I didn't tell you everything back there at Shanks. Bill's letter hadn't just asked me to meet him in New York. He gave me an ultimatum. Said he'd always been against me joining the WAC—said if I didn't meet him we were through for all time." The bathroom door flew open and Marie, wrapped in a dripping towel, confronted Jill. "Would it have made any difference if you had known, Lieutenant—tell me, would it?"

"You know it—"

"—wasn't in the rule book."

Another explosion rocked the ship, threw Jill back against a tier of bunks and sent Marie slamming into the open door. A huge knot raised almost immediately on her forehead.

Jill helped the dazed woman into a utility coat, snatched up her torpedo bag and helmet from under her bunk and, half hauling, half pushing, got her to the dining room.

Captain Trueblood rushed over to them. "What—"

Jill interrupted. "Ma'am, she fell—was disoriented."

"We have a medic here now. He'll check her over. But see if you can find a ship's officer and find out where we're hit. Are we going to abandon ship? Get me some information. These women should know something about what to expect."

"Yes, ma'am."

Jill bent over Brodzinsky, who was lying on a stretcher. "You okay now?"

Brodzinsky opened her eyes, her harsh whisper meant for

Jill alone. "Christ! Am I s'posed to be grateful 'cause you didn't turn me in to the captain? Get this straight! I'll *never* let you forget what you let them do to me."

Jill ran now from past failure, away from that unforgiving voice, to the sanctuary of the open deck. She edged, in a dark illuminated by gun flashes from the upper deck, along the bulkhead, careful to stay out of the crew's way, until she saw Dee Gleeson.

"Dee!" she yelled hoarsely.

"You shouldn't be up here. I'm taking a chance they'll forget I'm a woman and think of me as just another correspondent with the run of the ship."

WHOOP! WHOOP! WHOOP!

A destroyer passed close by at flank speed, depth charges pumping across its stern. A piercing shaft of searchlight on its bridge swept back and forth across the murky water. Gradually, Jill could see the shape of a conning tower emerge under the light.

The gun crew above cursed at their gun.

"Damn you! Range!"

"One twenty and closing!"

"Fire! Fire! Sink, you sonofabitch!"

Jill saw men tumbling like targets in a shooting gallery about the sub's deck as 20mm. tracers slammed into them. She saw the destroyer turn and bear down on the U-boat.

"Scratch one Nazi sub," a sailor yelled in a high voice full of uncontrollable glee.

"They're going to ram it," Dee shouted above the battle din.

Jill had never witnessed a moment of death before. She stared transfixed as the bow of the bigger ship crunched through the sub just behind the conning tower. In pieces, the sub sank like the stones she used to try to skip on the irrigation ditches back home. Only these stones were full of living men, some tossed over the side, where they struggled in the choppy waves, yelling words she could not hear, but whose meaning she suspected. For a moment she knew their panic. She had felt it before at the embarkation pier, but it had been momentary, not forever. These men were truly stepping off into the unknown before her eyes, and there was nothing she could do about it.

Suddenly, the unfinished business of her life—to beg Neil's forgiveness, to find Des, to grow older and more comfortable with herself—seemed more precious than it ever had. Shivering, she stood there, never more alive, the night air washing over her like the waves closing over the sub.

"Will they pick them up, Dee?"

"No." Dee's voice was flat and final. "If they stop dead in the water, they're inviting a torpedo. Probably more than one U-boat out there, you know."

Jill tried not to think of the alien voices calling through the night in their hated tongue, voices that begged for what she could not give. "Do you know how bad we're hit, Dee?" she asked, trying to close her mind to the men in the water.

"I heard the third officer say that an aft cargo hold had been hit and was flooded. Thank God it wasn't the troop hold."

They moved to the starboard rail, and Jill, looking over, saw a gaping hole at their waterline, faintly illumined by the bright ribbons of flame from two burning cargo ships. Compulsively, she scanned the flame-lit water for the telltale signs of a torpedo streaking toward them. It was obvious the cargo ships had been hit to create a diversion, pull off the destroyer screen so that the U-boats could get at the troop ships. They weren't yet safe. There might be other prowlers out there in the black night.

"Ladies, what are you doing on deck?"

Jill whirled to see Captain Hawkes in a freshly laundered uniform, followed by Number One. "Sir, Captain Trueblood sent me to find out if we're going to abandon ship."

The captain jerked his glance from Jill up to the radar swinging on the mast overhead. "Number One, have Signal report the first sign of bogeys coming in for the kill." He returned his focus to Jill and Dee. "Now, ladies, get below and stay there. Tell your captain that Jerry hasn't finished us. We've slowed to twelve knots, but we'll make headway until we're taken under tow. I'll buy you both a gin in Algiers, Saturday."

Jill wasn't reassured, but she saluted and left the deck with Dee. They had closed one blackout curtain and were about to step through the second when they heard the watch officer report to Hawkes.

"Sir, that Jerry fish flooded two compartments, we've got rudder problems and gas seepage from the storage tanks. If we're hit again—if there's a fire—"

"Right," the captain said. "May God be with us tonight."

Jill was frozen with one hand on the inner blackout curtain. Dee nudged her. "Are you going to tell that to your comrades?"

"No." Jill made her decision instantly. Right or wrong, she was the only one who could make it. "If we explode, it'll be over in . . . Why should they spend their last hours in fear?"

Making her way to the dining room, Jill reported, "The captain says we're going to be taken in tow."

One Wac pulled out a deck of cards and started dealing a game of acey-deucy. Minutes later a mess attendant served coffee and Spam sandwiches. The scene reminded Jill of one of those scary movies where the guests at the manorhouse go on doing ordinary things in the drawing room while the audience knows a mad killer lurks in the closet. But in this case she had chosen to be an audience of one. She had no one to share her fright. That aloneness was the worst part of the long night.

Shortly before six bells she stationed herself in the darkened gangway and watched the sun make the sky salmon pink against the azure sea. She knew now that they would make it. A light easterly breeze was blowing, but she shivered under her Mae West as she watched the Mediterranean rolling past the convoy. What an awful way to die—she relived the horror of the sinking sub—calling out to life that had already turned away. Suddenly the cut on her hand began to throb, and she made her way to sick bay to get it properly bandaged.

On the second morning after the *Canberra Princess* had been hit, the 59th WAC Signal Company was welcomed to Algiers at a dockside shed by the deputy chief signal officer, Allied Forces Headquarters. Jill stood in the back with a sense of movement which told her she still didn't have her land legs.

"We have a lot of work for you to do," the colonel said. "We can use the skills you high-speed radio ops, teletypists and cryptographic people bring us. The only thing I can promise you is long hours and far from ideal conditions—and a chance to kick the Nazi war machine in the backside. Are you up to the task?"

As one woman, the Wacs enthusiastically yelled, *"Yes, sir!"*

"Good!" the colonel said, beaming. "I'm convinced you will live up to the Signal Corps motto, which is—?" he raised his voice in a question.

Back came the strong, proud response: "We do the impossible and do it well!"

The colonel was pleased. "And now I'll turn this orientation over to your immediate superior, who will give you your permanent assignments." The DCSO then motioned toward the door, and Captain Desmond Stratton strode to the center of the room.

27

To reduce the use of precious cargo space, letters to the troops—called V-Mail—are microfilmed and blown up again after overseas transit.

ON A WINDY late-September evening, Max's chauffeur dropped Elisabeth at the Franklin Hotel after another Maryland weekend with just a few minutes to spare before her weekend pass was up. She was relieved. Of all things, she didn't want to have to answer to Captain Swearingen for late sign-in. She tried to keep a low profile in the company; the less anyone knew about her, the better. She didn't need to belong to any of the company cliques. Sure she'd had friends at OC, but that was different, once in a lifetime, and she didn't want or need to try to duplicate it.

In her box there was a picture postcard from Bunny saying that hello was all she had energy for after fifteen hours on KP, and six V-mail letters from Marne. She picked up the thin envelopes, climbed the single flight to her room and tossed them distractedly onto the small table to one side of her bed. Not now. She couldn't bear the memory of any other man to come between her and the still-warm impression of Max's arms. She relived his kisses, the salt tang of him in her mouth, re-creating a deliciously sensual mood.

Finally reality pushed against her. She flipped on her bedside radio and undressed as Frank Sinatra sang "You'd Be So Nice to Come Home to," singing along distractedly, " . . . you'd be all that I would desire. . . . " All her movements seemed unconnected when she had just left Max; she was not grounded, but like a whipping electric wire, full of raw current, landing capriciously here and there. Her sensual memory of him left her with no sense of control over herself, and certainly not over fate.

It was a presentiment of ill-fate that nagged at her, although she chose to think of it as conscience, a new idea altogether in her adult life. She supposed it was left over from saying goodbye to Jill earlier in the month. Somehow it always hurt her to have Page and Jill and Bunny think well of her. And then there was the pressing question of what to do about Marne.

Reaching for the letters, she saw that some were over a month old, while one had been written on September 10, 1943, a little over two weeks earlier. They were all numbered so that she would read them in sequence, and she picked up number one scrawled in Marne's big-fisted handwriting.

Somewhere in Sicily

Why haven't I heard from you? Only one letter has caught up with me lately—darling, I don't mean to sound angry, believe me I'm not—it's just that I don't think of anyone but you or anything but staying alive. You can bet I don't intend to die, that's not in my plans at all. You're in my plans—only you. I want you and want to tell you how much, but I don't want the censor reading about it.

This is capital H Hell. I slept in a barn last night and worse than the bombs and incoming 88s were the fleas. A whole Panzer column of fleas marched up and down my back until I thought I'd go crazy. And in between I counted eighteen air raid alarms. The Krauts sent in everything they had.

When dawn came there were four Tiger tanks lined up in front of us on the road. One of them had three white rings on its barrel, one for each Sherman he'd knocked out. I radioed the others to go for that sonofabitch, and we put him out of action for good.

Elisabeth picked up and discarded other letters riddled with holes where they had been censored, then Marne's last letter, which seemed to have slipped by the censors intact.

Somewhere in Sicily

Darling Elisabeth, do you know you're famous all over the 2nd Armored Division? I found a combat artist to paint your picture (from that old *Vogue* layout) on my lead tank the Lucky Liz. I kiss it every morning for luck. Don't laugh, darling. A guy gets superstitious fast in combat.

We've been on the move for days now—heading east—

Elisabeth turned the page over and saw that the next two sentences were blacked out by the censor.

. . . and now we're in a staging area.

If you've heard about that Patton flap—where he slapped the kid with battle fatigue—take it from me it's been exaggerated. He's the best damned armored commander in the world—that includes Rommel—and we can't win this war without him.

I detoured into a town on my way to a Divisional meeting. Since I got my Captain's bars, I'm in on a lot of the staff planning. The place was a smoking mess! The Germans left snipers behind and our dogfaces had to go down each street drawing their fire and flushing them out.

Another thing—if you hear anybody bad-mouthing "Tommy Atkins," tell them for me that these British soldiers are some great fighters. We've been bivouacked next to the "blokes" for the past few days, and they're first rate in my book.

I want you to know I honor my vows to you, and there are plenty of chances for girls here. Death may be all around me, but your love is sacred to me—you are my goddess, the only real thing in my life. I tried to make you feel that in the hotel that last weekend. Did I succeed? Write every day.

She felt an unfamiliar regret that she couldn't be the woman Marne thought she was. Loving Max to distraction had made her more tolerant of Marne's love for her. For a very brief moment, she toyed with the idea of being straight with her husband, of abandoning the charade of faithful, waiting wife—but only for a moment. She couldn't jeopardize a sure thing for Max—not yet.

But she knew vaguely as she went to bed that such a moment of emotional weakness had opened her mind to a fantasy of possibility. She *must* find a way to become a permanent part of Max's life, and then she would let Marne go gladly. Suddenly, she felt a blow of recognition, one she knew came rarely to people before it was too late to take action. What if Max was waiting for *her* to make the first move? What if he needed an unmistakable sign from her that she was his and only his? Elisabeth had known powerful—even brutal—men who placed an impossible emphasis on loyalty in others. She wondered if that could be what bothered Max—he thought she didn't trust him, didn't want him enough to risk everything. It was possible. Look at the way he referred to her as Mrs. Gardner when he desired to put distance between them. Could he want her to divorce Marne first to prove herself? In her life she had seen the improbable, even the implausible, come true often enough. *She and Max—together.* There had been things more unattainable in her life and yet by her determination she had made them otherwise. Drifting toward sleep, she wondered what she must do to show Max she belonged to him, only him.

Her chance came almost immediately.

"Elisabeth." Danny Barnes, thin to the point of frailty, was waiting for her as she stepped off the quartermaster-depot bus from the Franklin the next morning. "Colonel Nick wants to see the whole team in his office in thirty minutes."

"Anything important?"

"Looks like it. He's got three secretaries hopping from one file to the next, digging out every spec sheet and WAC clothing contract. And, by the way," he said and cast her his shy, intense smile, "these orders came down for you first thing this morning."

She held her breath. They couldn't ship her out. *They couldn't!* "What the hell are they?" she said, half frantic.

Barnes looked downcast. "Your promotion to first lieutenant came through. The colonel sent his personal recommendation after that job you did on the uniforms. Aren't you pleased?"

Relief filled her. "A promotion—oh, that."

"You really don't care?" He looked puzzled then, hurt even, because he'd been part of her success.

She slipped into the safety of her good-soldier role. "It's not that, Barnes. I just don't want to get shipped out when there's so much work to do here. You understand, don't you?" She needed him on her side. Together they formed half of the WAC uniform specialists' team, and Danny Barnes was the EM who could get things done for her. Master Sergeant Kuban spent most of his afternoons on various "official" expeditions that ended in nearby bars, while Captain Everson waited for Barnes and Elisabeth to come up with ideas that would guarantee he could sit out the war stateside.

Impulsively, she picked up the telephone on her desk to call Max, then just as quickly put it down. Max hated any hint of female possessiveness. He was a man, and men, no matter what they said, wanted to pursue. Some kind of leftover predator instinct, she supposed, but whatever it was, she wouldn't make the mistake of telephoning Max until she had something of importance to tell him. No matter how she longed to hear his voice, she must remain the assured, cool woman who had attracted him, a pose Elisabeth found it a growing struggle to maintain with him.

"Come on, Lieutenant," Barnes interrupted her train of thought. "Colonel Nick doesn't like to be kept waiting."

"Right behind you." She took her coffee cup and followed him, taking a seat in front of Nickolson's desk, which looked like a battleground for papers and official memos.

"Okay," the colonel said, "let's get to it," and he sat down on the edge of the desk. "I don't have to remind you that the substance of this meeting goes no farther than my door." He looked up, waiting for nods of compliance.

Did his eyes linger a fraction longer on her face? She wasn't sure, but the chilling memory of Madame Gabriella's steely gaze shook her for the briefest second before she smiled an innocent agreement.

The colonel shifted to pick up a manila jacket of papers. "The OQMG has handed us a big job, and as you can guess they sat on it so long they can't give us the time we need. We're directed to develop a WAC off-duty dress, summer and winter, for officer and enlisted. Captain, I'll need material specs from your team on each in two weeks."

"Very well, sir."

Barnes asked, "Colonel, what about the design?"

"I was coming to that. We'll go after the usual women's-clothing designers."

"Sir, may I speak plainly?"

"Yes, Sergeant."

"Colonel, I think we might be overlooking the talent we have right here at the depot. I mean—" Barnes paused, looking around at Elisabeth—"Lieutenant Gardner has made uniform sketches which I think are damned good."

Kuban interrupted, hung over but looking for a chance to show he was on top of the discussion, "Colonel, that's one helluvan idea. We'd save money and have a great story for the newspapers to boot."

"Worth exploring, Colonel," Captain Everson chimed in.

The colonel stared at Elisabeth for a moment. "I suppose we could include the lieutenant in the competition. What do you say, Gardner? Want to give it a shot?"

Was he kidding? To actually design a dress—no, four dresses, and see them turned into material, buttons and trim, to see them worn by women. Her designs. "I can't think of anything I'd like more, Colonel."

"All right, go to it. But, Elisabeth, I can't promise you more than equal consideration."

"Certainly, sir, I would want you to be fair to the civilians." Inwardly she smiled. That was waving the old school tie at a career officer.

Gradually during the meeting she had lost all sense of the danger she had felt earlier. She put it down to a natural tension, because thoughts of Max intruded now into her every thought and act—especially here at the depot.

The colonel continued, "Everson, I want you to get to work on the production schedule, and have it on my desk by the end of the week. We have to have designs, specs and material allocations ready for contract bids by early November."

"You'll have 'em, sir."

Outside the colonel's office Elisabeth threw her arms around Barnes and kissed him while the office Underwoods came to a standstill. "You're a darling for going to bat for me like that."

Stumbling, Danny backed away, a look of pure adoration on his face. She observed him more carefully than she usually did. He was infatuated, she could see that, infatuated in a strangely passive way, but Barnes was a man nonetheless and might want more from her than she could give. Christ! She'd have to be careful, she didn't want to encourage or discourage him. Damn! Here was *another* nice guy who wanted to adore and take care of her. It was amusing, after all. She seemed to attract men who needed a goddess. There was just no way to get rid of men like Marne and Barnes, not even in the Army. Irritated, Elisabeth sat down at her drawing board and picked up a charcoal for sketching. She had been nice to Barnes because she could use him, but she couldn't take seriously his response to her, because it was Max she wanted passionately, obsessively and miserably—the one man *she* couldn't fool.

That night she walked down Broad Street to a public telephone booth and dialed Max's Drexel Hill number.

She waited for him to pick up his extension.

"Elisabeth. What a pleasant surprise," he said in the breathy baritone that sent pinpricks of remembered pleasure through her body.

His measured politeness established a formal distance from her. She wanted to scream at him, tell him not to take that tone with her, but instead she said calmly, "I've only a moment, Max, but I thought you'd like to hear about an interesting new development at the depot." She waited. Damn it, she was always waiting.

"Yes," he said finally.

"The colonel gave my team a new project today—developing WAC uniform dresses for off-duty wear. And, Max, I'm going to submit designs for them—Colonel Nick agreed."

"I wasn't aware you were interested in designing, Elisabeth," Max said.

"I didn't know it myself until a few months ago," she told him, hoping he'd be impressed.

"Why are you telling me this?"

"I thought ... " She hesitated, knowing she was violating every army reg she could think of, and then began again. "I thought you'd want to know about a potentially large contract you could bid for."

She heard his deep breathing through the earphone. "Aren't you aware," he said, his voice almost lazy, "that you could be in serious trouble by giving me advance contract information?"

What kind of game was he playing? She was giving him exactly what she knew he wanted.

Then his voice became intimate, the tone he used when he was aroused. "Darling, I must go to Washington tomorrow for a hearing at the War Production Board, but I'll be back on Friday. We'll have dinner, then, just the two of us."

"I'd like that very much, Max," she said in a voice whose sensuality she could no longer control, suggesting plainly what she'd like much more than dinner.

"Until Friday, then."

She waited for him to hang up the receiver. He didn't. "Max, are you still there?"

"Yes."

"Why?"

"No reason, or at least none I want to discuss right now. I'll talk to you about it on Friday." He hung up then.

What did he want to discuss with her on Friday? Her hand shook as she replaced the receiver and caught her own reflection in the window of the glass booth. Her eyes searched the face to see if it knew something. Was Max going to ask her to marry him? Had her desire to help him get another contract finally convinced him of her love and loyalty? "Max," she said aloud, her voice seeming to come from the woman in the window, "I'll prove it!"

Elisabeth walked swiftly back to the Franklin Hotel and climbed to her third floor room. She had thirty minutes before she had to report for a tour as company duty officer. Pulling from her small writing table one of the tissue-weight V-mail sheets, she looked up the APO number, which she could never seem to remember, and began to write what she knew was a Dear John letter every patriotic American would despise her for:

> *Monday evening*
> *September 27, 1943*

MARNE:

I have fallen in love with another man and I want a divorce. Sorry, but there is no easier way to say it; the best way is straight out like that.

My mind is made up so please save us both embarrassment and don't ask me to reconsider. However, you should let me know whether you want me to file for the divorce or whether *you* want to.

By this third paragraph you should have begun to hate me for what I'm doing to you. I hope you do hate me. That would be the first wise reaction you've had to me since we met. I was never the woman or wife you thought I was. Believe me, this is the kindest thing I have ever done for you.

Hastily, she signed and sealed it, carried it downstairs to the orderly room and placed it in the pile of outgoing mail. She was on duty until midnight, but during those hours she wouldn't allow her eyes to stray to the letter box. She wouldn't allow her mind to question or look back. She must strip herself naked of her neatly guaranteed future for Max. It was a risk only Max could appreciate, a move that would convince him she wanted to belong only to him.

Max sat upright behind his great mahogany desk for some time, his right hand resting on the cradled telephone. He had no inkling of why he had suggested that some mysterious message would be given Elisabeth on Friday night. He supposed he was in love with the bitch and his senses had deserted him—a dangerous situation, since she seemed to be taking chances and losing her own well-developed sense of self-interest.

Damn! And Nick had been acting strange, too, lately—

standoffish. Did he know about the affair with Elisabeth? What did the colonel suspect? In any event, he'd be a fool to trust her now. When a vain, neurotic, selfish woman falls in love for the first time, she precipitates danger like loose cannon on a heaving deck. But, damn it, he needed her, just a few more weeks, months at the most. He must find a way to keep her loyalty just long enough, while gradually cooling the situation. When it was safe, he would see that she was transferred to the other end of the country. A word in the right ear would do it.

Anyway, the war would probably end in 1944 and the quartermaster stockpiles would kill the uniform-manufacturing business for years to come. He had already begun to plan his reentry into the postwar clothing business, when the homecoming GIs would quit making war and start making babies by the millions. Baby clothes, layettes, that sort of thing—*that* was where the smart money would be in the ready-to-wear industry, and for that transition he wouldn't need a has-been fashion model. That was not to say he didn't need a wife, but he needed one who would cover his wartime profits with a patina of respectability.

He rang for his butler.

"Yes, sir."

"Hinton, I'm driving to the capital tomorrow morning for three or four days. Pack the conservative pinstripes. No evening clothes this trip. I'll be dining at the Army-Navy Club, where tuxedos are considered downright unpatriotic."

"Very well, sir."

"Make it the gray pinstripe, Hinton. War profiteers don't wear gray, do they?"

"No, sir, they don't," the butler said, smiling at Max's little joke.

"And, Hinton, while you're about it, please see if you can get Miss Longley for me."

A few minutes passed. Max poured a large scotch. The telephone on his desk buzzed.

"Miss Longley on the line, sir."

"Thank you, Hinton."

"Kit, darling," he said.

"Max," the thin, reedy voice, product of several generations of gentry inbreeding, answered. "I don't know if I should even *talk* to you. You've been so naughty."

"A businessman's time is not his own, my dear. Surely you know there's a war on."

"Don't be tiresome, Max. I've heard you've been fighting on *quite* a different battlefield."

"Perhaps that is why you should pay special attention to me now that I'm home for good from the wars."

"*Are* you home, Max—for good?"

"Yes, most definitely, or rather I will be after a run down to Washington. I'm having a little dinner party this Friday. You could see how war-weary I really am, and besides, darling, I've arranged an amusing guest list. Will you come?"

"Yes, I'll come, if only to see this new Max for myself."

28

In September, German Colonel Otto Skorzeny, in a daring glider raid, rescues Mussolini, who has been imprisoned by the new Italian military government of Marshal Pietro Badoglio. By October, the dictator, accompanied by his mistress Clara Petacci, is set up in a German puppet government at Lake Garda. The Badoglio government is not given the status of one of the Allied Powers, but is classed as a "co-belligerent."

BY ONE O'CLOCK on the afternoon of Wednesday, October 13, Page felt that her stomach had started a war of its own. All morning she had been unable to take a break at one of the Pentagon's coffee bars, and she was well on her way to missing lunch.

The news from the army comcenter that the Badoglio government had declared Italy to be at war with Germany had caused a flurry of small celebrations all around the second floor from A to D ring, but she had not had time to participate. She had spent the morning polishing press releases for the all-states WAC recruiting campaign. A brilliant idea of Page's superior, Major Jesse Rice, the campaign enlisted women in their own state's training companies. The drive had given the WAC's public image a boost and also just about replaced the women who had chosen discharge during the conversion in July.

There were now 260 WAC companies, stationed in almost every command in the continental Zone of the Interior and the overseas theaters. These companies were doing work vital to the war effort from motor transport, postal service and parachute rigging to food preparation, supply and a variety of clerical and administrative work, but there were never enough companies to satisfy the stack of requisitions on Colonel Hobby's desk. And no one in the Director's office believed that the WAC could enlist the 600,000 women General Marshall had asked Colonel Hobby for.

Page wrote "30" on the last press release, marked the routing slip for mimeographing and distribution, and, still concentrating, reached for a cigarette.

"Oh, how soon they forget," a man's voice said in a familiar tone of mock self-pity.

"Randy!" His voice was deeper, but no older sister could forget a younger brother's teasing tone. Jumping up from her chair, she threw her arms about him. "Let me look at you." She stepped back, still hanging on to his hands. "You've changed so—it must be the Clark Gable mustache and the fifty-mission crush to your hat." She had instantly settled into the habit of easy raillery that was an affectionate shorthand between them. "I swear, Little Brother, I'd pass you right by on the street. The last time I saw you on leave from the Academy you were but a callow cadet."

"That was before I towed targets for aerial gunnery practice, Big Sister. Ages a man fast." He looked quickly at his watch. "Listen, can you get away for some chow? I've got to be back at Gravelly Point before four o'clock."

"Let's go." She jotted an explanatory note and left it propped on her desk.

On the way through the marble corridors, she pointed out

some of the Pentagon's landmarks. "That's Special Services right next door to us. Captain Wayne King, the bandleader, has his office there."

"Hobnobbing with celebrities must be dangerous work." He grinned. "Do you get hazardous-duty pay?"

"Funny boy! As a matter of fact, it has its moments of pure terror. Try coordinating a bond rally with Mrs. Winston Churchill, Jeanette MacDonald, and a dozen big brass all trying to stand next to them. I'd have never made it, but I worked with a great officer. You may have heard of him—" she was teasing again—"Captain Pat O'Brien?"

"Enough, you shameless name-dropper!" He sighed loudly. "There goes the hot combat-pilot image I was going to impress you with—shot down." His one hand spiraled down like a falling airplane.

They squeezed into the next elevator. "And this is the famous concourse," Page announced guide fashion when they reached the enormous expanse on the bottom floor. "The officers' dining room is over here. It's a good thing you came this month. Women officers weren't allowed to dine here until recently."

"Still leading the charge, Page?"

She grinned. "Now you sound like my friend Bunny. Little brothers should not be so perceptive."

"Just so you don't think yours is the only cross being carried in this war, let me tell you my own horror stories. You know the ninety-day wonders hate us West Point guys worse than they hate the Nazis! And the older Point men are unhappy because my class was commissioned in our third year so we could leave our Hudson River paradise to win the war for them. Everybody's somebody's scapegoat—and that's as profound as I'm gonna get this whole war."

They took their trays to a quiet table against the back wall.

Page had almost forgotten her hunger in the excitement of seeing Randy again. "Have you heard from Father?" she asked, spooning the split-pea soup she had ordered.

"Not since I went Air Corps over Armored and disgraced him."

"No, Randy, that's *my* special niche in his life. But you're wrong not to think he's proud of you. He is—tremendously so."

"He has one helluva way of showing it, Page. He even reamed me out in a letter which his adjutant signed."

"It's his way. I don't mean to play Can You Top This, but when I was in the hospital at Fort Des Moines—"

"In the hospital? I didn't know."

"Oh, it was nothing important, as it turned out. But let me make my point—Dad called the hospital head from London to find out about me. It never occurred to him to ask me directly."

"Why can't he talk to us, Page?"

"I think he's afraid of loving us too much, and losing us, like he lost Mother."

"They don't teach us Freud at the Academy. I'll have to leave the analysis to you Cliffies."

Page made a face, then said seriously, "He always thought you'd take his place, Randy. You know that."

"Look, he may have written the book of my life, but that doesn't mean I'm going to live it."

"What are you saying?"

"As soon as I do the duration and six months, I'm resigning my commission."

"Oh God! Why? I'd give anything—"

"Page, I knew it my first month at the Point. I don't want to spend the rest of my life in uniform, clawing my way up the promotion ladder. He loves it—damned if you don't love it, too—but I hate it."

"What do you want to do?"

"I don't know. I'm not a very ambitious guy, but I sure know I don't want any part of this life." He smiled, the wry sideways smile she had always loved. "Hell, Page, *you* were always a better soldier than I was, even when we were kids. Remember at Fort Sill when I used to make you and your girlfriends be the Indians, and you always won? The General just refused to acknowledge it."

Page smiled at the memory, but worried that Randy might make some headstrong announcement that would tear apart her family forever. But how much family was there to save? Randy would go his own way after the war; her father had always insisted on his own plan for her. When she thought hard about it, the only real family she had was the Army and her sisters in the Corps. She shook her head to clear it of the thought that had become more and more persistent, one she could not seem to rationalize away permanently—the thought of living a military life even after the war. Again she shook her head. But of course Paul was right. It was ridiculous to think of women soldiers in a peacetime Army.

Randy snapped his fingers. "Come back, Page, wherever you are."

"I was just thinking that you certainly have a right to lead your own life, Randy, but you don't have to tell him until after the war. Can't you let it go until then?"

He nodded reluctantly. "Still the mediating angel between the men in the family. I can't quite believe it yet—that you actually had the guts to defy him and join the Army."

"I surprised *myself*," she said, then changed the subject. "Now tell me all about flight school."

"Nothing much to tell. I like flying well enough. Bombers, really—B-17 flight school is where I'm headed. I'm not your hot-stick-jockey, fighter-pilot type. Yeah, flying's fine, I guess. We get the best food and the best girls." He reached into his inside blouse pocket and dropped a handful of pilot wings on the table, a mischievous grin lighting his face. "The girls are crazy to get pinned."

"Randy, that's terrible." But she laughed in spite of herself.

"Now," he said, finishing his apple pie and lighting a cigar, which looked impossibly adult against a face still carrying the round-cheeked remnants of boyhood, "tell me about your Wacs."

"What do you want to know?"

"You wrote me about the terrible time you were having with the rumor mill."

"Oh yes, that's always with us, but public acceptance is growing. Our new recruiting campaign involves local communities more, and that's helping people see that Wacs are regular women." She told him about all the press releases she wrote showing the diversity of women in the Army, ticking off a range of her stories that had been recently picked up by the wire services. "There's the private whose rheumatic-fever-control experiments at Buckley Field Hospital earned her a commission; the furloughed sergeant who couldn't sleep because the beds at home were too soft. Just yesterday I distributed a report from the Medical Corps giving Wacs with the

Fifth Army in Italy a first-class health rating. That's army code for assuring civilians that we aren't pregnant en masse."

Randy stubbed out his cigar. "Sounds like pretty tame stuff to me."

Though she tried for a lighthearted tone, she couldn't keep the bitterness and frustration out of her words. "Damn it, Randy," she said, lowering her voice, "it's what I *can't* publicize that the public ought to hear. You know that Washington is ringed with antiaircraft batteries, don't you?"

"Yes. I'd expect the capital city to be protected from air attack."

"And you think they're fully manned, don't you?"

"Of course, Page, they'd have to be. What is this, *The Sixty-Four-Dollar Question?*"

"What if I told you they weren't all manned, that some of them were wo-maned?"

Randy let out a low whistle. "You're the public-relations expert, but I'd say that's one helluva story."

"That's what's so frustrating," she told him, her chin propped on her hand. "The Army is scared to death of getting a negative reaction from the public, a-little-girl-can't-handle-a-great-big-gun stuff, so I can't mention it, nobody can. Just think, Randy, if flying was woman's work you'd never get the recognition you're due, you'd never be able to brag or pass out wings to every pretty girl you meet."

"Hey, take it easy, Page. Remember me? I'm just a poor flyboy on a stopover to see his big sister. I'm not responsible for the Army or the backward ways of the whole country." He reached for her hand. "Know what?"

"No. What?" she answered falling into a silly game they had played as children.

"You always were too serious, reading poetry and all, but now you're positively grim, a Janie-one-note. You've got to get out more. Have some fun. What happened to that Major Whatshisname? Can't he take you away from all this?"

She stopped smiling at the idea that her younger brother was giving her such mature advice, and a memory of Paul's goodbye filled her. "He's shipped out, Randy. I don't know where. He couldn't tell me, and I haven't heard from him yet."

"Liked him, did you?"

"Yes—a lot."

"That's tough, Page. But honest, listen to ol' Randy, now—I'm quite an expert on good times. This WAC thing is really getting to you. You're even beginning to sound like one of those Suffragettes, dressed in virginal white, chained to the White House fence. Why don't you try to get a furlough or at least take a couple of days on a pass? Do you good. I'll bet you've been working round the clock."

She had to admit he was right. In the month since Paul had left she had been working day and night six days a week, sometimes Sundays too. "I could take a couple of sunny days while Indian summer holds—maybe even play some tennis at the club. Are you sure you can't stay?"

"I'd love to teach you proper respect for my backhand, but I've got to report to Lockbourne in Columbus, Ohio, tomorrow. Besides," he said, his grin devilish again, "there's a girl at the Air Transport Command office out at Gravelly who's just dying for a pair of wings for her cashmere cardigan."

The short hour they'd had was gone, and they had talked about everything and nothing. The most important question—*Is this the last time I'll ever see you?*—she had never asked.

"Take care of yourself," she said, "take exceptional care of yourself, Little Brother."

He kissed her on her forehead. "Did I ever tell you you're some swell big sister?"

Page went with Randy to the main-floor entrance, and watched him start down the steps to the street below. She wanted to run after him, tell him why he was so precious to her. He was the only other person in the world who shared her blood and her memories exactly. But soldiers didn't run after other soldiers. Instead her eyes followed him until his uniform in the distance was indistinguishable from dozens of others.

29

Yes, I want the war to be over, just as keenly as any soldier in North Africa wants it. This little interlude of passive contentment here on the Mediterranean shore is a mean temptation. It is a beckoning into somnolence. This is the kind of day I think I want my life to be composed of, endlessly. But pretty soon we shall strike our tents and traipse again after the clanking tanks, sleep again to the incessant lullaby of the big rolling guns. It has to be that way.

—Ernie Pyle

"HAMMERSMITH, SECOND LIEUTENANT, Jill H., U.S. Army, WAC," she wrote in the guest book, adding an unaccustomed flourish under her neat signature, not to be outdone by the more elaborate European handwriting style just above hers in the guest book. She placed her Hobby hat on a marble table in the midst of what looked like an internationale of hats—a French general's, two British naval officers', one of them a Wren, and an AAF colonel's overseas cap.

"I have to pinch myself, Kaye," Jill said to her companion. "If I had a magic lamp I could never fantasize anything like the Palais d'Été."

"And those zouave officers," Kaye Young said, eying the swarthy pantalooned colonials striding about in their boots and tasseled hats, "all look like Turhan Bey in the Loew's Saturday matinee."

Jill laughed. "Come on, Kaye, you can take your pick of dates in Algiers. Besides, you don't even speak French."

"You know," Kaye said playfully, "that's not as much of a problem as you might imagine. I think I'll suggest to Dee that she do an article on nonverbal dating. I've always thought communication highly overrated—without words you just get down to fundamentals fast. Ugh! Me Kaye, you Tarzan . . . "

Jill giggled. "Sshhh! What if General Giraud heard you?"

Kaye simulated a shocked tone. "Sshhh yourself or *you'll* offend him! He's French, isn't he?"

Jill was amazed at the total transformation Kaye had undergone since they arrived in North Africa. While not exactly man-crazy, she certainly wasn't the angry, sarcastic woman she had been. Jill had asked her once about the change. "It's this way," Kaye had said. "I thought it was my fault when Dick wanted out of our engagement, but since I came here I've realized what a bastard he was—after all, forty thousand Frenchmen can't be wrong!" Jill knew there was a basic truth to Kaye's joke. Ten thousand men for every Wac in Algiers can work marvels for a woman's self-confidence. If Kaye had been jilted by one man, the cure seemed to be the droves of attentive Allied officers waiting to shower her with masculine attention in a dozen different languages. The cure, in fact, may have been too complete, because Kaye had taken a romantic's interest in Jill and Captain Desmond Stratton of late.

They moved into General Henri Giraud's receiving line. The commander of the Free French in North Africa was hosting a formal buffet at his headquarters; his spahi honor guard, swords drawn, stood just behind and to either side of him. Only in her wildest daydreams had she seen herself in the company of a famous French general, and now just two short months since the *Canberra Princess* had been towed into Algiers everything was coming true.

She stopped and stood at attention in front of the General. "Lieutenant Hammersmith, sir, Women's Army Corps, United States Army," she said. "Thank you for inviting us."

He lifted her hand and bent to kiss it. She felt his white mustache scratch her skin. "General Eisenhower has told me many times that his women soldiers rank with his best troops," he said in heavily accented English. "It is always my pleasure to pay homage to good soldiers."

She was overwhelmed by the warmth of his Old World courtesy. She caught herself almost dipping into a curtsy. Good God, would she never stop responding like a dutiful child? When would she grow up and leave the too self-conscious Jill behind?

"Thank you, General," she said. She drew herself up to his Croix de Guerre and stepped aside for Kaye.

"Lieutenant Kaye Young, sir."

"And what is your duty, Lieutenant?"

"I command one shift of the all-nation switchboard, General."

"Ahh, then it is to you we owe the good telephone service we have here in Algiers."

"Sir, that credit goes to my operators."

He nodded. *"Mais certainement!"*

Kaye joined Jill in the main room. "Not Jean Gabin, but nevertheless a handsome old lion," she said, relishing her newfound role as expert on the male sex.

"Hello, you two. I hoped I'd find you before I left."

It was Dee, followed by two army photographers.

Jill shook Dee's hand. "You're leaving? When? Can you say where you're going?"

"Tomorrow. Flying to London. My magazine wants me to write an article about GI Janes with the Eighth Air Force. Can I send you something from merry old England?"

Kaye laughed, "How about a nice cool fog?"

Jill frowned at Kaye's levity. "I wouldn't mind going with you, Dee. It's all over in North Africa. The war has moved on and left us behind."

Kaye rolled her eyes at Dee. "Does Rommel know how lucky he was to escape before Jill landed?"

Dee grinned. She was used to the constant ragging of soldiers. Shifting her gaze to the feast laid out for guests, she said, "Do mine eyes deceive me or are those *eggs* on the buffet table?"

"Eggs! Real ones?" Jill whirled around, scarcely believing it. Eggs were a precious commodity in North Africa—a medium of exchange far more effective in a bargaining session with native merchants than American occupation scrip. "I could eat a dozen, but we have to be on our party manners. Besides—" and she giggled at the idea—"my mother would find out."

"I know what you mean," Kaye said in mock seriousness. "Even oceans cannot dim the all-seeing maternal eye." Kaye's own eyes roved the glittering military crowd. "Look who's here, Jill, your *friend,* Captain Desmond Stratton—and he's heading our way."

"Where? Never mind, I don't care. Why does he have to show up and spoil things?" Jill asked, her slight overbite giving her mouth a pronounced pout.

She saw Dee glance a warning at her.

"I can't understand these two," Kaye said to Dee. "They're like two kids who punch and chase in the schoolyard, when all along the whole thing is about s-e-x."

"Damn it, Kaye, he'll *hear* you." Jill knew that the impasse with Stratton wasn't her fault. She'd tried several times during the last six weeks to tell him that she regretted not giving him a chance to explain back at Fort Des Moines, and that she wished now she'd answered his letters. But each time she tried, it hadn't worked; there was still too much anger and hurt between them. Besides, he was her superior officer at the com-center, and—at this thought she frowned to herself—he had obviously learned to keep a proper distance from junior officers. Still, everyone seemed to guess that they had known each other before, and she knew there was a noticeable tension in a group whenever they were together. Kaye certainly hadn't been fooled for a minute.

"Hello, Lieutenant Young," Stratton said to Kaye, and then with obvious deference, "and hello to you, Lieutenant Hammersmith."

"Sir!" Military courtesy demanded that Jill acknowledge his presence.

"Captain Stratton," Kaye said, glaring at Jill, "I'd like to introduce Dee Gleeson, the correspondent who was with us when we took the German torpedo."

"Hello, Captain—Stratton, was it?" Dee's observant eyes were traveling back and forth between Jill and Des.

Jill busied herself with the egg dishes on the laden buffet. A servant bowed each time she pointed to one, and she had to use sign language to keep him from heaping her plate to the point of overflow. Every minute, she was aware that Dee and Kaye and Des were chatting like old friends and that at one point Stratton threw back his head and laughed out loud. His laughter hurt her more than the unresolved problem between them. He had no right to laugh. After what he'd pulled at Fort Des Moines, perpetual hangdog guilt was more appropriate from him. She worked her way to the foot of the long table and examined a bust of Napoleon intently while she tried to eat. Damn Stratton! He'd even spoiled the first nondehydrated eggs she'd had since she left the States.

"Lieutenant?" The voice she welcomed and at the same time dreaded came from behind her, slightly hesitant—not really much like the one he used as chief of the army com-center in Algiers.

She faced him. "Yes, Captain Stratton." She would never let him know how ill at ease he made her.

"You don't have to stand at attention," he said. "We're not on duty."

And to Jill's surprise it was Stratton who seemed uneasy.

He looked at her and cleared his throat. "I see you are admiring the Little Corporal. I studied—" He saw the instant flash of anger in the way her small shoulders reared back. Damn! He'd forgotten her sensitivity about her size. How could he have made such a pompous blunder?

Jill interrupted just as Des stopped in midsentence. She owed him obedience, but she didn't have to take his condescension. "Captain, please spare me any wit about short people, Napoleonic or banty-rooster complexes, Lieutenant Half-Pint jokes or . . ." She finally ran out of breath.

Stratton flushed. "Now, *wait* a minute, Jill," he said, using her given name for the first time since Fort Des Moines. "It was an innocent comment. I was just trying to make polite conversation. Isn't this gathering supposed to promote goodwill among allies? When I saw you here, I hoped it would do as much for the two of us. But I'd probably get better manners from the Germans than from you."

"Manners! Are *you* complaining about *my* manners?" She tried to make her voice calm and cosmopolitan, but she felt a furious heat suffuse her face and give her away. "Why you're nothing but a—a—a coward!"

Instantly, she was sorry. Caution had failed her, and now she had gone too far.

Des felt hurt and disappointed. He knew she was stubborn, but he hadn't suspected she didn't know how to forgive. "That's ungracious. I wouldn't have thought it of you. Surely I can make no more explanation than I did in my letters."

"I—I never read them."

He took a step back, and, afraid he would leave, she put out her hand to stop him. "Will you tell me now what you wrote?"

He hesitated. "It's too late for most of it," he began, only to stop himself before he went further than he intended. "I explained why I couldn't tell the murder board that I was the one you were with that night at the Palm Bar. You see, Captain Dawson and I had girl trouble. That's not important now—what's important is that he was trying to get at me through you. Don't you see? Dawson thought you'd been with me, but he couldn't prove it. If I'd told him, he'd have thrown the book at the both of us—you know that."

"But—"

"No, damn it, Jill, this time you're going to hear me out. You can believe it or not, but I didn't care what he did to me—he'd have seen I was transferred to some dead-end desk job. But *you* he'd have washed out of OC school, and I knew that would kill you. Even after the hearing, Dawson was out to get me. Fortunately for me, Algiers was his idea of a backwater." He had told Jill the truth, at least as much of it as he could, and that was all he could do. He would never tell her how much he'd suffered those last few days before her graduation, or about the months when he had waited for her to answer his letters. Most of all, he'd never tell her that he had wanted her desperately, or for how long, and how many other women it had taken for him to get over the wanting.

Jill saw people staring, especially Dee with a strange, haunted expression on her face, but by now she was almost beyond caring. All the weeks of reporting to Des every afternoon before her shift, of signing for classified material and discussing priority coded traffic in a cool, professional voice; all the weeks of punctilious military courtesy observed, hiding her feelings—feelings she could hardly define herself: all that self-control suddenly collapsed.

She looked up at him, ready to move into his arms. At that moment he looked like the young officer in the mess hall her first day in the Army—the most beautiful man she'd ever seen. His teeth were white against his Mediterranean tan, his deep-gray eyes waited for her to speak.

"Oh, Des—you mean, you really didn't want to let me go through that hearing alone?"

He shook his head almost violently, his teeth clenched. "It nearly killed me. You looked so frightened. A dozen times I started to speak, but I couldn't take a chance on getting you kicked out. I had to hope you'd understand later. I knew how much getting your bars meant to you. Well, Christ, it was awful! I never saw anybody so brave—the way you stood up to Dawson. I tried to tell you the next day. I *did* tell you in my letters."

"But I've been here for two months. Oh, why didn't you talk to me about all this before?"

He smiled down at her, with something of the Des Stratton she remembered in his smile. "Listen, Jill, you've been here all right, but how was I supposed to pierce that armor you wear when you're around me? No, don't tell me now. We'd just argue about it. How about a truce—for the duration, Lieutenant? Or at least while we're both in this outfit. Maybe it's too late to be friends, but at least we don't have to be enemies. Is it a deal?"

It's not too late, she wanted to shout, but her pride nodded yes, and he left. Perhaps it was just as well. How could she be his friend? She had no strategies for casual friendship with Des Stratton. He aroused in her extremes of feeling, more than Neil, more than anyone ever had. He made her happy or miserable; she either hated him or was crazy about him. For the hundredth time, she wished she'd read his letters. Mother had always said her stubborn streak would be her ruination. Why hadn't she listened?

Absentmindedly, she forked some egg from her plate, only to put it down again. Des had hinted that his letters contained more than explanations. What had he written that he couldn't tell her now? As she watched his dark head disappear through the palace entrance, she knew she had forfeited the right to know all that those letters contained. Des had made it quite clear it was too late.

Kaye hurried over as Des made his exit. "What was *that* all about? The rest of the Palais d'Été couldn't tell whether you two were ready to make love or fisticuffs."

"Don't be silly, Kaye, and don't see romantic intrigue in every man–woman encounter." Jill was embarrassed to think that so many people were speculating about her and Des. "Captain Stratton was taking care of some unfinished business, that's all."

"Oh, *that's* what it's called these days."

Ignoring Kaye's sarcasm, Jill looked at her watch. "Oops,

I'm on duty in an hour. Say goodbye to Dee for me. Gotta run." Leaving Kaye obviously curious and unsatisfied, she did run through the marble foyer, through the double line of ceremonial spahis on white Arabians and out to the square.

Dee sat in front of the fountains in a jeep, the engine idling. "Hop in, Jill—I'm going your way."

"I'm not in the mood for a lecture, Dee." The testy remark was out before Jill could bite her tongue.

"Don't worry, I'm not wearing my Dutch Aunt hat today."

They drove along the teeming streets in silence. Jill longed for the emotional safety of the picturesque old school building that served as WAC barracks in Algiers.

Finally they drove through the arch into the compound. "Here you are, Jill. Goodbye—and good luck. You're a great gal. I only hope you learn that someday."

" 'Bye, Dee. Sorry I spoke out of turn back there."

"Forget it. Besides, you already know what I'd advise you to do, don't you?"

"Yes, I guess I do."

Dee put the jeep into gear and drove out the compound gate, waving just before she passed from sight.

Jill stood there listening as the particular whine of jeep tires faded into the afternoon. Dee believed in the miracle of romantic love, but Jill knew there would be no such miracle for her. In her life, love must be a duty she owed to Neil. She didn't deserve it for herself.

30

In a patriotic anti–black-market drive, fifteen million housewives sign a pledge that says: "I pay no more than ceiling prices. I accept no rationed goods without giving up ration stamps."

PAGE HAD NO difficulty getting a three-day pass for the last October weekend. The workload at the Office of the Director, WAC, had begun to scale down since the conversion to full Army status. From being the source of all command decisions over women soldiers, Colonel Hobby now had only advisory duties. Files and personnel were being rapidly deployed throughout the Pentagon. Page knew it would be just a matter of days, at most weeks, before she would be reassigned. She didn't look forward to the possibility of sharing the fate of one of her fellow officers: the former WAAC historian's invaluable collection of the beginnings of women's army service had disappeared into Army Service Forces files, and she had been relegated to a clerk's job. Damn it! Page knew she had so much more to give. She'd take any way out, other than trade on her father's position, rather than be stalled in a Washington back office for the duration.

For the first two days of her pass Page unwound from the tension of the past months, taking short naps and long walks in the glorious northern-Virginia fall afternoons. Other than a letter to Bunny, she tried to forget the war, especially now that Paul might be in it somewhere, but the radio and the newspapers wouldn't let her. She'd read somewhere that one third of all broadcasting was war news, and the estimate sometimes seemed low. Everywhere, the dial was full of news about a second B-17 raid over Schweinfurt and the capture of road junctions south of Rome by the British Eighth Army.

Even at the neighborhood movies, she had a choice between

two war films, *This Is the Army* and *Mrs. Miniver*. She decided against Helmut Dantine's sneering Nazi-pilot portrayal in *Mrs. Miniver* and settled for George Murphy's hoofing and Ronald Reagan's haircut—which reminded her so much of Paul's—and found herself enjoying the show although it resembled no army *she* knew.

On the third day, restless and tired of the inactivity, she took a taxi to the St. Albans courts, her Wilson racket under her arm. The gut strings were slack and would probably break at the first net volley. She signed the singles match card, and picked up a locker key at the tennis director's office.

The pro on duty was well over fifty. "Not many women playing today, miss, but I'll do my best to line you up."

"I'll play the lieutenant," Page heard a male voice behind her say, "if she'll promise *not* to take it easy on an old man."

She faced the voice. "I'd be happy to play, sir."

The man wearing a major general's two stars picked up his locker key. "You don't remember me, do you?"

"Begging your pardon, sir . . ."

"The Philippines. I was Lieutenant Colonel Cecil Willis then—the summer of 'thirty-six, a dance at the Fort Garfield O club. You were home from school and I was attached to MacArthur's staff on Luzón."

"I've heard my father speak of you, sir, and I know Major Paul Burkhardt, who was on your staff last year. But I'm sorry, General, I don't remember our dance; it was so long ago and there were so many officers."

"Never mind." He smiled with a hint of an old sadness in his eyes. "I remember *you*. I envied Dalt the prettiest daughter at the dance. Mrs. Willis and I never had children."

After changing into whites, they met at the court nearest the pool and began a warmup rally of baseline ground strokes. Page decided she liked him. A general who wanted a pretty daughter to dance with was an image that charmed her. But her own father had been proud of her looks, too; it was her ambition that bothered him. She wondered what General Willis would have thought of a pretty daughter who enlisted in the Army.

Within minutes, she liked the General even more, because he let her know he was trying very hard to beat her and played over his head, taking one of the three sets from her six–four.

Maybe here was a man who was blind to her sex and just looked upon her as a worthy opponent. Finally her youth and form triumphed over his male strength and single-minded determination. In the last set she rushed his weak serves and sent one after another down the line to his even poorer backhand.

"Good competition! That's what I like," he wheezed and plopped down onto the courtside bench beside her. Catching his breath, he asked, "Where are you assigned, Lieutenant?"

"In the WAC Director's Office at the Pentagon, sir." Under his questioning, she talked about the breakup of the WAC office, adding that she'd be reassigned before the beginning of 1944.

He wiped down his racket, enclosed it in its leather case and handed it to an aide. "Have you thought of overseas duty?"

"Almost every Wac wants to go overseas, General."

"Is that right? I confess I don't know much about the Women's Army Corps, although I will probably have enlisted women in my next command." He stood to go, and she immediately got to her feet.

He seemed to be evaluating her, taking her measure as she'd seen her father do with new young officers.

"How would you like to go to London as one of my junior staff officers?"

It was her turn to catch her breath.

The General went on, "It's an intelligence assignment, so you'll need a top-secret clearance. We can work out the details later, but I can tell you that the slot calls for a first lieutenant. Your father's there, isn't he? Well, this would be your chance to see him occasionally."

"General Willis, you don't have to offer me any inducement beyond the opportunity to serve with you overseas."

"That's fine—fine, Lieutenant. And if there are any unbombed tennis courts around, I'll see that you do. I hate golf—abominable, boring game—and that's all Ike and the others talk about."

Page stiffened. "Sir, I hope I will be judged by my work and not by the quality of my lob."

The General scowled. "Lieutenant Hannaday, that's a hair's breadth from insubordination, and I damn well don't need instruction in military ethics from you." His face suddenly softened. "But I did phrase the offer badly. I have a pretty good idea what kind of officer Dalt Hannaday's daughter is, so don't get me wrong. I mean to work your butt off twelve hours a day and *then* expect you to play three fast sets. This is no cushy posting I'm offering you. Do I make myself clear?"

"Yes, *sir!*"

Whew! She whistled under her breath as she watched the General head for the showers, with his aide hurrying behind. As barracks talk had it, she'd just been reamed, steamed and dry-cleaned! She wouldn't make *that* mistake again. But her head kept spinning for a different reason. In ten short minutes the rest of the war had been decided for her.

In a way, she hated the thought of leaving Colonel Hobby's office, but it was time for her to move on, to work for promotion and varied assignment experience. Suddenly, she was aware that she was thinking like a career officer. Perhaps Randy had been right; perhaps she had always fit naturally into military life without realizing it.

Now she definitely needed a swim to cool off. Changing to the one-piece swimsuit she'd tucked in beside her tennis dress, she walked back to the pool and dove in at the deep end, the cold water snatching the air from her lungs. Back and forth she swam, glorying in the way her body smoothly cut the surface of the water. There hadn't been much time for exercise since she'd left Fort Des Moines, and she'd missed the sense of physical power that using her body always gave her.

Exhausted now after forty laps, but refreshed, Page flopped into a deck chair and curled up under her damp towel, allowing the unseasonably warm sun, which was at its zenith, to toast her upturned toes. Drowsy, she thought of Paul that last night before he'd left. She knew she had been shameless, practically coaxing him to her bed. Paul, since the first time he'd cooked for her, had struggled for control, always careful to respect her, but that night she hadn't wanted his respect, she'd wanted him next to her, in her bed. Darling Paul. He'd wanted her, too—she knew it—but he'd insisted on being so protective of her.

"This isn't fair to you, Page. I may not come out of this war alive."

"You will, I know you will." Their arms were around each other's waists as they walked to the bedroom, their hungry mouths reaching for each other, their bodies moving swiftly, hips touching as their legs swung in unison. "But even if the worst would happen at least we'd have this night to remember."

"Darling, isn't that supposed to be the man's line?" Paul had laughed, she remembered, but his laugh was bittersweet.

Lying there in the dark, she'd said, "I do adore you so, Paul."

They'd made love to each other then. Vaguely, Page was aware that someone on the first floor was playing Bach—one of the Brandenburgs. And the organdy curtains undulating in a breeze at the window were as sensual to her as watching a log fire. Although she wanted to give her body totally to physical love, her mind was full of these unconnected emotional impressions, almost as if body and mind belonged to two different people.

That night she knew for certain that Paul was in love with her. He was open, easy to read; his love was writ large for anyone to see. And she knew she loved him, too, but not in the same way, more like fog dipping to touch the ripples of a lake—vaguely. Yet she spent hours dreaming of him and refused to think of life with no Paul in it.

"Page, love me."

"Oh Paul, I do, but then . . ." He had covered her lips with his fingers to still the torrent of confused words.

She'd felt his sadness, palpable in the room. "You don't really know me, do you, Page? I want you—God alone knows how I want you—but I feel like a blind man entering an unfamiliar room. Just when I think I have a firm grip on you, you elude me. You haven't decided what *you* want from life, and you especially haven't decided that you want to share it with me."

"Paul, give me time." She didn't want to hurt him. She couldn't bear to see him leave for overseas with things unsettled between them. But there were no choices. He had to go; she needed time.

"Page, I'm not a man who will settle for a crumb when I want the whole loaf." He'd smiled sardonically in the dim light. "You'll have to pardon the rotten metaphor, darling. I'm not quite up to verbal brilliance tonight."

"Professor, you talk too much," she said, silencing him with her mouth and her body.

Over a month had passed, but she still felt the frustration of that night. Why must Paul not be satisifed with anything less than her total surrender? What was it Saint Augustine had said? *Love means I want you to be.* Why couldn't Jimmy, and now Paul—or any man—love her like that? Why couldn't they be content to be in her life but not be all of it?

Rousing herself from the poolside chaise longue, Page lazily walked back to the women's locker room and stepped into a shower. She let the cooling water sluice down her body and wash away the painful pulses of desire that Paul's memory evoked, moving next into the outer dressing area, where she toweled herself dry until her skin turned a glowing pink. Voices carried to her from the adjoining lounge.

"My dear, where did you get those hose—they're silk, aren't they?"

"Yes, lovely, lovely silk. I got them"—the voice giggled—"from *Mr. Black.* He can get you anything from tires to a prime standing rib roast to mayonnaise for only about twice the OPA ceiling price. He doesn't bother with points, either, if you get my drift."

"Mother says a black-marketeer is as important today as a good bootlegger was in her day."

Page wasn't shocked. Illicit sales were unpatriotic but common enough, especially when people were making money and had no place to spend it. She suspected that the two women pledged at bond drives, rolled bandages, directed their cooks to save grease and thought they were helping win the war.

"Did you see Page Hannaday playing tennis?"

That's my name, she thought. By now, Miss Silk Stockings' voice sounded vaguely familiar.

The other woman replied, "Yes, I saw her with General Willis. I knew her only slightly before she joined the women's army."

"Well, my dear, I knew her. She was at Radcliffe—one class ahead of me. Did you know her mother was one of the Charleston Bidwells? I simply can't imagine *her* associating with all those whores and dykes."

Idly the second voice said, "And she seems so feminine, too."

Page was shaking with fury as she buttoned her uniform blouse and walked deliberately into the lounge.

"I thought I recognized your voice. Lauren Whitaker, isn't it?" She wanted to shout at the woman, but she was bound by a desire to defend, not disgrace her uniform.

"Why, ah, er—yes," Lauren Whitaker replied, turning to her companion for help. "This is Page Hannaday—you remember." She flushed, floundering.

Page never had more command over her voice, not even during OCS when she had faced the grading pencil of ancient regular army drill sergeants on the Dewy parade ground. "Lauren," she said, coldly furious, "I couldn't help overhearing your personal assessment of women serving with our armed forces. Now which is it this week—are we all whores or all lesbians? Of course, you're including the thirty percent of women who are married or widowed. And don't forget the ones who have sweethearts in Bataan death camps or dead in Sicily . . ."

Page heard her voice begin to quiver and prayed she would keep her composure long enough to say what she had wanted to yell to the world for months. "On my desk in the Pentagon, there are a dozen photos of a burial being held in North Africa—not startling news in itself these days until you notice that the pallbearers are women soldiers, maybe some of those same whores and dykes you were talking about."

Her tone was acid, and she ignored the shocked faces of the women she confronted. She knew she was close to breaking down; the frustration of months of combating the slander campaign, and Paul's long silence, had become a mountain of pain to which this nasty chitchat had added the last hurt. "So, ladies, and that term is so far from describing you it—"

"Now, just a minute!" Lauren interrupted.

Wanting to smash the regained superiority from Lauren's face, Page rushed on, saying aloud the words that had been forbidden her typewriter. "The next time you're slipping into your black-market silk stockings and passing crude innuendos about women in uniform, maybe you can manage one small thought for an American servicewoman buried under a white cross in the North African sand—a woman who won't ever feel silk against her skin again." She stopped, almost out of control, close to breaking down. "You bitches," she said, and now tears started which she didn't bother to wipe away. "You malicious bitches!"

Feeling emptied and clean, she heard Lauren sputter behind her, "Well, I've never heard such . . . such . . ."

The other voice broke in. "Oh, shut up, Lauren. Just shut up for once in your life!"

31

The Allied forces battle up the boot of Italy, sometimes literally inch by inch. After the Fifth Army captures Naples in October, the Germans fall back, fighting one delaying battle after another. British commander General Sir Henry Maitland Wilson describes it as a "slow, painful advance through difficult terrain against a determined and resourceful enemy . . ."

IN THE NOVEMBER days that followed General Giraud's reception, Jill found herself in limbo as far as Des Stratton was concerned. He was no longer an enemy to be watched and outflanked, but he was no friend to be sure and comfortable with either. Her answer to the dilemma was to be stiffly polite.

Des saw her behavior as confirmation that she could accept him as her superior officer while on duty, but that her belief he had played the coward was so ingrained she could neither forget nor forgive. Therefore he was careful to keep their conversations impersonal. They were both still walking on eggshells, he saw, but different eggshells. He didn't know what to do or what he wanted to do. Once, following their encounter at the Palais d'Été, he had a cup of hot coffee waiting for her when she came on duty. She had thanked him, and for a moment the vulnerable look of sweet innocence that had first attracted him appeared fleetingly to cross her face. But he hadn't made a habit of such attentions. It was just as well, since they both had limited time during shift change.

Each afternoon at four, Monday through Saturday and on

alternating Sundays, Jill reported to Des at the comcenter. He was businesslike, although occasionally thoughtful. She sometimes wished there was more time, but he always seemed so busy.

She picked up messages waiting to be encrypted, then locked herself into the code room with her shift of three EW code clerks and didn't come out until midnight or more often even later. The work was endlessly fascinating. It was her responsibility to take secret words and make them undecipherable by the enemy. After assigning code systems to each message according to its destination and classification, she sometimes thought about this new but hardly more comfortable relationship with Des—she wouldn't call it a truce, since it was more an armed standoff.

As the rotors in the code machines clicked to one of a possible million different combinations for each letter and number in the alphabet, and the sticky-backed tape spiraled out its scrambled five-letter code groups, she caught herself wondering if she would feel today as she had the time he'd taken her in his arms. The memory brought with it both physical weakness and a surge of feeling that— Always at this point, she stopped herself angrily. Kaye was putting these silly thoughts into her head with her teasing that Des was sweet on her. Desmond Stratton was her superior officer, and that was the only way she thought of him or wanted to think of him. There might have been something more possible between them once, but that was all over. He'd said so, hadn't he? They might no longer be enemies but they were far from—anything closer.

Besides, she had promised herself to Neil. They were high-school sweethearts, engaged to be married—despite what Kaye said about a silent fiancé being no fiancé at all.

There were lots of perfectly logical reasons why Neil didn't answer her letters. Her father had written about several reconstructive skin-graft operations for his face and hands.

It should be obvious, even to a skeptic like Kaye, that Neil was simply not up to the strain of writing. He did send for Bear whenever he was home on convalescent leave—and Bear was his link to her. After the war everything would be as it had been between them. After the war, she'd forget all about Des-

mond Stratton. When she was an old lady, rocking the afternoons away on her adobe patio, she'd probably even laugh
about him.

These reveries usually lasted no more than a few minutes
before she was interrrupted by a rap on the code room door. It
was often Des carrying an urgent decrypt just ripped from the
Teletype. Once she thought how symbolic it was that there always seemed to be a locked door between them.

On the morning of November 13, 1943, unable to sleep
while the Algerian cleaning women banged buckets and mops
outside in the hall, Jill sorted through some recent snapshots
to enclose in her next letters to Bunny and Elisabeth. Flipping
on the radio, she half listened to the news on Armed Forces
Radio. Fifth Army troops were engaged in savage fighting between Naples and Rome. Restlessly, she punched her pillow.
Italy, not North Africa, was where the real war was. *Damn it!*
Was she always to be a bystander?

Someone knocked. "Are you awake, Lieutenant Hammersmith?" called the company clerk.

"Yes, what is it?"

"Captain wants to see you in the OR as soon as you can
make it."

"Tell Captain Trueblood I'll be there in fifteen minutes."

"Yes, ma'am."

Jill needed the full time to get into a fresh uniform and try
to communicate in high-school French to the women outside
her door that they should clean her room while she was gone.
"Maintenant!" she repeated several times and pointed to her
room while making sweeping motions with her arms.

Gingerly she stepped along the wet hall floors in the officers' wing toward the OR. What could Captain Trueblood
want at this time of day? Was it Marie again? Damn! Now that
the private was back in her platoon, it was always something.
Last week it had been late sign-in from an overnight pass, the
week before insubordination to a noncom. Marie Brodzinsky
delighted in getting into trouble so that Jill would have to reprimand or restrict her to barracks. It was diabolical, that's
what it was. The more Jill was forced to punish Marie, the
guiltier Jill felt, and that seemed to be exactly what Marie intended.

Descending to the floor that housed the company administration offices, Jill sighed hopefully. Maybe it wasn't Marie this time. Maybe it was complaints from her night-shift workers about sleeping conditions. There was little she could do about that perennial problem either. It was impossible to monitor every Wac coming off day duty. Sometimes just the volume of well-intentioned *Ssshuush!* in the hallway woke up her code clerks.

She reported smartly, priding herself on punctiliously observing customs of the service. Overseas duty had not made her lax as it had some soldiers.

"Sit down, Jill."

"Thank you, Captain."

"How are things at the comcenter?"

It was unlike the captain to encroach on sleeping time for a chitchat. "Just fine, ma'am."

"Glad to hear it." The captain stood up and went to her window and looked out on the courtyard. "I've got news for you."

Involuntarily, Jill caught her breath. "It's not my family? Nobody's . . ." She couldn't bring herself to say the word "dead." She'd heard from others how the CO called you in and tried to break bad news gently.

The captain shook her head and moved to sit on the edge of her desk. "Nothing like that. No, this is good news for you, at least I think you'll take it as that. I know I'd give anything to be in your shoes."

"Yes, ma'am?"

Captain Trueblood looked as though she was savoring every word. "How would you like to be in the first contingent of Wacs to set foot on European soil? Strictly voluntary, now."

Jill was only partially successful in retaining her military manner. "Of course. Yes! What do I do? When do I go? Where?"

"I told Captain Stratton you'd feel that way."

"Captain Stratton. What has he got to do with this?"

"He's commanding a new signal contingent on orders for Italy, and he put in a written request for you. Paid you a high compliment, too. Said you were his best code officer, and the only woman he knew who had the nerve to pull off this assignment."

"*He* said that?"

"He did. Now let me tell you what you're in for. By the way, Kaye Young will be the other junior officer, with a first lieutenant from Casablanca as CO. Sixty code clerks, telephone ops and postal people will make up the detachment, all of you heading for Fifth Army headquarters in Italy. Conditions will be rough. You may eventually be living in tents right behind the combat troops—subject to bombing and shelling. It'll be dangerous. Are you still game?"

Jill could hardly believe she wasn't dreaming all this—at last she was going to get a chance to be a real soldier. "I wouldn't miss it for the world, Captain. That's what I joined up for. When do we go?"

"In a few days—by plane to Naples, then ground transport northeast to Caserta. I don't need to tell you there's an information blackout." The captain stood up and extended her hand. "Remember Wacs are guinea pigs in this. The Army wants to see if we can measure up when things get tough. If we can't, the Women's Army Corps will not get a second chance."

"We can, Captain." Suddenly Jill remembered Page's dragon, and her expression sobered.

"What's the matter—haven't had a change of heart, have you?"

"No, ma'am, nothing like that. I had a friend back at OC in Fort Des Moines who said the WAC would have to slay dragons before we'd be accepted as women soldiers. Maybe our dragons are in Italy."

"At least the first one is, Lieutenant."

Jill stood up at attention. "I'll make the Corps proud, Captain."

"I'm sure you will. That's why I agreed to *your* going, Jill. You demand a great deal from yourself and set a high standard for the EW. They may not always like it, but they admire you for it. Don't take it amiss when they call you Lieutenant Half-Pint."

"I did at first, Captain. I've—well, I'm tired of jokes about my size."

"They're not laughing at you, Jill. It's their way of showing affection, of letting you know they lay claim to you."

"Thank you for that, ma'am—and for your confidence in me. I'd die before I'd let you down."

32

During the second Schweinfurt raid in October, sixty Eighth Air Force bombers with over six hundred American airmen in them are shot down, wrecking morale and flyers' confidence in the ability of the B-17 to defend itself without fighter cover. Bomber Command in England temporarily abandons deep-penetration daylight raids over Germany.

ON SATURDAY MORNING, November 13, Page received her promotion to first lieutenant and her reassignment orders to the Chief of Staff, Supreme Allied Commander, in London. General Cecil Creighton Willis, Jr., COSSAC G-2, now with a third star, had also TWXed priority travel orders for her. By early afternoon Transportation had put her on alert for an early-morning flight.

"And, Lieutenant," the scheduling officer warned her, "if you haven't got longjohns, better get yourself a pair."

That probably meant the Greenland route. As excited as she was about going overseas, she wasn't exactly thrilled at the thought of flying the North Atlantic in wintertime.

Page cleared her desk and said goodbye to her co-workers and Colonel Hobby. As she left the Pentagon in the late afternoon, she blushed to remember how she had stammered with the Director, sounding like a gushy schoolgirl with a favorite teacher. How could Page say to the colonel that her words heard so long ago in those first days at Fort Des Moines, "You have a date with destiny," had come to hold a special meaning for her life, even beyond their original intent? She didn't understand this feeling herself, so how could she communicate it?

Through the rear taxi window, she looked back at the huge complex and knew that one door was closing. For eighteen months she had been a part of the idea of a women's army. Now she would become a part of the reality, one woman soldier among many soldiers, both male and female, on the front lines of the war. All her life she had been marking time, waiting for an opportunity to find out who Page Hannaday really was and what she could really do.

"WAC Detachment."

"Will you please call Lieutenant Gardner to the phone. Tell her First Lieutenant Hannaday is calling."

Page lit a cigarette and surveyed the living room full of half-packed boxes she was readying for storage. From where she sat she could see the open doors of the cupboard in the kitchen with its shelf of cooking spices that evoked a sharp memory of Paul.

"Page! Is that you—and with silver bars?"

"Hi, Elisabeth. It's me, silver and all."

"Congratulations. Nobody deserves it more, but I thought you said you'd never make first at the Pentagon, that all the rank was going overseas." Elisabeth paused for a moment. "Is that why you're calling?"

"You know I can't answer that. I just want to let you know that I'll be . . . out of touch for a while, but I'll write as soon as I can. Is everything all right with you?"

"Why wouldn't it be?"

"No reason—it's just that when we saw Jill off in New York City you looked so tired. No, more than that, and I really don't mean to meddle, Elisabeth—you looked almost haunted."

Elisabeth laughed, but Page heard a brittle quality, or rather a dry fragility that she would have suspected of anyone but Elisabeth.

"Page, you're becoming as melodramatic as Bunny"—with finality Elisabeth changed the subject—"have you heard from her?"

"I tried to call her earlier, but the CQ said she was signed out for the weekend. I'll—well, I'll just have to write to her."

Almost to herself Elisabeth said, "Two of us gone and two of us left. This goddamned war is nothing but one long goodbye."

"We can take it."

"You really believe all that gung-ho propaganda, don't you? I wish I had your faith."

"You do, Elisabeth."

"Oh no—only what passes for faith. But you see, I never believe in anything, so I'm never disappointed."

They said goodbye and promised to write and to take care of themselves. As she replaced the phone on its cradle Page wondered if either of them any longer had control over her own care. Despite her denials, Page sensed in Elisabeth's voice a frightening desperation.

Very early the next morning, Page was struggling with the clasp on her flight bag when her doorbell rang.

"It's unlocked," she yelled.

"If I'm too early," a voice said, "I can wait out here."

"Heavens, no. Come on in." A WAVE ensign appeared at her bedroom door. "Want to help me get this lock closed?"

The ensign took her hat off and threw it on the bed. Together they got both bags locked and pulled to the landing.

Page said, "I've left my forwarding address on the kitchen table. Well, I guess that's it. I'd better be off—D.C. taxi drivers, you know."

"What about all the stuff in the kitchen? There must be a hundred dollars' worth of spices in there."

"You keep them. They'll bring you luck."

"What? I don't understand."

"Never mind. See you around sometime."

The Wave, watching her as the driver helped with her bags, gave her a thumbs-up sign as Page turned to wave. "Keep your powder dry, Lieutenant," she called after her.

One hour later the door to the storage room at the Bolling Field flight-ops hut flew open suddenly and caught Page literally with her pants down. "Hey, wait a minute, I'm changing in here."

"It's okay," a woman's voice answered.

"Sorry, thought you were one of the ground crew," Page answered, her words muffled as she tugged on the zipper of her fleece-lined leather flight pants.

"Lieutenant," the voice said closer now, and Page saw two shoes planted squarely in front of her, "my name's Joan Wright. Looks like we'll be flying to Prestwick together."

Page flopped down on a bench. The tall brunette in front of her wore rumpled slacks and a belted blue blouse with pilot's wings over her left breast pocket. "Hello—Joan, is it?" Page was winded from her struggles. "Isn't that a WASP uniform?"

"Right—Women's Airforce Service Pilots. I've been detached for a month to inspect British women pilots in the Air Transport Auxiliary. From the look of your gear, you're going for more than a month."

"Page Hannaday," Page introduced herself, and shook the other woman's hand. "I'm going to be stationed in London."

"Not if you freeze before you get there. First thing on the flight plan is to get you suited up right. Take off your uniform down to your longjohns. Here, let me help you with those ankle zippers. Now put your boots on and zip them up."

Page stood up and took two steps in the awkward boots. "I feel like Frankenstein," she said, awkwardly lifting her arms in front of her.

Joan laughed. "You'll love them at twenty-five thousand feet. Now let me cross your pant suspenders twice or they'll keep falling off your shoulders and drive you crazy. Okay, now the jacket." Joan stepped back and surveyed Page. "You'll pass muster."

"Thanks to you."

A few minutes later the two women clomped out into the ops hut. The harried dispatcher motioned them toward an AAF captain with a clipboard.

"Lieutenant Hannaday? Joan Wright?" the captain asked, checking their names off. "I'm Captain Willo—Doug Willo. Your gear will be put aboard. Follow me."

Page walked behind him toward several planes parked on the Bolling Field tarmac. He stopped under the Plexiglas nose of a mammoth B-17G with the name *Flaming Mame* painted on its side along with an artistic rendition of a stripper caught in her act. It was the biggest plane Page had seen since she'd taken the Clipper to Manila years before. So *this* was what Randy wanted to fly.

"Sorry there wasn't room for you gals in one of the regular C-47 flights," Willo said. "We've got so much brass hopping over that anybody under colonel gets bumped. You won't find us long on comfort, but we'll do our best."

Page climbed in through the fuselage hatch and walked

forward past the waist gunners and onto the narrow catwalk over the bomb bay, then into the cabin. The captain pointed her toward a pull-down seat against the bulkhead behind the flight engineer.

"Whatcha flying, Joan?"

"Been ferrying PT-19s out of Hagerstown."

"Ever check out one of these babies? It's quite a thrill."

"You're telling *me!*"

"After we get up, I'll get the Chief"—Willo nodded toward the flight engineer's jump seat right behind him—"to let you have his seat for a bit."

"I'd love that."

"You had breakfast yet?" It was the young navigator calling up to Page from his plotting table below and forward in the nose.

"No. I didn't have time."

"When we're airborne and I've got a fix on our heading, I'll send you gals up some breakfast."

Leaning forward, Page adjusted her seat harness so that she could watch the co-pilot going over the checklist with Captain Willo.

"Free the controls," he said. "Rudder. Ailerons."

"Roger," Willo answered.

"Check magnetos on. Ignition left. Right. Both."

"Number one hydraulic pump switch on," Willo said.

"Start number one."

Over on the far left, Page saw the giant blades of the outboard Wright Cyclone engine shudder, cough and start to rotate.

"Pull auxiliary ground power plug," Willo told the Chief.

With brakes released, the Fortress began to move as Willo used the one engine to swivel the plane onto the runway. There the checkout procedure continued until all four of the engines were roaring, pounding, thundering through the vibrating metal skin under Page's feet. She had never felt the effect of so much raw power surge through her body before. No *wonder* Joan wanted to fly, she thought, to control such a behemoth and ride it through the sky like a modern Valkyrie.

Willo recited, "Fuel booster pumps on; fuel/air mixture in automatic rich; propellers in full rpm; engine cowl flaps open; wing flaps up . . ."

Page's rubber earphones crackled and she put them on. "Tower to Baker one three niner. You're cleared for takeoff."

Willo stood on the brakes, his left hand on the control yoke, right hand advancing all four throttles.

The Chief sang out, "Okay, you have full power."

Page braced in her seat against the bulkhead wall as the plane surged down the runway, gathering speed until Captain Willo pulled back on the control wheel, and with one last bump they were airborne.

Gradually the tension knot in her stomach disappeared and she was aware of a rarer emotion felt only once before, the day she first arrived at Fort Des Moines—the sense of adventure, of jumping with both feet into the unknown.

"First stop, Gander, Newfoundland," the navigator announced when they had leveled off at ten thousand feet and reached their 170-miles-per-hour cruising speed. He poured cups of coffee from a thermos and handed out brown bags. "Breakfast from the Greasy Spoon."

Joan complained as she opened her bag. "Oh no! Fried-egg sandwiches. Page, I hope you have a strong stomach. I could swear these eggs have been fried in olive oil *before* the mayonnaise was slathered on the bread."

"Don't worry, Joan. A stomach that has held SOS can handle anything."

"You mean Wacs eat ol' shit-on-a-shingle, too?"

"Do we eat it? Army cooks invented it."

After a few bites Page leaned back in her seat and closed her eyes, listening through her headset to the hum of the navigational beacon they were following. Once it stopped and her eyes flew open. "Anything wrong?"

"Don't worry," the radio op told her. "We're in the cone of silence—directly over the beacon. We're right on the beam, Lieutenant."

The engine's drone almost drowned out the beacon's sound in her earphones, the two together making a mesmerizing, mind-numbing hum. She couldn't read as she'd planned when she'd zipped an armed-forces paperback edition of *The Human Comedy* into one of the flight suit's deep pockets. She couldn't concentrate on plot and character in this din. Instead she drew out Bunny's last letter from between the book's covers.

November 5, 1943
Lowry Field, Colorado

GREETINGS PAGE,

Did I say I wanted to find out what it was like to be an enlisted woman? Ol' Bunny found out all right. I've pulled K.P. every week since I got back here. K.P.—take it from one who knows—is an army experience to miss & I mean MISS. Up at 4:30, stumble into my fatigue dress and Li'l Abner boots, trudge to the messhall in the snow and dark. I don't mean to sound like an orphan in the storm, but you get the picture—& that's only the good part. Next, a mess sergeant who looks like she eats Privates and Corporals for breakfast points at ME and says in impeccable English: "You girl there—you do grease trap." Sounds simple enough, but I'd "rather be in hell with my back broke" as one of my southern bunkmates puts it.

The grease trap in your typical messhall is located in the most inaccessible place in the kitchen—in a concrete bunker under the main sink drain. The only way to get to it is from a kneeling position. It's quite a ritual & goes something like this: down on your knees, drag off the heavy metal lid, dip off the coagulated grease (GOD! HOW IT STINKS!) and place in bucket, carry bucket to G.I. grease can.

By the time I finish this bit of torture (which the Sarge loves to watch an ex-officer do), I can't eat the chow they pile on my tray, & I spend the rest of the day dreaming up incredibly perfect murders which I want—oh so very much—to practice on the mess sergeant.

Other than K.P. I'm flying high—and as soon as I make sergeant I'll have too much rank for that duty.

You asked why they'd ship me back here as an EW when I'd been here before as brass. PULL, my dear Page—not mine, but my Colonel's, who tells me daily that he'd defy Tooey Spaatz himself for me. Old Harry's not a bad sort plus he's got a great thing going for him in my book— I COULDN'T FALL IN LOVE WITH HIM IF I TRIED. Not that he's not good-looking; and he's a damned fine air recon officer, but I've taken the pledge—

for life. You can't imagine how safe that makes me feel—or maybe you can.

Speaking of safe, Harry is keeping me off overseas levies now that I'm working with photo mosaics—the last three non-coms in my job were scooped up within a month of each other. I want to do what I can—you know that, Page, or why would I have re-enlisted?—but I can do it just as well in the good ol' ZI. I'll let Jill carry the flag and you can be the heroine. I'm too old to fight that dragon you're always talking about, even metaphorically.

I'm hoping to get a Christmas leave. My mama isn't well, now Angela's gone to California. Poor Mama. Two daughters married to a man she disapproves of—it's been too much for her. I don't hate Angela, you know that, Page. I don't feel anything. I just hope she has the sense to swallow her pride and come home when Johnny dumps her, and he will.

Enough and enough, dear friend. Can you believe it's been almost a year since we left each other at the Fort Des Moines train station? If the four of us have made it this far, 1944 will be a breeze.

> Love ya,
> BUNNY

Page smiled, a wave of affection overtaking her as she re-folded the letter and slipped it back inside the book. Here she was in a bomber over the winter Atlantic instead of packing for a skiing trip to Vermont; Jill was in Algiers instead of on a small northern-California ranch; Elisabeth was working in a warehouse in Philadelphia instead of looking out from the glossy pages of *Vogue;* but when all the world was topsy-turvy, Bunny never changed. We need such friends, she thought, for the energy they expend happily pursuing their dreams. And because they keep us from taking ourselves too seriously. No matter what her pain—and Page knew that Bunny had been betrayed as few women had—she kept on meeting life, connecting with it day after day. *God!* She was honest, and so sane, so absolutely steady, and she didn't even know it.

Page's earphones crackled with static interrupted by a voice: "Gander to Baker one three niner, do you read?"

"Roger, Gander," the radio op replied.

"Give me your position report."

Soon they were within sight of the runways, which slashed black lines through the dazzling white of endless snow as far as Page could see.

Joan shouted at her above the noise of landing gear coming down, "Storm's coming. The field could be socked in."

After they were on the ground the approaching storm was confirmed by the weather officer at flight operations. "We're going to catch the tail of it. May not get much snow, then again we may get enough to shut us down for two or three days. Hard to say. The billeting officer will take care of you."

Captain Willo got Page and Joan assigned a room at the visiting officers' quarters and invited them to relax at the O club later. "Hope you gals play pool."

Joan grinned. "I do. My dad taught me."

Page smiled, but shook her head. "My game's tennis, Captain. I think I'll just read, but thanks." She was unexpectedly tired. It's harder to be a passenger, with nothing to do, than a driver who's fully occupied.

"Suit yourself," Willo replied. "Come on, Joan, we'll do some hangar flying."

"Sure. Love it."

After a quick meal, Page struggled out of her bulky flying suit just as Joan returned to change for the officers' club. "With that weight off, Joan, I feel light enough to fly by myself."

"You get used to them."

"How long have you been flying?"

"Since I was thirteen. My dad was a barnstormer. He buckled me into a special harness when I was a kid. By the time my feet reached the rudders, he couldn't keep my hands off the controls. Natural, I guess. Ever heard of us? Wright and Daughter, Aerobatists—state fairs our specialty."

"No, I'm afraid not. When did you join the WASP?"

"Last spring."

"Like it?"

"Yes. Not because I want to blaze trails or anything, I just want to fly the kind of planes I've never had a chance to fly— P-51s and B-17s. Does that sound unpatriotic?"

"No, I think I understand. The country's full of women who

want to grab the opportunities of this war. Why not? Men have been doing it for centuries. What's the WASP military status now?"

"We haven't any," Joan said, frowning. "Jacqueline Cochran says General Hap Arnold is all for taking us into the Army Air Forces, but he's run into a snag in Congress."

"I was at WAC HQ in the Pentagon, and I know that Colonel Hobby agreed to WAC commissions for Wasps."

Joan shook her head. "No soap. Jackie wants to run the show for her girls, ya know. Well, one way or another, I guess we'll get in. The real problem is at the lower echelon—" and here Joan twirled an imaginary mustache like the villain in a melodrama— " 'How come a little slip of a girl like you wants to fly that big ol' plane?' " She grinned good-naturedly, and left for her date with Willo.

Outside, heavy snow was falling and a strong swirling wind piled it into instant drifts against the base buildings.

"Looks like we're going to be here for a while," Joan said hours later when she came in.

Page slammed her book shut. "Oh, damn! It's so frustrating to be on my way but not, at the same time."

"I don't blame Willo and the rest if they're not in an all-fired hurry. Pilots over Germany have a three-week life expectancy these days."

Joan draped her damp clothes over the bedstead. "Anyway, pilots get used to weather like this. I was delivering planes from the Republic factory last winter and got snowed in at Pittsburgh for three days with nothing on but my flying suit. Just once you should try to explain a woman wearing what looks like rompers with no luggage to a hotel clerk!"

Page laughed. If she had to be snowed in, she couldn't ask for better company.

She had been asleep for some time when she was awakened by a loud knock at the door.

"Lieutenant? Joan?" It was Willo's voice.

"What is it, Captain?" Page called.

"There's a brief break in the weather—a window we can fly through before the main storm hits. We gotta make room for the next flight comin' behind us. Suit up and meet me in the ops building in fifteen minutes."

Page struggled out from under the warm covers into the icy-cold room, quickly repacking the few articles she'd used the night before.

Joan shivered into her longjohns. "Brrr. I hate to sound like your mother, but you should visit the ladies' room before we take off and keep your liquid intake down during the flight. It takes twelve hours' flying time, and the only 'convenience' on the plane is a bottle with a funnel *definitely* not designed for female anatomy." Joan giggled. "A friend of mine nearly froze to death over Oklahoma when she had to drop her entire flying suit to use it."

By the time Page and Joan hurried to the runway, the bomber was warming up, the snow had stopped and the lights of snowplows traced narrow yellow paths up and down the runway. The crew chief buckled them in and showed them how to plug in their oxygen masks to the plane's main system. They would be flying most of the way at 25,000 feet, he told them, above the weather and square in the path of the best tail winds.

Captain Willo looked around at Page, his oxygen mask dangling. "Next stop Prestwick, Scotland, Lieutenant." He gave her the familiar thumbs-up sign.

Did she look frightened? Probably so, but it certainly wasn't over flying. She was ashamed to admit that the thought of the oxygen mask smothering her face for all the hours ahead brought back the old panic she'd felt in basic. But she'd conquered that fear and taken her place as part of the team; she would conquer it again.

When they'd been airborne an hour, the navigator handed a map up to Page. A long shallow upcurved line skirting south of Greenland and Iceland and ending to the north and west of Glasgow showed their course. It looked to Page as if they were flying across half the globe.

Hours later, she traded seats with the bombardier forward in the nose. They had long before outrun the dark and flown into the rising sun. Cocooned in her flight suit and helmet, surrounded by Plexiglas, Page felt none of the vibration she had in the beginning. The steady drone of the engines were an integral part of her now, like her breathing. She was in an immense quiet bowl, alone in its exact center, clouds below and ahead of her, and above her the top of the world was painted an incredible deep lavender.

Shortly after noon she took a few quick gulps of hot coffee, happy to replace the oxygen mask after quickly becoming lightheaded in the thin atmosphere. During these hours she thought of the twists and turns her life had taken during the past year. She thought of Paul and couldn't escape the happy feeling that he was coming nearer. Was he in London or on some chancy OSS mission?

It occurred to her for the first time how much of her own life in the past months had been the result of taking chances. Quiet Page, studious Page, obedient Page—all those things she had always been had been replaced by a person who took chances. She'd taken a chance by joining the women's army, by letting a strange major into her apartment in the middle of the night, and finally by joining General Willis' staff overseas. Each one had led her to this moment when she found herself perched in the nose of a Flying Fortress headed toward the maelstrom of war in the ETO. She would most certainly see her father again; but could they learn to be father and daughter in a different way? Could her father ever see her as a person separate from his wishes? And Paul—yes, she would meet Paul too. She could sense it. The two most important men in her life, both different, but both wanting her to be their own version of the perfect woman—they too would be part of this new adventure.

The intercom crackled. "Say, skipper, there's something wrong with the oxygen back here."

Willo answered, "I'll have the Chief check it out. It *is* pretty thin."

Page looked back and saw the Chief come forward.

Soon Willo's voice rang through her earphones again. "Goddamnit to hell, Chief. Ground crew at Bolling told us they fixed the *Mame.*"

Page heard Willo ask the crew chief to check the number of oxygen bottles stored in the cabin racks and in the tail section—racks that also held emergency flares and parachutes.

In a minute or two Willo was back on the intercom: "Pilot to crew. We've got walkaround bottles for an hour—then I'll have to take her down to twelve thousand."

The bombardier eased in behind Page and pointed up toward the main cabin. She crept past the navigator and regained her old seat. What happened when they descended to twelve thousand feet?

A familiar feeling of panic squeezed Page's chest. She knew it was more than thin air that caused her to hyperventilate; it was the old phobia—the mask was smothering her, claiming her. Minutes passed while she fought down the dizziness and sense of falling that threatened to overwhelm her. She admitted freely to herself the phobia she couldn't seem to be rid of, but gratefully she recognized the greater fear that saved her from cowardice—the fear of proving women were unfit comrades.

"I won't kid you," Joan told her, "there's danger of icing. I heard Willo tell the co-pilot that two planes in the flight ahead of us didn't make it."

"What happens if there's icing?" Page tried to sound matter-of-fact.

"You either get rid of it or you go in."

The next hour sped by. Page's mouth grew tender from sucking in pure oxygen. She kept her breathing shallow and minimized movement, but finally her bottle was empty, its comforting hiss stilled.

"Dropping down," Willo said, pushing forward on the controls. Clouds rushed past the windshield, enveloping them in bluish-white billows.

"Leveling off at twelve thousand," Willo said on the intercom.

"Outside temperature reads two degrees Fahrenheit, Skipper," the co-pilot said.

Page tapped Joan's shoulder. "Where does it ice?"

"Watch the leading edge of the wings."

At first Page thought it was just eyestrain and worry making ice appear where none truly was, but the longer she watched the more obvious it became that glassy white bulges had formed forward on the wings.

She heard the co-pilot report, "We're starting to pick up drag."

"Inflate her damned icebreakers, then!" Willo ordered.

Moments later chunks of ice cracked off the wings and flew past the windows. Relieved, Page leaned back and only then realized she had been straining against the harness, gulping to fill her lungs with precious air. But she had only a few minutes of relief. Almost at once the ice began to rebuild in bigger, even more bulbous chunks.

"It's too heavy, the breakers aren't working this time," the co-pilot said.

Willo answered, "I'm losing lift. Gotta try to get under this weather."

The big plane nosed down through the cloud cover. Page realized that her life was in danger, but her mind could not imagine the world without her in it. That must be what courage really is, she thought, a failure of the imagination.

At one point in their descent they broke through the clouds into dazzling sunlight, which glittered prettily on the ice-packed wings like some macabre joke. Page almost welcomed the fog that erased that picture, although she knew they must have lost more altitude than Willo had intended.

Suddenly in her headset Page heard a low, insistent, comforting hum that made her heart pound with fresh hope.

"Navigator to pilot," the intercom crackled. "We've picked up the Prestwick directional beam, Skipper. Give me two minutes and I'll have a revised ETA."

Page waited with the rest of the crew, watching the rigid arm movements of the captain which told her far more than the calm, professional voice of the navigator.

"Okay, here it is," the navigator said. "We've lost our tail winds and we're approximately three hundred miles, or one hundred eight minutes, out. With that ice we'll lose fifty feet every minute, which means we hit the drink nine minutes before ETA. If we lighten load by four thousand pounds, we *might* have the additional lift we need."

Page saw Willo's shoulders relax almost as if knowing the worst was a bigger physical relief than blind hope had been. "Captain to crew. You heard it, guys. If the ice breaks up as we drop down, then we won't have to clean house. If it doesn't, then we'll jettison everything we can just this side of the coast. I don't want to drop a fifty-caliber on a thatched cottage."

The crew checked in one by one, from the bombardier in the nose to the tail gunner lying on his stomach seventy-five feet to the rear.

Joan reached out to Page and gripped her sleeve. "It'll be okay," she said. "Willo's first rate, and that navigator is a genius coming right in on that radio beacon from dead reckoning."

Although Page heard reassurance, she also heard the concern in Joan's voice, the experienced pilot in her overcoming the desire to nurture. The minutes seemed to spin away out of her control. Page could see that the ice wasn't increasing, but it wasn't breaking up either, although the co-pilot had tried several times to inflate the rubber-coated icebreakers.

Below, between patches of thick fog, the flat gray ocean gradually broke into ripples that became waves as they dropped lower. Page wondered how long a fifty-thousand-pound plane would float or if it could float at all. How could she swim in this bulky flying suit? And if she took it off, how many minutes would it take her to freeze? The crew chief reached over and patted her shoulder. Did her fear show?

"Okay, Chief," Willo finally called from the cockpit when it looked as though they were within a few hundred feet of the water off the Inner Hebrides, "let's jettison the waist guns and everything that's not bolted down—ammo boxes, the lot. Jesus," Page heard Willo mutter then, "I'll have to sign my ass away on a statement of charges for this gear."

She pushed against hysteria rising from deep in her abdomen. Oh God, money—what a crazy, dumb thing to worry about at a time like this.

Then she felt a perceptible lurch. A little bound as if the plane itself wanted to live.

Joan, who was closer to the instrument panel and knew how to read the altimeter, reported regularly. "The rate of descent is slowing, Page. See the nose—tipping up slightly. I think the ice is melting—not much, but there's more lift. Feel it?"

Yes, she *could* feel it. The fog was thick now, and she couldn't see the entire wing span or the remaining ice, but she knew she felt the plane, which must be skimming the caps of the waves below, push more eagerly toward the Scottish coast. Ahead in the whiteness lay Prestwick.

The radio operator flicked the button on his microphone: "Prestwick tower, this is Baker one three niner, over."

Moments passed. "Roger, Baker one three niner, this is Prestwick tower. We're fogged in here. Visibility zero. What's your position? Over."

"Prestwick tower, I am about two zero northwest at two hundred contact. ETA in three minutes."

"Are you in distress?"

"Yes. Heavy icing."

"Baker one three niner, hold your heading for three minutes. We've got two guys with Very pistols stationed at the north end of runway. Crash truck standing by."

One minute. Two minutes. Page strained forward, her eyes searching the white blankness ahead for a light. Three minutes.

Willo said, "Gear down." The plane lurched. His left hand grasped the yoke of the controls; his right hand gripped the throttle. "Where are those goddamned flares?" Willo yelled into the microphone.

"Prestwick tower to Baker one three niner. We hear you but we can't see you."

Another agonizing minute passed while Page braced herself for a crash. She knew that the slightest miscalculation would send them smashing into the ground. They had to be hugging the runway by now, and with a sickening insight she knew that she too might embrace it totally at a blinding instant. Involuntarily her lids closed against the possibility, and almost instantly a sudden flash of light wrenched them open. There to either side of the plane's nose a beautiful red-orange shaft leaped through the fog and formed a brilliant arch over them.

"Full flaps," Page heard Willo shout as they dove through the arc of light and their wheels at last wedded the earth.

For a moment she clung to the rigid metal of the jump seat and watched as the plane maneuvered behind a jeep that mounted the sign "FOLLOW ME." She knew she had faced death, and discovered the depths of her own courage.

Sixteen hours later, Page stepped from the blacked-out overnight Glasgow-to-London train into Victoria Station. An RAF officer from her compartment deposited her bags on the platform.

"Let me help you with these, Leftenant, at least as far as the American transport office. Step this way."

He placed her bags inside the office door, returned her salute and hurried off into the crowds.

"Are you Lieutenant Hannaday?" a staff sergeant asked as she stepped into the office, which had an American flag draped across the window.

"Yes."

"Right," he said, picking up her duffle. "General Hannaday sent his car for you, ma'am."

"How did he know I was coming?"

"General Willis—"

"Of course."

"I'm to take you straight to Claridge's."

"Claridge's Hotel?"

"That's right, Lieutenant." The sergeant grinned. "And if you don't mind my saying so, you may want to powder your nose up a bit. The General has a little surprise party cooked up for you. Half the officers at COSSAC will be there to meet you, including one who told me to say, 'The professor cooks tonight.' Does that mean anything to you?"

Page laughed.

33

In late November 1943, the Big Three, Roosevelt, Churchill and Stalin, meet in Teheran to plan a second front in Europe. Russia agrees to declare war on Japan after Hitler is defeated.

IN THE DARK early-morning hours of November 17, Jill arrived in the Allied Forces headquarters at Caserta, jouncing in one of several two-ton trucks which had picked up the detachment of Wacs from the Twelfth Air Force base outside Naples. She was tired, weighed down by a barracks bag and an awkward bedroll, and everywhere she stepped her service shoes went almost ankle deep into chilling, sucking mud. The WAC billets had cold running water, but no hot water and no heat.

"Well, it isn't the Isle of Capri," she heard one of the EW say, throwing her gear onto a canvas cot, "but it's sure better than our guys have it up in the mountains."

"That's the spirit," Jill called out to her. "We're Fifth Army now." She hoped the women couldn't tell she was whistling in the dark. How were they going to work twelve-hour shifts and live under these conditions?

A few weeks later, writing to Page, she had completely forgotten her doubts.

December 24, 1943

DEAR PAGE,

I was so surprised to hear that you were in England. I can't tell you where I am—the not so sunny Mediterranean will have to do for now and the censor may not even allow me that much, but I can tell you that all the big dreams I dreamed back in OC at Fort Des Moines have come true. I know guys are getting killed and I'm sorry for that, but these are the most important days of my life. I'll never do anything again that will give me quite this feeling of accomplishment.

You'd be proud of these women, Page. Every one of them was given a chance to rotate back to easier duty and not a one wanted to go. These Wacs thrive on hard work and discomfort; the sick call rate is lower than in units stateside.

The other day a Signal Corps major called me from the comcenter to ask me what my women needed, as if he couldn't believe they were happy, or—anyway, what he wanted to know was how the women could display so much esprit after long hours and fatigue and all.

I told him the only thing I could—that when Wacs are considered to be useful and valuable members of the outfit, and command lets them know it, well, then nothing can shake them. He looked interested but, Page, I could see he didn't really know what I was talking about. Finally, he promised me some beauty parlor equipment just as soon as the generators could handle it. The EWs loved that and so did I. That's the point, isn't it? We can want to get on with the job, but we're still women—the two together are not in conflict.

Wish I could tell you about the Italian people here, but

that will have to wait until after the war—at Babe's. Don't forget.

Got to get ready for duty, and I want to write Elisabeth. Do you think she would send me some long flannel underwear? Oh, and before I forget, I should tell you that S. is my immediate superior here. He's not the man I thought he was. I still don't think I can trust him, not *that* way—you know what I mean—but he's a first-class officer and fair.

There goes Armed Forces Radio playing Crosby's "White Christmas" for the one hundredth time today. That's the cruelest song—someone always breaks down. Even I get misty-eyed and I *never* had a white Christmas in my life. Now I really have to double-time to work. Take care, Page. I wonder where we'll be this time next year.

Love,
JILL

Taking a quick inventory of the time, she decided she had time to drop a quick line to Elisabeth.

Christmas Eve, 1944
Somewhere in Italy

DEAR ELISABETH:

Sometimes it's uncanny how I seem to get what I wish for. Remember, I'm the gal who didn't want to be my mother's idea of a lady. Well, nothing genteel about me now. I'm sure my crinolined ancestors are absolutely twirling in their graves. I found a tailor who cut down a man's O.D. wool shirt and trousers for me. Haven't been able to find a pair of combat boots small enough, but I'm hopeful, or someday I'll disappear, worn service shoes and all, into a pothole. All of us dress this way—not WAC regs, but at least we don't freeze.

Speaking of freezing. Could you send me a pair of flannel longjohns? All I'm allowed is scrip so I'll have my folks send you a check.

Afraid you'll have to take me in hand when I get back to the States. What little sense of style I had is long gone now.

Write soon.

As she stepped outside the billets and returned the MP guard's salute, she could see in the northwest sky flashes of light, like summer lightning.

"What's that, Corporal?"

"It's the Long Toms, ma'am, pounding the German defenses up in the Mignano gap. Some Christmas present, huh?"

"If we can see them from forty miles away they must be blinding up close."

"You bet, Lieutenant. I wouldn't want to be one of them poor sonsa— Pardon, ma'am. Talked with one of them sad sacks on a 155mm. gun crew—he was pullin' some R and R last week. They stand in a three-foot pit, most times filled with water, wrasslin' those big shells and powder charges as big as fifty-pound sugar sacks. Nope, I wouldn't like that duty."

"Merry Christmas, Corporal."

"Same to you, Lieutenant."

She started down the short block to the communications area. From out of the dark a child's voice called, *"Buona sera, signorina."* And then the familiar child's plea of *"Caramelle, prego!"*

"Si, caramelle." She reached inside her battle jacket, the smallest made for the U.S. Army and still sizes too big for her, and drew out the chocolate bars and candy orange slices she'd saved from the mess.

"Mille grazie, signorina."

As she walked on, she heard them smack their lips.

There was no street in Caserta where she could walk without seeing the pinched white, hungry faces of Italian children, and the even more pitiful starving animals, pets no family could feed any longer. Their suffering was a reality of her great adventure that she didn't want to face. After all, it wasn't America's fault; if they hadn't followed their Duce ... She showed her identification at the barbed-wire gate to the com-center area and hurried over to the command van.

Desmond Stratton was waiting for her. "Merry Christmas, Captain," she said, her smile hesitant.

"Merry Christmas, Lieutenant."

He had tried to overcome their awkwardness with each other, but they were never alone, and the war intruded on every minute. "Sorry about this one." He pointed to a thick figure-eight roll of punched, coded Teletype tape. "This must be the nightly bad news. At least these families won't hear until after Christmas Day. They'll have that much."

She nodded, took the tape, unlocked the code room and went inside. Within minutes, Christmas 1943 was forgotten as the decoded nightly casualty list unrolled the names of the Fifth Army dead and wounded. At first, she tried to read the names, ranks, serial numbers, looking for one she recognized. What would I do if I found one? she wondered. Cry. Scream. She stopped reading and later mechanically pasted the message, now in the clear, onto paper, stamped it with a big red "SECRET" stamp and placed it in the locked headquarters pouch for AG Casualty Section.

These men, all these men—had some of them thought, as she had, that the war was the biggest thing in their lives, something they couldn't miss because the chance might not come again? Or were they just drafted, half hero, half scared, trying to stay alive and failing.

Jill heard a knock on the code room door.

"Yes?"

"Lieutenant?" It was Des. "Can you come out for a break— take a cup of Christmas grog with us?"

As soon as she could break away, she opened the door, stepped out and carefully locked it behind her. "Where's everybody?"

"You're too late—they've had theirs." He raised his cup and touched hers. "Anyway, Merry Christmas and Happy New Year, while we're at it. I'm going forward for a few days, so I'll make my year-end toast now."

She raised her cup and touched his. "Happy New Year. And—" Jill had let it go long enough—"I probably should have said something back in Algiers—you know, about requesting me for this duty and all. I mean I want to thank you for choosing me."

He looked at her, and the softness behind his voice belied

his gruff words. "I get the best man for the job—or woman, if that's the case—and you're the best code officer I've got."

"Thanks." She stood there, and though he had put down his cup, he did not move away. Unspoken words seemed to press down on her, his and hers, saying things she didn't want to hear. Embarrassed, finally, she gathered the incoming coded traffic and ducked back into the safety of the code room.

She was confused. Sometimes when she was with him she felt as if any moment she would explode with the tension. Later, she would deliberately avoid deciphering the minutes they'd spent together, because she refused to allow herself to think about him, to dwell on what might have been or could be. Nonetheless, as the sound of someone singing "Silent Night" came through the locked door something inside her, something embryonic, expanded and stole out of the solitude of her heart.

BOOK THREE

1944:
TO THE ENDS
OF THE EARTH

34

By early January 1944, eighteen hundred Wacs are as-
signed in the Mediterranean theater of operations of the
United States Army, called MTOUSA for short. Al-
though the bulk of the theater's women soldiers remain in
North Africa, several rear-echelon WAC detachments have
arrived on the Italian boot, most of them assigned to head-
quarters, ordnance, judge-advocate or adjutant-general sec-
tions. Some are Air Wacs serving at bases of the Twelfth
and Fifteenth Air Forces. By far the most forward Wac
unit is a small signal group moving up behind Fifth Army
combat troops within sound of the big guns, subject to air
raids and perpetual blackout.

MOVING UP MARKS a soldier's progress through enemy territory. For Jill and her Signal Wacs, moving up to Presenzano at
the base of the Mignano corridor in late January put them
only twelve miles behind the front lines, closer to battle than
any other women soldiers. Their big truck provided a bone-
chilling morning ride even with the canvas end flaps tied down
tight. It was their introduction to rugged combat conditions.

"How much longer, driver?" Jill stamped her feet on the
floorboards to keep them warm.

"Depends on how long the MPs at the crossroads take to let
us through. Believe me, I don't like it any more'n you do. The
Krauts just love to strafe convoys before breakfast."

They had been slowed to a crawl by a snarl of weapons carriers heading toward the front, red-crossed ambulances heading back with wounded for field hospitals, and even long lines
of mules backpacking rations for GIs holed up in the rocky
mountain defiles ahead, facing the Germans.

This was the real war. No more O clubs, regular hours or home-away-from-home quarters. The idea excited Jill, and she knew that her women felt the same way. Only two days earlier, on January 22, 1944, as the first news of the Anzio beachhead reached the Caserta Wacs, the detachment had been divided into forward and rear echelons. Stratton had again requested her to head the code operation and move with his command to the forward base.

"You sure, Lieutenant?" he had asked when he called her in. "Caserta will look like a posh resort where we're going. You'll be living in tents with mud for floors, cold rations, the lot."

"I'll go where I'm most needed, Captain."

"In that case, I have something *you've* needed for a long time." He reached under his desk and held up a pair of brand-new size-five combat boots. "French," he had explained. "Not exactly high style, but their supply sergeant's taken a very un-Gallic liking to Spam, so I made a swap." He thrust them toward her. "Here, take them."

She had cradled them like a precious infant in her arms. "Boots! I can't believe it. At least let me pay you for them."

"Forget it. I just didn't want to have to report the first case of Wac trench foot."

Now she looked down at the brown boots planted on the floorboards of the big deuce-and-a-half, caked with mud, but dry inside and sturdy. They were the sweetest thing anyone had ever given her—the man she had hated with such passion had become her benefactor.

Kaye had lifted an eyebrow when Jill showed her the boots, insisting that Stratton was a virtual fairy godmother, WAC style. "Mmmm, I wonder, Jill. What else do you suppose he could do with his *magic wand?*" And Kaye bent double, laughing at her own joke.

Even though her earthy humor was maddening at times, Jill would miss Kaye. She had a basic good sense and vulnerable sweetness that her bawdy jokes were meant to hide. That was the worst thing about the WAC—not the food or the home-sickness or the danger, but the making of close friends that you lived and worked and played with only to leave them behind or be left behind by them, suddenly and forever. First Page, Bunny and Elisabeth, now Kaye. Her bad penny, Marie, was the only Wac she seemed to be stuck with, no matter how many moves she made.

Now the sound of guns pounding up ahead told her she wouldn't have the luxury of time to miss anyone. The barrage grew louder as the truck's driver skidded to a halt on a deeply rutted, frozen road in the middle of a cantonment of pyramidal tents. Before she had a chance to step off the running board, a siren screamed in the frosty morning air.

"Get those women out of the back, Lieutenant," the driver yelled at her, abandoning the truck in midroad. "Hit the dugouts!"

Jumping out and dashing to the rear of the truck, the two tugged on the rope to release the flaps, Jill shouting all the while, "Come on, move, move, *move!*" She pointed the twenty-two women toward a series of large sandbagged foxholes behind the tent rows as heavy bombers swept in over the north end of town.

"You, too, Lieutenant!" the driver yelled and dove for the nearest bunker. "For Christ's sake, move your ass!"

She gulped down terror. "There's classified material in this truck, and I'm responsible for it."

A bomb hit in the town. Flames jabbed at the winter-blue sky, followed by a pillar of smoke. In a staggered pattern, the huge bursts marched route step toward the encampment.

A jeep slammed to a stop, slid the last few feet in the frozen ruts, and smashed into the front of the truck.

"Are you crazy?" Stratton called, waving his arm. "Get outa here now, and that's an order!"

When she didn't move fast enough, he half dragged, half carried her, until they tumbled down under the sandbags of an empty dugout seconds ahead of shrapnel pattering like a spring hail shower behind them.

She was embarrassed and thus furious. "I could be court-martialed if those code machines are tampered with."

"A corpse can't be court-martialed," he yelled back, fury etched on his tired, lined face. "Don't they teach you Wacs how to take care of yourselves in an air attack, or were you showing off, Lieutenant?" He felt a terrible anger at her. The tension between them for the last four months coupled with his fear for her exploded and demanded an outlet. He grabbed her by the shoulders, shaking her roughly, as they crouched there on their knees in the freezing mud. "Don't you ever take a dumb chance like that again or I'll send you to the rear! Do you hear me?"

Jill's teeth chattered as much from the damp as from the shaking. Cold and miserable, angry and amazed at his behavior and terribly aware of his closeness, she began a soundless sobbing, her courage draining away in the tears running silently down her cheeks.

Before he knew what he was doing, his arms had circled her shoulders and pulled her to his chest. Her helmet banged his as his mouth searched her face, tasted her salt tears and at last found her lips.

She heard him calling her name in the semidarkness, accompanied by the sounds of bombs exploding closer than ever, causing the earth to shake violently under them. He repeated her name as if it was food and he was starving, water and he was thirsty, medicine and he was sick, a map and he was lost, returning to her lips, kissing them tenderly, clutching at her with his hands. Instantly, she realized that none of what he was doing frightened her, or surprised or even shocked her. What did terrify her was the involuntary response of her own body, which pressed insistently, out of her control, into his.

"Never—never," he repeated the words of raw anguish, "take chances like that, and that's a direct order."

She nodded, too exhausted to protest, her head resting on his jacket, her nose sunk in the strange odor of it—mud, mildew from the constant damp, and a maleness, or what she thought was a fighting man's scent, the smell of fear and danger and something even more compelling and primitive.

Des shifted and leaned his back against the earthen wall opposite the entrance, pulling her with him. Again, she did not protest his encircling arm. This was no time for coy man–woman games. There was only reality here inside, while a few feet away bombs were exploding and ack-ack guns pumped out shells, adding to the sense of apocalypse. It wasn't even strange to be here in his arms. She could have been parked with Neil in her father's truck on her way home from a college dance, she felt so safe. But this was not Neil, this man who had kissed her and held her out of fear for her safety and, instinctively she knew, out of his own fear—this was quite a different man. More important, they had shared the fear of death on the battlefield, and it was a special bond, drawing them closer in a silent pact.

They pressed closer with each fresh burst of ack-ack. Jill clasped his big hand in both of hers, and could feel the steel in his fingers through the wool gloves they were both wearing. But, with all his strength, she felt his human need for reassurance, and she gave it to him with her smile in the half-light.

Minutes later the all clear sounded and they scrambled out of the dugout, Des reaching back a hand for her. She coughed, actually tasting the acrid cordite fumes of gunpowder wafting over the wreckage of the camp. There were many downed tents with piles of smashed cots and gear scattered about, but the comcenter truck was untouched, thank God. She knew she must see to her women, but she was reluctant to leave Des. She wanted to prolong this special connection, but felt equally awkward and embarrassed in the daylight. Did she salute the man who had just kissed her tears away?

Des looked down at her. What kind of hold did this woman have on him? Just like some kid, he got the shakes every time he was near her. "We've got work to do." He tried to make his voice matter-of-fact. "But I'll see you later at the officers' briefing."

"Of course." His businesslike tone brought her back to reality. He didn't have to spell it out for her. What had happened had been natural, but had obviously meant nothing to him beyond the need of a man and a woman to comfort each other in the only way they had.

Des saw her face lose its softness, and realized she had misunderstood his meaning—or had he not known what he meant until the words were out? But he knew now. "Yes, at the briefing, but afterwards too, for a long time afterwards. Look, Jill, there's no reason to keep on with . . ."

"With what?"

"With this pretense that we don't care for each other. It doesn't make any sense, not here, not when the whole damned world is blowing up in our faces." He took a short step toward her and gripped her arm. "Jill, darling, let's grab this chance while we can."

She knew exactly what he was saying. These were words she'd put into his mouth in her reveries, but now that she actually heard them she wished she were a thousand miles away.

Her promise to Neil was there between them, like some barrier, bigger even than the war. How stupid she'd been to dream that anything could come of... "Des, I can imagine what you must think—I mean because I was scared and, well, I let you...." She stumbled over the words, which sounded impossibly sophomoric even to her own ears. "Nothing's changed, nothing *can* change. There's still Neil, and I've promised, I *had* to promise ... Please understand, it has nothing to do with you."

He looked at her, and she saw in his deep-gray eyes first hurt, then anger. He saluted her and the salute was an act of proud repudiation of all he'd said. "That's right, Lieutenant, your private life has nothing to do with me," knowing his words hurt her, "but before you get around to choosing your china pattern, perhaps you'd better see to your troops."

He flung away from her, leaving her standing there alone. Suddenly she was aware that men were running past her and her women were crawling out of the dugouts. She'd have to pull herself together and get busy.

"Lieutenant," she heard Sergeant Harper's voice yelling to her through the noise and confusion. "Over here."

Jill hurried to where Harper, Brodzinsky and others bent over a Wac propped on a pile of sandbags by a bunker. The woman had a bleeding shrapnel wound on her left shoulder. "Hold still, this won't hurt," Jill said, ripping open her first-aid kit and pouring sulfa powder directly on the open wound. She applied a pressure bandage, and caught Marie's eye. "Brodzinsky, get a medic."

Marie stared at her, eyes wide, pupils dilated, her voice when she spoke rising to the edge of hysteria. "Two inches lower and she could have lost a breast! How many ways can this war take our womanhood?"

Christ! None of her women had ever had hysterics, and Brodzinsky was not going to ruin their record, especially when it might be just one more way to get even with her. Jill's voice was as cold as the white breath that hung in front of her face. "Private, you get a medic here on the double or you'll spend the duration wishing you had."

Instantly, the look of fear was replaced by hatred, an emotion Jill knew her nemesis could cope with very well, and Marie rushed off, returning in minutes with help.

Jill followed the stretcher bearers to the hospital tent, left Harper with the EW after the doctor described the wound as superficial, and ran to the comcenter truck to supervise its camouflage. Work was what she needed, grinding, enervating, numbing work to keep her mind busy so she would not have the time or the energy to wonder what it would have been like if she had said yes to Des—the one word that had tried to push past all the others, the word she had not allowed herself to say. She didn't know at what moment her body had betrayed her by wanting to make love with Desmond Stratton —maybe as long ago as OC training. She only knew she could never allow physical desire to make her fail her duty to Neil.

35

An appearance at New York's Paramount Theatre by Frank Sinatra causes thirty thousand teenage bobby-soxers to riot and takes seven hundred policemen to quell the disorder.

"HURRY, DANNY!" HER voice was low and excited.

"I am hurrying, Elisabeth—I'm not exactly an old hand at this." Danny grunted and motioned for her to move the flashlight to the right.

In spite of a nagging feeling that a thousand eyes watched her in the darkened office, so far everything had gone as they'd planned. Elisabeth was sure no one had seen them enter the administration building. She was surprised at how simple larceny really was. It didn't take grand strategies, just a little nerve. What was nerve but a lot of self-confidence? She checked the lighted clock on the colonel's desk: 0210 hours. They had twenty minutes before the patrol was due to make its rounds.

The tumblers clicked, and Danny swung open the safe door. "Here are the bids," he said, "right where the colonel left them this afternoon."

"Which one is Stryker's?"

"This one." He pulled a bound manila packet from the center of the pile. "I've got to put it back in the same place, just in case Colonel Nick remembers."

"Why would he, unless . . ." She left the question of the colonel's suspicions unasked. She must not upset Barnes, who was turning out to be a real nervous Nelly. But most of all, she knew she must not be silly. Why would the colonel be suspicious of his own people? Everybody knew that bid-rigging went on *before* bids were submitted, not after. That's what made this so safe, but, safe or not, this was a stratagem she knew Max would admire, and Max's admiration was what she must have.

Danny twisted around in the harsh glare of the flashlight to look up at Elisabeth. "Are you dead sure Stryker will give you the photos if we do this?"

"Do you think I'm lying?"

"Of course not, Elisabeth—I'd never . . ."

Elisabeth saw that his hand shook as he handed her the bid packets. She knew she'd have to handle him carefully; there might be a limit to his infatuation. Quickly, she untied the other bids and determined the lowest numbers, then took Max's bid and went to her desk. "How much time have we got?"

"Ten minutes."

Danny, using a delicate cleaning solvent that erased ink without leaving a stain, altered Stryker's numbers, and Elisabeth, slipping the forms into her typewriter, replaced the high figures with lower ones. Finished, she folded the contract and put it back inside the packet. "That's it, then." They returned to the colonel's office, stopping once to duck out of sight when headlights glared momentarily through the windows.

Danny carefully replaced the bids inside the safe and closed the door, twirling the combination knob counter clockwise. He turned a white face to her. "Let's get out of here."

They left through the offices into the adjoining warehouse and down the rear delivery ramp, stopping suddenly at the sound of voices.

Elisabeth grabbed Danny and pulled him back against the rough plank building into its shadows. Two guards with slung rifles were lighting cigarettes and griping.

"This is the goddamned boringest duty I ever pulled."

"You want excitement, dummy, why'ncha volunteer for combat. Me, I'm for walkin' these posts 'til the war's over—if I stay so lucky. 'Sides, I got some cute jailbait on the string and I ain't gonna leave the field to that skinny Four-F crooner Sinatra. Do you know what he's got that the girls go for? Shit—I don't for tryin'."

"Me neither. Didja try that warehouse door on our last round?" The soldier pointed a finger at the shadows hiding Elisabeth and Danny.

"Hell! What for? Who's gonna break in to *get* a uniform. All the Joes around here want is to get out of OD."

The guards crunched on through the soot-covered snow between the warehouses until their quarrelsome voices disappeared into the dark. Elisabeth and Danny, holding their breath, moved rapidly along the building until they reached the staff car.

"Danny, we shouldn't be seen together tonight," she told him. "Drop me at a cab stand and I'll make my own way to the hotel."

He nodded. "We did it. I—I can hardly believe we got away with it."

"Well, *believe* it. You're a very clever guy, Danny—and, oh, you kept that man Stryker from ruining my life. I'll never forget you, darling."

Even now, weeks later, standing in a public phone booth, Elisabeth could remember the triumph she'd felt that night. No man, not even Max—perhaps especially Max—could doubt her loyalty after the risks she'd taken for him, first giving up Marne and now ensuring he got a lucrative contract.

Elisabeth Gardner took out her compact and powdered her nose, a professional beauty's reflex before facing anything, in this case even before picking up the telephone to dial Max's Drexel Hill number once again. With one last glance in the tiny mirror, which she rotated in a circle the better to see all her features, she regained the look of assumed hauteur that had been her protective armor for most of her adult life.

The sound of his telephone ringing filled the cramped, dimly lit telephone booth and drowned the noise of passing traffic, of tires crunching February's refrozen slush.

"Mr. Stryker's residence."

"Hinton, this is Mrs. Gardner. I want to speak with Max."

She felt rather than heard his hesitation, no longer than a single pulse of the vein in her throat.

"I'm sorry, madam, Mr. Stryker is entertaining and cannot be disturbed. May I take a message?"

"You've taken a dozen messages! I want to talk to Max, and I want to talk to him *now*. You tell Max that for me."

"Just one moment, Mrs. Gardner."

She heard the receiver clatter against the table, and stamped her feet, knocking the snow off her service shoes onto the asphalt floor of the booth, where it melted and puddled while she waited, the telephone cradled against her ear.

"Mrs. Gardner?"

"Yes."

"I'm afraid Mr. Stryker cannot speak with you at this time. He wishes me to say he will be in touch in a week or so." The line went dead.

The bastard! He'd hung up on her.

How strange it was and how frustrating to be here in the same booth she had used to call Max so many times before, times when he had answered her call within seconds and welcomed her in that intimate, enveloping voice of his. How long now since she had heard his voice outside of the terribly formal meetings at the depot? Ten days? Two weeks? When this whole miserable WAC dress contract business had first come up, she had reluctantly agreed that it might be best not to risk being seen together outside the depot, especially since Max was convinced that there had been talk about them and that Colonel Nick had asked probing questions. Max had bluntly told her he couldn't risk a Federal investigation, not even for her. But that had been weeks ago, and after her designs, *her* designs, had been accepted for the new WAC off-duty dresses, and Max had won the contract, there was no longer a need for them to be apart.

She wasn't a naïve shopgirl. She had known when he arranged the cozy little dinner drama last fall with that stick figure socialite Kit Longley that she had a rival—a formidable one. He had told her that being seen on the pages of the Philadelphia *Inquirer* with a banking heiress was good for business, but he didn't really expect her to believe him. It was part of his game, the lion expanding his pride, lazily watching the females maneuver for his favor, waiting for one or the other to make a kill to feed his insatiable appetite.

It didn't matter. None of Max's society playthings mattered to her. *She* could give Max something none of them could, understanding that went right to the core of him. She knew his insides as she knew her own, the heightened sensitivity, the protective coldness, the boy's raw survival instinct turned to dangerous manipulation in the man. She understood his need to be powerful, to control, his almost religious desire to dominate everyone around him and yet to avoid any responsibility for those who surrendered their freedom to him. She knew all this, because she saw herself in Max. If she could only be alone with him, he would remember—she would make him remember! Still, a question nagged at her, tugged at her subconscious: Was understanding enough for Max?

She dialed Checker Cab, gave the dispatcher her location and the Drexel Hill destination. A half hour later, the taxi was headed toward the northwestern suburbs.

"Mind if I play my radio, miss?" the cabbie asked and held up a leather-covered portable already spouting war news.

"No, but please keep the volume down."

"I've got it all the way down."

She needed to think even though the reports of progress from the Anzio beachhead intruded Marne between her thoughts of Max and what she would say to him once she arrived unannounced at his home.

"Boy, our guys are really giving it to them, huh, Lieutenant?" And without waiting for her confirmation he launched into his own analysis of the war news. "Now if the Fifth Army can just get across that Rapido River and link up with the troops from the beachhead, we'll cut off the Germans' escape toward Rome and then it'd be a sittin' duck, whatcha call one of them open cities. We could just walk right in there. What d'ya think, you being in the Army and all?"

"I don't know. My husband may be there." What a stupid thing for her to say! Now she'd get endless reassurances, and prying questions. But the news from Italy had made her think of Marne, especially since there had been no news from him. Although she had told him not to reply to her letter—okay, she thought with a twinge, her Dear John letter—she had fully expected him to do so. But not one word had come through. She was aware that the driver was talking, talking . . . "Do you mind?"

"Sorry, lady. Whatever you say."

Say? Say? The word echoed through her consciousness. As she rode, she had no inkling of what she might say to Max. Maybe it wouldn't be necessary to say anything; perhaps he was even now waiting for her to make a move toward him, one that would assure him of his control over her, while leaving him free of asking her to come. She could play that game, if that's what he wanted; she could even fake losing, if that would really win him.

"Do you want me to wait, lady?" the driver asked her. "It'll be hard to get a cab out here later. Ya know we gotta save gas—can't come back till a fare's coming this way."

"No, don't wait."

Elisabeth pushed the bell button and heard faint chimes through the door. It opened, and Hinton, nonplussed, barred her way, but she brushed past him. "Tell Max I'm here," she said, tossing Hinton her winter uniform coat, a move that brooked no refusal.

"Please wait here, madam." He disappeared in the direction of the study, not bothering to hide his look of disapproval.

While he was gone, she was absorbed by the face in the foyer mirror, the high color accenting her cheekbones, the blue eyes wary, the nostrils of her expertly modeled nose pinched to narrow slits—the image of a self-satisfied composed beauty, given completely away by the erratic pulse beating in her throat.

"Mrs. Gardner, you're to go to the study."

She hadn't heard Hinton return. "Never mind"—she waved him aside—"you know *I* can find my own way."

The double doors to the study were closed. She opened both and stepped inside, hearing them close quietly behind her—of course, Hinton had followed her. Did he think she was going to steal the porcelain figurines?

The familiar furniture shapes, the predatory scent of leather and tobacco and brandy, the scent of Max, enveloped her, the open fireplace drawing the winter cold and hard resolution from her. A faint odor of expensive perfume lingered in the air—ah! the lion's lair had had a recent visitor. Her own senses, even the hair at the nape of her neck, was acutely tuned to the idea that a rival had been here, perhaps only moments earlier, and might still be here. Elisabeth whirled around, searching the room, defying it, like the fox in a steel-jawed trap ready to bite off its own leg to beat the trapper.

He entered from a side door, stepping toward her deliberately, his eyes seeming to bore into her as if he was determined to avoid the golden package she came in. "I'm truly glad you've come, Elisabeth," and his smooth voice enveloped and caressed. He motioned her to the sofa opposite him with elaborate politeness. "May I get you a drink before we get to business?"

"No, I don't need one, Max, but you go ahead if you do."

He sighed, but his eyes narrowed, pulling the corners of his mouth up, which was Max's look of admiration. "That's what I like about you, Elisabeth—right down to it. All right, then, let's don't spar. What do you want? Money?"

She looked at him crazily, shakily. "No."

"It's the sergeant, then, Whatshisname—Barnes?"

"No, he's never asked for money."

Max stood up and began to pace, to prowl up and down in front of her. "I don't want to know how it was done. I don't even care. Did I ever *tell* you I wanted you to tamper with the contracts? That was *your* idea."

"Max." She was weary of this. "Stop it! Don't play the innocent bystander with me. You knew I intended to get that contract for you any way I could—damn it, don't play this game with me. I'll play your other games, but not this one."

He stopped pacing and planted his legs apart like a sailor on a heaving deck. "What's Barnes's payoff?"

"There isn't any payoff. I told Barnes—well, I told him you had some compromising photos of me from New York and that this would buy you off."

"That's splendid! You tell this sergeant that I'm a two-bit blackmailer, so he risks prison and wants nothing for himself." In his anger, Max's vowels reclaimed a trace of their guttural heritage. She knew this was yet another betrayal he would unconsciously blame on her.

"Max, don't be so obtuse. He's in *love* with me. He doesn't want anything from me."

Max sneered now and his eyes lost all trace of admiration. "You're the blind fool, Elisabeth. Everybody—*everybody*—wants something, including you."

"I've asked for nothing."

"I didn't say you weren't clever."

Without pleading, she asked, "What do *you* want, Max—from me?"

He shrugged, his face perched on the icy edge of indifference, a look that cut deep into her soul. All her life she had dealt with men's emotions, her father's rage, a customer's desire, a husband's need to devour and own. She could cope with the gamut of male emotion, but not with this indifference of Max's. And she couldn't believe it now, especially from Max, the man she had responded to, felt more with than any other man. But when he spoke, he said nothing of what she wanted to hear. When he spoke, everything in her longed for him to stop.

"At first you amused me." He knew he had to make this convincing now, or he could be implicated in a government investigation, and everything he'd worked for would be lost, "My dear, you were—well, you were this marvelous, unexpected find, like a diamond in a coal mine, and, frankly, I thought you might be useful."

"*Was* I useful, Max," her voice was a single, flat tone, "was I useful in your bed?" It was the only place she could strike out at him, the only place he had really given her in his life.

About this he refused to lie; she deserved that much. "You know you are a magnificent woman, and I confess that I have missed you—no, stay where you are—I've missed your inventiveness is what I meant to say." He lowered his voice and she knew they were not alone in the house. "Kit is not your match in bed, no, not even close. But now—and I do regret it, Elisabeth—it is time to say goodbye, to be practical and recognize when something is over."

He sat down opposite her, crossed one muscular leg over the other. He could have just completed an important business presentation.

Max's civilized veneer and his callous confirmation of another woman in his bed goaded her to sarcasm. "You're not going to say anything so cliché as 'This is best for both of us,' are you?"

"No. I'm just going to ask you to leave, to leave and not come back." He still wanted her, right now more than he had realized he would, but she was too dangerous and the stakes were too high. He affected a look of boredom because he had to activate her pride before his determination failed him. Boredom with other people was something they had shared together; it was their private joke, something they had laughed about. More than anything, he knew, she would not be able to bear the idea that he could be bored with her.

Elisabeth saw his languorous disinterest, but she could not accept it. She stood up, unfolding her long legs in the one graceful motion her model's training had made second nature. Arousing a man had never been necessary before. Being the pursuer was not her role, and she played it badly. She crossed to the sofa and sat close to him, touching along the length of him, picking up his hands to guide them to his favorite places.

He fought for control. This was so much harder with her here than he had imagined it would be. "This is unworthy of you, Elisabeth. Why don't you go on back to your husband, and be a good little wife after the war?"

How she hated him for an instant! Even the gift of her security he threw back in her face. "You bastard." She hoped, nonetheless, to impress him with her loyalty. "I've already written and asked Marne for a divorce."

"You told him about me?"

"Yes—oh, not by name, just that I was in love with a man."

"That's very sweet, my dear, but you see it's impossible." He rose quickly and moved to a safer distance. "I'm announcing my engagement to Kit Longley next week."

"You can't do that!" She hadn't meant to sound so shrill, like a jealous shopgirl.

"Oh, but I can and I will."

"But don't you see, darling," and she loathed the pleading weakness she heard in her voice, "I've given up everything."

"Elisabeth, I never thought to play such a cheap scene with you, but since you insist . . ." He stationed himself warily in front of the large fireplace. The flames backlighted his hair, outlined his powerful figure, left his face in shadow, and then he pulled the ace he'd been saving from his sleeve. "Don't give me the 'I've sacrificed everything' speech. It's beneath you. Do you really think I don't know you were a common little thief at Gabriella's? Do you believe for a minute that I haven't had you investigated from the first, that I don't know you were Marco's slut, trading your body for every order of twelve-ninety-five dresses? Don't ever insult me by playing the wronged woman. Now I want you to leave, and I don't want you to return." He yanked on the tasseled bell pull, and Elisabeth, fascinated, watched it dance up and down like a jolly puppet.

She stood there for a moment, rooted, looking at the man she loved, the great complete love she had not even known she needed or wanted. "What did I do?" She was startled to hear these oldest and saddest of lovers' words come from her mouth.

"You did nothing," he said, as close to unhappiness as he was ever likely to let himself come. "Don't you understand? There was nothing you *could* do—nothing you could ever do."

It was one thing to lose a man because a new woman had taken your place, but, oh, to hear that your love had never had its chance and all the scheming dreams had been mere self-delusion—*that* hurt most of all. Max, in one short moment, had obliterated a year of her life as if it had never been worth living.

She walked then, a remaining scrap of pride moving her legs like a wind-up doll's, to the study doors, and out into the foyer. Hinton was waiting with her coat.

"The car will take you back, madam," he said, looking past her, talking to the ghost of a woman who had never really been there.

A sound on the private stairs beyond the formal drawing room caused Elisabeth to raise her head groggily. No one appeared but the emptiness of the space between was filled with the unmistakable authority of Kit Longley, her presence claimed even the air Elisabeth struggled to breathe. There would be no confrontation scene that Elisabeth could replay later in her mind, no chance to gloat over a telling verbal thrust. There would be nothing at all. The Longley woman belonged to a social class that simply ignored unpleasantness, particularly when it concerned someone outside their circle. To Kit Longley, Elisabeth knew, she no longer existed.

"Your coat, madam," Hinton's voice said again, slicing through Elisabeth's numbed senses. He opened the door, and a rush of cold February air enveloped her.

Behind her she heard footsteps echo and a door close. Her life as she had envisioned it had stopped abruptly, but the life of this house, of Max, proceeded smoothly with never a ripple to show she had been there. She could see him standing at this moment in front of the fire, vastly pleased with himself. How blind she had been not to really know him before, when now, suddenly, it seemed so obvious. For a man like Max, the greatest aphrodisiac wasn't sex or understanding as she'd thought—God! what puny weapons, she'd had. No, not even money or power drew him like acceptance; the *one* thing she couldn't give him. For acceptance he would sacrifice anyone, even her, perhaps, especially her, because she reminded him of what he had escaped. Oh, she hadn't counted on this, hadn't wanted to think beyond her passion, but there must come a time when men like Max wanted to forget they were ever on the outside. She stumbled getting into the car.

"Careful, madam," the chauffeur said, catching her by the arm.

Entering the car for Elisabeth was like crossing a mental threshold. Because sanity was so unbearable, her mind began to race into a fantasy faster than the Lincoln rolled down the curving driveway and out onto the street. With each mile, she rejected more of her sudden insight into Max's behavior, returning again and again to her need to believe that his desire for her would win over any obstacle. How could that dried-up old maid Kit Longley ever think she could satisfy a man like Max? Elisabeth laughed aloud, the high-pitched sound reverberating inside the limousine. She caught the driver's frightened look before she could stop herself from laughing wildly again. For some moments, she maintained a tenuous clutch on reality because what she really wanted was to scream, to crush something, anything, and she wanted most of all to *show* Max, to prove to him what a mistake he had made so that he would beg her to come back to him.

She was almost back at the Franklin before she realized the essential truth of what had happened to her—that she was more in love with Max than ever. Pride, revenge, her own safety, none of it really mattered to her. She loved Max, she ached with it, was sickened by it, exalted by it. These feelings of love had been so hard for her to find that she could not, would not, give them up. He had hurt her. Damn it, he had! But the pain of it had not killed her love. In her life, pain seemed the logical result of love. For Elisabeth pain and pleasure were inextricably mixed.

As the sound of tires crunching outside on the driveway receded, Max felt a momentary relief that Elisabeth was gone before a heaviness returned to sap the strength from his legs and slow his furious pacing. The bitch! A part of him was filled with rage at the threat she posed to everything he had worked a lifetime for, and a part of him felt utter and absolute emptiness, a part he had not known she filled until she was irretrievably gone. When Kit entered, he wanted to smash that smug expression from her face. Christ! Another woman demanding explanations.

"Darling—" he took her in his arms—"I'm sorry about this tasteless affair tonight. Believe me, I had no idea she would barge in like that."

"That doesn't worry me, Max, but the look on your face does. The truth, now." She firmly disengaged his arms and walked to his desk, carefully choosing a cigarette from the silver box. "Oh, one always sounds like Sam Spade in these matters. Does she have anything on you, as they say?"

"Would it make any difference if she did?"

"None."

"Then I don't know."

"Is that your answer?"

"Yes. What I do know is that she's like nitroglycerin. If she's not handled properly, she'll go off and do a great deal of damage."

"Then buy her off, darling. How much can she want?"

"No, my dear, money is not what she's after."

"Surely that little nobody didn't really think she could have you. Max, I think you better tell me all of it." Kit sat on the edge of the sofa Elisabeth had just vacated. "Sparing me the *amour*, of course."

Max heard her voice take on a note of ennui, a tone he had

always thought she hid behind, but now he wasn't so sure. Maybe her security was so unassailable that nothing really bothered her.

"Max, from the beginning."

He told her as much as he had to tell, with a growing admiration for the practical toughness he saw just below her surface, a toughness he had once assumed was simply brittle sophistication.

"Max, do you mean," her tone didn't betray the least inner turmoil, "she took it upon herself to tamper with sealed bids to your benefit along with this cohort sergeant of hers, with no encouragement from you? Never mind, I don't want to know if it's true or not."

"Why?"

"Don't you understand, dear Max? It doesn't matter to me *what* you've done. Anyway, what I think is beside the point. Frankly, my darling, not even my Great-Aunt Abigail would believe you, unless . . ."

"Unless what?"

"What is it the generals say—a good offense and so forth?"

He smiled and crossed the few feet that separated them. "What pretty scheme are you hatching?"

"Nothing at *all* pretty, I assure you, Max darling." She held up her face to him. "Kiss me."

He kissed her thin lips, but they remained lifeless and flaccid. He hid his disappointment expertly. He had discovered during their first night of lovemaking that Kit Longley was frigid. Not frigid in the usual sense of being repelled by the sexual act. That he could have accepted, perhaps even felt some compassion for. No, Kit Longley was fascinated by every kind of love between a man and a woman. She watched him when he mounted her, the way a breeder watches a stud stallion, judging, evaluating, calculating. They had made a mutual exchange of reputations, his as a lover and hers as a woman acceptable to the first families of the country. He had everything but a secure place in the world; she had everything but a sense of her own womanliness. Publicly they gave each other the one thing each lacked, privately they gave each other nothing.

He released her. She rose and moved to the telephone, picked it up and dialed. "Long distance?" he heard her say. "I want to place a call to Washington, D.C., person to person to Senator Davies Carleton. Tell him Kit Longley is on the line."

Max crossed quickly to the desk where she stood. "What are you doing?"

"Trust me and I can get rid of your little lieutenant, my sweet."

Intrigued by her self-assurance, he nodded yes.

"Uncle Carly?. . . . Yes, it's so nice to hear *your* voice. You've been neglecting me, and I may not forgive you. . . . Yes, of *course* I know there's a war on. Uncle Carly, I need a tiny little favor—well, it just means my whole happiness that's all. My fiancé . . ." She smiled at Max, who stood next to her. "Of course you didn't know I was engaged. That's what I'm calling to tell you. . . . The favor? Well, Uncle Carly, Max Stryker, my fiancé. . . yes, *that* Max Stryker, is being blackmailed by a Wac, of all things, who thinks she's in love with him and . . ."

Max smiled at her. So *this* was what it was like to be on the receiving end of the chain of privilege. How clever Kit was and how absolutely, perfectly old school, closing ranks to protect one's own kind. For the first time in his life, Max felt absolutely safe. Kit was right, of course, the best defense against the threat Elisabeth posed was to light the fuse and let it explode in *her* hand. Why would he expose Elisabeth if he weren't innocent? He was sorry for Elisabeth, sorry there was no other way. His mind wandered as it rarely did. What a fantastic woman Elisabeth had been, her body so golden in the Maryland sun—but that was not important now. With his ass on the line, he'd sacrifice hers without another thought. The world was full of women, wasn't it?

"And so you see why this Wac must be stopped from ruining Max's reputation, Uncle Carly. You know all kinds of generals at the War Department, so naturally I turned to you and not to Daddy. It would be just too embarrassing to tell Daddy about my fiancé's former *femme fatale*. You *do* understand. Tell me you do." Kit paused, listening, satisfaction obvious in her thin face. "Of course, you have my word that he is absolutely innocent. . . . I knew I could count on you." Adding in a little girl's pleading voice, "You will come down next week for the wedding. Yes, so soon, of course so soon. I wouldn't want a marvelous man like Max to slip through my fingers." Kit paused, listening. "Absolutely not, I won't reconsider. Max *will* be my husband. . . . Of course I'm not angry. Until next week then, darling." She hung up.

Here was a new facet of Kit's character, or lack of it. He had thought of her as a dilettante, bored and restless. He knew the type. They loved to circle around the edge of respectability only to dart back to safety if real scandal threatened. But not Kit. From the look on her face, the cat-in-the-cream delight in her eyes, he was forced to view her anew. He could see she was, in her own way, something of a rebel, too. Here she was, nearing middle age, and she'd chosen to marry an outsider, chosen to create a scandal in her society, and was obviously delighted to rub their noses in it. Formidable was the word for her, much more so than he had given her credit for being.

Max bent formally and kissed her hand. "Kit, I've underestimated you. You're quite a woman."

"Max, do you really mean that?"

"Come upstairs with me now, and I'll show you how much woman you are." She was the second woman he'd lied to that evening in curiously opposite ways. Telling Kit he desired her was as false as telling Elisabeth he didn't want her. "By the way, I thought we'd agreed to announce our *engagement* next week. What's this about a wedding?"

"I think it's better that we get married with a minimum of fuss. Big parties are so unpatriotic and all. Anyway, Max dearest, there is really no reason to wait, especially now, is there?" Kit picked up a cigarette and waited expectantly.

Max flicked the crown-shaped table lighter and lit it for her. "No, no reason to wait—especially now." He took her arm and they walked slowly to his private staircase. He wondered how long he'd be satisfied with his bargain.

36

In spring 1944, shipment of Wacs to all overseas theaters doubles, but the biggest jump occurs in female troops headed for the Pacific. To process women for overseas duty the Army Service Forces set up a special training battalion at Fort Oglethorpe, Georgia.

"ROUTE STEP—*HARCH!*"

Two lines of women soldiers in oversize fatigues spread to either side of the road, wet red Georgia gumbo sticking in great globs to their boots.

Bunny whispered over her shoulder to the woman behind her. "Vicki—how far have we come?"

"About five miles."

"I thought so—my feet hurt all the way to my hips."

"Hold on, Bunny"—Vicki giggled—"till we hit the obstacle course." She giggled again. "Then you can crawl on your big bazzooms."

"Ve-ry fun-ny!" Bunny sniffled, wiped her reddened nose gingerly with a Kleenex and plodded ahead, railing silently against the far-off brass who had dreamed up a combat course to toughen women, which meant they trained with inadequate equipment and clothing, resulting in a barracks full of head colds.

"Company—*halt*," the WAC sergeant yelled. "Fall out behind the obstacle course. This is your final run-through, so, *people*, give me your best. The CO and the battalion commander are watching from the bleachers."

The Wacs were lined up behind a long wooden obstacle with boards nailed in diamond-shaped patterns on a scaffold about a foot above the ground. The idea was to navigate it on the run without breaking a leg.

"*Go!*" yelled the sergeant.

Bunny brought her knee up high and jumped into the maze. As long as she had to be here, she wouldn't be last. Ouch! She could feel the skin scrape from her shin when she got too close to the forward edge. Jump. Concentrate. Jump, jump.

Cadre urged them on. "Keep moving, women. Down the nets next."

Her breath was coming in great whooshes from deep in her lungs; she welcomed the respite at the ladder behind the cargo-net scaffold. She jostled Vicki with her hip. "Now, keep your foot out of my face this time, PFC Victoria Hansen."

"Keep your face out from under my foot, Sarge."

Bunny scrambled up the ladder about thirty feet to the top, turned around backward and for a moment jabbed her feet against the cargo roping below, searching for a toehold, then down hand over hand, foot over foot, to the bottom. It was almost too real. With a dozen other women swarming down the netting, it heaved and yawed like the escape net over the side of the sinking ship it was supposed to simulate.

The training cadre stood at the bottom. "Move out! Move out, people. Gas training ahead."

Hardly catching her breath, Bunny ran on until she reached the barbed-wire obstacles, then loosened her gas mask from its pack and waited for the command.

"Gas!" somebody yelled, and tear-gas grenades began to plop around her. Coughing, she dropped to the ground, slipped into her mask, pulled the straps tight and winced as rubber met skin raw from exposure. She gave the face piece one last jiggle to make sure it was tightly sealed, and crawled forward. They'd been through this a dozen times. God! She was sick of it. As she scrambled through the white billowing gas clouds, stopping once to disentangle her sleeve from a strand of wire, she wondered whether Page had ever got over her fear of the mask. Damn! If Page Hannaday could take it, scared as she was, Bunny Palermo could stand a little discomfort, and she dug her elbows into the sticky Georgia clay.

Vicki flopped alongside as Bunny wearily reached the far end of the chemical-warfare course and pulled off her mask. "Gee, you look funny," the kid said, giggling, "like one of those African mudmen in an Osa Johnson movie I saw once in school."

"Oh yeah?" And with her clay-covered fingers Bunny reached over and deliberately painted mud cat whiskers on Vicki's face, which sent the younger girl into another spasm of giggles.

"Bunny!"

"Umm." Hands were shaking her. "Can't we win the war after I get some shuteye? I read where Hitler doesn't get up till noon."

"Bunny, wake up. Killer Crane has called a snap inspection in ten minutes."

"You're kidding—come on, you're getting even with me for the mud pack yesterday." Bunny opened her eyes and stared at Vicki Hansen in disbelief. "Not even Captain Crane would pull a surprise inspection on a warm Saturday afternoon with the Georgia sand fleas out for blood." But the frenzy up and down the barracks marked her words as wishful thinking, and she tumbled out of bed and began to pull on her uniform, thankful she always kept her foot locker ready for inspection, a trick she'd learned as an officer candidate.

"What did I tell you?" Vicki said triumphantly. "Looks like the Killer's struck again."

Bunny snapped her sheets tight, then drew her blankets taut and laid out the overseas issue on her bunk: steel helmet, gas mask, bandolier, first-aid kit ... She winced from the pain in both her upper arms and rubbed them briskly where they had been jabbed full of tetanus, smallpox and cholera vaccines.

Damn Lieutenant Colonel Harry Duquesne, she muttered to herself for the hundredth time. If she ever discovered he had deliberately put her on an overseas levy, she'd strangle him with her own two hands. She sighed loudly and shrugged.

It was too much of a coincidence that she'd been shipped out to Fort Oglethorpe for two months' overseas training in February, the week after he left for the Southwest Pacific. Instinctively she realized he had probably engineered her transfer. He had his good points, more of them than she'd found in any other one man—he was good at his job, with an air of calmness, thoughtful in his way—but Harry was selfish, though not at all in the same way as Johnny P. Harry knew how to take good care of his prize possessions, and his women. Only one thing bothered her. Harry was still married, although he had assured her his marriage was over long before they'd met at Lowry Field. She'd be glad when his divorce was final. She would never do to another woman what Angela had done to her.

She smoothed the wrinkles from her shirt and adjusted the four-in-hand. She had never learned to tie the knot so it didn't tilt crazily within minutes. As she pushed the tie up firmly against the collar stays her mind returned to its familiar haunting ground—Johnny P. She wondered how long she would continue to define her life by what he had done to her. With Johnny she had felt alive every minute, and every day had the potential for novelty, but she had paid a terrible price. With Harry, if she decided to marry him as he'd begged her to do—after his divorce came through—she knew she'd lead a moderately dull life, but she'd be safe. Harry would see she was never exposed to the slightest danger. He wouldn't take her to the brink of anything—passion or hurt—which made him the perfect lover for the kind of life she wanted. Life with Harry looked like a fair trade for love with Johnny. She wanted never again to be the victim of her own need to love a man. Not loving too much was what she wanted, and what she had with Harry, although she *was* fond of him.

And then she saw Captain Crane enter the barracks and float daintily between the bunks. Preceded by choking waves of gardenia perfume, she poked into wall lockers, asking EWs about their training in her high-pitched Alabama-belle accent, for all the world as if Scarlett O'Hara were doing a poor imitation of Captain Bligh. She was called "Killer" not because she was a tough CO, but for the same reason a fat man is called "Tiny." She was not a bad officer, just an earnestly inept one, and because she didn't really know how to command she often did the right thing at the wrong time to prove she had her bars on straight.

"Fall out in front of the barracks!" the first sergeant yelled.

"Oh Lord, now what?" Bunny muttered.

Vicki fell in beside her. "If she pulls my pass, I'll die. This is my last night to see Hans."

"Vicki! Are you still meeting that POW on the q.t.? If you're caught . . ."

From out of the corner of her eye Bunny saw the captain sweeping down the barracks fire stairs, holding her skirt with one hand as if she were wearing a dozen silk petticoats. How had she *ever* gotten troop command?

" 'Toon, ten-*shun!*"

Here it comes, Bunny thought. She didn't care for herself, since she had no plans to go anywhere. But poor Vicki was going to get restricted to barracks her last Saturday night in the States. Bunny knew that when she'd been CO the only reason she'd ever pulled a snap inspection was to shape up a platoon that had grown sloppy. But with this CO, who could tell?

"Ladeez," the captain yelled, straining her small voice to be heard to the last rank, "yoah latrines are lovely. Sergeant, y' may dismiss the women."

"Dismissed!"

Bunny and Vicki turned and headed for the barracks, running the last few steps, jostling each other to be first. Once inside, they collapsed against the wall, laughing helplessly.

Finally Bunny shook herself. "Did you ever hear anything like that? Ladeez—" she began a perfect imitation of the CO—"yoah latrines are lovely. Ah've never seen such gleamin' beauties in all ma borned days."

Tears were running from Vicki's eyes. "Bunny, I can't—really I can't understand the WAC. How they could give her a company when you couldn't get your commission back?"

Wiping her eyes, Bunny shrugged. "It's my own fault. I took a discharge, and you know the regs against direct commissions for civilians. I could have gone through OCS again, but I thought I'd see what I was missing with you lowly garbage queens."

"You don't have to pull KP now that you've made sergeant first class."

"Listen, kiddo, once you've had KP as many times as I have, it leaves a permanent mark, if not a permanent odor."

"I don't mind it so much, especially—"

"Especially when you can neck with a handsome Nazi in the storage room."

"That's not fair. Hans was never a Nazi. He told me he hated it, that he was glad he was captured."

Vicki had been in Bunny's second basic-training platoon at Fort Des Moines. She'd come a long way from the rookie who wondered if a kiss would make her pregnant, but she was still easily swept into a romance by a pair of soulful blue eyes or, for that matter, brown, black or green.

"Just don't be foolish, Vic."

"Oh, Bunny, you worry too much."

Later that evening when Bunny returned from playing the latest Tommy Dorsey V-records in the dayroom, she found Vicki sobbing softly into her pillow. "Come on, kid," she said, sitting on the edge of the girl's bunk. "What happened to your big evening?"

"You don't understand."

"I understand more than you know. When your love is new and you have to leave him, it takes a while to stop thinking about what might have happened if—"

"No, Bunny, that's not it."

"What is it, then?"

"Hans—he was different tonight when I said I was leaving. He . . .he . . ."

"He what?"

"Oh, Bunny, he said he hoped my ship would *sink!*" At this, Vicki began to cry anew, deeper sobs. "You were right. He really *was* a Nazi."

"He didn't mean it, Vic. He cares for you so much he probably just went a little crazy at the thought of losing you," Bunny lied. She knew she was lying, not only for Vicki's sake but for her own. She had pulled a curtain on her memory and wanted to leave it in the dark. How could she reach through Vicki's childlike vulnerability and tell her that some men who couldn't own a woman wanted no one else to have her, could even want her dead?

Vicki sat up. "Do you really think so?"

"You bet. Now try to think abut the adventure we're heading into. Tomorrow when we get on the train to California, all that crawling around on our stomachs in the dirt, the tear-gas drills, the cargo-net climbs, even when you stepped on my face—it'll *all* make sense. Now get some sleep."

It was out there, then; loving a man was out there, ready to pounce. She was wary as she undressed and climbed between the sheets. There was a trap she needed to avoid, must avoid, and that was the bittersweet attraction of love. Twice burned, she knew that the pain of betrayal wouldn't last forever, and

like the lemming Page had said she was, she was still capable
of fighting her way to the sea to drown in some pointless,
hopeless, ridiculous love affair. For a moment there was a
touch of suffocating panic until she remembered Harry, good
ol' safe Harry.

The next day, Bunny and the Wacs at Oglethorpe boarded
the train. On the fourth night they marched onto the troop
ship *West Point* bound for Australia. The GI's on the dock
serenaded them as they sailed from Oakland:

> *"The Wacs and Waves will win the war.*
> Parlez-vous?
> *So what the hell are we fighting for?*
> *Hinky-dinky*, parlez-vous?"

37

> *I don't want to walk without you, Baby,*
> *Walk without my arm about you, Baby.*
> *I thought the day I left you behind*
> *I'd take a stroll and get you right off my mind,*
> *but now I find—*
> *That I don't want to walk without the sunshine,*
> *Why'd you have to turn off all that sunshine?*
> *Oh, Baby, please come back or you'll break my heart for me,*
> *'Cause I don't want to walk without you, no siree.*
> > —*Frank Loesser and Jule Styne*

FOR THE NEXT days after Elisabeth's confrontation with Max,
her belief was that Max would send for her; it could only be a
matter of time. He could become engaged all he wanted, but
he would never be able to get rid of his need for her. Her own
physical desires created the logical runway from which she

flew every frail fantasy of hope. She had frequent headaches, until she began to fear them and would look for a codeine-APC pill as soon as she felt the pressure start to build in her temples.

"You're taking too many of those things, Elisabeth," Danny Barnes said from his desk opposite hers, and then asked, "What's the problem—everything's okay, isn't it?"

"No problem. Everything's fine." She was annoyed by his interruption, and even more by his proprietary manner.

"Stryker's not bothering you again, is he?"

"No!" she said, too loudly, then lowered her voice when those around them stared. "Don't ask me so many questions. My head is splitting."

"I'm sorry." Barnes glanced nervously behind him. "Have dinner with me after work. I think we'd better talk."

"Sure." Why not? What did it matter—what did anything matter without Max?

They drove in one of the olive-drab 1941 Fords assigned to the office to a small bar and café far enough from the depot to escape prying eyes. It was nearly empty. The surface of the long bar was flooded evenly with artificial moonlight from bulbs above the mirror. As she sipped a second double martini, Elisabeth's headache disappeared and she began to feel curiosity about the uniformed woman who faced her in the mirror, to be fascinated by the sight of her own suffering eyes.

"Thanks for this, Danny," Elisabeth said softly and motioned toward her drink.

"You never called me Danny before—like that," he said, his hand so near hers on the bar she could feel the heat radiating from his skin.

She patted his hand as she would have absent-mindedly acknowledged someone else's child.

He did not turn to look at her, but stared straight ahead, talking to her image in the mirror over the bar. "You don't owe me anything, Elisabeth, I know that . . ." His voice trailed off as he ducked his face behind his glass, which he held with both hands.

"That's not true. You've been terribly decent throughout all of this mess," she told him with a generosity that might have encouraged him if she had not been talking to his reflection, which distanced her from him, kept her safe from his caring.

There was no possibility that she could return his love with much more than an impatient tolerance. After Max, she had nothing left to love with.

"No, you don't owe me anything," he went on, "but I've got to know if I stand a chance with you. Wait!" He put his slender, sensitive fingers over hers. "Don't answer yet," he went on, desperation spilling over the words. "Believe me, I feel like ten kinds of a heel, with your husband overseas." He rolled the cold glass across his forehead. "But I need you—you don't know how much."

Ruefully, his lips tight together, he smiled and looked into his glass, and when she didn't answer he retreated totally: "Forget I ever said anything. It must be the booze talking."

After a silent dinner and two more drinks he put a tentative hand on her sleeve. "Elisabeth, I don't want to worry you, but I think something's going on at the depot."

An alarm jangled in her head. "What do you mean, going on?"

He shook his head in puzzlement. "I can't put my finger on it," he said softly, dejectedly. "Colonel Nick's attitude, civilians going through records, dumb questions—maybe it's nothing. But I want you to promise me that you won't tell them anything."

"Tell them what?" Elisabeth realized she was just a little drunk. Nothing Barnes said made sense to her.

Barnes rested his elbows on the table and his head between his hands. "Oh God, Elisabeth, I couldn't stand to go to prison—to think of you in the Federal penitentiary."

A shock of energy raced through her. Prison! She had survived so many false prisons—her childhood, cheap dress houses, her marriage, the Army. But a *real* prison with bars and worse—no she wouldn't, couldn't. There had to be a way, some bargain she could make. There was always some bargain a smart girl could make. Maybe she could turn Danny in. No, that wouldn't work. He could easily tie her to Max if he wanted to. But she must do something—tonight. She couldn't bear to think of being separated from Max for years, when he might come for her at any time.

Finally she knew what she had to do. Briefly she thought how much like a game of kick-the-cat this was. Max kicked her and she, in turn, kicked Danny Barnes. In love as in life, someone was on top, and in this case she meant it to be herself. Openly she watched Danny Barnes sitting so forlornly across from her. He was a nice kid, in this thing way over his head, but what could she do for him now? It made no sense for *both* of them to go to jail. Her life, her future, was at stake, and here, across the table, was the answer; and the only thing she had to do was turn the infatuation he felt for her into protective passion. The simplest task in the world with a young man like Danny Barnes, a man who, she thought, seeing him with clear eyes for the first time, might have a question about his own manhood. He was the kind of overanxious man who actually courted martyrdom. He wanted to throw himself at the lions to save her—and maybe himself.

Elisabeth shuddered. The shudder was from pure fear, not from the thought of giving up her body to Danny or a dozen Dannys. That would be something outside of her love for Max; she had always kept an inviolate core for herself—and now for Max. He was the only man who had shared or ever would share the essence of what was Elisabeth.

"Danny, darling," she said, her voice low and intimate.

Startled, he looked up.

Her eyes met his, pleading. "I'm so scared," she said, her voice miserable, and for once she told him the truth. "Don't leave me tonight, Danny. Hold me—hold me all night."

Danny drove feverishly to an auto court just over the New Jersey line, and stopped under a cheap sign blinking the legend "NEW BEDS AND GAS HEAT" in red neon.

Elisabeth waited demurely in the car with the motor running, listening to the high, clear notes of Harry James playing "I Don't Want to Walk Without You," from the office radio. She clenched her teeth—everywhere those damned songs about a guy going off to war and a girl waiting for him back home. You didn't have to go overseas to lose a love. She sang along, the words aching and bitter, "Why'd you have to turn off all that sunshine?"

Danny came back, key in hand, and parked the official car out of sight behind a line of trees. The room was shabby, the only light a small bedside lamp with a ship's wheel, its parchment lampshade a map.

Elisabeth knew she only had to convince Danny that what

he wanted to believe was really true—that he was an attractive, special man, a lover Elisabeth couldn't resist. The job proved harder than she imagined.

An hour passed. He perspired as he sat up on the edge of the bed, his hands on his forehead. "I'm sorry. I can't—I just can't . . ."

Surprised, she noticed he'd left his undershirt on. She hadn't felt the loss of his skin on hers. She pulled him down next to her and cradled his body. "Darling, you're exhausted and worried. I understand. Please—let's try again. Don't you know how much I need you?"

Despising him every minute, she helped him hold his erection. She had no sympathy for a man who got what he wanted and then didn't know what to do with it.

Later, he delivered her back to the Franklin. "Listen to me," he said urgently as she put her hand on the car door latch. "If you should be questioned about the contracts, don't tell them anything."

She gasped, and her terror was not affected. "Don't let them put me behind bars. If you love me, Danny, you won't let them do that to me."

He tightened his grip on her arm. "Elisabeth, I never thought I'd ever hear you say those words—they're worth everything to me. I'll take all the heat if it comes down to that. I would have even without—without tonight."

The next morning she arrived at the depot in the jitney bus just as she had for over a year. The other uniform-design teams were buzzing with the news that the short battle jacket worn by General Eisenhower, called an Ike jacket, was going to become an item of issue for all army personnel by the fall of '44. When Captain Everson asked her over her extension telephone to meet him in the colonel's office, she hoped, desperately, that the meeting had something to do with the new jacket. But the minute she stepped inside she realized that something far more serious was being discussed. Arrayed in front of her were Colonel Nickolson, Captain Everson, her own WAC CO and a strange civilian wearing a shiny gabardine suit. Without looking in his direction, she was aware that Danny Barnes sat in a straight-backed chair on her left. The colonel motioned toward a chair. As soon as she sat down, she realized that her back was to Barnes. She must find some way to signal him, to remind him of his promise.

Colonel Nickolson cleared his throat, several times, while all the others sat in silence staring at her. The colonel said, "Now, I hope it's clear," he humphed again, "that this is a damned unfortunate business," and here he looked hard at Elisabeth, "and damned serious. I don't know which of you two is to blame, but I intend to get to the bottom of this."

The colonel then introduced the civilian as an investigator from the office of the QMG in the Pentagon, and in a slightly softer tone said, "I want to hear your side, Lieutenant Gardner. Just start at the beginning and tell me what you know."

"Colonel, I'd be happy to cooperate with you and these other officers, but I haven't the faintest idea what you're talking about." She tried to gloss her words with the spontaneity and offhand openness she had always found so winning in her dealings with men, but she could not keep the deeply bitter tone from sounding through.

Colonel Nickolson grunted angrily. "Damn it, Gardner, you've been accused of altering the figures on sealed contract bids and then trying to extort five thousand dollars from Max Stryker when he rebuffed a—an amorous liaison."

Elisabeth was stunned. "I—what?"

Barnes shouted from behind her, "That's a lie! She had nothing to do with it. I've already confessed." He went on patiently, almost by rote, "*I* broke into the safe, changed the figures after the close of bidding, and *I* alone intended to hold up Stryker for money. She's innocent. I made her do it."

"Why?" Colonel Nickolson yelled at Elisabeth.

Barnes was on his feet behind Elisabeth's chair, his fingers gripping her shoulder. "Because she's in love with me." Barnes's hand tightened, and Elisabeth nodded yes, relieved but still not trusting her voice.

The colonel slammed his fist against his desk drawer. "Just how many men *are* you in love with, Lieutenant?" he asked her sarcastically. "No, never mind that. *Did* you try to extort money from Mr. Stryker? Can you answer that?"

"No, I did not," she said truthfully.

"Then please explain why Mr. Stryker has accused you of

attempted extortion and of trying to blackmail him and his fiancée, a Miss Kit Longley, when he refused to marry you after what he calls a shallow little affair. Not a very gentlemanly statement, that last, but one to which he has sworn."

Max had said that! How often they had lain side by side and he had told her that his other affairs were shallow and bound to end soon because they always had? She had always known that he felt the difference of their love, although she had been too careful with him, too aware of his power over her, to ever ask him for confirmation.

Elisabeth said icily, not accepting the contempt she saw in their eyes and not asking for their pity, "I cannot explain such statements. I deny them and I deny your right to make these Star Chamber accusations. I demand the right to legal representation—no! I demand a court-martial to defend myself." It was a desperate gamble, but something in the faces of all of them, from civilian to her commanding officer, hinted that they weren't as confident as they appeared.

Captain Everson, faced with the specter of battalion quartermaster duty on an atoll in the South Pacific, roused himself to his full military presence. "Sir, since Lieutenant Gardner is one of my team people, I take full responsibility—"

"Commendable, Captain," the colonel interrupted, "but not too helpful."

From the other end of the room the civilian investigator said, "We're not getting anywhere with this, begging the colonel's pardon. Let's look at the facts. Sergeant Barnes has already admitted to tampering with the Stryker bid, and infrared photography bears that out, so what we have in the lieutenant here is an accessory. The QMG is not interested in jilted Wacs—"

Barnes was on his feet again. "I've confessed," he yelled. "What more do you want? Leave her out of this or I'll withdraw my confession. Let her go and I'll plead guilty."

"Sit down," roared Nickolson. "I'll make the decisions here." And then, somewhat more calmly, he said, "Everson, take Barnes and Gardner to Warehouse 101 and hold them there until we finish."

For the half hour or so that they waited together, Elisabeth sat stiffly across a cutting-room table from Danny Barnes,

guard by a morose Everson. For most of her life she would
have lacked any understanding of the pure conscience of a
man like Barnes, one that said to him, This is what matters to
you—for her you suffer anything. Now she understood a little.
Hadn't she sacrificed her security, handed it to Max as the
most precious gift she could give him? But she would not be
led away like Barnes, surrendering her freedom, not now, not
for traitor Max, bastard Max! When the guardhouse MP came
to take Danny away, she let him go without a word, because
she had no words in her experience to praise his sacrifice.

Elisabeth's CO escorted her back to the Franklin Hotel.
"Consider yourself confined to quarters, Lieutenant Gardner," she said in a low voice so that the motor-pool driver
could not hear. "Believe me, I don't know the truth of this, but
you do not strike me at all as a naïve young woman. If I were
you, I'd feel bad about the sergeant—Barnes, was it? He'll be
lucky to get off with ten years at hard labor in Leavenworth. If
he's protecting you—well, you should be ashamed of yourself."

Elisabeth heard the captain delivering her lecture, unemo-
tionally. She was beyond shame. Instead, her mind repeated
one word over and over: Max! *Max!* His name raced through
her like blood pumping from an open wound, leaving her
weaker and emptier with every surge.

". . . and you a married woman," the CO went on.
"Gardner, are you listening to me? I said, Colonel Nickolson
doesn't want you back, and I'm recommending you for a general discharge—not an honorable, but a general. If it were in
my power instead of the colonel's, I would have you up on
charges, no matter how many senators want—"

"Senators?"

"Never mind, Lieutenant. You're to be discharged for the
good of the service. In my opinion, you have disgraced the
Corps and your uniform—and you a member of the first OC
class."

Elisabeth put down a highly unsuitable desire to laugh at
the officer. It was out of habit only, since she no longer had to
observe military niceties. "Well, then, you and I *both* will be
delighted when I take this uniform off," she answered her. She
meant what she said, every word of it, but she was not without
a twinge of regret when she thought that Page and Bunny and

Jill might hear and withdraw their friendship before she had a chance to explain. Again she would be alone and outside, and she steeled herself not to care.

Elisabeth stayed in her room during the following weekend, not wishing to face the stares and the whispers. The CO brought her meals to her on a tray, but afterward she could not remember what she had eaten. Her mind raced from scheme to scheme. At first she thought she might kill Max for what he had done to her, but soon she began to see ways in which he might have been driven to it by that bitch Kit Longley.

On Sunday afternoon someone knocked at her door. Opening it, Elisabeth saw one of the aircraft warning officers who lived in the room next to hers and had always spoken pleasantly to her. The woman paused awkwardly. "I thought you might like a copy of the *Inquirer.*" She placed the thick paper in Elisabeth's hand. "And, oh, I almost forgot—a . . . this letter for you was put into my box by . . . a—"

Elisabeth took the letter and closed the door as the woman stammered, "—mistake, and if you need someone to talk . . ." Elisabeth didn't want a friend, didn't need comforting, wanted to get nothing at all off her chest. If she was to be alone, she'd revel in her aloneness.

Seating herself in the wooden chair in front of the little oak table she used as a writing desk, she opened the large envelope with the Boston cancellation mark. In it Mrs. Elisabeth Gardner was informed that her husband, Captain Marne Pershing Gardner, had asked his attorneys to file for divorce on the ground of desertion, and to delete her as beneficiary in his will. In lieu of alimony, Captain Gardner had further instructed his attorneys to settle the sum of two thousand dollars on Mrs. Gardner if she was agreeable. After several paragraphs of legal language, Mrs. Gardner was instructed to sign and return the enclosed papers unless she planned to contest the suit.

She signed the papers, sealed the envelope and sent it to the mail desk in the orderly room. What difference did it make if Marne divorced her? Without Max, what difference could anything make? Besides, she could use the money.

Returning to her room, she idly turned the pages of the newspaper, flipping past the news of the bombing of fighter assembly plants in Germany, until Max's and Kit's faces leaped out at her from the main society page, with the headline: "Surprise Saturday Nuptials for Banking Heiress and Industrialist at Groom's Maryland Estate. Distinguished Guest List Includes Senator Carleton."

With self-protective logic, she decided she would not read the story now. Later was time enough, when she'd had time to think, to clear her brain and decide what to do. Three men, she thought—all three men in her life—gone. Marne, then Danny Barnes, now Max—bastard Max. She had sacrificed the others for him—damnable Max, darling Max. Of all the men in her life she had given the most of herself to him. She opened the *Inquirer* again and searched his face. Minutes later a smile formed, twisting her lips sensually, triumphantly. It was plain there on his too solemn face, terribly plain and easy for her to read: for all his other solemn reasons, Max had married the bitch to escape from her. Elisabeth's smile broke into a silent chuckle, and she spoke to his picture in her loneliness. *Oh, Max, you fool. Don't you know that the ghost of past love never quite dies? I will come back to haunt you for as long as you live.*

38

The Fifth Air Force in the Southwest Pacific produces the greatest fighter aces of the war. Captain Bill Shomo shoots down six Japanese fighters and one bomber in his first combat, while top ace Major Richard Bong claims a career total of forty enemy kills with his P-38.

THE FAST WALTZ beat of an Aussie band trying hard to swing drifted into the Brisbane bar from the public dance next door. Sergeant Barbara Patra LaMonica Palermo sat at a table with three other Wacs watching a continuous stream of GIs, ANZACs and Australians file in and out of the dance hall. She sipped slowly on XXX beer, her stomach finally recovered from the seasickness she'd experienced on the *West Point* as it wallowed its way to Brisbane through a succession of spring-time Pacific storms.

Now here she was, assigned as a darkroom chief technician—which wasn't her MOS, strictly speaking—replacing an Australian woman whose government wouldn't allow its female nationals to move up to the Solomons with American troops. Sensible government.

There was little chance she'd get to stay in Australia, although she planned to ask Harry one last time to try to keep her off the forward-unit list. She was near twenty-nine years old, too old for all this gung-ho stuff. Let the eager young kids like Jill get all the front-lines glory they wanted. She would never understand why so many Wacs wanted to be as close to the fighting as possible. There was a lot to be said for safe and dry.

"What are you muttering about, Bunny?" PFC Vicki Hansen asked, her foot tapping in time to the music.

"I was making a list of the joys of Down Under to write to some friends of mine."

"Name two good things about this place," demanded a red-headed tech sergeant.

Bunny frowned, pretending to think hard. "Well, Red, for starters, how about unheated barracks and bucket latrines?"

The woman laughed and raised her glass. "And let's hear it for outdoor showers."

"I can top that," Bunny said, warming to the subject. "I've saved the best for the last. Here's to mutton stew, mutton legs, even the mutton-fat muffins we had in the mess hall yesterday. Women of the WAC, I give you Australian mutton in all its indigestible forms."

With appropriate catcalls they downed the strong ale.

"Don't believe her," Vicki said. "I've known Bunny since she was my basic platoon officer at Des Moines. She barks a lot, but when it's rough going she's the one who keeps us all in step."

"You were an ossifer?" asked the redhead. "D'ja get busted or something?"

"Busted myself, so I could come out here and keep you

sheilas out of trouble." Bunny fell into her marvelous imitation of an eastern-Australian accent, "Mother Bunny to the rescue, mates."

"You ladies all alone?"

Bunny looked up to see two young lieutenants wearing the AAF winged star, which matched the patch on her own left arm. "Just four helpless women," she said in a dry voice, irritated once again that men of whatever age always considered women alone if they weren't with men.

Ignoring the remark, the two pilots pulled up chairs, motioned to the barmaid and sat down. "Why don't we go over to the dance, sweetheart?" the officer next to Bunny said, and pressed her knee with his.

"Haven't you ever heard of the nonfraternization rule, Lieutenant?"

"As the song says, honey, nothing can stop the Army Air Corps," he said and reached up to remove his silver bars, then unpinned his pilot's wings.

Warmed by the beer, Bunny was amused and yet drawn nonetheless to his careless virility, the intense directness of the man. Flyboys had a well-deserved reputation for raiding service clubs and sweeping all women before them. This one looked to be well practiced.

He leaned into her, his knee pressing hers deliberately. "Got a Jap Zero over Buna last week," he said in a confidential, strangely erotic tone that drew her imagination into the cockpit with him. "Dropped my belly tanks, spun in behind him and caught him smack in the canopy. He went into a dive—zingo!—and never pulled out. *Sayonara.*"

Despite herself, Bunny was attracted to the aphrodisiac of his battle language. His bold eyes invited hers to connect with his, compelled her to evaluate his masculinity. Although he turned to charm the other women, his sidelong glance told Bunny it was her attention he wanted. Something about him, she didn't know what, reminded her of Johnny, but then all men, except Harry, reminded her of Johnny.

Again he leaned toward her. "You're some hunka woman. You single, married or something?"

"Or something."

He grinned. "Aren't we all?"

Bunny responded against her will to his arrogant maleness;

an elemental feeling of recently repressed ecstasy rose to warm her olive-tinted complexion. Although she thought she'd killed it outside La Jeunesse that last day with Johnny and Angela, it was alive because she was alive. You idiot, she upbraided herself, you've spent all your woman's life preparing for love, and now you act like a surprised schoolgirl when some guy catches your eye. Nevertheless, she could not welcome desire's coming—not yet. She could not treasure and cherish it, and finally she could not let it happen even casually with the young lieutenant.

"Hey, Yanks," yelled the bartender. "Your Fifth Army just marched into Rome. Have a round on me before I call time."

Bunny could see that the other pilot was more than a little drunk and was keeping Vicki busy fending off his roaming hands. Then, weaving, he stood and raised his glass. "Here's to our guys in Italy—to all dumb dogfaces everywhere and all the bloody generals." He took a long pull on the bottle. "And especially to that sonofabitch MacArthur who doesn't care how many of us he kills."

"Shut up, Lenny!" the pilot next to Bunny said.

Two of the Wacs excused themselves and left, and Bunny stood up. "Coming, Vic?"

Vicki's amorous pilot answered for her. "Naw. You're staying with me, aren't cha, sweetheart?"

Vicki nodded, obviously under his spell.

Bunny walked to the door and out onto the crowded street.

"Hey, wait a minute, doll," the young lieutenant called after her. "Hey—" he grasped her arm, grinning—"what's your hurry?" His hand stroked her shoulder, and he looked her up and down with a collector's eye.

He was fun, and sexy, but she hoped she was past her need for either. "You're wasting your time, flyboy."

"Honey, I'd rather waste my time with you than *make* time with these other sheilas." He shrugged. "But a guy has to be practical. If I headed into the briny tomorrow, I'd curse my pure intentions all the way down." He looked at her with a half-leering, half-wistful smile. "Know what? You bring out my better nature."

"You're the first guy who ever handed me *that* line." Bunny was more than amused. God, this guy's attractive! she thought. But she boarded the bus to camp, waving until they turned the corner and he was out of sight. She'd made her bed with Harry, she thought, just the tiniest bit regretfully.

Later that night Bunny lay half asleep when Vicki came into the barracks.

The younger girl perched on the wooden edge of Bunny's bunk, as she often did after a date, her eyes brightly soft. "Oh, Bunny, he's really nice when you get to know him."

"Who's nice?" Bunny mumbled, her eyes half-closed.

"Lenny—you know, the pilot who was a little soused. We got some dinner, and he sobered up—told me all about himself."

Bunny was wide-awake now. "You be careful about dating officers, Vic. All an MP has to do is ask for his AGO card and *you're* the one who'll be brought up on charges."

"But, Bunny," Vicki wailed, "*you* date an officer."

"That's different. Harry's a colonel. MPs don't ask colonels for ID."

"Yeah—and you wear civvies and talk in that phony Australian accent. It's not fair." Vicki pouted. "Lenny says he thinks he's in love with me."

Bunny sighed, exasperated. "Listen to me for once, Vicki, will you? Some guys drink too much, some guys love too much, but the cure's the same. They sleep it off and in the morning they start all over again with a new bottle and a new girl."

Vicki's lips trembled, and Bunny could have kicked herself. "I'm sorry, Minnesota. What do I know? I'm a two-time loser. Maybe I'm wrong."

"Do you really think so?"

"You bet, sweetie. Now you go get some sack time and I expect he'll call you tomorrow."

Of course young Lenny wouldn't call, but Vicki would probably be starry-eyed over some other boy-charmer by midweek. She was so open to love, so painfully, wonderfully open. Like most women, Vicki had an amazing way of forgetting the pain and remembering only the pleasure. Bunny whispered into her pillow, *Oh God, why can't I?*

The next day, the man across the desk from Bunny was showing a mild distress, but she had to have an answer.

"Harry, I believe you when you say you had nothing to do with my being sent here—"

"Honey, if anything," the man reiterated his plea for belief, "it was the other way around. I wangled this assignment because I saw *you* were on orders to ship out."

"But why can't I stay in Australia instead of going to New Guinea? I don't want to be a heroine. If only MacArthur knew how really hopeless I am at roughing it. Why, if I don't get my nails done once a week, I'm disconsolate."

She watched his pleasant face across from her working on a careful and precise answer. Harry always considered his words, which was one reason he was one of the few direct commission officers MacArthur wanted for his staff, but it did make him appear a trifle pompous at times. It was particularly infuriating for Bunny, who was always shooting from the lip. His face was unlined except at the corners of his brown eyes. Despite the silver in his perfectly waved hair, he looked younger than his forty-five years, but he acted older. Ordinarily she liked his distinguished looks, so un-Italian and restful, and yet she could count on the very pleasantness of his face to make her remember uncomfortably the delicious agony of Johnny's.

Harry went on emphatically, "Bunny dear, the old man doesn't want Wacs at his headquarters. But beyond that, we're all going to move up, me included. He's asked me to head up FEAF air recon as soon as Hollandia is secured. It means a full-bird colonelcy."

Ordinarily she would have been impressed, but today wasn't ordinary. She was restless, and, frankly—yes, she admitted it—bitchy.

He cast an eye outside his office window to determine that no one was looking, then he gave her a long, slow, deliberate kiss. "Honey, I want you with me so that I can look out for you."

As disguised as it was, Bunny did not misunderstand. He wanted some word from her, some important sign that would confirm her need for him to be a man. But this special want of his, at that moment, outran her usual desire to fulfill it. Today she was petulant, frustrated; perhaps the intriguing flyboy of last evening had unsettled her, caused her to reevaluate Harry. Still angry, she raised her voice. "Ter-rific! Swell! So Mac-

Arthur himself wants me to be a jungle bunny. Oh, well, in that case . . ."

"Bunny, do be serious! I never know when you're joking. I hoped you'd be in a better mood, since I've had bad news about Louise, and I could use some kind words. She absolutely refused my last divorce settlement. My lawyer says we must start all over."

"Harry, I'm sorry about your wife, but I need to know if you're going to try to keep me off that New Guinea manifest or not."

"I'll do what I can—what I think is best for you. Have you forgotten that's what you told me you wanted?"

"No," she said, subdued, "I haven't forgotten."

He walked with her to the door. "Then leave everything to me, Bunny. You won't be sorry. At least we'll be together and that's the important thing."

On her way back to the darkroom, Bunny was disturbed by her resistance. To Harry. To her own memories that seemed to silently mock him as he loved her. Even more, she was upset by her behavior toward him. She had never been an unkind person, but Lieutenant Colonel Harry Duquesne at his best seemed to bring out her worst. There was something about her feelings for him that made her resentful. In almost every way he matched exactly what she had once told Page, Jill and Elisabeth jokingly was her ideal man—steady, loving, moderate in everything, with inherited wealth. After all, she was from an Italian immigrant family, and he offered her a life she'd never know without him. But now, after months of being promised to Harry, she walked along in the Australian winter June profoundly disturbed by the thought of marriage without love, although she'd told herself for ten months now that love had played her for a sucker for the last time. At least with Harry she wouldn't get hurt; like a professional gambler, she would make the smart bet and not give him anything she couldn't afford to lose.

But the question still lay unanswered in the back of her mind: Without the risk of pain—without, even, the possibility of anxiety—would such a marriage, despite mutual affection, be suffocating? Was it love at risk that gave a woman the feeling she was truly alive? She walked on, impatient with herself, willing her mind to cease its inquiry. Kicking the gravel at the air recon photo building, she decided she didn't want to know any more than she already knew about love.

When she walked in, the whole section was gathered around the radio. "Hello, Vic."

"Sshhu," Vicki said, her finger to her mouth. "Listen."

Radio Sydney reported in one bulletin after another that the Allies had opened the second front, landing in France and driving inland. Even the Germans were broadcasting that Allied troops were off the beachhead, and the news set off a sustained celebration in the building.

"Here's to June fifth, 1944," said the section chief, passing a brandy bottle liberated from some officer's bottom drawer. Bunny joined the others, pouring the alcohol into a pint of milk, a vile mixture GIs had picked up from the Aussies which looked absolutely wholesome if an officer happened on them unexpectedly.

"Make that June sixth, Sarge," someone said. "Remember the International Date Line."

"June sixth!" they all roared to the sound of clinking milk bottles.

Everybody agreed it would be over in Europe in a few months. Bunny thought of Page and Jill and was happy for them while being sad for herself. The Pacific war might go on for years. Sergeant First Class Palermo would probably be out here until she was a gray and wizened old lady.

In the midst of the revelry she went into the darkroom and shut the door. If she hadn't re-upped, she'd be making two bucks an hour in some war plant and spending her summer vacation at the beach. Yes, and feeling like a rotten shirker. So what was the difference between doing her bit at Lowry or Brisbane and doing it in New Guinea? None, she guessed. How bad could it be on the islands? She answered a knock on the door.

"There's a war on." Vicki held up a canister. "Rush recon film. Want me to take it? It's really my turn."

"No, I'll do it, Minnesota. You go enjoy the party before the OD comes around and breaks it up."

"That's swell of you. You sure?"

"Go!" Bunny pointed back toward the main room, laughing.

39

Bless them all, bless them all,
The long and the short and the tall,
Bless every blondie and every brunette,
Some we remember and some we forget.
But we're giving the eye to them all,
The ones that appeal or appall,
We stall and we tarry while they wanta marry,
But nevertheless, bless them all
                    —*Jimmy Hughes and Frank Lake*

PAGE TURNED INTO the New Bond Street crowds and headed toward Piccadilly. Although it was past eight on this early-June evening, double War Daylight Saving Time made it almost as bright as midday. She shifted her helmet and gasmask kit a more comfortable inch lower on her shoulder. Since the so-called "little blitz" ended in mid-April, she had never been without her steel pot. The memory of ricocheting rubble and having nothing on her head but a cloth overseas cap was a great reminder, although her father said the Luftwaffe was too decimated to launch more mass air raids on London.

She squared her shoulders at the thought of her father. Since the day she arrived in London, he'd been thoughtful and, for him, gruffly affectionate. There had been no major change in his feeling about her joining the WAC, she knew, just a temporary truce while he formulated a battle plan.

As for a woman, even his own daughter, having military ambitions, or career ambitions of any kind, *that* General Dalton C. Hannaday regarded as an illness for which he had to find the cure. His not-too-subtle prescription had been to arrange for her to meet every eligible staff officer in the ETO. Even Paul, although he wasn't regular army, was an acceptable escort if he could woo a recently headstrong daughter back to her former docile ways.

Smiling to herself, she looked to the right instead of to the left as she stepped off the curb into Piccadilly. It had taken her months, and not a few near-misses followed by Cockney curses, to become used to English traffic.

Straight ahead she could see one of the giant barrage balloons tethered to its steel cables. What was the latest joke on Americans she'd heard just the other day? If it weren't for the balloons holding England up, it would sink under the weight of all the Yanks. Interesting how the humor became more positive as everyone felt the big invasion day approaching. At least, this joke was an improvement over the tired music-hall one-liner that Yanks were "overpaid, oversexed and over here."

Not that she blamed the English. It couldn't be easy to host over a million and a half boisterous young men, most of them away from home for the first time. By proper British standards they were bold and brash, and they crowded Londoners right off their own streets. She remembered Ernie Pyle saying at one of her father's parties for correspondents that there were so many GI Joes around town an Englishman on some London streets stood out as much as a bowler and cane in North Platte, Nebraska.

But she had learned to love the real London in the past seven months, especially her two-room flat in Claridge Court, close to SHAEF's London offices at Norfolk House. She loved street barrows, the flowers in Regent's Park, a pub with a bright coal fire burning, sage-and-onion stuffing, dumplings and even meatless pasties. It was wonderful what English cooks could do with flour, vegetables and little else.

She *was* hungry. By her watch, it was almost twelve hours since she'd eaten breakfast. Page lengthened her stride, side-stepped a cluster of Royal Navy Wrens and descended the five stone steps into the White Horse Cellar pub. On the far side of the smoky, rectangular dark-paneled public room, Paul half rose from a table and waved her over.

Dropping her helmet and kit on a high-backed bench by the fireplace, she bent and kissed him on the cheek. Somehow, even with silver lieutenant colonel's leaves on his uniform, Paul managed to look professorial, his hair properly rumpled and his tie slightly askew, pipe clamped between his teeth. It was hard for her to think of him as a spymaster—a spook, he'd called himself—sending agents behind the lines, sometimes to their death. It must be difficult to weigh the intelligence gathered by dead men, even though General Eisenhower relied on it. Impulsively, she bent and kissed his cheek a second time. She knew that basically he agreed with her father: he too thought she should get ready to put her wartime adventure with the WAC behind her and marry him. She loved both men, her father and Paul, but how could she allow herself to be ruled by either? Then her mind circled back as it always did to the warmth of Paul's arms, a heat she was by now addicted to.

Page sat down opposite him, extending her long legs playfully between his. He smiled at her teasing. Yes, she knew she loved Paul, had known it for certain ever since she arrived in England. She couldn't explain this love, a love that wanted expression without permanent involvement; but then she hadn't really wanted to fall in love, especially now and especially not with a man who couldn't understand her needs no matter how hard he tried. Someone had once said that love lives only when the opposites meet. Page wondered if it would always be so.

"Hungry?" Paul asked.

"Something bloody awful," she said, smiling.

He beckoned to the woman behind the dark mahogany counter. "Page dear, I think you're going native."

"Could be I'm a throwback," she said. "One of my Tory Hannaday ancestors escaped back here after the Revolutionary War."

The bustling barmaid took her order. "Salt on your chips, love?" she said, used to American tastes.

"No, vinegar, please," Page said, smiling up at her, "and could I have one of those lovely pickled onions—" she hesitated and grinned at Paul—"that is, if you don't mind, Paul?"

Paul laughed. "Better make that two, then."

The woman winked at the next table, full of RAF men. "I think we should give this American lady a clap for knowing how to eat good English fare."

The men obliged and raised their pints to Page.

Page took a sip of Paul's proffered ale. "I'm glad I'm beginning to know how to speak the King's English," she said. "The first time someone said they were going to give me a clap, I was shocked. No, I take that back, the worst culture shock was on my first night here and my landlord wanted to know when he should knock me up in the morning."

Paul laughed easily. She couldn't concentrate when his eyes crinkled like that. It wouldn't be so bad to sit across from him at a table, like this one, for a lifetime. She must be crazy even to question it.

The airmen began to sing one of their interminable choruses of "Bless Them All"—a song no London pub in June of 1944 was long without.

The Wrens whom Page had seen outside walked in and seated themselves at a table nearby. They nudged each other and sang their woman's answer to the men:

> *"Bless them all, bless them all,*
> *The long and the short and the tall;*
> *Bless all the poor guys and those with the jack;*
> *Fact is we love every wolf in the pack.*
> *Oh, we've got our hooks out for them all,*
> *We're always at home when they call.*
> *They make our hearts tingle,*
> *They wanna stay single*
> *But nevertheless, bless them all."*

Bowing toward the women and with another pint all around, the men at the next table swung into a hearty chorus of "Kiss Me Good-night, Sergeant-Major."

"When you've finished eating," Paul said above the din, motioning toward her fish and chips, "I have something to tell you."

"Tell me now," she begged. "I hate to wait for surprises."

"It's not a surprise exactly. I won't be seeing you for a week or so," he said, dropping his voice.

She knew better than to ask why. Her months on General Willis' staff had taught her that good intelligence work was based on need-to-know. If she didn't need information to perform her duties, she had no right to it no matter who was involved.

Besides, she knew that the long-hoped-for second front was

imminent. She'd been with General Willis at the final Overlord conference at St. Paul's School only two weeks earlier.
Everybody had been there—the King, the Prime Minister, Eisenhower and dozens of Allied generals. The PM had given
one of his usual fighting speeches; the whole of England
seemed massed to descend on France as soon as Ike gave the
word. Somehow, Paul must be involved in the invasion. But
how?

Keeping her voice low, she asked, "Will you be in danger?"

"Page, you know I can't answer that."

She bit her lip. "I'll hurry and finish, then."

"No, take your time." And he raised his hand for another
pint.

"Paul," she said his name with an urgency that seemed to
surprise him, "walk me back to the flat, right now."

"All right, if that's what you want." He dropped a handful
of shillings on the table to pay for the uneaten food.

She gathered her kit and followed him through the crowd
to the door, which he held open for her. Worry lined the spot
between her eyes, a physical urgency hastened her walk.
As she placed her foot on the first step, Paul pulled her back
sharply. "What!" she said, annoyed to think he'd changed
his mind.

Paul pointed up to the street level, where a black Scottie had
just finished relieving himself against the railing post. A wonderfully tweedy woman with yellow teeth, seeing them duck
back to avoid a splashing, waggled her finger at the dog and
pulled him along by the leash. "Oh, Jasper," they heard her
say in a perfect Mayfair accent, "you've let down the side
again."

It was one of those moments when people aren't really supposed to laugh, Page knew, like during a prayer in church. But
she leaned, helpless with laughter, against Paul's rough wool
jacket. It was simply too ludicrous that an upper-class woman
scolded her pet dog in cricket terms, too fantastically silly
when Paul might be dead in a few days, when thousands *would*
be dead.

Together, through a warm dusk crisscrossed with searchlights, they headed through St. James's to Page's flat. Her
landlords, the Falconers, were discreetly absent as they

climbed the carpeted stairs to the third floor. Just inside her door, Page dropped her things on a chair and, without pulling the blackout curtains or turning on the lamp, began unbuttoning Paul's uniform.

"Page, I didn't tell you so you'd go to bed with me out of an excess of patriotism."

"Oh, Paul,"—she kept unbuttoning—"as Mrs. Falconer would say, save your breath to cool your porridge. When did you ever have to entice me to bed?"

Following her into the familiar darkness of her bedroom, the air muskily scented with Page's perfume, Paul protested again, "But this isn't fair to you, darling."

"Now, hush, Professor." She put her finger to his lips and, holding him, sank onto the narrow brass bed. "Let's not worry about what's fair. We have tonight. Paul, please don't waste it worrying about the future. Soldiers in wartime don't *have* a future." Through the open blackout curtains the last rays of June 3, 1944, cast their glow on his long limbs, his dear, sensitive face and tousled hair. If this was to be her final memory of him, she knew it would be difficult to live with this image, but she also knew it would not be impossible.

She let her hands follow her eyes and roam across his broad shoulders, past the beginning hint of a belly and down onto his muscled hips and thighs. "I want you, Paul," she said honestly, without a trace of embarrassment.

"Page—Page." His voice was ragged-edged with feeling, and he moved a leg across hers. "I don't understand a woman like you."

"Understand? Tonight's not for understanding, Paul," she said, running her tongue lightly, passionately, over his upper lip. Later, she knew, understanding would be important. When a man and a woman have a luxury of time, they can spend it on philosophy; when only minutes separate them from goodbye in wartime, those minutes must become an affirmation of the instant.

The early morning sun was streaming through the open windows, glinting off the two sets of dogtags hung over the bedside lamp, although it seemed but a few moments before that they had made love in the dark night. Astonished, she jerked awake. She lay in Paul's arms—their legs entwined in the closest embrace. He was still inside her, connecting her to him with his life-giving flesh, and she was reluctant to break the tenuous link. But her stirring woke him.

"Darling, I'm so sorry," he said suddenly and, fully awake, gently withdrew. "I could have crushed your leg. I was so tired that—"

"We were both tired, but fortunately not too tired . . ." Her voice trailed off at the memory of the breathtaking climax they had both reached a few hours earlier. "You wouldn't care for another bit of dalliance," she said, half mocking, half sincere.

He groaned. "Darling, I've only minutes . . ."

"Oh, Jasper . . ." she sighed, and, grinning he added his deep voice to her words, "you've let down the side."

He kissed her thoroughly. "If there weren't a million other reasons, I'd love you for that."

Grabbing a green Chinese wrapper from the foot of the bed, she stood naked and slipped it around her shoulders on her way to make tea on the two-burner hotplate in the front room.

Paul watched her leave, her chestnut hair burnished by the light slanting through the windows, that clean, All-American-Girl leggy look of hers transported in his mind for a moment to a faculty tea. How proud he'd be to have her as his wife.

Returning minutes later, she found him knotting his tie and tucking his shirt into severely wrinkled pants. "No cream, no sugar," she said with a deliberate lightness and handed him the large white crockery cup brimming with dark Ceylon and Indian tea.

Picking up her bantering tone, he returned, "You do that rather well, Page. Would you like to apply to be my batman? It could work into a great job after the war."

"I don't know." She smiled guardedly at him as he bent to tie his shoes. "What's the pay?"

Paul pretended to count on his fingers. "Well, nothing actually, but you'd get a raise every Saturday night."

Suddenly, Page couldn't stand the joke. She didn't want Paul to ask her again to marry him—not now. It wasn't that she didn't want to say yes, it was just that neither of them knew how much of life was left. It was crazy to try to live beyond today. It would be even crazier, Page knew, to try to explain to Paul that she dreaded the day she would cease to be a woman soldier. Yes, someday she would be a wife and mother like every other woman, but not yet.

"When do you leave on your mission? I'm guessing it's a mission."

"Don't sound so anxious to ship me out."

"Here's your hat," she teased, and then, embarrassed, she knew she had tried too hard to distract and the joke had gone brittle. In a way, she *wanted* him to leave now, not to go into battle or to be hurt, but to release her from the battle of wills they almost always fought when he was near, a battle that often left them both hurt and withdrawn. "Take care of yourself, Professor, and when you come back we'll take up right where we left off."

"What's happened to your maidenly modesty?" he teased, then held her tight against him. For a moment, she sensed a hesitation—no, a desperation. "Don't forget me," he pleaded, the final plea of every soldier facing the oblivion of death.

She opened her mouth to speak, but he murmured, *"Au revoir,* darling," and walked quickly out the door.

France! He must be going in ahead of the invasion. She knew that the OSS dropped teams of agents behind German lines. But why a high-ranking officer like Paul, an intelligence research and analysis man, on a field operation? It didn't make sense unless Paul's knowledge of German was critical, but she could hardly bear to think about what that might mean—contact with the enemy, probably, and, if caught, torture and death as a spy. She could already feel herself mourning him, but she shook off the morbid thoughts and stepped into the tub.

Within an hour she was at her desk, lost in the urgency of work. General Willis' adjutant stopped by to tell her to call the General at SHAEF headquarters in Bushey Park. She asked the operator for a line.

General Willis finally answered. "Page?"

"Yes sir."

"Let's scramble."

Page activated the scrambler button, listened for the echo and then said, "Scrambler on, sir."

"Right. Want you to plan for a trip south tomorrow—two days, probably. I want to be on top of it if there's a security problem. Pete Stark and Major Johnston will be along. Call

Portsmouth and get quarters—three rooms will do it. You'll be driver."

"Yes, sir. Should I drive out to Hampton Court and pick you up?"

"Early," he said. "Be here by daybreak and you can breakfast with us. I can promise you some real English bangers. How does that sound?"

"My mouth is watering, General."

Page heard an echoing click, turned off the scrambler and hung up. She knew she would have to work through lunch to clear her desk, but she was happy about the trip. It couldn't have come at a better time to take her mind off Paul and what might be happening to him.

By midafternoon she had routed all the urgent paperwork on her desk. She had nearly forgotten that it was Sunday and that the last few hours of the day were devoted to hearing complaints from the enlisted Wacs at the London headquarters or passing out reprimands, transfers, promotions, the work of a troop officer sandwiched between her round-the-clock G-2 staff duties. Fatigued, she read the memos attached to the four 201 files on her desk. Today of all days she had too many problems, some she'd rather not have to deal with. Two of the women had been reported as suspected lesbians by some other women in their section. There was no hard evidence, just embarrassing behavior. She decided to handle it by telling the women in a friendly way that there was talk and that she knew they would want to do something about it. "When you're young and far from home you can become more . . . more dependent on each other than perhaps you ordinarily would. I believe you both to be innocent of these charges," she said while one of the women sobbed, "but that counts for little when you live closely with so many others—and appearances count for everything."

Later, after a half hour of tears and denials, she almost looked forward to O'Conners. What would Bunny say now, Page thought smiling to herself, if she knew that O'Conners, the former Carmelite nun from her basic-training company, had discovered men? She stepped to her door and said, "Corporal O'Conners, please come in."

O'Conners reported.

"Sit down, Mary-Kate," Page said, O'Conners had a combative look on her face. Page sighed. The woman had been in three times in as many months to request permission to marry as many GIs—no, one of them had been a Free French sailor. Perhaps it was her convent breeding, but O'Conners expected every man she dated to marry her, and, according to the request for quarters attached to a marriage certificate in front of her, one of them finally had done it.

"I'm afraid I have to deny you a quarters allowance, O'Conners," Page said.

"That's against the Commandments, ma'am," O'Conners said, bringing the moral authority of her former occupation down upon Page and the U.S. Army. "God has ordained that a husband and wife should cleave together."

"In the best of worlds, I agree," Page told her patiently, "but at the present time marriages are being discouraged in the ETO. I have a directive forbidding separate quarters for marrieds." Page read the pertinent passage to O'Conners: "It has come to the attention of this command that husbands and wives are living together. This practice will cease immediately." Page suppressed a laugh. As regular army as she was, she had to admit that the order was a farce.

"Would the Army rather we *not* marry and live in cardinal sin?" O'Conners intoned in her best mother-superior manner.

As soberly as possible, Page answered, "Of course not. I will send your request up through channels with my recommendation to reevaluate the policy. Until we get an answer, I will grant you a weekend pass whenever your section CO can spare you. Congratulations, Corporal." She shook the woman's hand. "I hope you'll be very happy. Will you send Kaplan in?" she added, dismissing her before O'Conners could marshal all the saints behind her request.

One folder remained, with the name "Annaliese Kaplan" on it. Page wondered why Bunny's basic trainees seemed to end up in her command. But Kaplan was no O'Conners. She was a good soldier. A brilliant pianist and an accomplished linguist, she was now a sergeant and had worked at the German desk in G-2, monitoring shortwave broadcasts. Six weeks ago she had been ordered to detached duty somewhere, come to think of it—the orders had been unspecific—and she was now to be discharged. Page couldn't understand why, but the release had come from Colonel Hobby's office at the Pentagon marked "CONVENIENCE OF THE GOVERNMENT," and there was no mistake.

"Sergeant Kaplan reporting, ma'am."

"Take a seat, Annaliese. You'll need to sign all of these papers where the blue X is."

"Here?" Annaliese asked, and Page nodded yes.

Annaliese had little of her German accent left, and what she had lent a kind of throaty fullness to her English. Men probably loved it, Page thought. Looking at Annaliese from under her lashes while the sergeant signed her discharge papers, Page seemed to see her as a woman for the first time. Despite her poise, there was something demure about her, even in a khaki uniform, something still of the sheltered darling of the German privileged classes. Her figure was medium in build and height, but her eyes were startling, large and black, liquid and haunting. Errant wisps of very curly dark hair escaped their bobby pins and wandered from under the overseas cap. It occurred to Page that she had never seen Annaliese smile. But who could blame her? She had lost her fiancé in a concentration camp, didn't know the fate of her parents and had sacrificed her career as a pianist. What was left to a woman if love, family and work were gone?

"Is that all, Lieutenant?"

"Uh, yes, really. The exit physical has been waived. Here's your pay voucher. I guess that's it."

"Well, then—"

Page interrupted her. "I don't know where you're going or what you're going to do, but I wish you luck." Wanting to ask more about what she sensed was a mystery behind the woman, in the end she simply added, "I wish we'd got to know each other so very much better, but there's never time, and now . . ."

"I understand," Annaliese said, "and now there's no time at all. Thank you for your kindness. I will remember as long as—" She broke off in midsentence.

What had Bunny said so long ago—that Annaliese reminded her of Page? Odd, since they were nothing alike. Page stood and held out her hand, which Annaliese gave one sharp pump in the European manner. Page walked the other woman to her office door. "If there's mail before your orders reach the APO, where shall I send it?"

Annaliese returned to her desk, scribbled on a scrap of paper and handed it to Page. "Goodbye again," she said and disappeared down the hall.

Strange and courageous woman, Page thought, idly glancing at the paper in her hand. One look and she felt an almost physical shock hit her. It was the address, she knew, of OSS Special Operations in London. Paul's address! In a split second, the strangely intuitive feelings she had experienced during her few minutes with Annaliese Kaplan gathered like a fist and struck her. Without the slightest reason to believe so, she knew that somehow Paul and Annaliese would be sharing the same fate. A chain of longing for Paul tightened its hold on her, and she felt a surge of unreasonable jealousy.

Page closed her office door and leaned against it. She was being silly, putting nothing and nothing together and getting two. But as she left Norfolk House, and during the evening while she did her laundry and packed a few things for the trip to Portsmouth, she couldn't shake the image of Paul and Annaliese together—and in danger. By three in the morning, when she was inching through the rain and the wind, heading west along the Thames toward the General's cottage near Hampton Court, she had decided that her woman's intuition had been just a case of invasion jitters after all.

Paul looked at the luminous dial of his watch as the dropzone green light blinked on and off. It was 0300 hours and the Dakota transport had reached the DZ. He gave the line in front of his a tug and, finding it secure, pushed hard against the pack ahead of him and watched it disappear into the void before a sharp slap on his own shoulder sent him tumbling into the same empty dark.

A concussive shock shook him as his chute popped open. Holding on to the risers, Paul peered down into the French night below, trying to get his bearings as the moon passed in and out of the clouds. The wind was picking up, and cold drizzle peppered his face. He said a quick prayer that they wouldn't land in the flooded tank traps east of Sainte-Mère-Église. How stupid to drown in a few feet of water under the weight of his own equipment.

Only ten seconds had passed, he knew, by the time he could see the ground rushing to meet him. It was the only reception he expected—or wanted. The Maquis resistance fighters had not been alerted in advance because of the problem they'd had with double agents in this sector. Unbuckling his harness, he saw the billowing white of another parachute a quarter mile due west. Hastily burying the silk, he sprinted in a half-bent-over run toward the spot where he had seen his companion land. Giving one click on the snapper he had fished from a zippered pocket, he heard an answering click-clack.

"Anna?"

"Yes, Paul. Over here." The voice, speaking in French, came from a small stand of poplars.

"Where's your chute?"

"Here, under the brush."

"I'll bury it," he said. "Don't want the Germans to stumble across it. Stand watch over there by the hedgerow and give me one click if you hear anyone coming."

Quickly, Paul dug a hole with his entrenching tool, buried the chute, the shovel and both flying suits, stamping down the telltale hump of fresh-dug earth, then kicked dirt and leaves over it. Next he moved swiftly to the tall hedgerow. He knelt a moment. Every shadow, every rustle of leaves reminded him he was isolated from his own world, and that there was no turning back.

"Oh three twenty-one hours," he said to the woman, looking at his watch. "Damn the weather. We should have landed no later than midnight. We've got to move fast before daylight or a German patrol finds us breaking curfew." He pulled out a small square of silk from inside his heel and spread it on his knee. He pointed at the map shielding a penlight inside his jacket. "Anna, we're here now. We'll follow the hedgerow due west to this lane and then across to the farmhouse, about three miles in all. You know what you must do if we're separated."

"Yes," she said, and he could see the outline of her face, her great dark eyes concentrating on repeating the instructions she'd been studying for weeks. "If separated—or you're taken—I will go to the alternate safe house and wait for our troops."

"Right," he said, not knowing where the safe house was so he couldn't give it away under torture. He replaced the map. "No talking unless you have to, then *en français* only. Let's go."

The drizzle of rain increased as they made their way west, crouching twice to avoid being seen by passing patrols. Once the sudden kick-start of a German motorcycle stopped them motionless. Peering between the hedges, Paul saw that a soldier had paused to shield a cigarette from the rain, then ridden on.

Faint streaks of dayglow shone behind them before they approached the farmhouse. It looked deserted enough. With their backpacks and rough clothes, he hoped, if they were seen they would pass for hikers searching for a warm barn to bed down in.

He slid through the gate into the courtyard, Anna behind him. Nothing moved. The shutters were closed against the rain and the cold wind blowing east from the Channel. Softly, he knocked. Waited. And knocked again, this time a bit harder.

The door opened a crack, and a woman's voice said from the dark, *"Oui, qui est-ce qui est?"*

Paul said, " 'The long sobbing of the violins of autumn,' " the first line of Paul Verlaine's poem "Autumn Song."

A moment passed. " '*Blessent mon coeur d'une langueur monotone,*' " the woman's voice answered with the second line, and the door opened wider. *"Entrez, mes amis."*

Motioning for them to follow, she quickly mounted the stairs in the hall and opened the door to a small white-painted dormer room. "Be comfortable and rest," she said in English. "I will send a message to tell Centime you are here."

Paul took off his backpack and helped Anna with hers. "You might as well get some sleep if you can," he told her and pointed to the sagging iron bed and the ancient coverlet.

"I'll try," she said, but he could see that her nerves were drawn taut.

He admired her enormously. Although he had trained only intermittently with her during the past six weeks, he had seen how this shy and gentle woman had grasped the basics of a complicated intruder operation. The effort of skill needed to maintain their deception for even a short time would mainly fall on her. A slight mistake in detail or language, even a technical hitch no one had foreseen, could give them both away. It would be a bad death for him, he knew, but nothing compared to what the Abwehr or the Gestapo would mete out to Anna, a Jewish saboteur.

Thinking out loud, he said, "The trick is to maintain the illusion of being German."

"You forget," she said, "it is no illusion—I *am* German."

He longed for his pipe, but instead lit a pungent Gauloise he had been issued as part of his cover. "Just talking to myself, Anna. Going over every detail. Wondering if there is anything we've been careless about. Of course you'd have no problem being German." He smiled. "I wish we'd had more time to spend on this, to get to know each other better."

"That makes twice someone has said that to me in the past twenty-four hours," Anna said.

Paul frowned. "You didn't breach security?"

"No, not that. When I picked up my discharge yesterday, Lieutenant Hannaday said—"

Anna stopped, Paul knew, because his face had changed. *Some spy I am,* he thought, *when the mention of her name makes me as easy to read as an open book.*

Outside the storm quickened. Somewhere in the house a loose shutter banged loudly, a voice railed against it, and then the banging stopped.

Paul lay down on the floor, shoved his pack under his head and brought the image and the scent of Page into the room with him. *Darling, I'll make you proud of me. I won't let down the side.* This time the joke didn't make him laugh. Would he ever see her again?

40

Communiqué Number 1 received at 3:32 A.M. Eastern War Time, Tuesday, June 6, from the Supreme Headquarters of the Allied Expeditionary Force: Under the command of General Eisenhower, Allied naval forces, supported by strong air forces, began landing Allied armies this morning on the northern coast of France.

—Columbia Broadcasting System bulletin

"This is Richard Harkness in our nation's capital. If I had only one word to describe Washington this historic D-Day morning, that word would be that our nation's capital is confident. There is a feeling here that now the invasion is under way, it will succeed. . . ."

{Announcer} ". . . the German DMV Agency, . . . broadcasting a report that Allied tanks have penetrated several kilometers into France; that looks as if we are deepening our bridgehead. . . . And here's another bulletin, from a U.S. fighter base in England, which says that Thunderbolt pilots returning from the invasion area today reported that Allied troops are piling onto the shore of France . . . and that the skies are practically clear of German planes. And, uh, now, uh, here's another bulletin—just a second—here's one more bulletin that says big guns on the French coast opened fire across the Strait of Dover shortly after midday today. . . . And here's another one: The German High Command, in its first invasion communiqué, today said Allied forces suffered, uh, very heavy reverses in the Caen area of northern France, and it claimed that an entire regiment of paratroopers was destroyed in that sector. Our own communiqués have reported only light casualties, and we mustn't put too much stock in these German claims of 'wiping out whole regiments.' That's the usual Nazi trick. . . ."
—*National Broadcasting Company broadcasts*

ON MONDAY, PAGE reached General Willis' quarters—estate, really, since he had managed to snare the headmaster's house of a former boys' school with adjacent tennis courts—just as a soggy daylight began to break over the Chiltern Hills.

"The General has eaten, Lieutenant," his orderly said, and added that he had returned to his paperwork, leaving orders to call him after Page had breakfasted.

The orderly served her toast and orange marmalade, not made out of turnips but real prewar-quality preserves, two plump steaming bangers—a marvelous bland breakfast sausage she had learned to love—and a cup of strong tea, half hot

329

milk. "That's swell, Corporal," she said, guiltily remembering that few English and not too many enlisted ate so well. "I know most Americans don't, but I adore English breakfasts. They make up for all the boiled kidneys and brussels sprouts we eat for dinner."

The General interrupted, standing in the doorway, "Ready, Page?"

She stood as he entered the room and the corporal handed him his briefcase. "What route shall I take, General?"

"The Dorking road through Haslemere to Portsmouth," he said, already heading out the door.

Page dashed through the rain to hold his door, then quickly slid behind the wheel of the Chevrolet staff car with a three-star flag on its bumper and headed south. She moved along through heavy traffic. Every staff car in England seemed to be heading southeast toward the vast pre-invasion military camp that was cut off by security from the rest of England.

The General consulted his master map. "Turn east down here, Page, and stop at Ashchurch. I want to see if security is on its toes."

They drove down a narrow road, through the village with thatched cottages little changed since Bonaparte had threatened England. What had changed was the countryside, which was now one huge equipment parking lot. Page saw row after row of 105mm. howitzers, their covered muzzles pointing toward France. Beyond a peaceful farmer walking a huge plow horse, steaming in the chill rain, even longer rows of half-tracks waited their turn at war. Page knew from classified documents that over 320,000 different items, from tons of chewing gum to a stockpile of coffins at a camp in Dorchester, backed the troops ready to invade Hitler's Fortress Europe. Two guards flagged them down and, in spite of the three-star flag, asked for identification and checked it with headquarters. Apparently satisfied that his security regs were being followed, the General waved her back toward the Portsmouth road.

Rain continued to beat steadily against the car.

"What do you think, Johnston?" the General was saying, and without waiting for an answer he went on. "I think this time Ike's bought one. Look at it out there." He pointed out the window. "It's a goddamned monsoon. If we try to drop the

Eighty-second or the One Hundred First, the Heinies'll have 'em fried for breakfast."

Johnston agreed. "The weather does look bad. But the tough part is those agents OSS Special Operations dropped last night. If Ike doesn't give the green light to Overlord, then those two are going to be holding a very empty bag right in the middle of the German Army."

Momentarily jerking her eyes off the rain-washed road ahead, Page looked through the rearview mirror and right into General Willis' worried eyes. She had no more doubts then. Paul, and probably Annaliese too, had been dropped into France on some mission connected with the invasion. Their success, their very lives, depended on good weather. Page, with her eyes fixed on the road, said a prayer for Paul, and as if to answer her the wind shook the camouflaged Chevy and the rain slanted almost horizontally into the windshield. It was late evening when she finally reached Portsmouth, and the storm, if anything, was worse.

Paul had waited all day for Centime. To pass the time, he and Anna had gone over and over the mission until he had been afraid they would become overrehearsed. In this business, it paid to leave room for spontaneity. All afternoon the storm outside had banged against the shuttered windows. Paul sent a little prayer toward the sloping ceiling. *For Christ's sake,* he said, not a bit facetiously, *keep it up for a few more hours.*

Late in the afternoon, he heard a knock at the door and pulled his automatic from his jacket pocket.

"Ah oui," he called.

A low voice said, "Centime."

Paul opened the door. *"Entrez, monsieur—"* He stopped in confusion. Centime was obviously a woman and just as obviously carried a Bren gun pointed straight at his midsection.

Bowing slightly, he introduced himself and Anna.

Centime said, "We had no word from London that you were coming. How do I know that you are not Gestapo agents or *collaborateurs?"*

Paul understood her caution. "Because I have given the proper identification code, which means the invasion will begin within hours."

"Even that the Gestapo could have wrung from the real Colonel Burkhardt."

Paul had to make an instant decision of his own. He had to trust her or they would stand here playing games all night. "The Gestapo could not know the signal for French insurrection unless *you* have told them," he said and then recited, "*Le chapeau de Napoléon, est-il toujours à Perros-Guirec?*"

The muzzle of the Bren dropped slowly toward the floor. "What can we do for the Colonel and Mademoiselle?" she said, gesturing toward Anna.

"We need a closed German command car by seven tonight, taken in such a way that the Germans will not discover it gone until after dark."

"Before dark you will leave?"

"We must."

"The car, it will be here, Colonel."

"One more thing. There must be no *maquisards'* activities in this sector until after you see the first 'chutes. The German commanders must be lulled into a complete sense of safety."

Centime shrugged. "That will be more difficult, *mon colonel.* My people have waited over four years to fight *les Boches* in the open. *Mon Dieu, nous ne quittons pas maintenant.*"

"*Je vous dis encore: après les parachutistes!*" Paul said harshly.

She nodded. "Until later, then." And, tossing Anna a curt nod, she slipped out the door and was gone.

Paul smiled at Anna. "Thanks for having the good sense to—"

Anna dismissed his thanks. "I didn't think I ought to open my mouth and use German-accented French." She nodded grimly. "She might have shot first and apologized later."

By seven they were dressed and waiting, Paul in the uniform of a German major of the Panzerlehr Division, and Anna in that of a German woman signal auxiliary.

"*Herr Major,*" she said, opening the door of the staff car that had been driven to the rear of the barn and left idling with a full tank of gas.

"*Danke.*"

As they drove, they spoke only in German, as if the trees and the hedgerows had listening enemy ears. Paul knew they would reach the western checkpoint of Sainte-Mère-Église within minutes. It would be the first test of their disguise and their forged papers. His hand fingered the Schmeisser machine pistol holstered at his side. He had not told Anna—why add another terror to what she must be feeling?—but he would never let her be taken alive if he could get off one shot.

Paul gathered himself into a knot of concentrated energy as they approached the guardpost and slowed. The guard presented arms, and a *Feldwebel* left the guardpost, saluted Paul in the back seat and asked Anna for their pass.

Handing it over, she said something in a low voice that made the sergeant laugh. And then, louder, she said in a confidential tone that the weather was so bad she might get a night off after being on constant invasion alert for weeks. Paul had never noticed how seductive Anna's voice was, but the sergeant had and was leaning into the car admiringly.

"Was gibt es?" Paul said, his voice guttural and harsh with the long tradition of Wehrmacht command. "Do you insist on delaying me?"

The sergeant jumped to rigid attention. *"Nein, Herr Major!"* He signaled the guard to raise the red-and-white striped barrier bar.

Paul found himself gulping air in the back seat of the Mercedes. Without realizing it he had been holding his breath. "Do you have your bearings?" he asked Anna.

For answer she nodded, her own concentration total, and turned on the far side of the town square beyond the church. The clock on its steeple said 7:30.

He knew she had practiced this drive in her mind for weeks and was as familiar with the town as she was with the inside of her own room. Paul whispered, leaning forward, "Drive by 3 Rue du Grénadier slowly, and then circle back."

Anna nodded. *"Sehr gut, Herr Major."*

The house was shuttered against the weather, but light slipped between the cracks. Circling slowly, Anna came back and parked across the street. Paul looked at his watch. It was nearly 7:40. They had less than three hours to do their work and make their escape.

Anna got out of the car and knocked on the door of Number 3. Paul stepped out and, flipping his collar up against the rain, walked around toward the rear. Thank God, the back door wasn't barred. Quietly, he jimmied the lock and made his way stealthily down a central hallway toward the sound of voices.

"*Fräulein Nachrichtenobersturmführerin,* you must stay and have a drink to warm yourself on this cold night." A young signal captain with a bottle of schnapps in his hand was speaking to Anna, who threw him a dazzling smile.

"*Herr Hauptmann,*" she said, "you are most kind, but I do not mean to intrude now that I have directions."

A German woman auxiliary asked, "Where did you say you were stationed, *Fräulein* Lieutenant?"

"At the telephone exchange in Bayeux."

"That is strange, Karl. I thought I knew all our women at Bayeux."

At that moment, Paul stepped into the room.

"*Herr Major!*" The captain looked at the pistol in Paul's hand and then back to Anna, who now had her own Schmeisser leveled at them.

"Cover me, Anna," Paul said in English.

"*Mein Gott, Amerikaner!*" the woman gasped.

Paul bound and gagged them, and placed them side by side on a settee by the fire. "Okay, Anna, now it's up to you. You know what you have to do."

Anna reached into the case she was carrying and withdrew an official-looking German file stamped with the insignia of the Seventh Army, and spread the contents over a desk against the far wall. To make room, she pushed aside a vase of spring flowers, freshly picked and carefully arranged. Moving deliberately, she rang the communications central dispatch, asked for the signals officer in charge and, in a Bavarian accent, a perfect imitation of Colonel General Friedrich Dollmann's secretary's, told him she needed a clear line. While the General's real secretary watched her wild-eyed above the gag, Anna explained that the General was calling a *Kriegspiel* for tomorrow morning in Rennes. She said in a tone used to transmitting authority, "I must reach all division and regimental commanders within the next hour, or they will not be on time." She paused for a moment then said, "*Jawohl!*" She hung up.

Paul said, "What is it?"

"I don't know," Anna replied. "He said he'd call me back."

After interminable minutes, the phone rang.

Paul heard Anna explain again why she needed a clear, secure line to contact her General's commanders. It must be only a security call-back, to double-check the identification cipher Anna had given. If they had been changed in the last twenty-four hours—well, the jig would be up. He watched the secretary's eyes over the gag for some clue. Were they triumphant, knowing that the codes had been changed and the Gestapo was on its way? No. They rolled wildly from him to Anna and then pleaded frantically with the captain tied at her side to do something.

After interminable minutes, Anna nodded yes to Paul, and he relaxed the bunched muscles in his neck. "I have the line," she whispered, her hand over the amplifier.

Paul walked to the settee to check on the two prisoners. As he bent over the captain's leg bindings, a hand grabbed his gun hand, another hand pushed against his windpipe. In an instant, he saw that Anna had already made her first connection and was talking, so if the gun went off the Germans would be down on them within minutes.

Although the German captain's feet were tied, and he was still gagged, he had the strength of desperation. Paul managed to drop the gun in his hand and kick it across the room in Anna's direction. The damned Kraut knew he couldn't allow the sound of a gunshot to go out over the phone line. In an eerie silence they grappled on the floor.

Rolling free, the German scrambled on his knees for the gun not far from Anna's feet. Paul, even in his effort to stop him, wondered at Anna's continued calm voice while her eyes never stopped darting from one to the other of them, her own gun lying useless by her hand. Paul knew she was watching as he grabbed the German's neck in a commando hold and with his knee planted on the man's spine gave a sharp jerk—the sound of the cracking spinal column rang in Paul's ears, almost as loud as a gunshot. Breathing rapidly, he dropped the man's body and watched it fall, head wobbling, to the floor. The technique did not always kill, Paul knew, and he was prepared to use his knife, but the German captain lay still except for a twitching in his arm muscles. Paul shuddered convulsively, stood and walked to the General's secretary shrinking into the upholstered settee. She struggled as he approached to check her bonds. "Be still," he told her in a voice he hardly recognized, "and you will live. *Verstehen Sie?*"

335

Paul moved swiftly to the window, as much to avoid the eyes of the terrified woman as to guard the approach to the house. All was quiet, and the shadows that marched up the Rue du Grénadier were trees and shrubs, not goosestepping soldiers. He knew that if Anna could work undisturbed for another hour, maybe less, every German commander facing Utah Beach would be on his way to a war games council and miles from his unit when the invasion came. If he and Anna could bring this off, thousands of First Army GIs who would otherwise be dead would still be alive tomorrow night. As for him, he knew that the chances of his ever seeing Page again were— He wasn't sure, but at that moment he thought he saw one of the shadows detach itself from the courtyard wall opposite and slide behind the parked command car.

Page had dropped exhausted into bed after the grueling drive from London. By dark, the weather had miraculously cleared. Cheered by the thought that the invasion was on— Paul had a chance now, she knew—she had fallen asleep in her slip. She woke slowly in the pitch dark, thinking that she had been dreaming of driving and that the rumble she heard came from the sound of automobile tires on macadam. But quickly she became aware that the thunderous roar came from overhead and outside.

Raising the window, she identified the drone of aircraft, hundreds of them, a giant Allied armada of airplanes, flying east toward the Channel and France. In them, she knew, were some of the men of the 101st Airborne. While Ike visited the 82nd Airborne Division, General Willis had made a final two-hour detour to the 101st base before turning toward SHAEF headquarters at Southwick House near Portsmouth. She'd been so proud of the guys with their darkened faces, jostling for a better view of General Willis—and of her, she had to admit—joking and laughing. She had helped put the cocoa and linseed oil night camouflage on some of their grinning faces.

As soon as she stopped the General's car and he got out, they snapped to attention.

"Stand easy, men."

A young corporal had laughed. "General, we'll take your driver with us, if you can spare her."

"Don't let her hear you say that, soldier. She'd go in a minute."

Page leaned out the window to get a better view of the sky lit with the winking wing lights of hundreds of planes. Some of the men whose hands she'd shaken last night had only hours left to live. Which ones? The corporal? The gangly lieutenant who'd given her a letter for his girl in Boise? For an hour or more she sat on the window seat, watching the fanning contrails of the airborne invaders, wondering if Paul could hear them where he was; and wondering, too, when she and other women soldiers would go to France. Since the beginning of time, men had assumed that they fought wars while women wept. The WAC had changed all that—women in the ETO would not be happy until they too had crossed the Channel.

The next morning a sleepy-eyed Page joined a late G-2 staff breakfast. News was pouring across the Channel. The first still-damp photos of action on Omaha and Utah beaches were passed around the table. As she stared at them, at the bodies and the burnt-out wrecks, Page knew she would never again think of a beach as a place of yellow sand where children played, not after Omaha and Utah, Gold, Juno and Sword.

General Willis joined the table. "We've got a lodgement—holding a salient back from the beach to Sainte-Mère-Église," he said and dropped into a chair. "But the Eighty-second and One Hundred First Airborne have taken a shellacking to keep the heat off the beaches—long lists just beginning to come into AG Casualty."

Smiling faces smeared with cocoa flashed through Page's mind. But as she looked up at the General from the cup of hot tea she was nursing with both hands, there was only one unspoken, misty question in her eyes.

"Paul's alive, Page," General Willis told her. "He and his woman companion were among the first wounded brought out."

41

> *The liberation of Rome in no way slowed the Allied pursuit of the tired and disorganized German armies in Italy. . . . Armored and motorized units sped across the Tiber River to press hard upon the retreating enemy's heels. Five hundred heavy bombers joined with light aircraft to smash rail and road routes leading to northern Italy. . . . General Clark said that parts of the two German armies had been smashed. . . . President Roosevelt warned the people of the United States in a radio talk last night not to over-emphasize the military significance of the liberation of Rome. "Germany has not yet been driven to surrender," he said. "Victory still lies some distance ahead. . . . It will be tough and it will be costly."*
>
> *—Associated Press dispatch, June 6, 1944*

JILL STARED OUT at the bazooka-blasted rubble that had once been a village just off Highway 6 in the Alban Hills south of Rome. What caught her eye was not the destruction—she was used to that—but the wild summer poppies growing everywhere in the fields and on all sides, almost as if a grieving God had laid a wreath around the town.

It was hot and dusty, and she smiled to think that the longjohns Elisabeth mailed last February had arrived with the first summer weather. Some snafu at the Algiers APO. Wouldn't you just know it?

"Lieutenant—" her driver stuck his head out from under the hood of the jeep—"looks like I've got some dirt-fouled carburetor jets. Take me the better part of an hour."

Jill nodded. "Okay, Corporal Stanley, we might as well use this time to chow-down."

She walked back along the line of dusty trucks. "Harper, break out the C rations," she called up to the sergeant, whose legs dangled over the tailgate. "We've got an hour to kill."

"Ma'am, some of the women were wondering if we could go over into that grove of olive trees, try to get out of this heat."

Jill could understand why even the sparse shade under the soft gray-green trees looked so inviting. Three hours of jouncing in and out of shell holes in a stifling canvas-covered truck had been hard even on her hardship-hardened Fifth Army Signal Wacs. "Let me check with Captain Stratton. Wouldn't want to trip over any antipersonnel mines. I'll be right back."

Walking toward Des's jeep at the head of the small convoy, she was anxiously aware that it had been several weeks since they had spoken except as commander and subordinate. Part of the reason was obvious. Since the breakout from Anzio, the forward signal group had moved up twice, never in any one place for more than two weeks, living within sound of the big guns and always under blackout conditions. They had both been busy and then exhausted during their brief off-duty hours. Even the fall of Rome a few days earlier had brought only a temporary respite from the crushing workload.

But Jill knew that the rest of the reason for their aloofness from each other had nothing to do with the war or fatigue, but with Des's inability to accept the fact that she must be true to another man. She had tried to offer friendship. They had so much in common—every minute of their existence in Italy, their work, the food they ate, all of it the same. Clearly, this should form a bridge on which they could meet. But, oh no, not Des Stratton. He seemed to think she could put Neil and her promises to him into a little compartment in her mind and shut the door on them until after the war. Men could do that. She'd seen it happen dozens of times. Men left their wives and sweethearts in the ZI, and for a few weeks after they got to Algiers or Naples or some other foreign place they mooned around the barracks. But men just couldn't stand loneliness. Sooner or later, they put their love and values behind a partition for the duration and went after everything in skirts to fill the empty hours.

Perhaps Des's distant attitude was best. It took every ounce of her strength to fight against her feelings for him. If he had tried to persuade her . . .

Captain Desmond Stratton looked up from his map case. "Lieutenant?" He acknowledged her presence with what Jill thought sounded like exaggerated politeness. "I was just about to walk back to your jeep to see if you needed help. What's the trouble?"

"Sir—" she could keep her military distance, too— "carburetor jets—the driver says it will take about an hour. Do I have your permission to let the women eat? Over there." She pointed to the olive grove questioningly. "Is it safe?"

He pointed in turn. "See those sheep grazing there? If it wasn't safe, they'd be shish kebab by now. But I thought we could get a hot meal in Rome. There are several messes already operating, and the USO is set up."

"Captain, we can't make Rome before midafternoon. Besides, Wacs don't always feel welcome at the USO."

He slapped his map case against his leg. "I don't know why you gals can't get along together." He laughed, taunting her bitterly. "There are enough guys in the Mediterranean theater to go around."

Jill bit her tongue. The conceited dope. And anyway, how unfair! Her Wacs got along just fine with the British ATS women and loudly admired the brave Frenchwomen who were allowed even farther forward than the Signal Wacs.

"But if you can't, then go ahead," Des said and turned back to his map case, rudely dismissing her.

If I won't play his way, he won't play at all. Damn it! Why did it have to be so hard? Why couldn't a man do a job with a woman and forget about—well, forget about being man and woman? Damn it again. Why couldn't she *forget?*

Watching the small figure trudge back to the rear of the convoy, Des slowly unclenched his fist and smoothed the wrinkles out of the map he hadn't been aware he was crumpling. *Why did he act like such an asshole every time Jill got close? Well, he wasn't going to beg her. Only once in his life had he ever chased a woman, and his marriage had been an unmitigated disaster. If a woman didn't want him, he didn't want her. One thing for sure, he didn't* need *Jill. He was a conquering hero, and plenty of women went for that. Jill could hang on to her goddamned virginity till—* Des clamped his mouth tight shut, aware from the smirk on his driver's face, even though the man still faced front, that he'd been muttering out loud.

Walking back to her jeep, Jill gave a high sign to Sergeant Harper, and Wacs began spilling out of the trucks with their rations and blankets over their arms. "Harper," Jill told her sergeant, surveying the abandoned German equipment lying everywhere, "remind the women not to go souvenir hunting—it's too dangerous."

Soon the unit was spread out like a Sunday-school picnic on the grass under the trees, and the ration bargaining, a ritual at every mealtime, began.

"I'll trade an egg yolk and pork for franks and beans," called PFC Schultz, waving an OD can in the air to derisive hoots.

"Schultzy," said one woman, "here's some straight dope for you. I wouldn't eat egg yolk and pork for General Mark Clark himself."

Jill propped her back against the rough bark of a tree. "The captain says we could have a hot meal at the USO in Rome."

Schultz spoke up. "Lieutenant, they'd probably make us wash up the dishes for it."

"Yeah," said another, "they think we're here to do their dirty work for them."

"Just like," another chimed in, "back in Presenzano when the tents had to come down at moving time, they always managed to be somewhere else."

Schultz went on griping, with the other women nodding agreement. "They think we're supposed to do things for them because we're in the Army, but when we show up at the USO, then they say the clubs are just for soldiers. What do they think we are—clowns? Talk about having it both ways against the middle—"

"Okay, okay," Jill interrupted, not wanting the griping, a good safety valve in moderation, to get out of hand. "Go easy on that kind of talk around the captain. He's already got it pegged as sorority squabbling."

Leaning back again, Jill loosed the Fifth Army insignia green scarf around her neck. She felt the rough bark of the olive tree under her hand like a man's face stubbly with a couple of day's growth of beard. She closed her tired eyes. Oh, Des, why do you always misunderstand, almost as if you chose to? Maybe it had been her own fault, at least a little. Back there on the first day in Presenzano, in the midst of her first air raid, she had eagerly returned his kiss. She'd been caught by surprise, not just by the kiss, but by the explosion of feeling, the frantic rush of it that had touched her everywhere inside, and had frightened her—not of him, but of herself. It had not reminded her one bit of the hold-back kisses that Neil had given her. Somehow, from that one kiss, Jill knew that Des would never jump suddenly out of the truck while they were necking on the ranch access road and disappear into the dark, to return in a few minutes and take her home without touching her again. No, and she smiled at the thought, that didn't sound like Des at all. There was absolutely nothing safe about him, and something else Jill had figured out, with Des: it was everything or nothing. Okay, since this standoff was his choice, it would have to be nothing, then, because she'd pledged her life to Neil. *Couldn't Des see that it was all settled?* After what Neil had been through because of her, she owed him her love. She shifted uncomfortably on the hard ground. Already she knew that giving Neil all her life would be so much easier than giving him all her love.

Poor Neil! How could she have ever thought that the war was glamorous, exciting, not to be missed? What a naïve child she had been only two years ago—even a few months ago! The war was none of the things she had thought it would be. Mostly it was long hours of numbing work, it was writing ten-page letters to her parents and Neil, trying to keep some connection to a past that became more vague and unreal every day; it was staying clean in winter mud and summer dust—and for a woman soldier it was a fight not to live life on the outside, just for the moment, but to keep compassion and human sympathy alive, to keep broken bodies and broken towns from becoming so commonplace she would cease to care about anything very deeply. And each day hanging on to her humanity became harder. At Cassino alone almost 38,000 men had died. For what? She would never forget passing below the leveled abbey that under bombing and shelling had fallen stone by stone on top of the town clinging to the mountainside below. All those men . . .

"Lieutenant," Schultz whispered and jarred her from her reverie, "do you have your Colt automatic?"

Jill was instantly alert. "The forty-five? No, it's in the holster in the jeep. Why? What is it?"

"Something moving in those trees behind us."

"Stay down!" But when the women hugged the ground she reassured them, crouching behind her tree. "It can't be a stray German. They'd give this convoy a wide berth unless they wanted to surrender. Must be an Italian." She wished she were as sure as she sounded. *"Chi c'è?"* Jill yelled, knowing that wasn't exactly Italian for "Who's there?," but hoping it was close enough. Just then she heard the sound of a young girl's piping voice.

"Americana. Americana. Buon giorno."

Jill stood up and faced toward the sound. "Come out here!"

A very young girl followed by a large German shepherd stepped from behind the trunk of a gnarled olive tree and walked hesitantly toward them.

Marie Brodzinsky, who had taken up her usual place apart from the others, said, "Why, she's just a kid. Don't scare her."

Jill could see that the child was possibly ten years old, although it was hard to tell with some Italian children, especially when they were as scrawny as this one. For a moment, with that dog tagging behind her, she looked to Jill like a reincarnation of herself as a child playing with Bear in her father's orchards. "What are you doing here?" Jill asked, her voice kind, wishing she had her "Soldier's Guide to Italy" so she could look up the Italian words that were beyond her limited vocabulary.

The girl, her black eyes enormous as she spied the packets of food spilled on the army blankets, shook her head frantically. *"No Fascista, signorina* Lieutenant. Me demo-*cra*-cy."

"Sì." Jill nodded. Fascists in Italy were harder to find in 1944 than Hoover supporters in a 1934 shantytown. Jill pointed to her mouth and asked, *"Mangia?"*

Marie came forward with her mess kit piled high with Spam and rations and pushed it toward the girl.

Schultz said, "Cripes, Marie, she's probably crawling with lice and you're letting an Eyetie eat out of your—"

Marie said bitterly, "That's my lookout, not yours. Us untouchables have to stick together."

Jill saw Schultz shrug off Marie's words, but she cringed inside. Marie Brodzinsky was her personal albatross. From Camp Shanks to Algiers and up the Italian peninsula, Jill had watched Marie grow more bitter and suspicious, separating herself from the others, not forgetting or allowing them to forget, dragging the rape story behind her everywhere, and all the time watching Jill with a palpable hate. Sometimes it was almost more than Jill could stand.

At that moment Des shouted from the road, and she hurried over to see what he wanted. "Corporal Stanley has run into more problems on that carburetor," his voice matter-of-fact but not sarcastic as before. "I don't want to hold up the column any longer, so he'll follow as soon as he can. You can ride up here with me. We'll jump off in five minutes. Get your women moving."

She sighed on her way back to the olive grove. Des was in one of his all-business moods. The caring she had seen at Presenzano, the sweetness even, must have been her imagination. When he found she was not going to jump into the sack with him, he had changed fast enough. Her mother had been right about one thing, anyway—men were just after sex.

"Let's go, people," Jill ordered. "Marie, you can leave a box of C rations for the girl."

Marie said, sharply even for her, barely this side of insubordination, *"Her name's Tina."*

"Hurry it up," Jill said, ignoring the obvious insult to her rank since none of the others had heard it. She picked up her unused mess kit. She had eaten only crackers and had added concentrated lemon powder to her tin cup of water. This whole business with Des and then the girl had ruined her appetite.

She called to the child standing by the roadside watching the Wacs climb into their trucks. Jill took her C-ration stew, scooped it onto a spread-out ration carton and put it in front of the dog, whose wagging tail made her more homesick than she'd been for months.

"Grazie! Grazie!" The little girl's grateful look would haunt her later, she knew.

"Buona fortuna, Tina." What else could she offer? There were thousands of children wandering the countryside looking

for parents or food or perhaps for their lost childhood. War took most from children, she saw that now. But what could she do?

Jill retrieved her gear from the downed jeep and took a back seat in Des's command car, whose canvas top would be some protection against the sun and the dust. She took off her heavy helmet and liner and ruffled her damp, crushed auburn curls, letting her scalp breathe. Looking back, she saw that all the women were back in the trucks. The little Italian girl and her big dog must have faded back into the orchard. She thought she heard barking, but the sound disappeared when the women started a lusty chorus of "Duty." Des swung into the car and gave the hand signal to move on.

For the next twenty miles they rode through the war-ravaged landscape in silence. Des wasn't much on small talk, Jill knew. His erect shoulders looked stiff and unforgiving. She was surprised, then, when finally he turned and draped his arm over the back of the seat, with a determinedly friendly look on his tanned, dusty face that made his gray eyes look even lighter and his teeth even whiter.

"I'm sorry we can't have a tourist's look at Rome," he said, "but I must stop at Corps for orders, and then we'll have to go on or we won't be set up before nightfall. Okay with you?"

"Yes, sir." He didn't need her permission. "I never expected even to ride through the Eternal City."

"I was here before the war . . ." He seemed to be about to tell her about it, but changed his mind and became a commanding officer again. "The Germans are badly mauled, but they've set up a line centered on Lake Trasimeno about eighty-five miles north of Rome. Here's where we'll be." He traced with his finger on the map. "You can see that we have to get a move on to make it in and unload before dark."

"Right, Captain. I'm just here to follow orders." She could hardly believe it as she heard herself speak. His tone had been friendly. Why did she keep hearing herself say things to Des she did not mean?

He nodded, his mouth set. "Thanks for reminding me."

She stared at the back of his helmet. Even the slightest attempt at conversation turned into a sparring match. Most of the time it was his fault, but this time it had been hers. For the better part of an hour she tried to think of something amusing or even noncommittal to say, but his squared back made everything she thought of seem silly in advance.

They drove into Rome on the Via Tuscuiana and made for the Piazza Colonna, where XVI Corps headquarters had commandeered a fashionable hotel facing the square.

"Let your women take a latrine break inside—a few at a time," Des said, jumping to the sidewalk and tossing the words over his shoulder, "but I don't want anyone wandering off to see the sights."

He returned the two sentries' salutes and hurried inside. Harper appeared alongside and Jill repeated the captain's orders. She stared at the two MPs standing on either side of the massive doors with their brass shining and their belts and holster lanyards white enough to reflect the sun. Headquarters troops! She must look a fright with a layer of sweat and dust covering her face and clothes, but she hadn't the energy to move. There was something deeply debilitating about the tension between her and Des, something that sapped her body as well as her spirit. While it seemed to make Des more stiff, it wrung her out and left her limp. She thought again of putting in for a transfer. If she asked, she knew he'd give it to her, but she couldn't bear to think of her outfit going on without her, not when they'd come through so much together. No, she'd stick it out for her women. She'd just have to get better at avoiding him—and the stray sensual images of them together that intruded on her thoughts far too often.

A five-truck convoy with a command car in the lead circled the square and parked, the command car pulling alongside. "You gonna be there long?" a captain asked her.

"I don't know, sir."

She couldn't help but see the box full of single dog tags riding in the jump seat or fail to notice the Graves Registration designation on the trucks. Behind the trucks' tightly closed canvas side curtains, she knew, coffins were neatly stacked to the top. Instantly, it brought the price of war much closer to her than mere names on tape rolling from a code machine. She shuddered and felt between her breasts for the jingling lump where two dog tags rested against her beating heart.

By the time Des came out, the sun had swung lower in the west over Vatican City and Jill was stiff from sitting. It was apparent from his hurried manner that Des wasn't going to order a USO stop.

"Jesus!" He tossed a bag of sandwiches and a thermos into the rear seat beside Jill. "They passed me from one section to another. Christ, the Army never changes. Anyway, the real hangup is not good news for you, Lieutenant." He gave the driver an order to turn and parallel the Tiber River, heading north on Highway 1. "Believe me, I tried to talk them out of it—"

Jill broke in, "Talk them out of what!"

"They've captured fifty German women signal auxiliaries up north, and the Fifth Army Wacs are detailed to guard them until higher command decides what to do with them."

"German army women?"

"Yes. It hasn't been decided whether they're civilians in uniform or military POWs or what."

Jill grimaced. "What a mystery! A captured enemy woman in uniform *would* be difficult to fathom."

Des threw her a sharp look. "I don't want to get into the whole subject of the women-in-the-military with you. You've got your orders."

"Yes, sir." And whatever they were, she would carry them out. It wouldn't be easy playing nursemaid to a bunch of Nazi women after a twelve-hour comcenter shift, but her Wacs didn't wear the green scarf of the Fifth Army for nothing. Any job General Clark thought they could do, they would damn well do.

Along the highway north of Rome, smashed German troop carriers had been pushed into ditches and off into fields to make way for Allied traffic heading toward the front lines. Here and there and especially at traffic crossings when the convoy slowed to a crawl, Jill shuddered when she caught the heavy sweet odor of rotting flesh.

By 1800 hours on Jill's watch, they had passed through the last American checkpoint and found the forward communications command center. Her WAC unit was to be billeted in the offices of a former olive oil factory, while the German prisoners occupied the main factory building. MPs patrolled outside; her Wacs were to mount interior guard.

Checking her watch again, Jill signaled Harper to her. "Sergeant, the captain wants the switchboard and the code trailer operating by twenty hundred. That means we've got less than two hours to get settled in, detail the interior guards for the German women and have the first shift report to duty. Get going on those assignments and report back to me in thirty minutes. I'll want you when I go in to talk to the prisoners. Ask the women if any of them speaks or understands German."

Inside, she climbed a short stair to a windowed office. A door to shut. Hallelujah! Privacy. But it was not to be. The office door hung by one hinge, and the office itself showed signs of recent German occupation: pieces of gear lying about, a desk tipped crazily on three legs, ransacked files. Shoving a file drawer under the desk, she swept its surface clean with her hand and wearily tossed her kit on top. Time to write to the parents of each woman in her unit again. It consumed precious hours, but she wanted to explain to them somehow that, while the job was hard and dirty for the Wacs of the Fifth Army, theirs was a tremendous satisfaction. Never again, as women, would life inspire them to such an effort as this war demanded. Jill wanted people back home to know that as tired as they were, not one of her women had returned voluntarily to rear-echelon duty when given the chance. No, there was nothing glamorous or glorious about war, as Neil had tried to tell her. But these swell women? Well, *that* was quite another story.

Jill unfolded the legs of the canvas cot that supply had delivered and spread her blankets, then stretched out wearily, clothes, dusty boots and all.

Before she knew it, Sergeant Harper was shaking her. "Lieutenant."

Jill saw by her watch that she'd dozed off for about ten minutes. "Sorry, Harper." She sat up and for a moment she thought herself incapable of standing.

"You're worn out, ma'am. Why don't you let me take the first shift?"

Harper was at least fifteen years older than Jill but seemed as inexhaustible as a mother with a toddler. Good old Harper. Strong and kind. But she, Jill, was the officer in command of this outfit. "Nothing doin'. I want you to see that the women are as comfortable as possible." She stood and put her helmet on. "What's the water situation?"

"No hot, as you might guess, but we've got cold coming through the pipes."

Jill picked up her dispatch case and started down the stairs. "Anybody know German?"

"No one."

"Not Schultz?"

"No, ma'am. Said her ancestors came over a hundred years ago. Can't speak a word."

Jill grimaced. "Okay, we'll do the best we can. I don't want to use a male interpreter if I can help it. You know, female problems . . ."

Harper preceded her into the main factory workroom. A fruity, oily smell permeated the place, although the thick stone walls kept the interior temperature cool. Thank God for that. If this place were hot, the atmosphere could gag a person.

"Achtung!"

Everywhere down the rows of cots the gray-uniformed women jumped to rigid attention, reminding Jill of the snap inspections at OC school when the fear of washing out had been palpable in the barracks. Each woman had a silver badge embroidered on the right breast of her jacket and a gold lightning flash on her left sleeve marking her as a signal auxiliary. A German Army field cap completed the uniform.

Harper asked, "Any officer *sprechen* English?"

A woman stepped forward at attention in front of Jill and thrust out her arm at a rigid angle. "Heil Hitler!"

Jill was furious. "That's *verboten!* No more Nazi salutes. Is that understood? Do you speak English?"

"I speak, *Fräulein Leutnant.*"

"Your name?"

"*Nachrichtenobersturmführerin* Heidi Giesel!"

"Harper, look at the list of equivalent ranks."

"That's a lieutenant, ma'am."

"Right." Jill's voice was as impersonal and stern as she could make it. She was determined that her Wacs would never be accused of pampering German prisoners because they were women. There were already stories coming from the rumor mill that Axis POWs in the States were getting soft treatment—that Italian soldiers were being invited to dances and that a German camp had even struck for higher wages. True or not, this kind of talk didn't sit well with a dogface doing the fighting. It wouldn't help the reputation of Wacs either. "You will stand roll call and personal inspection every morning at zero seven hundred hours, and every night at eighteen hundred hours. At morning inspection, I will expect a list of all your women who need medical attention, after which they will be escorted to sick call. You will get the same rations we get and one hour of exercise outside the building under guard. Groups of six only. I want details of women to start cleaning up this place right now. Do you understand?"

The German officer turned and translated for the others, who had remained at attention while Jill spoke. "We understand." Her manner was meticulously military and correct, but defiance was written everywhere on her face.

Jill nodded, ignoring her manner. Although this woman looked like the same ones she had seen in newsreels gazing at Hitler with rapt adoration and raising arms in the Nazi salute, she could respect her military discipline. "Good! Give Sergeant Harper here a list of the personal essentials you need and we will try to get them for you, but you'll find that we don't have many ourselves. Any questions?"

A woman down at the rear shouted a question in German, which brought a sharp word of obvious rebuke from the officer.

Jill asked, "What did she say?"

"Your pardon, *Fräulein Leutnant,* but she asked if we would be exchanged."

"I don't know. That's being decided in Rome. You'll be here until then and I expect exemplary behavior from each one of your women." Jill made sure there was no mistaking her tone. She motioned Harper to follow her to the door. "I want their gear searched—yes, yes, I know the MPs did it, but we'd better do it again. We'll be harder to fool." She left by the doorway through which she'd entered.

Jill felt a little like a miner groping in a dark hole. There were no military regulations governing the treatment of enemy women soldiers by victorious women soldiers. She was determined to be fair but not to allow these Führer lovers to think they could take advantage of the Women's Army Corps. She could imagine how they felt, though; women captured in wartime had always had more to lose than their lives. She'd heard stories of retreating Germans raping partisan women as they lay bleeding from horrible wounds. Their own GIs crowded the streets of Rome, waving hundred-lira notes in every woman's face. The sooner these Kraut women were on their way to the rear, the better she would like it.

Walking back into the office side of the factory, Jill heard Marie's voice from inside one of the ground floor offices.

"Listen, if she finds out, she'll throw the book at us and the kid. She doesn't take a crap unless the regs tell her how to squat."

Jill knew whom Marie was talking about. Damn her. Why didn't she just let it go?

Schultz was talking. "She's regular army, sure, but she tries . . ."

"The hell she does," Marie said.

Jill turned the corner, stepping hard in her boots. She didn't want to overhear any more. The group of women closed ranks when they heard her footsteps, but not before she had seen what they were trying to hide from her and heard the soft high-pitched whine of a dog.

"Brodzinsky!"

"Yes?"

"How could you have brought that kid and her dog up to a forward area?" Damn! This was a command problem the book hadn't covered.

Schultz broke in. "Lieutenant, the kid's lost her whole family and just picked up this Kraut dog because she was scared to be alone."

Then Brodzinsky spoke up, her voice softer than Jill had ever heard it. "She's got no place to go but on the streets." There was a special pleading in her voice that had not ever been there even in the MP office back at Camp Shanks. "She'll have to sell herself."

The girl Tina pushed her way between the women. "Learn *inglese* vera good," she said and looked up at Jill, straining her thin little-girl voice, obviously trying hard to remember and speak the unfamiliar words. "Work hard, eat a little."

Schultz said, "Please, Lieutenant."

Jill bent down and scratched the dog behind his ears, knowing the very place that had sent shivers of doggy joy rippling down her own dog's back. "What's his name, Tina?"

"Charlito."

"Well, Tina, Charlito needs a good brushing. And, Schultz, you get over to the dispensary and get a little delousing powder." Jill turned to Tina and drew a locket containing Neil and Bear's picture from under her wool shirt, where it clinked comfortably against her dog tags.

Tina handled the locket as if it were the reliquary of a saint. "Your dog—*bellissimo,*" she breathed.

"He's old now, but when I was your age he was my dear friend—*mio caro.*" The child nodded solemnly and Jill knew she understood both picture and words.

"Well, I'll be a . . ." Brodzinsky said.

Jill ducked her head so that Marie wouldn't see the tears in her eyes. They were distilled from loneliness, her sense that somewhere between the child she had been—so much like Tina—and the woman she was she had learned some wrong lessons. Maybe what Dee Gleeson had been trying to tell her on the ship was that a woman's strength was not in perfection, but in compassion.

Her voice was breaking but gruff. "Brodzinsky, fix Tina up with some clothes and draw some rations for Charlito. I'll have to talk with Captain Stratton about it. We're breaking every security reg in that book you don't think so much of"— Jill couldn't help allowing herself the tiny hurt pleasure of showing Marie she had overheard her—"but I promise you we'll keep them safe until we can find the right place for them."

Jill looked up and into Marie's eyes. *Can't you tell that I'm trying to become a different person from the one who let you down back at Camp Shanks?* But aloud she said, "Okay, let's break this up. Night shift better move out on the double."

42

War bonds sell in denominations of $25 to $10,000, and America purchases $135 billion. Everyone participates in bond rallies and parties, including celebrities. Betty Grable's nylons are auctioned for a war bond pledge, so are Man o' War's horseshoes. Screen actress Hedy Lamarr kisses any man who purchases $25,000 in bonds, but one man faints before he collects.

WHEN ELISABETH RETURNED from her New York shopping trip on a hot mid-June day, she found the afternoon mail delivery shoved under her apartment door, a letter from Danny Barnes on top, only the second one she'd received since he went to prison. She had meant to answer the first letter, but whenever she thought of it she was plunged once again into those last terrible, near-crazy days when she had lost Max. In recent weeks, as she grew emotionally stronger, she hadn't thought of writing.

Dropping her packages, she kicked off her shoes and opened the letter.

*Fort Leavenworth
June 6, 1944*

DEAR ELISABETH,

Isn't it just the greatest news?—the Normandy invasion. You probably think that guys in here don't care, but a loud cheer went up when the word came in over the radio—some of us trusties are allowed to have radios in our cells.

More important is the rumor of a general amnesty, which some of the jailhouse lawyers argue is almost sure to follow as soon as peace breaks out. It happened after the last war, and they say it'll happen after this one— especially for guys like me in here for non-violent crimes. That's not the only rumor. One of the guards told me the draftboards are scraping the bottom of the barrel and that some of us might get a commutation if we volunteer for combat duty—and if we survive, a full pardon.

Sometimes I think I'd have a better chance to survive in combat than in here. I know I've only been here four months, but it seems like as many years. When I think about how long it could be before I see you—well, I try not to think about it or I'd be half crazy (like a lot of the guys in here) from waiting, and subtracting days from the years left on my sentence. I still can't believe they gave me fifteen years. Didn't my good service record count for anything? That means I won't get out of here until 1959, unless there's an amnesty and they release me. *Why can't they release me?* I'm hardly a threat to democracy.

Don't get me wrong, Elisabeth. I don't regret what I did. I'd do it again in a minute, especially if I thought I had a chance with you, if you gave me one word to help get me through this. I know you can't let your husband know now while he's in the thick of things. But are you going to divorce him after the war?

Lying here and thinking back on that year we knew each other, I know you never promised me *anything,* you're too fine a woman for that, but I believe you grew to *like* me and I know I worshipped you right from the first.

Besides that, I learned to understand you because I understand what it's like struggling to find a true self. Does it sound conceited to believe I know you? For instance, I understand that you need me to soften your own idea of yourself; I understand that you have a talent for design and a feel for material which *you should not resist.* You already have a sixth sense for fashion, and you can't *learn* that even at the Parsons School. Some people call it taste, but with you it goes farther than a model's knowledge of clothes. You have *it*—talent. After the war, you could be one of the new American designers who will take the place of the French (at least until they get back into production). I've known this for a long time and I've known

that I wanted to help you do it, be a partner in your life—
in your whole life.

Do I sound nuts scheming like this, considering where I
am? I've got all the time in the world to plan. And it's all I
do. It's a way of blotting out the present, this cell, the
other men, it's a way of being who I want to be and of
being close to you.

DANNY BARNES
3217-423007

His letter sounded just like him—not demanding or begging. She liked him for that, and so she *would* write today.
That much she certainly owed him for what he had done. But
that was as far as she would go. She didn't feel guilt. Guilt
over the past was something she had suppressed all her life as
a weakness, or for perfectionist women like Jill who made a
vocation of it. Anyway, she thought almost affectionately, taking out her writing materials, the little guy *was* different from
all the other men who had deceived themselves about her. He
had a quiet kind of dignity that shone in his letter even
through his obvious anguish. She liked that. But most important, he actually thought that her ideas were important. No
other man, not even Max, had thought so. Max had done no
more than flatter her when she proposed ideas, and then he
had immediately substituted his own judgment for hers. Poor
decent Danny in jail with men who could overpower his tentative sense of himself. Yes, she would write to Danny, maybe
even encourage him to think about a business partnership. It
was a harmless enough scheme. But it *was* a dream. Where
would she ever get the money to have a *couture* business—cutters, models, showrooms? Out of the question, but how exciting to think about! At that moment she felt a closeness, almost
a kinship, to Danny Barnes. But she must be careful to nix any
thought he might have of an unchanging partnership of love
that would put her into a jail she loathed more than he loathed
his. Only one man had tempted her, still tempted her, to forgo
her need for freedom and impose on herself the heavy chains
of loving another human being, of putting him first. *Max!*
As always when she thought of him, she felt his presence
near her, the rough brush of his jacket on her arm, heard the

special sensuousness of his voice that had persuaded her once of his passion and offered her an escape from the emotional isolation she had chosen for herself. Where had she gone wrong? She had been so careful never to test his love as she had tested the obedience of other men. A bitter smile twisted her lips. In her life she had used good men, then given herself to the one man who could use her. It's a B movie, she thought, and not a very good one—the hard, unfeeling lover, the heroine coughing her life out into a lace handkerchief. Impatiently she ordered her mind to move on: except for those first few hours after leaving Max, she had never been close to dying of love. Shaking off her reverie of Max, she wrote Danny a long letter, full of just the right mix of compassion and friendship without commitment.

"Mrs. Gardner?" Her name and a knock at the door came simultaneously.

It was the apartment manager from the first floor. "Yes."

"There's a gentleman—here from a newspaper, says he—wants to see you."

Why would a reporter want to see her? "Did you tell him I was in?" she said through the closed door.

"No. Said I'd see. Then the gentleman said if you was gone he'd just as soon wait until you came back." Elisabeth opened the door to the large woman, whose florid face was flushed from climbing three flights of stairs. "Said he'd camp out on the stoop till you came home," she puffed. "Seemed that determined, he did."

The landlady looked through the crack in the door until Elisabeth narrowed it even more. She had nothing to hide, but it pleased her not to satisfy the old biddy's curiosity. "All right, Mrs. Owen, tell him to come up."

After Mrs. Owen's lumbering retreat back down the stairs, she heard lighter footsteps start up. While she waited she listened as newsboys under her window shouted the headlines of the afternoon newspapers. "Troops move up from Utah beachhead!" they yelled in their soprano singsong. It was Friday, the ninth of June, and she had just enough left of the divorce settlement money to pay her rent for the next week.

Perhaps she shouldn't have taken the train up to New York and bought the Norman Norell original. No, damn it, she had been right. Her pre-WAC clothes taken from storage immediately after her discharge had felt as if they belonged to another body. All she had wanted was to shed her uniform and be Elisabeth again, but not in the old clothes. It had given her spirit an incredible boost to buy the figure-clinging beaded evening dress with thin straps that crossed halfway down her back, a dress that swept low on her spine, softly molding to her buttocks. No, she didn't regret the purchase. In the right clothes she knew she was more than a match for any woman in Philadelphia. In this dress, if she could see Max, and he see her just once ... By now Max must have had more than enough of that spavined, horse-faced bride of his. Elisabeth's self-saving vanity was unhampered by any doubt on this score.

A snap-brim hat shoved to the back of a balding head came into her view on the stairs, followed by a face and a short square body—the man was a cliché, a reporter from central casting.

"Mrs. Gardner?" he asked when he saw her at the open door. "Walt Fracas from the *Globe-Democrat.*"

Holding the door open for him, she said, "Come in, won't you," in a calculated voice, mixing just the right amounts of ennui and curiosity. She offered him a chair. Instead he dropped his hat into the chair, walked to the window and looked down.

Not turning around, he asked, idly playing with the window-shade cord, "Think your husband's armored division is in the Normandy breakout, Mrs. Gardner?"

She was startled at his information. "He was transferred to England, but ... I don't know ..."

"And how about you, Mrs. Gardner?" he said, facing her. "Wish you were still in your country's uniform in this hour of triumph?"

On guard, she flared at him, "Now wait a minute! You have your nerve, walking in here and asking me personal questions. Maybe you'd better state your business and leave." But Elisabeth was wilting inside despite her apparent righteous anger. *What was his game?*

The reporter shifted his feet and put his hand over his heart. "Now, don't get huffy. Hear me out before you kick me out."

Elisabeth said stiffly, "Go on."

"In a nutshell, I'm working on a big story, a national story. We're after the war profiteers, the businessmen growing fat while our boys fight and die in the foxholes—making plane parts that fail under stress, selling substandard food, that sort of thing."

She didn't reply, but she was listening, trying to jump ahead of him to find an answer to the question he hadn't yet asked.

"I think you can help us with this story, Mrs. Gardner." Elisabeth opened her mouth angrily. "No, no, hear me out, because my paper is willing to pay you handsomely for that help."

Interested but wary, Elisabeth asked him, "Pay for what?"

He got up and walked around her small living room, picking up her things and then putting them down, like a small-time appraiser ready to offer her an insulting lump sum for the lot. "You're a smart lady, Mrs. Gardner, and I can sure see you're a woman any man could go for," he began in a soft voice that steadily rose in volume, "but, if you don't mind, let's cut the bullshit!"

She was silenced, staring at him, wondering why she always seemed to find herself in the clutches of sleazy little men who wanted something from her; someday, she vowed, she would have the position and money to protect herself from the Walt Fracases of the world. But most of all she was quietly raging at Max, who could have protected her from all this and had not done so. Why should she protect *him* now? Because, of course, that was what this weasel was getting at.

Putting on his hat, Fracas sat down on the chair opposite her. "That's better. Don't suppose you have a drink." He looked at her face, which was taut with rage. "No, I guess you don't. Okay, to get down to it, we want the goods on your old boyfriend Max Stryker—er, contract manipulation, cost overruns, the rotten material he used for arctic clothing, everything you know."

Relieved, Elisabeth smiled at him. By telling her he thought she knew so much, Elisabeth knew he really didn't know much about her at all.

He went on. "And there's a hundred dollars in it for you if you give us the right dope."

She laughed aloud. "Even if I *knew* what you want, and I don't, I'd never sell it so cheaply."

Angry now, Fracas said, "Don't pull that know-nothin' stuff

on me. I have a source inside the QM depot who told me all about the doctored bids and the dumb kid who took the fall for you. And, Mrs. Gardner, I've got someone who's willing to swear you were Stryker's whore."

Stung, she raised her voice. "Go ahead, use it. I *want* you to use it, and then I'll sue you and your paper for every dollar I can get." She gambled that he didn't know Marne was divorcing her. "My husband will never allow his name to be muddied by—"

Fracas put up both hands to stop her. "Okay, okay, I believe you."

"Now get out of here," she said, knowing she had the upper hand for a moment. She stalked to the door and wrenched it open.

He walked through, then turned on the third-floor landing, smiling with what she imagined he thought was pure charm. "Listen, Mrs. Gardner, we got off on the wrong foot here. Maybe if we—"

She wasn't about to relinquish the power she'd gained over the situation. "I'm not interested."

"But I bet you can use a little money," he insisted in a wheedling tone, "what with your hubby away and all. I have an idea I can help you out, if you will agree to help me out."

"No!"

"Just go to a party, the Debs' War Bond Ball tonight, with me. He'll be there. Stryker, that is."

Max? She could see Max tonight. Suspicious, she said, "How do you know he'll be there?"

"The women's page editor always gets a list of guests for these society bashes."

He's got me, she thought. To see Max she'd have to play along with this creep. But, still unsure, Elisabeth asked, "What would I have to do?"

"Not a thing but be seen with me. You see, Stryker knows we're looking into his affairs. Now, if he saw you with me, he'd get worried, and worried men make mistakes. He'd think—well, you know what he'd think."

"What if he thought nothing? He'd see a casual acquaintance at a ball with a newspaperman, that's all."

"Then the *Globe-Democrat* would be out fifty dollars."

She smiled at him pleasantly. "One hundred dollars."

"Okay, one hundred," he snapped. "It's formal. You got a formal dress?"

"Oh yes, Mr. Fracas, I've got a dress, a very special dress."

He started down the stairs, then stopped. "Seven-thirty. Sharp!" he called.

Elisabeth Gardner nodded absently, her mind racing ahead. In four hours she would see Max. She had planned such a meeting in her imagination hundreds of times; too bad she wouldn't be on the arm of a smashingly handsome millionaire, but to Max that short dump of a man, Fracas, might be the most threatening man in all Philadelphia tonight. Max might think she'd turned on him, but so what! He'd turned on her fast enough. For a few minutes she vacillated between the old physical desire for him and the new ache for revenge. Then her inner woman's voice spoke and she responded—it was the only language she had ever learned. *I must wash my hair, steam the Norell. I will be beautiful. Independent. And mysterious.*

She could see him seeing her for the first time in months, and in her mind he came to her, begged her to forgive him, and then he *acknowledged her* and only her, before all the others.

With one sweeping glance, Elisabeth saw that the ballroom contained one near-antique Molyneux dinner gown, a sprinkling of uninspired lace evening dresses from Chanel, a marvelous prewar Elsa Schiaparelli straining across a dowager rump, several Gabriellas she recognized from the '42 collection, the last one, but she saw nothing to match the slinky chic of her own gown and form. Thank God she'd had the discipline to resist the starchy army food that had wrecked so many Wac figures.

She looked down at her escort, who was running his finger inside a too-tight collar, his evening clothes giving off a pungent odor of mothballs. "Now what?" she asked, relishing the thought that she felt more at home in these social surroundings than he did.

"Now we hook our fish," he returned. "Let's circulate, and when Stryker spots us I want you to appear to be deep in conversation with me."

"Isn't that a little childish?" She was becoming suspicious of the entire scheme. "Max isn't a fool, you know."

"You let me worry about that. You just do what you're paid to do."

"Fine," she agreed, amused by his confidence, "but couldn't I be a conspirator with a glass of champagne in my hand?"

Fracas snatched two glasses from a passing waiter's tray, and as she sipped the wine her eyes, which had been ceaselessly searching since her arrival, picked Max out of the crowd. He hadn't yet seen her, so she had a chance to watch him unobserved. He stood in a small group beside his wife, who wore a tight sleeveless gown that tended to show her overlong neck and thin arms to disadvantage. Inbreeding, Elisabeth thought, sipping again, is not an unmixed blessing. And Max? He stood at Kit's side, aloof from the babble, looking tired, new lines in his face. *Good,* she thought. *Good!* She choked off the vindictive cry of grief below her voice box before it gathered a sound. *I hope you suffer, you bastard. I hope you think of me every time you get that skinny slut in . . .* Impatiently, she pushed at her hair swept high and to one side. Well, he'd made his bed. *Oh, Max—and I could have been in it with you.*

"Okay, Mrs. Gardner," she heard Fracas say, "go into your act."

The dancers swirled by to the dated rhythms of a society orchestra. Elisabeth said, "I'm thirsty," holding out her glass.

"Nix on that," Fracas countered, "I need you sober."

She let the remark go by. Stupid man! As if she could ever be a drunk. She'd even tried the solace of alcohol after Max's marriage, but she had lacked the two requisites of the successful drunkard, the ability to drink through a hangover and the desire to destroy herself. She hadn't survived Kopperstown, Pennsylvania, Marco's Fashions and the Women's Army Corps to end up selling herself on the street for a drink.

"Talk, damn you," Fracas stage-whispered. "He's looking at us."

Knowing that Max's eyes were on her, Elisabeth, her hand shaking imperceptibly, smoothed her hair again and sipped at her empty champagne glass, extending her right leg slightly to enhance the long leg line and cup the dress even more tightly under her derrière. She could have been posing for magazine photographers, and she was pleased with the living picture she had just drawn for Max's eyes. "Mr. Fracas," she said to the squat man with a forced smile, all animated attention, "do tell me about your fascinating work, running around spying on people, rummaging in wastebaskets, peering in public toilets—"

Angry, he said, "None of that smart stuff, now!"

"Careful, Walt dear. Max might think we don't get along too well and, poof, there would go your slimy scheme, which to my mind is already shaky." He forced a smile and she began to enjoy herself just the slightest bit more. "And, by the way," she said lightly, "I want the hundred now."

"Now?"

"That's right. Now. You see, I don't trust you. What's to stop you from refusing to pay after we leave here, pocketing my money and, if I complain, telling your boss I'm a liar? So, I'll take it now, if you please, or I'll make one hell of a scene and walk out; Max would think I refused you and you'd lose your game of nerves."

A smile on his face, Fracas, the image of foiled villainy, fairly snarled at her, "Do you think I carry a hundred on me?"

Smiling pleasantly back at him and raising her empty glass in a mock toast, she said, "Yes, I think you do." She gathered herself noticeably to move away.

"Wait. You can have it."

"Now," she demanded.

He palmed the bill and she slipped it into her evening bag, and, without missing a beat, she talked on animatedly for the next fifteen minutes. From side glances, she could see Max not watching her, but from the flush on his tanned neck she knew he was aware of no one else in the huge room.

A short runway was pushed to the stage, followed by Mrs. Too-Tight Schiaparelli at the microphone gushing the rules of the bond auction. The poor debs of 1944, she explained, were patriotically sacrificing their coming-out parties to help the war effort and would auction their dances for war bond pledges. "But before we begin"—the woman was standing too close to the mike—"our own Neddie Brockway, now Captain Brockway of the Army Air Corps, will tell us how our boys in uniform need our help to win through to the final victory."

"Okay," Fracas said through the applause, perspiring from his effort to be sociable, "that does it. Stryker's got the idea all right."

Outside he said, "I'll take you home."

"No you won't. I'll pay for my own cab," she said, rushing to get away from the loathsome little man. "By the way, don't ever bother me again. If you do, I'll tell him—tell Max—you're just fishing, that you don't really have anything on him."

Congratulations, she told herself as the Yellow Cab made its way through the Philadelphia streets to the working-class fringe of Chestnut Hill where she lived, you were more important to Max tonight than that bitch he married. He doesn't know that you've been loyal—that Fracas didn't get a thing. It must be driving him mad. Wonderful! Delicious! But as much as she tried to hold on to the idea that Max had a good scare coming, the old pain enveloped her, the simultaneous feelings of resentment and frustrated longing for him, not as he was but as she wanted him to be. And over it all there was a nagging sense that the whole evening had not been quite what it seemed.

Late the next morning, she was propped up in bed. She had written a letter to Bunny at Lowry telling her about the war bond ball—the parts she *could* tell. She smiled at herself for what she considered outrageous sentimentality. There was a tiny compulsion within her, almost always controlled but not yet uprooted, that wanted to open up to her friends. She had felt it at OC, and each letter from Page, Jill or Bunny seemed to resurrect it.

"Shit! To hell with introspection," she said aloud, and, grabbing a pencil from the night table, she began to sketch some of the clothes she had seen the night before, experimenting with shoulders and hemlines. She was lost in concentration when the door buzzer rang. Throwing a red-and-yellow heavily embroidered silk wrapper over her nude body, she opened the door.

A delivery man said, "Mrs. Gardner—package for you. Sign here."

The man carefully put the small box on her table and left.

Opening it, she found an antique cloisonné bowl on which an intricate design of bright butterflies and flowers formed an elaborate pattern; attached to the encircling blue ribbon, an envelope—inside, a card that said: "I had forgotten that you are the most exciting woman in the world. I must explain, must see you. M." Even without the card, she would have known the sender. Every other man who aspired to be different thought it *de rigueur* to send a woman yellow instead of red roses or a self-consciously understated single pink rosebud; such a gift as this one, Elisabeth knew well, could only have been sent by someone whose hard-won taste required him to find truly original expressions of it.

A brown rectangle fluttered from the envelope to the floor. Picking it up, she saw that it was a train ticket for the afternoon *Washington Limited* dated Saturday, June 17. One week. Only one week, she thought, until I can show him he's been wrong—so wrong.

43

Two days after the fall of Rome, the Fifth Army takes Civitavecchia, thirty-nine miles west northwest. Within two weeks the British drive on Perugia and the Fifth pushes hard against the German line centered on Lake Trasimene.

ON HER SECOND week in the abandoned olive oil factory in the hills north of Rome, Jill sat at her desk catching up on unit paperwork and writing a letter to Kaye Young, now stationed at Naples. The Wac billets had been bombed there recently, but characteristically Kaye had written that "only the ceiling and one wing" had fallen in. Jill chuckled, remembering Kaye's marvelous gift for comic understatement. Only, indeed! This was the same Kaye who had jumped "starkers" out of a shower room window and into a foxhole during an air raid. "I'd die if I got killed with no clothes on. How would I explain it to my mother?" Jill missed her friend. The rules of command and rank made friendship with the EW impossible, and Des certainly refused to fill that bill.

Sergeant Harper stuck her head around the sagging door. "Lieutenant, that German officer wants to talk to you again—privately. Says it's important. Won't tell me what she wants."

Jill frowned at this fresh problem with the prisoners. "All right. Bring her up here."

A few minutes later the woman reported stiffly, but minus the Nazi salute. "*Nachrichtenobersturmführerin* Giesel."

"Yes, yes." Jill recognized the ranking officer of the German women POWs who had acted as a translator. "What is it this time?"

"The food, *Fräulein Leutnant*. My women are used to hot food with sausage and vegetables. They will sicken on this." She flung a C-ration carton on the desk. "The Geneva Convention clearly states prisoners are to be given food that—"

Jill hated the woman's arrogance. "*We* eat those rations," she explained, reining in her impatience, "until a field kitchen can be set up. You see, Giesel, Americans do not steal from the people of Italy."

The German woman bristled. "The Italian people are traitors. They deserve no better. The Führer says our Wehrmacht can take whatever it needs."

Impatiently Jill waved her hand in dismissal. What was the use of arguing with a fanatic Nazi? Then, quite suddenly, the woman changed her tack.

"Excuse me for my bad manners," she said, smiling, her rosy cheeks and milky complexion the image of good health. "That is expected of me, but I—"

Jill interrupted, "I'm afraid you don't understand. Whether you ask politely or not, there *is* no other food to be had until the field kitchen comes up. Now I think you better get back to your—"

"I had hoped we could talk one to the other as women soldiers."

"What about?"

"Of course we have heard about the American army women, *Fräulein*, but we do not know about your training."

"I don't have time now—"

"German women are required to give a *Pflichtjahr,* what you would call a duty year, to the Fatherland. First I was a nurse's aid in the Red Cross, then I was selected for transfer to the Giessen Signal School—"

"Yes, I see, Lieutenant Giesel. I'm very interested in all this, and I'll be happy to talk about it later, but—"

A roar filled her ears, and a shattering of glass. The pane of the tilted door to the office collapsed and scattered on the floor. For a mad millisecond she was back on the *Canberra Princess,* until she saw the smile on Giesel's face, the stiff-armed Nazi salute and words her battered eardrums couldn't hear.

"Harper!" Jill yelled, and a scared Harper dashed up the steps and into her office. "Watch this prisoner, and don't let her talk," she said and ran swiftly down the steps and out of the building. To one side of the factory, an inferno leaped skyward where she had seen a small gasoline-can dump earlier. A German POW lay dead on his back, while a GI in fatigues, darkly outlined against the orange flames, writhed in a frantic dance, his clothes ablaze. Jill rushed forward, her short legs leaping over jerrycans with their sides blown out, oblivious of any danger, her entire attention focused on the burning man. Ripping off her jacket, she beat at the flames with it, putting out the fire on his legs only to see it crawl up his back and burst out anew.

The heat! She could scarcely see. The fumes! Her throat. She dropped to her knees, overcome, unable to hold him in his frenzy to escape the pain. His screams filled the night. "Oh, God, *help!*" The man was burning to death in front of her. It must have been like this for Neil. She felt rather than saw someone rush past her and forced her eyes open against the smoke. "Marie!"

"Get back!" Brodzinsky yelled at her and threw herself on top of the blackening man, beating on the flames with her hands wherever they erupted, smothering them with her body.

Jill must have fainted momentarily, because the next thing she knew corpsmen were bending over the moaning soldier, cutting away smoldering rags of clothing, injecting him with morphine. Others were busy with entrenching tools, shoveling dirt on the flames.

A soldier took her arm and led her toward the ambulance. Marie went before her, walking in a daze, holding her blackened hands like two charred steaks in front of her, skin hanging in strips. Dear God, her hands were burned terribly.

Jill stopped in front of her. She felt cold—shock, maybe—but not confused. "Marie—" she choked, her throat raw—"that was the bravest act I've ever seen." And then, somewhat lamely, she added, "And I'll see that Captain Stratton puts you in for a medal."

As if she hadn't heard her, Marie asked, "How's the guy? Alive?"

"Yes, thanks to you. He owes you a lot, Marie—and so do I."

A corpsman interrupted them and helped Marie onto one of the two stretchers in the ambulance, her head facing toward the rear doors.

"Marie, I . . ." Against the shouts and the running feet all around her, Jill struggled to say what she had wanted to say for so many months, since that night in the provost marshal's office at Camp Shanks. Marie would probably be sent back to Algiers to the hospital and then home or to a reppel depple for reassignment. They would never see each other again. "I was wrong at Shanks and, what's worse, I wronged you. I thought—oh, I don't know what I thought being a good officer was all about. But I want you to know this. I believed you, even then, though I tried not to." Jill's voice trailed off. What else could she say?

"You want me to forgive you, Lieutenant." Marie's voice was blurring from the morphine. "Well, I can't—anyway not right now. I've lived with my hatred for so long, I almost think I need it. But I'll tell you one thing—" the words were running together—"I've got my pride back. A man took it, now I took it back—from a man."

"Yes." Jill nodded, the tears starting. "Oh, yes, you did that."

"Tina—the kid—look after her."

"I promise," Jill said.

Marie was still muttering, but now unintelligibly, when the doors shut on both soldiers, woman and man, rescuer and rescued. As Jill watched the ambulance drive away, she accepted for the first time in her twenty-three years that she could live with an unforgiven fault, one of the most difficult things any woman, especially a perfect little lady, could do.

"Are you all right?"

It was Des asking the question. She hadn't seen him drive up.

"Shall I get a medic?" he said, his eyes wide with concern.

She held her palms up for him to see. "A few blisters, but not even worth treating."

"The hell you say. Those are nasty-looking."

"I can't leave now."

Despite her denials, Des called, "Medic!" Then, to her: "Are you strong enough for a reprimand?"

Jill was shocked at his words. "A what!"

"One of *your* prisoners somehow passed that Kraut POW a grenade which he threw into the gas dump while their officer was distracting you." Again he was her commanding officer.

Jill, exhausted as she was, exploded. "Knock it off, Des," she said, not caring how unmilitary she sounded. "My Wacs were responsible for guarding the prisoners from the inside of the factory, and your MPs were posted on the outside." Getting her nerve up, she continued, her pulse speeding, "Now, if I'm right, Captain, the dump which went up was on the outside. It looks like we share equal responsibility for this fiasco."

He glared at her, and then his face relaxed in a surprised grin. "Okay, Spunky, what kind of report *should* I write?"

"That you're sending the German women to Corps in Rome, where all those rear-echelon goldbricks can watch them, where the big brass will have to make a decision they don't want to make—and send them by the first available transportation." Catching her breath, she went on, "And, furthermore, that you're putting Corporal Marie Brodzinsky in for the Soldier's Medal."

"You would send such a report, just like that, huh?" Des said admiringly, and he held tight to her smoke-blackened sleeve, almost as if to reassure himself that she was still there, as the medic came up to examine her hands.

44

In 1944, railroads log three times their prewar mileage, carrying two million soldiers a month. Civilians are often grateful for standing room; the better seats can sell at a scalper's $50 markup.

WHEN ELISABETH, WEARING a cool emerald linen suit, stepped from the crowded club car into Washington's Union Station on June 17, Max's chauffeur was waiting.

"Good afternoon, Miz Gardner, ma'am," he said just as if he had never driven her home half hysterical months earlier. "This way, please."

From the train station, jammed with servicemen on the move between camps or to a port of embarkation, they drove through the heavy downtown traffic, then crossed into Virginia and stopped on a quiet Georgetown street lined with red brick town houses. Entering a rear alley, Max's man pulled into a garage and preceded her across a miniature paved courtyard lined with pots of bloom and into the house. Max waited comfortably in a sunny solarium in the rear, a shaker of martinis set out on the white wicker table.

He didn't speak, but poured her a drink and handed it to her. Tanned, handsome, smiling—the perfect host. She suppressed a bitter cry of rebellion at the bright pleasantness of it all, because she was determined to keep her cool dignity, not to betray it as she had done that winter night in his study. Seating herself, she half turned on the padded sofa to look out into the walled courtyard, the gin and vermouth searing her throat. *I will not mouth inane greetings. I will not make it easy for him.*

He said, "I meant it—the card."

Steady-eyed, she looked at him, stubbornly refusing to help.

He sat down in a nearby floral-patterned chair and leaned back. It was all he could do to keep from grabbing her; she was incredibly lovely sitting there, flashing hatred and desire at him. He would have to move carefully; show no weakness or she would devour him like a barracuda. He smiled again and swirled his drink. "What is it you want?"

She laughed, a sound incompatible with the pain of his being so near to her. "Perhaps you forgot, Max. *You* invited *me* here," she answered him, her voice as detached as she desperately wanted it to be.

Looking across at her, a questioning frown drawing a straight line between his eyes, he said, "You're not going to believe that this has nothing to do with that reporter—"

"That's right. I'm *not* going to believe it."

He continued coolly despite her interruption, "—but that it has everything to do with seeing you at that stupid ball, remembering you in my arms, knowing what you do to me."

Suddenly she could stand it no longer and the hurt fury spilled from her mouth. "Don't try to play me for a sucker again, Max. I swear that for the rest of my life I'll never trust my feelings. You taught me well. I know what you want from me; you want to buy my silence with a half hour of your precious time in bed—poor love-starved Elisabeth, you think. To hell with you!" The rhythm and cadence of her own anger, the memory of his betrayal, the ache of her loneliness, were all there in that speech. She saw him cover his eyes for a moment. Could the great Max Stryker be embarrassed or, more to the point, uncertain what to do next?

"You've changed," he said and his voice was softer than he wanted it to be. "You're harder." He saw her toss her head, her hair falling to one side of her face, sarcasm distorting her sensuous mouth. "Believe me or not as you will, but I asked you here because I haven't been able to forget you. I thought I could, but I can't forget what we had."

"Banking heiresses make chilly bed partners."

He chose to ignore her. "At least believe I tried to forget. There—isn't that what you want to hear? Doesn't every woman want to believe that a lover is forever haunted by her memory?"

It was a protest all the more convincing to her because it revealed his struggle. Somewhere deep inside her, surprise was gathering, and a faint, crazy hope.

"There," he said again, "now I've said it. That's as close to the truth as you'll ever get with me."

She spoke, sparring with him as she never had before. "To return the compliment, Max, you've changed, too. Now you're much more transparent than you were when you wanted the Army to do your dirty work for you and send me to prison. Don't you think I find it a tiny bit hard to believe that this yearning for me overwhelmed you only *after* you saw me with Walt Fracas?"

He looked intently at her, wondering how much he *could* tell her, then drew back before he went too far and she pounced.

She could see deep inside him to a tiredness, and other things she could hardly believe were there. Did she see regret, sincerity, for God's sake, the last emotion Max Stryker could fake?

"I thought you might be hard to convince." He got up, crossed to the door into the house, opened it and called, "Come in here."

A moment later, Walt Fracas stepped into the room, resplendent in a new Palm Beach white linen suit and a panama. Doffing the hat, he said, "Good afternoon, Mrs. Gardner." He stood there, blinking in the sunlight.

"Elisabeth," Max said, "I want you to meet my new director of public relations."

She caught herself, but it was too late. A small cry of consternation escaped from her and then illumination. Fracas had used her to get to Max. Of course. She had been the bait all right, but not for a story about war profiteers. The bastard had been for sale, and her appearance had upped the ante for him.

"Max, you used to buy better people," she said, happy for the opportunity to despise both these manipulators in one sentence.

Max smiled at her. "Think what you will, but I have been negotiating with Fracas for more than a month. And I was going to offer him twice what I did. Bringing you to the ball was an unnecessary little piece of blackmail, and he paid dearly for it. A woman with your background should understand a man like Fracas. At sixty-five dollars a week, he had gone as far as he could at the *Globe-Democrat.*" Max turned his sardonic eyes toward Fracas. "For the two hundred I'm paying you, you'd sell out your paper, wouldn't you, Fracas? Hell, you'd sell your sister and throw in your mother."

"Whatever you say, Mr. Stryker."

Max excused himself and followed Fracas into the next room.

"Maybe I oughtta been in the movies, Boss," Fracas said, palming the hundred-dollar bill Max handed him. "Do you think she bought that newspaperman-on-the-take story?"

"That's none of your business. Now make yourself scarce."

Max paused for a moment, absentmindedly tucking his shirt into his pants, before reopening the door. Yes, his plan had worked like a dream. When he'd decided that Elisabeth must be in his life again, he'd needed to test her loyalty. Did she still love him? Sure she'd taken Fracas' money—who wouldn't take easy money?—but the most important thing of all was she had refused to inform against him.

He stepped through the door and moved to a bright floral-covered ottoman and sat down. "Now do you see that I have no need to silence you? Can you get it through your lovely head that I may have wanted you—for yourself?"

Who did he think he was—handing her love back to her and then taking it up again whenever it pleased him? Impatiently, she opened her purse, extracted a cigarette and tapped it against the table, aware of an unbearable tension which seemed about to divide her in two. "My dear Max," she said, giving a bitter, passable imitation of Kit Longley's Main Line accent, "whatever would your wife say if she could hear you now?"

In two long steps he crossed to where she was and sat down, grasping her arm in the vise of his hand. "I have no illusions about you," he said, his words falling like pieces of gravel. "You're a beautiful fuck-up. You fucked up your modeling career, your marriage, the Army, you may even fuck me up, damn it." He growled like a cornered animal and kissed her angrily, biting, bruising, sucking, the fury of his desire throwing her back upon the sofa. Then came a mutual snatching, ripping, tossing of clothes until, locked naked together, they rolled upon the reed mat on the floor, the sexual tension of months compressed into seconds, the molten core of her radiating intense heat through her body to his. She strained upward to meet him as, cursing frantically, he flailed and probed for her center. Raising her buttocks, she grasped him in her fist and guided him home. He wants *me,* she thought. Only *me!*

She lay in a sprawl of arms and legs, his face buried in the tumble of her hair spreading from her like a golden fern. Minutes passed before she became aware of the scratchy reed weave under her body and stirred reluctantly.

Max rolled up on one elbow. After the swift violence of their lovemaking, he seemed rested, no longer tired, sure of himself. "I want *you,* Elisabeth," he said the words she had waited so long to hear. "I thought I had what I wanted, but it's not complete without you. I don't like this feeling, so don't get any ideas that you can push me further." He had to stop, had to make himself stop because he was saying too much, giving her too much—like handing a gun to a killer. "Let's just say I've found a way to have you."

She opened her mouth to say something, but he battered her lips with a kiss.

"No, don't say anything. Listen to me. I can't marry you." He frowned at her look of rejection. "No, don't kid yourself— you're a bitch, but you're an honest bitch, and marriage is not what you really want. You've had marriage, and where has it got you? It's not for you. Christ, haven't you learned that yet? Do you see yourself in an apron in my kitchen, handing out cookies to the kiddies? Don't be stupid. This is what we have, great sex, maybe the best sex the world has ever known. You'll have the finest clothes, an allowance, any goddamn thing you ask for."

She felt terribly cold. "Do you mean, sir, that I'm to be your mistress?" she said, her line deliberately yanked from a Victorian novel, striving for a sardonic tone and failing.

He shifted his bulk and stood up, looking down at her. "That's what you were *made* for," he said, and pulled on his rumpled gabardine slacks, slipping his polo shirt over his head. "You need to be pampered, and I want to pamper you. You want fine things—" He broke off and pulled her to her feet. "Come on, I want to show you something."

Naked, her hand in his, she followed him through the little house and then up the stairs, watching his buttock muscles play under the cloth of his well-tailored pants, remembering the feel of them as they knotted, straining, under her hands. He wants me, she thought, that could be enough.

Leading her through a bedroom door to the right of the second-floor landing, he threw open the closet. "I had them all moved here from Whiskey Hill," he said, watching her.

Her clothes. All the clothes—the Mainbocher suits, the Gabriella afternoon dresses—everything he had bought for her.

"Cover yourself," he said, a pleased smile on his face, "or you won't make your train."

Lovingly, she slid into a pale-blue Adrian with one-sided draping, consciously admiring her silhouette in the mirror across from the old-fashioned fourposter. "What train?"

Max, admiring her from behind, said, "Of course you can stay if you like, my dear, but I must drive back to Philadelphia tonight and we must not be seen together." He looked honestly regretful. "I would much rather have a small dinner here alone with you, but important guests are coming . . ." He left the rest unspoken because he knew she understood no matter how she might try to deny it. But, just the same, he was on his guard now, not against her but against any detectable softening on his part, which he knew she would despise. He reached into the top dresser drawer and withdrew a thick batch of stapled papers. "Here," he said, tossing them on the bed, "for you."

She picked them up. They were a property deed made out in her name, with a description of the lot and the location.

"This house is yours, Elisabeth." He took her in his arms. "I'll come as often as I can, and occasionally we could go away, after the war—the Bahamas, Mexico. We *must* be discreet, that's why Washington and not Philadelphia. Kit must never know it's you." His mouth grazed along her neck, his lips firm and full on her skin. "She may know there is someone, I don't care and she won't care, but she can't know it's you—*you* she'd resent. Understand? I'll see that your things are moved up here whenever you're ready."

Suddenly Elisabeth felt exhausted. The restless nights of the last week as she had waited to see him again, the interminable train ride, the sight of him holding out a martini, cool and desirable in the reflected sunlight, the way he had ripped the passion from her body, and now this offer to share *part* of his life with her. "Let me get this straight, Max." She didn't even try to hide the bitter irony she felt. "You want me to live in this chintz haven waiting for you to ride up and claim me in the off hours between business trips."

He made a face. "I wouldn't put it that way, and you can furnish this place as you desire. When I'm here, believe me, I'll be all here—all for you."

He was offering himself, not as she had wanted him, as his wife, mistress of Whiskey Hill, the socially prominent Mrs. Max Stryker on his arm at all the best parties, but she could have *him* with his arms around her, his warm skin melded to hers, she could have him some of the time, through some of the dark nights. The bastard! He was greedy, selfish, but she could understand that because she was those things herself. With the fingers of one hand she riffled back and forth through the clothes hanging in the closet. A defiant thought settled in her mind: *Then why can't I have him, as he has me?*

"Max darling"—she caressed his back with both of her hands, kneading it in sensuous suggestion, using her strength in the way she knew he liked—"once you told me to go back to my husband and be a good little wife. Well, what if I tried to make it up with Marne and he was stationed in Washington after the war? This could be our own little sanctuary away from responsibility and dull, gray marriages."

Max pulled back out of her arms, a sharp, sudden lurch like a slap in her face. "There's no time for bad jokes, Elisabeth."

"Joke?" she asked, understanding him but refusing to understand as well. "I'm offering you what you offer me."

He was wary now. "What's your angle? Christ, Elisabeth, I need you here, I need to *know* you're here. You've won, can't you understand that? Share you? What kind of man do you think I am?"

Salt tears stung behind Elisabeth's eyelids, but she would never give Max the satisfaction of knowing that she was a woman like other women after all, that she wanted him the way other women wanted their men, not after she had convinced him she was capable of ignoring her own feelings.

"Max, do you think I could live here like a hermit, never being seen, or doing anything, never having a purpose? I could be a designer, I could—"

"Now you're talking like that sixteen-year-old girl from Kopperstown, Pennsylvania. Don't be naïve. I'm offering you the only *real* life you can ever have. You won't have to play games with me, we know each other like no other man and woman have ever known each other." He looked at his watch and frowned. "I must go. Think about it, Elisabeth. Promise me to think about it." He kissed her again, his tongue touched her lips, her tongue, in a dozen places, sparking her desire, and then he was gone and she was left staring at the steadily blurring fourposter. Damn him to hell! He had offered her half of everything she had ever wanted out of life, more than any other man. Why wasn't it enough?

Later, that night, opening the door to her Philadelphia apartment, she stooped to retrieve a yellow envelope from the floor. She read:

REGRET TO INFORM YOU YOUR HUSBAND CAPTAIN MARNE
P GARDNER WAS KILLED IN ACTION TEN JUNE IN FRANCE
DETAILS FOLLOW.
WOOD ACTING THE ADJUTANT GENERAL

Marne dead? That big young body quiet, empty of life? His ambition, his love for her turned to hatred, gone too. Elisabeth was surprised that losing a husband she hadn't loved could make her feel such a dull sadness and regret, an emotion rare in her life. Maybe Max was right. She fucked up people's lives, but none more than her own. She had toyed with the idea of winning Marne back, it might not have been too difficult, but even that chance to turn to the once known, the safe, was gone now. Rage bubbled up in her. God damn it! Would she always have to make her life fit a man's need, as a tool for her father's ugly passions, as Marne's dream of a family matriarch, as Max's mistress-in-waiting?

She was confused. Her whole scheme of life was crumbling. Did she really want Max's vision of her future, his idea of her *real* life? No matter how much she loved him, she knew she could never depend on him. Could she learn to depend on herself?

45

In a twenty-four-hour period, June 15–16, two hundred and forty-four V-1s are launched from the German-held Pas-de-Calais against London. V-1 rockets kill 5,479 people and destroy 1,104,000 houses, schools, churches and hospitals.

A COLUMN OF orange and blue flame towered over the buildings ahead of her. Page could feel the huge explosion radiating shock waves under her feet. What was it the Germans called them? *Vergeltungswaffen*—vengeance weapons to get even for D Day. Involuntarily, she ducked as a bomb exploded ahead of her. By the time she reached the site, a smoldering double-decker bus was being evacuated. Rescue workers carried a wounded woman, moaning in a soft, high-pitched voice, on a stretcher past Page from the bus to a waiting ambulance.

Dodging from house to house and leaping over heavy fire hoses, Page, close to choking on the dust, raced on toward the Hyde Park Underground shelter. A pile of rubble blocked her way, and momentarily she leaned exhausted against the lamppost, surveying the street. She would never get used to what bombing did to a street, the empty husks of row houses, their exposed wallpaper stained by weather, a bathtub tilting crazily from a second floor. Looking into these empty homes, once clean and warm and full of people, filled her with an incredible loneliness. After a minute she ran on until she reached the shelter. A woman crashed into her, bumping a pram down the Underground steps while holding her baby on her hip.

"Here," Page said, "let me give you a hand with that."

"Thanks, love. Now, mind your own step."

Page found a niche between the stairwell and the ticket

booth, parked the carriage, took off her helmet, and lit a cigarette with shaking hands while the mother fussed with the
baby.

The woman asked, "Will you hold this bottle, Leftenant,
while I change Colin's nappy?"

Page smiled, the ordinariness of the scene calming her. "Of
course," she said and then thought how incongruous her
pose—a woman in uniform with a baby bottle held aloft to
keep it from being jostled by the pressing crowd. She finished
her cigarette just as the wailing sirens sounded. "All clear,"
she said conversationally.

"There have been so many alarms since yesterday," the
young mother said, "that I'm confused whether it's the alert or
the all clear. The *Times* called those pilotless bombs Herr
Hitler's secret weapon. Maybe I should send Colin to my parents in High Wycombe. What do *you* think, being in the forces
and all?"

"I'm as much in the dark as you are," she answered not
quite truthfully. Intelligence had known about the V-1s for
months, and the air forces had been pounding their launching
pads in France. What was worse, she knew, there was an even
more powerful jet-propelled rocket weapon at Peenemünde on
the Baltic that the Germans were sure to use to terrorize London civilians and try to break their spirit.

"Name's Pamela, Leftenant," the woman said, rocking the
pram compulsively back and forth, forever jiggling her child
as most young mothers did. "It's the bloody way they buzz
louder and louder like giant wasps and then just stop, in midair like, and fall straight down without a sound. It's enough to
give one heart failure to hear an engine cut off."

Page made a sound of agreement and gave her an American
cigarette. "I must get back to duty, Pamela." Seeing the
woman look apprehensively toward the steps to the street
level, Page added, "But why don't you stay for a while until
you're sure there won't be another alert."

"Take care, Yank," the woman called when Page reached
the stairs.

Page hesitated, then turned. "Pamela, take Colin and go to
your parents for the summer if you can."

She was happy to escape the dank, human odors of the Underground. Outside she could breathe fresh air, although even

here the air was filled with bricks newly turned to dust. Page took a detour back to Norfolk House to avoid the rubble she knew would fill the streets ahead. Picking her way around fire hoses and ambulances, she thought of the frightened young mother she'd just left in the tube. Page could understand why Londoners had cracks in their stiff upper lips these days. Everyone had been so euphoric on D Day only two weeks ago; not only because final victory was in sight but because, with their French airbases captured, the Luftwaffe bombers would soon be gone from English skies. Now there was a new threat—terrifying bombs that came day or night in all kinds of weather, high-explosive bombs that could be seen and heard. Page knew she wouldn't want to see the bomb that had her name on it.

She returned the salute of the guard behind the sandbagged entrance to Norfolk House, went to her small office and turned the light on. "Oh, sorry, sir."

General Willis opened his eyes from the club chair she had purloined from the anteroom. He looked at his watch. "Don't worry, it's time I'm off. Have to take catnaps when I can, and I thought no one would look for me in here."

The General had puffy bags under his eyes. He had probably been getting no more than three or four hours' sleep since she'd driven him back to SHAEF from Portsmouth the day after D Day. All the G-2 staff had worked round the clock several times since that day, and she herself had curled up in her leather club chair for more than one exhausted catnap.

"Page," the General said, straightening his tie, "I want you to change your billet to the Allied Women's BOQ in Bushey Park. Help us get ready for the move to France. The whole of SHAEF will shift headquarters as soon as we take Paris."

"Yes, sir," she said, hoping her regret at leaving her Claridge Court flat didn't show on her face. "Does that mean Wacs will be going to France, sir?"

"That's a matter of dispute, as you know, Page. Some staff organizers say that if women were captured they might be ill-treated, and even you have to admit that's a possibility."

Page agreed it could happen. "Any soldier captured in wartime can be ill-treated, General."

"Page, you never will make allowances for women being women. The real question is whether women can live out in the open in tents under harsh field conditions—cold rations, mud, rain."

Page started to respond, since every letter from Jill in Italy talked about just such conditions, but the General interrupted her. "I know, I know," he said, smiling, "Girl Scouts do it all the time. Well, I suspect you gals will win in the end. Can't do without you now, and things can't be more dangerous in France than they are in London today."

He heaved himself reluctantly from the comfort of the soft chair and picked up his hat and kit. "Report at oh eight hundred day after tomorrow, Page, and if you can squeeze out a few hours why don't you run down to Kent—here's the address—and say hello to your friend Paul Burkhardt. The doctors say he can have visitors now."

For a moment she had an ungenerous thought. Was General Willis playing matchmaker in her father's stead? No, she decided, he was a man who asked a lot from his subordinates but gave them extra consideration when he could, too. The important thing was that Paul was getting better. At first, when she had known he was in England in the hospital, and he hadn't contacted her—well, it was tight security, of course, but she had been dreadfully afraid he was badly wounded, maybe beyond the doctor's ability to repair, although they did wonderful things with smashed faces and— Abruptly, she swept from her mind the sudden image of Paul's pleasant face mangled beyond hope like Jill's Neil.

By evening she had cleaned out her files, sealed the boxes and marked them for security delivery to Bushey Park. The following morning, she had packed her personal belongings, seen them on their way to the BOQ, and was headed southeast into the Kentish countryside.

Page covered the forty miles to Tunbridge Wells in two hours, good driving considering that the roads were jammed with troop trucks and equipment all converging on the Channel ports. It was lunchtime when she parked in front of the old stone spa building now serving as an Allied hospital. A nurse led her down a long stately hall and pointed to Lieutenant Colonel Burkhardt's room. "Thank you, Sister," Page said.

Knocking, she heard Paul's voice tell her to come in. She hesitated and knew why. It was because she had not cried for

Paul. Tears in his name would have been welcome. They would have washed away all doubt, left her naked without the uniform that identified and increasingly defined her, tears would have left her truly Paul's. Then she could have known once and for all whether what Paul had once said was true: "Page, be very sure that you are not hiding in your uniform, using it as a cocoon to escape life as it really is, as you and every woman were meant to live it." Of course, at the time, she had told him she was certain she was not hiding and, at the time, she had meant it. But she had wondered since then whether he was right and, she, maybe, was only afraid that, after a short maidenly struggle, she'd let him rescue her like some hero of old. Whenever she thought about Paul, her mind circled and circled again back upon its own thoughts until tears, except of frustration, would have been impossible.

She opened the door. Annaliese Kaplan, wearing a hospital robe, sat beside Paul's bed, her left arm in a sling, spooning lunch into Paul's smiling mouth. Paul, thinner, his face pale, was in a body cast from neck to hips. One long leg, from which he had the covers tossed back, was swathed in bandages.

"Page!"

"Paul, darling," she said, and went to the bedside opposite Annaliese, bent and kissed him lightly on the lips. Although she was sure it didn't show on her face, she was a bit upset with herself for that proprietary gesture. How could she have made such an adolescent move? The kiss had "This is my man" written plainly on it for Annaliese to read, and Page could see by the woman's next move that she had comprehended clearly.

Annaliese rose. "Paul, I'm supposed to be having my nap now after lunch," she said, and then, smiling at Page, she added, "Sister on this ward is a martinet, worse than any drill instructor at Fort Des Moines. You'll excuse me, please."

Ashamed of herself and confused by her own feelings of competitiveness when they were so unnecessary, Page said quickly, "Oh, do stay."

"No," Annaliese said softly and slipped out.

Hesitating only a moment, Page followed her into the hall. "Annaliese," she called after the retreating figure.

Slowly the woman turned as Page came up to her. Page

didn't know exactly what she wanted to say, but in the end Annaliese spoke first.

"He's a wonderful man. You're very fortunate."

"Yes, I know." What a limp remark! She wanted to say something important to Annaliese, but she didn't know what it was.

"I'm happy that you know." Annaliese smiled, her mouth a sad little wrinkle as she continued down the hall.

Page watched her. What had Bunny said so long ago at Fort Des Moines? "She reminds me of you, Page." But how? Then suddenly Page understood the puzzle, the nagging feeling of simultaneously identifying with this woman and yet being her rival. Annaliese was not Page as she was, but her other self, the self she might have been, the self she tried to be—ready to do a job if needed, but yearning to live only in and through the man she loved. Annaliese was Page without doubts, without the call to adventure, the need for action in her daily life; Annaliese was Page with the desire to know what every day would be like for the rest of her life. This look at her other self, her conventional self, was disquieting. The peace of normality, of belonging happily to a man, tugged at her despite her crazy dreams of a military life.

Thoughtfully, she returned to Paul's room and pulled a chair to the bedside and sat down.

Paul stared at her for a long moment. "She's a courageous woman, Page."

"Tell me about it, Paul."

"I still can't reveal much, but I *can* tell you that Anna stayed at her post with me while we were being attacked. She probably saved several thousand lives."

Page leaned forward. "You were attacked by German troops."

"Waffen-SS troops."

"SS! How did you get away?"

Paul smiled ironically. "The German signal people had the jitters and, well—Page, you aren't going to believe this, then again *you* probably would—a suspicious woman Maquis leader had followed us, and she helped us hold them off until our paratroops began to land." He shook his head in mock disbelief. "I seem to be fighting this war with women, don't I?"

He said the words lightly, so that he wouldn't think how close he had come to shooting Anna to save her from the SS. If Centime had delayed another minute . . .

"How bad are your wounds? And don't tell me they're only scratches."

"Believe me, I won't. They're damned painful. I've got a broken collarbone, crushed ribs, and I might have a permanent limp from this slug in my leg. That ought to get me some attention when we go dancing at the Savoy."

Relieved by the lightness in his voice, she said, "What makes you think, Colonel Burkhardt, that I want you to have any more attention than you're already getting from certain quarters?"

Paul, wincing from the effort, reached for her hand. "When I thought maybe I wouldn't make it back, it was you I regretted leaving the most."

"And not the lovely Annaliese?" Page couldn't believe she heard herself saying such a petty thing. "Paul, forgive me. What a stupid joke!"

Paul gripped her hand tighter, excitement lighting his usually calm dark eyes. "I can't believe it! Are you really jealous of Anna, Page?" Without waiting for her to answer he went on, "Well, that's about the best news I've had in a long time. It can only mean that you—that you—" Paul broke off and pulled her weakly to him. He kissed her not as a sick man would, but as a drowning man would gasp a last lungful of air.

Breaking away, Page said, "Paul, if this is an example of the stamina of the American fighting man, I can only wonder that the war hasn't already been won."

But Paul wouldn't allow her light repartee. "Page—marry me?"

"How can I say yes, Paul? SHAEF will be moving as soon as Paris is secure." But then how could she say no and regret it the rest of her life?

"After the war," he persisted.

On her way back through the green English countryside toward Bushey Park, Page knew she must have known he would ask her. Hadn't she given him every reason to believe that she had changed her mind, that she wanted to make certain he was hers? As the smoke from the bomb fires of London rose in the east, she turned into the giant tent encampment that was SHAEF, her words to Paul echoing in her head: "Yes, Paul, the day this war is over, I'll marry you."

Page checked into the Allied Women's BOQ. British and French women officers shared these quarters with American Wacs.

"Right down hall, third on right," the young British WAAF subaltern told her when she asked for her room assignment. "And here's telephone—no, two telephone messages for you."

"Thanks," Page said. "May I use this phone?"

"Sorry, Leftenant," the DO said in a broad Yorkshire accent, "that's summit I can't do—'ficial business and all. Try booth right out door. Must 'a missed it when you came in—usually a line out there in t' evening."

"Right."

The first message was from her father and didn't require an answer, since it was in the form of a command. Dinner with Lieutenant General Dalton C. Hannaday, it said, 1930 hours, Friday, 23 June, 1944, in his quarters.

The second was from a sergeant at the 22 Upper Berkeley Street enlisted women's quarters. She dialed the London number.

"Staff Sergeant Douglas, please. Lieutenant Hannaday here."

Minutes passed while the duty NCO went to find Douglas.

"Sergeant Douglas, ma'am. Thanks for calling back."

Page opened the door to the stuffy booth for a breath of air. "Before I forget, will you do something for me, Sergeant?"

"Sure, if I can."

"Are you still assigned to the APO postal directory?"

"Yes, ma'am."

"Could you trace some letters for me?"

"That depends on a lot of things."

"I'm trying to locate a Lieutenant Elisabeth Gardner at the Franklin Hotel detachment in Philadelphia. I haven't heard for several months, and I'd like to know if she's still there."

"I'll send a tracer right away, ma'am."

"Thanks, Sergeant. Now what can I do for you?"

"Lieutenant, I know you don't have any responsibility for the enlisted women in London anymore, but I thought you could help."

"Help how?"

"Three EWs were wounded by a buzz bomb two days ago on their way to the South Audley Street mess. Nothing fatal, but they're all in the hospital."

"Give me their names, Sergeant and the next time I'm in London I'll pay them a visit."

"Right, ma'am. That's fine, but that's not what I called for. It's their Purple Hearts. This morning a colonel came by and pinned medals on all the Joes wounded in the air raids, but our gals were skipped over just like they weren't there. Ma'am," the sergeant said, her voice rising in righteous indignation, "that's not *fair!*"

"Sergeant, did anyone ask for an explanation?"

"Not right out, ma'am, but one of the nurses said she guessed Wacs weren't supposed to get wounded."

Page tried to keep the fury out of her voice. "Thanks for letting me know about this, Sergeant. I'll do what I can."

"I knew *you* would. Thanks, Lieutenant."

Page rang off. Damn! Those women soldiers lying in a London hospital had as much right to a medal for their wounds as male soldiers. A woman's flesh torn by shrapnel was indistinguishable from a man's, her blood from his blood. Page began to quickly make a mental list of people she could contact: the WAC ETO staff director, General Willis, even her father . . . For the first time all day, Paul was pushed to the back of her mind.

Friday evening at precisely 1930 hours she presented herself in a fresh Class-A uniform like any other junior officer at one of her father's command-performance dinners. Since Wacs couldn't carry umbrellas, she was grateful to the orderly at her father's front door who dashed out with one to the sedan. Another unseasonable North Atlantic storm was blowing in, the twin of the one that had almost canceled the Normandy invasion.

"The General's in his study, Lieutenant Hannaday," the orderly told her, putting her wet utility coat on a hanger. "Go right on in."

Page heard her father's voice through the sliding doors separating the outer foyer from the rest of the house. "Barneville on the Cotentin peninsula was captured yesterday, and that protects our west flank and isolates Cherbourg. We'll have it in a week. Isn't that what your intelligence boys think, Cece?"

Page heard General Willis' voice next. "Maybe ten days, if we can keep Rommel's Panzers busy before Caen."

Page slid the door open. "Good evening, Father."

General Hannaday beamed at his daughter. "Gentlemen, my daughter, Page, the best little soldier in the family, I might add—she's on Cece's staff," he announced to the others in the room.

Smiling politely, Page kissed her father's cheek, but she wasn't fooled by his introduction. She knew he pretended to others that his daughter had his blessing simply to save himself the embarrassment of admitting that General Dalton C. Hannaday couldn't control his own women.

Page moved about the room after greeting General Willis. It was comfortably filled with 1920s English furniture, complete with antimacassars and a brass dog on the hearth. One large log burned the chill from the room. Major General Charles Eliott Baker, an infantryman, and a captain from his staff completed the group. Page accepted a whiskey and chatted with the captain, who said he couldn't wait to get to France.

Page nodded agreement. "I'm looking forward to crossing the Channel myself."

"Miss Hannaday," he said patronizingly, "I'm sure we can find more pleasant jobs for our auxiliary ladies than the discomforts of a combat zone."

"Sir," she said, emphasizing the military courtesy since he had treated her like a debutante at a tea dance, "the WAC hasn't been an auxiliary force for almost a year."

Her father joined them. "Captain, you'll find my daughter is extremely loyal to her Corps, and you'll get no farther than I have trying to explain to her that war is no place for women." Warming to the attentive captain, her father went on, "During a global war such as we're fighting, women in the Army may have a use, I'd be the first to admit I was wrong about that earlier, but I try to caution my daughter against excessive involvement in a temporary military expedient. There'd be no place for women in a peacetime Army."

The captain looked from daughter to father and very obviously wished he were elsewhere. "Very interesting, sir."

Page was furious with both of them, but, like a good junior

officer, hid her feelings from superiors. "That may be, Father, but since I *am* in the Army, you would expect me to do everything I can for my enlisted women."

Looking puzzled, her father nodded yes. "I've relieved more than one subordinate for failing his men."

It had been almost too simple to lay the trap. "Then if you had men wounded in line of duty who had not received their proper recognition, you'd do something about it."

"What's this, Page?" General Willis interrupted, "Wounded men not recognized?"

"That's right, sir," she said carefully. "Army personnel wounded in the bombing last Friday who were deliberately passed over for Purple Hearts at a hospital ceremony."

"Whose men are they?" her father asked. "The regulation clearly states that all personnel in zone of combat . . . If some soldier's Congressman gets hold of this, somebody's ass is gonna get kicked."

"That's what I thought you'd say, Father. Three enlisted Wacs were wounded—"

General Hannaday's mouth dropped open.

General Willis laughed. "At ease, Dalt, she outflanked you on that one. Page, give us the particulars and we'll see whose snafu this was."

An orderly summoned them to the small dining room furnished with a fake Queen Anne table and chairs. The captain was treating her as if she had bubonic plague, so her father held her chair for her. "Where," he whispered, none too good-naturedly, "did you learn your tactics?"

"From you, sir."

Just seated, Page heard a commotion in the hall behind her and turned to see her brother walk through the door, bomber jacket, fifty-mission crushed cap and all. "Randy!" she cried and threw herself at him, so happy to see him that tears glazed her eyes.

"Gentlemen," her father said, "my son, Lieutenant Randall Hannaday of the Eighth Air Force bomber command."

Randy, an army brat, wasn't overwhelmed by a roomful of brass, Page could see, any more than she was. After correct good evenings according to rank, he was barely cordial to the captain, who was West Point class of '42, a first classman when Randy had been a plebe.

"A bastard," Randy told her from behind his hand.

She was full of questions as they sat down at the table. "When did you get to England? Where are you stationed? How many missions have you flown?"

"Whoa!" he said, and ticked off the answers. "I've been here a week. I'm stationed in Suffolk near Stowmarket. I've flown one milk-run mission to France and I have a forty-eight-hour pass because we're in a four-day storm pattern—and, Big Sister, I've been calling you in London for three days."

"I've been transferred to Bushey Park," Page explained.

The orderlies served bully beef disguised as a passable *boeuf bourguignon*, dehydrated whipped potatoes, the ever present brussels sprouts, and brandied canned peaches. The generals discussed grand strategy, the necessity for a second-invasion strike at the south of France, a quick march up the Rhone valley, a link-up, then on into Germany. General Willis gave a sketchy report of a sea battle in progress off the Philippines where our carrier aircraft were shooting up the Japanese.

"Yeah," General Baker said, "those Nip tin cans are sitting ducks for aircraft, but in the ETO it's the foot-slogging dogface who's going to win this war."

"Don't forget the tankers, Chuck," General Hannaday said. "As soon as we break out of Normandy, we're going to ride over those Heinies all the way to Berlin. No trench warfare this time."

Baker turned to Randy, his voice relaxed from the wine. "I suppose, young man, you'd say none of us would get very far without your air cover, wouldn't you?"

"No, sir, I'd have to say it's going to take all of us to beat the Nazi war machine."

Baker, who had emptied his wineglass twice already, didn't look satisfied with Randy's answer. "You don't sound like one of those glory-hog flyboys to me. After the war you should transfer out of the Army Air Corps and get into a real man's army."

Page saw Randy gulp his own wine and, careful to avoid his father's eye, say, "General Baker, after the war I don't plan to do anything of the kind. I'm resigning my commission."

She'd known it would happen sooner or later, only she had convinced herself it would be later. Everyone at the dinner table froze. Oh God! Randy had the very young's idea that honest and open confrontation could illuminate any problem, overcome any objection. Page looked at her father. She had seen that hurt, uncomprehending, angry look only once before, when she had announced she was joining the women's army.

"Randy," General Hannaday commanded, "we'll discuss this later in private."

Although Page wasn't looking forward to the battle, she longed for the dinner to end, and it did with polite excuses of duty's call following an hour of strained conversation.

After the others had left, Page quickly excused herself and went upstairs to the bathroom. She flipped a comb through her thick chestnut hair, its bright tones highlighted by the summer sun, and studied her face in the mirror. It was the face of a woman who had learned not to get between the differences of two men, not to try to become their voice of reason, their referee, their mother, satisfying neither and afterward feeling the frustration of having in some way made things worse when she had only wanted to keep the family peace.

Angry voices climbed the stairs, Randy's denying the validity of his father's idea of life for himself, the General's voice mocking Randy's maturity. She stood it as long as she could, longer than she had ever done before, and then she raced down the stairs and into the study. Her father's face was a picture of disappointed rage, her brother's of aggrieved individualism.

The General shouted on sight of her, "Christ, what have I done to deserve two such children? My coward son wants to throw away the brave traditions of a century of Hannadays, and my daughter wants to be a woman soldier!"

"One hundred years of butchers is enough," Randy yelled.

"Father! Randy!" Page said, aghast at the wounds they were inflicting on each other. "Paul Burkhardt and I are engaged," she said suddenly, as if instinctively knowing the very words that would stop them. "We're to be married after the war."

Both men looked at her.

Her father grunted. "Well, at least I have *one* child who knows her natural place in life. The professor, huh?"

Randy said abruptly, "I'll see Page to her billet, Father."

While her brother got her coat, she kissed her father on the forehead. He sat staring morosely into the fire.

"You may go now, Lieutenant," her father said as if she were the lowliest officer on his staff.

Heedless of the pelting rain, she ran to her car. "Drive for me, Ran—please."

"Sorry for that back there, Page," he said, taking a deep breath. "Look! In bomber command I could get it any time I go on a mission. If I don't have much time, I'm not going to live a lie with the old man. It had to come and it was never going to be any easier."

She nodded, her head splitting miserably from more than the argument, from more than the wine.

"Forgive me for thinking only of myself, Big Sister," Randy said, circling the car back on the road she indicated. "I forgot—congratulations! When do I meet the lucky bridegroom?"

For answer, she began to cry, the long, shuddering sobs she hadn't cried since she went away to school for the first time, a friendless army brat. She felt as she had then—suddenly, terribly and completely alone.

Randy shifted, uneasy, behind the wheel. "What's the matter, Sis, bride's jitters already?" he said in a determinedly light but still puzzled voice.

Minutes passed before she could control the deep wrenching sobs. "Ran, I can't explain it to you—maybe most especially not to you—but I . . . I have two loves."

"Christ, Page," her brother said. "You mean you're engaged to one man and in love with another?"

"No, it's not two men. I love Paul deeply—yes, I do—but I'm my father's daughter, too. Don't laugh, Randy, but . . . *I'm* old army, I'm the flag waving at retreat, I'm troops marching. I even believe in recruiting posters. Remember when we were little and Dad took us to Saturday-morning muster on the parade ground?"

"I remember."

"Remember when he'd stand there, so straight and tall and handsome in his uniform, and take the salute? I thought he was the most wonderful man in the world, and I wanted to be just like him."

"I didn't know you felt that way; I was just a little kid."

"And—something I've never told anyone—when I went away to school, at five every evening I'd hear the clock strike, and I'd ache to be back on the post, to hear the retreat cannon go off, see the flag lowered and carefully folded. I'd always stop on campus and stand at attention. Oh, I'd pretend I was looking at something, but I was really trying to be a part of the Army wherever I was."

"Sis, I—I never knew."

"God help me, Ran, but all this runs in my blood so strong and I *must* learn to live without it or lose Paul—and I love him."

He leaned over and gave her a brotherly brush on her cheek. "It's a nutty world, Big Sis. The General has got everything he ever wanted in a son—in you."

46

Broadway musicals play to standing-room-only audiences in 1944. Mexican Hayride *at the Winter Garden features Bobby Clark, June Havoc and Cole Porter's songs. At the Imperial Theatre* Song of Norway *includes the hit tune "Strange Music," and at the Adelphi Theatre Nancy Walker appears in Leonard Bernstein's* On the Town.

ELISABETH WAS CAUGHT in the noon-hour haze of late August on New York's Seventh Avenue, jostled by workers and bosses as they rushed from tall buildings to catch the few rays of sun that managed to break through the humidity. She felt supremely at home, as much a part of the human traffic of this street as the handtrucks and taxis were part of the automated traffic. She knew that the Garment District had been called a jungle and perhaps it was, but if it was she intended to be a tigress in it.

She had tried to but could not remember when she had first known she would return here to design clothes. Danny Barnes hadn't put the idea into her head; it had been there, maybe for years, hidden from sight like a hibernating crocus bulb under the snow ready to push up and burst into bloom at the proper time. That time had come when she received Marne's government insurance money, the $10,000 that, if she watched the pennies, could give her a modest start. The irony attached to the money had not escaped her. The man who had dreamed of her as some mother/goddess, the man who, she learned, had been unable to file the final divorce papers, by his death had provided the seed money for her independence from men like him. It was her truth and she saw it clearly, so she accepted the faint twinge of regretful memory for the fallen Marne as her truth, too. She could acknowledge it and at the same time be happy about the money.

Turning right off Thirty-eighth Street onto Broadway, she headed for her sublet near Herald Square, stepping into the street to avoid the double lines waiting at Walgreen's for a ration of two packs of cigarettes.

During the past week she had explored the Garment District from Fortieth Street to the low Thirties and a block or two on either side of Seventh Avenue, getting to know each building as she never had done when she worked for Gabriella. She was patient. Sooner or later she would find just the right loft for her workroom. Until then, she must ground herself in a crash course of art history, the principles of design and a knowledge of fibers and how to adapt them. After that she would learn everything she needed to know about the production end of the fashion apparel business.

The intensity of her ambition clutched at her. Several times during the past week she had weakened, wanting to scurry back to Max's arms, but she could not let herself. Elisabeth had nothing but contempt for self-haters, even the ones who fought it. Years ago she had decided that the only way she could survive in the world poor, female and beautiful was to never doubt her right to do whatever she wanted. Never.

Something about the hot, muggy day reminded her of the afternoon two weeks before when she had told Max of her decision. The Washington heat had been oppressive that weekend, and her complaint about it had brought a promise from Max to have air-conditioning installed in the town house after the war. "I'm not going to live here," she had announced, as surprised as he at the vehemence in her voice.

He had sat down on the fourposter, irritably slapping at the folds of the dressing gown that partially covered his nakedness. "Your husband's dead; you have no ties," he'd said enumerating the details of her availability. "Christ! Freud was right. Who knows what a woman wants?"

She had put out her hand and grasped his shoulder to keep him from turning away in anger at her words. "Max, I want to try to be a designer." He opened his mouth to argue, but she rushed on. "I said *try.* If I don't make it I'd be content with whatever life we could have here together."

Max had been furious at the idea that he could come second in any woman's life, but he had grudgingly acknowledged that they could be together as often in New York as in Washington. In the end, although he adamantly refused her one penny's worth of financial support, he was still magnanimous for Max. "I don't want you to have any doubts. And when you've got this childish fantasy out of your system" —his confidence in her ultimate failure almost sabotaged her resolve—"you'll see I know you better than you know yourself."

She had been satisfied with that. The old Max would never have seen the need to indulge her in her own way. For that matter, she knew, the old Elisabeth wouldn't have asked.

Entering the canopied door of her building, she let herself into her ground-floor apartment, stripped and lay across her bed, exhausted by the crowds, by the humidity and a little by her own audacity. *I can't do it. It's too hard. Too much against it. Max will win in the end, and maybe I really want him to.* She realized she was breaking her own rule against self-doubt, but she had worked so long and so hard for Max's approval that without it she felt unsure. She argued on with herself, but she always came back to the idea of Elisabeth Gardner, fashion designer.

On impulse, she threw a wrapper loosely about her shoulders, sat down at her drawing table and pulled out a piece of stationery. She didn't know what had made her send Page's last letter back marked "Addressee unknown," or what now made her write except that Page was one of three people in the world she could trust.

August 25, 1944

DEAR PAGE,

I'm out of the service—discharged. I'm not pregnant or anything. Someday I'll tell you my side of it if you want to know. Until you hear it from me, don't believe any lies.

Today, the radio is full of stories about the Allied march into Paris. If I know you, you won't be far behind. You always did seem to know just where you were going.

I used to envy you that. Now I have something I want very much. (Maybe you had something to do with it.) I'm studying and working hard to become a fashion designer. It's not easy. Not that I haven't done difficult work in the past—when I think of what I went through at Fort Des Moines!—but this is different. Success doesn't depend so much on what I do as on what I am, I mean what kind of talent I have inside me.

Remember when the four of us used to talk in the barracks about all the things we wanted? Well, I thought some man would give me everything, now I want to get one thing for myself. I can see you smiling at me for being sentimental. Don't you dare tell Bunny. But say hello to her and to Jill when you write them.

Elisabeth put the fountain pen down and blew on the last few lines, which were still wet. She felt foolish, as she always did when she caught herself being honest. It had happened so rarely in her life that she was wary of the feeling—somehow secretive, as if she had done the wrong thing.

She lay down once again on her bed, angry at herself, and puzzled. Why did she have this need to confide in Page like some silly shopgirl seeking sympathy from another over a lunch counter? She had always known that friendship, for her, was a snare. When she'd left Fort Des Moines, she had rejected any lurking need for it. Elisabeth's mind turned on these questions, until, finally drowsy, she fell asleep.

The telephone roused her. A sudden August shower had

cooled her room, a temporary breeze billowed the organdy curtains and blew across her bed. It was almost as if the room breathed.

Her voice muffled, she said, "Hello."

"Darling." It was Max. His voice caused her cool, damp skin to prickle.

"Are you in New York?"

"Yes. I'm going with a theater party to see *Mexican Hayride* at the Winter Garden, but I'll plead an early meeting and beg off El Morocco afterwards. I should be at your apartment by eleven-thirty. We'll have a bite together."

Elisabeth couldn't help herself. "Literally?"

Max laughed. "You have an almost ribald sense of humor, Elisabeth. You must read Boccaccio." And in a quasi-serious voice, "But you must also learn to curb such enthusiasms on the telephone."

"Then, Max darling, what *will* we talk about?"

"Tell me about your day."

The questions she'd had earlier about him, about anything, vanished. Only Max—seeing him, being held in his arms— mattered. Only within the sound of his voice was she real, only with him did pleasure have a chance to outlast pain. That was her truth.

She cradled the receiver between the pillow and her ear. "Max, I've got so much to tell you." Enthusiasm broke through caution. "I've been over every inch of Garment Town—"

"Listen," Max broke in, his voice carelessly hurtful, "I'll say this just once. I don't want endless, girlish gush about your *career*. I just want you to get it over with as fast as possible—to come to your senses. I won't open any doors for you." He stopped and she could hear his measured breaths. "One thing I did do. I closed one old door. Marco's put the arm on Joe Bonine." She started to interrupt. "No, don't thank me. I wanted to protect that beautiful face of yours, from purely personal motives. I must hang up." And she could almost see the dark concentration of his face, the pulling away from her. "My party is at the door. I'll see you later, and wear the Norell—this time just for me." He hung up.

She sat up in bed wide awake, her thinking a series of fragments of what she must do to prepare for him. Champagne.

Food. Bath. Dress. Wait. Damn! Max went to see a hit musical while she waited like the mad wife in the tower for a midnight visit.

Elisabeth cradled the hard black telephone, surprised that the tears and frustrated shivering she never gave in to were so close to the surface. Wouldn't Max be surprised if he could see *this* Elisabeth Gardner? *To hell with it!* She would show him the face he wanted now, but at the same time she would see what she alone could accomplish. Then she would show them all—her father, Madame Gabriella, Page, Bunny, Jill, even Colonel Nickolson and Danny. And especially Max Stryker.

47

During the 1944 American-Australian offensive against Hollandia, New Guinea, 3,300 Japanese are killed and 600 are captured. More than 7,000 enemy soldiers flee into the jungle, heading for their base at Sarmi 145 miles to the west. Only 500 of them make it; most dying from wounds, starvation and sickness.

ON AUGUST 25, 1944, Bunny and her group of Far East Air Forces Wacs took off from Brisbane for the next stop, Hollandia, on the north shore of New Guinea, about eight hundred miles beyond Oro Bay. They were the first WAC detachment and the one to be closest to combat in the Southwest Pacific area.

Bunny walked down the C-47's benches facing each other, checking to see that her women were buckled up. "Look," she ribbed them to distract the ones with takeoff jitters, "when the jump light goes on, I want everyone to form a line *in front of me.*"

"Go on, Sarge," the group razzed back. "Anyone from New Jersey goes first."

Vicki took up the banter. "They're going to set us down nice and easy, you'll see. There are a thousand GIs to every one of us. We'll be like Dorothy Lamour on a desert island."

A howl went up from a corporal near the tail section: "In this getup? Have to be a pretty desperate GI to mistake my winter coat with liner for a sarong!"

After the thrill of takeoff, they quickly became bored with the steady engine drone and began to doze or write letters to pass the time. Hours later, they arrived in a downpour that stopped abruptly as they clambered down the ladder hooked to the plane. Swirls of steam rose from the ground, from their wool clothes and backpacks, from the metal plane. Bunny had never known such humidity, so thick every breath was almost liquid.

"Ma'am," she said to Captain Mary-Ellen Bright, "if we don't remove our coats and packs, some of the women will faint."

"Right, Sergeant, and I'll find out where our transportation is." Perspiring, the captain headed toward the ops hut, walking a gauntlet of curious soldiers.

Bunny heard a gasp behind her.

"Bun-ny!" Vicki said in a shrill, scared singsong and pointed to the tail of the plane.

From around behind the tail section walked a native wearing a heavy shell collar, a white shell disk in his nose, a belt of beads and nothing else. "*Olman,*" he said, hitting his arm. "Camels," he said, pointing to Bunny.

Was she supposed to give natives cigarettes?

Before she could decide what to do, he reached out and touched the Hobby hat hanging from her cartridge belt, giving her the universal shrug and raised eyebrows that meant curiosity. Bunny took off her helmet and placed the Hobby hat on her head. The black man's eyes opened wide, dancing with covetousness, and he threw her an enormous toothy grin. He removed one of the shell collars that circled his throat and pushed it toward Bunny.

"Better give it to him, Palermo," one of the women snickered. "He doesn't have a heck of a lot more to take off."

"Stand easy, and don't interfere with international diplomacy."

The exchange was made. Bunny tied the heavy shell collar

over her uniform, and the native strutted away, the Hobby hat perched on top of his elaborate hairdo.

"Do you think we've started a fashion trend?" Bunny asked, barely able to keep from laughing until he was out of earshot.

Vicki joined in. "He looks better in it than we ever did."

Three trucks drove across the packed earth airstrip and stopped in front of the cargo plane. A soldier jumped from the cab of the lead truck and crossed the area with a casual, long-limbed walk that became a swagger only when Bunny noticed a cigarette dangling confidently from the corner of his mouth.

"Welcome to paradise, ladies," he drawled in a deep, easy baritone, giving them a calculatedly boyish grin, which was, Bunny could plainly see, all the more irresistible because of the effortless male assurance behind every gesture of his rangy, muscular body. "Breckinridge T. C. Smith, of Tennessee, currently private in the AAF, at your service," he said and swept his helmet into a magnificently cavalier bow, exposing damp blond curling hair that would have melted the hardest female heart.

Bunny saw that her women were entranced by the display. The same women who had had their pick of GI dates for months now seemed shy, high-strung, aquiver over a handsome guy with a well-timed gesture. Her sixth sense, and all her other senses as well, detected a lady-killer. Well, *she* wouldn't fall for his Rhett Butler charm.

She said in a crisp sergeant's voice, consciously pulling rank, "Private, your paradise feels more like a steam bath. We'd like to be on our way to the WAC area, if you don't mind."

Bunny could tell she'd embarrassed the others with her brusqueness, but there was no going back. "Hansen, get the captain, will you?" she asked, seeking to break the last remnant of the spell this man's abundant sexuality had cast.

He stared at her with just that bittersweet air, that how-could-you-misunderstand-me-so look, that reminded her hauntingly of Johnny. She could see that battle had been joined, that behind his startlingly blue eyes he welcomed her indifference as a direct challenge to his manhood.

"Let's go, Sergeant," the captain said, arriving with the field transportation officer.

The GIs gathered in a circle around the small group of

women, leaped to carry their duffle bags and eagerly helped each Wac hampered by a tight skirt into the trucks. Bunny took a seat in the cab of the second truck, and Private Smith climbed in behind the wheel.

"Thought you were driving up front," she said, noticing an unfaded patch on his shirtsleeve where a tech sergeant's stripes once obviously had been sewn.

"No, *ma'am*," he said, exaggerating the "ma'am" in a slow Southern way. "Since I assign drivers, I gave myself this *particular* truck."

Bunny pretended she didn't get the emphasis, although she suspected he felt her discomfort whether she showed it or not. Either was a point for this kind of man in a game of rough-and-tumble wits. "Do privates command truck assignments in Hollandia?" she jabbed at him.

"Well, Sergeant, these stripes just come and go so regular like that the motor pool officer don't pay them no never mind."

"Were you busted?"

"You could call it that, ma'am. You see, I had a little jungle juice distilling last week and the old man stumbled on it during a snap inspection."

"Too bad."

Private Smith smiled. "It doesn't matter a hoot because—" he kept her guessing for a few moments why it didn't matter while he negotiated a turn in the winding road—"I supply the officers' club with the best high-proof stuff they can get this side of Kentucky mash. When they run out, I'll get my stripes back."

All this was imparted in a matter-of-fact voice that had no air of bragging or toughness about it, but instead a touch of great good humor. Bunny began to be unsure, to think she might have made a hasty evaluation. He was an operator all right, the kind of enlisted scrounger the Army produced in war or peace; a finagler who supplied off-limit luxuries seemingly out of nowhere and nothing. Was he a threat to her? Or just a poor Southern boy trying to stay alive and make a few bucks at the same time?

"Got a cigarette?" she asked, calling a temporary time out.

"Sure. Luckies, okay? Go ahead and keep the pack. They're free."

"Free?"

"That's right. Fags are free because some Jap patrols are still holding on up in the hills. That means Hollandia is considered a combat area. When it's secure you'll know, 'cause we'll have to pay a dime a pack."

They drove out of the jungle into a clearing at the foot of the Cyclops Mountains. Two rows of tents were pitched a little distance from a corrugated-tin-roofed building.

Smith pointed to the building. "That's the Jap officers' mess hall over there, and," he added with a show of pride, "your tents have wooden floors. That's first-class barracks in New Guinea."

He jumped down from the truck and helped Bunny carry her duffle bag into the first tent. "You gals stow your gear where you want it, and I'll be back with everything you need in a couple of hours."

"How did you get to be in charge of this detail, anyway?"

"Well, ma'am," he said with a trace of what sounded to her like self-satisfaction, "I lost the Wac lottery."

"The Wac lottery?"

"When you got ten thousand guys all wanting to meet sixty Wacs, well, you can see that my lottery—"

"Your lottery—you mean you sold chances to meet the plane?"

He shrugged. "Of course."

"But you said you lost."

"Only in a manner of speakin'. I bought one winning ticket—promised to cut the guy in on my first batch of mash. So then I guess you could say I sort of won after all."

He grinned at her from the step on the truck, a languid, cocksure curl on his lips that was wildly irritating to her. That was why she was surprised when she felt an involuntary smile tug at her mouth.

"That's better, that's a lot better. As my Granny Smith would say, 'That covers the thing from A to Izzard.' Now I've got to skedaddle, if you want me back with your chow."

Vicki Hansen watched the truck jounce back down the road that was little more than two ruts cleared of underbrush. "Hubba, hubba! He's some smoothie!"

"You said it. Whew! What a line."

"Bunny, I thought you were awful mean to him and so did the others. We were talking about it coming out here. Never saw you turn on a guy like that before. The heat got you?"

"Forget it, Vic. Guess I'm just seeing ghosts where none exist." Bunny wished she felt as sure as she sounded. Then why shouldn't she be sure? It was a big base. She'd probably never run into Private Breckinridge T. C. Smith again.

Captain Bright stuck her head through the tent flap. "Palermo, as soon as you're unpacked, meet me in the mess hall."

"Yes, ma'am. Give me five minutes."

Bunny spread her blankets on the cot and unpacked her duffle bag. All of her clothes had a musty odor about them. There were no bureaus and no rods to hang anything on.

Vicki Hansen wailed from the back of the tent, "Bunny, where are we going to put things? There's no furniture."

"Let's ask Breck Smith," someone suggested. "He said he would do anything for us."

Bunny muttered under her breath, "I'll just *bet* he would," and, knowing she was unreasonable, quickly headed for the tin-roofed mess hall.

The captain was waiting for her, poking through debris. "Sergeant," she said, "I'm putting you in charge of assigning details to get this mess hall cleaned up. It must be ready for our Wac cooks by the time they arrive in two weeks. You can make up a detail roster and I'll see it's posted."

"Yes, ma'am." Bunny eyed her surroundings skeptically, looking at the wrecked tables and kitchen equipment. "Can I have the women do it in the evenings? When it's cooler, I mean."

"That's a good idea, Palermo. And you can requisition some men in here for the heavy work, too. That accommodating private said he'd see we had all the volunteers we needed. Look, I'm going to rely on you until I get a regular first sergeant. I know the T/O calls for more rank, but I can't get you a promotion right now. Think you can handle it along with your darkroom duties?"

"I'll certainly try to."

"Good. I appreciate this, Palermo. A woman with your background, first OC class and all—well, I rely on you even though I know you didn't exactly volunteer for this duty." The captain's voice trailed off as she moved toward the door and a dozen other command responsibilities.

A few minutes later, Bunny retraced her steps to the tent to get her clipboard and roster. It would take her an hour or more to make assignments. Some of the heavier equipment would have to be moved by men. Why not ask Private Smith—Breck, Vicki had called him—to get some muscle for her? Speak of the devil! The sound of grinding gears and squealing brakes told her he had returned. Through the tent flap she saw him unloading K-ration cases with two other GIs, his cigarette dangling from his mouth, several Wacs giggling like cheerleaders on the fifty-yard line whenever he looked their way. Oh, to hell with them, she thought, more than a little surprised that she was so thin-skinned about the private and his cheering section.

Vicki appeared a few minutes later. "Bunny, Breck wants to see you."

"I'm busy."

"He said you'd probably say that, but he only wants a few minutes."

"Damn it, Vic, I don't have time to play games with him."

"He said you'd say that too, and to tell you it was strictly business."

Out of excuses, she put down her rosters and went out to the unloading area. "If I wasn't getting paid so much for this job," she grumbled at Vicki, "I'd quit."

He was waiting, lounging on a tailgate, his fatigue hat pulled over his eyes.

Bunny asked, "You wanted to see me?"

"Yes, *ma'am,* very much," he answered, his voice insinuating a meaning she chose to ignore.

"Well?"

"Here's your rations for the next few days," he said in a businesslike voice that, if anything, was more mocking to her ears than before. "I've brought your Atabrine so that you can have nice yella eyeballs like the rest of us, and . . ." He ticked off a number of necessities—salt pills, a Lyster bag for drinking water. "And for you, Bunny—that's your name, isn't it?— I've got some blackberry jam and crackers."

Bunny thanked him. "We'll *all* enjoy the jam, Private," she said pointedly and handed the jar to Vicki, who was watching this exchange with her mouth half open.

"Oh, *thank* you, Breck." Vicki's pretty little face radiated her habitual wonder at the eternal inventiveness of men.

Breck jumped down and put a hand out to stop Bunny. "What's your hurry? Wait a minute. After you gals chow down, I'll take you to the quartermaster salvage dump. There's enough there," he said, challenging Bunny, "to make even you smile, Sergeant."

"We'll see," she said, finding it impossible to stay mad at him. She walked over to the K-ration cases and picked out one of the square boxes. "That's what I was afraid of, beans and weenies. Do you think you could get us more stew or canned beef the next time, Private Smith?"

"Breck, my name's Breck, Bunny." He threw Vicki a dazzling smile and then went on in the unctuous voice of a travel guide, "And that's what I'm here for, ladies, to make your stay with us in beautiful Hollandia the high point of your Southwest Pacific tour."

Bunny smiled at his antics. "Sorry, Breck, if I've made some wisecracks."

"Well, that's mighty *decent* of you, Miss Bunny." Breck went into his Southern-rube routine, which Bunny already suspected was something he hid behind. "As my Granny Smith always says, 'What's bred in the bone'll come out in the flesh.' "

He walked over to help with unloading the other trucks while Vicki turned from his departing figure to Bunny, her eyes envious. "Gosh, listening to you two is just like watching a Spencer Tracy–Katharine Hepburn movie."

That evening as Bunny sat in the ruined interior of the former Jap mess hall, she had to admit to herself that Breck made good on his boasts. He wasn't just a blowhard. Their trip to the QM salvage dump had scavenged large hinged wooden boxes, crates, tin cans, nails and broken office furniture, enough to make their tents more homelike and the orderly room a functioning office. Breck had promised to rig a shower the next day and show them how to wash their clothes in cold water and press them under their mattresses by sleeping on them.

She was just winding up the detail list—benches and tables to be salvaged, stoves to be junked—when a noise from the kitchen distracted her. Perhaps she had jarred something loose as she poked around or maybe Vicki had come in the other door. "Vicki. Is that you?" Vicki didn't answer. "Victoria Hansen, you're too old for hide-and-seek!" She smiled in the direction of the noise, but no Vicki stepped out of hiding. Her imagination was playing tricks on her, or the jungle noises, the native drums in the distance, or the oppressive humidity even after dark had her hearing things. Bunny bent to the lists on the clipboard. The flight, the tension between her and Breck, squaring away the tents and now this weather—all of it had sapped her energy.

She heard no further sounds, but she gradually became convinced, without raising her head, that she was not alone in the mess hall. Jungle fever, she thought, trying to josh herself out of the mood, but she could not. The sense of being stalked was too strong in her, strong enough so that she slowly edged her hand toward a loose two-by-four that had once braced a mess table.

For several minutes she sat, tensed, her hand closed around the makeshift club, its solid construction and sharp angles comforting her. Then she saw him, or rather she saw his shadow in the faint light of the camp lanterns filtering through the windows. He was making his way around the perimeter inside the mess hall, edging toward her. Now the light from her own lantern glinted off the bayonet of the rifle he held in one hand pointed toward her. His bloodied other arm dangled loosely at the side of his tattered Japanese Imperial Army uniform. He drew closer to her almost as if he were shy with this enemy woman soldier standing in his mess hall. She saw his lined face, short black hair, fevered eyes, straight white teeth clenched, the lips pulled back, old sweat staining his collar salt white.

He waved the rifle at her and said, his voice low, taut, questioning, *"Onna no heitai?"*

She rose from her seat, looked at him, numb with helplessness. He was very close now. She raised the two-by-four. He wavered, and she realized he was terribly sick; then he jabbed at her with his bayonet. She felt a numbing sting, then saw a dark wet trickle of blood run down her arm. He dropped to his knees with a soft little thud, the rifle weaving back and forth in front of her.

"Don't, please don't," she pleaded, knowing he was about to shoot her.

His head lolled to one side and his voice was harsh and desperate. *"Okuni no tame,"* he gasped, *"nara yorokonde shinuzo,"* and brought the gun up against his chest to steady it.

Her mouth was cottony dry, her tongue refused to form a scream. Then she heard his teeth snap together, followed by the *thrump* of her two-by-four hitting his head—or was it the other way around?

"Are you okay?" Suddenly, Breck was speaking urgently beside her. Did he always turn up when a girl was in trouble? She'd have to ask him that sometime, she thought, her mind in a silly torpor.

"How did you get here?" she began.

He gently loosed her fingers from around the two-by-four and threw it under the table. Then he held up her arm to inspect it, opened his musette bag to retrieve some sulfa powder, and sprinkled it on the wound. "We're walking guard all night until we can get barbed wire up. One of the guards saw this guy sneaking in"—he motioned to the Japanese on his knees slumped forward on his rifle in an almost prayerful position—"and thought it was one of our randy guys plannin' to do some impromptu courtin'. When we realized what was goin' on we had to get in position to get a clear shot, 'cause if we'da missed, we were afraid he'd shoot you before we could get off another round. I was just ready to squeeze the trigger when you let him have it."

Suddenly weak and nauseated, she asked, "Is he dead?"

"Yes. But from the looks of him he was mostly dead already. Now I'd better get you to base hospital so the doc can look at that arm."

"Thanks, Breck, I . . ." she said, aware that other Wacs were crowding outside against the windows, all talking at once.

"Don't pay it no mind," Breck Smith said, a mock grimace on his face. "When we put the WAC area off limits, we mean it."

"You're screwy, you know it," she said, holding on to him as they made their way through the crowd to his truck. In her pain, she could see him clearly as he really was. He was athletic, not predatory; his eyes twinkled and his mouth was droll, not calculating. He laughed easily and often, and his voice was the kind of soft, gently mocking adult voice that children loved.

"Right you are, Bunny dahlin', and I expect I'll get a whole lot crazier before this is over."

He means the war, she thought, but she didn't ask him as he helped her climb into the deuce-and-a-half, which he slammed into gear. They raced through the night to the base hospital.

———————— **48** ————————

General Charles de Gaulle enters Paris at the head of Free French forces. The German garrison commander, General von Choltitz, surrenders in the luggage office of Montparnasse Station after defying Hitler's order to destroy Paris.

ON THE EVENING of Friday, August 25, Jill turned the old-fashioned brass key in the door to lock her room in the Excelsior Hotel. Rome! She could scarcely believe that she had awakened to the sound of the bells of Santa Maria Maggiore dueling with those of Saint Paul's Outside the Walls, that she had lunched at a sidewalk café on the Via Veneto and viewed the majestically crumbling Roman Forum from the terrace of the Piazza del Campidoglio. Now, dressed in her Class-A uniform for the first time in months—it felt like a clinging satin gown and her dog tags like the most translucent rope of pearls—she walked to the mezzanine and descended the staircase to the lobby feeling like royalty. A countess at the very least.

Des was waiting at the bottom, brass insignia glowing, wearing a new uniform which fit his tall, lithe form like the most elegant white tie and tails. "Is Tina asleep?" he asked, but his admiring eyes were riveted on her.

"Yes." She was pleased by his genuine concern for Tina. An emotional response to the tiny cheerful girl and her huge dog had been one of the few things they had ever agreed on. "She's stuffed full of *cioccolata* and worn out from the excitement of seeing a big city for the first time. I spoiled her today. I'd be a terrible mother."

"I don't think you should judge your capacity for motherhood by Tina. Not many twenty-three-year-old mothers have twelve-year-old daughters. You're more like a doting aunt."

As they moved toward the huge revolving doors, Jill had no reason to quarrel with what he said or to look for some ulterior motive. Since the terrible night of the explosion two months earlier, they had drawn closer into—well, she thought of it as a working partnership to help Tina. Anyway, what Des said in a casual way was true: she *was* foolish to fancy herself Tina's mother. But insanely she'd begun to hope since she promised Marie to care for the girl that maybe she *could* be her mother, in a real sense—that she could adopt her and take her home to California with her after the war. If she and Neil couldn't have children—well, Tina could complete their family. She liked the picture of the three of them on the ranch. It gave her plans for her life with Neil more substance. She had even written to him about it, but had received no answer to this or any of the other letters she wrote faithfully once a week. Continuing to believe that she and Neil would share their lives after the war had become a pitched battle between her determination and his silence. But her determination remained strong because she fed it with all her perfectionist's belief that only she had harmed Neil and only she could save him. She needed her strong will for more than her struggle to keep Neil in her vision of life; she needed it to balance her physical desire for Des Stratton, which was even stronger than it had been at Presenzano.

Des was speaking to her as they walked toward his jeep. "Jill, I've made an appointment for you to see the sisters at the displaced children's orphanage."

"When?" She instinctively resisted the idea, even though she had agreed when they started for Rome that it would be best for Tina to be turned over to her own people, at least temporarily. The child couldn't continue to move up behind the lines with the Fifth Army Signal Wacs.

"Tomorrow afternoon."

"So soon?"

"It's the last day of our three-day pass. Besides, the longer you're here with her the harder—" He interrupted himself and handed her into the jeep. "Listen, Jill, tonight is the only night we'll have in Rome for God knows how long. Let's make the most of it. Have fun. Get drunk. Forget the war. We could even let go and pretend to be just two ordinary people, a man and a woman—a guy and a gal . . ."

She laughed, wary, but having fun already. "Okay, I get the idea." There was something so appealing about his request that she didn't want to listen to her better judgment. He seemed to be offering so much, maybe a real friendship was possible after all.

Des swung into the driver's seat and bent to turn on the ignition. "How did the hotel take having Charlito as a guest?"

"He didn't sign the register," she returned, "so they don't know for certain that they have a furry guest. But I think they're suspicious, especially since they heard my GI blankets barking on the luggage cart."

They bantered about the dog calling room service for a bone and putting his paws outside at night to be shined with her shoes, and as they drove down the wide main boulevards they were laughing, carefree. At that moment, unbidden, her mind questioned her commitment to Neil, because she was terribly conscious of feeling nothing tangible, physical, for him, and intensely aware of every movement of this man beside her.

Des pulled up to a club displaying an off-limits sign although several high-ranking men with girls on their arms were on their way inside. He leaped lightly down and came around to help her. "Now I know what you're thinking, Miss Rule Book, but it's either this or the O club and a whole evening with some fat Finance Corps major telling us how tough the war is." He put up his hand to still the protest he expected. "Everybody goes here. It's the most popular R-and-R spot in Rome. As your commanding officer, I *order* you into this clandestine speakeasy. Think about it, Jill, a den of iniquity, and it's all ours." She had never seen him so full of fun, so much like the carefree college boy he must have been.

Why not? Just this one night she'd forget she was descended

from eight generations of honorable Virginia Henrys and be a girl on the town with her guy. She left her hand in his and they descended into the noise. Wispy clouds of blue smoke hung over the dance floor, and ringed around its walls were wine-sodden GIs, some in various stages of falling down.

Des found a small table, so small their knees touched underneath. "What do you want to drink?"

"I don't know," she answered above the din. "I've tried Chianti, but it's too sour."

Des nodded and caught a passing waiter, who soon returned with a colorful red-and-blue bottle.

"You'll like this," Des said, pouring her drink. "It's Cinzano, a sweet vermouth, and the Italians have it for a cocktail, like we'd have a Manhattan, but watch out for it or you'll have a hellish hangover."

She sipped it. Then took a swallow. Sweet with bitterness lurking under the aromatic taste—like a cough medicine, but not like one. She had never tasted anything like it.

"How do you know so much about Italian wine?"

"I was here before the war, one of those guys who shipped over on a cargo ship and hiked around Europe after college trying to hold off growing up." He raised his glass and touched hers. "Here's to dumb kids who, for one short summer at least, think they have all the right answers."

"Dumb kids," she echoed the toast, remembering her own childish sureties. "Did you ever grow up?" It was a tease, but the Cinzano had put an edge on it.

He shrugged. "Like most guys, I guess, not without a struggle. That's why I acted like such a horse's ass at Fort Des Moines. When the war started, my divorce from Lois had just come through, and I wanted to fight—someone. I applied for a direct commission thinking it meant a command, and I ended up hutting women soldiers around Iowa. None too graciously, as I recall."

"None too. For a while it looked as if you thought we were the enemy."

Impulsively, his hand slid across the table and touched hers as it had two years before at the Palm Bar in Des Moines. "Jill, let's not be enemies ever again. Let's be friends."

"I'd like that." She took another drink, and he refilled her glass. Unreasonably, she felt sad that he'd given up any thought of romantic feelings, but she realized that this would make it easier for her—eventually.

Des smiled, making small talk. "Ever hear from those OC friends of yours?"

"Oh yes, especially Page and Bunny, though not from Elisabeth that much."

The room rocked to the last of a dozen ribald verses of "Dirty Gertie from Bizerte" until a burst of applause forced Jill to focus on the small dance floor in front of them. Good, she thought. Dancers. Anything would be better than more "Gertie" or another wheezing waltz from the house band, a saxophone-accordion duo that was laboriously working its way through "In Dreams I Kiss Your Hand, Madame." "Des, is there a worse musical sound than accordion and saxophone?"

"None." He smiled and then, at the fanfare, put a finger to his lips. "Ssshh, Apache dancers."

"I thought they were French."

"No, they're all over Europe in dives like this one."

Jill watched the men in the room respond to the sensuality and violence of the couple on the dance floor. And she could see why. The dance was about war, not the one being fought to the north of them, but the war between men and women and the fear on first one side and then the other of losing control of one's body and one's self. Was this the kind of overwhelming physicality that men wanted, that Des wanted? Fascinated, she wondered if she might not want it, too.

Following the dance, the woman performed alone, or almost alone, doing embarrassing things to a chair, accompanied by wild cheering. Jill felt her face flame.

"Sorry, Jill," Des was saying. "Now I can see why this place is so popular. Do you want to leave or can you take it?"

"I'll stay as long as you want to."

"That's my spunky exec. What you need is another drink and she'll look live Pavlova."

"I doubt it. Those guys," she said and pointed at the crowds of soldiers around the dance floor, "they're pie-eyed, and they *know* they're not watching a ballet."

He laughed. "You're right, but don't blame the men for drinking. It's one of the two ways to live with fear."

She looked at him, his face only inches from hers. "Don't tell me what the other way is." She tried to be offhanded, but it was a feeble attempt. "I think I can guess."

He drew even closer, dropping the light tone of the evening. "I'm not sure you *can* guess, Jill."

"Oh, I'm not a complete innocent, you know."

"Aren't you? It's been my experience that women who lack innocence never need to tell a man so." His words were clearing a small space around them, cutting through the smoke and the noise and the jostling bodies, enclosing them in the smallest of worlds. He said, "Shall I tell you about you?" and then went on without waiting for her to answer. "Right now you're having fun with me, but you won't know it until tomorrow or even weeks from now. You have never allowed yourself to feel in the present. Think about it. This boyfriend of yours—you love him now in memory more than you ever did when you were with him—"

"Wait a minute." She had to interrupt him, but, at the same time, she was unwillingly fascinated by his words.

"Let me finish—and you have some idealized dream about sacrificing your life for him after the war."

How could she have been such a fool as to think they could be just friends? "You don't know what you're saying. I owe Neil some kind of life. It was my fault that he enlisted and is crippled."

"You mean that you, you alone, are responsible for the war? Wake up, Jill, to what you're doing to yourself. You were young and you made a mistake. I don't know who made you think you had to be Little Miss Perfect and pay for your mistakes forever—that *you* had to take responsibility for everyone's life but your own. Listen," the words seemed to tumble out of his control, "someday you have to wake up out of that dream world. You can't go to bed with that memory of yours forever, lavishing all your love on stray kids and mutts. You're going to have to find out whether you can love a real man who will love you back."

Jill took a larger than normal swallow of her drink. There was no sharpness to what Des was saying, nothing veiled. He meant exactly what he said. She could respect him for his honesty, even if she couldn't allow herself to agree with him. "And you think you're that real man?"

"I could be, and you know it! I didn't imagine that kiss back in Presenzano."

"I'm sorry for that."

"Don't ever apologize to a man for kissing him."

"Don't lecture me. I'm not a child. You refuse to understand that I can have a deep sense of responsibility for what I did, responsibility that I can't avoid—don't want to avoid. Oh, what's the use?"

Des had turned to his drink and rolled it distractedly back and forth between his hands, the glass clicking against his class ring, his eyes staring at the dance floor now full of couples swaying to the strains of "Sorrento." Jill was sorry for her outburst. She wanted to take his hands in hers, to tell him that nothing was his fault, that there was so much he didn't know. But before she had the chance, the band stopped playing and hit a loud chord.

"Attenzione, signore e signori," a man said, holding up his hand for quiet and then continuing in broken English, with a rising inflection. "Today, twenty-fifth August, zi Allies marched inside Paris." Then, amidst the cheers, he conducted the band with a corked wine bottle in the opening but scarcely recognizable chords of "La Marseillaise." The man bowed ceremonially, then shouted, bottle on high, "Down with all *Fascisti.* To final victory!"

Jill and Des stood and raised their glasses with the rest, toasting victory.

Des said, "Let's dance."

She couldn't fool herself. It was wonderful to be in his arms again, and yet to be safe from any idea of his that she could belong to him, that anything could happen between them that she couldn't walk away from. To her credit, she saw her own dishonesty. *I can't accept anything from him, not even this night in Rome, if I can't return the gift.* He moved in a rhythmic two-step, the only step possible on the crowded floor, and she gave herself up to the beat that communicated itself from his body to hers.

"Hey, Nursie!"

The drunken call came from a table nearby. She knew that the yell was for her, and ignored it.

The same slurred voice called again. "Hell, that ain't no nurse—it's a WAC officer."

She was facing him now: a weaving red-faced T/5 whose friends were trying to pull him back into the crowd.

"How come *they* get bars, walkin' aroun' lording it over us noncoms?"

Des put his arm around her shoulder and spoke to the man's buddies. "Better take this man out before the lieutenant here prefers charges, because if she doesn't I'm going to have this guy's ass hauled to the nearest guardhouse for the duration."

"Never mind, Des." She was aware that the man's sentiments were probably shared by half those present.

One of the group, not much steadier than the rowdy noncom, said, "Sorry, Captain, ma'am, he's leaving," and he wrestled his buddy out the door.

Jill started for their table, aware that some of the people had not even heard the fracas and that some had looked on with curiosity and then returned to their fun. And, strangely, the ugly incident hadn't upset her too much, either.

Right behind her, Des said, "Wait here, I'm going to get that bastard's name and unit—"

"No! Drop it, Des. There was a time when that kind of talk would have really bothered me, but I know the kind of job I'm doing—that all Fifth Army Wacs are doing in Italy."

"Okay." He held her chair for her and sat down opposite, throwing her a quizzical glance. "In some ways you have grown up, haven't you? Self-confidence even becomes you, makes that cute mouth of yours even cuter." He saw he'd embarrassed her. "I guess I can tell you now—hell, yes, this is as good a time as any—I put you in for the Bronze Star for your part in the dump explosion."

Jill was overwhelmed. A medal for bravery? "But, Des, it was Marie Brodzinsky, not I—"

"She's up, too, but surely you know you initiated the action that saved that man's life. If that wasn't above and beyond, I've never seen it."

He paid for a new bottle of Cinzano to take with them as she gathered up her shoulder bag and fastened the strap under her left epaulet. *A medal for bravery!* Did she really deserve it? She had rarely been proud of herself, and she found it so hard to start now.

Twenty minutes later, after they'd looked in on Tina and found her sound asleep with Charlito on guard at the foot of her bed, Des opened his door at the Excelsior and paused to let Jill step ahead of him. She stood on the threshold, uncertain.

"I shouldn't be here, Des," she told him, looking around his room.

"Why not?" He brushed past her and stepped inside. "It's early and Tina's still sound asleep."

"It's not that, it's . . . well . . ."

"Okay, I get it. Mama told you never *ever* to go to a man's room unless there were fifty people there. Right? Look—" and he swept his hand around the room—"not an etching or a knockout powder in sight."

"It's not that and you know it. Why won't you make an attempt to understand what I'm saying? If I come in—oh, what would you think it meant and what would it help?" She didn't tell him that she was more afraid of her own behavior than of his.

He crossed to the sink and rinsed two glasses and poured some of the sweet wine. He handed her a glass and sat down on the edge of the bed, patting a place next to him for her. "Come on, Jill, sit down, for Chrissakes. Don't start acting like a kid now." He could see her bristle. "I mean let's just have a nightcap together like two adults. I'm not going to defile your virginity."

He saw her take the dare, close the door, and sit down stiffly on the edge of his bed. He leaned back against the pillows and stared up at her. Damn it! She was a lovely woman, a miniature wonder, and there was nothing he wanted to do more than defile her virginity immediately and all night through. Oh, it wasn't that he didn't respect her ability and her courage, but it was wartime and they were being bombed and shelled several times a week, so what did those old senior-prom rules of the game count for in Italy, 1944. "Relax, will you? If I just wanted sex, there are easier ways to get it in Rome."

"I know that." She looked at him, her eyes troubled, nervously licking her full upper lip in the most maddeningly provocative way he'd ever seen.

"Look, Jill, I didn't mean to hurt you. Damn, I'm sorry. Sorry. *Sorry!* That's all I ever seem to say to you. I don't mean to snap at you, it's just that you make me feel like some ogre ready to jump any helpless maiden in distress." Irritated at himself as well as at her, he threw his head back, and it connected with the heavily carved headboard with a resounding crack. "Ouch!"

Jill automatically reached toward him, stretching herself across the bed to him. "Oh, Des"—her voice trembled with the effort of not loving him, and the tremor raced through her— "I'm the one who's sorry."

"For what?" He sat up, kneading his head, his face a contrast of anger at himself and frustration with her. "For not loving me, when I need you so much?" He realized how childish he sounded, demanding her love because he needed it, but he couldn't think straight.

"Oh, Des," she whispered, her voice sounding miserable.

Forgetting the pain in the back of his head, he captured her face between his hands and kissed her, a brushing kiss that barely touched her lips. Then he moved his mouth back again, and back again, until he felt her relax and then begin to strain toward him. He increased the pressure of his mouth against that pouting lip, and her body tensed all along its length. Damn! He'd known it all the time. She acted like a little puritan, but she had the devil's own responses. But now that he had her in bed wanting him, something made him want to pull back.

Jill could not breathe. His kisses were the only ones in her life to which she had responded with her whole self, not just her nurturing, caring self, but with her woman's body, with the deepest nature of a woman. At that moment she was more frightened of Des—and of herself—than she had ever been.

In a panic, she pushed at him and, up on her knees now, tried to back away, but the soft mattress seemed to roll her toward him.

Now, up on his knees, too, he knelt in front of her, his eyes glazed, his fingers beyond his recall, and hastily loosened her shirt buttons. He dropped his head and kissed the cleft between the mounds of flesh; he kissed them right and left, quickly before she could cover them, kissed the warm swelling softness of her breasts. They were surprisingly full for such a little woman.

She was crying without a sound. She appealed to him. "Don't let me do this. Help me!"

He heard her but didn't want to acknowledge the real meaning of her words. "Jill—Jill, do you know that I adore your body?" he asked and urgently pushed his painfully swollen and throbbing body against hers. She must feel it, too. If he was right about her, if she was a full-blooded woman who cared for him, she would want to save him from this pain. She'd help *him,* damn it!

They fell down upon the bed, lying full length, holding tightly together. She was saying his name over and over, moving against him, her fingers grasping and regrasping the material in the back of his shirt.

He knew he could take her now without asking, but a nagging something, some misguided chivalry or supreme self-assurance, forced him to say the words that broke his absolute hold on her. "Jill, tell me you want me to make this moment perfect, that you want this as much as I do. Tell me you want me to make love to you right here—now, in this bed."

With a cry of recovery as if she had come from a deep anesthesia, "Oh, no—*no!* Darling, Des, I can't. I promised."

Supremely frustrated, he threw himself over on his back. He hadn't felt so near to tears since he was a little boy. "You shouldn't play the *femme fatale,* Jill," he lashed out bitterly, "you're not the type."

Tears were caught just under her eyelids and she didn't know how long she could hold them back. Once she began to cry, she might never stop. It was so unfair of Des to blame her when she had no choice. "I wasn't playing, Des. I know you're mad, but you must believe that I was honest. I really wanted you then—I've wanted you for a long time, I want you right now." She stopped and looked at him, and even he could see that she was desperately unhappy. She whispered, "You don't believe me."

He still wanted to hurt her to soothe his own pain. "Why should I believe you? Your whole *life* is a lie." Even as he said it, he knew he did believe her, and hated himself for trying to make her feel guilty. Oh God, it was too easy to make this woman feel guilty, because she wanted to. And more than that, it was a cheap way to get a woman into bed. Damn it anyway! With a city full of easy sex, he had to want a professional virgin. No, that was unfair. She had passion all right—it was her damned sense of duty. Oh hell! His voice shaking but softer, he said, "Okay, Jill, I'll just chalk it up to a case of mistaken identity. I must be stupid to think you really cared for me the way I want you to."

"Des! Don't ever say that again. You're not stupid. Can't I make you understand? I do care for you, but I was brought up with a set of rules. Maybe they're old-fashioned, but I can't give them up because they're inconvenient."

He stared at her across the rumpled blankets. "You care for me? But you're saving yourself for someone else, a guy who doesn't even write you—hell, someone who may not even be capable of being a husband to you. I don't get it, Jill. Why do you insist on throwing your life away, *my* life away, when I love you?" The instant he said it, he knew it was true. He'd pretended to himself that he was just trying to score with her, but he'd loved her all along—in Des Moines, in Algiers and to distraction since Presenzano, all the way up the mud, dust and blood of the Italian boot.

"I—I do love you too, Des," she said shyly. "I've known it for a long time, and if this were a peaceful world and I'd never sent Neil off to . . . well, if things were different, there'd be a chance for us."

"But that's just it, Jill. Why won't you deal with reality? Things *aren't* different. The world's at war and we love each other—maybe we shouldn't, but we do—and, damn it, *we're* here right now."

"I'm not able to think that way, Des. I wish I could. Don't you see that the easiest thing in the world for me would be loving you?" She got up and buttoned her shirt, glancing tearfully at the red stain of wine on the bed where her drink had spilled. "Don't you see that this is the hardest thing I've ever had to do?"

He had run out of arguments. Talking to her was like trying to change history. *You did a good job, Patrick Henry: give her duty or give her nothing.* "Okay, you're an honorable woman who sticks by her promises even when they hurt everybody. Is that supposed to make me feel noble for having lost you? Well, it doesn't. You can sleep with your righteous rules, I can't."

She hated this—hated it even more because she knew that by crossing the few feet that separated them, she could change the look on his face and wipe out the fire burning in her own body. But she couldn't take that walk.

417

With one last look, the saddest Des had ever seen although he was too wrapped up in his own misery to acknowledge it, she opened the door and stepped through it.

"Jill?"

"Yes."

He was forced to talk to her back, because she didn't turn. "You think I'm jealous of this Neil. No, don't deny it, I know you do. I'm not jealous, you know. I wouldn't be Neil for a million bucks. You're going to make him pay for your sacrifice—you won't intend to, but you will. Maybe you have already. Yeah, maybe he *wants* you to let go of him and you won't."

Her shoulders slumped, but without an answer she closed the door and was gone. He rolled onto his stomach, to subdue the throbbing between his legs that had started when he first touched her. Okay, to hell with her! But the memory of the kisses she'd returned pounded in his head. What could he do about her, with her, without her? Where in hell had Jill learned to shut out all but sacrificial feelings? A moment later, he heard her door open and shut down the hall.

When Jill closed the door, she leaned for a moment against it, alive in every cell of her body, but exhausted in a way she had never been from overwork on the front, almost as if she had been opened up, emptied out and then been zipped shut again. She was a different woman from the one she'd been earlier in the evening, so long ago now. The best part of her she had left back there in Des's room. Why, oh why, did she feel so weak with him when she knew herself to be a strong woman? When had she perverted her strength into a hopeless search for an idea of perfection, pleasing nobody, not Neil, not Des and, most of all, not even herself.

Tiptoeing to her side of the bed, careful not to disturb Tina, Jill began to undress, fighting desperately not to remember the way Des's hands and mouth had felt when he had sought her breasts, and losing. Oh God! How could her promise to Neil be strong enough to hold her? She gripped the table to keep herself from running back to his arms, to beg him to take her into his bed and do with her what he wanted—what *she* wanted.

Raising her eyes, she saw propped against the lamp a V-Mail letter addressed to her from her mother. How had it followed her to Rome? Probably someone on leave from the company had brought it to Rome and deposited it with the clerk at the Excelsior.

Opening the one-piece envelope and letter, she began to read. From the opening sentence, she held her breath. Her mother cautioned her for several paragraphs not to blame herself, to be brave, to talk to the chaplain. She scanned quickly down the page and came to the reason. The word leaped out at her. Suicide! Neil had committed suicide, she read, and began to understand as she read, jumping from one sentence to another: ". . . Sunday morning . . . family at church . . . despondent . . . locked the garage . . . started the car . . . found dead . . . had Bear with him. . . ."

Bear! He'd killed her dog. Why?

A note, a note. Had he left word for her, something she could live with? She read the letter again, every word, slowly. *Oh, Neil, you couldn't have. Not that final punishment. Is my guilt so great?* But he had. Neil had left life without a word for her, taking Bear, the one thing in the world they had both loved together. She would live the rest of her life knowing he had not truly forgiven her. Oh, she could understand his anger. She had understood since she'd seen him so broken and frantic at Oak Knoll Hospital. After all, she'd sent him to war for some childish idea of glory when he didn't have to go, and he'd come back mutilated, his face and his soul charred. But this! She couldn't comprehend the hatred with which he had left her, to die without releasing her from her promise.

Slowly, with growing horror, Jill knew that by his silence Neil had taken her promise with him—and with it the rest of her life?

She heard a door slam down the hall and she realized dully that it was Des going out. She knew also what he was going out for, and she couldn't blame him. She had hurt him as much as a woman could hurt a man; she had rejected his love and his body. Funny, she had hurt Neil by *not* rejecting his body. Nothing she had ever done was right for anyone. She had hurt those she loved, and most of all she had hurt herself almost past enduring, trying, always trying, to please, to be what she thought others wanted her to be.

The sobs were tearing at her throat now. Fully clothed, Jill lay down on the bed and Tina stirred in her sleep. *Oh God,* Jill prayed, *help me to understand what I have to do to make things right.*

But she didn't really believe that her prayer would be answered. How could it be when, with Neil barely in his grave, she had been with Des, rutting like an animal in heat in his bed and responding to his hands and kisses as she never had to Neil's?

49

The opening of the road to Paris costs the Allies dearly. The Normandy campaign losses stand at 16,138 British and Canadian dead and 58,594 wounded, 20,838 Americans dead, 94,881 wounded. But Germany pays heavily, too, with 200,000 men dead and wounded and another 200,000 captured. On the German home front all theaters and nightclubs close, vacations are eliminated and students mobilized.

"LIEUTENANT HANNADAY," THE cigar-chewing driver said, "this ain't gonna be no sightseeing tour. The Red Ball Highway into Paris is one-way and we don't stop for no man—no lady either, if you get my drift."

"I get it, Corporal. You won't have to stop for me."

"Right! Next stop Pa-ree!"

The big two-and-a-half-ton truck wheeled out of the Le Havre dock area crammed full of General Willis' personal files and office equipment, headed for the new G-2 office at SHAEF in Versailles. In the week since Paris had fallen on August 25, SHAEF headquarters had started operations right across the street from Louis XIVth's palace. MPs flagged them onto the Paris road, and they headed southeast into the Seine Valley countryside. A breathtaking sight unrolled before Page.

She was not overwhelmed by the tall trees lining the two-lane road or the farmhouses, some with gaping shell holes, but by the amazing mounds of gear, *acres* of neatly aligned trucks, jeeps and bulldozers, *mountains* of rations. "Corporal, I've never seen anything like this, not even in the south of England—mile after mile of supply dumps all the way to Paris. This is the first time I've been absolutely sure we're going to win this war. How could Germany hope to match this?"

The corporal grinned proudly, chewing on his unlit cigar. "You got a good eye for a lady, Lieutenant. The Red Ball Express's gonna win this war. We'll just bury 'em in materiell," he said, pronouncing the word the army way. "We have orders not to stop rollin' except for gas and repair. Usually have a guy ridin' relief—don't need 'im on this short haul. Yep! We keep 'em goin'—the guns, the tanks, the dogfaces."

The corporal fell silent, and she amused herself by counting "Kilroy was here" signs, some in the most unlikely places. "Look"—she pointed at one on a bridge pylon in the middle of the Seine.

"Some Joe musta hung upside down on a rope to paint that one," the driver said with the amused toleration of one good old boy for another.

Something about his attitude reminded Page of what Bunny had written from New Guinea about a soldier named Breck. The man sounded attractive but a real wheeler-dealer. She hoped Bunny wasn't falling for the guy. The letter had been a little too offhand even for Bunny. Hadn't two Mr. Wrongs been enough? Some lines of Thackeray's—probably from *Vanity Fair*—floated up to her conscious mind: "It is strange what a man may do and a woman yet think him an angel."

She wondered what it would be like to love a man the way Bunny could—totally, blindly, with her whole being, wanting nothing else. She sighed.

"Not that much longer, Lieutenant," the corporal told her, mistaking the sigh for fatigue and double-clutching around a slower truck.

And he was right. Soon they were in the city, on the Rue de Rome, then turning onto the Boulevard Haussmann.

Excitedly, Page asked, "Are we anywhere near the Champs-Élysées?"

"Don't worry, Lieutenant," he said, reversing his earlier no-tour stand, "you're gonna get the twenty-five-cent tour before I take you out to Versailles."

At the end of the Boulevard Haussmann Page saw the Arc de Triomphe, standing massively astride the Étoile, where the twelve major avenues of the Right Bank came together to form a star. The corporal laid on his horn and took a complete turn around the arch and then headed down the chestnut-lined Champs-Élysées, weaving through the bicycles, waving at gendarmes in their posts, until the Obelisk in the Place de la Concorde loomed above them.

"I thought there'd be more traffic," Page said, "horns bleating and all that."

The corporal shifted his mangled cigar. "The Frenchies don't have any gas. The Krauts looted everything when they left—stoves, food, clothes, even their bathtubs. But it's still a great town for a pass—Pig Alley and that big nightclub where the gals are half naked. Sorry, Lieutenant."

He swung the truck southwest and drove the twelve miles to Versailles in good time even for the Red Ball, as if the thought of tonight's visit to the Folies-Bergère to hear Mistinguett sing "I Want a Millionaire" lent wings to his wheels.

A week later, Page was working late and listening to the BBC Home Service's report of the first supersonic V-2 rocket attack on London. She shuddered. The new flying bombs were even more dreadful than the V-1s. They flew over three thousand miles per hour and gave no warning at all. Paul was in London for reassignment, she knew. Surely, she comforted herself, God had not saved him from one German weapon to kill him with another. And yet she knew the god of war did just that, was doing that on the front lines this minute.

The telephone rang. "General Willis' office, Lieutenant Hannaday speaking."

"Page!"

"Paul? *Paul* darling, where are you?"

"At the Hotel Meurice."

"Here, in Paris?" she said, unable to believe it. "I had you dead in London under a V-2 rocket."

"Yes, it's terrible. I've been listening to the BBC, too." He lowered his voice. "Page, I've been reassigned to SHAEF, G-3 staff."

"Paul, that's wonderful, but why Plans and Operations?"

"Not now—later. When can I see you? Tomorrow?"

"Yes, tomorrow's Saturday. I'll come to the hotel as soon as I can."

It was late afternoon before she reached Paul's hotel. She had walked from the Étoile toward the Rue de Rivoli and was somehow depressed in spite of looking forward to seeing Paul again. Paris was not the joyous city of the songs and the movies. Grim, hungry people hurried through the afternoon showers. Fresh flowers lay incongruously in the center of a street—carefully bypassed by the bicycle traffic—or at the foot of lampposts, testament to the death of a resistance fighter on that spot during the liberation of the city only days before. A woman about her own age or a bit younger had slunk away into a side street on her approach, the head scarf not hiding her shaven head, evidence of having loved an enemy soldier.

She saw him as soon as she walked through the revolving doors of the Meurice. He detached himself from a group of officers and strode under gleaming chandeliers across the lobby, his limp still noticeable.

"Page, I thought you'd never get here." He kissed her despite curious stares. "Let's get out of here for a while."

They walked to Fouquet's on the Champs-Élysées and took a table outside close to the wall, secluded from sidewalk gawkers and yet open to the fresh air of a Paris newly scrubbed by rain. He ordered red wine for both of them. *"Deux* Beaujolais, *garçon."*

"Paul," she said, sipping the tangy, full-bodied red, "how did you manage this assignment? I was certain they were going to send you stateside or at least keep you in London."

"So was I, darling," he said, stretching his wounded leg straight in front of him, rubbing it vigorously. "This time last week I had orders for the Farm in Virginia. I thought I'd have to sit the war out, teaching young spooks the spy business."

"What changed things? I know you have great powers of persuasion, but . . ."

"Wish I could add to that reputation, but it was Anna who saved me again."

"For what?" She knew she shouldn't ask.

"It was something Anna developed—a new twist on black propaganda."

"On what?"

"I can't tell you exactly, but I had the qualifications needed." He placed his cap on the table, running his fingers through his thick waving hair in a well-remembered reflex. "Anna's a marvel, really."

"What did she develop?" A hint of sharpness invaded her voice, although she tried to keep it casual. Paul didn't seem to notice.

"Propaganda," he began as if he were lecturing his classes at Rutgers, "is an effort to supply seemingly authentic news to the enemy that we want them to know. If the enemy soldier knows it's from us, then that's 'white' propaganda. But if he thinks the news he hears is from his own people, but it isn't, then that's 'black' propaganda. We use fake German radio broadcasts, newspapers, leaflets; we use truth, half-truths or lies to convince the German soldier to stop fighting."

"I think I see. How clever Annaliese must be. I wouldn't have thought it of her."

"Oh, Anna can fool you all right. She can go from *agent provocateur* to a typical German *Hausfrau*—as you'll find out."

Startled, Page said, "She's in Paris?"

"Of course. She's at the Meurice, too. We're going to develop the psychological-warfare division together. We'll be coordinating with G-2, so I'll be around Versailles for some time. Mind being stuck with me?"

"Of course not, darling." She was determined to quiet the jealous suspicions of Annaliese that rose suddenly out of her uncertainties. Page believed that Paul loved her, but there was something buried deep in her woman's psyche that made her fear the competition of other women for her man. She didn't like or understand this feeling. Maybe it started, she thought, when we had to have a man to hunt meat for our cave or we starved, or maybe it comes down from medieval times when we women got a husband or disappeared into a convent. Whatever the cause, Page vowed to herself she would never play that stupid game. She wondered if this ancient curse on her sex had been one of the reasons she had finally accepted Paul's proposal at Tunbridge Wells. No—Paul himself was quite reason enough, and then seeing him wounded had made her realize she truly loved him. But when she allowed herself to think about it, she wondered why the price of love was so high for her.

"...and, darling, we *can*," Paul was saying. "Don't you think so?"

"I'm sorry, Paul, what were you saying?"

"I just planned our entire life together," he said ruefully, and took her hand gently in his. "I won't say it all again. You'll just have to live it to find out."

Her voice was urgent almost to desperation when she leaned forward and put her cheek to his. "Let's go back to your room now," she whispered, "and go for dinner later." Only with Paul's arms around her, his body feeding her body with his love, could she stop the questions that rose unbidden. Only in his arms, she thought, could she reaffirm the need for love's protection her sex had sought for a million years.

50

SOMEWHERE IN THE PACIFIC—An exhilarated pilot of the Thirteenth Air Force came back from a P-38 attack on the Philippines with a story that tops all others of Filipinos waving happily to flyers making low-level raids.

He said he was flying low when he passed over a Filipino girl. He says she tore off her sarong and waved it at him. The intelligence officers who heard his story say it may be so, but they think it's a case of wishful thinking.

—Yank, the army weekly, November 17, 1944

BUNNY SWUNG HER legs to the floor and slipped on her boots after shaking them for hidden lizards. Her GI pajamas were plastered to her body from the steamy jungle heat that prevented her from sleeping for more than a few hours a night. Picking up her cigarettes, she walked as softly as combat boots on creaking wooden floors would allow and sat down on the steps in front of the tent, hoping to catch a random breeze.

The WAC area had changed considerably over the two months since they landed in early September. A fifteen-foot barbed-wire fence now surrounded the compound, covered with burlap to discourage the caravans of off-duty GIs who hooted and cat-called their way around the perimeter, especially when Wacs were on their way to the outdoor showers. To ensure their privacy from the rear-echelon boys, they had found a secluded pool fed by a small waterfall behind the WAC area and had swum, bathed and washed their hair there until a nest of pythons had been discovered nearby and the pool was posted off limits. With a small, tired movement Bunny pushed back the damp dark curls that clung to her even damper forehead. That was AAF efficiency for you. Never fix anything you can put off limits.

Bunny pulled her nightclothes away from her body, allowing a wisp of a cooler breeze to pass between and touch her skin. She had to admit there had been positive changes in living conditions too. The mess hall—she shivered at the never-to-be-forgotten memory of the thud of wood against the Japanese soldier's head—was first rate, if you didn't mind a steady diet of bully beef, and they had their own beauty shop with a hose-rigged washstand courtesy of Breck Smith.

There wasn't much Breck couldn't do. He had a cool, assured way of sizing up a problem and then solving it. He liked to put on that dumb hillbilly act of his, but he was one smart cookie.

Bunny lowered her head and rested it on the back of her laced-together hands atop her knees. That was the trouble, maybe he was too smart for her. She had told herself almost since the first day that an affair with Breck would be impossible, that she had no time for and indeed no interest in passion, but every time she was with him she was forced to confront something she found terrifying in herself, and that was her own potential to love and feel deeply.

Peering between her fingers, she saw a trail of bugs marching single file under the steps, like little insect zombies in the jungle night. *God, how I wish I could just shrink down and get in that line and never have to worry about feelings again.* Breck and Harry. Harry and Breck. The two men made her feel violently opposite things at the same time; and then her mind fought itself, rarely giving her any peace. No matter how many arguments she used to convince herself that Harry was the man to give her the safe, uncomplicated life she wanted, no matter how many times she tried to avoid Breck, she was forced to acknowledge the daily, hourly, almost-moment-to-moment waste of her loving womanhood, and to admit in the remotest corner of her mind that Breck had begun to intrude persistently into her thoughts.

"Can't sleep," Vicki murmured groggily, sitting down next to Bunny, tucking her pajama legs into her boots to ward off attacking mosquitos. "Whatcha thinking about?"

"Nothing much."

"Says you. He's made you like him better than that stuffed-shirt colonel of yours, hasn't he?"

"Let's just say I appreciate his good points." Bunny knew that by "he" Vicki meant Breck.

"Don't beat around the bush with me, Palermo. And don't treat me like I was a kid or something." Vicki slapped at a mosquito. "Did you bring your jungle cologne out with you?"

"Nope, forgot it."

"Bugs love me—" Vicki scratched at the bite—"I attract them just like you attract pain."

Bunny jerked upright. "What! What's that you said?"

"Nothin'. Oh, I don't know. Just being a smart-ass, I guess. It's this damned heat." Vicki rose and stretched. "Guess I'll give that cot another chance. Wish *I* could get Breck to get *me* an air mattress like yours. Guess I don't rate." She shuffled back inside the tent, trailing crankiness.

Attract pain. What had Vicki meant by that? What could a kid from Parkers Prairie, Minnesota, know about anything? Love was a marvelous game to her. She'd learn, given time, that love was an illusion, an unpardonable lie men told to women and women longed to believe. Few women knew that; only one other she'd known had understood, and that was Elisabeth. Although she had guarded the secrets of her personal feelings, Bunny knew that if any woman had looked clearly under the false face of love it had been Elisabeth.

Bunny walked back inside the tent to her cot and lay down on the air mattress. The feel of it holding her body softly brought back Breck's mocking face as he delivered it to her from "a midnight requisition." "Damn you," she whispered into the humid dark, "damn you, Breck Smith—get out of my brain."

Later that morning Tech Sergeant Breckinridge T. C. Smith sauntered away from his desk in FEAF headquarters at 0930 hours, stuck a card with a leaf colonel's insignia on his windshield, which precluded its being requisitioned by any lesser rank, drove the jeep he had more or less permanently liberated from the motor pool toward the southern edge of the base, and turned down an inconspicuous lane. He jammed the jeep into second gear, momentarily looking up as a wave of fighters headed northwest for the Philippines.

To be free of duties at such an early hour was not unusual for him. He knew from sheer instinct that now that he was the reinstated noncom chief of Base Special Projects division, FEAF headquarters, Air Planning Group, his absence from the office on base business was expected and not especially missed. The lieutenant colonel in charge, a fiftyish moving-and-storage entrepreneur in civilian life, had no more information or authority than he, Breck Smith, decided was necessary to get a particular job done. Agreeably the colonel spent most of his nights at the area officers' club soaking up combat stories to tell after the war, and most of his days on a cot in his office, a fan whipping the warm air over his khaki shorts. Breck and his colonel formed a special kind of military partnership. For Breck's part of the bargain, his organizational abilities and keen judgment of men had gathered into one temporary building behind a row of parked planes at the end of Hollandia's longest airstrip the grandest bunch of AAF scroungers, comshaw artists and red-tape cutters in the whole Southwest Pacific war zone. The division hummed along smoothly when private projects called Tech Sergeant Smith away.

No one had ever defined the precise duties of the office or the protocol he was to use. In point of fact, almost all requisitions were passed by word of mouth, since they were usually unauthorized—a relaxing recreation room for one outfit, food and strong drink for an officers' celebration, a spring-cushioned bed for a one-star. Most ground command officers at

FEAF knew of his outfit, and each gave tacit approval, knowing it likely they would sooner or later desire his services for a special project of their own. In return, it was understood that he could make a reasonable profit from certain concessions, mainly a poker club he called the Four Queens, operating just off base. For months this had proved a practical arrangement for everyone, because the Army, in war or peace, prized men like Breckinridge T. C. Smith as secret military weapons and he knew it. For all such irregular operations only one rule was observed, the rule of official blinders. Breck knew that if he ever became an obvious embarrassment, forcing the brass to acknowledge the real purpose of his military existence, the give-and-take arrangement would end and he would be the goat.

On this November 1944 morning in the middle of the steamy equatorial summer, Breck whistled as he twisted the wheel to keep from becoming mired in the mud that grew deeper with every downpour, and he thought about Bunny. He stopped whistling, a grin spreading across his face, which was deeply tanned from a combination of tropical sun and Atabrine. He had rarely felt so good, especially this early in the morning.

He pulled up to the steps leading to the front door of the Four Queens and ran a critical eye over the place. For the first time he saw the accumulation of rusting junk and busted Jap plane parts. Stepping inside, he frowned at the beat-up tables, the shaky folding chairs and the finger-smudged Vargas Girl pinups.

"All right, Mac, cut the action," he told a corporal running a crap shoot. "That's all, fellas," he said to three Seabees playing twenty-one. "We're closing down today. Getting some heat from the provost." He knew that would send them scrambling.

Corporal Andy McBride looked worried. "What's up, Smitty? The friggin' major was just in here yesterday playing low-ball. Won a big pot, too, just like you wanted."

"Never you mind, Mac. I got somethin' bigger than dice or cards cooking—bigger than anything."

"Bigger than gambling? Ain't nothing bigger, not in the friggin' SWPA."

"You let me fret about that, Mac. I want you to get on the

field telephone. Get Bob from Base Electrical, Eddie from Engineers and—" Breck thought a moment—"and Frenchy and Gunner from the office. Tell 'em to make sure the colonel has enough booze and then get here on the double."

During the next hour, Breck methodically evaluated the Four Queens inside and out, and the lists he was making grew longer and longer.

Mac found him as he stood at the rear of the building. "All the guys are here."

"Roger! Let's go." Breck gave the perpetually worried Mac an enthusiastic shove.

Master Sergeant Bob Bryant from Base Electrical saw Breck first. "What the hell's this all about, Smitty? I gotta get back to my shop. Those dumb draft board shits they're giving me don't know their ass from a solenoid."

"Yeah," said T/5 Edwards, "I left my baby-faced loot reading FMs. By now he's got a hundred better ways 'n me of doin' every goddamn job on the base."

"Rest easy, guys." Breck made a circle with his forefinger over the group, and Mac poured drinks all around. "I've got a plan, so listen up, and then if you don't want in . . ." He shrugged. The men settled back and tossed off his latest batch of four-star premium. "Look around you, men." Breck waved his arm around the room. "Tell me, what's missin'?"

Master Sergeant Bryant looked. "Nothin'."

Breck shook his head. "Now, that's where you're wrong, Bobby boy. Look again and you'll see that there are no girls."

"Girls?" Frenchy asked. "Why?"

T/5 Edwards agreed. "We don't need girls to play poker. You know how women play poker?" he asked. "They play dime store."

"What the hell's dime store?" Frenchy asked.

Eddie answered, with a look of supreme disgust, "Fives and tens are wild."

The men groaned and Breck motioned to Mac to pour another round. "Hold on, fellas. We don't need girls to play poker with. Remember girls? They're soft and you can dance with 'em, and moon with 'em—and whatever else you smart guys can think up." Breck had their attention now and they were also a little tight, since Mac had been pouring doubles, maybe close to triples. "You know the score. The FEAF Wacs can only go out in a group and only to recognized base activities which have been cleared with their CO twenty-four hours in advance."

"Yea," said Gunner. "You'd think they was a pack of lade-da virgins or somethin', and some of 'em will never see thirty-five again."

Breck was annoyed. "The hell, Gunner. You want out of this deal?"

"Bite mine! I never said I wanted out."

Eddie spoke up, "Clam up, Gunner. Yeah, Smitty, we're with you so far."

"Okay, then." Breck was secretly pleased at the men's response, but just in case one small doubt remained he had a clincher. "From this day on, the Four Queens will be known as the La Conga Club." He looked around at their puzzled faces with a confident grin. "Why? Because, gentlemen of the Army Air Corps, women are crazy for Latin dances. The beat hots them up until—well, my Southern upraising don't 'low me to dwell on all the possibilities, but my Granny Smith always said"—Breck ignored the groan at the mention of his grandmother's name—"that a gal at a town dance on Saturday night is apt to kick over the traces, and it don't make no never mind if she's pretty as a speckled pup or ugly as homemade sin."

Bob, Eddie, Frenchy, Gunner and Mac shifted their feet nervously, and Breck pressed his advantage. "Look around you—does this look like a club that would entice the lovely ladies of the U. S. of A.'s Women's Army Corps? No, gentlemen. Base Special Projects division is shamed! Whose dances get the Wacs?" he ticked them off on his fingers. "The One Hundred Second Seabees with their flush toilet in the ladies' room; the control tower group with their Glide 'Em Inn and their damned eight-piece orchestra."

Mac interrupted. "But Christ, Smitty, where are we gonna get a friggin' toilet and a friggin' orchestra?"

"Ah, that's just it. We've got somethin' better; we've got booze to trade, and my New Guinea Four Star will get us everything we can't scrounge. We can turn this dump into a showplace, a goddamn South Seas Stork Club." Breck could see Gunner still wasn't with him all the way.

"But where the hell's the money in it?" Gunner asked, protecting his ten percent of the gambling take. "Girls is nice, but they don't bring in the payday boys pantin' to get rich."

Breck knew he had them all now. *"That's* where you're wrong, Gunner. The La Conga will be a high-class joint. We'll have a back room where the games'll run just as they do now, only in fancier surroundings. The ladies will be guests at our Saturday night hoedowns in the *main* ballroom, which you're sittin' in right now. We'll get guys in here with their tongues hanging out, just to see something in a skirt, guys who never held a pair of jacks before—*and don't know what to do with them.* Then it's up to you boys to see they get in the right game."

Breck looked around and saw their faces become suddenly, wildly enthusiastic. He got out his list. "Here's what I want each of you to do, and you got four days to do it in."

With typical GI grousing they took the lists, swearing they couldn't get half the stuff, and left on their scavenger hunt.

At the door Gunner turned. "Hey, Smitty, how do we know we can get the Wacs to come?"

"Just leave that to me. I'll take care of the WAC captain. Since I helped her fix up a beauty parlor out there she thinks I came down outa WAC heaven."

The men hurried off, leaving Breck alone with Mac at the bar. "What's the *real* pitch, Smitty?" Mac asked. "Not getting some new boys in the friggin' games. It's that WAC sergeant, that looker, Bunny, you're always hangin' around—that's it, isn't it? You're doing all this to get your hands on her, huh?"

Breck's face lost its relaxed air. "Don't bother trying to figure it out, Mac. Hell, I can't hardly figure myself out. Let's just say I've been sitting across a mug of coffee from her in the WAC mess hall and *accidentally* bumping into her at the recon photo lab long enough. I want to get down to some serious conversation—and if you tell those bozos I said so, I'll swear you've gone nuts from the jungle juice."

After Mac had left with his list, Breck asked himself Mac's question. What the hell did go with him? Why was this woman any different from any of the others, all more amenable than she was? He couldn't explain the way he felt about Bunny with any of his usual confidence. He only knew, and was confused by knowing, that nothing mattered when he wasn't with her, not the still, the gambling, the scams—none of it.

51

*In November 1944, American planes raid Tokyo for the
first time since Doolittle in 1942. Led by Dauntless Dotty,
111 B-29s bomb the Musashi airplane engine plant.*

WHEN BUNNY HEARD the knock at the darkroom door that
November Friday afternoon, she thought it might be, no, she
hoped it was, Breck. She hadn't seen him for two days, but
most of the women in her tent had made it a point to pass
along gossip that Breck was up to something impressive, even
though no one knew exactly what it was. He'd been seen hauling an amazing assortment of gear out toward the Four
Queens—the place every Wac knew about and was dying to
see. Someone had said he was even trying to buy live fish.
Bunny had observed aloud that the last thing Breck Smith
needed was *more* live fish, since he had dozens every payday.
But, as usual, any joke about Breck, no matter how mild, had
brought her tentmates to his defense. The man who had made
their lives easier could do no wrong.

Again there was a knock.

"Red light's on," Bunny called through the darkroom door.
"Out in a minute."

It was Harry who answered in his formal head-of-FEAF-
Air-Recon voice, "Take your time, Sergeant Palermo."

She couldn't help feeling disappointment. *Come off it,
Bunny! You're not one of those foolish, romantic women who
fight off the perfect man because they don't feel like a bobby-
soxer every minute.* Besides, she told herself, Harry was a
pleasant and practiced lover, so she had no complaints.

Bunny worked quickly, and in another minute she turned
off the red safe light and opened the door of the windowless
darkroom. "Your prints are ready, Colonel Duquesne."

His uniform was freshly pressed, without perspiration marks. "May I come in and look at them?" he asked.

"Certainly, sir. But"—as he started to close the door—"please leave the door open. It's hotter than Jersey City in August in here."

"Quite right, Sergeant Palermo." Harry stepped back out again and spoke to the desk corporal on duty. "Can you get two cold Cokes for us, and one for yourself, Corporal?" he said, tossing him three nickels.

"Yes sir, thank you, sir."

Stepping back inside the darkroom, Harry, who had just neatly rid himself of any observers, held her for a moment against his crisply ironed shirt. "You're looking beautiful today." He kissed her. It was a nice kiss and ordinarily she would have enjoyed it, but she fended off further attempts by busying herself with the print cutter. She was just not in the mood for Harry this afternoon—it was too hot, and, well, she was not in the mood. More and more, lately, she had felt anxious when he was near her, wishing him gone, wanting to get away, like someone who had been snowed in all winter and had cabin fever.

"What's the matter, Bunny?" Harry said, planting himself in front of her so that she had to face him. "Are you ill? I think I'll ask Colonel Jamison at base hospital to give you the once-over. Is it that bayonet wound, or is it some female thing? Louise always got like this when . . ."

"It's nothing—or it's everything. The heat, the air raids, the bugs, the lizards."

"I know what you need," he said, a smile of discovery on his face. "Some R and R—just the two of us. This Saturday night, about eight. I'll have my adjutant call your CO and tell her you have special duty. I haven't seen you for weeks, and we'll have this place to ourselves. I'll even arrange for dinner—leave it to me, I'll take care of everything."

Bunny nodded, overcome suddenly by emotional lethargy. Maybe it would be good for her to be alone with Harry. She had always enjoyed their quiet evenings together. She might recapture the serenity he'd given her in the beginning back at Lowry; silence her misgivings. She smiled gratefully. "I'll be here Saturday night—about eight."

"That's my girl! And I've had some good news about the divorce. It looks like I've finally got Louise where I want her—she gets the New York town house, I keep the Connecticut place."

"Here's your Cokes, Colonel."

"Thanks, Corporal. Give one to Sergeant Palermo, and you can have mine. I've got to go." He moved to the cutting board. "These prints dry enough for me to take now, Sergeant?"

"Yes, sir, if you handle them carefully."

"Good. Thank you for your quick work," he said, leafing through the prints. "By the way, Sergeant, have a look at this pommel. Isn't it a beauty?"

Bunny saw the corporal smother a smile that proclaimed the enlisted man's never-ending amusement over officers' doings. In his spare time Harry was writing and photographically illustrating a book on the infinite variety of Japanese war swords. He must have bought, bartered for or confiscated every Japanese sword in the whole of the SWPA, and his collector's vanity convinced him that after the war the book would be a publishing sensation, maybe even a Book-of-the-Month Club selection. Harry wasn't the only officer collecting enemy souvenirs, but his out-of-character enthusiasm had a strange effect on her. Instead of adding an intriguing new dimension to his personality, it forced Bunny to face the possibility that what she had taken for self-assurance was merely self-importance. Could she live with a man like Harry without laughing at him? But she couldn't think about that too deeply. She had safely made her bed with Harry and was determined to lie in it. As silly as she knew it sounded after two failed marriages, she still thought marriage was for keeps. This was it! No more chances if she messed up this one.

Bunny glared at the smirking corporal, who retreated out the door. "It's a magnificent pommel, Colonel."

"Thanks again, Sergeant Palermo," in a voice loud enough for the corporal to overhear. "I'll have more film ready on Saturday evening. Rush job. Okay?"

"Right, sir."

He winked confidently and squeezed her arm, and, nodding with pleasant imperiousness to the corporal at the desk outside, left with his handful of prints.

Bunny put the darkroom in order. She was glad Harry kept her busy with the extra jobs. There hadn't been much air recon work for her since the Leyte invasion nearly a month earlier. Most of the photomontages were being handled at the forward bases; even the B-29s on raids over the Japanese capital returned to bases in India. As for what his wife, Louise, might or might not be getting ready to do, she'd heard all this before. It was a charming compliment to her in a way, but Harry read just what he wanted to read between the lines of his lawyer's letters. There was no doubt in her mind that Harry felt a— what could she call it?—a mature affection for her in addition to a sexual attraction. And until recently she had returned it in kind, even reveled in her ability to master this new, moderate way of loving. This Saturday perhaps she'd regain that feeling.

Quickly, Bunny looked at her watch: 1650 hours, only ten minutes to retreat. She'd have to hurry. The WAC detachment was the only FEAF outfit to stand formal retreat and guard mount every evening before chow. Captain Mary-Ellen Bright insisted on it because some Air WAC directive from Washington had noted that it increased morale in observant detachments. Bunny surmised that occasional three-day passes in a rear area, which were not available for female troops, would do a hell of a lot more for morale than a ceremony attended by half the mosquitos in New Guinea.

By 1710 hours the hand salute had been rendered, the flag lowered, and the last scratchy strains of "The Star-Spangled Banner" wheezed from the ancient wind-up Victrola. The company was ready to be dismissed when the captain, instead of returning to the orderly room, announced, "People, I'm flying to Brisbane to meet with the WAC staff director tonight. I'll be back in a week, so if any of you want me to bring you some personal items, let me know in the next half hour. On another matter, I'm sorry to say I've had some reports of recklessness on the part of some of you. As of now, I want you all to *pay attention* to the order to head for shelter or hit the foxholes when the siren goes off. The provost marshal tells me his officers have to personally order you to take cover. I know there are standing water and bugs in the holes. That's unpleasant, but it could be even more unpleasant if you allow danger to become so routine you do not take proper air raid precautions. We've already had a close brush with the enemy." Here the captain looked at Bunny. "One is enough." Captain Bright started to dismiss the troops and then, as if to underline what she'd said, added ominously, "A word to the wise."

Vicki caught up with Bunny on her way to the tent to get her mess gear. "Wow! Was she ever steamed. Know what that was about? This afternoon I didn't want to cuddle up to a bunch of black water beetles when the Osaka Express came over. Why should I? The Japs never hit anything—just make a lot of noise trying to keep us from working." Vicki took short, quick steps to keep up with Bunny. "Isn't that how we'll win the war—keep on working?"

"You don't have to convince me. The captain's the one who's going to come down on you with both feet. But really, Vicki, promise *me* you'll take more care. Don't be so dumb you think nothing will ever happen to you. Let me tell you . . ." Stepping into their tent, Bunny rubbed her arm gingerly where the small bayonet scar showed puckered red. Then she pulled down her sleeve, buttoned it against mosquitos in spite of the heat and picked up her mess kit from the orange crate next to her cot.

"Does it still hurt?" Vicki asked as they headed toward the mess hall. "The wound, I mean."

"Only when I'm alone or with someone."

"No, I mean really."

"Sometimes, kiddo." Bunny added melodramatically, "I'm agoin', gal, but afore I go . . ."

Vicki giggled. "What, Ma?"

"Promise me you'll keep the farm and stay away from two-legged male critters."

"You mean like yonder Breck there." Vicki pointed toward the palm-lined mess hall.

"Ah, my favorite brunettes," Breck said when Bunny and Vicki joined the line winding out through the mess hall screen door. "I have a treat in store for you and the other lovelies of the Hollandia WAC detachment. Listen, can you hear it?"

A young corporal beside Breck explained, "It's the fri—the new La Conga orchestra."

Breck made the introduction, "Andy McBride—Mac—my right-hand man. Andy, meet Bunny and Vicki."

"What's the La Conga?" Vicki asked.

Breck answered, "Why, Vicki honey, only the greatest nightclub this side of El Morocco. It has the biggest dance floor outside Roseland and the hottest band since B.G. But that's not the best part."

Bunny said with exaggerated disbelief, "There's *more?*"

"The best part is that all Wacs will be the guests of Base Special Projects for the inaugural dance."

From inside the mess hall Bunny heard the La Conga band playing a passable version of "Brazil" although the drummer hit his rim shots just off the beat. But what the band lacked in talent was more than made up for by volume.

"Well, what do you think, Bunny?" Breck asked.

The band finished its number and immediately struck up "That Old Black Magic" with a rumba beat.

"I think Xavier Cugat is probably tossing his maracas off the Waldorf-Astoria roof garden this minute."

"Okay, so they're not as good as the Glide 'Em Inn bunch, but the La Conga Club makes that place look like a pig waller."

"Don't you guys listen to Bunny," Vicki said. "I think the band's swell."

The foursome made their way through the chow line and sat down at a trestle table as the band broke into "Frenesi."

"Don't they play anything but a Latin beat?" Vicki asked.

Mac looked at Breck and then back to Vicki. "Don't you like that kind of music, Vicki?"

"Oh, I adore it," Vicki said and moved her shoulders under her khaki shirt in time to the enthusiastic rhythm.

Mac looked at Breck. "Hot dog!"

"But, Breck," Bunny broke in, "you know the regs—Captain Bright has to approve all party requests in advance."

"Leave her to me, sweetheart. I'm going to go charm her right after chow."

"That may be too late. She's off to Brisbane this evening."

Breck jumped up. "Hold my place, Mac. I'll be back in two shakes."

"I think we should go to the La Conga," Bunny overheard a Wac at the next table say, "after all he's done for us."

"Yea," said another voice. "Besides, I heard Breck's place is something special."

Breck reappeared, looking uncharacteristically despondent,

and edged past the chow line that was snaking alongside the steam tables.

"The captain's gone, but not before she cleared the control tower group for tomorrow and the Seabees for next Saturday."

"Oh, I'm sorry, Breck," Vicki said, her voice apologetic.

Bunny felt Breck's frustration. Or was the frustration her own? Still, she had not planned to go to any dance, no matter who had it. She had promised Harry she'd be at the photo lab Saturday night. "I'm sorry, too, Breck." And she *was* sorry. For an instant, she imagined what it might be like to move, sinuously swaying, across a dance floor in his arms.

Breck slicked his hair off his forehead and it immediately curled and fell forward again. "Don't pack away your dancin' slippers just yet."

"But, Breck, I won't be going to any dance tomorrow night," she said matter-of-factly. "Colonel Duquesne wants me to open the lab and run a roll of film for him."

Later that evening, Mac shook his head violently from side to side. "Jesus, the guys are gonna be friggin' mad, after all the friggin' trouble." He looked sideways at Breck, who was sipping some day-old four-star premium at the new bar in La Conga, something he rarely did.

Breck stared thoughtfully at his drink. "You know, Mac, the girls aren't going to like this stuff straight. I want you to get around to all the mess halls tomorrow early and get all the canned orange juice you can come up with. Got that?"

"Sure, Smitty, I got it, but what's the friggin' use? The girls can't come."

Breck smiled, a slow confident grin. "That's right, they can't come, but that's not the same as *won't* come."

"I don't get it. You mean you thought up a way to beat out the friggin' control tower guys and their Glide 'Em Inn?"

"Uh-huh—a surefire way, Mac."

"Come on, give," Mac said doubtfully.

Breck picked up a deck of cards and shuffled them expertly, riffling through them until all four queens were laid neatly on the bar. "Here's our Wacs, and here"—he moved an ashtray and spread out the four jacks—"are the control tower group, who just don't happen to have any wheels assigned to their outfit. Get it, Mac?"

"Nah."

"Okay, let me lay it out for you." Breck was working it out in his head as he went along. "Now, if these jacks don't have wheels they're going to have to go to our old buddy Sergeant Murray at the motor pool. And what will friend Murray give them but the dirtiest, ugliest wrecks ever got together in one bunch, absolutely guaranteed to break down halfway to the WAC compound."

"Say, that's a friggin' dirty trick."

Breck was the picture of injured innocence. "War is heck, my friend."

"Yeah—well, I don't want to be around when those guys catch on." Mac poured himself a generous drink. "But that still doesn't mean we can get the girls for *our* dance." He was puzzled again. "Or does it?"

"Mac, use your brains. They're expecting a convoy of trucks at nineteen fifteen hours"—Breck turned the jacks face down and dealt up four kings—"and, by God, Mac, there'll *be* a convoy. We don't want a bunch of disappointed gals, now, do we?"

Mac grinned, delighted. "Naw, Smitty, we sure to friggin' hell don't want that. But what about your—what about Bunny?"

Breck looked around at the La Conga dance floor still in the process of last-minute renovations, and for an instant imagined Bunny sitting at one of the tables. "Mac, old buddy," he said, revealing a palmed ace of hearts, "that's when a guy has to pull out his ace in the hole."

On Saturday afternoon the makeshift WAC beauty shop was crowded. Bunny knew she had never appreciated the sheer luxury of having her hair done as she did at Hollandia, where the women in her tent took turns being the beautician under Bunny's instruction. Two sinks, served by a rubber hose with a clamp to shut off the cold water, an assortment of waveset and lotions, a prized shipment of the latest Rayette home cold waves, curling irons heated on a camp stove, and wicker chairs that Breck had found God knows where: what more did La Jeunesse have than this? Bunny had brought the requisite helmet full of warm water, which she had set in the sun until it reached lathering temperature.

She had blissfully surrendered to a scalp massage when Vicki stuck her head inside the tent and called her name. "Here—but I refuse to move. MacArthur himself couldn't get me up right now."

"How about Colonel Duquesne?"

"How about him?"

"Here's a note from him that was dropped off at the OR."

Bunny pushed the towel from her eyes and held the note up to read it.

With obviously suppressed curiosity, Vicki inquired politely, "I hope there's nothing wrong with the colonel."

"No. He was called to an emergency staff meeting at Humboldt Bay. Doesn't know when he'll be back."

"Then you're off duty tonight. Come on to the dance. You *know* you'll enjoy yourself after you get there."

"Why not? Thanks." Bunny hummed a bar of "Don't Get Around Much Anymore." "I'd hate to be all dressed up in my best khaki pants and combat boots with noplace to go."

Vicki sighed wistfully. "Don't you wish we were going to Breck's new club? Don't you think Mac is awful cute? Such a gentleman. Remember how he made sure the band was playing the kind of music I like?"

At precisely 1915 hours, the Wacs walked carefully on the duckboards laid out on top of the muddy path to the gate. Up drove a convoy of freshly washed trucks, engines purring, driven by soldiers in clean uniforms who had gotten so close to their razors their faces glowed pink in the headlights.

"What's *your* names?" demanded one of the Wac cooks of the drivers. "Are you guys new to the control tower group?"

Remembering the dictatorial authority of Wac cooks during her own KP days, Bunny balefully observed that they'd all have made inspired grand inquisitors.

"Name's Gunner," the lead driver said. "We're . . . new replacements. Climb in, ladies, the party's about to begin."

Grumbling, the cook allowed herself to be helped into the truck with the rest.

For twenty minutes they jounced inside the truck until Bunny said, "These fellas must be taking the long way round to the Glide 'Em Inn. I can't tell *where* we are." The truck turned off the main road. Bunny could see lanterns hanging from the trees, illuminating the tangle of vines that held the jungle together. She heard the sound of music up ahead.

Recognizing the tune, all the women in the lead truck sang along in broad Caribbean accents, "Drinkin' rum and Coca-Cola, go down Point Cumana. Both mothah and fathah, workin' for the Yankee dol-lah."

Bunny laughed out loud, an absolutely crazy idea forming in her mind. "He *wouldn't* dare," she said aloud.

Now Vicki caught on and stuttered, "You don't mean—we aren't going—this can't be the—"

"I *do* mean, we *are* going, and this *is* La Conga," Bunny said as the truck stopped next to a large concrete patio.

Breck, Mac and dozens of other spick-and-span GIs caught the bewildered Wacs as they jumped down from the tailgate.

"Remember, ladies," Breck said as the host, "the guy who catches you is your date for the evening."

The angry Wac cook stood on the tailgate. "You guys can't do this. Why, it's kidnapping!"

Breck swept her his cavalier bow, winking at Bunny. "Nothing of the kind, I assure you, ma'am. The control tower group had truck trouble, and we're standing in for them like good buddies should. Now—"

"It isn't authorized," the cook insisted.

"Aw, forget it, Cookie," a soprano voice behind her commanded. "The rest of us are dying to see the place."

Breck grinned at them. "Listen, if you don't like it here, you can leave quicker'n a bride and groom after the weddin'. Come on, let me show you La Conga."

Bunny jumped down into his outstretched arms, and, tucking her hand over his arm, he led her, followed by the rest, around the patio pots planted with clumps of kunai grass, pointed out the fish pond, and finally took them up the steps and inside the club.

Bunny was astounded. The dance floor of smoothed-out concrete in front of the La Conga orchestra was a good four hundred feet square, and above it, draped from the ceiling, hung a canopy of opened silk parachutes colored robin's-egg blue and orange, illuminated by soft indirect light. A rope draped with silken tassels a foot long fashioned from shredded parachute cords separated the dance floor from an elegant bar stretching across the rear. Behind it hung an oil painting of an exotic nude. Bunny was sure she had once seen it in the attack group's dayroom.

Breck interrupted the Wacs' oohs and ahhs. "And for those occasions, ladies, when you desire to retire to the powder room . . ." He waved his hand toward the side door labeled "Salle de Poudre." Frenchy opened it proudly to expose a walkway with a laced-palm-frond roof, protection against sudden downpours.

Bunny squeezed Breck's arm. "You—you're crazy. Crazy but wonderful—you've thought of everything." She didn't even bother to keep the admiration out of her voice.

Breck smiled, the image of the gracious host. "And now the first drink is on the house—a special libation from that master mixologist Corporal Andy McBride in honor of our guests, the FEAF Wacs."

Behind the bar, Max ladled glasses of purple liquid until every GI and Wac had one. "To La Conga," he said, his glass raised in Vicki's direction.

"La Conga," everyone in the room toasted and drank.

Vicki coughed, her face turning red. "Jesus," she said, "what *is* this purple stuff?"

Mac shrugged in Breck's direction. "I did what you told me, Smitty, only I couldn't find enough orange juice, so I put in grape, lemon, pineapple—everything."

Breck went to the center of the dance floor and held his hand up for silence. "Ladies and gentlemen, the first prize of the evening—one cloud-soft rubber air mattress—goes to PFC Vicki Hansen for naming our La Conga cocktail. I give you— the Purple Jesus!" He led the applause. "And now, for your dancing pleasure, the La Conga orchestra, just returned from a triumphant engagement at the New Guinea Astoria roof jungle."

There was a rush of soldiers toward the few unattached Wacs, but Bunny saw only one shouldering his way toward her, was caught by his eyes, by his utterly effortless masculinity, and, without any urging or awareness that her feet were moving, she was carried with the crowd toward Breck. They met at the tasseled rope, she on one side, he on the other. Instead of bending to unfasten it, he reached for her, placed his hands on each side of her waist and lifted her over, holding her exuberantly aloft for a moment as if he wished to present her to the gods of La Conga.

Suspended, she felt the steady pulsing of blood through his hands, and felt her own heart quicken as she slid down into his arms. *Uh-oh, Bunny—wait just a minute,* she thought, her mind racing. *You've finished with all these emotions. You like the security of being Harry's girl. No more disenchantment, no more betrayal, no more sabotaged joy—not ever.*

Her voice sounded strained even to her own ears: "We Wacs appreciate all you've done for us, Sergeant Smith, but it's poor business, isn't it? I mean, aren't you losing a lot of money turning the Four Queens into a dance hall?"

Breck's eyes questioned the sudden change in her as she strained back against his arm. "That's mighty nice of you to worry, Miss Bunny"—his drawl was mockingly defensive— "but if you'll look around you'll see that the card room in the back is getting a lot of patronage." He pulled her toward him gently until her head rested against his shoulder. The band played a slow bolero version of her favorite Helen Forrest song, "More Than You Know," and Breck hummed a bar or two in a mellow baritone. "Do you disapprove of gambling on moral grounds?" He had dropped his broad drawl for speech that had only slightly slurred vowels.

"It's unpatriotic to take a guy's pay." She could hardly believe the self-righteous sound of the words.

"I see. Well, Sergeant, I don't agree with you. Men are going to gamble in New Guinea for lots of reasons—they're bored, they're lonely, they're scared of getting killed. They're going to do it in the barracks or on the job if they have no other place, and that's going to mean big problems between guys who have to live and work and fight together. So I built a place they can go to, where they'll get a fair run of the cards, have a drink, a place where they can forget for an hour or two that they're in a stinking island jungle full of malaria, bombs and Japs."

"You almost have me believing you're part of the USO war effort." Bunny desperately tried to protect herself from him with flippancy, but her tightly reined determination was crumbling. "Breck, I'm sorry—I've got a big Italian mouth. Forget about the crack that you took a guy's pay. It wasn't fair of me. I've heard how you've helped Joes in trouble. Let's drop the subject. Okay?"

Breck wasn't ready to drop it. "While we're on the subject of character, since you've examined mine, let's take a look at yours. As Louella Parsons would say"—and now his cocksure grin was upsetting her as much as his words—"what WAC sergeant is romancing an AAF colonel long after she's fallen in love with what handsome Southern nightclub owner?"

She stopped dancing so abruptly that Vicki and Mac, who had been behind Breck, bumped into them.

"Sorry, folks. The lady's overheated," Breck said. "Let's go outside and cool off, Bunny." He steered her out to the patio. "Come on, I want to show you my fish pond."

Bunny allowed herself to be propelled reluctantly to the pond's edge. Looking into the water, she saw the two of them close together and drew away from him to a safer distance.

"Look at that red fish over there." Breck pointed to a brilliantly striped fish. "Didn't know if he was going to live for a day or so—didn't know if he could adapt to the change from river to pond. But he did, and now he's thriving. The others— well, they died because their predictable little lives changed and they just gave up, didn't have the courage of Red Stripes over there. They just kept on insisting their lives couldn't change, and it killed them."

In the dim light of the patio Bunny saw other couples standing close to each other. Breck slipped his arm around her waist and drew her toward him. "How much courage have you got?"

"Breckinridge," she said, trying for her usual wry tone but giving his name an involuntary caress, "I'm a two-time loser in the love game and I can't stand the pain. I don't want to swim in your pond—I don't want to take any more chances."

"You want an insurance policy? Bunny, I can't give you that—but I can give you the way I feel about you and this. . . ."

If this was happening to Vicki, Bunny thought, I'd call it one hell of a fish story. But it wasn't happening to Vicki, it was happening, and happening quickly, to her. Suddenly, she could see that the safe life she'd planned with Harry—a moderate little love—wasn't just a practical response to pain, but a void.

Breck's lips touched the hollow of her neck and moved insistently along her cheek, leaving a trail of kisses, while her lips were parted, waiting and eager for him to reach them. But he stopped just short of kissing her mouth. "Open your eyes, Bunny. Wake up. You're not the first woman who's loved a man she shouldn't have loved." Damn Vicki and her gossipy tongue. Bunny just had time to think before Breck said, "Maybe the third time is the charm." And then he stopped any arguments reasonable or otherwise with his kiss. She tried to hold back a little longer, to think that if she wanted him he must be dangerous, to think he was too handsome, too glib, just like Johnny—ready to take her love and use it against her, to make her a victim and then taunt her with her own weakness. She was afraid to love him because this kind of risky love had always made planning and good sense impossible in her life. While her mind frantically searched for a way to avoid the change he demanded, her body yielded to the uncontrollable pleasure of being in his arms, and helplessly she felt herself tumbling toward surrender.

The sound of squealing brakes forced them apart. The patio was bathed by headlights, and confused couples shielded their eyes from the sudden brightness. Bunny saw Harry jump from an MP command car with a major beside him. Behind his car a string of battered trucks drove into the clearing, filled with men she recognized from the control tower group.

Harry strode up to Breck, who released Bunny as if he was in no hurry at all. "Technical Sergeant Smith," Colonel Duquesne said, the words frozen in fury, "you're under arrest for running a gambling game, selling alcohol to enlisted men, fraudulently luring an officer from his post, stealing a picture, and taking a WAC detachment to an unauthorized dance."

"You left out not sending my granny a Christmas card."

"Major"—Harry jerked his arm toward the provost marshal—"take this man into custody under double guard until I prefer charges, and post this damned place permanently off limits. Sergeant Palermo, you'll ride back with me."

52

By December 1944, Third Army Commander General George "Old Blood and Guts" Patton, Jr., makes daily news. On the first of December his forces reach the River Saar, on the third it captures the main bridge over the river at Saarlautern, on the sixth it enters Sarreguemines on the Moselle, on the seventh it penetrates the Siegfried Line northwest of Saarlautern.

"LIEUTENANT HANNADAY!" THE unmistakable voice of Lieutenant General Cecil Willis echoed and reechoed through SHAEF's main G-2 offices.

Page stood at her desk and buttoned her jacket. Outside she could see a sleety December rain slanting into headquarters' windows. Inside, the section's Christmas tree blazed with lights that one of the Wacs had received in a package from home. She checked her hair in the mirror taped to the side of the wall, rearranged a few errant strands, wiped a carbon smudge from her cheek and walked rapidly to the rear of the large office, and opened General Willis' door. "Yes, sir, you called for me?"

"Yes. Come in but leave the door open." General Willis jabbed his finger at the papers in front of him. "I'm not convinced that the MO unit has any value, even though I think Burkhardt's a good man. Morale operations—playing sad songs for the enemy, for Christ's sake. Anyway, how can we tell if it's effective without interrogation of enemy POWs right after they're captured? Not weeks later when they've had a chance to compare notes with other prisoners."

Page was quick to defend Paul. "The radio broadcasts have gone quite well, I understand sir. *Volksender Drei* has been jammed repeatedly by the Germans. At least their High Command considers the station dangerous." She wasn't exactly questioning the General. She'd been around the Army long enough to know that generals never had to explain themselves—didn't even have to be right, for that matter—and that *she* had to accept his views without question.

General Willis grunted acknowledgment of her defense. "Now they're broadcasting poetry besides playing records by Marlene Dietrich and Greta Heller—pure fluff."

"I think the idea is to make their soldiers homesick, so nostalgic they won't want to fight," she said, and bit her lip because she had so quickly forgotten to keep her opinions to herself.

"I *know* what the logic is, and I appreciate your loyalty to Burkhardt, but, hell, all soldiers are homesick—ours too. Front-line soldiers won't turn tail and run just because they're homesick." The General checked his appointment book. "Nothing that can't wait. That settles it then, I'm going up to the front for a few days, and if I don't see results . . . Let's see . . ."

His voice was booming. Page wondered why he was shouting.

". . . tomorrow is December fifteenth. Call Eighth Corps and tell them to isolate their next prisoners from the other POWs for special interrogation when I get there. Call Burkhardt and tell him I want him to go as interpreter. Too much security at stake to use lower-echelon people. Give him a chance to see firsthand what his work is accomplishing. Got that?"

"Yes, sir, I'll contact Colonel Burkhardt right away," Page said and hurried from the office.

She cleared the General's schedule through Sunday, called the forward command in Belgium, then asked the SHAEF operator for Paul's office. Annaliese answered.

"Good morning," Page said courteously, always a bit uneasy, even guilty, with the woman—as if she were constantly being confronted by the image of herself deeply in love with Paul. "May I speak to Colonel Burkhardt?"

"Yes, he's here, Lieutenant. Oh, before I call Paul to the telephone, I—congratulate you on your engagement. I've meant to many times, but . . . Paul told me about the university where he teaches, and the town. You will be very happy."

Page didn't miss the tremor in Anna's voice. "Thank you."

Paul came on the line. "Yes, Page." He sounded busy.

"I'm calling for General Willis, Paul," Page announced to make it obvious she would not call during duty hours for a chat.

"Of course, darling. I'm just in the middle of checking tonight's broadcast script. A record we expected from New York didn't arrive, and— Well, tell me what the General wants."

"He wants you to accompany him to the front; Middleton's Eighth Corps headquarters in the Ardennes."

"May I know why?"

"He's made no secret of it, Paul. He's growling like a wounded bear around here, saying he is not convinced the Morale Operations unit is doing the job. He probably wants to divert the funds to less subtle propaganda. Anyway, the only way to find out, he says, is to interrogate freshly captured Germans before they get a chance to mix. I'm afraid he wants to see for himself."

There was a long moment's silence at Paul's end.

"I'm sorry, Paul darling. I know how hard you've worked."

" 'Mine not to question why . . .' " Paul quoted, the "do or die" of the soldierly lament hanging in the air between them.

"Don't ever joke about dying to me. You've already given me enough scares for one war."

"Then we must forget there's a war on tonight, and I know just the place near the Boulevard Saint-Germain—a tiny jazz club in a medieval dungeon."

"Sounds intriguing, Paul. Meet me at the SHAEF bus stop at Rainbow Corners at nineteen hundred."

"That's the Red Cross Club, isn't it?"

"Right, it's closer to the Meurice than the Étoile transportation stop, so you won't have to walk so far. I know your leg bothers you more than you say."

They said goodbye. For a moment Page delayed returning to work, stared down at the mountain of papers on her desk. Every day brought her closer to the day when she would become Paul's wife, closer to fulfilling her promise to share his life and hold it as dear as her own.

When she was in his arms desire made her content, but when she was alone again plaguey questions came unbidden to the surface. Was it possible she would not be happy living Paul's life? Was it possible—despite the happiness that Anna-liese assumed and so obviously believed—that desire, liking, even love were not enough for a lifetime? Yes, she adored Paul, but whether this alone was enough for her was an unsolved mystery. Sometimes she thought that love was not her strongest impulse. What then? The alternative was to live a life no other woman had ever lived before—a military life that Paul kept reminding her was not even possible. Page felt snared in the dilemma of Matthew Arnold's line—what was it?—"wandering between two worlds, one dead, the other powerless to be born."

That night he was waiting when she stepped from the SHAEF bus in front of the Red Cross Club. The sounds of Glenn Miller's "Tuxedo Junction" beckoned to passing GIs, many of them combat troops on R&R from the front. Two buddies with their arms around each other staggered near the corner, yelling, *"Couchez-vous?"* at every passing French girl.

"Let's walk," Paul said, and steered her away from the crowd. He seemed moody, withdrawn.

It had been a gray, cold evening, unsoftened by snowfall. A few hearty *boulevardiers* sat in the sidewalk cafés, muffled against the cold, sipping hot strong coffee substitute. Although the lights of Paris were still dimmed by the necessity of war, the smell of roasting chestnuts from vendor carts near the Pont-Neuf conjured up the romance of the city for Page, and affectionately she squeezed Paul's arm.

He smiled down at her, his trouble momentarily forgotten. "Shall we take the Métro now? The leg is just a little stiff tonight."

"Does the wound still hurt, Paul?"

"No, not pain. It's just that this leg"—he rapped his left thigh—"feels about twenty years older than the other one."

They descended into the next Métro station. Warm, moist air full of human scents rushed up the steps to greet them, bounced off the glistening tile-lined corridors and followed them into the electric car as the door clanged shut behind them. They got off at the Saint-Germain-des-Prés exit, walked down the boulevard and turned onto a darkened side street in the heart of medieval Paris and down the worn stone steps of Musée des Trois-Mallots.

Page was delighted. "Oh, Paul, what a treasure! How on earth did you ever find it?" They had entered a stone cave, smoky, full of wailing soprano sax and jammed with uniformed representatives of every Allied force in France.

"I stumbled on it exploring the Left Bank one day. I had an idle hour and you were on duty. Out of curiosity, I dropped in to see the dungeon and get out of a sudden shower, as I recall. This place is a museum by day, you know. The manager here is a fascinating man, used to be *maître de chai* for Rémy Martin before he retired."

Page smiled wryly. "It is appropriate for a cellar master to end up being a cellar manager."

They stopped at the bottom of the stone steps and waited to be seated.

"Oh look, Paul, there's Annaliese with a Free French officer. She's seen us. Shall we join them?"

Paul looked uncomfortable. "Would you mind if we didn't? I'd like to have you to myself this evening, and—you'll laugh at this, Page—when you and Anna are together . . ." Paul stopped, uncertain. "Let's just not mix business with pleasure tonight."

Page nodded. So Paul felt it, too. A strange kind of division, and yet a sameness, between the two women.

Through the blue haze of cigarette smoke, the elderly manager approached. *"Bon soir, colonel,* it is delighted to see you again,"* he said in polite if ungrammatical English.

"Good evening, Monsieur Saint-Honoré," Paul answered and shook his hand. *"Permettez-moi de vous présenter* Mademoiselle Hannaday."

"Enchanté, mademoiselle," the aged man murmured, bending over her hand. "Follow me, *s'il vous plaît."*

He showed them to a small banquette in the rear of the underground room under a chiseled stone wall that curved outward behind them, signaled a waiter and whispered an order. In minutes the waiter returned with a dusty bottle of Rémy Martin cognac marked *"extra vieille."*

"Monsieur et mademoiselle, I blended this myself some years ago, and hid it from *les Boches."* He then wiped the bottle with

a practiced flourish, decanted it, and poured the amber liquor into a warmed snifter, which Page cupped in her hands, sipping. The tiny sips flooded her mouth with insistent, pervasive flavor.

"Monsieur Saint-Honoré, this is exquisite. I've never tasted anything like it."

The old cellarer beamed. *"Bon, merci,"* he said, and, adding to her glass, he bowed and left.

"What an interesting man," Page said, relaxing against the back of the banquette. "There is something absolutely fascinating about people who love what they do and are very good at it." She saw Paul's face drop its smile of pleasure. The moody look returned. "What is it, Paul? What did I say?"

He was silent for a moment, and then, his eyes miserable, he said, "Is that so important to you?"

"Is what so important? I was just making an idle comment." The low, sweet notes of "I'm Coming, Virginia," the old Bix Beiderbeck solo, twined around them as Paul looked at her so intently he could have been trying to see under her skin.

Abruptly he spoke, as if he had been holding back a secret part of himself for a long time. "I will never be one of those men of action you admire—" He shook his head to stop her interrupting. "No, hear me out. I'll go back to teaching after the war, maybe become head of the romance languages department before I die, but most likely not. We'll live in a fishbowl academic community with an insular mentality."

Page saw his face recede from her, although he hadn't moved.

"I'm not denying it's an unexciting life. It suits me fine, but if it made you miserable, if you stayed with me only out of pity—*God,* how I'd hate that."

"Paul, *what* is wrong with you tonight? I adore you, you know that. You're depressed over your work, that's it, isn't it? You know Willis. He could be using this MO business as an excuse to get to the front, to put a cluster on his DSC. Oh, Paul, you know what an old firehorse he is." She felt like the boy with his finger in the dike stanching the flow, only somehow she had punched the hole. She had never dreamed that Paul—sweet, matter-of-fact Paul—would tune in to her deepest doubts, hear whispers of the subtle, mostly unspoken questions of her own mind. But he must have. Suddenly she hated her own uncertainty. She would never want to hurt him. Never! He deserved so much better from her.

The manager returned. Page blessed him.

"Colonel, would Mademoiselle like to see *la musée?*"

Paul looked at Page. "It's a bit grim."

Nothing could be more grim than this, she thought, thankful for any diversion. "I'd love to see it."

They followed Monsieur Saint-Honoré down a tunnel farther underground until they came to an ancient planked door. He opened it. Light bulbs, strung on bare cords across the chamber, cast an eerie white glare over the gray stone interior.

Grim was hardly the word for it, Page could see. The museum was the repository of ancient torture instruments so beloved of summer tourists. An iron maiden stood against one wall, coffin for how many medieval Parisians, she wondered, its spikes ingeniously placed so that they would not kill immediately. An iron spiked boot, thumbscrews and a gruesome assortment of pincers and probes hung around the stone walls. "What was this used for, monsieur?" she asked, gladly focusing her attention on an innocuous-looking hole in the worn stone floor under which she could see flowing water.

"*Ah oui,*" he said and pointed to the block and tackle on the ceiling. "If the tongue, she was not loose, then the poor victims were hung upside down and dipped into the Seine. Since the river was the sewer for all the city, some thought it the worst torture of all." He laughed at the joke, which he had probably repeated daily for years.

Page shuddered from the damp, and Paul asked her if she wanted to leave. But before she could answer, she noticed small barred openings in the wall. "What are those, *monsieur?*"

"Cells, *mademoiselle.*"

"Cells? But they're not big enough! No one could live in there." The holes carved out of the stone wall were barely big enough for a person to sit in if he bent double. "You don't mean that people were kept in there?"

"*Oui.* The poor unfortunate ones were, for years, and when they got out they walked like this." He bent over and crept crablike close to the floor.

Page looked at the tiny cells in a horror so profound, so personal, it was almost like a sentence on her. She could not imagine a life so constricted, so devoid of anything but the effort to survive and, having done that, to be left at the end with aged, shriveled flesh—with nothing. Before she could stop herself, she blurted out her horror, "A life like that isn't worth living, in a cage, like an unreasoning animal. I'd rather the iron maiden and get it over with!" That is your truth, she thought. She glanced quickly at Paul, too late. He had frozen at her outburst, and on his stricken face she could see he had made a connection she hadn't intended. Or had she? Her head was spinning. . . .

Their host looked concerned. *"Mademoiselle* is ill?"

"No, *monsieur,"* Page said thickly, "I'm just tired. Please forgive me."

"Bien sûr," he said.

But Page knew, as she and Paul returned to the nightclub to retrieve their coats, that it did matter. It mattered very much to both of them. She saw that it mattered to Anna, too, who watched them leave, frowning questioningly.

Paul barely touched Page as they retraced their steps from the Boulevard Saint-Germain and he put her on the late bus to SHAEF. "I'll see you when I get back from the front."

"Oh, Paul, please—we never quarrel."

But he left her and walked in the direction of the Hotel Meurice, his body bent into the night.

A soft snowfall had begun to cover the city of lovers.

53

Hitler's personal plan to halt the Allied progress into Germany calls for a surprise panzer thrust through the Ardennes, a sector used to train green American replacements and refresh exhausted combat troops pulled back from the line. Thickly forested, the Ardennes is infiltrated by SS men disguised as GIs.

PAGE WAS IN the deepest part of sleep an hour before her alarm was set to go off on Friday, December 15, when she awoke to a knock on her door. "What is it?" she questioned, her voice muffled by her pillow, happy to be awakened from a horrible dream—Paul had been torturing her, while she wore a black mask over her face. Shivering, she dismissed the images from her consciousness and called, "Come in."

The duty officer opened the door and stuck her head in. "Just took a message from General Willis, Hannaday. He wants you at Orly as soon as you can make it. Says he's holding the plane. If you're going to London will you bring me back some Bowsers?"

Page struggled upright. "He wants me at Orly *now?* Are you sure?"

"Sure I'm sure. Who else would he want in these billets?"

"Okay, thanks. But don't get your mouth set for English toffee—that's not where I'm going."

She dressed quickly in jacket and slacks and threw underclothes and two shirts into her musette bag. She nixed her wool dress uniform coat in favor of her utility coat with a zipped-in heavy fleece lining. Rugged and bulky, still it shed everything from rain to hail and she didn't have to endure that awful wet wool smell.

A staff car waited outside the Allied Women's BOQ, and

they made good time through the deserted predawn streets of Paris. The reddish gold of daybreak was hovering at the end of the runway where a Dakota waited, propellers turning. "Here you go," the flight chief said, pulling her up and into the plane as the blocks were snatched from under the wheels.

General Willis motioned her to the seat beside him in the rear. Paul nodded from his seat forward. Willis had the contents of his dispatch case spread on the seat opposite. "There are fresh reports of company-strength probes by the enemy in the Ardennes, and I think they bear on Fifth Corps's preparation for an offensive on the northern flank. I want Ike to have an overall intelligence analysis by afternoon. Sorry for the early-morning roust, but I didn't think you'd gripe. You'll be farther forward than any Wacs, except maybe Bradley's— something to tell your grandkids." He reached for a cup of coffee the crew chief poured from a thermos, then fell silent over his map case as the plane became airborne, circled Orly and headed northeast. "Take this down and see that it's encoded top secret and sent priority as soon as we land."

When the Dakota had reached cruising altitude, Page and the General were hard at work on the report. Several times Page stole glances at Paul, but he appeared to be asleep. Was he truly tired, or was this Paul's way of showing her that he was on his guard? Strange—two people who liked each other, loved each other, instinctively knew the most painful places to probe. She shivered, feeling the cold rejection of his silence this morning as he must have felt the rejection of her words last night. This tension between them made it more difficult to finish the work at hand. Just as she began to pull the General's words together she would lose the sense of them and have to begin again. The doubts that were growing between her and Paul crippled her concentration.

At last she finished and marked the message for transmission from VIIIth Corps communications. By the time they landed, the quiet was embarrassing her and she had decided Paul was sulking. As they stepped onto the tarmac, irritation began to take the place of embarrassment. After all, what had she done last night but react to a vicious form of torture? Why should she feel guilty for his suspicions? Two could turn a cold shoulder as well as one.

In the staff car that picked them up, she was the punctilious junior officer deferring to the colonel; they could have been strangers. She noticed that General Willis threw sharp glances at both of them, then joined the pointed silence, exasperation added to the other tensions on his face.

The road to Middleton's headquarters was lined with civilian carts piled heartbreakingly high with household goods and with the very old holding the very young, moving toward the rear. It was bitter cold. Ahead of her, Page could hear the sporadic boom-boom of artillery. As they neared headquarters, companies of GIs just pulled from the murderous Hurtgen Forest fighting to the north bivouacked by the road, resting and cleaning their weapons for the push through Belgium into Germany.

Once inside the headquarters building, Willis learned that General Middleton was inspecting forward command posts but had left orders for his intelligence officer to give General Willis any help he asked for.

"I want a room to interrogate the prisoners you're holding for me," Willis snapped.

Although he was always a bit abrupt, Page could tell that the General was more than usually impatient, and she suspected the cause. Damn! She had gone to such great lengths to prove herself a hard-working junior officer no different from any of the General's male staff. Now she had jeopardized all of the months of good work by allowing male–female troubles to interfere with a soldier's first military duty, which was never to allow personal considerations to surface. An army brat was *born* knowing that much! Although General Willis had always been supportive of women soldiers, such behavior was bound to confirm his gravest doubts about the ability of men and women to work side by side. She would have to try harder than ever to regain his confidence.

The General issued orders nonstop. "Page, you get that message off to SHAEF and hold yourself ready for another report. Captain—" he indicated Middleton's G-2 staff man— "see that the lieutenant here has a room to work in and get her some hot chow. The colonel and I could use some, too, and make the coffee hot. Okay, start the parade. And I want those Krauts marched one at a time straight through the headquarters and back here to me. Let's overwhelm 'em. Most are privates who've never been in a higher headquarters, let alone talked to a general. You'll find"—this time he was speaking to Paul—"that old-fashioned psychology works, too. Scare the piss out of 'em, I say."

Page gave the signal officer her message, waited for it to be encoded and got the transmission confirmed by SHAEF. "Thanks, Captain, I may have another, or several, later."

"Anytime, Lieutenant. Everthing's quiet in this sector. The weather's closing in. Germans won't start anything this close to Christmas."

Tired from the loss of sleep, Page napped on a cot in General Middleton's office until Paul shook her. "We've got another report for you, Page. Are you up to it?"

"Of course." She forced herself to ignore the back he immediately turned to her. How could she fight his ghosts for him? She could barely face her own. But still he was a haunting presence in the room even after he'd shut the door behind him, as if he had been standing over her, watching, before she woke.

Page hurried to the rear room—which had once been a storage room, by the look of it—in the provincial French hotel now turned VIIIth Corps headquarters. General Willis waited. He looked tired and haggard. At fifty-three, he had added ten years of lines to his face since she'd first met him, some, Page could see, within the last few hours.

"Close the door, Lieutenant, we don't want to feed the rumor mill out there."

She did, and took a seat at a table piled with empty coffee cups, K-ration biscuits and ashtrays. The General handed her a sheaf of scrawled notes written on the back of yellow message forms.

"Can you make any sense of these?"

"I'll try, sir."

"Something's going on over there." He pointed to the east. "They're up to something. Burkhardt, do you agree?"

"Yes, General. The answers are too pat, almost rehearsed. I think these men allowed themselves to be captured to feed us info to lull us into a false sense of security."

"Now, why do you think they'd do that?"

"Only one reason. They want us to think they're planning

something in this sector, but they're really going in some other place—the same strategy we used on them on D Day, General."

"Maybe, but maybe old Fritz wants us to think just that. Maybe he's telling us the truth because he figures we won't believe him in a month of Sundays. Page."

"General."

"I've already told the colonel and I'll tell you. The quarrel about the Morale Operations psychological-warfare unit was a smokescreen. OKW knows who Paul is—hell, the German high command knows what I have for dinner every night by midnight, at least we have to assume they do. What I'm really here to do is to check out some rumors we've had about panzer movements, troop concentrations, across the front lines in Belgium and Luxembourg. Are they going to hit and run—for a holiday home-front morale booster—or are they going to counterattack in strength? We didn't think they could do it, but now I'm not so sure." He rubbed his cheeks, already dark with stubble. "Let's add it all up and see what we've got."

For the next two hours Page worked with the General and Paul on the report until she had the substance of the interrogations on paper. Paul seemed to be relaxed with her; perhaps his coldness had been connected with the General's questioning his work after all.

"Now send that on to Ike and we'll see what he says." As the words left his mouth, the General was already heading for the cot that Page had vacated.

Within an hour SHAEF CINC had replied, summoning the General back to Paris for a top staff meeting early the next morning, December 16.

"Damned fog closing, Burkhardt," General Willis said. "I'll send the plane back for you when it clears, but try to get a more accurate estimate of enemy strength by tomorrow, the earlier the better."

"General, I think Lieutenant Hannaday should return with you. I'll use a headquarters clerk."

Page stood to attention. "General, I think I could be of help to Colonel Burkhardt, if you won't need me."

General Willis shrugged into his blanket coat with black lieutenant general's striping on the sleeves. "Okay," he said doubtfully, "but be careful, and when Burkhardt says you leave, then *you leave*—none of those women-soldier arguments of yours. And, Burkhardt, don't go below division. It's too risky. Wouldn't the Krauts just *love* to get their hands on you two?"

They watched the General climb into his staff car, saluted and went back inside out of the cold and the gathering fog.

Paul spoke first. "While you're sending the General's ETA to SHAEF, I'll get on the field telephone to the One Hundred Sixth at Saint-Vit and Twenty-eighth Division headquarters so they'll know we're coming. They'll have to send out patrols to get prisoners tonight."

Page heard a softness in his voice, an unspoken plea for understanding, of what she did not know, but she did understand that it had to do with her. "Paul, I'll get this off and then maybe we can find a corner—talk things over."

"Not tonight, Page, not until we get back to Paris. This is not the place. I can't think; we might both say things we don't mean. Anyway, I'm tired and I want to make an early start tomorrow—five o'clock. Can you be ready?"

"Yes, of course I can." She too knew how to tend to business.

Early the next morning it was snowing, visibility was poor, and they didn't leave until after daybreak. Reports had come through from both divisions that the enemy was attacking in force through the forested Ardennes area, but they looked like strictly localized engagements.

Middleton's aide stopped them as they were leaving. "Colonel, the General insists you have a first-class sharpshooter as a driver. Hold up a minute and I'll get someone from the rifle company out back."

Within minutes, a man trotted up, checked the safety on his rifle and climbed into the driver's seat.

Paul got into the back seat with Page. "Let's go to Twenty-eighth Division headquarters first," he directed the driver, then said to Page, "Their patrols bagged some prisoners last night." He settled heavily into the backrest and pulled his helmet down over his eyes.

Just like her father, Page thought, Paul could sleep his way through emotional problems, while she seemed to need to suffer every twinge. Women were happiest, she remembered someone had said, when they were ankle deep in their sub-conscious. Not even a uniform changed that. She sympathized with Paul—anxious about his work, about her—but she couldn't understand the purely male desire to escape from almost all emotional examination.

Fog lay between the trees on either side of the snow-covered road when the driver stopped to check the road signs. "She-it." He rubbed his cold hands together. "I coulda sworn the Twenty-eighth was that way."

Paul sat up. "What is it, soldier?"

"Colonel, I came through here yesterday, and, well, I thought we made a right turn here. Now the sign points straight ahead."

Just then Page saw a jeep detach itself from under the trees beyond the crossroad. The driver wore a white MP brassard and a shiny white helmet. "Ike's little snowdrops," the GIs on leave in Paris called them. He highballed a salute, just like someone fresh from stateside.

"May I be of assistance to the colonel."

Page saw Paul's mouth twist slightly in amusement at the formal request. "Yes, Sergeant, you can help us find the way to Twenty-eighth Division headquarters. My driver here seems to think the sign's wrong."

"No, sir, just came from there myself, sign's right on the money." The sergeant smiled at Paul and shrugged toward the driver. "Hey, Mac, it's easy to get lost in this fog, but if you drive straight ahead you'll hit them right on the kisser. Okay?"

Paul nodded and returned the sergeant's salute, then motioned to the driver to continue.

"That's one odd GI," Page said, looking back as they left the MP behind. "What a strange mixture of stilted English and slang. Wonder what part of the States he's from."

Paul nodded, but his mind was obviously not on her remarks as he watched their progress through the thickening fog. Up ahead for the next few miles they could hear the explosions of heavy mortar shells. "How far now?" he asked the driver.

"Dunno, sir. Can't make out any landmarks in this peasoup; can't be more'n a couple miles, though."

They came upon a squad stretched on each side of the road.

461

Paul tapped the driver on the shoulder and told him to stop at the head of the column. A very young second lieutenant walked over and reported to Paul.

"How far to Division, Lieutenant?"

"Sorry, sir, we're replacements and we're lost." The lieutenant got out his map and traced a route with his forefinger. "Map's wrong, too, Colonel."

Paul reached for the map. "Does it show a right turn back there at the crossroads?"

"Yes, sir, it did, but the MP said it was wrong. Said to go this way and it would cut miles off our march—"

As he spoke, the sound of a machine gun's steady tat-tat-tat followed by the thunk of bullets ripping into the metal of their jeep hit Page's ear. Paul shoved her face down into the leather seat.

"Get down!" he yelled in a strange, shrill voice that surprised her.

All around her she could hear the screams and animal grunts of men mortally hit. A grenade exploded in front of them and she heard its fragments thunk against the front seat. What was Paul saying? The noise, the confusion. She couldn't think.

"Get out of here," Paul yelled in her ear, pushing her. Half falling, she dropped to the frozen ground and raced the few steps to the side of the road, jumped into the brush with two GIs and dug her body into the embankment. She was surrounded by the whine of bullets, so intimate and personal compared with the distant thunder of London's bombs. She was trembling.

"Oh, God," one of the soldiers rasped, "they've got a halftrack with a flamethrower."

Page could hear the squeal and squeak of tank tracks on the road, bearing down on them.

"We've got to knock it out before they use the flamethrower," the lieutenant yelled, and, racing along the side of the road, he threw grenades at the tank treads. One, two, three explosions rocked the ground under Page. The smell of cordite stung her nostrils, smoke drifted into her eyes, but she couldn't take them off the scene in front of her.

The Germans were still firing from inside the—what had she heard them called?—*Schützenpanzerwagen*. Firewagon!

The name held terror in it for every dogface. Was this the fire-breathing dragon she'd talked about so blithely back in the safety of OC barracks, she thought crazily—the one she would have to slay before she could call herself a soldier? Suddenly, the firing stopped. The silence was more ominous than the expectation of searing flame or the crack of rifle shot had been. She stretched out her hand to a fallen carbine and knew that if she had to she could use the short-barreled semiautomatic. Bless General Willis for insisting that all members of the staff, even Wacs, fire the .45 automatic and the M-1 carbine for qualification. Bless him again, she prayed, for defying orders that Wacs not have weapons training. What had he said?—"In a tight spot you can't throw your typewriter at the enemy." Picking up the rifle that one of the dead had dropped, she checked the clip to see that it was loaded and then lay against it, hugging it to her urgently as if it were her lover, gaining strength from the cold metal and the smooth pressure of the stock against her cheek. If she had to, she would shoot.

The soldiers beside her opened up, and Page, without thinking, cool, steady, squeezed off round after round at the firewagon camouflaged with fir boughs. Under this covering fire she saw the lieutenant and a sergeant dash to the side of the disabled half-track and lob grenades inside it through a rectangular opening in the front. A hideous orange flame burst through the slit and curled its tentacles down the sides and up along the turret. She cheered as it burst apart.

The soldier next to her yelled at the half-track as if it were human, "Burn, you sonofabitch!"

Paul dropped breathless at her side. "We've got to"—he gasped and swallowed air—"get out of here, Page."

Page wondered if she could answer. She suspected that if she tried to say anything it would be a shriek. Surprisingly, she heard her own steady voice. "What do you want me to do?"

"There must be troops coming behind the half-track, Tiger tanks too, maybe—so this way is blocked. Best thing—get back to Eighth Corps fast. Our mission—to confirm German attack plans. Looks to me like they're confirmed. Now we've got to let Corps know about German infiltration—dressed in our uniforms, speaking our slang. But first"—he gripped her shoulder where she lay—"I've got to get you out of here."

"Paul, we can do it." She was pleased that a kind of calm,

463

like the center of a great storm, filled her. She might collapse later, but right now she felt she could do anything he asked.

"I'm going to make a dash for the car, turn it around. Then you run like hell when I give you the signal, and jump in."

Before she could say more, Paul was running in a crouching weave toward the jeep. He pulled the dead driver from behind the wheel and then gunned the car toward her.

"Now!" he yelled.

She was in the front seat beside him before she realized she was still hugging the M-1 to her, sling wrapped around her arm to steady it for firing. Behind them the small-arms fire picked up again until it too faded into the deathlike quiet of fog and forest.

"Paul," she asked as he maneuvered along the rutted road, "what are we going to do if those Germans masquerading as MPs are still at the crossroad?"

"We'll have to bluff it out, there's no other way."

Page shuddered from the cold and from the sight of congealing blood on the dashboard.

Paul slowed as he approached the junction. She knew he'd decided not to run it for fear she might get hurt. She gripped the weapon tighter, holding it low out of sight. Paul unsnapped the squarish holster containing his .45 automatic, and they glided to a stop in the middle of the crossroad.

For a moment, Page felt an almost palpable joy to see that twenty or so GIs were encamped by the road among the fir trees, with a cardboard fire going, cooking 10-in-1 rations. They had manned a deserted German pillbox, and it looked as though they were digging in for the winter. But fifty yards beyond, on the road toward VIIIth Corps, she spied the enemy "MPs," and her breath escaped her in a cloudy whoosh.

"Paul, look down there."

"I see them, and they see us." Just then the "MP" jeep had started down the road toward them.

About fifty feet away the jeep stopped; the German disguised as an MP sergeant got out and walked toward them. Page was acutely aware of a battlefield second sight: she saw every step the sergeant took while simultaneously seeing the comrades he'd left in the jeep readying their automatic weapons. If she hadn't known they were the enemy, she wouldn't have seen this preparation, just as the soldiers beside the road had glanced up at the MPs and then gone back to preparing their meal. How could she alert them without getting everyone killed?

The "sergeant" saluted. "What's the problem, Colonel?"

Did he sound suspicious?

"Got lost back there, Sergeant." Paul's voice was just the right friendly superior-to-subordinate tone. "Guess we'll go back to Corps and wait for the fog to lift."

"Thought I heard firing from the west," the sergeant said. "Did you run into any trouble—and, say, where's your driver?"

Paul had slipped his .45 automatic out and now raised it into the "sergeant's" view. "Freeze! Don't make a move or you'll never see home again."

How long Paul could hold him without raising the suspicions of the Germans in the jeep Page couldn't guess; she just knew she *had* to do something. She couldn't start shooting; the Germans would kill her and Paul and half the GIs now hunched around the fire eating their rations. She remembered a bull session back at Des Moines where she, Bunny, Jill and Elisabeth had talked about what they'd do if they were ever in combat. She'd had a lot to say then, but now she couldn't remember a word of it.

There was no chance she could outshoot the enemy. What could she do? And then she remembered that women in the Maquis often acted as decoys while demolition teams worked right behind the Germans' backs. "Don't move, Paul," she whispered. Slowly, she got out of the jeep and stretched her arms over her head, wiggled her shoulders and, taking off her helmet, shook out her hair from under her watch cap. She must draw all eyes away from Paul. Walking toward the huddled GIs now staring up at her from their mess kits, she raised her arm in a carefree wave, ruffling her hair again, and hoped she looked as though she were on an afternoon stroll through the Bois de Boulogne. A half minute or more elapsed, and she knew she didn't have more than seconds left before either the "sergeant" or his comrades would make a move. In a low voice, which she tried to project harder than she ever had since she was in OC at Fort Des Moines, she said, "The MPs are Germans in disguise—shoot them! The MPs are Germans in disguise—*FIRE!*"

She dove into the fir trees and rolled behind a tree trunk as the GIs opened up with everything in their arsenal, drawing fire upon themselves, away from Paul. An American machine gun fired a staccato *put-put-put* to her left, and the MP jeep, which had turned and gunned off down the road at the first rifle report, swerved and overturned in a ditch. The one German who managed to jump clear was cut down before he'd gone three steps.

American soldiers approached Paul's jeep, where the disguised German now stood with his hands up, a dour expression on his face. "How did you know?" he asked.

Paul pointed at Page as she ran up. "She knew."

A young private standing with his gun barrel resting against the German's neck looked at her in obvious admiration. "Goddamn, ma'am. You ever want to change outfits, you can join us."

"Yeah." His buddy nodded. "That was some walk you took!"

Page laughed, the incredible energy she'd felt flowing away, leaving her limp. "Guys, when you started firing it was the sweetest sound I'd ever heard."

They invited her to share their rations, and as an afterthought, "You too, Colonel."

Paul looked at his watch. "It's almost zero eight hundred and we've got to get back to Corps. You soldiers be careful of any MPs on this road."

"Right, sir," the young private said, grinning. "We're always careful of MPs."

Paul nodded. "While you're at it, better question anyone who comes along in an American uniform." He put the German into the front seat and motioned Page into the back. "He's your prisoner, you take him in."

Picking up the M-1 from the floor, she trained it on the German's back, with the muzzle just touching.

"Colonel," the man said in English, "does the *Fräulein* know how to use that rifle?"

Paul jammed the jeep into gear. "*Kamerad,* you'd have to gamble that she doesn't. Is it worth it when you could sit out the rest of the war?"

Page never took her eyes off her prisoner all the way down the road to Corps, in spite of the increasing numbers of soldiers and vehicles heading toward the front who stopped to stare at the sight they made. She was aware that during the action she hadn't had time to analyze her own feelings, and now all those delayed emotions rushed in upon her: intense fear of death, followed by a rage that anyone would try to take the life she alone owned, and finally a rush of pure joy—not just because she was alive, but because she'd won. She'd tweaked the dragon's tail.

Paul pulled up in front of the former hotel; the street in front of VIIIth Corps headquarters was alive with soldiers on the move. Page's arm muscles ached from holding the carbine steady for so long, but she wouldn't lower it until she was finally relieved. Weary beyond anything she had ever known, she surrendered her M-1 and climbed down from the jeep.

"Christ, didja see that?" she heard one GI standing nearby say to another. "A goddamned colonel driving an MP with a Wac riding shotgun on him." He reached across his chest and scratched his armpit. "What the hell kinda war is this, anyway?"

54

Major Glenn Miller, director of the USAAF band, is missing and presumed lost on a cross-Channel flight from England to Paris, December 15, 1944.

BUNNY SAT DOWN hard on her air mattress, squeezing the last bit of air out of it to make it fit inside her bedroll. "There," she said in Vicki's direction, "I think we can get away with taking it if we roll it flat between the blankets. Anyway, we all weigh less than we did when we got to Hollandia, even counting the beads and bone carvings we traded for—"

"Sarge, listen." A woman near the tent entrance was monitoring the shortwave radio. "It's Tokyo Rose."

The last driving notes of Glenn Miller's "Chattanooga

Choo-Choo" vanished into a friendly American girl's voice: "Any futile hope you may have had of the Reich's collapse must have faded with the Germans' surprise counteroffensive in the Ardennes. Brave panzers and Wehrmacht soldiers have penetrated American lines and are this minute driving you Americans back all along a front stretching from Spa to Luxembourg. Before I get to some of your favorite GI jive, I understand that the Wacs are being sent up to the Philippines. You guys may think this is a nice Christmas present. Well, we have a nice Christmas present for *them*. Of course they won't get there."

Bunny laughed along with the rest of the women in the tent. "Wanna bet, Rosie?" she yelled at the radio set. "Just like we were never going to bomb Tokyo or take Saipan."

Vicki added, "Or Guam."

Captain Bright stuck her head inside the tent flap.

Bunny saw her first. "Atten-shun!"

"As you were. Carry on with your packing." The captain threaded her way toward Bunny's cot through duffle bags piled in the aisle. "Palermo, here are the 201 files for your group and the orders attaching you to the GHQ WAC at Tacloban. The rest of us wish we were going to Leyte with you."

"It won't be long until everyone moves up, ma'am."

"You're right." And the captain walked down the aisle shaking hands and wishing them luck. "By the way, Sergeant," she said, passing Bunny's cot on her way out, "don't take on any Japs single-handed this time." She lowered her voice. "At least not before Christmas, when a certain unit of First Corps is scheduled to be pulled back to Tacloban for replacements, along with a special friend of yours."

Breck! In spite of his having carried her Wacs off, Captain Bright had come to his defense last month, submitting an account of his invaluable additions to the FEAF Wacs' comfort and efficiency. Who knew but what she'd helped get Breck and the others a lighter punishment, although no one at FEAF but Harry had really wanted a general court. And since Colonel Duquesne couldn't prove that Breck had sent him on a wild-goose chase to Humboldt Bay, even he had to settle for reduction in grade and Private Smith's reassignment, along with his whole Base Special Projects group, to a Sixth Army line outfit.

"What was the captain whispering about?" Vicki said.

Bunny didn't know whether to repeat it or not. The news might send Vicki into raptures over Mac and bring down a host of unanswerable questions probing her own feelings about Breck. Still, she didn't have the right to keep such news from her. "I don't know where she got her information, but she says that Breck and Mac's outfit will be in Tacloban for Christmas."

"That's swell!" Vicki's mouth dropped wide open in joyous surprise. "Isn't that swell?"

Bunny's voice was flat. "Yes, swell."

Vicki slipped an arm through her pack and backed up to Bunny for help in settling it comfortably on her shoulders. "Listen to you," and she imitated Bunny's tone, " 'Yes, swell.' Don't you care? He did it for you, you know that? Gee, if I had a guy that crazy about me, I'd—"

A shout from outside halted Vicki's daydreams temporarily, "Fall out! Truck's here. Hurry it up."

Within an hour they had taken off, the big Sunderland flying boat spraying water high into the air before it banked on a north-northwest heading that would take them south of the Carolines and into the Leyte Gulf by midafternoon. A sudden tropical downpour thundered on the plane's roof, but Bunny did not have that comfortable protected feeling she remembered as a child in her room at home. She had not felt any certainty since that night at La Conga when her plan for a safe future had all but dissolved in Breck's arms. And Harry hadn't helped her with his insufferable pomposity. He had actually offered to forgive her and had insisted that his timetable for their life together could go forward. Did she really want to spend the rest of her life making love to a man who synchronized his watch with hers every morning? She thought about Harry's love for structure and the discipline of schedules, his iron resistance to the surprises of life; the very qualities that had at first made her prize a life with him looked now very much like a living death. Had Breck opened her eyes or had he just confused her?

"Think Tokyo Rose knew what she was talking about— about us, I mean?" one of the women asked Bunny.

"How could she? It was just one of her bad jokes."

Finally, Bunny dozed. It was the first time in months she'd been cool enough to drop off to sleep this side of exhaustion.

She awoke when the plane banked to one side, pressing her helmet sharply against the back of her neck.

Looking out the window, Vicki complained, "Leyte looks like just another jungle island to me."

"So, wha'dya expect?" called a voice from down the aisle. "Bermuda?"

"Aw, your mother wears combat boots!"

Bunny said, "Keep it down to a dull roar," and looked at the mottled green island passing beneath them. The shore was lined with LSTs and LSMs, the beach jammed with equipment and with lines of men passing materiel hand over hand to waiting trucks. The bay loomed below, and minutes later they taxied to an unloading dock.

As the plane wallowed to a stop Vicki said, "So much for Rosie's latest prediction," and, gathering her gear, she clambered down the steps.

They formed up and marched beyond the dock area to the trucks just off the beach waiting to take them to their new station.

Suddenly Bunny could hear the high whine of diving fighters. "Take cover!" she yelled, and ran for the first foxhole, threw down her duffle bag and dived into two feet of brackish green water. Looking back, she saw that Vicki was staring into the sky, making no move toward shelter. *Oh Christ, the girl didn't believe she was mortal.* "Vicki," Bunny shrieked, "get to cover!"

Vicki waved nonchalantly and ducked under a truck.

Another Wac jumped into the foxhole, sending a spray of water into Bunny's face. "Now what do you say about Rose, Sarge?" she puffed.

"Yuck! My apologies to Rosie," Bunny wheezed, pulling her head deep inside her helmet, the slimy water oozing down inside her boot tops.

Bursts of firing danced in from the docks, seeming to whiz just inches from Bunny's head. She heard the gentle *plop, plop, plop* of bullets hitting the sand fifty feet in front of her, and the labored engine noise of fighter planes pulling up after a dive. Moments later, the scream of diving planes began all over again, this time with the steady *POM, POM, POM* of ack-ack following them. A cheer swelled from the Joes in the brush, and, twisting on her back, she saw a smoking fighter spiral toward the jungle. Then another was hit, the shell ripping off a wing, and it started its ungainly head-over-tail fall from the sky.

Bunny saw Vicki crawl out from under the truck, stand up and cheer. The Wac in the foxhole yelled, "Sarge, they got two of them!" and shouted defiantly in the general direction of Tokyo, "Did you see that, Rosie?"

"Come on, come on," Bunny said, struggling upright under the weight of her waterlogged pack, her uniform filthy where she had rolled in the muck. "Let's get our gear together and get out of here. Rose could have the last laugh if they come back."

Bunny rushed toward Vicki. "Damn you, Vic! If you ever pull a dumb show-off stunt like that again, I'll put you on report—I mean it."

Vicki shrugged. "At least I'm dry," she said and stomped forward to open the door of the truck cab. The driver, nearly cut in two by big .50-caliber bullets, fell out on top of her, smashing her to the ground. She screamed, struggling to get out from under the awful weight. Several GIs ran forward, pulled him off and laid him next to the truck.

Bunny knelt by the girl. Blood was everywhere on her uniform, her hands, her face. Vicki was gulping convulsively, screaming silent screams. Bunny shook her. "Stop it! Stop it! There's nothing you can do."

"Oh, Bunny," she cried, tears mixing with red blood and dripping pink from her cheek, "God, I didn't think—oh, get this blood off me!"

During a muddy hub-deep ride up to Tacloban, Vicki sat in dazed silence staring at the sky, and Bunny knew that a part of Vicki Hansen was gone forever, maybe the best part, the part that laughed at death.

Bunny reported to the WAC lieutenant in charge, handed over the 201s and was shown to dormitory-type billets in an abandoned mission school, formerly Japanese officers' quarters. "Look," she said to the nine Wacs in the group after they had gotten Vicki to bed down the hall, "four walls. Did you ever think being closed in would feel so good?"

"Never," one Wac, stripped to her underclothes and dog

tags, said. "I used to tell my mom I'd go crazy if I didn't get out of the house. Boy, is she in for a surprise when I get home."

"When I get home," another took up the theme, "I'm going to have clean sheets every day, and fresh fruit for breakfast, and two-hour tub baths . . ."

"And food that doesn't come from green cans," Bunny added. "Okay, kids, I hate to break up your favorite game, but here's orders: the lieutenant told me we could have Christmas Day off to sightsee in the town, go swimming . . ." Nine Air Wacs sent up a cheer. *"But . . ."*—they groaned in unison— "there's always a *but* in the Army, and this one is that we'll all have to work twelve-hour shifts for the next eight days helping the GHQ Wacs get caught up on operations and casualty reports."

A T/5 said, "That's why we're here, gals, to unchain a guy from his typewriter."

"I better never run into Miss Giles, my high-school typing teacher, again," one woman said in a murderously vengeful tone. "She assured me that forty words a minute was my ticket to a well-paid job in clean, professional surroundings."

Within an hour, Sergeant Palermo made up the barracks detail roster, posted it and settled in. The photo lab night team didn't expect her until after chow. She checked on Vicki, who was sleeping soundly after two codeine APCs, then stared out at the compound, which looked very much like the playground of the parochial school she had attended in Bloomfield so many years before. But she wasn't thinking of home, at least not the way the other women were. Other questions filled her mind. Would Breck come looking for her here? He had been shipped out so fast they hadn't had a chance to see each other. Would he feel the same when they met again? And why did she care what he felt? Damn it! It was true. She wanted to see Breckinridge T. C. Smith. Standing there in the fading light, parrots squawking in the mangrove trees outside the walls, Bunny knew she wanted to see him more than she had allowed herself to realize.

55

*Christmas Day, 1944: Russian tanks besiege Budapest.
Allied planes fly six hundred sorties over the Ardennes, and
drop relief supplies on Bastogne. Americans secure Leyte Island in the Philippines.*

AT TACLOBAN, THE eight days before Christmas—long, exhausting days and nights of work, their monotony broken by
frequent air raids, washing laundry, eating, sleeping—passed
slowly. It was plain to Bunny that she and the rest of the Wacs
were slowly losing their health and their spirit. Three GHQ
Wacs had been sent back to the evac hospital with a diagnosis
of general debilitation. Of the ones on duty, several had skin
fungus infections; and some others were scarcely holding ma-
larial symptoms at bay with daily doses of Atabrine.

The worst problem was never drying out. Uniforms were
musty and moldering, shoes had to be cleaned and put back
on wet. She had complained to the lieutenant. "Ma'am, we all
need shoes. Some of the women have to tie theirs on their feet,
the leather's so rotten."

The lieutenant agreed, with an exasperated slap at an insect.
"I've ordered them, Sergeant, again and again. USASOS says
they've been shipped, but they simply never get here. I think
one carton of WAC field boots just gets misplaced somewhere
in this mountain of war materiel all around us."

WAC supply had been a farce since Des Moines, and they
all knew it. But Bunny put on a funny face when she reported
to the FEAF Wacs that they'd have to make do with their
Class-A service shoes when their Li'l Abners fell apart. "We've
given our boots to the war effort. For all I know they're being

lobbed by mortar into Jap bunkers or dropped out of bomb bays on Manila right now."

On Christmas Eve, two hours before she was due to report for duty, Bunny made her way through the tropic evening to the Tacloban cathedral square. It was the first mass she'd attended since she was on leave and went at her mother's insistence, how long ago?—nearly eighteen months now. She found herself not in a familiar little parish church full of first- and second-generation Italians, but in a large provincial Philippine cathedral with black-shawled townswomen and with dozens of other Americans in uniform.

After she had touched the stations of the cross with holy water and dropped all the pesos in her pockets into the poor box, she sat down on an empty cot in an alcove chapel that sheltered some wounded GIs. The man on the stretcher in front of her had terrible burns, his eyes wide but unfocused in his drugged daze. His head was wrapped around with two-inch bandage except for his eyes, nose and mouth; his arms to his elbows were thickly wrapped, covered by a gauze sleeve slip-knotted once below the fingers, reminding Bunny of two giant white salamis.

She knelt and crossed herself. "Pray for us," she responded as the priest said the litany. And she prayed for the man on the stretcher, *Let him sleep through the pain.* She rested her head on her clasped hands. Then suddenly she knew why she had come to this sanctuary: the silent prayer, the one unspoken, was for Breck. *God, don't let anything happen to him.* She swallowed hard, squeezed her eyes shut against the tears and slipped as naturally as she had as a troubled child into the Hail Mary.

The murmured words comforted her, the power of forgiveness and certainty in their repetition flowed through her. She did not hear the rustle of fatigues, the scuffle of boots or the scrape of M-16 against bandolier nearby.

"Say, honey, don't I know you from Hollandia?"

Her eyes flew open at the sound of his quiet question. He stood gaunt and unshaven in the shadows a few feet away. Laughter welled up and she suppressed it with her hand, but not before he'd seen it. She got up and walked toward the rear with him. "How did you get here?"

"Vicki told me where to find you."

"No, I mean how did you get to Tacloban?"

They stopped. His face was outlined in a slanting beam of pale light from some high window.

"Walked, sweetheart. I'm a ground pounder now—and that suits me just fine, since the ol' USAAF can't take a good joke." Breck grinned the same slow, careless grin, but there was a poignancy to it that matched the dark hollows under his eyes. Bunny had never before seen eyes so tired. She wanted to cradle him in her arms while he slept the night away.

They walked slowly to the entrance, their hands occasionally touching as if by accident. Two soldiers lounged outside, eating roasted sweet potatoes called *camotes*. The square was filled with vendors hawking milkfish, chicken stuffed with spiced meat and vegetables, and roast pig from street carts.

"Bunny, you remember Frenchy and Gunner?"

"Hi, fellas." They were carrying native thatch and a thick piece of bamboo. "What's that—portable camouflage?"

"Never you mind," Breck said. "You'll find out soon enough."

An air raid siren wailed, the third that day. With her hand now firmly in Breck's, Bunny and the three soldiers jog-trotted from one dugout to another back to WAC quarters. The all clear sounded; a false alarm, or the planes had passed over to attack another target.

Vicki and the other women emerged from the bomb shelter and greeted Breck like a hometown guy they hadn't seen in years. Vicki threw her arms around him, and Mac, who had gone straight to see her, said in pretended alarm, "Hey, don't forget whose girl you are!"

"Who said I was *your* girl?" But her eyes teased his, and he put his arm around her waist and squeezed it.

Bunny could see that Vicki had fallen in love with Mac, not the easy postadolescent attachments of a year ago, but a woman's love. How natural it was for Vicki to just let go of all past disappointments, to believe that this new love was real.

Vicki bent over to examine the thatch and bamboo that Gunner and Frenchy had dropped on the paved courtyard. "What's this for?"

Breck grinned. "Well, I just thought of you poor deprived

little gals so far from home, and I thought you ought to have a jungle Christmas tree."

Bunny pointed at the fronds and the bamboo. *"That's* a Christmas tree?"

Leaning his rifle against the wall of the reception room just off the court, Breck, with help from Mac, Frenchy and Gunner, tied the thatch to the bamboo trunk. Then from a pack he took several pieces of scrap aluminum—pieces of downed Jap planes—crudely cut into star and angel shapes and hung them on the branches. "There you go," Breck said. "Santa Claus has come to town."

Bunny looked up at him, her great dark eyes soft. "That's ingenious, Breck. I don't know what to say."

"Well, what do you know? As my Granny Smith would say, the poor girl's flabberstricken."

One of the Wacs produced some warm Cokes. "Not a Purple Jesus," she said, grinning at Mac, "but there's a war on."

Someone began to sing, "Silent night, holy night . . ." Outside, the sun dropping down on the western horizon beamed through the windows and glinted off the metal ornaments.

"You off duty tomorrow, Bunny?" Breck asked.

"Yes."

"Spend it with me?"

"Yes."

56

The 101st Airborne and 10th Armored Divisions are com-
pletely surrounded at Bastogne by Von Manteuffel's Fifth
Panzer Army. On Friday, December 22, the Germans de-
liver a surrender ultimatum, to which Commanding Gen-
eral Anthony McAuliffe replies, "NUTS!" Patton's Third
Army tanks break through on December 26 and relieve the
garrison.

THE BOY-SOPRANO voices swelled into the cavernous ceiling of Notre-Dame-de-Paris as Page put her hand over Paul's. She was overwhelmed by the feeling that God was in the cathedral this Christmas Eve midnight of 1944.

"Don't you feel it, Paul?"

"I feel you here close to me."

And she felt close to him—their souls were touching. It was the first time they had touched anywhere since that night an eternity ago—had it been only ten days before?—at the *musée*. They had ridden in silence back to Paris from the Ardennes, napping, in the command car, since there had been no break in the weather and planes were grounded. In all those hours, Paul had only once spoken: "You were magnificent back there."

"No, Paul, I was so scared, I didn't know what I was doing."

But he hadn't accepted that. "No other woman could have done what you did, not even Anna."

Page had tried to explain that many other women could have done what she'd done, that women too did what had to be done in wartime, even when they risked their lives, whether it was the ATS artillery batteries around London or the women partisans in mountainous Italy or Russian women combat pilots.

But Paul hadn't wanted to hear about them. He had insisted that, no, she alone was special, different. She knew he wanted her to be special because he loved her, but she saw that it made her less than human, too. By claiming superiority for her he confirmed the sense of unworthiness that had plagued him lately. At the same time, he prepared his male ego for the worst. For mortal man to lose a goddess was no disgrace. She saw all this clearly and had not been able to change him. But what about *her* motives? Was she lying to herself, too—holding on to Paul and their wavering dreams, even here in France's premier church? These questions haunted her as they stood to sing the "Cantique de Noël."

Two rows ahead of her, the terribly tall, hawk-nosed figure of General de Gaulle rose head and shoulders above the crowd. His head was bowed; she supposed he prayed for La Belle France as Germans poured back into his country through the Bulge. Page prayed, too, for the GIs massacred by fanatic SS troops at Malmédy, for her brother flying over Germany every night. Then she prayed a prayer she knew had been heard by these immortal stones for centuries, surely since the Crusades—the prayer of a soldier for comrades. "Keep them safe," she whispered, her mind full of the images of fresh young replacements fighting the firewagon and of the begrimed squad at the crossroad, bending over their cardboard fires, eating K rations in the winter cold. "Keep them safe," she prayed, "or don't let them know what hit them."

57

A killer typhoon of 150-miles-per-hour winds batters the U.S. Third Fleet in December, delaying the attack on the Philippine island of Luzon.

BUNNY SMILED, HER eyes closed. She could feel the heat of the sand beneath the blanket radiating up and into her body, cool now from her swim and the wetness of her makeshift bathing suit—a cut-off khaki shirt and skirt, with wool underwear. Breck was bare to his slender waist, his pants legs rolled above his knees.

"A dollar for your thoughts." Breck looked down at her, his blond hair curling wet over his forehead, bits of sand clinging to his shoulders.

"You're overpaying." Still smiling, she opened her eyes, feeling young—and playful too, like the child she had once been on a Sunday outing to the beach. She saw Vicki and Mac wading in the shallows, jumping the low breakers flowing onto the shore lined with coconut palm. Turning onto her stomach, she reached for a handful of coarse, damp sand full of tiny shells and let it sift through her fingers. She felt incredibly lazy, and yet she couldn't deny the physical energy beneath the surface, the result of having Breck's body so close to hers.

"I want to know, Bunny, what you're thinking." He enunciated each word, although his tone was light. "I don't have time to come courting every Sunday, to meet your mama and your papa and to chase you round your front-porch swing." He traced a circular pattern with his forefinger on her arm. "It's not that I can't tell t'other from which, as my Granny Smith always says—I know how to treat a woman, if you'd let me show you." He flashed her a grin.

"I bet you do." The words she said were sarcastic but without malice. "I'm curious, Breck: why do you play the rube?"

His grin widened. "For fun, sometimes, and then to give people what they expect, and . . ." He thought a moment and grew more serious. "Maybe partly out of habit, too. You know, you're asking for the story of my life," he said, and then, thinking aloud, he added, "and it's time for that."

He had lost both parents to influenza and had been raised in the clean poverty of an eastern-Tennessee mountain cabin by his Granny Smith, a combination midwife and chicken farmer. "There warn't no high school, Bunny gal—and I did talk just like that once—but out of Granny's egg money and working for my board and room I got through a Murfreesboro high school. From there, well, I had some luck—won a tobacco company scholarship to Duke University, where I was a second-year law student when the draft caught up with me. A story as old as Saturday matinee at the movies: a mountain boy, living by his wits in the big city." He squinted against the glare of sun on sand, a trace, but only a trace, of sadness in his tone. "Now, I want to hear about you and your family. My granny's letters keep asking about your family. She sets great store by a gal's family."

"You wrote your granny—your grandmother. About me?"

"Sure. Told her we wanted the old pioneer's cabin for our honeymoon cottage."

"Breck! Don't—"

"Okay, if you want to go to some fancy place, that's all right, maybe even Myrtle Beach"—he ignored her attempts to interrupt—"but you ought to see the cabin before you turn it down. My great-grandfather brought his Virginia bride to it a hundred years ago. They planted a walnut tree by the stoop and now it shades the whole little hollow. Acsah was her name, and a wedding-ring quilt she made is on the bed. Don't think she'd mind a bit if we slept under it—not that you're going to get cold."

She looked at him and was startled once again by his blue eyes, huge clear circles of blue that pulled her until she felt she could let go and tumble forever into them. Despite his gambling and his deals, she sensed an honesty; somehow she knew his show-off manner was a cover for his openness. There was no pretense in him; he was a whole, happy man.

"Listen, Breck, why can't we just have a few laughs and let it go at that?"

He stared at her as if she'd violated some important rule of his. "But laughter and love go together."

She looked away. Oh, if it could be true . . . But it couldn't, because it never had been for her. She looked straight at him. "Look, you're a wonderful guy, I can't deny that, but I've told you, I'm bad news in the marriage department. Believe me, I'm doing you a favor. I know I've made the right decision."

"What decision's that?"

"I've agreed to marry Harry Duquesne."

"You've *agreed,* you say. That's not love, that's a business deal."

"Okay, have it your way. Harry and I are right for each other, don't you see that? I can be his new acquisition, and he can be my security. If you really knew me, you'd know I've had all the romance I want for one lifetime." She didn't allow herself to feel the unbearable pain of what she was saying. She had to hang on to the memory of the mess she'd made of loving a man, of the brief passage when her life had been ensnared with Johnny Palermo's. But that time seemed so unreal, here on this sunny beach, a bright time out in a hellish war. She and Breck were two people in faded khaki, playing at being in a world gone momentarily sane again.

"That doesn't explain anything," he said, his eyes locking stubbornly on hers.

"What should I explain?"

"Why you keep talking about that jerk Harry, when it's Johnny Palermo that's made you so suspicious of my loving you. That ex-husband of yours, damn him—you're going to let him win, aren't you?"

Bunny scrambled to her knees. "Breck, stop it! Vicki didn't know the whole story. You don't know what you're saying."

"I know you've got me pegged as another phony." He shoved his hair off his forehead and slicked it back, looking very much the way he must have as a small boy.

She shook her head at him, she couldn't tell herself whether in anger or agreement. "Let's not argue," she said, "let's just—"

Breck jumped up and danced around her like a madman, waving his arms and yelling, "Let's *do* argue, Bunny—let's yell, scream. If we've only got an hour or two, let's at least be honest with each other."

Suddenly he dropped down on the blanket beside her and pulled her to him. "No joke, this is the truth and you're going to hear it. At first, I couldn't understand why a girl, why *you,* hated me at first sight. It had never happened to me before, and I was determined to win you over just to keep my record perfect. But somehow I got caught in my own trap. I began to see through that tough pose of yours, and I kept liking what I saw, more and more. You're wonderful—sweet, funny, sad . . . Did you hear what I said a minute ago? I want to marry you. I want to love you and feel you loving me. I want to take you to a cool cabin and lay you down on my great-granny's quilt. Half the time out on patrol, I can't tell the difference between the malaria and my memory of you that night by the fish pond."

She felt an old emotion, one she had sworn never to feel

again. This is a moment a woman could build a love on, she thought wildly. She couldn't let it happen. She squinted from the sun, teasing, her face inches from his, and let her sardonic sense of tragedy, especially of her own little tragedy, come to the surface. She laughed. "We've both got a high fever, Breck. Better double our Atabrine or—"

With a groan half laugh and half frustration he pulled her lips down onto his in a very much different kiss from that patient, exploratory one on the patio of the La Conga Club. This time his mouth was urgent, drawing the breath from her, sending her senses to full alert, starting her legs tingling.

Bunny pulled away from him, breathless, undecided, pushing on his chest with one hand, pulling at his arm with the other. *Oh, I could make a miserable mistake with this wise, foolish, tormenting, sexy man.*

"Open your eyes, Bunny," Breck drawled. "If you're praying for help, I won't need any."

Suddenly Bunny was furious, the safest of all emotions when she was next to Breck. "You—you conceited—wolf!" she stammered, searching for a stronger word as she scrambled to her knees.

Breck laughed and jumped to his feet, pulling her up, his laughter growing.

Bunny felt outrageously silly. "You—you said you won't need any *help,*" she sputtered, and a laugh broke through, joining his until, clutching each other hysterically, they fell in a jumble of arms and legs on the blanket.

They lay there, catching their breath, giving in to the giddy moment of joyous release, until finally it was spent and they lay still and silent. She rested her hand in his lightly and innocently as if they were kids on a first date. Down the beach, past a boy riding a carabao, she could hear Vicki and Mac in a noisy mating battle, splashing water at each other, rolling in the sand, indulging in the physical play that postponed sexual intimacy, the intimacy that threatened her now. Breck's hand left hers and moved up her arm, slid under her neck and rolled her body against his, cradling her head on his shoulder.

They lay there touching along the full length of their bodies, the rich blue Philippine sky turning dark, the sun drifting behind thick clouds. He kissed her again and then again. Her heart pounded where he touched her breast. A glow spread over her body, the old erotic warmth teasing her in the old way, but fulfilling her in a new way.

The rain came fast in huge drops, forcing them reluctantly apart. Snatching up helmets and gear, they ran toward a grove of trees already sheltering Vicki and Mac and a colony of chattering monkeys.

"Hey, you two," Vicki said, "what's the big joke? We could hear you laughing all the way down the beach."

Bunny looked at Breck, and they burst into laughter again. Now she didn't remember or care what they laughed about. It was enough just to laugh.

They put their shoes and helmets on, and all four dashed along the road toward Tacloban, challenging one another to a race. They arrived out of breath and found Gunner and Frenchy waiting outside the R&R barracks.

Gunner yelled, "Jesus, you guys, we're pulling out early." He waved his arm at them. "Come on, Skipper wants to make San Miguel by nightfall. That means we'll be back hunting Jap snipers by tomorrow night."

"Osifers!" Mac hissed. "Don't they have no respect for Christmas? Or a guy's date?" he added with a longing look at Vicki.

The rain was pelting Bunny in spite of the sandy blanket she held over her head. Breck stood in front of her, rain running off his helmet in an imperfect sheet around him.

"Get my stuff in the barracks, Gunner. Please give me another minute, and I promise I'll clean out the rest of the Jap stragglers single-handed."

Gunner hooted, promising to relay the offer to the captain.

"Listen, Bunny." Now Breck's hand gripped her shoulders until she was sure his fingers had marked her for life. "Johnny's not going to beat me and neither is his stand-in, Harry."

Bunny opened her mouth to say something.

"No, don't argue with me, there isn't time. Don't you get it, yet? *We're important.* You and I. Can't you see, we're as right as two peas—"

"In a pod," she said, holding the soggy blanket over his head now, looking up at him, a damp smile on her lips.

Breck nodded. "You said it, sweetheart—in a pod. Can't you see how crazy you are about me, how much you want to marry me?"

The platoon sergeant was shouting for the men to form up on him.

Breck spoke faster, half shouting above the rain and the noise. "If we don't get hit by another typhoon, we'll be going up to Luzon soon, but I'll come back—" Gunner and Frenchy were pulling Breck and Mac toward the platoon, whose formation was almost complete.

Bunny couldn't ask, When will I see you again? Women weren't asking that in the Philippines in December 1944.

But he sensed her unspoken question. "Darling—this war can't go on much longer," he called to her, stepping backward, one hand on each side of his mouth to make his voice carry through the downpour. "Then we'll have forever. Say yes."

She was wet through to her skin; the rain pelting her face made her blink. She stared after him, wanting to say yes, wanting to shout *Yes,* but she allowed the moment to pass, in an act of self-possession she regretted bitterly as soon as the truck carried him down the road and into the jungle. Was it possible that this time she had made the wrong decision for the right reason?

58

In Italy the Fifth Army stalls in November during a last attempt to break through the German Gothic Line just ten miles short of the Po Valley. Every soldier, man and woman alike, is disappointed. After Allied troops roared across the Arno River, swept through Pisa and raced past Florence with the Germans running before them, they thought that the Italian campaign might end before Eisenhower reached the Rhine. But it was not to be.

BY THE END of December 1944, Jill and the forward element of Fifth Army Wacs were living in tents fifteen miles north of Florence. As Sergeant Harper put it, "Another freezing cold, rainy, muddy winter in sunny Italy."

Stalemate! Jill suspected that every combat soldier longed for it until it was actually on him and then it proved to be the worst duty of all. The waiting was interminable and they couldn't hope for movement now until spring.

Thank God, that Kraut field marshal, Kesselring, had left so much of Florence intact. With communication traffic, both in code and in the clear, at a low level, all her women were on reduced shifts and had weekly passes into Florence, the loveliest city Jill had seen in Italy. The only physical evidence of war were the pontoon bridges across the Arno to replace the ones the Germans had blown.

Sergeant Harper stuck her head inside the flap of Jill's tent. She was smiling. "Lieutenant, we're leaving for the ceremony in five minutes. Don't forget."

"Thanks, Harper." Jill smiled back. It was Harper's little joke. As if she could forget. She'd remember today for the rest of her life—the day she received the Bronze Star from General Mark Clark himself. Photographers from *Stars and Stripes* and

Yank would be there, and afterward there was to be a reception. Too much fuss over a little thing. She hadn't been courageous when she ran to the burning soldier after the explosion. As a matter of fact, she hadn't even thought, just reacted. That wasn't courage, but training.

Jill was aware of a deep embarrassment at this recognition, and that feeling puzzled her. All her life she had tried to push herself in front of the line, to show everyone that as small and young as she was she could do the job whatever it was, and now that she had actually accomplished her dream she felt a profound humility. Every woman in her unit deserved a medal for the work she'd done. It wasn't fair to them for her to be singled out.

An hour later, she crossed Florence's Ponte Vecchio, the only bridge the Germans had left standing. Even the Krauts had been unwilling to destroy the ancient medieval bridge with its tiny shops clinging precariously to its sides. Once across, she turned her jeep left and headed for the Piazza della Signoria, where she reported to the parade commandant and took her place near the steps of the Palazzo Vecchio, which towered over the square.

Troops filled three sides of the piazza as her group received the signal to march to the reviewing stand on the palazzo steps, where General Clark and his staff waited. She was last in line, almost disappearing behind tall GIs. While she waited for the citations to be read and the medals to be pinned on the soldiers ahead of her, she remembered other formations so long ago at Fort Des Moines—formations when she had suffered agonies of wondering if she could possibly measure up in this man's army. *I wish Page and Bunny and Elisabeth could see me now.*

Finally, Mark Clark, tall and lanky, young for a general and, she thought, good-looking, stood in front of her. Her forehead came to the bottom row of campaign ribbons on his chest, but his face was serious—and yes, she could see respect there—as he looked down at her.

The adjutant said, "Attention to orders." He cleared his throat and read, " 'For meritorious service while serving as a member of a forward unit of Signal Wacs detached to the Fifth Army, Mediterranean Theater of Operations, Hammersmith, Jill Henry, First Lieutenant, WAC, displayed personal characteristics of clear vision and exemplary personal courage in helping to rescue a soldier from a burning gasoline dump at the risk of her own life.' "

General Clark bent to pin on the Bronze Star. "Congratulations, Lieutenant Hammersmith. The Fifth Army is proud to number such soldiers as you among its ranks. You are a credit to the Women's Army Corps."

"Thank you, sir," she replied, saluting, unable to keep the shivers of pride from flooding her whole being. The medal swayed with every breath she took, as if to remind her the United States Army had put its stamp of approval on her, no small achievement, even she, so quick to be self-critical, had to admit.

Jill executed a right-face and filed with the others up the steps of the palazzo to watch the march-by in their honor— Italian alpine troops in feathered caps, Indians in turbans, Moroccans, Anzacs from New Zealand, several headquarters companies of Fifth Army GIs, and, best of all, passing in review, her own small detachment of Wacs, wearing the green scarf of the Fifth Army, stepping smartly along the piazza in front of her. She saluted their colors. It was a moment she knew she would remember always. Only one thing would have made it a perfect day, but she did not see Des anywhere among the reviewing party.

After the parade, General Clark took her in tow. He insisted she share his staff car to the reception and seemed to be showing her off to the international crowd in the drawing room of the Palazzo d'Ordella like a delighted uncle whose favorite niece had just taken a first-in-show.

"Lieutenant"—he looked back to see that she was indeed behind him—"I want you to meet our hostess, the Marchesa Helen d'Ordella de Castel Fantini." He rolled the noble name off his tongue with the obvious delight that Jill had noticed even the most republican of Americans took in the idea of European nobility. "Now I'll let you two get acquainted, if you'll excuse me."

When the General stepped aside, Jill saw a tall brunette without a trace of gray, a still-handsome woman in her fifties. "At last I get to meet the brave woman soldier," the Marchesa said in a voice so loud it boomed into the far corners of the large room. Normally Jill would have withered with embarrassment, but the woman smiled so sweetly that she smiled back and took the glass of wine a servant offered.

"Thank you, a . . ." She let her voice drop, unsure of using the title.

The Marchesa laughed. "Call me Helen. Have I finally lost my Western twang after thirty years in Italy?" She lowered her voice so that only half the room could now hear her. "You know, before I was the Marchesa d'Ordella and so forth I was Helen Packard of Cody, Wyoming. Ever been there? Just outside Yellowstone—God's country, my papa used to call it. But here I go, rattling on about myself when this shindig is to honor you and the other medal winners."

Jill was a little overwhelmed by the Marchesa Helen d'Ordella de whatever the rest of it was. An Italian noblewoman who talked like Annie Oakley. An American living in Florence for thirty years and obviously married to Italian nobility. How romantic. And how contradictory.

"And now that I've met you"—the Marchesa took her arm as if she were an old friend—"I can see what Desmond Stratton has been raving about these past weeks."

Des! How did she know Des, and what had he been saying about her?

"Captain Stratton is my commanding officer." She put handcuffs on her voice, as she always did when she talked about Des.

Surprisingly, the Marchesa threw back her head and laughed. "Oh yes, he's that." Her eyes sparkled. "He's a very commanding officer and very much like someone I once knew a long time ago—wars ago." The Marchesa stopped smiling. "Well, that was then and this is now," she sighed, temporarily distracted by some memory Jill couldn't understand. "I never thought I'd live to see the day that Florence was full of Americans. But I'm keeping you from the others who want to meet the brave WAC lieutenant." She patted Jill's arm. "Come for tea tomorrow at four. I'm aching for a nice sit-down with another American woman."

"I'd love to."

And with a friendly nod, the Marchesa went to greet her other guests. It was then that Jill noticed Des across the room staring at her.

He walked toward her. Jill held her breath. They so rarely said a word that didn't have to do with a package for Tina or comcenter operations. "You've met Helen, I see. Quite a woman, isn't she?"

"She's a fan of yours, too."

Des nodded. "You know, she's flat broke, in spite of this palace. She's turned it into a *pensione* for Americans on leave. I come here every chance I get, and we've grown to be like old friends. I guess she's spent most of her life trying to keep this place from tumbling down so she'd have something to pass on to her son."

"But what about her husband?"

"Oh, he died in the First World War, shortly after they were married."

Jill was genuinely moved. "How terrible for her."

"She's a hell of a woman for doing her duty"—his voice now as guarded as her own, but with its accustomed sting. "You two ought to have a lot in common."

As if he felt he might have gone too far, Des started to leave on a jaunty note with a two-fingered salute, but Jill stopped him. "Wait. I must thank you again for putting me in for the medal. It was—well, it was a high point of my life."

"Forget it, you had it coming. By the way, that corporal—Brodzinsky, wasn't it? She got the Soldier's Medal in Algiers last week. And you'll be happy to know that her hands are going to be all right, a few scars maybe, but no loss of function. They've shipped her back to the ZI for skin grafts."

She thanked him politely for telling her, and he moved off into the crowd as others came up to congratulate her and shake her hand. Her tongue ached to call him back, to ignore everyone but him, but she couldn't. He had acted properly, exactly the way a commanding officer should toward a subordinate on such an occasion. That was all she was to him now. That was what she'd wanted and that was what she'd got.

The next afternoon, promptly at four, Jill parked her jeep in front of the Palazzo d'Ordella, pulled the bell chain and was ushered into the sitting room of the Marchesa's private apartment on the third floor.

"Come, sit over here." The Marchesa indicated a small settee in front of the fire where tea had been laid. "Put your coat right there on the arm where it's handy. These old places have sudden drafts swirling about and no central heat. I'm used to it, but my American guests are always freezing."

Jill did as she was bidden, glancing about the room at its plush draperies, the faded Aubusson carpets and the portrait of a darkly handsome young man in an Italian uniform of the last war. Her husband, probably.

The Marchesa followed her eyes. "My husband, Giancarlo. He was killed shortly after that portrait was painted. I was six months pregnant. But we won't talk about sad things. Desmond tells me you're from California. Tell me about your home and your family." The older woman poured a cup of steaming strong tea and held it out to Jill, motioning for her to help herself to some rolled almond cookies on the table.

Before long Jill found herself chattering like a schoolgirl invited to a favorite teacher's house. It was important to her that the Marchesa like her—no, more than that, understand her. Whatever Des had told her . . .

As if reading her mind, the Marchesa asked, "Now what about my handsome friend, the captain? You have every right to tell me to mind my own business, but I get the distinct feeling that he hankers after you."

Jill smiled in spite of herself; the direct manner and the Wild West language were so out of place in these Old World surroundings. But when she tried to find an answer, she couldn't. "I'm sorry—a—"

"Now, make it Helen," the Marchesa insisted.

"—Helen, but it's too complicated to explain."

"I understand." The Marchesa shrugged. "Forgive me, sometimes I just forget myself. We Westerners are not the strong, silent types we're made out, you know; we love to gossip and pry. Comes from too much solitude with only animals to talk to."

"No, please—it's not that I *won't* tell you, Helen. I don't think I know how to tell you. I truly love Des. I don't deny it even to myself, but he and I disagreed about what's right and what's wrong. When I came over here I was engaged; my fiancé had been horribly wounded." Jill poured out her story to the Marchesa, at the same time trying to be fair to Des. "And so, you see, now that Neil is dead, I can't go running to Des when I hurt him so—and I don't deserve . . . Oh, what's the use? It hardly makes sense."

After the torrent of words and feelings, they both sat silent for a few moments, until Jill noticed that the other woman had tears in her eyes. "I'm so sorry, I've upset you. Perhaps I'd better leave."

The Marchesa loudly blew her nose into a delicate lace handkerchief. "You'll do nothing of the kind, my child. Now just give me a minute." She breathed deeply and regained her composure. "You've awakened feelings I thought were dead, and now I find they were merely sleeping. Oh my—" she stared hard at Jill—"you *do* remind me so much of myself at your age."

Jill was astonished. "Me? Why, you're tall and —"

"No, no, height hasn't anything to do with it. We may look different, but, believe me, we're cut from the same cloth." Her hands quieted on her lap, and her voice dropped in volume and had a youthful sweetness to it.

Jill thought this must have been the way she sounded as a young woman fresh from the States, caught up in a filthy war.

Helen was still talking. "It was 1915, when I came over as a nurse. I thought it was a great adventure, but it was only a great slaughter not much different from beef butchering on my papa's ranch. Only these were men. One of the wounded was Giancarlo d'Ordella. I nursed him and married him. He died without seeing our son."

"Where's your son now?"

"In Germany. They took him as a labor conscript to ensure my cooperation."

"I'm sorry, Helen."

Helen seemed not to want to hear, impatiently waiting to return to another time. "After my son was born, I came to my husband's family in Florence. Here I met Richard Brodie, an attaché at the American consulate. I didn't want to renounce my citizenship, and he helped me. I don't know how it happened, but we fell in love, more deeply in love than I had ever imagined I could be. It's not that I hadn't loved Giancarlo in a way—he'd been wounded, he needed me, and I was just the gal who could fix everything. If I hadn't been that type, I wouldn't have come over here to run the war, would I?"

Jill nodded with a wry smile, recognizing the similarity.

The Marchesa went on. "Finally, I had to make a choice, and I chose to stay on. You see, I had promised Giancarlo I would see that his child got his proper inheritance." Her voice was very soft now. "Richard went home alone. Oh, it sounds archaic and melodramatic in 1944, but in those days heritage and titles meant something."

"But, Helen, you kept your promise and you did what was right."

The Marchesa raised her hand from her lap in a small gesture of futility. "Yes, I knew my duty and did it, but at the time I didn't know about all those years of nights I'd be alone wondering about Richard and his life, imagining him with a happy wife and children. You see, Jill, a man like Richard wanted a woman who wanted *him* above all else—above all ideas of duty and martyrdom, no matter how attractive that idea can be for some of us women. Where do we get it—" she shook her head in wonderment—"this desire to give our lives to a dead dream? No, Richard wouldn't buy any of it. His idea of life was simple: a man and a woman fall in love and they don't allow anything or anyone to come between them ever." She stopped for a deep breath and looked at Jill, who understood now why the Marchesa had thought they were so alike. "What I didn't know when I was young was that such a decision is never finished and done. There are no neat endings in real life. Only in the movies is everything tied up into tidy packages. The wondering goes on and on. Some days I think I was right, and some days I bitterly regret my bargain. But I will tell you this. Nothing in my life made up for losing Richard, not my son, not position, not the approval of others, not even my own smug righteousness." She got up and moved to Jill's side on the settee. "Oh, my dear, be very sure that you can live without Desmond all the days of your life, before you discard him in some imitation of guilty sainthood."

Jill was sobbing. "If I only could, but it's too late. He hates me now."

Suddenly Helen seemed to get her voice back, and with a hearty laugh she boomed into the farthest corners of her suite, "Well, if that's hate, I'll take it over any other man's love. My dear, not a week ago a very miserable young captain sat where you sit now and poured out his love for you to me."

Jill was shocked. "Did *he* ask you to talk with me like this?"

"Not in so many words."

Jill sniffed, her tears receding at the thought. "I would think he would have too much pride."

The Marchesa laughed again. "You are so *very* young, my child. The lover too proud to fight for his woman is a figment of the romantic novelist. A man like Captain Desmond Stratton would go to any lengths to win the woman he loved."

BOOK FOUR

1945:
THEIR EYES
HAD SEEN
THE GLORY

59

On New Year's Day, 1945, the approaching victory in Europe found a war-weary Women's Army Corps facing two final problems: maintaining efficiency and readying for troop redeployment to the Pacific theater. Their crusading spirit, which had once dreamed of breaking down military barriers, had faltered. Most Wacs now knew they'd remain second-class soldiers until they shared combat with men. Even the most noncombatant male stateside supply clerk, stacking linen in a warehouse, ranked in the military and public mind far above a Wac under enemy attack. Of the early enlistees who had fought public slanders and longed for full recognition, most had by now given up the idea, shot down by a battle fatigue of hopelessness. One Wac wrote Colonel Hobby: "We don't want appreciation; we only want to go home."

IN THE PHILIPPINES by Monday, January 1, Bunny and her unit had news that the hidden snipers and last holdouts on the northwest side of Leyte had been cleaned out and the island had been declared secure. But there was no time to celebrate the end of one action, since it was obvious to everyone, from commanders on down to Wac privates, that another big operation was about to begin.

"What about it, Bunny?" Vicki demanded that afternoon in the dayroom over a rare iced Coke. "Is this it, for God's sake? I mean will it all be over in 1945?"

"MacArthur tells me less than he tells you," Bunny flipped back at her irritably, and then was ashamed. "Oh, I don't know, kiddo. The Japs aren't going to lie down and let us have Manila, and they're certainly not going to step out for rice cakes while we walk into Tokyo." She exhaled in despair. "There's bound to be a big fight. I'm not sure they know how to quit."

Vicki's lower lip trembled, although it was obvious she tried to hold it firm. "God, Bunny, I don't think I can stand to think I'll be here for another New Year's Day, or that Mac will have to fight for another year." Tears poured from her eyes past her determination to hold on to them. "He's got only so many chances. He'll be hit for sure."

Bunny put her arm around the younger woman's shoulders, but she couldn't think of one comforting word that rang true. Which of them knew what the next day would bring? In this crazy war, life was lost at the far reaches, through a five-hundred-pound bomb or a one-ounce bullet, a thirty-foot python or a tiny mosquito. It was useless to try to make any sense out of it, and she had given up trying. What worried her today was whether any of those extremes would find Breck. He was just the type to take chances, to wear his mortality lightly.

"Oh—I forgot," Vicki added, rubbing her eyes as she dug into a fatigue pocket. "Letters for you."

The first, a month-old letter from her mother, told her that Angela was home—pregnant; that Johnny Palermo had run out on her, taking the little money they had left. Mama had used some of Bunny's allotment to buy Angela a bus ticket home from California, and hoped Bunny wasn't angry. The letter was an I-told-you-so which Mama had a right to. Mama had been right about Johnny, not once, but twice.

For a short moment Bunny's mind was crowded with old, ugly images, but she no longer had trouble shrugging them off. Angry? At Angela? No, she felt no more anger. She had been freed of her anger at Angela when her love for Johnny Palermo died in those minutes outside La Jeunesse. Angela was a victim of her own weakness, a weakness, after all, that Bunny had shared. No, anger wasn't what she felt for Angela; pity, maybe, but without responsibility. She wished her sister no further harm, but she felt no love for her, either. She was a part of something dead, and so Angela was a little dead, too. In a way, Bunny was comforted by these feelings. She had moved on in her life and was trying to leave old pain and old hatreds behind. That must be what the word "maturity" means, she thought.

The second letter, on official U.S. Army stationery, was from Harry, now Brigadier General Duquesne, telling her that Louise had started divorce proceedings and that he would see her soon. Reading the familiar phrases, she told herself it would be so easy not to think, not to feel, to just let Harry take care of blocking out a new timetable for her future. Old pain may have dissipated, but its lessons were still with her.

More pleasant were letters from Page in France and Elisabeth in New York City. How had Elisabeth managed to wangle a discharge? Page didn't seem to know, either. Bunny sat down and wrote to Page, and with the few minutes left before she went on duty she dashed off a short note to Elisabeth:

> *Somewhere in the Philippines*
> *New Year's Day, 1945*
>
> Hi! It looks as tho' I do get around, but I could have skipped this particular tropic isle. I'll trade you some of this incessant rain for some good ol' stateside snow anyday.
>
> Can't tell you what I'm doing—all very hush hush—when this war is over I plan to spend the rest of my life without keeping one single secret.
>
> Thanks for the picture of the Jersey side of the Holland Tunnel. Just what a homesick gal needs for the New Year. Yipe!
>
> We're working day & night so don't worry if you don't hear for awhile.
>
> Bye for now,
> BUNNY

One day followed another, scarcely distinguishable from all the days she'd spent in one island jungle or other with one exception: Breck was almost constantly on her mind.

On Wednesday, January 10, Bunny was asleep, the mosquito netting pulled over her face and shoulders, when the sound of the dayroom radio woke her up. Armed Forces Radio was broadcasting a delayed episode of *The Lux Radio*

Theater, which had once been her favorite, but not now when she needed rest so desperately. She was about to yell a mild obscenity about the ancestry of inconsiderate Wacs when a news bulletin interrupted her. The Sixth Army had landed in Lingayen Gulf on Luzon only about ninety miles from Manila. Casualties had been moderate, although Japanese *Shinyo*-class suicide boats had attacked the invasion fleet during the night. Breck! He must be on the beach now, and he *must* be safe—he *must* be safe.

Bunny tried, but couldn't sleep again. Vicki came in and flopped onto her bed, lighting a Camel, the aromatic odor reminding Bunny she hadn't had a smoke all day. She stuck one arm from under the netting and was fumbling on the overturned ammo box that served her as nightstand when a Wac from casualty section came in.

Vicki sat upright, turning pale under her tropic tan. "Had any news about C Company, Second Battalion?"

"Yes—some."

"Is Mac listed—Private Andy McBride?"

"I know Mac." The Wac paused. "No, he's not listed." Looking Vicki in the eye, the Wac cocked her head toward Bunny.

Bunny saw them both. "Breck?"

"Yes," the Wac said.

Bunny asked the worst question first. "Dead?"

"No, Sarge, he's not, he's ... "

"Wounded? How bad?"

"No, not wounded."

Bunny swatted frantically at the prison of tangled netting, becoming more and more ensnared. "For the love of Christ, tell me, *what's happened to Breck?*" Her voice was a wail.

"He's missing," the Wac said as Vicki untangled Bunny from the netting, then put out her arms as if to a small child. "Gee, I'm sorry, Sarge, Breck's presumed captured."

I can imagine no better way to begin the New Year for Wacs than with the news that the Distinguished Service Medal is being awarded to Colonel Oveta Culp Hobby, Director, WAC. . . . The citation said, "Without the guidance of precedents in United States military history to assist her, Colonel Hobby established sound initial policies . . . The high standards of conduct and discipline, the efficiency, and the devotion to duty exhibited by members of the Women's Army Corps, both overseas and in the United States, testify to the character, ideals and leadership of Colonel Hobby." The only quarrel a Wac can find with this is that Wacs have known, for two and a half years, that she wore a DSM—if not on her coat, in her heart.

—*Letter to staff directors,*
January 18, 1945, from Air WAC Lieutenant
Colonel Betty Bandel

PAGE KNEW THAT the last leg of her flight from Paris was almost over when she felt the landing gear of the C-47 lock into position over the small Des Moines airfield. It had been more than two years since she and Elisabeth, Jill and Bunny had left by train—or two days, or two centuries. The woman who had been Second Officer Page Hannaday that winter day in 1942 seemed as close as yesterday and as distant as someone she had only read about, familiar and yet a stranger. So much had happened to her in the intervening years, to every woman soldier, so much.

Only Paul hadn't changed, he was ever and always Paul, moving assuredly from day to day even on D Day when that day might have held death for him, loving his idea of her and his idea of love, yes—but not knowing her, not as she wanted to be known. Paul, who believed he had a lover's authority over her life. Although Paul had made emotional demands on her, she, unlike other women, had made none on him. How much like her father she was, she thought ruefully, although she had suspected it almost from the first day she'd put on the WAC uniform.

What did she want from Paul, from any man? She wanted to love and be loved, but to keep a special freedom intact. Page shrugged in self-derision. Not in this world, she thought. There was only one way to have Paul—his way, as a wife, mother of his children, supporter of his work. But this was woman's age-old compromise, and she would just have to learn to live with it. It was beyond her imagination to see herself without Paul at her side.

Lieutenant Colonel Hannah Parker Neilson, WAC staff director for the ETO, looked at her, smiling, as Page turned away from the tiny window. "Lieutenant, you know what they say about talking to yourself."

"Sorry, Colonel—just thinking out loud about this place."

"How does it feel to be coming back to Fort Des Moines?"

"Like coming home, ma'am."

The colonel nodded in agreement. "Yes, this is where we all started."

As it happened, it had been Colonel Neilson's personal request for her to represent SHAEF Wacs that had brought Page this far from the war to attend the meeting of WAC civilian advisers and high-level WAC staff officers from all the major commands, the meeting everyone thought would be the last one of the war, maybe of the WAC.

The wheels touched down, squealed, rolled and stopped near the control tower. She saw a group of olive-drab sedans head toward their plane. "Colonel," she said, pointing out the window, "here comes our transportation to the post."

The long trip from Orly was over. It had been uneventful flying halfway around the world; certainly nothing like her B-17 flight to Scotland. It was during the long flight that Page realized that she had been living in a world of action and that it was inaction that was stressful for her. Again she was forced to face the idea of how like her father she was. He had always been so restless between field exercises, so eager to leave for a new posting, and she had always resented it, never understood it until now.

"Ride in my car," Colonel Neilson requested. "We'll talk about the speech you're going to make tomorrow."

Page frowned. "I wouldn't exactly call it a speech, ma'am, just some remarks about the morale of the Wacs at SHAEF in Paris, and at the forward headquarters in Reims. I think it's important to let them know that our women are anxious to be part of the Army of Occupation, that we want to finish the job alongside the men."

Colonel Neilson nodded and reached for her coat across the narrow aisle. "You may get questions about demobilization from the civilians," she said, tugging her Ike jacket waistband over her skirt top. "In particular, the Wac wives of soldiers coming home after Germany surrenders. There's going to be a point system, and the Army is trying hard not to send ETO troops out to the Pacific. Some men will come stateside and be stationed near their homes and discharged outright. We're already granting discharges to a Wac if her husband has been wounded and can prove he needs his wife at home to care for him. But the question everybody's going to ask is, What about the ex-soldier who just wants his wife to be home when he is, or the ETO Wac who has as many points as the GI who's rotated ahead of her?"

The plane steward threw the door open, and Page, the colonel and her aides were on their way down the steps and into the waiting cars.

Page leaned back, exhausted, into the scratchy upholstery. Dazed from lack of sleep and the seven-hour time differential, she wondered if there was a conspiracy to chip away at the Corps until it was gone. But, responding to the colonel's questions, she said, "We all enlisted for the duration plus six months, ma'am. ETO women don't forget that."

"Not all Wacs feel that way."

Page shifted her dispatch case. "Maybe not, but I supervise the WAC mail censor from SHAEF G-2. A few weeks ago one of the EWs wrote home, evidently in answer to a letter she'd received from her parents. The gist of it was that they'd decided she'd been overseas long enough and wanted her to come home. She told them that when she griped, it was only a soldier's right to blow off steam. Don't take me seriously, she wrote, because I want to stay as long as the emergency exists, and believe me, Colonel, she knew that meant six months after the defeat of Japan."

"Tell them that tomorrow, Lieutenant. We've got the afternoon slot right after lunch," the colonel said, staring out the window as they drove through downtown Des Moines. "It's like another world here, isn't it?"

That was exactly what Page had been thinking. They could have been in a time machine, the difference was so blatant. The image of a snowy Ardennes crossroad came sharply back to focus in her mind. "To look at this place, these people, you wouldn't know that half the cities of Europe are rubble, that the walls of London buildings are propped up with posts like so many brick tents. The pilot told me Dresden was destroyed the night after we left Orly. But these people are all so—so fat and so clean!"

The colonel answered, "Lieutenant, don't make the mistake of thinking they don't know there's a war on. This is the fourth year of war for them and they're just as war-weary in their way as we are."

"You're right, ma'am. It's just that I've seen too much."

The next morning, Page dressed to radio news that paratroops had retaken Corregidor. She ordered breakfast at the officers' mess from a mimeo menu dated Friday, 16 February, 1945, then reported to the post theater for the first day of the three-day conference. The seats were filled with women and a sprinkling of men in uniform. She'd never seen so many WAC majors and lieutenant colonels. If a buzz bomb dropped on this building right now, she thought, it would wipe out the entire leadership of the Women's Army Corps. A number of distinguished civilian women who made up the National Civilian Advisory Committee sat in the audience. She recognized the author Dorothy Canfield Fisher, educators, a doctor, civic leaders, businesswomen and a prima ballerina. In the front row sat Mary McLeod Bethune of the National Council of Negro Women, who had been instrumental in opening the women's army to negro women.

There was Colonel Hobby, thinner, tireder and grayer, but wearing the red, white and blue ribbon of the Distinguished Service Medal. She was the first woman ever to receive it.

Page took a seat beside Colonel Neilson in the front row and settled in for all the welcoming speeches, wondering why she felt so alien, as if she no longer belonged in warm, safe buildings with clean, well-fed people.

The training-center commandant called Fort Des Moines the first military academy for women—which would surprise any West Pointers, Page thought—then introduced Iowa's Governor Blue, who used the charming phrase "sisters-in-arms." After the Governor, Colonel Hobby told them that women were no longer perceived as "playing soldier" but were greeted everywhere with the accolade "good soldier."

The audience applauded enthusiastically, and Page joined in politely. It all sounded grand, but she had been in the field too long to indulge in much wishful thinking. Sure, Ike and General Marshall praised the Corps, but down from that military Olympus the thoughts of line officer and dogface alike would have made the General Staff blush. Practically all the GI comment about the WAC in censored letters home was negative. Wacs were insulted on the street, denied promotion and supervisory positions over men. And far too many people, military and civilian, still assumed that Wacs were just a little something extra for the boys on Saturday night. What the WAC needed, Page was convinced, was not more empty kudos but a permanent and recognized place in the Army—not just for the war emergency, but to build the peacetime army, too.

But the more she listened, the more her spirits sank. No one, at this conference anyway, was planning for the Corps to be around after the war. Recruiting was now at maintenance levels, and most of that was confined to medical-technician companies. The head of WAC recruiting told them a recent poll indicated most civilians thought Wacs should help nurse the wounded after the war. This was dismal news for Page, made even more so because as she looked around the auditorium she didn't see that it incensed the women there. Something in Page rebelled at the thought of the WAC as a corps of nurses' aides.

After lunch, Lieutenant Colonel Neilson was called to the podium on the small stage. She was a striking, no, commanding woman—tall, strong-featured, with her red hair in a two-sided pompadour caught up in a roll above her collar in the back. This was a woman who was at home with English society or eating rations out of a mess kit in a WAC tent encampment in France. Her silver leaves and Pallas Athene insignia caught the theatrical footlights. Page felt a stir of anticipation.

"Only a few days before I left my headquarters in Paris," the colonel began, "the news came that a certain WAC unit had been bombed out for the second time. I am proud to say that I have never received a report of a Wac losing her head during the worst raids. Personally, I think every one of our women who came through the blitzing of London by V-one and V-two rockets should have the Bronze Star—maybe several of them."

Amen to that, Page thought.

Neilson went on, "During a raid, there is a natural instinct on the part of both GI Joe and GI Jane not to let the other see fear."

Page was pleased at that. So much, then, for all the argument that women soldiers in danger would become hysterical, or that men would become so protective of them they'd neglect their duty.

The colonel was saying, "I wish every detachment overseas had the same barracks the WAC has here at Fort Des Moines. But that's not possible. When a company moves up to a new site, officers and enlisted alike must roll up their sleeves to make the place livable and free of nasty surprises. One detachment commander cleaning her own quarters saw she had inherited a bed—a soldier's most prized possession in the field. But as she pulled back the covers she found the upper half of a dead German soldier."

Some of the women in the audience gasped at the macabre image. The colonel paused, and if she had more tales in this vein she skipped over them to a recital of supply problems and job satisfaction. Page began to read over her notes until she heard her name called.

"First Lieutenant Hannaday," Colonel Neilson said, "will give you a picture of the morale and off-duty activities of WAC troops at Supreme Allied Headquarters. Lieutenant Hannaday."

Page walked to the stage, spread her notes and put her hands on the lectern. There was nothing daunting in these rows of faces, not for someone who'd faced a *Schützenpanzerwagen* in the Ardennes.

"Today," she began, her voice strong, "I want to tell you what the WAC is accomplishing at SHAEF and how we keep our morale strong."

Page enumerated the Red Cross and Special Services activities, the WAC service clubs, places for dating like the new Hamburger Date Club for both GI and Wac just opened in Paris. She talked about sightseeing arrangements for leaves and passes, about week-long courses at nearby universities. "We have recently begun to play basketball in Paris with French women's teams," she said, "although they play by men's rules and we had to learn to play on a full court."

She was coming to the end of her prepared notes. "I want you to be aware that a Wac's life overseas has its pleasant moments, but these come only after some pretty hard work. During rapid advances or emergencies such as in the Bulge last December," she said, "Wacs work seven days a week, often around the clock. When I can, I check our field units, and I'd like to tell you about one in particular. You'd think that Paris duty is the best there is, but for AG Casualty in Paris you'd be wrong. It's true they work in clean uniforms at the Hotel Majestic on the Avenue Kléber, but their duty is as tough in its way as any. During the Ardennes fighting, their IBM machines whirred night and day, and the cards, one for each wounded, MIA and KIA, mounted in stacks. I talked with one young officer—she'd been catching catnaps on a sofa, fully dressed—and she told me that it got to all of them sooner or later, that each card was a GI just about their age." Page saw some tears in the upturned faces, and thought to end on a happier note. "But when our troops are advancing rapidly as they are now, Wacs have time off and they are provided with as many relaxing activities as possible."

Page was finished. She gathered her notes and took a step from the lectern. A smattering of applause had begun. Suddenly, she knew she could not leave without saying what needed to be said, a plea for the Corps that no one else seemed ready to make.

"Just a moment! I have a request from Wacs overseas," she began again, standing exposed to the audience without a lectern to hold. "I can best make my point by telling you about a visit I made to the Panthéon in Paris. On its walls, there is a series of paintings depicting the life of Saint Genevieve, whose motto was: 'What I promised, I will do.' We Wacs in the ETO want you to help us honor our promise to do our job until the end of the war." Someone in the audience coughed pointedly, but Page plunged on. "Don't think we want to be pulled back home before the job is done. And after the war? What about afterwards? Some of us want to serve with the occupation forces in both Germany and Japan—and we want to serve equally with our brothers-in-arms."

She saw that what she had said had caused both male and female officers to shift uncomfortably in their seats, but she pressed on. "There is one more request that I bring to you, not from all women overseas, but from some of us." Out of the corner of her eye she saw the moderator moving toward her. "Please, let me speak!" The vehemence of her plea stopped him momentarily. "Don't sidestep the question of a permanent Corps after the war." Her audacity had them now, and she drew in a deep breath. "All of us in the ETO know and accept that winning the war in Europe and then in the Pacific is our first mission. But what is to happen to the Corps afterwards? Will it disappear into the history books as an interesting wartime experiment, or will we become a permanent part of the Army in peacetime?" Page saw one of the general officers motion to the moderator and knew she only had seconds left.

A tremor of passionate concern replaced the voice control she had displayed. "Why *not* a permanent Corps?" she asked, her eyes holding each of theirs. "For you to ask less for us who have given so much—yes, for the Wacs who gave their lives for their country—is to deny the worth of WAC achievement in every theater of war around this globe. If you grant less than permanent status, you denigrate the sacrifice of so many women soldiers who courageously endured bombings, shellings, privation, cold, bad quarters and years away from their homes just like their brother soldiers. Don't reward us by turning your backs on our request. Give us what we've earned—a permanent peacetime Women's Army Corps."

Short of breath, she stopped. The moderator rushed to the

lectern, signaling an end to her speech. Proudly, Page strode through the charged silence toward the audience to regain her seat.

"Just a minute, Lieutenant Hannaday," a woman's voice issued from the rear. "Are there women," she said, "who would choose to make the Army a peacetime career, forsaking marriage and family? It's true that married women with no dependants under age fourteen can now serve, but there would be no need for such leniency in peacetime. Before this war, army nurses were discharged when they married."

Another female voice took up the challenge. "I, for one, have always assumed that outside of wartime emergency a married woman's natural responsibilities would be incompatible with military duty. No husband wants his wife parading around an army camp while there are dishes in the sink and diapers in the pail."

Page nodded, exasperated, but determined to hold her own. "It's true that most GI Janes, like GI Joes, want to become just plain civilians again, but there *is* a nucleus of women who want to stay in and lead the military life, and again I beg you, do not ignore them. With all due respect, they deserve better from you."

There was a buzz of low conversation as Page, exhilarated, found her seat, but it soon became clear to her that her words had not sparked a debate or even a discussion. The conference plodded on according to the agenda, and the afternoon ended with a film *The Returning Soldier,* to Page's mind an incredibly optimistic look at demobilization.

At 1650 they were dismissed until the next morning. As she stood up, stiff from sitting most of the day, Lieutenant Colonel Neilson was called over to a group of officers near the stage.

"Well, Lieutenant," she said, gathering her briefing materials, "you certainly let the bees out of the hive. There are some things best accomplished behind the scenes. Besides, I thought you were engaged to be married."

Page nodded. "I am, Colonel, but . . ."

"I see," the Colonel said.

Page wondered what she saw. Even though she wouldn't personally benefit, she had a right to fight for what she believed. Surely the colonel knew she was no idle rabble rouser.

That night she was leafing through a month-old *Life* magazine when a familiar image leaped from a page reporting on Congresswoman Clare Boothe Luce's tour of the Italian front north of Florence. Jill! Almost unrecognizable in muddy fatigues and helmet; still, there she was, no mistaking the set of that mouth. God, she looked great! Carefully Page tore the photo out, wrote across the margin: "Our girl made *Life* magazine!" and slipped it into an envelope she'd just addressed to Bunny. Lord knew when her letter would find her. Poor Bunny. It was so obvious from her letters that she was crazy for a guy who was now a prisoner of the Japanese. Thank God Bunny didn't read all the horror stories in the stateside newspapers.

On an impulse, Page went to the telephone and tried to call Elisabeth in New York, but long-distance circuits beyond Chicago were busy. Coming back to her room, she decided to send Elisabeth a short note, telling her about Jill's instant fame in *Life* and asking her to write soon. Elisabeth worried her. The postal tracer from London had turned up information that Lieutenant Gardner had been discharged; the inquiry had then been forwarded twice, finally reaching an address in Georgetown, Virginia, only to be returned marked "ADDRESSEE UNKNOWN." After that Page had given up hearing from her, but a few days later a letter—well, a note really—had arrived at Bushey Park. Just like Elisabeth to do the unexpected.

Depositing the letters in the orderly room mailbox, Page wondered whether she should brave the Iowa winter wind for the second showing of *Laura* at Post Theater Number Two or settle for a drink at the officers' club. She had just spent a fruitless hour second-guessing herself. Perhaps she had been premature, her natural caution told her; no, she decided, it was the kind of rock-the-boat question that had to be asked. She'd had to speak up or live with a sense of failing the women who'd asked her to speak for them. And what about their morale? Didn't it deserve a boost? Before she could continue in this vein she heard several loud voices outside in the hall, then a knock on her door.

"Come!"

The door opened on four young officers Page had noticed seated together in the officers' mess after the conference. Since they had been whispering and looking at her, she thought they were comparing rumors, which were the leaven of every mess hall meal.

"Excuse us, ma'am," said the first woman inside, a young blond second lieutenant with none of the sheen worn off her gold bar, "but we would like your permission to talk with you."

"All of you?" Page wondered if the tiny quarters would hold them.

"Yes, Lieutenant."

"All right, but it will be a bit of a squeeze in here."

They crowded in and carefully closed the door.

"Here," Page said, standing, "two of you sit on the bed."

Two women sat down, the other two shifted their feet and looked at the blond, indicating she should speak.

"Well?" Page said.

"We heard what you said today, ma'am—at the conference."

Page nodded. "Yes."

"How many women at SHAEF feel that way?" the blond lieutenant asked. "We didn't know there were any others. You see, we've been trying to—to—"

One of the women on the bed jumped in. "What Murray means, Lieutenant, is that we've been trying to find out what will happen to the WAC after the war and been put off. Mind if I smoke?" Page handed her a butt can. "They tell us that winning the war is what's important; they tell us not to worry our pretty little heads; they tell us that maybe we'll be able to join the reserve. *Maybe!* We don't want to wake up someday and find the Corps gone."

Murray spoke up again. "That's why we're here, ma'am. We thought you could tell us what we should do."

How could she tell them what to do with their lives? She wore Paul's engagement ring on her finger. She was still too separated—her heart pledged to him, her mind pulling against her promises.

"What can I tell you?" she said, the excitement nevertheless creeping into her voice. "I'm just a message carrier."

"Begging your pardon, Lieutenant," Murray said, moving toward the door.

"At ease. I didn't mean that. The truth is, I believe deeply that the Corps should become a permanent part of the Army and I'm glad there are others, especially here on the only training center we have left. You know, don't you, they're closing Oglethorpe as soon as the medical companies go through."

"Yes," Murray answered, "we're all expecting reassignment here since there are so few basic companies in training. Now tell us, Lieutenant Hannaday, *what can we do?*"

Page answered them, surprising herself, because she did know just what they should do. "In the first place, you've already done something. As of now you're in touch with the SHAEF Wacs who want a permanent Corps." She scribbled her APO address on a sheet of WAC stationery and handed it to Murray. "Whenever you hear something you think we ought to know, send it to me and I'll pass it on, and we'll do the same for you." They nodded eagerly.

Murray spoke up, "And we can write to other WAC detachments in the ZI wherever friends are stationed. Once we know if there are others who agree, we'll be able to take action together. That's always more effective."

"What about the big brass, Lieutenant?" the blond asked Page. "Your father's a general officer. Won't he help?"

Page shook her head no. "We can't count on anything from that direction, I'm sorry to say, but Ike is another matter. He's *for* us. You know he has a WAC aide, Lieutenant Summersby—"

A snort of disgust came from Murray. "Yes, we've *heard* all about that Englishwoman. Colonel Hobby fought against her direct commission."

Page shrugged. "That may be true, but Kay has probably done the WAC more good than anyone else. She's a damned good soldier, and she speaks up for us. I think partly because of her influence, Ike never fails to give his women soldiers their due, and since you came here and asked me, I have to say that I think General Eisenhower is the only hope we have of permanent status. I'm praying that Kay can get me in to see him when I get back to Reims. Don't you realize that when we win in Europe, Ike, as supreme commander, will be able to write his own ticket?"

Murray nodded. "I believe that, Lieutenant, but tell us what we can do here in the States after we identify those who want a career in the WAC."

"I think," Page said thoughtfully, "it would be futile to write to congressmen. They'll take their cue from the heads of services and the theater commanders. I do think we have to let Colonel Hobby and the WAC staff directors know how we feel. They're sensitive to letters from the field."

"Okay," Murray said, "that takes care of the ZI and the ETO. What about the other overseas theaters?"

Page said, "I'm writing to a friend in the Philippines and one in Italy—the more widespread the support, the better. Remember, our friends don't necessarily have to want to *be* in a peacetime WAC themselves to support those who do." She chewed on the pencil she'd been using to take notes. "And if any of you know women in the WAVES or the Marines, let's get them in on it, too. For some crazy reason, the Navy has always been more receptive to women than the Army. Can you believe it, with their hidebound traditions?"

They shook hands all around, and in their faces as they filed out Page read hope and determination. Murray turned at the door. "Lieutenant Hannaday, is it true you were fired on in the Battle of the Bulge?"

"It's true."

"Were you scared?"

"I returned fire."

"Did you really capture a German prisoner?"

She laughed. "Not quite."

"Would you have killed him," Murray asked, "if you'd had to?"

Page had answered the question for herself as soon as she had been relieved at VIIIth Corps headquarters, slowly unlocking her forefinger from the trigger of the M-1 and easing the safety on. "Yes, Murray, I would have. We're not given combat training, but when you're in battle you only remember that others count on you to act like a soldier."

Murray nodded shyly at Page's answer. "I always wondered, you know, if it were me . . . Well," and she backed down the hall a step, "we'll be in touch with you as soon as we have something to report." She started down the hall again and then turned once more. "Tell the SHAEF Wacs about us?"

Page waved. "You bet I will." Closing her door, she lay down once again on her bed. Listening to these women had left her elated, renewed after the negativity of the conference. "Paul," she wondered out loud, saying to the ceiling of the small bare room what she had never dared say to him in person, "how can I marry you and leave the Corps just when it needs me most?" But what choice did she have?

Late that same evening, she was humming the haunting theme from *Laura* when the duty officer appeared at her door. She was not particularly sorry or surprised when the DO handed her the freshly cut orders canceling her temporary duty and ordering her back to SHAEF two days early. She had done what she had been assigned to do, and more. The surprise had not been what she'd said, the surprise was in how she felt about it.

Long after she was Paul's wife, she could be proud she had helped to keep the Corps alive for other women soldiers. At least she'd have that much.

61

ADVANCE HEADQUARTERS ON LUZON, MONDAY, FEB. 19—Seven thousand persons, including patients, internees and civilians, both American and Filipino, were freed as American troops seized the Philippine General Hospital . . . where fanatically resisting Japanese fought back against an ever-tightening ring that was steadily pushing them into Manila Bay. . . .

—The New York Times

Manila Bay is described as now open to American naval vessels.

—Columbia Broadcasting System bulletin

ON MARCH 7, 1945, Tech Sergeant Palermo sat cross-legged with sixty other Wacs beside a modern blacktop highway outside Manila. The roadway had served as a landing strip for the GHQ and FEAF Wacs flown up from Leyte. It was jammed with jeeps, trucks and GIs jostling for a place amidst wrecked cars and hoards of refugees with their belongings desperate to get back to their homes in the city. In the hills to the north, she could hear heavy artillery fire routing the last enemy resistance. Dead Jap soldiers still lay along the road, blackened and bloated, some writhing with fat white maggots.

Vicki plopped down beside her. "Ugh, the smell is awful!" When Bunny didn't answer, she asked, "Are you all right?"

"Yes." But she wasn't. For hours now she had been wondering if the retreating Japs had left Breck dead by some roadside in northern Luzon, his beautiful body food for maggots. She couldn't shake the picture from her head.

Vicki persisted, "You don't look so good, Bun. Maybe you ought to report on sick call when we get to our billets."

"The medics don't have a pill for this sickness," Bunny answered, her shoulders sagging lower. Then, needing to change the subject, she asked, "Did you hear the lieutenant say where we were going to be billeted in the city?"

"No. Rumor has it we were going to MacArthur's summer house, but the First Cav used it as a target when they shelled Manila." Vicki snickered. "Somebody pointed it out, and they just leveled it. You know how they hate MacArthur. Wow, I wouldn't want to be *that* artillery spotter."

The detachment lieutenant came up behind her. "Hansen! Don't pass on such stupid crap."

Vicki looked embarrassed. "No, ma'am."

"Sergeant Palermo," the lieutenant continued, "we're going to be taken to La Salle College in the city, so get your people together. You're still assigned to us for quarters and rations until I get new orders from FEAF."

"Yes, ma'am." Bunny saluted after struggling to her feet. Even with the stench, she wanted to sit there forever. *I'm so tired,* she thought, and put out an arm to steady herself against a tall cedar tree.

"She's got some nerve," Vicki whispered, still smarting from the CO's chewing out. "All the damned brass stick together. Little tin gods!" She waited until the lieutenant was well out of earshot before speaking in a normal voice. "Bunny, did you hear that when MacArthur came ashore on Leyte he walked *on top of the water?"* Several of the EWs sitting nearby laughed and were reminded of their own favorite MacArthur jibes.

Bunny smiled, but refused to be pulled into the conversation. She was strangely lethargic. Even laughing took too much precious energy.

The truck to their new quarters made its way through the crowded streets to what the GI drivers called "Atrocity College." The acrid odor of creosote and delousing powder hung in a miasma over the place.

"Just cleared the bodies out yesterday," one driver volunteered. "Wanna see the torture hooks where they hung people up?" he added, sounding like some macabre tour guide.

Bunny answered with a shudder that was half revulsion and half feverish shiver, "No, thanks, Corporal, we'll skip the scenic tour. We could use a hand with this gear, though." She realized she was tired to the bone with a fatigue that couldn't be cured by a night's sleep. And no wonder, she thought, twelve- and fifteen-hour work shifts or around the clock, week after week, followed by sleepless hours on her cot wondering where Breck was or whether he still existed at all. If only she could know for sure. But what did it matter? Hadn't she denied him a place in her life? Even if he lived, she might never know it, might never see him again. And if he died ... if he was already dead ...

Inside the former college, she quickly assigned the Air Wacs to their block of rooms. "Let's dung this place out," she said, looking wearily around at the debris piled everywhere, remembering how many times in the past year she'd said the same words. "Just look at the flies!"

Vicki said, "Damn! I hate those black furry flies most of all. Gimme a nice clean lizard anytime." She just stood in the middle of her room, arms hanging at her side, eyes suddenly listless.

"Come on, Minnesota," Bunny coaxed. "Don't you feel it? This is the end of the line. I don't think we'll ever move up again. One more time now, Vic. Come on, gals, let's all police this stuff." She knew she was talking as much for herself as for Vicki and the others. The interminable heat and humidity, the never-ending battle operations piling one on the other, the awful living conditions had sapped everyone's energy. The spark of instinct that made women care where they lived and how it looked had been eroded until it wouldn't take much to extinguish it altogether.

The next morning Bunny reported to the bullet-scarred tin building at Nichols Field, which had been designated as a photo lab and office. She helped the guys prop up broken desks and chairs and set up crates for photo files. They turned fragments of exploded shell casings into ashtrays and paperweights. She had barely set up the darkroom equipment when a civilian combat photographer appeared at the door.

"Sarge, will you run a few rolls for me?"

When she had completed the negatives he asked her, "How about giving me contact prints on these two here in the middle? How long will it take?"

"Do you want enlargements?"

"No."

"I can have them for you in three quarters of an hour. Fast enough?"

"It'll do, Sarge. Mind if I stay in here and watch you print?"

Nodding, Bunny set to work making the positives. Turning the safelight on, she exposed the print paper to the negatives, lifted them with tongs from one tray to another, first into the developer, then stop bath and fixer, and finally slid them into the wash. She could see that they were dramatic shots of Americans freed from the Jap internment camps.

"Cabanatuan," he said pointing to the emerging photos. "What a hellhole! Those poor guys are near dead. I'm afraid some of them aren't gonna make it even with the best food and medical help."

She wanted to escape from the pictures of living cadavers, because she knew it gave her another vision of Breck's fate. "Let's wait outside until they come out of the soup," she told him. "I'll blot dry so you can be on your way."

He lit her cigarette while they waited in two shaky chairs outside the lab. "Pulitzer Prize winners," he said, jerking his thumb toward the darkroom door. "They're good if I do say so—and, with my boss, I may just have to nominate myself." For a second he seemed ready to launch into a story about the stupidity of photo editors, but instead leaned his chair against the wall and quizzed her with the usual questions, mainly why-in-hell-would-a-girl-like-you-want-to-join-the-Army?

No thoughtful answer had ever convinced or satisfied a guy,

from buck private to correspondent, so she gave him the answer he would understand. "What, stay behind when all the good-lookin' guys were heading for tropical isles? You know what the song says, the ones at home are either too young or too old, too gray or grassy green."

He looked at her uncertainly. "Damned if I know why, but I think I've just been razzed." He flapped his arms, trying to dry out the fresh shirt that already was showing half moons of sweat. "I'm goin' home next week. Anyone you want me to call?"

She gave him her mother's number. "When you were at the camps," she asked him, sorry now that she'd flipped off at him, "did you run into any captured GIs?"

"Sure," he said.

"A private Breck Smith, Breckinridge T. C. Smith—tall, rangy, a fast talker?"

"Do you have a photo?"

"No. Nothing."

"Where was he captured?"

"Shortly after the landing on Luzon."

"Naw, the guys I ran into had been on Bataan and Corregidor, way back in the beginning. This Smith a relative or one of the guys you followed to this tropical paradise?"

"A—a friend."

He took off his cap with its correspondent's insignia and wiped the sweatband with his handkerchief. "Listen, Sarge," he said and cleared his throat, his tone conciliatory, "I hope your Private Smith comes back safe, but . . . Well, you just got to understand the Jap mentality. See, they think that if a soldier allows himself to be captured instead of committing suicide he's not much of a man, they think he's less than human, and—well, damn it, they're likely to treat him that way. I hate to say this about your friend, poor sonofabitch, but I heard the Japs put all the POWS they could cram onto old cargo ships and sent them off to the main Japanese islands."

Slowly she turned her head and looked out over the activity at the airbase. Dozers, cranes and heavy equipment were at work everywhere. The war had its own momentum, it didn't stop for pain. She knew that the correspondent had got up and strolled away a few paces. He came back and sat down.

"Hey, look here," he said, his voice friendly. "Is this friend of yours a smart guy?" She nodded. "Well, if he's got you to come back to, I'd be willing to bet my Pulitzer he'll make it back okay."

"Sure," she said and put out her cigarette. "If he's in Japan, he's got the corner on the geisha concession by now." Suddenly she felt an almost overwhelming rush of affection for that image: Breck the scrounger being pampered from head to toe by tiny kimonoed beauties, Breck in any setting, but Breck *alive!*

"What the hell," he offered. "That's a girl." And he gave her a thumbs-up sign later as he dropped the prints into the seat beside him and jammed his jeep into first gear.

That night the detachment commander came to warn them to stay on the boards laid to the outdoor latrines. "The sappers are coming to clear out any mines the Japs might have laid as soon as possible, but until they can *don't step off the boards.*"

Later Vicki called Bunny to her room. "Bun, I've got the most incredible cramps, and it's not the curse, I've already made four trips to the latrine. The last time, there was a line out there." Vicki's hands clutched at her stomach. "Nobody had the runs until she came along warning us about the latrines. You don't suppose the Wicked Witch of the Southwest Pacific put a hex on us?" she said, and gritted her teeth against another contraction. "I just know I'm going to fall off the boards next time, and" —she started up from her cot in a rush—"I almost don't care if I do. I'd rather die than this," she wailed and made a dash out of the room.

During the night three more FEAF Wacs came down with dysentery, and by morning they were so weak that Bunny had to call for transportation out to the base dispensary. "No room for them here," the doctor told her. "Take them back to their quarters and try to keep them from getting dehydrated, and give them paregoric." He put his face close to hers and peered into her eyes. "How do *you* feel, Sergeant? You don't look so good."

"I'm okay, Major. Just tired."

For the next week, Bunny worked days at the photo lab and was on-call night nurse for the Wac victims of the black flies and filth of the reconquered city. By the time the others had mended, and gangs of laborers had cleaned the La Salle College campus, thoroughly fumigating the area, Bunny felt continuously dizzy, trembly all over, and she couldn't stop perspiring although the temperature was only seventy-eight degrees, a mild day in Manila.

She asked the recovering Vicki, "You and the others gonna be all right tonight, kiddo? I—I think I'll go to bed. If I got it, the paregoric isn't helping much."

"Bunny! What a lousy break. Just when everybody's all over it, you get it. I'll help you out to the latrine. Just lean on me."

Bunny was reeling. "No, no—I don't have to go there. Just get me to bed—I feel like I'm falling."

Minutes later, maybe hours, she was aware that Vicki was standing over her, fuzzy others in the background. "She's burning up," someone said.

She heard her own voice as a kind of crackling, like crumpled paper or a fire. "Just sleep . . . dance a Lindy . . . tomorrow. Arghh . . ." And then the retching and gagging took over her body. Finally she was wrung dry of all juices, her insides brittle, flaming. Her teeth began to chatter; they clattered until her jaws ached.

Sometime later, Bunny saw Vicki advancing and receding over her. "Take it easy," Vicki said to two corpsmen wrapping her in blankets. "She's so sick!"

They transferred her to a stretcher; she thought her skin was being flayed from her body with their every touch. "No—no," she heard the crazy crackling voice with the New Jersey accent again. "Be okay . . . just need rest." From an incredible distance a man's voice, a soft Southern drawl—no, it couldn't be Breck, Breck was dead and she was going to him, but the voice went on, insisting, "What's the sergeant's name?"

"Bunny."

"Easy does it, Bunny," the man's voice said. "You got a doozy of a case of dengue fever. Get yah to the Philippine General. Docs'll fix yah right now."

62

President Roosevelt died yesterday afternoon, suddenly and unexpectedly. He was stricken with a massive cerebral hemorrhage at Warm Springs, Ga., on the eve of his greatest military and diplomatic successes—the impending fall of Berlin and the opening of the San Francisco Conference to set up a World Security Organization that would make the world free from martial and economic strife. . . . About 2:15 Eastern war time he said, "I have a terrific headache," lost consciousness in a few moments and died at 4:35. He was 63 years old.

Harry S. Truman was sworn in as President at 7:09 o'clock last night, and a few minutes later Mrs. Roosevelt left for Warm Springs.

Some 500,000 American soldiers of the Third and Ninth Armies, and thousands of tanks, sped along a 150-mile front toward Berlin and Leipzig.

In Italy . . . the Fifth Army . . . made good gains and was eleven miles from La Spezia.

Japanese planes resumed their suicide attacks on American ships off Okinawa . . . The Americal Division invaded Bohol, last of the enemy-held central Philippines.
                              —The New York Times, *April 13, 1945*

BUNNY DREW IN a deep breath and opened her eyes. *Alive!* She was still alive. After that burning, freezing hell, after the days when she hung on to her shaking self to keep her body from falling through an endless emptiness, she could at last see and touch. Her hands explored her body without recognizing the empty bag of bones and dry skin as Bunny. She smiled faintly through cracked lips. She'd finally lost the rest of the pounds she'd put on at OC—and more besides. But was *this* diet necessary? Couldn't she just have gone on the Hollywood plan like everybody else? She lay still again.

Gradually, a conscious feeling of admiration for her physical self overcame her. This was the real Bunny. This body that had betrayed her in the past had brought her through hell alive—she fell back after trying to sit up—if not kicking.

A voice calling her name came through the door across the room, which was all white—dazzling white walls, white bedsheets, and a woman attached to the voice in a white starched nurse's uniform. Bunny's eyes devoured the brightness after the days—weeks, maybe—spent in darkness.

"How do you feel today?" The woman's softly accented voice hovered over her head, followed by a hand on her wrist taking her pulse.

"I don't know. Like I'm here and not here. It's funny ..."

"That's the fever."

"How long have I—?"

"It's Friday, April thirteenth. You've been here over five weeks."

Bunny looked at the face behind the voice and started in recognition. It was the face of the geisha in her fever dreams, the one who had smilingly served a reclining Breck while concealing one of Harry's swords in her kimono. Bunny had screamed at Breck to be careful, but he had not heard her or seen his danger. And then she had been pulled by a terrifying force she couldn't name, spinning into a pit of black, lonely space. Each spin had taken her deeper toward some place where she knew Johnny Palermo would be waiting. She could hear him laughing as he had laughed that last day at La Jeunesse, a laugh full of hatred and triumph. Then, with her last energy, she had reached back for help and grabbed a hand in the dark. It was Breck's hand, stretching through the black void, pulling her back to life.

"Temperature's normal," the nurse was saying, shaking down a thermometer. "Feeling hungry?"

"Just incredibly empty, Nurse," Bunny answered, her voice sounding like a child's version of her own.

"I'm Nurse Chung—Antonia. Filipino, Sergeant. I always make sure the GIs know that right away. Some of them think they've been captured when they come out of it on the fever ward." She laid out a clean cotton nightgown and handed Bunny a hand mirror. "You had quite a bad case of dengue. Want to fix yourself up for your visitor? Maybe that Breck you called for during the worst of it."

"But . . ." Bunny began weakly. "Breck here?"

Nurse Chung gave Bunny's cover a last tug as she left. "I'll give you ten minutes before I let the General in."

Harry! No, she couldn't deal with Harry. She couldn't think. But did she have a choice? He was here. She lifted the mirror. Accentuated by a wild halo of black curly hair, her huge dark, blue-rimmed eyes stared back at her from above sunken cheeks. Her fleshless face looked naked, defenseless. At that moment she would have welcomed back all the lost pounds.

Then Harry's healthy face was there at her bedside, asking polite questions just as if she had been his secretary or a favored family retainer, until the two staff doctors, fussing over a general officer in their hospital, left the room. She looked at him. He hadn't changed in four months; if anything he'd become more himself. The single silver star in the precise middle of his epaulets suited him perfectly.

"Bunny, darling—don't we look well this morning." He bent to kiss her forehead. "I've just ordered your doctors to give you anything you want. Turned heaven and earth to get on the old man's inspection trip when I heard you were ill. Malaria, was it?"

"Dengue."

"My God! I've said it before, this is no place for our American women—said it a hundred times."

Bunny decided to let that remark pass. Harry had always thought the WAC had been created expressly to bring Bunny to him. He must be talking to hide the shock of seeing her like this. She had to keep Harry from slipping into a fantasy of their future together. The only way she could deal with him, do what she had to do for Breck and for herself, was to be honest right from the start. "Harry, I look awful and feel awful."

"Nothing of the kind. I've told you before, my dear, I like

your wild, earthy qualities—so different from any woman I've ever known."

Bunny took what felt like a plunge into cold water: "Harry, I'm sorry about what happened that night at Hollandia—"

A line creased Harry's unlined forehead. "My dear, I told you at the time to say no more about it. It's over and I'm willing to forget it. These things happen in wartime when women are far from the civilizing influences of home." He took his pipe from his pocket and, after a lengthy ritual, lit it; the familiar sucking noises grated on her nerves.

Determinedly she continued, "I'm sorry because I hurt your feelings, but I'm not sorry about Breck."

Harry swiped at a live ash that drifted down his tie, and got up to walk to the window, the lines around his eyes deepening. "I find you with an enlisted man, in a compromising position, the man is a Class-A screw-up—now you tell me you're not sorry!"

"Harry, do you know he's been captured, that he's probably dead?"

"Many better men are dead, too." But the color came up in his cheeks. "How do you know that?"

"I saw him at Tacloban." Her voice began to sound stronger and clearer to her. She had to sound like herself or he would never believe her.

His face was an unyielding mask, his words measured. "Bunny, you promised me you would never see that man again."

"No, Harry, I never made such a promise."

"It was implicit in my forgiveness, and you know it," he said and moved back toward her bed, his pipe held firmly in midair. He looked down at her, and then his features broke into a smile. "Bunny, you're making a bad joke, aren't you? I can never tell when you're being wonderfully impulsive."

Her tense body sank wearily back into the mattress. He would not believe her, not become angry enough to let her go unless she told him the truth, every bit of it. He was a wall and she had no way of getting to the rest of her life as long as he blocked her from whatever the future held—even if that future meant pain and risk.

Harry sat on the edge of her bed and picked up her hand. "Let's not discuss this old business," he said. "You haven't even asked about my news. Louise is in Reno this instant getting a divorce! What do you say to that? Your Harry called her bluff. Told her she'd get nothing if she played rough with me. She knew she'd gone too far. I'm no woman's fool."

Despite Harry's control, Bunny could see how angry he was by the pulsing vein in his throat, and she knew that his anger was not all aimed at his wife. "Please, Harry, no more."

"Of course, darling. You're tired. I'll come back later."

"No, Harry. I don't want you to come back later; I don't want you to come back *ever.*" He gave her a sharp look and held up his pipe as a shield to stop her words, but she plunged on. "I'm sorry, Harry. I'm sorry I can't love you, and I'm sorry I can't marry you. I thought life with you was what I wanted, but now I know it isn't."

Harry was shocked and unbelieving. "You can't mean you want a life with that hillbilly private!"

"I'm in love with him. He doesn't know it; he's probably dead, but I'll always be in love with him. I don't want anything if it can't be with him. Don't you see"—and she said it as much for herself as for him—"I'm ready to throw away everything on just the chance that someday—"

"You've still got a fever. You don't know what you're saying."

"But I do, Harry. Maybe for the first time in a long time, I know exactly what I'm saying. I've been telling myself for so long that love like that was too risky, and I couldn't stand the uncertainty, the pain of it. But I was wrong. What I really can't live with is something less." Harry looked as though she'd hit him, but she was convinced that the truth about the way she felt was the kindest of blows. "Oh, Harry, I wish I could be what you want, but I can't. I know now that I never could have been. I would have made us both miserable."

His composure was betrayed by the flush creeping up his face from his collar. "How *can* you, after all I've done?"

"Harry, what have you done? You wanted to divorce Louise long before you met me."

He jumped up, crimson now, the distinguished silver-haired general just as angry as any private rejected for another man. "I should have known—you low-class . . . preying on decent family men." He moved rapidly toward the door as if to put a distance between himself and any more words he didn't want to hear. His voice shook with outraged manhood. He yelled, "You Wacs are all alike. I should have listened when everyone told me what bitches you were. I won't forget again, you better believe it." At the door he hesitated and, with a murderous look, growled, "You look like an old hag, know it? *If your redneck lover comes back*, he won't want you. Know why? I saw it on his transfer papers." Harry's voice rose in triumph. "He's six years younger than you are!" With a look of satisfied spite, he leveled one last epithet, "You cradle robber!" Then he slammed the door so hard her bed shook.

It hadn't been easy. Harry had reminded her of a cobra, weaving above her to his own frustrated music. She closed her eyes, and her hands shook slightly as she smoothed the sheets tight around her body. She felt the pain of having hurt another human being, but then a long, shuddering sigh relieved the tension of these last minutes, and she opened her eyes. Knowing Harry, she was sure that even now he was busy armoring his memory with his own version of classic female betrayal and adding the experience to his wartime collection, like another samurai sword with a slight but interesting defect in the pommel. As for her, she was free, free to wait for Breck. To wait, perhaps forever.

Moments later Nurse Chung appeared with a tray. Despite Harry's upsetting exit, the odor of food made Bunny ravenous.

"That wasn't your Breck—the General," Nurse Chung said, and rolled the bed up so that Bunny could eat.

"No, Antonia, the General was another man, someone I once thought was the right man. My Breck is someone I thought was the wrong man, but he—" It was so complicated even for her that she stopped with a little shrug.

The Filipino woman smiled. "You know, there's an old Chinese saying in my family—we have one for every possible occasion. It goes: When the wrong man does the right thing it will turn out wrong, and when the right man does the wrong thing it will turn out right."

Bunny thanked her. "There must be a Granny Smith in every family."

"What?"

"Just a private joke, Antonia." But Bunny couldn't stop the little tug of joy at her heart. It continued through the first meal she'd eaten in many days and through the drowsy time afterward. That was Breck all right, the right man always doing the wrong thing. How did it go? When the right man does the wrong thing it will turn out right—turn out right. . . . The words repeated over and over in her head like an echo in a bottomless canyon. And then, with a certainty that exploded inside her, she knew he'd be coming back. How could she have doubted it? Somewhere he was waiting as she was waiting for this filthy war to be over, and when it was she would never leave his arms again. She dozed a minute, then jerked wide awake again. Six years younger? Was that really true or just Harry's male vanity lashing out at her? She had never thought to ask Breck his age. Would it matter?

The hatch opened, letting in a cleansing draught of sea air that revived Breck momentarily. He saw a leering face at the opening.

"You Plesident dead, GI," the words came spitting down on him. "We win war now. *Baka* Loosevelt dead!" The hatch slammed shut again, and he heard the lock bolt jammed in.

The man propped against the bulkhead beside him said, "Smitty, do you believe that about Roosevelt dying?"

"Maybe. He looked sick in the last Quebec Conference picture I saw, but we sure aren't losing the war. We may even have taken Manila by now."

"What the hell good does that do us? We're never gonna get back alive. Look at us! We're the walkin' dead already. And, shit, Smitty, you ain't even walkin'."

Breck rolled over on his good side; the sharp pain of his movements brought back the free-floating feeling that always preceded a blackout. But he didn't lose consciousness. *Good,* he thought, *I'm hanging on.* "What've I got to walk for, Buddy," Breck asked, a grin replacing the grimace, "when I can ride this luxury liner all the way up to Emperor Hirohito's front porch?" But the gung-ho effort cost him. His head sank back onto the metal deck, his left arm, immobilized against his body with strips of bloody fatigue jacket, throbbing with every pulse.

Breck refused to consider the possibility that he had been wrong when the Japanese doctor wanted to amputate a few days after his capture. The man—not a bad egg as Jap officers went—had insisted the arm should come off. Bone splinters could cause an abscess, he'd said, and anyway the arm would never be useful again. "No, no!" he'd yelled, struggling on the stretcher, until a Jap guard had menaced him with his bayonet. He'd been desperate. "Listen, Doc," he was half raving by then, "I've got a girl—what a girl! With a girl like that a guy has to have two arms to hang on to her." He'd fainted, but when he came to he'd been outside the surgical tent, on the ground, with both arms. One of the guys on this tub was a corpsman. "Medic," he'd yelled in the dark that first night, "what do I do?" Keep the arm quiet, came the answer, so the bone chips wouldn't move around. Jesus H. Christ, it hurt. But he still wasn't sorry.

The hatch opened again, and the guard lowered a bucket with their one meal of the day. The stench of it overpowered the smell in the hold of festering wounds, unwashed bodies and open bucket latrines. The man next to him took Breck's tin and crawled to the food along with the others and handed Breck his cup before dipping in with his own. Damned if he hadn't slopped hogs with better chow. Hell, during the Depression his granny's chickens ate better; but the thin rice gruel and chopped fish heads kept him alive, and he had to stay alive.

The man next to him spoke. "Where do you think we are, Smitty?"

He felt stronger; the vile stuff had life in it. "You got me. Let's figger it out. We were on this tub for at least two weeks before we sailed, maybe closer to three. We've been sitting in this harbor four more weeks. We can't have reached Japan, or why the hell wouldn't they take us off the *Honshu Maru* to a POW camp? That means we stopped short of the main islands." Breck gave his left arm the smallest tug to find a more comfortable position and winced at the pain. "Okay, now we can hear big guns—naval guns. Seems to me like the Jap captain of this leaky tub put in for repairs or provisions on his way home and got caught by one of our invasion fleets. You boys'll have to check this out with our friend Chet Nimitz, but I think we're probably in some harbor on Okinawa."

A rat the size of a three-month-old kitten ran along the deck in front of his feet. He kicked at it, and the other men cursed. It was the same rat some of them had been trying to catch for days, to eat. He'd endured too much to die from eating rat.

Breck knew he wouldn't eat rat no matter how hungry he got. Too dangerous—diseases. . . . He slipped off into a troubled sleep.

One day and night merged into another while they wallowed at anchor. The fish heads grew fewer, the stench more unbearable. Two men died, both in one night, and a detail of their comrades, themselves half-dead men, was chosen to drag the two bodies up the ladder and put them over the side. The men buzzed with information when they climbed down from the main deck.

"You were right, Smitty, it's a small harbor," one told him. "We're the biggest thing sitting here. Others mostly fishing boats, and I could swear I saw some destroyers on the horizon."

Breck asked, "Ours?"

"Don't know. Think so, or else why would these brave sons of Nippon be playing hide-and-seek?"

Hours later, Breck roused himself from sleep. The sound of big guns, bombs and ack-ack was much closer. Were they being attacked by American planes? Had he survived this long to be killed by his own guys? The cadaverous, half-insane men around him cursed their dilemma, caught like him between the desire to see this tub blown straight to the depths of hell and the primal urge to live any life, even this half-life.

The hatch flew open, flooding the hold with strong sunlight. With his fingers, Breck held his watering eyes open against the glare, and saw armed sailors crowd around the ladder, yelling down at them, motioning for them to come up. *How could he get up that ladder?*

"Come on, Smitty," one of the burial party said, "I'll give you a hand up. The air up there is so sweet you can eat it."

Afterward, he didn't know how he'd made it. The man above had tugged on his good arm, while the man below had pushed on his butt, but it seemed to be Bunny who urged him on. Her face was everywhere he looked; the sweet confusion in her eyes on the beach at Tacloban, her goodbye radiant with unspoken promises, preceded him up the ladder, dulled the pain, gave his body strength.

They were herded, staggering, toward the bow, where Breck could see the battle raging in the distance like it was a Movietone News film back home at a picture show.

"Christ, oh Christ, look at that," someone said in a hushed, prayerlike tone.

Jap planes were howling out of the skies from every angle, diving right into the destroyer outside the harbor.

The guards sent up squeals of laughter. *"Kamikaze! Kamikaze!"*

Breck could see that the destroyer was damaged, a fire was raging, but it was far from knocked out. A smokescreen billowed around the ship, but a snapping breeze blew it rapidly toward the island. The gun muzzles on the DDs pointed everywhere. *There!* Breck saw an incoming Jap plane take a direct hit and disappear into shrapnel in a burst of red flame and black smoke. He suppressed a cheer which would have earned him an instant bayonet thrust.

All around him swirled activity, which told him the ship was weighing anchor, getting ready to sail into the battle. *Damn!* Not even a fanatic Japanese merchant captain would sail unarmed into that hell out there. He decided that if he got the chance he'd go over the side, take his chances in the water. Even with one arm it was a better chance than he'd have on this half-wrecked one-stacker. He braced himself against the rusty rail.

The little ship hugged the shoreline when it broke out of the harbor. Breck saw one of the ship's officers rush toward them with an American flag. They were forced to hold it up over their heads. Now the captain's tactics were clear to him. The ship would make a run for it while the Jap suicide planes kept the destroyers and their escorts busy, and if that didn't work the captain obviously hoped any American carrier planes that showed up would see the men holding up the flag and take a guess at its meaning. As a gambling man, Breck could admire a pure bluff when he saw one.

Boldly the ship sailed full ahead for Japan, three hundred miles to the north. No American plane even made a pass at them, and the ship slipped behind a squall line and squeezed unnoticed between the American picket ships. Breck and the other POWs stood for hours in the bow, wet, cold, but somehow more alive than they had been for weeks.

"We're invading Okinawa," Breck whispered to the others as they huddled together against the spray from the open sea. "Our guys'll be set to invade Japan next."

Soon the other men took up his whispers and they circulated among the huddled few. *Won't be long now. Hang on. That's what we got to do, no matter what, we must stay alive because we're all going home.*

Do you hear that, Bunny? Breck shouted silently back over the stern toward the Philippines. *I'll be back and we'll be together.* And the half-crazy hope warmed him, healed his spirit and settled deep inside him as he was prodded down once again into the grim hold of the *Honshu Maru*.

-------- **63** --------

War bulletins, Thursday, April 26: Russian and American troops link up on the River Elbe. Hitler dismisses Göring for proposing a separate peace. The Fifth Army captures Verona on the Italian front. President Truman opens the United Nations conference in San Francisco. Three hundred fifty RAF Lancasters blast Hitler's mountain retreat at Berchtesgaden. XXIVth Army Corps advances on Okinawa.

FOR THE LAST time as her imperfect self, Jill Henry Hammersmith listened intently. Every word of the chaplain shimmered through her the way the bright late-April sunlight streamed in through the huge drawing-room windows of the Palazzo d'Ordella. The phrases he spoke enveloped her in their ancient meaning: "You, Desmond, and you, Jill, having come to me signifying your desire to be formally united in marriage and having assured me that no legal, moral or religious barriers hinder this proper union, I command you to join hands."

Jill felt Des take her hand in both of his and knew that she and he were, at this moment of symbolic union, being reborn. For a crazy instant, Jill tightened her hold on Des's hand, feeling that if she should ever let go now she couldn't live but, mutilated and incomplete, would bleed and die. She shook her head slightly, no more than a shiver, and the unwelcome image was gone. In its place came a new surety. With Des by her side, she was more than she had been. This moment held more of the perfection she had sought than she had ever known.

Des was saying, "I do," his eyes proud and passionate on her white veiled face.

The chaplain continued, "Jill, in taking the man who holds your right hand to your lawful and wedded husband, I require you to promise to love and cherish him, to honor and sustain him in the bad that may darken your days as in the good that may light your ways, and to be true to him in all things, until death alone shall part you. Do you so promise?"

With her eyes misty on Des's face, Jill said, "I promise."

Then the solemn requirement of the chaplain echoed about the room, "I charge this group assembled that if any know why these two should not be joined together in bonds of holy matrimony, let him speak now or ever hold his peace."

Jill half expected a voice which sounded like Neil's mother's to cry out against her, *Stop! This woman tries to build happiness on another man's grave. For ruining one life, she forfeits her own.* But the dissent was in her own imagination. There was no outraged cry, no sound except the concerted breathing of the people in the vaulted room as the chaplain continued the service. Her tense arms sagged in relief, and she felt Des grasp her more tightly. Now nothing could possibly come between them ever again.

Des stood straight and tall in his best uniform. Jill, in white parachute silk hemmed in Venetian lace—topped by a veil from Elisabeth airmailed all the way from New York, and with the fragrance of Chanel sent by Page in a diplomatic pouch from Paris enveloping her—held tight to him at the foot of the broad, curved staircase with an enormous Canaletto brooding over the scene. In the hush, Jill heard the sacred words that would echo through the rest of their lives, "By the authority vested in me, and in the presence of God and these assembled witnesses, I now pronounce Desmond and Jill man and wife."

As Des lifted her veil and tipped up her face for his kiss, it was a picture of him she knew she would carry in her heart forever. This man who had been in turn her enemy, her commanding officer and her heart's tormentor for almost three years was now her husband. With his lips on hers, she knew she would beat the awful legacy of guilt bequeathed her by Neil's death; she could learn to live in the present if it took every ounce of strength she possessed. Even in the midst of her wedding day, she instinctively knew that happiness was not guaranteed because she'd made a decision to be happy. She'd have to work at it, take control of it, make it happen.

Des whispered, "Mrs. Stratton. Nothing will ever separate us again. Promise?"

She could feel his breath warm on her ear as he held her before relinquishing the moment to the pressing crowd. Jill repeated her vow, "Until death alone shall part us, my darling," and then they were parted by the wedding party surging forward to congratulate them.

"Jill." The girl dressed in a diminutive version of Jill's own gown and carrying a bouquet squeezed through to a place at Jill's side.

"Tina, honey, stay here with me."

"You are *bellissima*," the young girl said adoringly, and then with the fatality of childhood whispered in Jill's ear, "I will be ugly when I grow up, and no one will marry with me."

Jill laughed and whispered back fiercely, "*Cara mia*, you are beautiful, and you will marry a prince."

"But I don't want a prince," Tina said earnestly, "I want a captain like Des."

One thing Jill knew as she hugged the little girl to her. She would teach Tina to believe herself worthy of accepting love when it came to her. Tina would not make her mistake, as Jill herself would never forget this lesson again. Oh, she was bubbling over with newfound wisdom to give Tina, but the most important idea of all was that it was never too late to change. Still Jill sighed, remembering that Helen had said there were no endings in life.

"My dear," Helen stage-whispered at her side. "This isn't a wake, remember, but your wedding day."

Jill erased the little frown of unwelcome memory and smiled. "Helen, I almost feel you should stand here with us to accept the congratulations. If it weren't for your—"

"Yes, I know. If it weren't for my nosiness, you were about to say."

"If it weren't for your caring, I was about to say."

Helen looked pleased, but said, "Nonsense! You two bring out my maternal instinct, and besides, it's wonderful to be treated like a wise matriarch by the young. A mother rarely gets to play that role with her own child."

Jill suspected that Helen had done far more for them than most delegates to the United Nations were doing for the world at that very moment in San Francisco. After the day when she received the Bronze Star, Helen had invited her and Des often to the Palazzo d'Ordella for musical evenings—like Helen herself, a curious mixture, of Aaron Copland and Vivaldi. Then, slyly outmaneuvering their vociferous objections, she had seen to it that they had the time and the place to court each other like any two young people during the early Tuscan spring of 1945. Later, having watched the magic of love at work, Helen had offered them wedding, wedding supper and honeymoon in the palazzo. All this, Jill knew, while Helen waited for word of her own son's life or death as Allied troops liberated one German labor camp after another. In many ways the Marchesa reminded Jill of Bunny when they had been green OCs at Fort Des Moines. Both Helen and Bunny had a bighearted courage that helped others far more than it helped themselves.

Des took Jill's hand again in his as supper was announced, and insisted they sit together on the Marchesa's right instead of being separated, as was custom, by the width of the table.

Des looked, admiring, at the table. "Helen, you have worked miracles with this food." Holding Jill's hand, he kissed the Marchesa's gallantly, "Ahh, it's an imperfect world. If only I were allowed two wives."

Their wedding supper was delicious. Prosciutto wrapped around figs, pasta cooked with fresh spring vegetables, a rack of lamb, deep-fried zucchini tossed with vinegar, and an almond and pine-nut *torta* which Jill fed to Des and he to her, for, as Italian as was the cuisine, their guests clamored for the old American wedding custom.

But, tempting though the dishes were, Jill managed only a bite or two of each one. Her mind was on her wedding night.

What had Des said in his anger at the Excelsior Hotel that night in Rome? "You're not the type to play a *femme fatale.*" Then what type was she? Would she be able to give him what he wanted, what all men wanted? Although their kisses and touching had come almost unbearably close to complete fulfillment in the last days before their wedding, the truth was that she was a near-twenty-four-year-old virgin. Her lack of sexual sophistication had always seemed appropriate with Neil. But how could she hope to please a man like Des Stratton, who was far more a man of the world?

The Marchesa stood at the head of the table and raised her glass. Everyone stood. "Long life, health and happiness to Jill and Desmond Stratton."

"Long life," the guests echoed.

Sergeant Harper, Schultzy and the other women in her unit, the chaplain, some men under Des's command plus a few from Fifth Army headquarters, and finally Helen and little Tina, all were smiling at her and Des. Even Charlito, alert to the bowl of table scraps being gathered, seemed to beam approval. These familiar faces were a real family and meant far more to her this night than all the dead Henrys of Virginia. *See, Des, I can live in the present,* she thought, smiling up at him.

"It's time, Mrs. Stratton," he whispered. It was obvious he enjoyed saying her new name. He stood and led her into the drawing room, where, with Helen and Tina on either side, they said good night to their guests; Des to the grins and pokes of the men, and Jill to the shy looks of the Wacs in her unit.

"All the best, ma'am," Sergeant Harper said, wringing her hand. "We'd about given up on you and the captain."

And then the last was gone. Through the open doors, Jill could see the long table being cleared and Charlito, well fed, asleep underneath. Des put his arm possessively around her shoulder.

Helen took Tina by the hand. "Tina, how would you like to sleep in the big bed with me tonight?"

Jill could see that the girl was thrilled. This was not the first time she had slept in the Marchesa's room. When Helen had arranged for Tina and Charlito to leave the orphanage in Rome and stay with her until Jill and Des could legally adopt the girl, Tina had often felt lonely and been invited into Helen's big bed.

"Now all of you come with me," Helen said, and, giving Jill and Des each a lamp, she preceded them up the grand staircase to the second-floor guest wing. She opened the door, kissed them and, taking the sleepy Tina by the hand after a second round of good nights, left with the girl for her apartment above.

"Sleep well, Helen," Des called after the retreating figure.

"Thank you," Jill said, "for making our wedding so beautiful."

Helen stopped with Tina on the curve of the balastrade and smiled down at them. "No, I thank *you,*" she boomed, "for allowing me to be a part of your happiness. But as for making your wedding beautiful, oh no, my dears, that is for the two of you to do." She continued climbing then, her lamp casting its light both before and after her.

Des closed the door to their room.

"I think she is so sad, Des," Jill said.

"I don't. She's tough and smart, but, what's more important, she wouldn't want us to spend a minute of tonight analyzing her life."

Jill smiled. "No, not Helen."

Giving her a light kiss, Des crossed to the fireplace, already laid against the chilly Florentine April night, and lit the fire. Then he loosened his tie and sat down in a fireside chair and patted his lap.

Jill had been standing just inside the door. She didn't know what she should do next, take off her wedding gown or what. At least she should remove her veil.

Des patted his lap again and chided her, "Didn't you just promise to obey, woman?"

"I don't remember that part, Desmond Stratton."

"Well, you'd better," he said and jumped from the chair, crossed the room, picked her up in his arms and returned to the chair all in the space of a few seconds.

"Des, you'll tear my veil," Jill said, laughing and out of breath.

He reached to her hair and fumbled with the pins until the veil came loose and floated to the carpet like jettisoned wings.

Then he buried his face in her hair and took a deep breath. "Jill, I don't think this is really happening. I'm afraid I'll look up and find I've been lost in a book and this happy man isn't really me, but someone else."

"Des, you're not imagining anything. It's really you and me and we're really married." She teased him, "I thought you were the practical one."

Des held her tight and said, "And I thought you were the one lost in fantasy."

Jill kissed his cheek and snuggled deeper into his arms. "I think that we've grown to be a little like each other already. Have you heard that the longer two people are married the more alike they become? It didn't happen with my folks." Each year her parents had grown in their differences: her mother became more a martyr to her unfortunate marriage, her father more defeated, frozen out of his patriarchal authority by his lack of illustrious forebears; and little Jill, immobilized in the middle, unable to please one without betraying the other. "Will we really become more alike as we grow older?" the grown-up Jill asked now.

"Yes, sweetheart, we will. It's not that we'll change so much, become different people or anything, it's just that we'll become more truly who we are by taking a part of each other for our own. Does that make sense?"

She nodded. "Wonderful sense," she said as his arms tightened around her and his lips found hers in a long, questioning kiss. Jill knew that the time she'd been dreading and longing for had come. She was embarrassed. In a small voice, she asked, "Do you want the bathroom first?"

They scrambled to their feet, and with a shyly formal politeness Des said, "Please, you can take it first."

Later, she lay on the four poster in the lacy gown Helen had given her and waited for him. In a way, she knew she would never feel more his than she felt during the ceremony, but in another way, which she had not yet experienced, she knew there was one more bridge to him, and that she would cross it as they made love. But, for these last few minutes alone, she was two women, both her old self and Des's wife, and yet not one or the other.

Jill waited for his touch, imagining what was to come. She

felt a welling forth of love that was different from anything she had ever felt for Neil. How could she have thought that her need to repair Neil's life was really love? For love she'd needed a partner, a shareholder in life.

"Are you having second thoughts?" Des was standing beside the bed.

"No, I was thinking how much I'm going to love being married to you." With those words, a surge of eagerness to know his body came to her.

She watched as he banked the fire and threw aside the silk dressing gown; then, shyly closing her eyes, she felt him slip into the bed beside her. His mouth touched hers and then quickly left to travel about her face and neck, randomly, with no apparent purpose except to know the hollows and ridges and corners, as if to seek out every last place she might be hiding, there to chase her toward the sunlight.

Almost immediately and together they unveiled themselves to each other, stripping away every superficial layer. First went Jill's nightgown and Des's heavy silk pajamas, next their ranks and positions of authority, and finally, for Jill, a lifetime of rules and strictures.

"Darling Jill, I never thought I'd be saying this, but I'm glad we waited for our wedding night. It's old-fashioned, and maybe a bit crazy in the midst of war, but now I know what a special gift we're sharing." The fire crackled softly and he saw her body before him, tiny and perfect.

Then Jill opened to Des. Seeing nothing but his face, hearing nothing but his words, she was totally connected to his love and, through him, to the core of life within herself. All the poisonous voices that had whispered since she was a child, "You're not good enough," fell silent. In the face of Des's love for her expressed through his words and his body, she realized she would never listen to them again.

Afterward, as she lay beside him, wrapped in his arms and legs, his wonderful mouth still and not insistently caressing hers, she thought how apt the whole idea of making love. Where there had been none before, where, in fact, there had been mistrust and even fear, they had made a love happen, taken a feeling and molded it into a living, lasting thing. She and Des might have children of their own in the future, but a child would not be their first creation; their love would be.

Des stirred beside her in a way she intuitively knew was a prelude to loving.

He whispered, "I didn't hurt you, did I?"

Jill said, moving closer to him, "How could you?"

"I love you, but I want to be careful with you. You're so small . . ."

For the first time she could remember, she didn't bristle at a remark about her size. In her own new awareness, she knew that Des valued her as she was and that he was only showing his care for what he prized. She no longer had to be on her guard for the innuendos that seared and lasted in memory for a lifetime. She felt herself equal to him. "You won't hurt me, my darling," Jill said, "unless . . ."

"Unless what?"

"Unless I thought you weren't going to make love to me again tonight."

"No chance of that, Mrs. Stratton," Des said, eagerly kissing her. "By morning you will be the most married woman in Florence."

Once more, joined completely, Jill felt herself accepted, enjoyed and cherished. A flame burned within her, set by Des's torch, whose heat enveloped her and lighted the things she knew, perhaps had always known, but now she knew that she knew them. For a moment, she felt what it was to be a very old woman who, at the end of her life, knows her truest feelings and does not need to do anything about them. Jill simply accepted herself as Jill.

Across the room, the coals in the fireplace glowed on, now and then throwing off a brilliant spark.

Germany surrendered unconditionally to the Western Allies and the Soviet Union at 2:41 A.M. French time today. . . . General Eisenhower was not present at the signing, but immediately afterward General Jodl and his fellow delegate, Gen. Admiral Hans Georg Friedeburg, were received by the Supreme Commander. They were asked sternly if they understood the surrender terms imposed upon Germany and if they would be carried out by Germany. They answered Yes. . . . After having signed the full surrender, General Jodl said he wanted to speak and received leave to do so. "With this signature," he said in soft-spoken German, "the German people and armed forces are for better or worse delivered into the victors' hands. . . ."

—*Associated Press dispatch, May 7, 1945*

THE EARLY-MAY sun was bright, the air like warmed cognac full of the heady scents of Paris, as Page drove toward the Hotel Meurice from Orly. Her plane from Reims had been late. Everything was late today, May 8, because, she supposed, after five long years and eight months of war all Europe had a right to slow down, to cram into one day all the forms of happiness it had not celebrated for so long. As she approached the Étoile, flocks of bicycles swooped down on her small Citroën at a wave from the gendarme, and to her left the elegant Avenue Foch was being swept by blue-coated street cleaners. All Paris seemed full of movement. For Paris, for Europe, this was a transitional day, the last day of war and the first day of peace. Page knew it was that kind of day in her life too. Today was the day she had promised to marry Paul.

She had parked on a side street near the Meurice. Now the concierge spotted her as she walked through the hotel doors. "Lieutenant," he called, bustling toward her, "Colonel Burkhardt asked me to give you this as soon as you arrived."

"Merci, monsieur."

The note was short. "Darling, Anna and I were called out to St. Germain. It must be the surrender, but no official announcement yet. If it is, I'll have to get it on the air. There must be isolated German detachments holding out everywhere. Meet me at Fouquets. I'll try to make it by late afternoon."

She walked down the Champs-Élysées to the restaurant where they had met so many times before, and saw that their favorite table against the wall was taken. It was right, somehow. Today of all days, it was time to come out of seclusion and join the flow of life at the edge of the street. Here and there, groups of people were arguing about the latest peace rumors, unwilling to accept them without confirmation. Page didn't blame them. There had been two weeks of false starts to the celebration of peace, and since Hitler's suicide last week in the Führerbunker in Berlin the whole world had held its breath.

She knew that this time the rumors were true. From her office window she had watched Colonel General Alfred Jodl last night step out of his car at SHAEF's forward headquarters in Reims. In the sparse light of electric bulbs strung in the courtyard of the red brick industrial school, she had seen him hesitate a moment before ascending the steps, then disappear inside to sign the surrender. It was strange, she thought now, that there had been no cheers. Everyone had just gone to bed, not knowing what else to do now that life wasn't dedicated to ending the war, knowing that their lives were about to change drastically, and having forgotten what life in peacetime was like.

But it had been earlier on the preceding evening that perhaps the most memorable moments of the day of German surrender had come for her. She had picked up the telephone in her office, thinking General Willis was calling from London. "Kay Summersby here, Page. Can you come now?"

"Now? But the Germans—"

"Believe me, now is best. The General is waiting to hear

from the German High Command. He can use some distraction. Can you come?"

Page didn't argue. She'd been after Kay to arrange this meeting for almost three months, but, with the front changing almost hourly, Ike had had no time for lieutenants with postwar problems. Crossing the courtyard, she smoothed her uniform jacket just as Kay opened her outer office door.

"Go on, love. And remember, don't back down. He may test you, but he likes a woman to stand up to him."

Page knocked on the inner office door.

"Come in."

"General Eisenhower, Lieutenant Hannaday has permission to—"

"Yes, yes. How's your father?"

"Well, sir, but wanting to get out of London."

"It won't be long. Give him my regards when you write." He picked up a yellow pencil and looked at her expectantly. He had a reputation for wanting clear, concise reports with no frills. "Now, Kay tells me you speak for a group of ETO women who want a permanent women's corps after the war."

"Yes, sir, and our group is in touch with other women in the Southwest Pacific, Mediterranean and China-Burma-India Theaters as well as most of the Zone of Interior commands."

He was still measuring her, but she knew it would take him only seconds to make up his mind. This is the man, she thought, who quietly gave the D Day go order in the midst of a hurricane. He wasn't flamboyant like Patton, or cerebral like Bradley, but she felt herself in the presence of a man who knew how to use power, perhaps the only man in the world who could save the WAC.

"If you've got so many women behind you, then why doesn't this come to me through the WAC staff director in Paris or from your Colonel Hobby? The chain of command is there for a reason, Lieutenant."

"Yes sir, but that takes time. General, it seems to the women who sent me that the higher commands are so wrapped up in demobilization problems—well, they're afraid the WAC could be gone before anybody paid attention to questions from women soldiers."

The General tapped his pencil and turned to look at the situation map behind his head, showing the latest spearheads deep inside Germany. "Lieutenant, are you speaking for a group of Wacs or are you speaking for yourself?"

She took a deep breath. "Both, sir. I want to be a member of a permanent Women's Army Corps, but—I'm to be married."

He flashed her a smile that suddenly made him look younger and quite handsome in spite of the lines of fatigue under his eyes and beside his mouth. "Congratulations, Lieutenant. If you'd said different, I think I would have given a month's pay to be there when your father found out."

"Begging your pardon, sir, Wacs are grown women. What they do with their lives is up to them, if you will help make it possible." Page was angry, with a desperate kind of anger that made her take uncharacteristic risks. This might be the last chance the WAC had before the Corps was dismantled with the best intentions. "General, I thought you were our friend and would agree that we'd earned a place in the Army." He sat up straighter, if that was possible, and tapped his pencil faster on a neat stack of messages before him. Some spokeswoman she'd turned out to be. Now she'd really blown it. She'd be lucky to get away with her first lieutenant's bars.

He got up from his straight wooden chair and came around the desk. "And of course you're right, Lieutenant," he said as he escorted her to the door. "You *can* count on me. I'll do all I can to see that the Army welcomes those women who want to stay after the war."

She stopped suddenly. "Thank you, General, but—but we want more than a holding action. We want a viable Corps, with recruiting and training centers."

He frowned, with his hand on the doorknob; he looked at her, and then a slow, wide grin grew from the frown. "You're Dalt's daughter, all right. Full regular-army status, that's what we'll go for. Okay, Lieutenant?" He'd nodded, serious now, shaking her hand. She hoped he hadn't noticed her hand was shaking already.

For the past twenty-four hours, she'd been going over and over in her mind the words she'd said to the Supreme Allied Commander, and she wished she had marshaled better arguments. Still, the outcome couldn't have been better. Ike was really on their side.

Signaling to the waiter just stepping from the main Fouquet

entrance, she ordered a glass of Calvados. When it came she sipped at the apple brandy, watching, under her lashes, two lovers tête-à-tête at a table in her line of vision. Their fingers moved together, laced one through the other, twining and re-twining in a seemingly endless effort to get closer still, to lose their separate identities, to meld flesh. Their knees and toes touched under the table, Page saw, as the man lit a cigarette, exhaling smoke about the girl like cloudy kisses. It was love she watched, pure unabashed love with all its passion and tension.

For her, love seemed to be all complexity and goodbye. The word startled her, but for the first time she knew the truth of it. Europe was at peace, and now Page felt the serene warmth of inner peace flood her being. Suddenly, she was sure what she wanted, with a surety that was like an old friend, for it had been a part of her since her first day at Fort Des Moines. She had tried so hard to become the woman she thought she should be that she had nearly erased the woman she really was. She breathed deeply, and knew she must draw on all her courage, for she was saying goodbye to the kind of love most women wanted, that a part of her wanted. Somehow she would have to make Paul see that it was her doing and none of his; make him see it so that bitterness wouldn't haunt him for the rest of his life.

"Page!"

It was Paul calling. He stepped to the sidewalk from a Renault, driven by Anna, who was smiling at him.

"Darling," he said and placed his hat on the table, running his fingers straight back through his hair so that it lay in smooth layers against his head.

Page knew she would always remember just such small details about this day.

"I'm so glad," he said, his smile radiant. "I thought I might be too late."

"For what?"

"The announcement. The government is about to make it official, and I wanted to be with you. Since we were there almost in the begining, it's right, don't you think?"

At that moment, just at dusk, three planes with American markings zoomed low over the Champs-Élysées, just above the treetops. Paul and Page stretched to see them drop flares as they pulled up over the Place de la Concorde at the foot of the wide avenue. Then the planes turned and repeated the maneuver, heading back toward the Étoile. A growing murmur from the gathering crowd caused both Page and Paul to turn their heads simultaneously toward the Arc de Triomphe, where huge flags of all the Allies were being unfurled.

Loudspeakers blared. *"Attention. Attention. La guerre est terminée."* Then the opening notes of "La Marseillaise" seemed to come from every mouth. People sang with tears unashamedly running down their cheeks.

It was official, then. The war was over. Hordes of French civilians, Americans and Allies in uniform swarmed onto the Champs-Élysées from every building, every street. Page felt herself and Paul being swept up by a solid mass of joy. She was danced around a table by a Frenchman who kissed her heartily on both cheeks, his words lost in the uproar. Traffic stopped, even bicycles moved only inches at a time.

Paul put a protective arm around her and pulled her back into the now empty downstairs barroom of Fouquet's. "Happy new world, darling," he said, kissing, hugging, squeezing her tight, all at once. "Let's make plans—let's talk—let's go to the Meurice and make love—or we could get married right now, today. There must be a way to do it."

She had never seen him so carefree, so like a child, wanting everything at once. It was all the more painful because she knew she could give him nothing but an honesty that would wound him.

"Yes, Paul," she said, "let's do talk. Are you going into Germany? Do you know where?"

He squinted across the table at her. "Do we have to?" he said, cranky as a boy denied his party. "Oh, all right, yes, I'll be going in within the week. I don't know where—Frankfurt, probably. You know we planned to use Wiesbaden as a headquarters, but that bombing mistake in February . . . The I.G. Farben building is largely intact in Frankfurt, and it's the only one that'll hold us."

Page looked at her hand in his and slowly pulled it away. "Will Anna be going with you?"

"Of course."

"I'm glad."

"What does that mean? You're going, too."

She inhaled, and the breath trembled in her chest. "Yes, I'm going, too, Paul, but not with you."

"Fine," he said, dropping his eyes. "You can come later."

"I will come to Frankfurt later, Paul, but not to be with you, not to marry you."

He moved the ashtray in line with a card advertising Martell's. "Fine, then, after that."

Sometimes Paul baffled her. She would explain herself, and then he would go back to his original premise as if she'd never opened her mouth. It wasn't that he didn't listen attentively; it was that he didn't hear her.

"I want to stay in the Army."

A sharp laugh and he settled back against the red leather booth. "Of course. We're all going to have to stay until the Pacific thing is over."

"After that—" she struggled to overcome his inability to accept her words, an inability that raced toward her like a tidal wave threatening to engulf her—"after Japan surrenders, I want to make a career of the Army."

"That's insane," Paul said too loudly. A waiter with his ear to the radio, taking it for a summons, left the bar and headed for their table. Paul waved him away. His voice lower, he said again, "Page, that's insane. It's one thing for you girls to have your meetings, to write your letters, but it's—" he broke off, not knowing the words for such folly. "Page, there are no plans for any WAC presence in the postwar Army. Don't you think I've checked? Everyone I've talked to thinks it's a lark. People are laughing at you, damn it, Page, they're laughing."

"I saw Ike yesterday."

"You what!"

"He's going to help us all he can. Maybe people are laughing, but it's what I want to do with my life, even if it's only a hope."

He looked at her, and his eyes accused her of what her own mind called her. Betrayer! "You said you loved me, and I believed—no, I still believe you."

"I do love you, Paul. I think I always will, but not in the way you want me to. Maybe someday a woman can be a soldier and married too, but that's not possible now—and it would never be possible with you."

Bitterness corroded his voice. "Don't bother to tell me you'll always love me. I hate you for saying that. What *good* is such love? An empty promise." His hurt tore at her. "How could I have been so wrong about you—about us?"

"Don't, Paul. Yours was the right love; I was the wrong woman." She bent toward him, her heart breaking at what she was doing, had to do. "Paul, Anna is in love with you."

He lashed out at her, "Goddamn you, Page. Don't you dare tell me what woman to want."

Suddenly she saw the arrogance of what she'd said. "Sorry, Paul," she whispered. "It was incredibly insensitive of me. It's just that I care so much about you . . ."

As she talked, trying to help them both through these terrible minutes, she could see he was passing by stages to the point where his male pride would overwhelm hurt, disappointment, even love. He was pulling the pieces of himself together, until they looked on the outside like the old Paul, but on the inside formed a new way to make sense of the unthinkable.

He stood up, rigid, pulling at his jacket, more soldierly than she had ever seen him; now nothing left of her Paul. "Do you want me to walk you to your car?"

"No. Please, Paul, don't leave like this, without understanding."

He didn't answer her plea. "You're making a mistake, a big mistake, one you'll regret. You have some pioneer-woman dream, you want to blaze new trails. You forget something— you'll be *alone,* trail blazers always are. Is that what you want from life? Let's say you get your wish and the Wacs become regular army; it won't be like this—Paris, London, Washington. You'll spend your life on run-down old posts, waiting for promotion." His low laugh came, hurting her with its harshness. "And all the time they'll despise you for what you do, the Army, civilians, the press. I didn't offer you an exciting life, Page, but, goddamn," his voice choked on the word, "I could have given you better than that."

The despairing dark eyes, emptied of light and illusions, would haunt her, Page knew. "I know you could, Paul, and I tried to want it."

"As you tried to want me?"

Oh, why was it so hard to explain that the parts can be true and yet the whole a lie? "Paul! Don't do this to yourself, and to me. I did want you—do want you. That's real. Believe me!"

"Christ, Page, that's what makes it all so hard to understand. I *do* believe you."

He left her there and walked through the open doors of Fouquet's into the night-lighted ecstasy of the boulevard.

She watched him shove his way through the happy crowd. She knew he would never turn around now. They had both gone too far.

------------------------------ **65** ------------------------------

A fashion show for the returning servicewoman was held at the Junior League Auditorium in New York. As reported in the weekly newspaper The Service Woman, *wardrobes for business, homemaking and country living were shown by* Vogue, Harper's Bazaar *and* Mademoiselle, *all designed to cost less than the average of $200 in mustering-out pay.*

Designer Sally Victor showed her hats, Claire McCardell a bathing suit and Vera Maxwell tailored suits for every figure. Since many postwar plans include Lohengrin and orange blossoms, Madame Eta draped a white satin wedding gown.

ELISABETH SAT AT her worktable, the May sun bouncing through the skylight of the empty Manhattan loft she had just leased for a year with the last of Marne's insurance money. The noise outside on Thirty-seventh Street, midblock between Sixth and Seventh Avenues, was deafening and had been accelerating since the Germans signed the peace treaty yesterday. Today, Tuesday, May 8, the open *New York Times* on her drawing table bannered victory in Europe, and President Truman had broadcast an official proclamation. Times Square was now impassable; the blowing horns, the impromptu parades and the tons of scrap paper fluttering down to the streets had put Elisabeth's normal haunts off limits. Christ! And she had planned to take the bus down to Worth Street to look at some new woolen blends.

Max had told her once that she was emotionally uninvolved with the war, that her life ran parallel to it without touching it. But Max was a cynic. Of course she was glad the war was over, or at least the European part of it. Danny had written from a hospital in France several weeks earlier, but she hadn't responded, hoping he wouldn't try to contact her. Both Page and Jill had written from the ETO, and he had asked them to look her up when they came through the port. Elisabeth shrugged, a rueful smile pulling at her mouth. So much for her firm rule of leaving the past in the past. But they might not even know she'd been kicked out of the WAC; she had told them only that she'd been discharged. Or maybe they did know. It was a small Corps and news traveled every time someone was transferred. "Hey, Page, didn't you use to be friends with Gardner at first OC? Did you hear she got caught in some kind of blackmailing scandal? Nearly got the guardhouse, I hear, but she probably pulled some strings." Had they believed the worst about her? Christ! What could it matter? She didn't need friends; that part of her life she'd just have to put behind her.

But there was another reason to be glad the war was winding down. No clothing designer faced with L-85, the government edict fixing maximum outside garment measurements, could be unhappy that the end of cloth rationing was in sight.

"Mrs. Gardner?"

She stopped tapping her sketching pencil and looked up from the chaotic scene on the street below. "Yes, Sophie," she answered the diminutive seamstress she had hired last week because the woman had once worked for Sally Victor.

"I've finished the last dress you cut and I'd like to have the rest of the afternoon off." Sophie explained, tearfully, that her family was going to synagogue to pray for her younger brother in the Pacific.

Elisabeth was annoyed. The surrender news seemed to have ravaged her day. And it was a great excuse for this girl to slack on the job. Gabriella would have sacked her *toute suite!* The war had simply ruined all the little seamstresses. Too many had taken over jobs they hadn't the self-control or the brains to do. "Go on"—she allowed the girl to see her irritation—"but I don't pay for prayers, just first-class sewing."

After the girl had left, Elisabeth worked and reworked the troublesome sketches for her Tuesday-night art class. Suddenly she threw her pencil down and held her head in her hands, giving way to a rare moment of defeat. She had to admit that her drawing skill hadn't improved nearly enough: even worse, she didn't seem to be able to get her design ideas on paper as Gabriella had done so easily. She felt panic rush through her arm every time she picked up her drawing tools. Damn! She could almost see the triumphant look on Max's face. Angry, she crumpled the unfinished sketch and threw it violently against the wall. As was her habit when she was frustrated with fashion sketching, Elisabeth picked up a pair of scissors and began to furiously, but expertly, cut fabric on a dummy. Pen and ink were so sterile; sometimes she had to get away from them. She needed to—there was only one phrase—make love to the material, according to the way she saw the weight, the pattern and the color, pinning and draping and adding details as she went along. Engrossed, she didn't hear the sound of footsteps until they were at the turn of the landing. Sophie? The stupid girl had thought better of her time off, had she?

The door opened, and a slightly built infantryman stepped through, leaning heavily on a cane. "Hello—Elisabeth."

"Danny! I hardly recognized you." It was true. He was very thin, and had a different look from the earnest young tailor she had known at the QM depot, or the frantically inept lover of that last night before they were caught. What was it? The combat infantryman's badge, the Purple Heart and the row of ribbons and battle stars on his uniform or something more. There was a remoteness in his eyes, a distance that is instantly established between people who have seen war and those who have not. Beyond that, his face told her nothing about why he was here.

"You want to sit down?" she asked, noticing how heavily he leaned on his cane

"Yes." He sat on a folding chair, looking around. "You're going to do it, aren't you?"

"I might," she said, afraid to commit herself until she knew exactly how much he wanted of her, "but it's hard, because I simply can't draw well enough." She indicated the piles of crumpled paper around her drawing table.

"Who told you you had to be a fine artist?"

"Gabriella could make charcoal and paper do anything she wanted."

"That's not you. Look at the way you're handling the material." Elisabeth had never stopped running her fingers sensually over the cloth as she talked with him. "You're a tactile designer, and a visual one, able to put line right onto the cloth. Elisabeth, you're a sculptress in fabric."

She laughed out loud. Of course! She didn't need easel, paper and pencil. With her scissors she could release the dress locked inside her fabric. She didn't have to draw it, it was there waiting for her. Why hadn't she seen the obvious instead of trying to fit herself to some established way? She buried her face in the green satin, touching and being touched.

Danny slumped in his chair.

"I've got a pot of coffee on in the back," she said, suddenly aware that his face was white. "Or maybe you want lunch? There's a place just down the street. Or I could call a deli—although all the delivery boys are probably out celebrating."

"No thanks. I just need to rest here a minute. I only got out of the hospital yesterday."

And you'd like to rest in my bed, Elisabeth thought, consciously edging away from him. Danny couldn't play the wounded veteran here; she didn't have time to nursemaid old lovers. But she couldn't afford to make him angry. He could still go to the authorities—cause trouble. "How nice of you to come straight to see me," and she intended her voice to dismiss him pleasantly from her life. "Are you sure you wouldn't like that coffee?" She saw him flinch, then stand.

"I think you've got the wrong idea, Elisabeth. I'm not here to collect. You don't owe me anything. I knew exactly what I was doing back in Philadelphia."

Elisabeth's mouth tightened: "Do you have to bring that up?"

Danny swayed and put both hands on his cane. "I only plan to bring it up once. I had a lot of time to think in prison and then in combat. A cell and foxhole are very much alike, you know—the only way to stay alive is to think yourself out of it. I know what happened at the depot—you and Stryker."

She squared her shoulders defensively.

"Elisabeth, it doesn't matter. Don't you see? I *know,* and it doesn't make any difference." How could he make her understand that he knew her better than she knew herself, that he saw and grasped how she could have fallen under the thrall of a man like Max Stryker? How could he protect her from such men and yet spare her sensitive pride? "I still want to be a part of your life"—he looked into the shrouded blue eyes that had been his hope through France and into Germany—"and I believe you need me to help you. I have the head for business details that you can't be bothered with. I can check out garments for cost, availability of material, salability and profit. I know how to be a workroom foreman, to placate skilled patternmakers and seamstresses; you won't have the patience, because you're a creator." He repeated the simple words again, "You need me."

"I don't love you."

"I know."

"But you think I'll grow to love you, is that it?" It always was.

"No. Well, once I hoped for something, but not anymore. Now I just think you're a smart investment. Helping you do what you want to do is good business, because I'm convinced you're going places. Can't you just accept that?"

His face reminded her of the saints aching for martyrdom in the stained-glass windows she'd seen at church as a child. Why not let him work as long as he expected nothing? "Strictly business?"

"Strictly. I've got five thousand dollars in back pay and savings to invest."

"What do you want for it?"

"Twenty-five percent. I'd be a minor partner."

She could see the obvious advantages. "You could stay here," she said, pointing toward the rear of the loft. "Fix yourself a little room back there with partitions and all."

"That's fine with me. It'll be good to have somone in the place, especially close to the spring showing in October."

"Hold on. You're going a little fast. How can I be ready with a spring 1946 line in five months?"

He limped to her work table. He looked stronger to her. "You *can* be ready, if you stop trying to be Michelangelo," he said, picking up her rough sketches. "You could go on trying to improve your drawing forever, but look here." Danny stepped to the draped mannequin she'd been working on. "When you translate your ideas into material, there's not a fine artist to beat you. Oh, you're ready to go, all right." He stopped, exhausted from the effort.

She laughed. "Maybe you *should* be my business agent, but . . ." She shrugged, not wanting to show any concern about him. Men always thought simple curiosity meant you wanted to go to bed with them. But she *was* curious. "I don't understand, Danny. You've got your family's business to go back to in Chicago. No, better still, now that you have a full pardon, you could work anywhere you wanted to for good money. What do you *get* out of this?"

Danny's shoulders slumped. "I think you're a good investment. And as I've told you, Elisabeth—twice—*you need me.*"

For an instant, even though she was standing by her own work table in her own place, she felt like a stranger. She didn't even understand this language. Then why should she? Maybe he was telling the truth, or nearly the truth. What did it matter? He had the money she needed. And he was right about one thing: he could handle the business end, and that would give her more freedom than ever. And why *not* have a spring line ready for the fall market week? The audacious idea excited her as one never had before. This time next year there would be an Elisabeth Gardner line, and one day there would be an Elisabeth Gardner dress hanging in every fashion-conscious woman's collection in America. She decided at that instant. "Okay, but I run the design end. Is that understood?"

He nodded.

"I've got my own ideas, and I won't change them for business reasons. I'm not interested in making all women look one way—I had enough of that in the WAC, I'm interested in creating clothes that women will want to possess as beautiful objects in themselves, clothes that never subordinate a woman, but celebrate her individuality." She'd been rehearsing that little speech in her mind for her first press interview and she saw she had impressed him, but she was also aware of her own deep response to the words. Ah, the truth made the cleverest lie. One level deeper in her mind another monologue was playing. *Okay, I'll take him in, since I have to, but only for as long as I need him. I'd make the devil a partner if it meant I wouldn't get stuck back in the pack of ordinary designers for years. Everybody's going to hear about Elisabeth Gardner—and soon.*

"Elisabeth, I'll take that sandwich now."

She put her hand on his arm solicitously. "Can you make it to the deli?"

"Sure."

She grabbed her hat and gloves, and threw him an extravagant smile. "Let's go, partner."

"You look like you could use something to eat, too," Danny told her, eying her ultraslender form, still touched with magic for him—the only woman who had ever bewitched him.

They walked down the stairs and jostled their way into the street, and he forgot about the throbbing in his leg. Someday, Elisabeth would realize how much she needed him, and he could wait until she did. What she said was true. He was a first-class tailor, and his family did want him back in their business. But that was a job, not a reason to feel alive every day. Every man had to have one deep purpose, one thing he could do that no one else could—and his was saving Elisabeth. Oh, he'd called it helping, because she didn't know how vulnerable she was, and he didn't ever want her to know. He would allow nothing to break that magnificent spirit of hers. Yes, she'd used him to help another man; but something had made her do it, something even beyond Max Stryker, some old concealed hurt, something unfathomable, stark and awful that he could only guess at. Nobody knew that about Elisabeth except he. She wore so many veils, no one could ever guess. But he had guessed. When he was honest with himself, he knew he clung to her for selfish reasons too. She was the only woman who had made him feel like a real man after those animals in prison had— He clamped his mind shut against the memory. In the end it would be simple. Elisabeth needed him and he needed her. Need was an irresistible aphrodisiac. That was why he was certain that one day she'd come to him as if she was coming home. Smiling, he let her take his arm as the light changed and he limped across busy Seventh Avenue.

66

In Italy, Allied troops break through the last German defenses in the heavily mined Apennines, storm the Alpine wall guarding Austria and capture one million enemy troops. Mussolini and his mistress, Clara Petacci, are shot by partisans, and their bodies hang upside down in a Milan square, mutilated by a mob.

JILL SAW THAT Des was shaving in front of a mirror attached to his tent's center pole when she ducked under the flap. "Good morning, Captain, darling." She stood on tiptoe to kiss him on the nape of his neck where his undershirt quit and his warm skin began.

He grinned at her through the shaving cream. "Lieutenant, do you know that you just broke every reg in the manual?"

"No excuse, sir." Jill grinned back. "I'm ready to take my punishment."

"Okay," Des said and wiped wisps of lather from his sideburns. "You're confined to our room at the palazzo for the weekend, where I will think of several interesting ways for you to redeem yourself."

With a womanly confidence she hadn't known before her marriage to Des just four weeks earlier, Jill slipped inside his arms. She exchanged no love words with him. None was needed. They shared the memory of hours of pleasure and the certainty of more this weekend, their last in Florence together before the Fifth Army moved on to Austria to become part of the occupation forces. For a few days after Germany surrendered they had lived in fear of separation. Strong rumors had circulated that all Wacs in Italy were to be shipped home. But then General Clark had personally called Colonel Hobby in

Washington, asking for permission to take his Wacs on to Austria.

Des frowned slightly into the mirror, concentrating on the tough hairs under his chin. "I wish you didn't have to go up to Battalion."

"No way out of it. You know these Army Security Agency types. When Arlington Hall gets on a retraining kick . . ." Jill left the rest up in the air. Des knew as well as she did that now that the war was over some of the forward cryptographers were careless. Last week a message had gone out to SHAEF headquarters half in code and half in the clear, compromising a worldwide system. She was sure this last mistake had brought the ASA civilian hotfooting it overseas to jerk them out of what he probably imagined were endless armistice orgies.

"I know." Des's tone was grumpy. "Now that the shooting's stopped, we're going to have these stateside experts swarming all over us. Fortunes of war," he added, his old grin returning. "Guess I'll have to punch my own TS card and stop bitching." He dipped his razor into his shaving water. "Why don't you leave early and come back sooner?"

"Thought I would. Should be back in plenty of time for dinner. Why don't you go on into Florence and visit with Tina and Helen, and I'll come straight to the palazzo."

Playfully he linked his arm with hers. "If you're real good, I'll take you sightseeing this weekend."

"Thought I was restricted to quarters."

"You are restricted to being with me, exclusively, Mrs. Stratton." He grinned down at her, looking silly with shaving cream drying on his cheeks. "But don't you think we ought to get out and see more of *Firenze* before we ship out? What if your mother asks you, 'And what did you think of the famous Ghiberti bronze doors, daughter?' "

"I'd tell her I was too busy making love with my commanding officer."

He laughed, excitedly, the result of their sensual banter. "Sure you would."

Des followed her out of the tent in his undershirt. "Say, Jill, let me get a driver for you, then you can enjoy the scenery and think of me."

Jill climbed in. "No time now, darling. I want to get this over." She put the jeep into first gear.

Des waved his olive-drab towel at her when she looked back before turning onto the Pistoia road.

It curved and climbed sharply toward the Apennines ahead of her on what she thought was a perfect end-of-May morning. She caught herself thinking of the crazy words to the Merry Macs record Schultzy had played in the dayroom until the grooves turned white. It was something about mares eating oats and lambs eating ivy, and then, unable to contain the bouncy, happy fun of it, she sang the jumbled words aloud.

Shifting down into second gear as the turns grew tighter, Jill stopped singing suddenly, remembering the old wives' admonition to expose an unborn baby only to what you wanted to be its lifelong influence.

"Do you like 'Mairzy Doats' as your first lullaby?" she asked, looking down and felt a little crazy talking to her stomach.

She didn't know how, but she had known she was pregnant almost at once. So much for being surprised by the doctor like in an Irene Dunne movie. The fourth morning of her honeymoon, she had felt a lightheadedness, a kind of delicate spinning sensation distinct from the giddiness of loving and being loved by Des. Her breasts had been tender, and an immense inner-wellness had filled her, as if somehow what was growing in her womb was a great medicine.

And then, right from the first day, she'd known that the tiny human she and Des had created was a girl. Why was she so happy at the thought of a girl? Didn't women want firstborn sons? She shifted into third on a straightaway and laughed aloud again. Her feelings were so on the surface these days that reading them was the easiest thing she did. Of course she knew why she wanted a baby girl—she and Des together had created a little girl more perfect than she had ever been.

It took her longer to reach battalion headquarters northeast of Pistoia than she'd thought. The ASA man had been waiting impatiently. He was carrying a security-reg binder with each section neatly partitioned by a different-colored tab. Uh-oh, she was in for it.

"Lieutenant," he said and leafed through the binder, index finger jabbing as he talked, "this code room has violated more security measures than . . ." Unable to come up with an analogy superlative enough, he expelled an exasperated breath between clenched teeth. "We better start with the basic lessons for these guys. Do you know they're carrying the safe combination around in their wallets?" She opened her mouth, but he plunged on. "Oh, that's not the worst of it. They have no double checks. The operator who assigns the system encrypts and checks the punched tape—all of it himself. If the Germans had held on another month these guys would have handed them every top-secret message in the ETO!"

Jill reluctantly agreed with him, while resenting his attitude. His palpable anger was the result of working in white-walled, brightly lit, inspection-clean comcenters. He didn't have the least idea what cryptographers at battalion and company level had to put up with: bombings, shells screaming in, thirty-hour shifts if a push was on.

But as the afternoon wore on, she began quietly to work out new procedures that reconciled the problems of working in the field with the needs of security.

At the end of the day, the ASA civilian complimented her. "You know your stuff, Lieutenant, and you kept me from making too big an ass of myself. If you want a job after the war, let me know."

Jill almost wished he hadn't said that. It's all too wonderful, she thought. How can I possibly deserve all this happiness? And then, unbidden, a memory from her childhood came back to her. Once, she had received a lovely new doll as a prize for perfect church attendance, but her mother had made her place it in a barrel for the poor. "Any common person can give away trash," her mother taught her. "I want you to learn that a real lady gives away what she wants to keep herself." But Jill had learned another lesson. Try as hard as she could, she never was able to accept the good she'd earned. Even as she thanked the ASA man, she knew that somehow she'd never enjoy what he'd said. For every new good that happened, one old good was taken away. She shook her head vigorously to clear it of the old, negative thinking, and discovered that she was tired and sleepy besides. She hadn't realized it before, but readying the detachment for the move into Austria had cut deep into her sleep.

" . . .and I agree that you should take the crypto sergeant

back to headquarters, Lieutenant. He can use familiarization training on that new high-speed Teletype."

It was after seven by the time she was back on the road. "I'll drive, Sergeant," she said, "since I know the road and I'm in a hurry."

"Got a heavy date tonight, Lieutenant?"

"You bet, the heaviest." She grinned sideways at him, relieved to be on her way, "We've only been married a month."

"Lucky guy."

They drove on into the balmy twilight air, the jeep a part of the winding mountain road and the violet sky. She yawned, swerving the car, and shook her head to clear her vision.

Squirming around in his seat, the sergeant asked, "Lieutenant, are you sure you don't want me to take the wheel?"

"What's the matter, Sergeant," she said, a little cranky, "you got something against women drivers?"

She saw that he looked away sheepishly. She had hit the nail on the head that time. Some men . . . There was no real need for her to relinquish the wheel. She was never too tired to drive. As a matter of fact, she was exhilarated at the thought of seeing Des and telling him of his child, which she knew she could keep from him no longer.

They drove in silence for some time, and she regretted her sharp words. "Sergeant, see"—she pointed off to the right at the lights of Prato—"we're more than halfway to Florence. There's a shortcut up ahead about half a mile—save us fifteen minutes."

Soon she turned onto a narrow dirt road, which still hadn't been cleared of all the equipment the Germans had abandoned on their flight north, but she was making good time. Even the sergeant must be able to tell that much. Involuntarily, her eyes closed against an oncoming light that appeared suddenly around the bend ahead. A car. Coming fast— straight for them. "Wrong side, you fool!" she shouted, and swung the wheel hard, skidding off the far shoulder of the road to a tiny clearing below as the car sped by.

The sergeant gripped the dash. "Christ Almighty, that was close!"

She willed her hands to stop shaking before the sergeant saw them, and jammed the jeep into second gear. Slowly, she started up the slight incline that would bring them back to the road. Suddenly, she was the center of a world of thunder and lightning. *Mine!* She felt a terrible force shaking the jeep. The steering wheel went loose in her hands as the tires left the earth, merging with the air. In the next interminable moments, her body was ripped from the driver's seat.

She lay on her back against the embankment, while a tire rolled noiselessly down the incline below her. All sound was now cut off from her. The mangled jeep burst into flame, and she felt its warmth against her face, but she couldn't hear the crackle of fire. *Sergeant,* she called or thought she called. . . . She was sure of nothing, except that she *couldn't* be dying. If she were, she would be thinking of her mother and father, or Neil—Bear would be there, and Des too. Her life from the beginning would flash before her eyes. That was the way it was when someone died. Everyone said so.

She saw the sergeant. He couldn't blame her. *Not my fault, Sergeant!* She must be screaming at him. He crawled toward her around the burning jeep. She watched him, bleeding, drag his misshapen leg behind. She thought to go to him, to help him, but when she tried to stand nothing inside her moved, nothing worked. Something was wrong. *No, no, stay calm.* The quiet was the only thing that frightened her, because she could *see* the sound all around. The sergeant's mouth was open, yelling at her, and the extra gas cans were exploding in the jeep. She was watching a giant picture, like the one on the staircase at the palazzo. Then another image filled the canvas of her mind: a picture of a man and a woman being married while the colors melted and blurred.

A wave of sensation began to creep up her body, leaving emptiness behind. *Des, this is so silly. I'm not even tired now. I can't die.*

The sergeant bent over her, talking to her, and she explained to him why he must get out of her way so she could get up. She had to meet Des! Why, the sergeant was crying. A big guy like that.

In every part of her that could feel, she raged at the unfairness of it: to come through the war, to find Des, to begin to find herself, and now to die. She would go to Neil after all. What kind of God would do this to her?

Then a terrible concentration controlled her pain. She had heard about such things from women who had given birth.

Perhaps death had been growing inside her all this time, just waiting to be born.

She had to make the sergeant hear her. *Tell Des, tell him . . .* Oh, she had promised until death alone should part them. *Tell him I tried,* she thought she said, but she could not be sure he understood. *Somebody please understand me,* the words coming now as a soundless anguish, *Oh, please, God, I need more time!* Then her last heartbeat pounded under her breast.

67

I'll be seeing you in all the old familiar places
That this heart of mine embraces all day through.
In that small café, the park across the way,
The children's carrousel,
The chestnut trees, the wishing well. . . .
I'll find you in the morning sun, and when the day is new
I'll be looking at the moon, but I'll be seeing you
                    —*Sammy Fain and Irving Kahal*

DES AND THE Marchesa had finished dinner and put Tina to bed when the messenger came from Fifth Army headquarters. Seated in the garden, listening to a popular song on Armed Forces Radio, they both heard Des's name spoken through the open French doors. "I must see Captain Stratton, at once," the urgent voice said.

Although he had been angry because Jill had stayed at Battalion and hadn't telephoned, the tone of the voice he heard told him what he had not considered. Jill! Something had happened! He jumped up and ran for the door, meeting the lieutenant with the duty-officer armband halfway.

"Captain, there's been an accident just off the Pistoia road—she hit a land mine."

"Jill?"

"Yes. Lieutenant Jill Stratton."

I'll find you in the morning sun . . .

Someone switched the radio off. "She's . . . ?" He couldn't bring himself to say the awful word. It tempted fate; it ended every desperate hope.

The officer bowed his head. "Yes, sir. I'm sorry to have to tell you that the lieutenant—your wife is . . . dead."

Des crumpled to a bench on the terrace. They had come through so much. To *this!* He felt cut apart from himself. What would he be without Jill? Finally, he asked, his voice a monotone of despair, "Where is she? I want to see her."

Helen, tears in her eyes, took his arm. "I'll go with you."

"No—Helen—please. I'll go alone."

Shifting his feet, the duty officer said, "Perhaps you'd better wait until tomorrow, Captain."

Des's head wobbled from side to side, almost as if he couldn't control it. He started for the door. He had a right to see her. It was their last weekend together in Florence.

The hospital morgue staff stared at him when he signed in. "I'm here to see Mrs. Desmond Stratton." The defiant meaninglessness of the words struck him hard.

A white-coated Medical Corps major took him inside to a table where a small body lay under a white muslin sheet. The doctor drew it back, and there was Jill's face, her eyes closed. A tiny red scar on her cheek was the only perversity that death had left on her young skin. Otherwise, Des could see no sign of injury. There were her auburn curls in disarray, as he'd seen them so many times, her upper lip so extravagantly full, almost ready to pout or taunt him. He'd looked at so many dead faces in this war. But not Jill's—no, he refused . . . Now his disbelief returned full force and he jerked his eyes up from her still form to the doctor.

"I'm sorry, Captain," the doctor said and picked up a clipboard. "Broken neck. Head injuries. And multiple internal injuries—a rib pierced her left lung and the hemorrhaging was—" The doctor broke off abruptly. "Would you like a sleeping pill, just for tonight?"

Des shook his head. "Did she suffer?" He almost strangled on the words.

"No, if it's any consolation, there wouldn't have been any

pain. The sergeant with her said she never said a word. She died instantly without knowing what had happened to her."

Oh, God! A scene from Fort Des Moines flooded his mind. "Wait until this war is over, then judge us," he heard her say. Des shrieked silently at the memory. What more could they have asked than what she gave?

Gently Des covered her marble-white face, and walked quickly from the room. Fleeing the lemony antiseptic smell, the perfume of death he would always remember, he slammed himself through the doors into the warm Tuscan night. He wanted to yell at the city, at the war, at the world; he wanted to bang his head against something, he wanted to feel physical pain to blot out the anguish that squeezed his chest until he could scarcely breathe.

Helen was waiting outside in her car. "Forgive me for following you. I'll take you wherever you want to go."

His voice choked. "To the camp. I don't think I could bear to sleep in our room again."

Softly, Helen said, "But Tina must be told, and she'll need you."

He didn't want to acknowledge her words. How could he help anyone? The one woman he wanted he couldn't ever have. He longed to invite feelings to overwhelm him, to give himself over to grief. But in the end he remembered his responsibility to the child. "Yes, Helen, you're right, of course."

Helen gave the driver orders, and the car rumbled across the Ponte Vecchio and turned toward the Palazzo d'Ordella.

"It was instant," he told the Marchesa, who dabbed at her own tears in the dark of the car. "She didn't suffer."

Helen nodded. "I'm glad, but what about you? You are suffering and must let it out."

A terrible sob wrenched at Des's throat. "If only I had gone with her. It's my fault. I should—"

"Desmond, you must not betray Jill like this." She rushed on over his strangled cry of protest. "Yes, betray all that was right between you. It's so easy to feel guilt. It's so cowardly—please forgive this bluntness, dear Desmond, but it *is* cowardly to accept unearned blame, to find the quick answer to the question of why this terrible death happened. It's so much harder, my friend, to understand that there is no answer to the randomness of death. There is no such thing as fair or unfair.

Jill was your wife, but she was also a soldier caught up in a world war. There is no more random death than the one on the battlefield, wherever or whenever it is."

Anger rushed through him, and he felt like silencing her. "Don't you dare tell me she's with God, that she's happier now. *I won't believe it!* She wanted to stay with *me.*"

"No, I would never say she wanted it this way. I'm angry too. I hate God when He takes those I love. Acceptance comes much later—understanding sometimes never comes."

Des slumped forward and put his face in his hands. "I don't know how I'll live through tomorrow."

"None of us ever knows, but we do it. And you will, too, Desmond. Life insists on being lived. As long as we breathe, we have no other choice."

68

Dachau. Bergen-Belsen. Buchenwald. Treblinka. Ausch-witz. The discovery of Hitler's "Final Solution" horrifies the world. A grim Eisenhower assigns former SS guards to bury their victims and clean up the camps. Most Germans deny they knew of the slaughter, but Dr. Gustav Schuebbe, former head of the Nazi Annihilation Institute, speaks for the unrepentant: "I still maintain that, just as one prunes a tree—by removing old, undesirable branches in the spring—so for its own interest a certain hygienical supervision of the body of a people is necessary from time to time."

PAGE WAS GLAD to be leaving Germany. If SHAEF had not been disbanded by July 1945, she'd made up her mind to ask for a transfer. Being in Germany did something to her soul. Not because it was a defeated, utterly destroyed country, but because of the hatred, hatred as pervasive as the stench from thousands of bodies trapped under the Frankfurt-am-Main rubble in the summer heat.

"Wait here for me, Corporal," she told the driver of the high-wheeled troop carrier that had been assigned to take her to the airbase. "I won't be long. Keep an eye on my gear."

"Sure thing, Lieutenant." The corporal eyed the children edging toward the vehicle and unloosed his holster flap.

Even children, Page knew, would steal, kill probably, for something, anything, to trade for food. Every morning there were stories of GIs out after curfew found dead or mutilated. No Wac went anywhere alone. Movies were attended in groups with armed guards.

Page climbed the stairs of the Park Hotel for her final appointment with General Willis and stepped around a civilian mopping the landing. He threw her a look of purest hate. When she first encountered such feelings, she had thought it was her victor's paranoia, but now she believed that the hatred existed. She felt his eyes bore into her as she continued up the stairs. And he was one of the lucky ones: he had a job and could eat and feed his family. Not many Germans were hired by G-5 military government, and then only as manual laborers. Until they went through the de-Nazification process, there was no trusting them. There it was again: suspicions eating at her. Yes, it was time for reassignment.

At a desk on the third-floor landing, Page saw that a Wac T/5 was on duty. "Lieutenant Hannaday to see General Willis."

The Wac checked her daybook. "The General asks you to wait, ma'am. He's in a staff meeting and will be out soon."

Page looked at her watch. She had a little extra time. Picking up the latest *Stars and Stripes,* she sat down, but could not keep her mind on the news from the Pacific and a long story about a dream house for the future. Tonight she would be in London for a showdown with her father. She didn't want an open rift with him, but she wasn't going to give in now, not now when she had already paid such a price; when Paul had paid, too.

The T/5 called, "Lieutenant, the General is back."

Page walked through the door and saluted. "I want to thank

you, sir, for allowing me to serve on your staff these past two years, and for giving me a chance to succeed or fail on my own merit."

The General rose and waved her to a chair. "Now, none of that formal stuff, eh? Let's have a drink." He poured two small schnapps. "We're old comrades now, Page."

Page thanked him and sipped at the liquor. "I have one favor to ask of you, sir."

"Hell, Page, I'm way out in front of you." He grinned at her. "Every general officer in occupied Germany *knows* what you and your group want. And you know I'll do everything I can. The day your ZI orders came down, I wrote to Marshall in Washington and told him that Wacs had been invaluable in whipping the Nazis." He chuckled. "Did you know the Germans are even saying that? One of those lousy *Herr Reichsminister* guys—Speer, Albert Speer's his name—said if Germany had used her women as we did they would have won. I put that in my letter to the Chief, too."

"Thank you, General. I hope you told him we want more than reserve status. We want regular army . . . "

"I gave him the whole scoop, Page. Now enjoy your leave in London, and don't be so serious all the time. Hell, a young, fine-looking woman like you should be out on the town— Sorry, Page. I forgot about you and Burkhardt. Fine fellow. Anyway, tell your Wacs to stand on their record, Lieutenant. The WAC has made an excellent contribution and, believe you me, America, the Army and the Congress will recognize you for it."

"Thank you, sir," she said, shaking his outstretched hand and stepping back to salute. She knew that General Willis believed what he was saying; she only wished he was right, but she knew also it would take more than wishes. America longed to get back to the status quo and wouldn't continue a radical experiment with its womenfolk without a lot of arm-twisting.

The T/5 looked up when she opened the door to the hall. "Good luck, ma'am. Will you be anywhere near Fairmont, West Virginia?"

"I'm going to Washington for reassignment. Do you want me to call your family?" She already had a list of parents and husbands to call.

"Would you, Lieutenant?" The T/5 wrote a name and address hastily on a buck slip and handed it to Page. "Tell them I'll be home soon."

"Glad to." Page tucked the note in with her orders and turned, to come face to face with Paul.

After two months, she hadn't really expected to see him. All those first days in Germany, she had looked for him in offices, in messes; even one terrible day at the Aglosterhausen children's DP camp she had thought she saw him in the crowd. Page had imagined what she would say and what he would answer, but now she was totally unprepared and fell back on the rules of etiquette.

"Hello, Paul." She was aware that the T/5 was idly listening, but the old warmth crept into her voice. "How are you?"

His answer sounded mechanical to her ears. "I'm fine. And you?"

"Leaving for the ZI today via London."

"Give your father my regards, please."

"Of course."

They stood facing each other, and Page could see they had been too much to each other—too much happiness, too much grief—to part as friends. The intimacies they'd shared were too near the surface, yet now forever beyond reach. There could be no closeness, because they could not use the lovers' language that had been theirs alone and thus they had no words to use. What had been alive and precious was now dead and despised, and had to be.

"And Annaliese," Page asked politely, but admitted privately to her old curiosity, "how is she?"

Paul looked at her and brushed his hand across his eyes as if unwrapping a bandage from an old wound. "Anna and I are getting married August twentieth in Nuremberg," he said distinctly, giving each word its full weight.

"I'm happy for you, Paul, and for Anna." She said it and meant it at the moment, although she couldn't help wondering what she'd feel on the twentieth of next month. An unbidden thought intruded: *So soon. You could forget so soon?*, but she said, "Paul, I must be going."

He held out his hand, and in some strange way it was opened to her as he wasn't. This hand knew things about her that no one else knew. She took it, aware of his every finger on hers, and, hesitantly, they smiled, sharing a moment that someday, when they finally resisted the tendency to push it away, would be important to them.

"Goodbye," Paul said, and there was pride in his voice, and finality, as he moved past her toward the desk. "Colonel Burkhardt to see General Willis," she heard him say as she started down the stairs.

The corporal was waiting below. "Hey, Lieutenant, if you're gonna make your plane, I'm gonna hafta drive like hell."

And he did, speeding past the badly damaged *Bahnhof,* although it didn't matter, since no trains were running. In some places streets had not been cleared, and in some sections Page had to hold a perfumed handkerchief over her nose to mask the awful odor of dead bodies trapped under fallen buildings. Everywhere whole families were living in the rubble, suffering dreadfully. She was appalled, but still she had not forgiven them. How could she, or any other American?

Once, shortly after arriving in Germany, she had tried to understand them. The young woman who did her laundry was pleasant and willing, but when Page had questioned her about her Nazi party affiliation she had said she had been a Nazi only for convenience. Oh, that one innocently given plausible reason had damned her, damned them all whenever Page remembered Dachau as it had been before the SS prisoners began to fill in the sunken graves of their victims. These Nazis of convenience had done that; they had scooped up blond, blue-eyed babies all over Europe, playing out their insane dreams of Aryan purity, babies who would never find their homes or parents again. It was fitting that the Nazi boot had come to rest on their own necks. There was a moral gap between the Germans and the rest of the world, an abyss so wide and deep as to be uncrossable. Hate might be the only reality, the only meeting ground.

The car came to a clearing in the rubble as they reached the suburbs. On the approach to the Autobahn, Page was horrified to see a man in a tattered Wehrmacht uniform down on all fours eating grass.

"Forget it, Lieutenant," the corporal said, picking up speed. "I saw a soldier eating a raw cat when we marched in here. Gave him my last Hershey bar, too. Know what he did? He ate it and then he spit on me, the bastard!"

As they sped toward the airbase, Page wondered if she would ever forget the sights and the smells of a people destroyed by evil, whose deeds had built barriers between themselves and decent people. And she wondered if her generation would ever stop blaming them for what they had done.

"Corporal, do you think they'll ever recover, the Germans, I mean?"

"Maybe," he said, "but not for a hundred years!"

She was glad to be leaving it behind. Paul and Anna and others like them in the military government, the war crimes tribunals and UNRRA were going to try to put a continent back together again. Compared to theirs, her job didn't seem so tough, and yet she wondered if hers might not take longer. Anyway, she was tired; like any soldier in the ETO she was tired in her bones and wanted to go home, to recover her spirit. She and a few other women soldiers like her, probably no more than ten percent of the Corps, had a job to do if they were to be accepted as full members of the Army and nothing less.

And then as they stopped for cross traffic near the airbase, Page saw a laughing GI on a motorcycle, a *Fräulein,* her skirt hitched high over her shapely legs, riding behind.

The corporal saw her staring and shrugged. "That's different, Lieutenant. That's men and women, and some of them Schatzies ain't bad."

Page nodded that she understood, and she did, but not in the same way the corporal meant. Hate can't last, she understood. It's too hard for human beings to live with. UNRRA, war crimes trials, all that by itself wouldn't rebuild Europe and dig Germany out of the rubble. Just a little time and our human need for reconciliation, to let go of hate and hang on to each other in the night—that's what it will take, she thought, as they turned onto the airbase.

That evening from Croydon Airport outside London she made her way once again, as she had done almost two years before, to Claridge's. This time no champagne party with legions of handsome young officers awaited her. This time when she knocked on the door to Lieutenant General Dalton C. Hannaday's suite, he was alone.

She motioned for the porter to drop her gear, tipped him and watched the door close behind him.

"Come in here, Page," her father called.

The small sitting room was dark.

"Turn the light on," he said. "I didn't realize the sun was down. Now that we're not on War Time it gets dark earlier than it should."

She crossed to the chair where he was slumped, a whiskey in one hand, kissed his forehead and sat down on the sofa. He had aged, his hair thinning back and so much grayer than she remembered. Then she noticed through the door to the bedroom that his bags were half packed on the bed.

"On your way to Germany?"

"I'm on my way out," he said, his voice harsh as he got up, went to a bar cart and dropped more ice cubes into his drink, spilling the whiskey over the side.

"What do you mean, Dad?"

"Out means out! Out of the Army! Out to pasture! Retirement!" His shoulders slumped forward as he regained his chair.

"I'm—so sorry, Dad."

He didn't seem to hear her. "All the dreams, the big ideas ... Did I ever tell you I planned to make Chief of Staff, the first tanker to do it? Not now. Everybody knows Ike can have it anytime he wants it." His voice was a monotone, as if he had lost the authority that had been as much a part of him as his arm. "No more war. No fourth star. No Chief of Staff. It's finished. End of the line."

She had never seen him like this. She had come prepared to fight him for the right to live life her way, and instead of the giant she remembered he was a pitiable shadow with no fight left in him. Suddenly Page began to tremble. She gulped air, dizzily. Terrified, she saw her life being smothered by her father as the gas mask had smothered her face. She saw how easy it would be to slip into the role of nurturer, to give up her life in an effort to distract her father from the pain in his.

He coughed. "Wouldn't be so bad, maybe, if Randall carried on"—he was not even struggling to conceal his despair—"but I guess this is the end of the Hannadays in the U.S. Army."

"No it isn't." She bent forward eagerly until she could have touched him, willing him to really listen to her words. "I know you don't understand this, don't want to understand—I'm a big girl and I can live without your understanding—but for your sake I wish you'd realize that somehow, some way, you gave me what you have." She stood up straight and tall in front of him, a little misty-eyed because he looked so broken. "You gave me my love for the Army. You! I wish you could be proud of that." Impulsively, she knelt on the floor and threw her arms around his knees as she had so often done as a child. "Oh, Dad, try to be proud of me."

He raised his chin off his chest. "Proud?" He slurred the word. "What have I got to be proud of? I raised two children—one a coward, the other a . . . a goddamned freak."

She heard the bitterness behind the hateful words, the feeling that he was useless now the Army didn't want him, the disappointment in children who refused to share his dreams. She heard it, but, as she rose and picked up her gear, she knew she would not give her life in apology.

"I'll write, Dad," she said and left him, his eyes closed against the light.

69

At 10:45 o'clock this morning, a statement by the President was issued at the White House that 16 hours earlier—about the time that citizens on the Eastern seaboard were sitting down to their Sunday suppers—an American plane had dropped a single atomic bomb on the Japanese city of Hiroshima, an important army center.

What happened at Hiroshima is not yet known. The War Department said it "as yet was unable to make an accurate report" because "an impenetrable cloud of dust and smoke" masked the target area. . . .

President Truman solemnly warned: "It was to spare the Japanese people from utter destruction that the ultimatum of July 26 was issued at Potsdam. Their leaders promptly rejected that ultimatum. If they do not now accept our terms, they may expect a rain of ruin from the air the like of which has never been seen on this earth."

—The New York Times, *August 7, 1945*

BUNNY TYPED "28 August, 1945," on the requisition form at the photo lab, then dropped her hands into her lap and stared at the lined paper. Since V-J Day she'd been afflicted with a disease far more debilitating than dengue fever. This new ailment, which almost every GI and Wac in Manila had contracted, was called postwar lethargy. The war was over. It was over in Europe and now in the Pacific since those atomic bombs were dropped on Hiroshima and Nagasaki. New requisitions, work, even the Army itself didn't make much sense to her. Going home was the only subject anyone had talked about since the night of August 15, when victory over Japan had been celebrated.

Every soldier and sailor in Manila had gone wild that night. Vicki had run outside the billets in her pjs, screaming, yelling, jumping up and down. Trucks and jeeps drove at breakneck speed up and down Dewey Boulevard. It seemed the whole world was drunk on San Miguel beer that night. She had walked the thronged streets with her friends—women she'd lived and worked with, and nearly died with, for two years— watching the crowd, gone crazy with happiness, surge around her. But through it all only one question formed and reformed in her mind: Was Breck alive? No one knew when U.S. troops would go into Japan and bring out our men who'd survived. And now, almost two weeks of interminable waiting after V-J Day, she still had no answer.

The phone rang on the section chief's desk. Bunny looked around, but knew he had probably left on a PX run. She stepped to his desk and picked up the receiver, "Photo lab, Sergeant Palermo."

"Bunny?"

The impact of that voice calling her from her fever dreams sent her whirling back to the endless dark space of her illness, and she dropped weakly into the desk chair. She was surprised as the pain swelled. This was not what she had expected. She could not allow herself to believe that this voice wasn't her memory playing cruel games: if she let herself go and believed, the pain would come again as it always had, only this time it would be infinitely worse. But the question had to be asked. She pushed away the shield she'd used to protect herself from taking such risks and plunged into the dark. "Breck?"

"So you still remember me," she heard him say with a tone reminiscent of the beach near Tacloban, the voice that had a tease in it.

Tears of happiness came. "Oh, darling, you're a man impossible to forget." With those words, she felt belief arrive, and her world come together again. "Where are you? Are you all right? Are you coming to Manila?"

"Whoa! One question at a time. I'm at Atsugi Airfield right outside Tokyo. The Japs brought us up from Yokosuka three days ago, and our troops just came in and took over, God love 'em all."

His voice faded, almost disappearing. "Breck!" she yelled into the mouthpiece. "I can't hear you."

". . . flying out to the States today. They want to hold us until the brass hats can give us medals, but we told 'em we'd do bad-ass things in front of the cameras if they didn't get us out of here *right now.*"

"Where are they taking you?"

"To Walter Reed—"

Bunny sucked in her breath. "A hospital?"

"Now, don't get upset, it's just a little arm problem. Won't interfere with my loving, as you will soon learn, my pretty."

"I love you, Breck. In my mind I've been telling you that every minute since you left me back at Tacloban."

"You poor kid. Guess I'll have to marry you."

"What do you mean, *kid?* Breck, why didn't you tell me you were only twenty-four?"

"Why? That's old enough for what I have in mind. Anyway, what's age got to do with love?"

"But in six years, when you're thirty, I'll be thirty-six."

"Bunny, you can be downright exasperatin'. You're some woman, but you can't be everything. You'll just have to let me be the younger one in this crew. When I was a kid wanting everything, my Granny Smith used to tell me I couldn't be the bride at every wedding and the corpse at every funeral."

Bunny laughed. "Breck, you're crazy, but that still doesn't answer—"

"Tell me, how old do you plan to be in six years if we don't get married? Look, honey, we'll work this out later. With you for a wife, I'll probably age twice as fast—" Bunny heard some other voices. "Look, I've got to give another guy a chance at this telephone. I'll write you as soon as I get stateside."

For an instant, he sounded so close she wanted to get her hands on him and never let go. "Darling, I'll write you today, and I'll get to you as soon as I can."

"When?" Breck said.

"Soon. I need forty-five points for discharge and I've got over fifty."

The connection faded and she heard his voice, but not his words. "What? Breck, what!"

"Bunny, say what you said before—say it again, louder."

"Breck," she almost yelled it, "I love you." The line clicked.

70

Allied leaders headed by MacArthur accept the Japanese surrender aboard the battleship Missouri *in Tokyo Bay on September 2. One day later, General Yamashita formally surrenders all Japanese forces in the Philippines. The enemy suffers more than 450,000 casualties in the retaking of the islands. Of 62,143 U.S. casualties, 13,700 are dead.*

LATE IN SEPTEMBER, Bunny, now high on the discharge list, was packing for the ship when a lieutenant in Transportation called. "Palermo, if you can be ready in an hour, you can fly home fast. Get you stateside by day after tomorrow."

"Sir, if I can't finish packing in an hour, I'll leave the rest."

She threw her gear into the duffle bag stenciled with her name, rank and serial number, left her air mattress on another woman's bed and a quick goodbye note in Vicki's room. Vicki would find it when she came off duty. There wasn't time for more. In the Army the dearest friends, closer than sisters one day, said goodbye the next. There had been so many leavetakings—Page, Jill, Elisabeth and now Vicki. Bunny added a P.S. to her note: "You and Mac come for a visit when Breck and I get settled."

On October 12, 1945, fourteen days after leaving Manila, civilian Barbara Patra LaMonica Palermo walked down the long tiled hall toward the solarium at Walter Reed Army Hospital in Washington, D.C. She wore a flowing red wool dress belted around her slender waist, a large black felt picture hat over her pompadour and the highest heels she had been able to find at Garfinckel's department store. Tech Sergeant Palermo was gone. She was plain Bunny again. At the end of the corridor, she saw him waiting for her in the doorway, his arm held up by a braced cast in front of him. Breck, with that roguishly confident, wonderfully cockeyed grin on his face; Breck, just the way she remembered him and always wanted him to be.

"What kept you?" he called to her.

She quickened her steps toward him, although her feet, used to the wide, flat, strong support of field boots, were killing her. She grinned in spite of it. It was a marvelously civilian kind of pain.

He called again, "What kind of milk-run shuttle did they put you on?"

"Got bumped." She rushed toward him faster to close the space between them. "Bumped in Guam, in Kwajalein, in Honolulu. I could have swum the Pacific faster!" She was laughing at him. He was laughing at her. And at last no more space separated them.

He swept her into the warmth of his body to one side of his cast, his good arm holding her tight against the rough cloth of his army-issue bathrobe, his lips thrillingly close to her ear, and she heard him say again the first words she'd ever heard him say, only this time they were for her alone. "Welcome to paradise, lady."

71

America is at peace for the first time in almost four years. At Willow Run, where a new B-24 bomber had rolled out every hour in November 1943, the runways are empty. Everywhere people say, "Bring the boys back," and "Take off all government controls." Most of all, Americans want to go on a shopping spree with the $140 billion in savings and war bonds they have in their pockets.

ELISABETH GARDNER COLLECTIONS. Elisabeth noted with satisfaction the sign on the third-floor plate-glass window visible from Thirty-eighth Street. The same legend in smaller print with the words "Third Floor Front" beneath was repeated on the street door to the stairway. Climbing quickly, she walked behind a fitting-room screen and hastily changed the figure-revealing black dress to which clung the overpowering flower stink of Gabriella's funeral. The bitch was dead. Elisabeth had known for some time that her former boss was spreading lies where it could hurt her, with buyers and with other couture houses. Well, no more.

Elisabeth had even managed a tear at the right moment, sitting next to the *Women's Wear Daily* editor. What a story: ex-model turned designer distraught at the idea that beloved mentor would not see her first collection. It had a ring to it, she thought, and so apparently had the editor, since Elisabeth had seen the woman furiously taking notes after she'd gone forward to lay a dozen roses across the coffin.

Elisabeth slipped into a flowing wraparound dress which she had designed as a work costume and crossed to her office. With Madame gone and Joe Bonine silenced, thanks to Max, there was no one left from her old life who could challenge her. Not even the buyers of cheap knock-offs would bother her in the grand circles she planned to frequent.

Danny Barnes knocked. "Elisabeth?"

"Yes, come in."

He stuck his head inside the office door, dapper in the thin mustache he had grown. "Do you feel like handling a problem? I know you're all torn up over the funeral, but—"

"What is it?"

"The tube top for the strapless-bodice dress—"

"The stretch-bandage war surplus."

"Yes, it hasn't come in yet, and the skirts are ready to attach." He looked down at the order forms in his hand and stepped all the way inside. "See, Elisabeth, the delivery date is October 12, 1945, plain as day. They couldn't have mixed it up."

"Can't you take care of this?" she said impatiently. "Did you call the supplier?"

"That's just it, Elisabeth. He gave me the runaround. And he's not the only one. You know the cotton-mill people delayed shipment to the dyers again." He looked puzzled and tapped the invoices. "If I didn't know better, I'd think some-one was trying to sabotage half our orders."

"Don't exaggerate, Danny," she said, trying to maintain the optimism she'd brought with her from the funeral. "Who'd do such a thing?" Could Gabriella be reaching out from the grave to ruin her after all? Of course not. She shrugged off the thought; Elisabeth Gardner didn't believe in spooks. "Danny, it's easy to explain. Everything's up in the air now the war's over. The mills were stockpiling enormous amounts of cotton for use in the Pacific, and now they've got to dump it. Why wouldn't our money be as good as anyone's?" She clenched her fists, thinking of her checkbook. "And speaking of money, how much do you estimate the show will set us back?" Whatever it took, she knew she'd get the money if she had to hock her fur coat, even though Max would be furious if she didn't wear it this weekend, and even more furious that his gift had supplied financing he'd refused to give.

"I'll have the figures for you this afternoon, Elisabeth. Right now, I've got to keep those seamstresses happy," he said and hurried off toward the rear of the loft, where the cutting tables and the sewing machines were located.

Elisabeth made a sharp turn and headed for the partitioned space facing on Thirty-seventh Street, which she had made into her private office. A thousand details needed her attention, and this was the place to take care of them. Around the walls, which she had painted a creamy white, hung her best finished color croquis, sketches of all the designs with which she hoped to storm the fashion world: her clinging jersey day dresses, the little high-waisted Empire with fitted sleeves, and her favorite, the dramatic greatcoat trimmed in leather. For evening, she had invented—that was the only word—a silk satin gown with a folded bodice from which a woman's shoulders and neck emerged like a swan's. The whole mood was one of elegance. Clothes like these would take women far from the square-shouldered, straight-skirted styles of the war years. Her intuition told her that women would reject mannish, tailored suits for the most feminine dresses they could find—*her* dresses.

Taking fresh sheets of special vellum stationery from a box, Elisabeth began to address the invitations. They were printed, not embossed because it was too costly, and each had a personal handwritten note. They would do nicely. Maybe next October or the year after she would be a member of the New York Couture Business Council and part of their press week special showings, but for now she'd be her own publicist. She wrote quickly to *Vogue, Harper's Bazaar, Mademoiselle,* the New York papers, the big fashion names at Bonwit's and Saks, everyone in the business she could think of. She needed lots of free publicity first, and that would bring in the buyers later with their order books open and their pencils sharp.

The next two weeks flew by in a flurry of last-minute details that became major problems. The room she had wanted at the Waldorf for her showing was unavailable, forcing on her a take-it-or-leave-it upper-floor conference suite. The pianist she'd wanted didn't return her calls; the best show models were already engaged by the big-name couture houses. It seemed to Elisabeth as if every door in Garment Town had a "Keep Out" sign on it where she was concerned.

Jauntily Danny suggested, "Why don't we ask Cole Porter to come down from the Waldorf penthouse to play for us?"

"I'm not seeing the humor in this, Danny."

"Okay, I've got a better suggestion. If we can't have a top pianist, let's pretend we didn't want one. I know a young woman, a student."

Elisabeth raised her eyebrows at the idea that Danny knew young women students. A bar girl was no problem, but she didn't want him to practice what manhood he had on a little music student ready to give up Carnegie Hall at the drop of a white picket fence. She needed Danny, more—she was suddenly aware—every day. Perhaps she would have to give some thought to tying him up—a contract, maybe.

"Met this girl in the Automat," he explained. "She plays the harp beautifully. We'll just change the theme to 'Fashions Made in Heaven,' see?"

Elisabeth snapped, "Of course, I'm not stupid."

"As for models," Danny, smiling at her feistiness, went on, "why don't you be one of your own models?"

"The hell—it's not done. Why, I'd—"

Danny nodded. "—be different."

"You're right, Danny boy. You have clever instincts, partner." Remembering his little musician, she brushed his cheek with a kiss. "So they'd think I was a showoff, so what! A former model wearing her own designs—it could get me a few extra column inches of print, and that's as good as orders any day."

In spite of the hectic activity of the last days before her opening, Elisabeth felt a new sensation, almost of clairvoyance: she saw a picture of her life in which she shared its excitement with Max, but this picture was at odds with life as she was living it. The too-brief hours they spent together were full of talk of Max's idea of their life together, as if her work didn't exist. Months ago, his words had ceased to make any sense to her, but she had continued to pretend to believe them, rather than fight him. Once she'd made it, she knew, he would be excited by her success.

The great evening arrived. "This is it," Elisabeth said, sounding as jumpy as a bombardier over the target. Danny piled the last of the dress boxes into the cab. "The Waldorf, driver," she directed.

Leaning back into the seat, she took a deep breath. She'd thought of everything. Her opening was the night *before* the major house showings, so she wouldn't compete with the established names. That was the single advantage to being outside the organized fashion business; she didn't have to play by their rules, and the fourteen-hour advantage would give the fashion editors plenty of chance to think about her designs before their deadlines. Suddenly, she caught her breath. "Christ! Danny, what about an iron and an ironing board?"

"Housekeeping at the hotel will have them in the dressing room."

Fiddling with the hand strap above the window, she ticked off her list: "Hairdresser and makeup?"

"They should be there now."

"Buffet?"

"Calm down, Elisabeth. The catering staff was working on it this afternoon."

"They'd better have it on time, Danny boy," she said, her face grim. "No second chance for me. I don't have a dime left."

"Elisabeth, you're going to be an enormous success tonight."

She walked through a side entrance of the Waldorf and into

the elevator, into the dressing room and then to the connecting door to peek into the main room. Twelve small tables with angel-topped flower centerpieces had been placed about the room, and a buffet table stood to the side with white-coated servers poised behind. "Danny, come here." He averted his face from the three models in various stages of undress and came to her side. She said, "There's only four people out there and I don't recognize any of them. What time is it?"

She felt a strong, comforting pressure on her arm as he moved to look through the crack.

"It's early, or it's traffic—holding them up." She suspected that his voice was deliberately nonchalant. "Elisabeth, those people are always late. It preserves their independence. Remember, they know we need them more than they need us."

Elisabeth whispered, "Shit."

Behind her, the hairdresser, a small Frenchwoman, screamed at one of the dressers who had slipped a dress on without help and loosened a model's carefully plaited coil of hair.

"Shut up! *Taisez-vous!*" Elisabeth yelled at her in her best Gabriella imitation. Everyone was on edge, so she dared not allow this woman to set off a shouting match. Why, she asked herself, weren't there more people out there? Just the freeloaders and the curious alone could have filled the room and gobbled the food. Damn! Shell games on the sidewalk drew a bigger crowd than she did.

Oh, Christ! The harp music started and she began to hope. Maybe she'd pull it off yet. *Get out there! Start talking. Show the bastards.* Order and discipline began to impose themselves from somewhere deep inside her. Smiling, she stepped through the door.

In less than an hour it was over. Danny arranged the major dresses in the small collection on mannequins and displayed them about the room. He said, "There'll be more coming."

"Oh sure. Eight more people will flood in. We couldn't stand another crush like that last one." If Danny sugarcoated one more thing, she'd strangle him. Her body was rigid as she sat at a table, the food Danny had placed before her getting cold.

"Listen, Elisabeth." Danny sat down. "Didn't you hear what the assistant buyer for Lord and Taylor said?" She didn't answer, and he rushed on. "Said if this show had been well covered, your greatcoat would have been knocked off in twenty-four hours."

"Assistant buyer—so what!"

"I'll tell you so what. This buyer said she'd talk to her boss, Dorothy Shaver, about you. That's a pretty good so what! And we have one order, don't forget. The buyer for Lillie Rubin in Miami Beach was crazy about the folded-bodice gown. That's a very influential store. Elisabeth, snap out of it. It's not like you to give up."

"How the hell do you know what I'm like?"

Suddenly, Elisabeth was furious at him. She couldn't stand another minute of Danny's eternal optimism. She refused to spend even a fraction of her life playing Snow White to his Dopey. She wanted to slap that earnest, helpful gaze right off his face, choke those hopeful words that only made her feel worse than she already did. But she didn't dare because she knew she needed him too much. He'd been right about that, anyway.

Danny's face turned angry when he looked over her shoulder. "What's *he* doing here?"

She saw Max at the door. Max! Here? He had come to help her after all he'd said. "Danny," she said, her face intensely alive for the first time in days, "see that all the dresses are packed in their boxes and taken back to Thirty-eighth Street."

"Don't you get it yet?"

She brushed him aside and walked toward Max, smiling at him. He picked up her arm, placing it through his. "Your friend there," he indicated Danny, "won't take this opportunity to get even with me, or save your honor?"

"Who, Danny?" she said distracted by Max and the way he brushed his mouth across hers. "He's harmless." She took a deep breath and relaxed a little. "I'm surprised, but enormously pleased, Max. I didn't expect you to come. But you've missed all the fun. Reporters, a buyer from Lord and Taylor ..." She stopped, realizing that she was gushing, and that he had a peculiar look on his face. They walked, mechanically. Downstairs. Through the lobby. Max tipped the doorman and handed her into the cab; she heard him give the driver her apartment address.

Elisabeth leaned against his shoulder. He'd come to her

opening. In the end what was important to her had mattered to him. She felt the side of her that pressed next to him glow warmly against the soft material of his dinner jacket.

"Is this enough, Elisabeth?" he said, his voice as thick as velvet, as the cab turned into Broadway.

"Enough? Of what?"

"Has tonight convinced you that your dream is a nightmare? Look at you. Even in this light, you look exhausted. Don't tell me you've become one of those dreary Greenwich Village types who is willing to sacrifice her looks for art. Don't tell me, because I won't believe it."

Abruptly she sat upright. Why was Max talking like this? How did he know things had gone so badly? Stray questions from the past weeks flashed by her mind. Delayed shipments. Stalling. Mixups. She'd put it all down to the madness of a large part of Manhattan simultaneously getting ready for market week. Now she wasn't so sure.

"What do you know about tonight, Max?" she said softly, allowing him to see a faint disappointment. "No, don't analyze my ambition, just give me the truth."

Max stretched his legs full length in front of him, and she saw the muscles knot under the good cloth on his thigh.

"Elisabeth, you know what I believe about you and me, and that's all you need to know. I'd do anything to force you to see what a myth you've invented." He sighed heavily. Elisabeth was sounding more and more like a wife, someone whose feelings he had to protect. Damn it! *His* happiness was her job, not some two-bit design house, undercapitalized and bound to collapse at the first market downturn. He was bored with this continuing argument. He couldn't understand why he just didn't deliver an ultimatum and quit playing games with her, but knew he'd have to keep tight hold on this desire, or he could lose her. He had to give her just enough rein to taste freedom, but keep her unsure of him so she would always run back. "Why is it that every metropolitan reporter dreams of owning a small town weekly"—he took a deep breath and exhaled noisily—"and every fashion model dreams of being a designer of couture?"

"Why don't you answer me?" Elisabeth said.

"Why should I? I did what was best for your own good, since you don't seem to know it anymore." The cab pulled up to her building entrance. "Hear me, Elisabeth. You, of all people, know how to play rough. If you can't take this disappointment, and I don't think you can, then it's best to find out now. I did you a favor."

Feeling frustrated and resentful, like a younger child told she couldn't play with older children, she snapped at him, "I get it now. It wasn't Gabriella. It was *you*, the great Max Stryker, putting the muscle on suppliers and—"

He added sardonically, "—renting your room at the Waldorf and buying off where I couldn't scare off."

The driver had come around to let her out, but she hadn't finished with Max. "That's not fair."

"I'm never fair when it might interfere with what I want. By the way, talk of fairness is silly coming from you." Max felt himself growing steadily more depressed at the idea that this time he'd gone too far with her, but he couldn't let Elisabeth see his caring or she'd pounce like a shark on a blood scent. He had been so sure she'd realize the hopelessness of her situation and run back to his arms. And then fear hit Max hard, a fear with a name on it. He knew that the time would come when he would need her and she would not come. She was growing stronger, and with strength he could lose her. He wanted to end this conversation and settle the problem in bed where they would both think more clearly. "Sabotaging your show wasn't so difficult. Believe me, my dear, you were doomed to fail in this town. No one who counts is interested in your dreams of fashion glory. Pretty little talents like yours are a dime a dozen."

Elisabeth needed to change the subject, to stop him, to leave. Max wasn't listening to her. He never would listen. If she wanted him, an important part of her life would exist in a limbo of silence between them. If she wanted him.

With a swirl of skirts, she climbed out of the cab and stalked regally to her apartment. Behind her, she could hear him laughing. Damn him! Damn him straight to the hottest pit of hell!

Her telephone was ringing as she inserted the key into the lock of her apartment door. Dropping her bag on the bed, she picked it up. "Hello."

"Elisabeth? Are you there?"

It was Danny. "Yes," she said.

"Elisabeth Gardner Collections isn't finished. I've got a small inheritance from my uncle, and some ideas that I'll tell you about tomorrow."

His voice was spilling out of the telephone at her. He wanted to rescue her. Momentarily, misery attacked her as it always did when some man like Marne—no, this was Danny—wanted to care for her, smother her with his love, own her. Max had been right about one thing; marriage, at least what most women thought of as marriage, wasn't for her. But Danny might have his uses. For one, he would make a conveniently undemanding husband, and marriage would be the least expensive contract she could offer. Danny was saying, "Elisabeth, I was worried about you. You were so depressed and, well, you know who clobbered us, don't you?"

"Yes, I know."

Danny paused. "I guess this means you're through with him." He waited again. "Doesn't it?"

Elisabeth stood absolutely still, the need in her pounding like a huge hammer, every throb a substitute for Max's body. It was irrational, this sexual need for Max, like a virus that attacks only the strongest and least vulnerable and leaves weaklings untouched. It is only the supremely certain, the arrogant, who can be devoured by their own sensual emotions. "Danny, I'm tired. Let's talk about this tomorrow." She hung up softly.

She stood very still with her hand on the cradled telephone receiver. Max had taught her a lesson tonight; not the one he'd meant to teach, but one far more valuable. Damned if she wouldn't have him *and* her work—Danny too—keeping them separated in neat little compartments, taking out first one and then the other as it suited her. That was how Max lived, and that was how she'd live. He'd been a good teacher. She smiled ironically, picked up the telephone again and dialed Max's hotel suite.

He answered, "Hello, Elisabeth."

"You smug bastard."

"Agreed."

"Max, once you said we made great sex together."

"Is that what you want?"

"Why not?"

"Then I'll expect you within the half hour."

Elisabeth slammed down the receiver. Then she smiled

again, this time with the ice-cold clarity of one who not only gets the joke, but instigates it; a most secure smile. Damned if she wouldn't see that it took more than an hour to get to his hotel.

Lazily, she walked about her apartment, examining items she already knew well. She had never before kept Max waiting. This was only a small triumph, but she recognized it as one and knew Max would, too. She wondered if she would take back little increments of time for herself until she would need to give Max nothing.

72

The Women's Army Corps had never before known a peacetime Christmas. The Wacs, and their predecessors the Waacs, spent the wartime holidays behind the fighting fronts as drivers, switchboard operators, stenographers, airplane mechanics, laboratory technicians, and clerks. One hundred thousand strong on V-E Day, they had earned 314 medals and commendations, including 23 Legion of Merit awards and fourteen Purple Hearts. Seventeen thousand Wacs served overseas. One hundred eighty-one died.

This week the WAC was half demobilized. Only 50,000 women would wear khaki for the holidays, all but 3,500 of them in the United States. Those overseas, the Army said, would be home by April. The future of the corps was still in doubt. . . .

—Newsweek, *December 24, 1945*

"NEXT STOP DES MOINES, five minutes." The train conductor's singsong echoed down the day coach and roused Bunny from a restless doze. She sat up, rubbing her stiff neck muscles.

Breck stood and stretched his long limbs. "Honey, I never knew I had so many aching bones."

"Is your shoulder all right?"

"You'll be finding out how all right it is," he threatened her with a salacious grin.

Soon the train lurched to a stop. Breck retrieved his shaving kit and Bunny's train case from the overhead rack, and they moved quickly past the sea of high-backed green coach chairs to the rear of the car.

"Watch your step." The conductor courteously touched his cap and held out his hand to help Bunny find the step down to the platform. "Sir," he said to Breck, "I want to apologize again for that reservation mixup. These things happen. Seems like more foul-ups during this holiday rush—first Christmas after the war and all. I hope you and the missus will have a happy holiday."

"He has no idea how happy it'll be," Breck whispered so that only Bunny could hear him.

She asked as they walked toward the terminal, "Nothing else *could* go wrong now, could it?"

"Nothing, sweetheart. Everything's already happened."

"Granny Smith must have a saying for a situation like this."

"That she does. She'd say that we'd come out with the hind teat every time."

"Is that something like the neck of the chicken?"

"Right, only on the other end. I see I'm going to have to give you some anatomy lessons," he said seductively.

Bunny knew they were each trying to handle their frustration with a light touch for the other's sake. But it hadn't been easy. For two months after their marriage in the hospital chapel, Breck's slow recovery from operations to remove deeply lodged bone chips in his shoulder had kept him from getting a weekend pass out of Walter Reed. Then Page's telegram had come a few days before his discharge, telling Bunny that the reunion at Babe's was on for Christmas Eve, 1945. Happily, Breck had planned their belated wedding night in the swankest Pullman compartment on the train to Des Moines.

Breck shook his head from side to side in disbelief as they headed toward the waiting room. "I still can't understand how they misplaced our reservations."

Bunny sighed. "Darling, it's over now. We're here, and I plan to make up for lost time." He straightened his snap brim hat, and she saw again that confident, all-male, cockeyed grin she'd fallen in love with back at Hollandia—oh yes, it had been that first day, she knew now.

Breck stopped at the waiting-room entrance and put his hands on her shoulders. "Say it again."

"Right here?"

"Here and now."

Bunny laughed, hoping he would never get tired of hearing it. "I love you, Breck."

"Bunny, you should laugh a lot. No more sad smiles."

"No more sad smiles," she echoed.

While Breck went to check with baggage claims for their luggage, Bunny walked around the familiar station. It was three and a half years since she'd arrived with the first OCs on that hot, humid morning in July 1942, and exactly three years tomorrow since she'd waved goodbye to Page and Elisabeth and Jill. Jill! Little Jill. News traveled slowly to SWPA. One Wac had learned of her father's death two months late from an old Chicago newspaper wrapped in another woman's package from home. And Bunny hadn't heard about Jill's death in May until Page had written her at Walter Reed months later. Jill's letters had stopped coming, but Bunny had naturally supposed her marriage to Stratton and the move up to Austria had left her no time for correspondence. She ached at the thought of Jill, dead in a strange land, and so senselessly—coming through the whole war, most of the time within the sound of battle, to become a postwar statistic. God, how she wished she could tell Jill how much she'd always admired that thrust-out chin. Too late now to tell her anything. Why do we always know what we want to say when it's too late to say it? Bunny wondered.

Across the waiting room she saw Breck beside a redcap with their luggage wave to her, and her thoughts brightened.

"Iowa Hotel," Breck told the cab driver. He held her hand as they traveled the snow-covered streets through the clear winter twilight. "This get-together tomorrow means a lot to you, doesn't it?" He'd been watching her stare out the window, and thought he saw a hint of tears in her eyes.

"Yes, though it's not much of a reunion. Jill's dead, and Elisabeth probably won't come even if Page can reach her—you know she got booted out of the Corps—so it'll be just Page and me." She squeezed his hand, trying to make him understand. "It's hard to explain. It was special in those early days—what we were doing with the WAC, the four of us, so different and yet like sisters. You don't understand, do you?"

"No, honey, but if you do it's enough for me. I don't have to know everything you know; I just have to care about your knowing."

God, how she loved him for that. "Darling, it's like—well, seeing this place for the last time is my real discharge from the WAC. After I leave here, I can really start my new life with you."

He smiled down at her. "I understand. I feel that way about my great-granny's cabin, you know the one I told you about at Tacloban. When we get there, then I'll know I'm really home."

He kissed her cheek, and Bunny felt his breath hot against her skin. She asked wryly, "Are you sure that's all you're thinking of?"

For reply, he moved closer and put his arm around her shoulders so tightly she knew he would never let go.

Bunny signed the register for both of them, since Breck's handwriting was still shaky: "Mr. and Mrs. Breckinridge T. C. Smith, late of the Southwest Pacific theater of operations."

On the way to their room, Bunny whispered, "You never told me what the T.C. stands for."

"No names. They're my mama and daddy's initials. You wouldn't want to call me Thomas Catherine, would you?"

"I don't know. It sounds kind of cute."

Breck aimed a playful slap at her derrière, but Bunny danced sideways.

Breck grinned. "Just wait until I get you alone."

The bellhop put their bags down and unlocked number 212. "You two newlyweds?"

"No, we're old married folk." Breck plucked the key from the boy's hand, gave him a quarter and shut the door on his puzzled face.

They looked at each other and broke into laughter.

She slipped inside his arms. "Breck, promise me something. Promise me bellhops will always think we're newlyweds."

He kissed her as though he couldn't get enough, lingering over her lips, tasting, teasing, learning.

Bunny's heart was beating so fast she almost couldn't

breathe. "Breck, wait! I have to clean up after that long train ride."

"That's a good idea." He swung open the bathroom door and saw a shower. "Hot dog!" he said, setting the water temperature. "Back on Hollandia, I used to see you head for the shower I built for the Wacs, and I'd dream about being in it with you."

She pushed him playfully, feeling sixteen again. Breck did that for her. His delight in life and in her made her feel younger than she'd ever felt. Her Breck was one of life's optimists, and he'd made her one, too.

Leaving their clothes in one pile on the bedroom floor, they raced for the shower, trying to edge one in front of the other by bumping hips, and arriving simultaneously, laughing and out of breath, under the stream of warm water.

He pulled her wet nakedness to his and buried his head in her shoulder. "I love you, wife."

"Touch me, Breck."

He ran his hands down her back and cupped his fingers under her swelling buttocks. With a shiver, he felt himself harden and rise.

"Oh," she moaned softly and strained toward him.

Breck held himself in check. He had waited for her for a year and a half, and he'd be damned if their first time would be a quick probe, over in minutes. He leaned his body away from her, and saw that her eyes were closed, her mouth ready, the water sluicing down her outline, cleansing, revealing her lovely form. "I think we better not forget what we came in here for," he said, his voice hoarse.

Bunny's eyes opened, squinting against the coursing stream. "*I* haven't." Her voice was low, and he didn't mistake her meaning.

He laughed again. "Don't you think we ought to soap up?"

"Bre-eck, damn it! Haven't you got your priorities wrong?"

"Maybe. My Granny Smith has a—"

"Oh no. If she's got a saying to cover this situation, then I'm going to have to revise my opinion of your sweet old granny."

He pretended to ignore her. "Granny'd say, 'Never stop a plow to catch a mouse.'"

She grinned. "That's what I call one smart lady."

"Now, wait, Bunny darling. Before you get yourself in an

uproar, why don't you see what I have in mind." He took the soap from the dish, tossed the wrapper beyond the curtain, and moved the bar in circles over her shoulders and around each breast, dropped his hand to her stomach and then lathered the triangular nest of dark, tight curls above her inner thighs.

Breathing quickly so her breasts thrust rhythmically toward him, she said, "Darling, let me soap you." Bunny took the bar from his hand and sudsed his shoulders and the blond hair on his chest, careful to avoid the red, welted scars of his wound. His nipples hardened under her hand, and as the soap ran down his body she licked his small hard nubs and made wet circles around them with her tongue.

"Bunny!" He leaned against the shower stall, his eyes closed, his penis growing harder and larger. "Know something, honey? For the rest of my life, whenever I smell Ivory soap, I'm going to get a hard on." He rolled his eyes heavenward, grinning at her now. "Do you know what that means? I'll get kicked out of grocery stores, pharmacies, restaurants . . ."

"Oh Breck, you wonderful nut."

He reached behind her and turned off the water. Holding her hand, he stepped out and grabbed two towels.

They dried the moisture from each other, playfully toweling the tender parts, vigorously rubbing backs and legs, until they were pink and flushed with warmth. Then Breck dried her dark curls. Overcome by their sensuous silliness, Bunny delicately hung a towel over Breck's erection. With a whoop, he picked her up in spite of his wound and, kicking wide the bathroom door, carried her to the bed.

Bunny looked up at him, and Breck saw trust and love flood into her eyes, and, not surprisingly, a simultaneous mischievous smile pulled up the corners of her mouth. "Are you finally ready to plow?" she asked, affecting exasperation.

Breck dropped laughing on the bed beside her. "Oh, am I ever ready to plow!" He rolled gently on top of her, and her mouth was open to him, and as he kissed her his tongue tangled with hers in a frantic reaching for first depths.

Bunny knew that all of her was open to him, and not even the smallest memories of Johnny crowded out the large ones they were making together. She was eager to receive him, beyond eagerness.

As he strained above her, enclosed in a hot delight, the sensation of her pulsating center brought a fleeting memory of the plunging bow of the *Honshu Maru,* and he saw himself looking back toward the Philippines, promising himself a night like this. But, oh, even in his longing he hadn't known how wonderful loving her would be. All those months in Japan the thought of her had kept him alive, and now he meant to repay her with the energy of his life.

For one tiny moment, as she rose to meet his thrust into her, Breck's words on the beach at Tacloban returned to her. Laughter and love, he'd said, go together. And with her lips parted in a loving smile, she gave herself totally to both.

At one o'clock on the afternoon of Christmas Eve, Captain Page Hannaday sat alone upstairs at Babe's, waiting for Bunny. Only two or three other uniformed women were in the restaurant, which had been recaptured once again by Des Moines civilians.

Fort Des Moines was now a major Wac demobilization center, and Page had the necessary but painful job of presiding over the discharge of the majority of the Corps. Everything in the WAC had changed since first Germany and then Japan had surrendered. In July, Colonel Hobby had taken terminal leave due to ill health, the very day Page left Frankfurt. Then Colonel Westray Battle Boyce became the new Director of the WAC, but despite her name she seemed to have no desire to fight for a peacetime Corps.

Page took the dusty bottle of champagne from the center of the table, reading the four faded names written on the label, and placed it in an ice bucket. All that fall after V-J Day, many of the top Wac officers had wanted the Corps to go out with all flags flying at some big ceremony to mark its end. But a few thousand women soldiers, like her, were hanging on as long as possible, hoping Congress could be persuaded. She had to admit that until this past month a permanent WAC had not looked likely.

But in November, Page and the others had taken heart. Lieutenant Colonel Mary Hallaren, former ETO Air WAC staff director, had been appointed WAC deputy director at the Pentagon, and, even better, Ike had become Chief of Staff at the War Department; both of them were strong advocates of a peacetime WAC.

"Page, is that really you with captain's bars?"

Page looked up toward the familiar voice near the stairs. "Bunny!" It was her friend, radiant and smiling. "My God, Bunny, you've changed." The eyes that had once mirrored deep pain no matter how much she clowned sparkled vibrantly now with—there were almost no words for it—belief, hope, joy, and something more Page couldn't put a name to, an aliveness of some place that had been dead. Page was amazed to feel her own eyes fill with tears. Was this what marriage did for a woman? Was this what she'd sacrificed?

"Changed, have I?" Bunny threw her arms around Page, laughing. "Is that a polite way of telling me I'm over the hill?"

"Don't be silly. I've never seen you look so fantastic, truly."

Bunny looked around. It was funny how a place that held so many long-ago memories could be disappointing. Oh, it wasn't that you couldn't go home again. You could, easily, but only as a stranger. Everything was the same and nothing was the same; those early days of the war, the jukebox pounding "Coming in on a Wing and a Prayer"—it was all shadows. In a vague way she resented it; coming back to Babe's was like taking a memory out of mothballs, a memory that no longer fit who she was now. "Page, speaking of change, this place sure hasn't changed. I get the feeling I'm going to have to hurry back to the post to make bed check or Sergeant Wolford will have my hide." She sat down at the small table. "Wonder what ever happened to the old sarge."

"Don't you know? He spent the whole war at Fort Des Moines, and then retired to Florida last month."

"Poor Wolford. That's what I call poetic justice."

"Oh, you wouldn't have recognized him toward the end. He thought the WAC had been his idea all along, called us 'my girls.'"

"Remember how scared of him Jill was? I wish she could hear this." Bunny had been avoiding Jill's name, but now that it had been said there was no going back. "It could have been me, Page—so easily on Hollandia, in the Philippines . . ."

"Yes, I know what you mean. It could have been me in the buzz bombing, at the Ardennes . . . Do you ever ask yourself why you're living?"

"No, Page, not anymore. I know why."

"Yes, I know, too, but Jill also had a reason to live—"

Both of them had been so intent on their conversation that they had not heard footsteps stop near the table.

"Am I really invited to this old vets' reunion, or not?"

"Elisabeth!" Page and Bunny exclaimed together.

How like Elisabeth, Page thought, to show up, without notice, then challenge us and get it over with, just in case we'd changed our minds about her. She even held Page's telegram in her hand as proof she had a right to be there. "I'm glad you're here, Elisabeth," Page told her and meant it. If possible, Page saw, she was even more stunning than she had been three years ago. The classic face, the shrouded seriousness of her eyes, the sense of inner turbulence that touched everyone, but that no one dared try to touch.

"This chair has your name on it," Bunny said, pushing a chair from under the table.

Elisabeth sat down. When Page's telegram had come, she had planned to ignore it—after all, she lived in another world now—but had found it impossible. Something drew her to this place, to these women, something about her deepest self she didn't understand, didn't want to understand lest it change her direction, because, right or wrong, she wanted to go where she was going. "Don't make the mistake of thinking I'm here to apologize for disgracing the uniform. And don't think I'm sorry I got kicked out of the Corps; it was the best thing for me."

Page regretted Elisabeth's mood. "You're here because you belong here, because we want you to be here."

"That goes for me too," Bunny said.

"I guess I'm here for Jill. I hadn't heard—until you . . ." Elisabeth laughed, a low self-mocking laugh and stared sadly at Page. "Remember that first day at OC, when we got off the truck together and stood under a tree trying to cool off? Jill was wearing that awful peplum dress, and I told her a short girl should never wear a peplum. Now, *that* I'm sorry for, even though it was true. Anyway, I can't stay long. My husband is waiting downstairs."

Bunny looked puzzled. "Your husband! I thought Marne was—"

"Yes, killed. I've remarried."

Bunny looked more puzzled still. "To that guy you almost . . ."

"The guy I almost went to jail for?" Elisabeth finished Bunny's question and noticed from the flush on Bunny's face that she knew she had no business asking. "You might say that I have him where I want him."

"I—I'm sorry. It's none of my business."

"That's right, but since you're interested in my setting the marital record straight, this husband is also my business manager and partner." Elisabeth hesitated, shrugging. "It's a marriage of convenience, really."

Bunny laughed now, that impudent teasing laugh that had echoed down the barracks of OC. "Aren't they all? I thought going crazy for the rest of my life without Breck would be damned inconvenient."

"I'm glad you're happy." Elisabeth smiled at the irrepressible Bunny, beginning to feel comfortable with these women, an old comfort she hadn't truly felt in three years. "Are we going to drink this thing," she said, gesturing toward the bottle, "or just look at it?"

Page nodded. "Our 'last survivor' bottle—sure, that's what we're here for."

"Hold on," Bunny said, "I'll get some glasses." She came back with four glasses, and knew that the others saw but said nothing, and neither did she. It was one of those dumb, sentimental gestures that belonged in a moment like this. She held up the bottle. "Page, you open this thing. You probably had lots of practice in France."

"Right," Page said lightly. "Champagne with our K rations." She began working the cork out of the dripping bottle. "I remember the night we signed this. Remember how excited Jill was? Said we'd come back here and swap war stories like some Gary Cooper movie."

Bunny nodded, " 's funny. Now all we can talk about is her."

Page poured three glasses of champagne, one for each of them. "Here's to Jill—sweet, simple, hardheaded . . ."

"To the kid," Bunny added, "fiercely loyal, confused, crazy, my friend."

Elisabeth drank without saying a word.

They were all three silent for a while, staring into their empty champagne glasses. There seemed to be nothing more to say.

Then Page broke the silence. "Oh, I almost forgot. This package came from a friend of Jill's a couple of months ago, and it's for all of us." She took a letter from her purse and put the package down onto the table.

Bunny stared at it. "What is it?"

Page opened the letter. "This will tell you all I know. It's from an American woman in Florence, a Marchesa d'Ordella, who signs herself Helen." Page began to read.

"DEAR FRIENDS OF JILL

"Many times Jill spoke to me of you and how much your friendship meant to her. She was a special person, and I miss her. By now you know that Jill is dead in a most tragic mishap. Her husband, Des Stratton, has gone on to Vienna, and asked me to pack her belongings and send them to her family. Before he left, he specifically asked that I send Jill's medal and citation to you. He said you'd know what to do with them."

Bunny's hand stole toward the package and disclosed a velvet-covered box. Inside lay a Bronze Star with ribbon, the citation folded neatly underneath. She unfolded the paper, read it and then passed it to Page, who gave it to Elisabeth.

"What do you know?" Bunny said. "The brave little . . . "

Quietly, Page filled their glasses a second time.

Bunny was awash in memories. She could hear Jill's voice saying, *Let's make a pact to return here—say, the Christmas Eve after the war is over. Whoever shows up gets to drink the bottle in memory of the others.* Then she heard her own voice answering, *You've got some imagination, kid. We're all coming back. . . .*

"Elisabeth?" a man's voice called from the staircase. "We'd

better hurry if we're going to make our connections to Chicago."

"Okay, Danny." Elisabeth impatiently put him off with a quick look. "Wait for me downstairs. Well . . ." She gathered herself as if she was going, but she didn't move. She was oscillating between a desire to leave and one to stay. Something held her, something unfinished. "Might as well kill it—" she bit her lip at the word—"the bottle, I mean."

Page nodded. She refilled their glasses and poured the fourth glass this time and set it across the table in front of the empty chair. She didn't feel there was anything overly dramatic or symbolic about the act; it just seemed right, since Jill was there in Babe's all around them. "Where to now, Bunny?" Page asked.

"Breck and I are going to visit his family in Tennessee—a wonderfully wise grandmother who has the perfect answer for every situation. Can you see a Bloomfield Italian Catholic living in the Bible-thumping Baptist Belt, the wife of a Tennessee hill country lawyer?"

Page winked at Elisabeth. "We can see that, can't we?"

"Okay, you two, but for the next year or two Breck'll be at Duke, finishing law school, and I'll be one of those vets' wives *Life* magazine loves to write about, living in a tin quonset hut." Bunny grinned at both of them. "Guess what. I want kids—a houseful. Can you believe it? I'll be Mother Bunny for real. What about you, Page?"

"I'm hanging on. Only a few more months and Congress will be making the WAC a permanent peacetime army corps, but you two know that old story."

"Page," Bunny asked, "do you ever have any regrets about your—about Paul?"

"Yes." Page sighed, a long, slow exhaling. "I knew I would, but I also knew I'd regret it more if I didn't try to find a life in the military service. I just had to choose the regret I could live with best. Funny, but that's something Jill wrote in one of her last letters to me. I've never forgotten it." She raised her hand as if to say something else, but let it fall, and turned her attention to Elisabeth. "What about you, Elisabeth?"

"You know I have my own design house now"—Elisabeth had not been caught by surprise, having rehearsed on the train—"and a really successful first showing of my line a couple of months ago. Afterwards, a buyer at Bonwit's in New York recommended me to Monogram Studios, and here I am on my way to Hollywood to do the clothes for the next Vera Hruba Ralston musical."

Bunny didn't believe all of it. She suspected that Elisabeth jumbled the true with the untrue until it all sounded false. "Vera Hruba Ralston," she said, grinning. "Sounds like a Hungarian breakfast cereal."

"Okay, she's not Rita Hayworth. Do you know how hard it is to break into that town? Other designers have waited their whole lives." Elisabeth was surprised that Bunny's joke had angered her, and more surprised that she had shown it. She wanted to be known by these women—these friends—but not to be found out; to be accepted, but to remain a blank page. "Damn it, Bunny, someday you'll have an Elisabeth Gardner original in your closet, if you're lucky enough to afford me."

Bunny nodded and smiled her soft self-mocking smile. "If I thought I'd look like you, Elisabeth, I'd hock the family jewels for one of your dresses."

Page drained her glass. "We've all changed so," she said softly.

"How?" Bunny asked. "I'm still the same."

"Oh, I don't mean outwardly, I mean . . . Take Jill. She was little more than a scared child at OC, yet she became a courageous woman who saved a man's life and even gave her own."

"I see what you mean," Bunny said. "When I joined up, I thought I'd made a dumb hash of my life, but I went on to show good judgment and make decisions others relied on."

"And I learned to rely on myself," Elisabeth said, thinking aloud.

"Elisabeth!" the slender man with the Zachary Scott mustache called impatiently from the stairs.

She stood. "I've *got* to go."

Page looked at Bunny, and Bunny nodded. Page picked up Jill's Bronze Star and handed it to Elisabeth, who automatically extended her hand to take it, and then pulled back as from an electric shock.

"What's this?" Elisabeth asked sharply, anger masking disbelief.

Page answered. "It's yours. Jill would have wanted you to have it."

"You're crazy. How do you know that?"

Bunny broke in, "It's true. In her last letter to me she wrote that she wished more than anything you could have seen her get her medal. Damn it—take it! In Hollywood you'll need all the courage you can get."

Elisabeth reached with both slender symmetrical hands, in an act of delicate intimacy, and took the case with Jill's Bronze Star. "She said that?" she asked, and then she walked, dazedly, to the stairs without looking back or saying goodbye.

"Elisabeth," Danny said, "what's wrong?"

She walked past him and started down the stairs. "Why should anything be wrong?"

"Oh, nothing." He fell in behind her. He had never seen her tears before.

Page watched the two heads disappear. "Did Jill really write that, Bunny?"

"No. But it sounded like her, don't you think? She always worshiped Elisabeth. Me, I'll never figure Elisabeth out. There's something about her—oh, not just the comradeship of OC, something more that I love in spite of myself."

"I know. I feel the same way. Marne, this man she married, the other man she almost went to jail for—there are almost too many reasons for her acting the way she does, and yet none of it explains . . . She's a mystery. Let's hope she makes it in Hollywood—Elisabeth will starve without recognition."

It was time to leave. It was a time for ending and beginning. They stood up and smiled at each other, and hugged affectionately.

"Page, you'll write and visit soon."

"Of course, and you?"

"You bet. I'm sorry you won't get to meet Breck this trip."

"I'll have that to look forward to."

"Page, you didn't say back there. How have *you* changed?"

"I haven't. I just discovered what had been there always."

"Page, I hope you slay your dragon."

"You remember that?"

"Page, be happy."

They walked away together down the stairs into the holiday crowd. A full glass of champagne sat in front of the fourth chair on the now empty table behind them, its bubbles slowly evaporating.

Page caught a taxi to Fort Des Moines, arriving just after four in the afternoon. "Stop here, driver," she said as they began to circle the Dewy parade ground. She paid him and he left her standing on the north approach road, on the spot where, on a hot, humid July morning in 1942—a world war ago—she and hundreds of others had become the first women soldiers. And over there on the now snow-covered acres of Dewy, they had won the green guidon which Jill carried so proudly. Would this ground ever echo again to the sound of women's marching feet, to a band of sisters?

She pulled her uniform coat up around her throat, and as she walked toward the colonnaded headquarters building she watched the Christmas tree lights twinkling in the family homes on officers' row. Something, a memory of Paul, caught in her heart, and ached there. Dearest Paul. There would be other men in her life, but from the beginning she would always know there would be an ending with each of them. Never would she know the love that comes to a man and a woman after years, after reaching and stretching to meet each other; sharing joy and sadness. She would never nurse a man through a bad cold, or spend hours patiently sitting with him watching their daughter's piano recital. No one ever again would know all her faults, and love her for them. That part of her life was over when Paul walked out of Fouquet's that night in Paris.

Walking faster toward the WAC BOQ, she saw the flag billowing atop its pole, and a group of soldiers heading for the PX. She thought, *This is my home, my real home; my husband, children, family.*

Her hand on the barrack door, she turned for another look at the parade ground, so haunted now with the ghosts of people gone from her life, sparkling in the late winter afternoon, tranquil and beautiful.

Tomorrow she would help process more women from soldier to civilian. Every day she became more aware how all these women had changed from the ones who had arrived in the early days wondering what would be expected of them. They had new skills, new resourcefulness. None of them wanted to return to the way things had been, not after earning the same money as men for the same job, after assuming new responsibilities. Someday, these women would make a differ-

ence in America—oh, maybe not these same women, but they would teach their daughters, the new generation of women to come, what they had learned as women soldiers.

And then, with tremendous force, she was struck by an answer to the question she had been thinking about since her first day at Fort Des Moines. In the coming years, these ex-Wacs would teach their *daughters* to slay dragons; these women returning to civilian life would be catalysts passing on what Wacs had learned in North Africa, Hollandia, Italy and Germany and on drill fields and in offices of five hundred army camps. The daughters would be able to slay all the mythical dragons women had been controlled by throughout history.

A fever of triumph suffused Page's face because she knew that, like Jill, Bunny and Elisabeth, thousands of women had learned there was nothing they couldn't learn, from firing an ack-ack gun to changing a truck tire, from courage and discipline to decisiveness and self-reliance. And for all time the girl babies soon to be born would kill the false dragon that women could not rely on one another, because women in uniform had been comrades.

For the first time Page knew that the Corps would never end, that the Wacs heading into civilian life would be a continuing part of their country's history. *Oh, Paul, you were wrong. The WAC won't be a footnote to history. We'll change history.*

A winter hush settled over the post, a cold sunset preceding a glittering Christmas Eve sky, and on the horizon she saw the moon's image rise just where it should. Captain Page Hannaday opened the door and stepped into the warmth of the barrack.